φ
500

B7

CLAIR DE LUNE

Books by Pierre La Mure

MOULIN ROUGE
BEYOND DESIRE
CLAIR DE LUNE

CLAIR DE LUNE

A NOVEL ABOUT *Claude Debussy*

PIERRE LA MURE

Random House

New York

BEFORE
MORNING

"IF YOU LISTEN TO MY SONG, I'LL DO ANYTHING YOU WANT."

He waited for an answer, but the young woman continued to ignore him. Grownups, he thought, could be very trying.

"Please, Aunt Tavie, come and listen to it." And since he was only four and a half and had not yet learned to be modest, he added, "It's beautiful. Even better than the one I made up yesterday."

She went on gazing into the vanity mirror, her flexed finger pressing a velvet beauty spot against her cheekbone.

Beauty spots were the rage in Paris in that spring of 1867. The Empress herself had launched the fad. Now, no elegant woman would have been caught dead without at least one or two beauty spots on her person. They came in all colors, shapes and materials and were worn on cheeks, neck, shoulders. Sometimes in obscure, unexpected places.

"I'm sure you'll like it very much." This in a coaxing whine he had always found effective.

Still no answer.

He was getting peeved. What was the matter with her, why didn't she give in? She would, anyway, she always did . . . Oh, well, he was in no hurry. Let her have another five minutes.

With the implacable patience of children he waited, whiling the time away by watching her reflection in the mirror: the long-lashed brown eyes gleaming in her pale oval face, the glossy auburn hair that swooped over her ears and coiffed her head like a tight-fitting bronze helmet. Yes, Aunt Tavie was very pretty. Very nice, too . . . But those five minutes must be up. Time for another try.

"Please, Aunt Tavie." Discreetly he tugged at her sleeve. "It's the most beautiful, the most—"

Suddenly all was thunder and lightning. She swirled on her stool, frowning and flashy-eyed.

"I declare you're the most aggravating little boy in the world!" She still held her finger to her cheek, which gave her an unfamiliar, vaguely ferocious look. "I have a mind to take you across my knee and give you a good spanking.

Ooh-la-la, she really was mad! There had never been talk about a spanking. A few *claques* on the *derrière,* yes, but never a spanking. This was no time for protests. Only silence and lowered lids.

"I swear you'd make an angel lose patience!" Already her anger was ebbing. "Stop pestering me or we'll be late at Madame Schneider's."

She stopped. He looked so small and heartbroken, in his black velvet suit and white starched collar, that she fought an impulse to take him in her arms. Instead she swirled back to her mirror.

"I don't want to hear another word, understand?"

The next few minutes went by in pregnant silence. Gingerly she tested with her nail the adhesiveness of her beauty spot, ran a wet fingertip over her eyebrows.

"Why don't you play it for Catherine?" she suggested, as a peace offering.

Catherine was the maid, and who wanted to play for fat, old Catherine? . . . "She's busy in the kitchen."

"Then go and play it to Linne."

Linne was the cat. Occasionally he played his tunes for her, but in the present circumstances the proposition was an insult. "She's out in the garden."

Again silence fell between them. At last she rose and walked to the mahogany armoire.

"I'll tell you what we'll do," she said, standing before the full-length mirror and putting on her small tricorn hat. "If you are a good boy, you can play your song for me when we come back."

It wasn't what he wanted, but it was better than nothing. "Then you'll let me play it as much as I want?"

She gave herself a last look, ran her hands down her hips to smoothen the flounces of her crinoline skirt. Then she turned around and squatted before him.

"Yes, my little Claude, you can play it as much as you want."

Lovingly she brushed back his black curls into a semblance of order. "And all your others, too."

He flung his arms around her neck. With a soft squeal of delight she hugged him, tenderly pecking his cheek.

"All right, let's go. I hear the carriage downstairs." She rose, took his hand, and together they started toward the door. "But remember, I want you to be a good boy at Madame Schneider's. The first thing you must do when you see her . . ."

Hortense Schneider was a popular actress and the most famous cocotte in Paris. As the star of Offenbach's operettas she worked hard and earned four thousand francs a month; as a courtesan she earned a half-million a year and worked much less. She was the undisputed queen of Paris' demimonde. Her specialty was vacationing monarchs. In that line her masterpiece, so to speak, consisted in having been at the same time the mistress of both the Czar and his son, the Grand Duke Wladimir, without either of them suspecting the other. Since then her acquaintance among royalty had become so vast that she had been nicknamed *le boulevard des Princes*.

A plump, vivacious woman, she had bright, calculating eyes and an even more calculating brain, eight dogs, the most famous pearls in Europe, and two buoyant rose-nippled breasts that were forever threatening to spill out of her bodice—and sometimes did. When this happened she casually would pat them back into place while going on with the conversation.

In spite of this, Hortense had a strong sense of propriety. Secretly this most illustrious of cocottes hankered after respectability. Her functions were as proper and as dull as those of a duchess. Had she been an honest woman, she would have given literary teas.

When she spied Claude and his aunt standing hand in hand in the drawing-room doorway, she popped a last bonbon into her rosebud mouth and heaved herself out of the sofa.

"There you are," she cried, hurrying toward them. "And what a pretty child!"

She kissed Claude on both cheeks, declared he was the most adorable boy in the world, and taking his hand, led him to her sofa.

"How old are you, *mon petit chou?*" she asked, sitting him next to her.

Four and half! Why, he was almost a big grown-up man! And what would he do when he was a big grown-up man? An officer perhaps? One of those dashing guardsmen that galloped around the Emperor's carriage? Or perhaps an admiral in a beautiful gold-braided uniform?

Already some of the women in the room were coming toward him, gliding in their billowing skirts, like animated bells. Drawn by some forgotten motherliness they circled around him, smiled at him through their painted lips, reached out their bejeweled hands to pat his cheek. Was he yet going to school? Did he know how to read, how to count up to ten? Had his aunt taken him to *L'Exposition* to sail on the big lake or ride the funny little donkeys?

Politely he answered their questions, tossed them smiles, eager to please his aunt, whose anxious glances he caught from across the room.

At last the ladies returned to their groups, resumed their attitudes of mundane boredom. Claude burrowed against his hostess, rested his head on one of her exuberant breasts. Thus, comfortable and a little sleepy, he munched the bonbons she slipped in his mouth and patiently waited for the function to end.

Suddenly, eyes wide and mouth open, he sat up and stared at the doorway, where the scrawniest, baldest, funniest-looking man he had ever seen was standing, peering short-sightedly into the room. In his light-blue velvet jacket, orange vest, yellow trousers and pink tie he looked like one of the *Nouveau Cirque* clowns, dropping in on Madame Schneider unexpectedly. A gold pince-nez forked his long thin nose; enormous side whiskers streamed down to his chest, where they mingled with the brown fur collar of his overcoat. It made you laugh just to look at him.

"Monsieur Offenbach!" tooted Hortense, hurrying toward him. "I'm so glad you came."

From his seat Claude watched the clown bend over her finger tips, then, still swaddled in his fur coat, follow her into the room. At once the atmosphere seemed to brighten. Everyone, it appeared, knew the funny-looking man. Everyone smiled at him, shook his hand. The ladies gave him their brightest smiles.

Having led the guest of honor from group to group, Hortense returned to her sofa and her bonbons. Offenbach sat down at the piano and absently began running his spidery fingers over the keys. Stealthily Claude slid from his place and unobserved made his way to him. For a moment he stood near the piano, mesmerized by the funny man's playing.

"And what is your name, little boy?" asked the composer, grinning between his long side whiskers.

Claude ignored the question. "Me, I can play, too," he said excitedly in his piping treble. "I make up songs. I made one up this morning. Want to hear it? I'll play it for you."

So saying he gave the pianist a hard shove that sent him tottering on the edge of the stool. Clutching the keyboard for support, Offenbach struck a loud dissonant chord that crashed through the room. Conversations stopped, a lady let out a cry.

Bedlam followed. Claude felt himself jerked away by a furious, sputtering Aunt Tavie, who stammeringly apologized and declared he was the worst little boy in the world.

"He just wanted to play his little song," said Offenbach, "and I didn't get off the stool fast enough, that's all."

The drive back home was gloomy and silent. Dinner, usually a happy, chatty affair, came to an end in a strained mutual reserve, each avoiding the other's eyes. It wasn't until she had tucked him in bed that the tension between them relaxed and their relations improved. For a minute she sat on the edge of his narrow bed, her folded hands bathed in lamplight, her face in the shadows.

"You were a very naughty boy," she said, still trying to sound stern. "How could you ever do such a thing? And to Monsieur Offenbach, of all people!"

She still pretended to be angry but already he could feel the loving impact of her eyes.

"I just wanted to play him my song," he said, peering at her over the brim of the blankets.

Impulsively she bent down to kiss him. "All right. Everything's forgiven. Tomorrow I'll listen to your song."

It was wonderful to be kissed and loved again. Everything was back to normal. "And all the others, too?"

"Yes, little rascal." Happily she rubbed her nose against his. "You can play me all your other songs and as many times as you want. And you are not a naughty boy, you are the best little boy in the world, and I love you very, very much . . ." She gave him a last tender squeeze. "Now go to sleep."

♦

She returned to the dining room, noticed that the table had been cleared, the ceiling lamp lowered. In the small fireplace half-charred logs burned silently, without flame. In the amber dimness of lamplight the room seemed smaller than it really was.

She sat down by the fire, rested her elbow on the arm of her chair. With a smile she recalled the afternoon's incident. Nobody had been hurt and it was rather funny if you thought of it. Probably Hortense would never invite them again, but what of it? A few years ago it might have meant a great deal, now it meant nothing.

As a matter of fact, she didn't quite understand why she had accepted the invitation at all. A week or so ago the actress had spied Claude and herself having a little afternoon pastry at Rumpelmayer's. She had sauntered to their table, greeted Tavie effusively, although they had not seen each other for several years, and invited them both to her next reception. Why had she accepted? Perhaps because she remembered what an honor it was to be invited to Madame Schneider's. Perhaps because she wanted to parade her happiness, show off her little Claude, enjoy the women's envy . . . Whatever it was she had soon discovered her mistake. Even before the piano incident she had felt ill at ease among these famous cocottes. Their mansions, their jewels and furs left her indifferent. She no longer belonged to their world; it seemed almost incredible that at one time she had.

No more incredible, however, than the fact that only a few years ago she still was Marguerite Debussy, the daughter of a Montrouge carpenter, a nineteen-year-old girl in thick woolen stockings and wooden shoes who every morning at six ran to the factory before the whistle blew and they shut the gate.

Neighbors did not understand why she sat eleven hours a day hunched over a long table sewing buttons for nine francs a week.

"Your daughter is much too pretty to do that kind of work," they said to her father. "You'll see, one of these days she, too, will cross the City Gate and you'll never hear from her again."

To get peace from envious girls and ruttish males she married a tinsmith by the name of Roustan. He turned out to be an alcoholic brute who staggered home drunk on Saturdays and beat her without mercy. After one year of this existence she finally did cross the City Gate and lost herself in the fastness of Paris.

Homeless and half starved, she chanced to meet an amiable young rake, who fell in love with her, bought her clothes and set her up in a dainty apartment. He also taught her table manners, corrected her most glaring grammatical errors and gave her a semblance of mundane polish.

"Now all you need is a new name," he said, enjoying his Pygmalion role.

She agreed. It was a question of both prudence and decency. As Madame Roustan, she might bring her husband to her door; to call herself Marguerite Debussy was to disgrace her poor but honorable family. Hector suggested she take the name of Octavie de la Ferronière, whose portrait by da Vinci hung in the Louvre.

"She was the mistress of Francis the First," he explained, and although she had given him the syphilis from which he died, she had loved him tenderly. "You look very much like her, and since the dear lady has been dead about three hundred years, I don't think anyone will object to your taking her name. Therefore, I, hereby, christen thee Octavie de la Ferronière."

As such she was launched upon the midnight set. For six months Hector enjoyed her favors as well as the envy of his friends. Then, having gambled and lost the family's last banknote, he sent a bullet through his tiny brain and unobtrusively departed from the scene.

Without difficulty she found a successor. Then another, then another. At twenty-two she was a well-established demimondaine.

Then, one day, she met Achille Arosa.*

A quietly handsome man with onyx-black eyes and a short black beard, he looked like an Italian poet. She was surprised to learn that he was born in Paris and was a financier. He and his brother lived in Saint-Cloud, Paris' most exclusive residential suburb, in a huge turreted house amidst the paintings they collected and where they entertained society people as well as musicians and artists, even penurious Impressionists.

She fell in love at once; he, by degrees. What had begun as a light-hearted caprice turned into a real love affair; in time a sedate, almost conjugal liaison. She vanished from the Café Anglais and other nocturnal haunts. Soon she was forgotten; some thought her dead. She merely was happy: content to wait for his visits, drive occasionally to Saint-Cloud, spend with him a few winter weeks on the Riviera, in his beautiful, secluded villa in Cannes.

At times, however, she felt lonely. Arosa was no idle playboy, like her former gentlemen friends. He was an executive with business and social obligations. It might be after midnight when his carraige halted at her door and, still in evening clothes, he let himself into her apartment. Sometimes he was tired or worried, and would sit by the fire with her for a moment before driving back to Saint-Cloud. Sometimes he could not come.

Marriage, of course, was out of the question, since she was already married and divorce did not exist. Even if it had been possible, she would not have let him ruin his career on her account. Bankers did not marry demimondaines. Nor did they marry carpenters' daughters. Thus she lived in a vacuum: separated from her former colleagues, shunned by honest housewives.

One day, in a gust of loneliness, she ventured back to Montrouge, where she found her father at work in his little shop. He took her in his arms, wiped the tears from his eyes and made her sit by his workbench as she had when she was a child. He did not ask questions, but gave her the family news. She learned that during her absence her husband had finally brawled himself out of Montrouge and, to everyone's relief, disappeared. As for her brother Manuel, he was as usual out of work.

"He's too proud to be a carpenter. What he'd like is the kind of job where money falls in your pocket. And the fool wants to get married!"

* Achile Antoine Arosa was born in Paris in 1827. His father, Francesco, was a Spaniard; his mother, Ann Gundey, was English. It was his elder brother Gustave who arranged for Gauguin to enter the brokerage business, at the Bertin Agency.

Thereafter, she often went back to her father's shop that smelled of wood and resin glue. She saw her brother Manuel again. Although she did not think much of him, she slipped money into his hand. He appeared grateful. Once they drove back to Paris together. On the way he told her about his plans. He had found a nice girl, Victorine. Not a beauty, quite plain in fact; but serious and hard-working. She would make him a good wife, but a man must support his wife and he was out of work. The reason he was out of work was that he didn't believe in working for others. You never got rich that way. The thing to do was to have a business that worked for you. A little shop for instance . . . And by chance he knew of a little crockery store in Saint-Germain-en-Laye, the prettiest town, only twenty minutes from Paris. A real gold mine and at a bargain. Nothing to do but sit behind the counter and let the money roll in.

"After all, people have got to buy pots and pans, don't they?" he said, turning his heavy face to her. "If only I could get that little shop I'll marry Victorine and settle down."

Octavie spoke to Arosa, and Manual got his shop. He married Victorine and took his bride to Saint-Germain, to a small apartment over the gold mine, at 38, rue du Pain. Nine months later, to the day, he was the father of a boy.*

The first time Octavie saw the baby, he smiled at her from his crib and she lost her heart to him. When she held him in her arms her latent motherliness surged within her. After that his image haunted her loneliness.

Meanwhile her sister-in-law was pregnant again, this time with a daughter, Adèle. By the time the couple celebrated their second wedding anniversary, a third child was on the way. No argument, Manuel was a proficient man in bed. Unfortunately he was proficient nowhere else. Under his guidance the crockery shop was declining at an alarming speed. Apparently no one needed pots and pans. The household's conditions grew desperate.

Again Octavie came to the rescue. She suggested that the shop be liquidated and the family move to Paris. Before the departure, however, her nephew must be baptized. He now was two years old and she wanted him to be a Christian. She also wanted to be his godmother. Since she was paying for everything, the parents raised no objection.

But Arosa did. When she asked him to be the child's godfather, his reply was a firm no. He did not mind buying the crockery shop for her nitwit of a brother, but he drew the line at personal relations.

* Manuel Achille Debussy was born in Montrouge on May 10, 1836. His wife, Victorine Josephine Sophie Manoury, was born in Paris on October 28 of the same year. The marriage took place on November 30, 1861. Their first child, Claude Debussy, was born on August 22, 1862.

For the first time Octavie insisted. She nagged, she begged, and in the end she won. On July 31, 1864, a black-curled two-year-old heathen stood in the Saint-Germain between his godparents: Achille Antoine Arosa, banker; Octavie de la Ferronière, without profession. He was duly anointed and entered into the Catholic faith under the names of Achille Claude. Octavie felt a thrill of triumph. In her head whirled all sorts of plans.

A few days later the Debussys moved to Paris, just in time for Victorine to go into labor. A second son, Eugène, made his howling entrance into the world, spent his short time on earth yelling and keeping everyone awake, and died in the torments of meningitis before he was six months old. But already, with the genetic intemperance of the poor, Manuel had made up for the loss. Victorine was pregnant again.

Strangely, she felt no gratitude toward her sister-in-law. Scrawny and sallow-faced, she envied her beauty. Duly wedded, she condemned her standing as a rich man's mistress. It took all of Octavie's courage to go to rue Clapeyron, where the Debussys had settled, but she climbed the five spiraling flights of stairs and defied Victorine's surly glances for the sole reward of spending a few moments with her nephew and godson. She brought him toys, played with him, and whenever she felt herself unwatched, hugged him with all the passion of her repressed motherhood.

Claude, as she called him, now ruled over her heart. He filled her thoughts when she sat knitting by the fire; he smiled at her in the darkness of her sleepless nights. It was unfair, she told herself, for her brother to have four children while she did not even have one. With each visit her yearning increased. Soon she was unashamedly bargaining with her brother for the privilege of occasionally taking the child home with her. Manuel haggled, but gave in, glad to get rid of this silent, secretive child so unlike his other children.

"He's a strange boy," he complained. "Always in a corner somewhere by himself, never saying anything to nobody."

With her, Claude behaved differently. He laughed, played, talked like a chatterbox. He was the most love-hungry child she had ever seen, stopping sometimes in the middle of a game to run to her and clasp his little arms around her neck. At first she had feared that Arosa might object to the boy's presence. To her delight he welcomed it.

"He keeps you busy," he remarked with a smile. "And obviously you two are very much in love with each other. You can have him around as much as you want."

She needed no more encouragement. To her, Claude's visits were always too short. He himself seemed to guess when the time came to return to his parents' home. His ebullience vanished. Silently he pressed himself against her, clutching her hand. One day, as she was taking him back to rue Clapeyron, she made up her mind. She wanted him all to herself, and said so to her brother. The negotiations went on for some time. Finally, on the promise of financial assistance, Manuel consented.

"Just bring him to see us once in a while," he demanded.

It was now four months that Claude had been living with her and the wonder of it still made her heart swell. It was an endless joy to have him around, listening to his babble, watching him hoist himself on the piano stool and make up his little tunes; to play with him in the little garden at the back of the house, tuck him in bed at night. No longer was she lonely. She had the love of the man she loved, she had her little Claude. What more could she want?

♦

Life went by, unhurried, carefree, swathed in love. Weeks, months. A year; then two. A third one began. Claude remained engrossed in the process of growing up, each day bringing another discovery. His existence revolved around his aunt. They played together and together they worked, for she had started teaching him the alphabet. Occasionally they drove to Saint-Cloud to visit Godfather Arosa in his beautiful home, or to Montrouge to visit Grandpapa Debussy in his little carpentry shop. And now and then, reluctantly, to rue Clapeyron for a brief, uneasy visit with his parents.

On his seventh birthday he rode on a carrousel. Then they went to a puppet show and later to Rumpelmayer's, where he made a pig of himself and ate a plateful of cream puffs, with the result that in the evening he had a terrible *mal de ventre* and disgraced himself by crying "like a baby."

That winter, as usual, he accompanied his aunt to Cannes, a wonderful place where it almost never rained and you could see the sea. In Cannes they lived with Godfather Arosa in a big white house with a red roof. It had a garden, much bigger than the one in Paris. In it he played hide-and-seek with his aunt or ran his hoop.

Twice a week, after lunch, he took a piano lesson from a sad-looking Italian teacher, while Aunt Tavie and his godfather sat on the terrace enjoying the winter sunshine: she, in her large-brimmed straw hat; he, in white pongee suit, smoking his cigar and reading the Paris newspapers that arrived at the house every day.

"Doesn't he play well?" she remarked one afternoon, raising her eyes from her knitting.

He lowered his newspaper and listened for an instant to the sound of piano scales that came out of the open window.

"He plays exactly like a seven-and-a-half-year-old child," he said with a teasing smile. "I played about the same when I was his age."

"Don't you think he has talent?" she asked, a little ruffled by his casualness.

He took another leisurely puff. "If you nurse secret aspirations for him to become a concert pianist, please dismiss them for his own good. In Paris alone there are hundreds of splendid pianists who are starving to death." With a wave of his cigar he stopped her protests. "And since we are discussing his future, don't you think it would be a good idea to send him to school?"

"School! But he's still so young! Besides, I'm teaching him his letters."

"I know, but I'm afraid he won't go very far in the world just by knowing the alphabet."

Gently he explained that on their return to Paris, Claude should be entered in a good school where he would be taught grammar, history, mathematics and various other necessary things.

"We'll see what dispositions he may have," he went on. "If he has none, we can always make him a banker, like me."

For Claude that winter wore on, like the previous one, in unclouded happiness. He played in the garden, took his piano lessons with Maestro Cerutti, made friends with Sven, a Norwegian carpenter who lived down the road, and went fishing with his godfather along the Estèrel coast.*

Then, shortly after Christmas, he noticed a change. Godfather seemed worried, angry about something. Sometimes he crushed his newspaper and flung it aside. Often he paced up and down the terrace smoking furiously, his hands behind his back. At dinner he either did not speak or launched into tirades about something called war. War, it seemed, was approaching, and Godfather said it was about the worst thing that could happen.

"The fools, the fools!" he shouted one day at dinner, slamming his fist on the table. "Don't they see they're playing right into Bismarck's hand? Don't they know the Prussians are ready and we aren't?"

A few days later they were at the station boarding the express for Paris. Good-bye, Cannes! Good-bye, Sven; good-bye, Maestro Cerutti; good-bye, sunshine and flowers and lovely sea! . . . The next morning he was back in a grim wintry Paris, with patches of snow on the sidewalks. In cafés people computed how many days it would take the brave French *pioupious* to slaughter the Prussians and enter Berlin.

It was too late in the semester to enroll Claude at school.

---

* This Norwegian carpenter left a deep impression on him, for many years later he still remembered and wrote about him.

"It doesn't matter," Arosa said. "With all this talk of war, he wouldn't learn anything, anyway."

Joyously she agreed. But Claude, she said, missed his piano lessons. Couldn't he go on with his music?

"By all means," he said, and smiled. "There is no reason why he can't have a serious profession and still play the piano. In fact, I may have the perfect teacher for him."

He then told her about Madame Mauté, a superb pianist who had been a pupil of Chopin.

"She's coming to the house next Sunday. Bring Claude, and we'll have him play for her. If she feels he has real talent, she might be willing to give him lessons. We'll see."

♦

Madame Mauté was impressed. She wanted to start the lessons right away, but her daughter Mathilde was getting married in June.

"Until then, *mon petit,* I'll be too busy," she said, patting Claude's cheek, "but we'll start right after the wedding."

Unfortunately, in June, Mathilde came down with scarlet fever, and her wedding was postponed. So were the lessons.

By now Paris was a bedlam. Everyone was talking war. The French and Prussian press insulted each other daily. In Paris and Berlin clergymen told their congregations that God was on their side. As for the population, they had seen so many parades, sung so many martial songs, drunk so many patriotic toasts, that there was nothing left for them but to go to war.

By mid-July all hopes of peace were gone.

Late one evening Octavie heard the click of Achille's key and ran to the door. At the sight of his rumpled clothes and haggard, grimy face she stopped short.

"Forgive me, darling," he said, so wearily she thought he was ill. "I haven't slept or washed for two days."

Taking his hand she led him into the dining room, made him sit in her own chair by the open window.

"War will be declared tomorrow," he said in a toneless voice.

For a while he remained silent, breathing heavily, gazing at the calm July sky, deep-purple over the roofs. From the street below came the muted screak of a cricket. She sat opposite him, her hands in her lap, gulping her fear, waiting for him to speak.

"You know what I think of it," he went on, without looking at her. "It's absurd, unnecessary and will end in disaster. But my country is in trouble, and I must go."

He spoke quietly, as if he no longer felt any emotion. In a flash she remembered the dinners at Cannes a few months ago when he had shouted, waved his fork. Now he looked like an old man, a tired old man.

"For the last two nights my brother and I have been working at the office. Now all is in order, our clients are safe—"

"When . . . when are you leaving?" she heard herself ask.

"In the morning."

After that she didn't hear clearly what he said. She sat staring at him, motionless as a statue except for a slight trembling of hands and lips. She didn't appear to be aware of it, and this weird, uncontrolled quivering emphasized her immobility, the masklike rigidity of her face.

So it had come . . . Occasionally she had tried to guess how their affair would end. Most probably he would come one evening and tell her he was getting married, explaining he was past forty, wanted a family of his own, and since they couldn't marry . . . She had been prepared for that, had even learned the words she would answer: "Of course, darling. I understand, you don't have to explain—" At other times she had imagined—almost hoped—the end would come in the heat of a quarrel, with the shrillness of angry words echoing for months in their minds. Perhaps it would be better that way. Anger beguiled pain. It helped a little to hate—not much, but a little . . .

Instead, the end had come in a way she hadn't foreseen—quietly, without tears or anger, in a drone of barely heard words about war, duty to one's country, the hope it soon would be over. It had come not in winter or spring, as she had sometimes fancied, but on this summer night. Gently, like a rope-soled assassin in the hush of her lamplit dining room. And with only the tiny sob of a city cricket to weep over it. The injustice, the heartbreak and finality of it.

"Please, darling, listen to me." His voice tore through the web of her thoughts. "Listen carefully, for we have very little time left. I don't know how long this war will last but I've made provisions— Are you listening?" His voice was almost sharp.

"Yes, darling."

"I've made provisions for you and Claude." From his coat pocket he pulled a bulky envelope. "Whatever happens you'll both be safe. This will see you through."

The following day war was declared. For a fortnight the boulevards resounded with the strains of military bands, the tramping of departing soldiers, the cheers of the crowds. One morning Claude saw the Emperor riding through the boulevards with his staff of gold-braided generals, on their way to the front. No denying it, war was exciting. Secretly he calculated that next month he would be eight, and if only the war would last another ten years he still might be able to get into it.

A very dull and depressing summer followed this exhilarating start. Instead of the expected victories, all that arrived from the battlefields were trainloads of wounded soldiers and news of fresh defeats. No one sang or danced in the streets any more. In August, Madame Mauté's daughter got well and was married. Two days after the wedding Madame Mauté herself fell ill. Again the lessons had to be postponed.

The following month hell broke loose. The Emperor surrendered his army and was taken prisoner. The Empress fled to England. France was proclaimed a republic. Octavie prayed that the new government would end the war. Instead, having lost all chance of victory, they decided to go on with it. No more letters from Arosa arrived. Was he wounded, was he dead? Like hundreds of thousands of women she wept the silent tears of war. The Prussians were now racing toward Paris. Just before the siege began, Catherine, the maid, announced that she was leaving for her native Brittany.

"At least you won't have to feed me," she said as the stagecoach left.

In October, Madame Mauté got well and at long last the lessons began. By then the Prussians were encircling Paris and shelling it to their heart's content. You could hear the crash of the bombs, see the columns of smoke rising in the air. This, Claude thought, was quite exciting, but it did not affect the piano lessons. Between him and the white-haired lady a bond of affection and understanding had formed immediately. She was amazed to see how quickly he learned.

"You are a born pianist," she remarked one day. "Monsieur Chopin, my teacher, would have been pleased to have you as a pupil, instead of all the silly girls he had to teach."

Suddenly, in November, war showed its true sinister face. The weather turned so cold the Seine froze solid, and people cut the avenue trees to make firewood. Then hunger came onto the scene. Women queued for hours in the snow for a tin cup of milk, a handful of beans, a half-pound of gray puttylike mush called *pain de guerre*. In December the zoo animals were butchered. For outlandish prices you could get a giraffe steak, a zebra cutlet, a bear's heart. But soon even these couldn't be found. People ate cats. Then they ate dogs, then rats. Old men and women dropped dead in the streets from hunger.

Now and then the French troops made some heroic and useless sortie that always ended in tragic retreat, and heaps of fine young men stretched out in the bloodstained snow, looking glassily at the sky.

"It won't be long now," Aunt Tavie said one day. "The war will soon be over.

She was right. The war—if you could call it that—lasted only a few more weeks. By the end of January an armistice was signed and peace negotiations began. In March the Prussians marched into Paris and gallantly marched out the next day.

It could have been the end, the long-awaited end. But no. The French Communists, the *Communards,* as they were called then, decided this was the perfect moment for a revolution. They seized the city and proclaimed *la Commune,* a communist, anarchist Republic. And so another war began, a civil war this time, between French Republicans and French Communists. Again Paris was besieged, but now by French troops. Street by street the Republicans reconquered the city. No quarter was given on either side; prisoners were shoved against a wall and shot. When it became evident the end was near, the *Communards'* rage turned against the very stones of Paris. They tried to burn their own capital—and nearly succeeded. For two nights and two days Paris was a gigantic pyre.

Then finally the last shot was fired, the last man killed. Charred ruins ceased to smoke, corpses and debris were hauled away. Cautiously one morning a bistro opened. Then two, then three . . . Again there was the rumble of milk carts at dawn, the smell of freshly baked bread, the tinkle of early Mass bells; later on, the cries of pushcart venders, the haggling of housewives. At night streetwalkers again paced the sidewalks. In the gentle spring of 1871, Paris once more was rising from her ashes.

◆

For Octavie the war had not ended, it never would. No more news had come from Arosa. She went to Saint-Cloud and found that his house had been burned to the ground. The money he had left had dwindled alarmingly. There could no longer be any possibility of sending Claude to a good school. There was just enough for the bare necessities. With economy they might live, both of them, for another year or two. After that, God would provide . . .

The following two years were among the most turbulent of France's turbulent history.

The war had ended and so had the revolution, but politics went on. Any day the Republic was to be abolished and monarchy restored. The government kept troops alerted, ready to crush any insurrection. A fever of conspiracy gripped the Parisians. Long-cloaked men ducked furtively into doorways, whispered passwords. Overworked police spies neglected their wives. In cafés fellow conspirators winked at one another over their *apéritifs,* while in dank cellars amateur assassins toyed with time bombs. The very air buzzed with explosive secrets. Like a giant mother-hen Paris was hatching a thousand plots.

Through it all Claude was learning to play the piano. He played quite well by now. Madame Mauté declared that soon she would not have anything more to teach him.

"I don't know whether I taught you too well or you learned too fast, but here you are, a ten-year-old—pardon me, ten and a half!—and already you play the piano better than I. I don't see why you keep on coming here."

But every afternoon, promptly at two, he was back, always hungry for more knowledge, eager to go with her on another junket through that wondrous world of music she had opened to him.

"Well, what shall we play today?" she would say, the moment he arrived. "Shall we have a little Beethoven or Schumann, or Bach?"

After an hour of this she would declare recess and walk to the bow window. There they would have tea and biscuits while chatting pleasantly, like old friends. She knew amusing anecdotes about great musicians and would tell him how the great Johann Sebastian Bach, who was a humble choirmaster, had once flung his wig at the organist; how Beethoven spilled his inkwell into his piano, flooded his apartments, wrote music on the walls ... Sometimes a faraway look would come into her eyes, and leaning back in her chair she would reminisce about the days—long, long ago—when she was a young lady and Monsieur Chopin was her piano teacher. How he drank hot chocolate during the lessons, beat time with his cup. How he warned his pupils to use the pedal sparingly and how he would press his finger tips to his mouth each time he coughed.

"And he coughed all the time, the poor man. He was dying of consumption and should've stayed in bed, but he was poor. Only the rich can afford to be sick."

Occasionally she would ask him to play his latest "compositions." Excitedly he would wait for her to ensconce herself in the armchair, pat a pillow at her back, then finally he would start. When it was over she would shake her head and say, "I can't decide whether you should become a pianist or a composer. Oh, well, when you are at the Conservatoire, your professors will know what's best for you."

From then on she often talked about the Conservatoire. There he would receive the finest musical education and at no cost whatever. The government paid for everything. Naturally it wasn't easy to get in, and he would have to work hard. But she felt sure he would make it.

One afternoon, during recess, she suddenly rested her cup of tea on the table. "Instead of always talking about it, why don't we go and look at it? It's not far from here."

A moment later they were hurrying down the street: he, in his red-pomponed beret and knee-length trousers; she, in a majestic, wind-swept ensemble of flowing veils, multicolored scarves and long-fringed shawls. And on her head something that looked like an inverted flower pot and had been, twenty-five years ago, a dashing bonnet.

"Well, there it is," she said as they reached rue Bergère. "Look at it."

It was one of those warm summerlike days that sometimes come in late autumn. Sunshine gilded the forbidding wall. In the entrance doorway a uniformed concierge stood under the limp flag, twirling his mustache.

Like a Roman statue Madame Mauté held out a draped sleeve and pointed to the building.

"That's where you belong!"

With beating heart he gazed at the grimy stone walls. So this was the Conservatoire! There they taught you everything. How to become a great pianist, how to write music, so that you could jot down any tune that came in your head . . . Of course it was terribly hard to get in, but he would . . . he would . . .

From that day on he worked harder. Now he spent nearly all his time in the living room practicing at his piano. Even the lessons, with their leisurely teas and chatter, became mere relaxation periods in his grueling, self-imposed schedule.

"Now don't work too hard," warned Madame Mauté. "You know I want you to get into the Conservatoire as much as you do, but you needn't kill yourself. Go out in the park with your aunt, it'll do you both good. She looks peaky to me."

But when he returned home he gave his aunt a hasty kiss and hurried back to the piano. She would have liked him to cuddle, tell her, as he used to, about the lesson, the people he had seen in the street. But he was a big boy now and he had nothing in his head but the Conservatoire. . . .

And so, stifling a sigh, she followed him into the living room, took her place by the window, content to be near him. Patiently she listened to the monotonous rippling of scales, smiling at him whenever their eyes met. At times she crumpled her knitting in her lap and looked at him. She noticed the tenseness of his face, the ever-increasing sureness and speed of his hands. And a soft pride would sweep over her.

And so it went, week after week, month after month, until a certain day in spring.

"Don't take off your hat," Madame Mauté said when he arrived, and he noticed that she was wearing her flower-pot bonnet. "We're going to see Monsieur Marmontel. Personally I think you're ready for the Conservatoire, but I want his opinion. I told him about you, and he's waiting for us."

That afternoon he returned home earlier than usual and in such a state of excitement that he collided with his aunt when she opened the door.

"Aunt Tavie! Monsieur Marmontel said I played beautifully, and in October—"

"I can't make head or tail of what you're saying. Let's go to the kitchen and there you'll tell me everything."

She made him sit across from her at the table where she was shelling peas. "Now tell me who is this Monsieur Marmontel."

He was a friend of Madame Mauté and a professor at the Conservatoire. More than a professor, the head of the piano division. He was very tall and thin and had no hair on his head.

"He kept pulling his beard while I played—"

"Never mind the beard. What did he say?"

"After I finished he turned to Madame Mauté and said, 'Madame, this child is a prodigy. In two years he'll be ready to give concerts.' And in October he wants me to pass directly into his class, the advanced piano class. Isn't it wonderful?"

She was smiling at him, forgetting to reply to his question. No, he never would be a doctor or a lawyer or even a banker, as Achille used to say. For better or for worse he was born to be a musician . . .

"What are you thinking about?" he asked.

"How wonderful it is and how proud of you I am."

She was seized by a coughing spell, a dry soblike cough that creased her face with pain. He watched her shoulders tremble with each new spasm, the beads of perspiration glisten on her forehead.

"What is it, Aunt Tavie? You're sick?"

Finally she caught her breath and forced a smile to her lips. "No, darling. Just a little cold."

◆

From the moment Claude guessed that his aunt was ill his boyish universe of trust and security burst like a punctured toy balloon. Yet he resolved he would not betray his fears or let her know he had discovered her secret. She, too, endeavored to keep the truth about her health from him as long as possible. Thus out of mutual love they entered into a piteous comedy of mutual deceit. When she told him she had caught a cold but the doctor had said it soon would pass, he pretended to believe what she said.

"Of course," he said, "you'll be all right."

As spring bloomed into summer his words seemed to come true. She coughed less; a semblance of color returned to her cheeks. He discontinued his lessons and they went out together in the afternoon. They sat in public parks and watched children play. Sometimes they preferred the quiet of a small neighborhood square with a fountain or a statue of some general in the center. Sometimes they watched a street singer warbling his lungs away to a handful of *midinettes,* sometimes an acrobat in pink tights and handle-bar mustache. On his birthday they went to the circus and laughed at the clowns' antics. Once they took the horse trolley all the way to Montrouge and went to see Grandfather. They also visited his parents. But most of the time they stayed by themselves, enjoying the warm summer sunshine, sitting on public benches and watching the never-ending spectacle of Paris.

But early in October the rains came and they remained at home by the fire, listening to the drumming of rain against the windowpanes.

"Just the same, we had a good summer, didn't we?" he said, and she replied they certainly had. "The best ever."

On October 22, two months exactly after his eleventh birthday, he passed the entrance examinations of the Conservatoire and was assigned to Monsieur Lavignac's elementary solfeggio class and Monsieur Marmontel's advanced piano class.

Thereafter his life, until then so calm and sheltered, became a whirl of new places, new regulations, new faces. On lesson days he went out of the house early in the morning, clutching his brand-new solfeggio manual, the hood of his pelerine pulled low over his eyes. Unaware of the pelting rain he would hurry through the bustling streets, and when at last he reached rue Bergère, he would sprint the few remaining yards, dash through the broad archway and burst into the school's courtyard.

In the hierarchy of the Conservatoire he and his classmates occupied the lowest rank and were variously known as the little ones, the small fry, the runts, the snotty ones. But they ignored the disregard in which they were held, and a month after their admission, talked the school's slang and aped the manners of their elders. The Conservatoire itself, so august a few weeks ago, was now *le Conserv;* its eminent frock-coated and top-hatted professors mere *profs.* "Look! That's Durand, the harmony prof. Ooh-la-la, they say he's a regular *canule* . . . That's Victor Massé, the composition prof . . . That's César Franck, the organ prof . . ." Then the bell would ring. In a trampling of nailed soles the students entered the main building, climbed the wide stairs and trekked along the corridors to their respective classrooms.

Many interesting and funny things happened in the solfeggio class and Claude told his aunt about them. But he did so without pleasure, watching her face, waiting for the next coughing fit. For she had started coughing again. More than ever . . . Again fever made her eyes glow as if there were a fire behind them. And it was getting more difficult all the time to go on pretending that all was well and her cold would soon go away.

One night in December she heard him crying in his room.

"What is it, darling?" she asked softly, resting the lamp on the night table. "Having trouble at school?"

He did not reply, and she sat on the edge of the bed, watching him sob on, his head buried in the pillow.

With a swift, youthful motion he turned around and flung himself in her arms. "You're sick, Aunt Tavie. Very, very sick!"

Then in a gasping stammer he told her how he had pretended to believe she only had a cold but had known she was ill since that afternoon in the kitchen when he had told her about his visit to Monsieur Marmontel.

"I don't want you to die, Aunt Tavie." The words came out in a wail of despair. "I don't want— I don't want—"

She hadn't seen him cry like this since he was a small child. All his brave resolutions of self-control had broken down. His heart brimmed over with grief. He no longer cared about anything, didn't even trouble to wipe the tears streaming down his cheeks.

He pulled away from her. "I won't let you die." Under his night-shirt she could feel his body grow tense with determination. "We'll fight together, we'll fight so hard you'll be all right again."

Overnight he became the man of the house. He appointed himself her nurse, gave her her medicine, made her go to bed early, some-times even before he had finished his homework. He forbade her to prepare his morning *café au lait,* tartly informing her that if she did he would not drink it. He appropriated her alarm clock and rose at dawn. Before going to school he went to the bakery shop, started the stove, ground coffee, lit the fire in the dining room so that the room would be warm when she came in. When he returned from school he put a new log in the fireplace, tucked the woolen blanket around her knees. If only he could keep her alive until summer. Then their friend, the sun, would come to their rescue, chase the fever away, bring the pink back to her cheeks. Again they would sit in sunny little squares, watch carrousels and acrobats. She would regain her strength.

She, too, fought as well as she could. Youth, she told herself, had tremendous reserves of vitality, and she was still young. At times foolish hopes flashed through her mind like flocks of joyous singing birds. Thus it went for three months. Then, one February morning, she knew it was all over. Neither her youth nor medicines nor Claude's attentive nursing would help. Life was ebbing out of her. Quietly but irresistibly, like water from a cracked vase. Every gesture cost her an effort. Even her heart seemed to beat more slowly, as if warning that soon it would stop beating altogether. For a moment she lay in bed, breathless with fright, sheathed from head to foot in a filmy shroud of cold sweat. Then her terror melted; in its place came peace.

She still was calm two evenings later. During dinner Claude told her about a hilarious incident that had happened during the solfeggio class. She laughed softly, asked questions, and they had a lively conversation not only about school but about various other subjects. Dinner over, she sat by the fire, and he tucked the blanket around her knees. Then he cleared the table and started doing his homework.

Slowly she glanced about the room. It hadn't changed in all these years. The ceiling lamp still made its circle of yellow light on the table. The clock on the mantelpiece still ticked on, like a brave little heart. Everything was as it had been that night when Achille had come to tell her war was about to be declared and he was leaving in the morning. She hadn't died then because you didn't die from grief—at least not immediately. And then Claude had been there, clamoring for attention and love. He hadn't given her time to brood, remember, keep the wound open. Gradually time had done its healing work; Achille had become a memory. Whether dead or alive he had vanished from her life and she had accepted his disappearance and come to love Claude twice as much. One love, she had learned, could fill a heart as much as two.

"Time for your cough syrup," he said, pushing back his chair.

Already he was pouring the medicine into the spoon with the gravity of a pharmacist measuring a prescription. "The doctor said every two hours. Well, there it is."

Obediently she opened her mouth, swallowed the medicine.

"Now you must go to sleep for an hour," he said.

She closed her eyes, pretended to doze off. He watched her for an instant, then went back to the table.

Claude, beloved Claude . . . He did not know the battle was lost. He would not know until tomorrow, when his father came to fetch him at the Conservatoire. At first she had planned to tell him everything, explain why she was going.

It would only hurt him and serve no useful purpose. How did you explain to a child you were going away to die? . . . Tomorrow would be soon enough.

He turned away from his book, looked at her from his chair. "Are you really asleep?"

She smiled, keeping her eyes closed. "Of course I am. Can't you see?"

And with the unquestioning faith of children he believed her and returned to his work.

Book One

LOVE
COMES
TOO SOON

CHAPTER

1

THE FOLLOWING AFTERNOON HIS FATHER WAS WAITING OUTSIDE THE
Conservatoire. As they walked toward rue Clapeyron, he told Claude
that his aunt had been called away. Then, without a pause, he
changed the subject.

"Me and you are going to be friends," he said. "It isn't every boy
that gets into the Conservatoire at eleven. No, sir. Pianists, they are
one franc to the dozen, but prodigies, they're rare as hen's teeth."
He ran his finger over the fringe of his mustache and went on,
"Now all you've got to do is win First Piano Prize at the end of the
year, and me and you are on our way. Of course it'll mean hard
work, but you can do it if you set your mind to it. Every day, when
I return from the office, I'll help you."*

And so it began. Scales, trills, arpeggios. Hour after hour. His
father standing by the piano, a watch in his hand. "Good. Now,
a little faster." Sometimes he would be pleased. His eyes would
gleam with anticipation. "First we give a concert in Paris. Then
London. Those rich milords, they pay anything to hear prodigies.
Then Vienna . . ." Somehow he had read about Mozart's childhood

* After years of chronic unemployment, Manuel had at last found his niche in
the world. A few months before, he had begun work at the Compagnie
Fives-Lille as a *garçon de bureau,* a combination janitor, filing clerk, receptionist, messenger and handyman. He occupied the same position for thirty-three
years, until 1906.

concerts at the Austrian Court. "Then Russia. That's where the real money is." He would close his eyes and in his mind he would hear the bravos, see the flowers tossed on the stage, and imagine himself in fur coat and top hat signing contracts, shoving fistfuls of banknotes into his pockets.

But soon he noticed that Claude, instead of playing better, played less well, less fast. "What's the matter? Can't you play faster?" And again Claude would tackle the chromatic, run his small hands over the keyboard until his head throbbed and his aching fingers stumbled over the keys.

At the end of the year he did not win First Piano Prize. Life at home became a torment. Gradually "the Mozart dream" was festering his father's brain, turning him into a senseless brute. Now he held a watch in one hand and a ruler in the other. The vision of those banknotes eluding his grasp sent him into paroxysms of rage. "Faster, *nom de Dieu,* faster!" Down would come the ruler, like a red-hot iron, and for a moment there would be nothing but pain and the welling of tears. And anger, the helpless anger of a child, turning to hatred, holding back the tears, choking back the sobs.

It went on like this for two more years. But neither ruler, nor slaps, nor Sundays at the keyboard did any good. With grieving heart Monsieur Marmontel saw his star pupil turn into a dazed, drowsy youngster who fell asleep during lessons and no longer played the piano well. The magic fingers Madame Mauté had trained with such loving care had been ruined. The boy who at eleven was a prodigy could not even win an Honorable Mention at fourteen.

Finally Manuel Debussy admitted defeat. "You'll never amount to anything. With luck, you'll wind up playing the piano in a café."

♦

The year after his father lost interest in him, Claude won a Second Piano Prize. But by now it was too late. He was no longer a prodigy, but a frightened, taciturn adolescent withdrawn into his loneliness. At home he felt like a stranger, unloved and in turn unloving; at school he became an unruly student who arrived late and collected demerits. His maladjustment found some sort of relief in rebelliousness. He vented the defiance of a repressed and unhappy youngster on harmony and counterpoint. When he learned that parallel fifth chords were to be avoided, he studiously crammed his homework with them. Expecting no affection from anyone, he shied away from the companionship of his classmates as well as the sympathy of his teachers. Like a whipped dog, he distrusted friend and foe alike.

Two more years passed, and now he was sixteen, then seventeen. Somehow he squeezed through the periodical examinations and escaped being dismissed from school. Occasionally he would accomplish some musical feat that stupefied his teachers, then relapse into his perverse indolence.

Out of school he was secretive and malcontent. Since he had failed as a child prodigy, his parents now expected him to contribute to the family budget. At his age, his mother told him, a boy was an apprentice in some trade and brought money home on Saturday. He could go on with his music, if he liked, but he must pay for his keep. To earn money he tried giving piano lessons to neighborhood children. Between classes he went from house to house, climbed ill-smelling stairs very much like his own, rang bells and with pounding heart waited for the door to open. Then, quickly, hat in hand, he recited the well-rehearsed speech. "Pardon, Madame. Would you like your child to play the piano?" Usually the door was slammed in his face. He walked up to the floor above, rang another bell, tried again. Now and then he was let in and lessons were arranged. In this manner he acquired a few pupils at half a franc an hour. If their parents happened to own a piano, he taught them at their houses. If not, they came to his. For convenience he was given his own room at the end of the corridor. There his piano, an upright, rather dilapidated Blondel, was placed. And there he slept, worked and gave his lessons.

Sunday was the week's worst day. It never ended. He left home early and loitered along the streets, looking in shop windows. He strolled along the Seine, browsing through the bookstalls, buying for one sou or two some dog-eared book which he read on a park bench, or, when it rained, in the waiting room of a railway station, beguiling his hunger with a thick slice of bread and a bar of chocolate. He returned home as late as he could, when he knew that everyone had gone to bed.

At the Conservatoire things were coming to a head. He now was finishing the various preparatory courses: harmony, counterpoint and sight reading. At the end of the year he would have to quit school unless he could be admitted into one of the three composition classes that prepared students for the famous annual contest of the Grand Prix de Rome.

Unfortunately the composition classes were open only to students who won at least one first prize in one of the preparatory courses. His chances of winning anything, let alone a first prize, were practically nil. That year his scholastic record was even worse than in the years before. His demerits made an impressive column in his file at the censor's office. At his last meeting with this official he had been told that he was tottering on the brink of expulsion. "My only satisfaction," remarked the censor, "is to think that next year you won't be here any more." With a sort of numb fatalism Claude went on, month after month, without visible improvement. He expected the worst, and all signs pointed out that he would get it.

One morning in June, only two weeks before the school's annual closing, he dashed out of the harmony class with his usual speed. The noon bell was still ringing and already he was halfway down the corridor when he heard someone running after him and calling his name.

"Professor Marmontel wants to see you," puffed the concierge.

"Me? What for?"

"How should I know? He just said he wants to see you."

"Now?"

"Yes, now. Hurry up. Presto, allegro, alegrissimo."

After thirty years as chief concierge, Lescot had become familiar with musical terms, as well as everything else at the Conservatoire. He knew all the school's secrets, from the professors' marital problems to the scholastic and disciplinary status of every student.

He caught the look of hesitation on Claude's face and added with a warning frown, "I wouldn't try to run out, if I were you. You've got enough discredits as it is."

Reluctantly Claude turned around, shambled to the piano room. "You asked for me, Master?"

The old teacher nodded and went on sorting the papers on his desk. After a while he locked a drawer, slipped the key into his vest pocket and considered Claude in thoughtful silence. Slowly he scanned the troubled, handsome face, the extraordinary eyes, jet-black and watchful; the mane of unruly curls; the threadbare suit, the hands defiantly shoved into the trouser pockets.

"How old are you, my boy?" he asked at last.

"Seventeen and a half, Master."

"Are you through with the year-end examinations?"

"Almost. Only sight reading, and it's scheduled for Tuesday."

"How have you been doing?"

"Not so good, I'm afraid."

"But, my boy, don't you know you can't enter composition if you don't win a first prize? What will you do if you are dropped out of school?"

"I don't know. I'll go on giving lessons, I guess."

"What kind of lessons?"

"Piano lessons. I've been giving piano lessons in my spare time. I don't like it much, but I've got to help my family." His defiance was melting before his old teacher's kindness. A timid, boyish smile came to his lips. "My biggest trouble is that I am so young. So I tell them I've won First Piano Prize at the Conservatoire. They don't really know what it means, but they're impressed. I hope you don't mind, Master."

"No, my boy. I don't mind. Tell them anything you want."

He paused, looking dolefully at Claude. Here was the most talented, most promising pupil he had ever had and he had been ruined by stupid, greedy parents. And now he was going from house to house, peddling lessons . . .

"Have you any plans for the summer?" he asked, coming out of his thoughts.

"No, Master."

The teacher picked up a letter from his desk. "I've just received this letter from Madame von Meck. She is a very rich and rather eccentric Russian lady who travels all over Europe with her family, her retinue and three musicians who play for her every afternoon. She needs a pianist for the summer, and I should like to recommend you."

"Thank you, Master."

"It would give you a chance to travel and get away from your family. And she pays very well."

The following week Claude won first prize in sight reading and thus became eligible to enter one of the composition classes in October. He also received a letter from Madame von Meck's secretary, instructing him to report to the Grand Hotel at Interlaken, Switzerland, where Madame resided at the moment. Enclosed were a month's wages, and the money for a first-class train ticket.

He gave the wages to his mother, secured a passport and left for Interlaken, where he arrived late in the afternoon.

♦

The little Swiss town was buzzing with summer trade. On rustic terraces overlooking the lake, blond-braided waitresses scurried about, carrying steins of foamy beer on their trays. Mountain climbers, their knapsacks on the ground, sat around pinewood tables, discussing tomorrow's excursion. Tourists crowded gift shops, bought cuckoo clocks and hand-painted wooden inkwells.

None of this plebeian jollity reached the Grand Hotel, standing aloof and stately on the hill amidst its manicured, melancholy garden. There, on the balustraded terrace of her suite, a gaunt gray-haired lady in a white cashmere shawl and black taffeta dress sat in a wicker chair, a book open on her lap, her mastiff at her feet; and, standing at her back, a huge Cossack bodyguard, bearded to the eye, his astrakhan bonnet on his shaven head, his silver dagger in his belt. Silent and perfectly immobile, except for the slow motion of her hand bringing her long ivory cigarette holder to her lips, Nadedja Philaretovna Frolowsky von Meck was enjoying the splendor of the Alpine sunset in the privacy of the very rich.

Slowly, as if with regret, she took her eyes away from the Jungfrau, surging across the lake like a bloodstained arrow, and considered Claude with the meticulous yet detached attention she would have given a new footman.

"So, you are the young man Monsieur Marmontel recommended." She spoke in excellent French. "How old are you?"

"Twenty, Madame."

"He tells me you are an excellent pianist. I hope, however, you are not one of those keyboard acrobats that are turned out every year by the Conservatoire." She took a leisurely puff from her cigarette holder. "Do you read music well?"

"Oh yes, Madame. I just won first prize in sight reading. If you want to see it I have the diploma in my valise."

His eagerness brought a faint smile to her thin lips. "I soon shall see if you are as good as you appear to think you are. By the way, are you familiar with the compositions of Piotr Ilyich Tchaikowsky?"

His puzzled look told her he was not. Her eyes narrowed in anger. "The greatest musician who ever lived and you've never heard of him! What do they teach you in that stupid Paris Conservatoire?"

"I am sorry, Madame," he said on a sudden inspiration. "We haven't yet begun the study of Russian composers."

This seemed to placate her somehow. For an instant she considered him through the smoke of her cigarette.

"In the morning you will give a piano lesson to my daughter Sonia. I must warn you that although not yet fourteen, she is very glib and resourceful at inventing excuses for shirking her work. You will have to be firm. Every week you will report to me on her behavior and progress."

In the afternoon, she went on, he and his two colleagues would play for her the various compositions she selected. This concert would take place in the drawing room of her suite, but not in her presence. She did not like watching musicians at work.

"It disturbs me from enjoying the music. I shall listen from my sitting room."

With an imperceptible flip of her hand, as she would dismiss a servant, she signified that the interview was at an end. Without another glance at him she returned to the contemplation of the Jungfrau, now lilac in the darkening sky.

Claude's arrival created little stir. Just another wage earner in the swarm of secretaries, footmen, chambermaids who gravitated around Madame von Meck. He made friends with his two fellow musicians. Pahulski, the violinist, was a flaxen-haired Pole who had been one of Tchaikowsky's pupils at the Moscow Conservatory. Danilchenko, the cellist, had a short beard and wore flowered vests. After the afternoon concert the three of them would walk down to the village and drink beer in picturesque inns.

From his two friends Claude learned that Madame von Meck was probably the richest woman in Russia.

"She owns two railroads," explained Pahulski, who had been with her the longest. "She used to manage them, too, but now her son Wladimir is in charge, though she still keeps her eye on the business. Now and then she drops in at the office in Moscow and everybody shakes in his boots."

Abruptly, one morning, orders came down to pack. With speed born of long practice ikons came down from the walls, samovars disappeared from the tables. The paintings, photographs, bronze statues and numberless knicknacks Madame carried with her wherever she went were carefully crated and removed from the premises. Once again the von Meck caravan was ready to take to the road.

Their first destination turned out to be Arcachon, a summer resort in the southwest of France, where Madame happened to own not one but two villas, which, however, proved inadequate and were soon abandoned. Again they were on their way, this time to Rome. On a torrid August afternoon the von Meck special train entered the Eternal City.

The marble fountains, the ocher-walled *palazzi*, the jet-eyed, slow-moving women, the beggars, the ruins—Claude loved them all. With his two fellow musicians he wandered through dim and narrow streets festooned with laundry lines, ate spaghetti in cool *trattorie* that smelled of wine, onions and olive oil. In the evening they loitered at cafés where Romans, fresh from their siesta, fanned themselves with their hats while eating pink ices.

Then it was Naples, with her bay, her smoking Vesuvius, her mandolins, her begging laughing-eyed urchins. Then, back to the Hotel de Russie in Rome for another week.

Despite its swift and constant changes, life within the household followed a rigid pattern. Somehow, at whatever the cost, pianos were always found and moved in. The afternoon concert in Madame's empty drawing room took place with clocklike regularity. Claude had soon discovered his employer's passion for Tchaikowsky's music and he played it with romantic fervor, delighted when, the concert over, he came into her sitting room to receive her instructions and found her dissolved in tears, her handkerchief rolled into a damp ball in the palm of her hand. "You played very well today," she would say. He sensed he was entrenching himself in her good graces.

The only cloud in his life was his relationship with Mademoiselle

Sonia. He had been warned she was glib and lazy, but he was not prepared for her genius of cunning. Nor the pale golden glint of her hair, the length of her eyelashes and the disturbing mobility of her brown eyes, which could be mirrors of innocence one moment and dark pools of mischief the next.

After the first lesson it was clear she was determined to drive him mad. Oh, she was respectful, most respectful . . . She called him *Monsieur le Professeur*. Whenever she struck a wrong key, which was most of the time, she endured his reproaches with an air of long-suffering saintliness.

"Please, *Monsieur le Professeur*, don't hate me," she would murmur in her caressing, faintly accented French. "I know Maman has told you horrid things about me, she does the same with all my tutors. But I'm not as bad as she says. I swear by the Black Virgin of Kazan I'm doing my best."

But she wasn't, she wasn't even trying.

"Mademoiselle Sonia," he said sternly one morning, "if you don't apply yourself, I shall have to report you."

She tossed him a look of anguish. "If you do, I'll kill myself."

It was maddening. Whenever they played four-hands her fingers would somehow get entwined with his. Inadvertently she would dislodge his foot from the pedal or she would nudge him with his hip. She would apologize, berate herself for her clumsiness, swear by the Black Virgin of Kazan it all was an unfortunate hazard—and do it again five minutes later.

In August the von Meck household landed in Venice. Madame installed herself in the royal suite at the Danieli while her retinue invaded the rest of the hotel and proceeded to turn it into an outpost of the Russian Empire. Basil, her chef, charged into the kitchen, hurled some terrible Russian curses at his Italian colleague, smashed a vast amount of crockery and sent the poor man flying at the point of a roasting spit. This done he hung an ikon on the hood of the stove, burst into full-throated song and plunged into the intricacies of Madame's dinner. Upstairs, on the two highest floors, samovars gurgled. The fragrance of Russian tea wafted through the transoms. Ostap, the Cossack boyguard, unpacked his balalaika and sang mournful love ballads while gulping vodka.

Claude's relations with Madame improved daily. She commended his talent for score reading, his rendition of Piotr Ilyich's music. Sometimes she left him the choice of the next day's program. Occasionally she asked him to play for her in the evening. Then this hard, imperious woman became gentle, almost affectionate.

"My little Bussyk," she would say, "you play very well indeed."

To please her he wrote a four-hand transcription of *Swan Lake* and even started work on a trio.*

One afternoon he found her in a state of acute perplexity, fitfully tapping a visiting card in the palm of her hand.

"If I had known the Wagners were in town, I never would have come," she said, while he waited for her instructions.

"The Wagners" turned out to be Richard Wagner and his wife, Cosima. That morning Frau Wagner had left a card at the hotel, and etiquette demanded a return call. The prospect disturbed Madame and put her in a fretful, loquacious mood, unlike her usual haughty reserve.

"I don't like either of them," she went on.

She felt the need of talking and did not dismiss him with a few clipped words about the next day's concert, as she usually did. With surprise he discovered that his recluse employer, who never saw anyone, never went anywhere, possessed a vast amount of information about the famous couple. Her dislike toward Cosima was mitigated by a grudging admiration for her superb disregard of conventions. Twenty-five years younger than Wagner, Cosima von Bülow had abandoned husband and children to follow the composer. She had lived with him six years and borne him three children before the thought had struck either of them to regularize their affair. This, Madame felt, required a considerable amount of poise and strength of character.

"Of course," she added with a slight sniff, "her mother did the same with Liszt. This might explain it."

Toward Wagner, however, she felt nothing but unmitigated contempt.

"He is a crook, a hypocrite, a coward, a liar and a cad," she snapped. "All his life he has been mouthing high-sounding phrases while extorting money right and left, cheating everybody and betraying his friends."

She could not say a good word about the man. He had stolen the wives of friends who had come to his help. His vanity was so monumental that he had taught his parrot to cackle, "Richard Wagner is a great man!" He was ugly; he was small, almost a midget. He had some revolting skin disease and scratched himself constantly. He wore outlandish clothes and lived in grotesque surroundings.

"Once, in Munich, he received me in his house on Briennerstrasse,

* In a letter to P. Tchaikowsky she wrote: "My little Frenchman has written a very nice trio. . . . He reads music wonderfully. . . . He has a very frivolous nature, quite French, but his heart is very kind. . . . Music is his only interest in life. I'm sending you this arrangement of your dances from the *Swan Lake* to give to Jurgenson for printing. Please don't put M. Debussy's name on it— for he might be scolded at school."

reeking of snuff and perfume, dressed in pink satin trousers and a yellow silk dressing gown adorned with pearls and an ermine collar, explaining that his skin was too delicate to endure the contact of ordinary fabrics. Later he showed me his Graal Room, a horror walled in pink and yellow satin with artificial roses on the ceiling. Personally I think he is a lunatic, but Piotr Ilyich, who is the kindest and most generous man, says that he would have become a fine symphonist, if he had not wasted his life on those absurd operas of his."

Suddenly she seemed to notice Claude standing before her. "Do you know any of them?"

"No, Madame. They're forbidden at school. One of the students was expelled for bringing in the score of *Lohengrin*."

She resumed her tirade. Then, having made clear her antipathy for the Wagners, she decided she would return Cosima's call.

"I want you to come with me," she said, returning to her usual imperious manner. "Be ready tomorrow at three o'clock."

With the familiar wave of fingers she sent him on his way.

"This is only a courtesy call," she said the next afternoon as they boarded the waiting gondola. "We shall stay only a few minutes."

She opened her black parasol and remained in frowning silence as they glided by the *palazzi* along the Grand Canal. The visit had been duly arranged the day before between the parties' respective secretaries, and the doors of the Palazzo Vendramin opened, as if by incantation, when the gondola slid to a stop in front of the *palazzo's* landing.

A liveried footman bowed the visitors into a marble hallway, took Claude's hat, and ushered them into the Meister's study. This done, he bowed again and withdrew, leaving them in a huge, dim room with narrow stained-glass windows, crowded with a profusion of pseudo-Gothic furniture and bric-a-brac of all sorts. Claude had a glimpse of an enormous, heavily carved desk, a grand piano, also heavily carved; a suit of armor complete with plumed helmet and crested shield, altar candles in their gilded holders, gold chasubles in a glass cabinet, pewter beer steins, a bolt of purple brocade on a bishop's chair, a marble bust of Beethoven; and unexpectedly, on the walls, a butterfly collection. The ensemble gave an impression of studied, theatrical disorder and uncertainty of taste.

"Perfectly dreadful," hissed Madame under her breath.

The door opened. In an aromatic cloud of snuff and rose lotion, Richard Wagner trotted in, hands outstretched, followed by a huge dog.

"*Chère Madame,*" he exclaimed, kissing the lady's finger tips, "*quelle délicieuse surprise!*"

Although forewarned, Claude was startled by his short stature, emphasized by the huge, handsome head. Wagner did not wear the pink trousers and yellow robe of the Munich days, but a sedate maroon smoking jacket and a black velvet beret.

"Cosima will be delighted to see you," he gushed on. "We see so very few people!"

Madame muttered a few words and introduced Claude. The composer deigned to extend his hand and launched at once into reminiscences.

"Ah, Paris! I was living at 31, rue du Pont-Neuf, in the house where your great dramatist Molière was born. Now it is doubly famous."

Chuckling at his own sally, he sat down on a thronelike chair in which he almost disappeared. He ordered his dog to lie down at his feet and resumed the course of his memories.

"Yes, Paris is a lovely city, but cruel to poor artists. Nowhere are creditors so heartless. I even grew a beard to elude mine . . . It didn't help. And let me tell you that your debtors' prison is very dreary and damp!"

Again he let out a merry chuckle, like an old sea captain recalling long-past storms. For an instant he gazed dreamily ahead while scratching the back of his hand.

"I am sorry the French do not appreciate my music. They are parochial and detest foreigners. But you'll see, they'll come to it in a few years. I have already many admirers in your country."

The dog growled and Wagner leaned down to pet him.

"Lie down, Pheps."

Pheps subsided and the Meister resumed his one-sided conversation.

"Do you love dogs? I simply adore them. Once I had a dog that howled when I played the Pilgrim's Chorus from *Tannhäuser*."

Again he chuckled and brought a pinch of snuff to his nostrils. Without a pause he pressed on, talked about his love of animals, spoke of those he had used in his operas. Horses, of course. Dozens of them. Dogs also. A swan in *Lohengrin*, a bear in *Siegfried*. Doves galore. Even a ram, even a snake.

"Even a toad!"

He might have gone on like this forever, but Cosima made her entrance, tall and stately in black taffeta. The moment she arrived, Wagner seemed to shrink. His jovial garrulity deserted him at once. He remained seated on his chair, like a timid child, smiling and speechless.

While pouring tea Cosima complained of the many tasks that fell upon her. There were so many letters to write. To publishers, orchestra conductors, Bayreuth executives. And, of course, the thousands of persons who wrote the Meister from all over the world.

"Isn't that so, Richard?"

Obediently he nodded.

Yes, the lot of a genius' wife was a hard one. She must spare him burdensome details so that he may be left to his exalted thoughts. So many people wanted to tell him their admiration, pleaded to be admitted, begged to speak to him. At least see him, get a glimpse of him.

"Why, if I didn't keep watch, he wouldn't have a minute to himself. Isn't that so, Richard?"

Before leaving, the visitors were treated to a glimpse of the Meister's bedroom, which had been decorated, under his supervision, in blue silk draperies to evoke the Blue Grotto. Then they trooped to the small garden with its marble bench and the old yew trees. There, she said, the Meister spent many hours by himself, away from the clamoring mob of admirers, in silent communion with the Muses.

"This is his favorite spot." With a quick proprietary glance she added, "Isn't that so, Richard?"

The Meister nodded.

Farewells were exchanged on the floating platform. The usual things were said. With mutual insincerity, hope was expressed for a new encounter in the near future.

A minute later the gondola was on its way back to the hotel. On the *palazzo's* landing Cosima and her husband were receding with each scooping of the single oar. She, tall and erect; he, stooped and looking very small at her side. For a while they waved limp hands, then they re-entered the house.*

For Madame the visit had been a strain. She did not listen to the gentle flapping of waves against the slender hull and paid no attention to the splendor of Venice glowing in the sunset.

"All this twaddel about shielding him from his admirers!" she sputtered irascibly. "The truth is that he is an incorrigible old lecher, and she is afraid he might find some little baggage to his fancy. Incredible as it may seem, this midget has broken many women's hearts. But now he has a wife who is on to him, and he doesn't have a chance to misbehave. Those libertines always wind up by marrying women who make them pay for what they did to other women."

So apprehensive was she of another visit from the Wagners that on her return to the hotel she ordered immediate departure.

Two days later they were installed at the Villa Oppenheim, a

---

* The Palazzo Vendramin, where Wagner died, is today Venice's broadcasting station. The little garden is still there, but the yews are gone.

huge villa on Via dei Colli, a short distance from Florence. For a week the house buzzed with activity. Carpets were laid, paintings hung, pianos tuned, while below, in the garden, hedges were clipped, paths sanded, white furniture scattered over the lawn. And far from the house, in the most inaccessible part of the garden, Sonia set her croquet hoops.

"Please, *Monsieur le Professeur,* come and play with me this afternoon," she whispered as they were playing a Mozart sonatina.

"Please, Mademoiselle, pay attention to the music. Or I shall be forced to report you."

Instead of the look of anguish he expected, she said, "If you tattle on me, I'll tattle on you."

He turned to her, every inch the professor. "And what, may I ask, will you tattle about?"

"That you are only eighteen and you told Maman you are twenty. She hates liars."

"How . . . how did you find out?"

"I had Ostap search your valise. He showed me your passport."

He gasped. How had she dared do such a low, underhanded thing! Passports were very personal. "I'm ashamed of you, Mademoiselle."

"Then you don't have to come and play croquet with me." A tear plopped down on her hand which was resting on the keyboard. "I'll play my myself."

He could have faced threats but not tears. "Don't you see I can't," he said, handing her his handkerchief. "What would your mother say?"

"I told her it would give me a chance to practice my French and she said you could play with me."

And so, that afternoon they played croquet, and every afternoon after that. Sonia proved an excellent, if somewhat petulant, teacher. "No, silly, that's not the way to hold your mallet. Here, give me your hand." Whatever little remained of his professorial prestige crumbled away. You simply couldn't be a professor one moment and a pupil the next. Soon they were exchanging confidences, laughing like the youngsters they were. She began calling him by his first name, then, one day, she announced she would call him Volichka.

"That's what I call my big brother, Wladimir, who is in Moscow. I love him very much."

Between games they sat on the grass under a broken-nosed statue and she told him about the pranks she played on her tutors and governesses, and the estates her mother owned all over Europe. The one she liked best was Brailov, in the Ukraine. It had a nice river and a huge forest.

"Perhaps we'll spend next summer there and we'll go in the woods together."

Summer, that year, would not die. October had come and the sky still remained blue and cloudless. Already he should have resumed his studies at the Conservatoire, but under the pretext of finishing his trio he had prevailed upon Madame to write Monsieur Marmontel asking for a fortnight's extension leave, which had been granted. Now even this was coming to an end. Nothing could be done, he must go.

Sadly he took leave of the members of the von Meck retinue. He had a parting drink of vodka with Ostap, who almost crushed him in a final embrace. He promised to write his two colleagues, who, in turn, promised to keep in touch. Madame received him with kindness, expressed herself satisfied with his services and promised to send for him again next summer.

The following morning, as he was packing his meager belongings, the door opened and Sonia stole into the room.

"I couldn't buy you a present because Maman never gives me any money, but I brought you this."

Shyly she held out a small object wrapped in newspaper. It was an ikon of the Virgin of Kazan, grimy with age and soot.

"I stole it from Basil's kitchen," she said simply. "I want you to have it, so you won't forget me. You won't, Volichka, will you?"

He shook his head. She kissed him quickly on the lips and fled out of the room.

◆

It was nearly midnight when the train clattered into Paris. Before leaving Florence he had telegraphed his parents the hour of his arrival, but no one was waiting for him at the station. Valise in hand, he stood under the outside marquee amidst the hubbub of arrival, the calls of luggage porters, the shouts of cabmen maneuvering their horses alongside the curb. It was drizzling, and for an instant he debated taking a fiacre. But fiacres were expensive, especially at night. He raised the collar of his overcoat and plunged into the glistening darkness of the street.

He was tired and drenched to the bone when he reached rue Clapeyron. His arm ached from the weight of his valise. Rain trickled down his neck. He groped through the hallway, greeted by the familiar stench of dankness and stale cooking. He struck a match and began climbing the stairs.

Nothing had changed. He was home.

"We got your telegram," his mother informed him the following day, "but your father's got to be at the office early and he needs his sleep. Besides it was raining."

He said he understood and had not expected anyone to meet him.

For an instant she watched him eat his morning soup, her sallow, bony face softened in a perplexed gentleness.

"I want you to know I appreciated the money you sent this summer," she went on. "I wished I could've stretched it so you didn't have to pay for your keep during this winter, but Adèle got sick and we had to have the doctor. Then the landlord has raised the rent."

This was a bitter disappointment. He had hoped he would not have to give lessons.

"I see," he said quietly. "I'll try to do my best."

That day he went to the Conservatoire to enroll in one of the composition classes.

"I'd like to be in Monsieur Massenet's class," he told the registrar.

"Naturally!" The official let out a sarcastic snort. "Everybody wants to be in Monsieur Massenet's class. Unfortunately, it's already full. All I can do is get you in Monsieur Guiraud's class. And don't look so disgusted. With the kind of marks you have, you're lucky they let you in composition at all."

Claude left the registrar's office in a disgruntled mood, but a few days later he had no more regrets. Of course, Monsieur Guiraud did not have the prestige of Monsieur Massenet, who was a famous opera composer and wore a monocle, but he was a good teacher, young and easygoing. With his straggly beard, his rumpled clothes and flowing tie he looked more like a Montmartre bohemian than a professor at the Conservatoire National de Musique. Even when he corrected your homework in front of the class, he did so in a way that you couldn't get mad at him. As profs went, he was a pretty nice one.

Between classes Claude looked for work. But he no longer went from house to house, seeking piano pupils. He was seeking employment as a part-time pianist in a café or dancing studio. He scanned the newspaper advertisements, and one day he read about an opening as a part-time accompanist in a singing studio. Wages: sixty francs a month.

He ran to the address and was ushered by a buxom maid into a small office crowded with potted palms and oriental bric-a-brac. There he was received by the singing teacher, Madame Moreau-Sainti. For a while she squinted at him from behind her desk, looking in her black taffeta dress like some speculative crow.

"I'm afraid you're too young," she said at last, not unkindly. Then as if she were reluctant to dismiss him without even giving him a chance, she added, "Have you had any experience as an accompanist?"

"Not as an accompanist, Madame, but I've been studying piano for many years at the Conservatoire."

"I'm sure you are a fine pianist. But pianists, as a rule, don't make good accompanists. They always think they're playing a Liszt Hungarian rhapsody and drown the singer."

"I play very softly, Madame. I assure you, Madame, if you'd only give me a chance—"

There was in his voice the pleading urgency of those who cannot afford to be proud, and she felt sorry for this youngster, so attractive, so eager and obviously so poor.

She remained silent, her fleshless hand arched against her cheek, and for the first time he noticed her spectacular ugliness. This kindly woman was the victim of an unjust fate. Her nose was too long, her mouth too thin, her chin too pointed. In addition she was cross-eyed.

"I wish I could help you," she said finally, "but you're really too young."

His heart sank. She wasn't going to give him the job. "Please, Madame. You'll see, if you give me a chance—"

"How old are you?"

"Twenty-one, Madame."

"Come on, tell me the truth."

"Eighteen."

"Eighteen!" she repeated under her breath. "And you have to earn money as well as follow your classes?"

"I have to." His hopes were rising. If only she'd let him talk, he might arouse her sympathy. "You see, Madame, I am the eldest and I must help because Father doesn't earn much and my brothers are still too young to go to work. And then—"

She let him talk, barely listening to his piteous, all too familiar story. Too many children and not enough money . . . There were thousands of families similar to his in Paris. The father, some white-collar nonentity; the mother, tired-faced, tired-limbed, worn out by a lifetime of household chores. The whole family squeezed into some four- or five-room apartment . . . And amidst all this shabbiness, this mediocrity—this handsome, lustrous-eyed boy of eighteen.

"And now what do you want to do? Become a concert pianist?"

"Oh, no, Madame. I'd like to be a composer."

"My God, what a profession! Isn't it very hard to earn any money as a composer?"

"Yes, but if you win the Grand Prix de Rome—"

"Isn't it frightfully difficult?" Like everyone in France she was awed by this most famous, most arduous of all academic awards.

"It is, but I still have two years." He smiled, and his smile enchanted her. "Maybe, if I work very hard—"

"That's just it. How will you be able to work if you come here every day?"

"I'll work at night."

She winced, angry at him for bringing his poverty into her cozy, cluttered office. "You are a most interesting young man, but, as I said, you're too young. Much too young."

His knees almost buckled under him. It all had been in vain. She wasn't going to give him the job after all . . . "Please, Madame!"

The words came out of his misery, like a call for help. "Please, Madame, give me a chance."

She hesitated, then she said, "All right. I'm an old fool, but I'll give you a chance."

"You will? You really will?" Rapture illuminated his face.

"Yes, I will . . . Mind you, it's just a try. I don't think you'll be able to fill the position, but I'm going to take a chance. Now listen, you must be here every day from five to eight."

"Yes, Madame. From five to eight. That's fine. My last class ends at four."

"And remember, no smoking in the music room."

"No, Madame. Of course not. Smoking's bad for the throat."

"And no talking with the pupils. Understand?"

"Yes, Madame. I understand perfectly. You can rest assured—"

Already he was bowing, fumbling with his hat, anxious to be off before she changed her mind. Halfway across the room he stopped and turned around. "I forgot. When do you want me to start?"

"Tomorrow, if you can."

"Certainly, Madame. I'll be here. Without fail. You can depend on me."

His words trailed after him.

She watched him dash out of the room. Eighteen! She could have a son his age. She was a fool to give him the job . . . What would her pupils say when they saw this youngster? Well, let them say what they wanted . . .

She pulled a handkerchief from her sleeve and defiantly blew her nose.

◆

He ran down the stairs in a clatter of hobnailed shoes, racing along the corridors between floors, afraid she might call him back. When he reached the street, he stopped in the doorway, panting, tugging at his tie. He had the job! Sixty francs a month, more than he had ever earned with lessons. Maman would be pleased.

Before him the avenue rumbled with the bustle of late-afternoon traffic, the pounding of hoofbeats on the wood pavement, the bells of horsecars, the whistles of gendarmes. The forlorn November day was dissolving into a clammy fog that blurred the street lights and the carriage lanterns.

He found his family having dinner in the kitchen, his father sitting at the head of the table.

"Did you get the job?" asked his mother, as he walked in.

"She said she'd give me a chance." He took his place at the table and began ladling soup into his plate.

"How much will you get?"

"Sixty francs a month."

"Sixty!" Manuel Debussy dabbed his moustache with his napkin. "I always said there's money in music if you know how to go about it."

Claude felt his eyes on him, heavy with rancor of the vanished Mozart dream.

"I must be there every day from five to eight," he said, to create a diversion.

His mother leaned forward across the table. "Did you ask for an advance, like I told you?"

He remained silent, his spoon in mid-air.

"Well, did you?"

"I'm sorry, Maman. I forgot."

Silence fell around the table. Until two years ago, he would have been slapped for that, now they did not slap him any more, but everyone's eyes focused on him.

"So you forgot," said his father with ominous calm.

Claude recognized this tone of voice. In the old days it preceded the slamming of the ruler on his knuckles.

"I'm sorry. I really am, but she almost didn't give me the job and—"

What good does it do to be sorry? Your mother told you to ask for an advance, because she needs the money—and you forgot!" His face had turned a purplish red. "How'd you like it if she forgot to cook your dinner?"

"I'll ask her tomorrow."

"And don't forget it."

They finished eating in silence, eating with the grudging reverence the poor give to food. At dessert his sister Adèle created a brief diversion by quarreling with her younger brothers over her portion of marmalade. For an instant the kitchen resounded with the shrillness of their young voices, until their father rapped on the table.

"Enough of that," he grumbled benevolently. "You three stop fighting and eat what your mother gives you."

The disorder subsided at once. Like a benign autocrat he ran his bulging eyes over the table. How sweet after the day's servility at the office and the rebuffs of superiors, to be master in one's home, to lay down the law, if only to children . . .

Dinner ended in silence. Manuel Debussy drained his wine, crumpled his napkin and rose from the table, announcing that he was going to take a breath of fresh air. They all knew it meant he was on his way to the corner bistro for his *café-rhum* and game of bezique with neighborhood cronies. They watched him struggle into his overcoat and chorused their *"Bonsoir, Papa"* as he stepped out of the kitchen. At once the younger boys dashed out of the room. Claude remained seated, watching his sister and mother clear the table.

"Want me to help with the dishes?" he offered.

"We go faster by ourselves," his mother said, walking to the sink. Without pausing, she went on, "If you're going to work till eight every night, you won't be home for supper. I'll leave something for you on the stove, so you'll have something to eat when you come home."

"Thank you, Maman."

He could not find anything more to say. She had slapped him too hard and too often as a child. There had never been love between them. Now they were strangers. A few times they had groped awkwardly toward each other, but it was too late, and they were too far apart. She belonged to a world of artisans for whom work meant manual toil and regular pay. Music was too alien for her to understand.

He lingered at the table a moment longer, feeling unwanted and useless, watching his mother shuffle about in her worn slippers. Finally he got up, said, "Good night, Maman! Good night, Adèle!" and went to his room.

He closed the door behind him and made his way to the window. From his pocket he took a cigarette. Two cigarettes cost one sou, and whenever he could he bought a pair which he smoked as a gesture of defiance, an assertion of independence. He struck a match and the sulphur sizzled in his cupped hands. Around him the room leaped to a brief, blazing life—its narrow cot against the wall, the washstand, the piano, the small table littered with books and music paper. Then the match went out, and darkness closed in again.

He stood in front of the window, smoking, watching the tip of his cigarette blink red in the windowpane like a distant railroad signal. His thoughts wandered back to his interview with the singing teacher. God, how ugly she was! But she was nice, she'd given him the job. At least he wouldn't have supper with his family any more and his father wouldn't humiliate him at the table, like tonight . . .

Why was he so different from his brothers, from everyone in his family?

From the nearby railroad station, the whistle of a departing train drilled through the night and brought him back to reality. He turned around and lit the lamp on the table. He sat down, took his counterpoint manual; then, tilting his chair back against the wall, he began preparing his lesson for the next day. Squinting through the smoke of his cigarette and stifling an occasional yawn he analyzed several examples of invertible counterpoint and learned that double counterpoint offered only two possibilities—the original and its inversion—whereas triple counterpoint offered six possibilities—the original and five inversions. He found the subject rather unexciting. Not difficult really, but boring. Then he studied examples of double counterpoint in connection with double fugue and found them still more boring. Rules, rules, rules. You couldn't do this, you couldn't do that. Why? Because it was forbidden. Why was it forbidden? Because the Masters had said so, and that was that.

He tossed the book on the table, stretched out with a long grunt of fatigue and ruffled his curly hair. His eyes turned to the window, and for an instant he listened to the gentle drumming of rain against the windowpane. There was music in the rain, if you listened closely. Not the kind the Masters had written, with a lot of triple counterpoint and all that. Another kind. Soft, liquid, without any rules . . .

Come on, there was no time to think about that. He was getting sleepy, and he still must do his homework and write six variations on a theme by Beethoven, with modulations in the diatonic, chromatic and enharmonic classes. This also was a bore, but it couldn't be helped . . . He took his pen, hunched over his music paper and jotted down the theme. Then he began searching for his harmony manual through the jumble of books, music scores, pencils and empty match boxes on the table.

His eyes fell on a battered volume of poetry he had bought in a bookstall along the quays. He opened it at random and half aloud read "Nuit d'Etoiles," by Theodore de Banville. He shut his eyes as wisps of sound arose in his brain, faint at first, but growing more distinct, becoming music, then melody, then song. For a while it filled his whole being. Then it vanished.

He opened his eyes, snatched a sheet of music paper and hurriedly noted down the melody. In the silence of his room, time stood still. Nothing existed but the enchantment of his own music. It was past three o'clock when he came out of his trance.*

---

* Debussy dedicated "Nuit d'Etoiles" to the singing teacher, Madame Moreau-Sainti. It was the first song he ever sold. He received fifty francs for it. Published only many years later, the song earned a fortune for the publisher.

Suddenly he remembered his homework.

"Oh, my God," he muttered, "he'll be mad as a hornet!"

He returned to Beethoven's theme, but his lids were heavy, gritty with sleep. The staves quivered before his eyes. His brain, a moment ago so alert, was now sluggish, drained of thought. For a while he fought the creeping numbness, trying to remember the rules of diatonic modulation. It was no use. Everything whirled in his head.

All of a sudden he toppled forward on the table, and with his face buried in his arms, fell asleep.

He was right. The next day Monsieur Guiraud was mad as a hornet.

"I will have a few words with you after class," he said.

The class over, Claude walked to the teacher's platform and waited for the lecture to come. From his desk Monsieur Guiraud frowned down on him, rubbing his bearded chin. Unhurriedly he scanned the pale handsome face, the tangle of black curls over the enormous, strangely convex forehead. Beethoven's forehead, he thought . . .

"Well, now tell me why you didn't do your homework," he began.

"I started to, Master, but I fell asleep."

"And you fell asleep because you were tired, and you were tired because, instead of studying, you probably wrote some silly little song." A web of fine wrinkles fanned out of the corners of his eyes. "Do you know why I know? Because I used to do the same thing when I was your age. Now show me that masterpiece of yours."

Sheepishly Claude pulled the manuscript from between the pages of his composition manual and held it out to his teacher.

"It's good," said Monsieur Guiraud after reading it. "A little immature, but good. The melody is fresh, and there are some original harmonies. But you'll never win the Grand Prix de Rome by writing songs." He saw the flash of wonder in Claude's eyes and a smile came to his homely, sensitive face. "I know, it's not easy. But I won it, and you can do the same."

He paused and began sorting the books on his desk.

"Also, I've noticed you don't mix with your classmates. You should make friends with them, have a beer together at the café, damn Beethoven and Bach and the profs. We used to do that when I was a student and they still do it, I am sure. Don't live too much in yourself, it's not good at your age. Now, run away and do your homework in the future."

"Yes, Master."

One minute later he was out of the building, hurrying to the singing studio. Things had gone better than he expected. Monsieur Guiraud was really pretty nice . . .

CHAPTER

THEREAFTER HE WENT EVERY AFTERNOON TO MADAME MOREAU-Sainti's and assisted her pupils in the art of *bel canto*. Most of them were middle-aged ladies who studied singing to fill a few hours of their time. Patiently he watched them do their breathing exercises, listened to their scales, their preliminary mimimimimis and tralalalalas. He grew used to the agitated bosoms, cavernous mouths howling fortissimos and puckered lips purring dolcissimos. He survived numberless renditions of Gounod's *Ave Maria* and Carmen's *Habañera*, as well as pastorales, lullabies, serenades, operatic arias and drawing-room romances. When Madame Gibet bleated about withered rose petals in yellowed love letters, the piano all but wept under his fingers; but when Madame Druchon, a hot-eyed, bilious housewife, bellowed about kiiiiiiiii-sses in the Sahaaaaaaa-ra or in the moonlit gardens of Istanbuuuuuuuuul, he provided the proper sensuous, passionate musical background.

Madame Moreau-Sainti drenched them in compliments. "Your legato, my dear Madame, is simply exquisite. Absolutely professional . . ." Or, "Today you sang even better than usual. Your high notes were pure crystal . . ."

After lessons she sometimes chatted with Claude. "You've got to encourage them," she would remark. "Most of them know they are about through as women and they study singing as they dye their hair or have massages, as a last attempt to attract some attention, receive a few compliments. It makes them feel young a little longer. It's really rather sad."

They were becoming friends. He no longer winced at her ugliness. Behind her disastrous face he learned to see the mind that was keen and the heart that was kind. They sensed each other's loneliness, and it created a bond between them. Occasionally they dined together in the small dining room adjoining the studio. In time she told him about herself.

"If I were a writer," she remarked wistfully one evening, "I would write the story of my life and call it 'The Story of an Ugly Woman.' "

Because of her looks her life had been a long, silent martyrdom. She loved children but when she tried to pet them they put out their tongues at her and ran. At school her classmates had sharpened their young claws on her. Her husband, a devout and promising colonial official who had married her for her dowry and a chance to practice the virtue of chastity, had found himself unable to endure the daily sight of her and had taken to drink and riotous living before dying from remorse and absinthe in a Tunis brothel.

The shock of his death and the discovery that he had squandered her fortune had caused her to lose her hair. This final visitation had almost broken her spirit. For a while she had contemplated suicide. Being a brave as well as a sensible woman, she had bought a wig instead and gone to work. In ten years she had become a successful singing teacher.

"I've done well," she went on, "but I think I will retire in two or three years. I'll buy a little house in the country with a nice garden. A garden is the nearest thing to a child. It gives you almost as much worry and as much joy. And it never leaves you."

Now he saw very little of his family. It was long past dinnertime when he came home. In the kitchen he found the stew that his mother left on the stove for him. Absently he wolfed it down on a corner of the table, washed his plate and tiptoed to his room. His home became a mere lodging, a place to work and sleep.

He followed his teacher's advice and made friends with some of his classmates and students from the other composition classes. He now had a little money of his own and was able to join them in a glass of beer in bistros near the Conservatoire. He took part in their discussions, damned Beethoven and Bach, called them "old perukes" and declared war on harmony, counterpoint and all musical rules. Together they sometimes went to the Opéra, where a box was reserved for the composition students of the Conservatoire.

In the spring Madame Moreau-Sainti raised his salary to seventy francs. He did not mention it at home, and with the money bought a beautiful Japanese print, which he tacked on the wall of his room. Early in June she closed her studio for the summer and made him promise to return in October. As they were saying good-bye she slipped a fifty-franc note into his hand.

"This is a little bonus." She smiled. "You've done very well."

He had never had so much money and he immediately bought another, much more expensive, Japanese print.

A week before the annual closing of the Conservatoire, he received a letter from Madame von Meck's secretary. Again he was informed that Madame was pleased to engage his services for the next three months and expected him to join her as soon as possible.

This time at her Brailov estate, in the south of Russia.

◆

Brailov was more than an estate, it was almost a small province. It spread for miles in all directions. It included several villages, a private railroad station, an ancient monastery, deep trackless woods, green pastures, a lake, a river, wheat fields that stretched out endlessly to the horizon; and in the middle of all that, a regal white marble palace rising amidst an intricate pattern of sanded paths and flower beds aigretted with gushing fountains. Two miles from the mansion, on the bank of the river, there was another, smaller, self-contained estate with a picturesque country house that was used as a guest cottage. It was called Simaki.*

Madame seemed genuinely pleased to see Claude again.

"My little Bussyk, I've missed your fine piano playing," she said with a pale smile. "Now remember, you must be firm with Sonia. She hasn't made any progress since you left."

He had just returned to his room when Sonia burst in panting, her blond braids flying.

"Oh, Volichka, my dove, I missed you so! I thought of you every day. Kiss me."

He complied. Several times and with increasing pleasure. She looked even prettier than the year before. She had grown a good deal. Her hair had turned the color of champagne, her brown eyes had become softer.

---

* It was at Simaki that Tchaikowsky resided when he was Madame von Meck's guest in June, 1879. From there the "beloved friend," as she called him, wrote her every day, sometimes twice a day, sending his letters by his valet Alexis, but never addressing her in person. During the twelve years of their friendship they exchanged thousands of letters, reciprocated formal bows on two occasions, but never spoke a word to each other.

Tchaikowsky's Fourth Symphony is dedicated to Madame von Meck, who helped him financially and thus permitted him to devote his full time to composition.

"That's enough," she said, pushing him away. "Now listen, Maman said it was all right for us to have French conversations, and we'll talk French together. But not here; in the woods, where we won't be disturbed. Tomorrow I'll come and pick you up after the concert."

She did pick him up the following afternoon and led him through the forest to a mossy nook which could be reached only by crawling through heavy shrubs.

"Nobody will find us here," she explained, lying down on the ground. "Besides, Ostap is watching. If someone comes, he will whistle and we will escape."

Ostap, she went on, was her slave. He belonged to her, body and soul. As a child she had bounced on his knees and played with his fearful silver dagger. He would do anything for her without any question.

"He loves Maman, but he loves me even more."

From then on they often went to their mossy retreat. There they lay, side by side, innocent and happy, their fingers entwined, listening to the ripple of the river and the rustle of leaves.

He grew used to her long, meditative silences followed by explosive outbursts of speech.

"It's really very simple," she declared suddenly one afternoon.

"What are you talking about?"

"Love, naturally."

Love, she explained, was a mysterious, irresistible force. When two people were born to love each other, nothing could tear them apart. They simply had to live or die together.

"Romeo and Juliet, for instance. My English tutor told me about them. Well, they were born for each other. We are like them, aren't we, Volichka?"

He had never thought about it, but he said they were, they certainly were.

"If life separated us, I'd kill myself," she continued. As he remained silent she turned to him, somewhat impatiently. "And you, would you kill yourself?"

Of course he would. But did she have to talk about death and killing themselves and that sort of thing? Love was something pleasant, to be shared and enjoyed.

"And you're absolutely right about our being born for each other," he went on, his hand creeping gently toward her breast. "We just can't help ourselves."

It was then that he got his first slap.

"Now, why did you do that?" he protested.

Petulantly she told him that he was just like all Frenchmen, who, everyone knew, were lewd and disgusting, interested only in bad things.

She then treated him to a lecture on the two kinds of love. The bad kind concerned itself with the body, which was a mere shell, perishable and worthless. It provided some fleeting moments of pleasure, but it really meant nothing. In short, it was the wrong kind of love.

"That's the kind you like," she said pointedly.

Then there was a good kind. It consisted in looking at each other, holding hands, listening to the birds and the beat of their hearts, exchanging kisses, but nothing else, lying side by side in the woods, as they did now. It was a communion of souls.

"That's the kind I like."

At once he was converted. She was absolutely right. From now on there would be nothing between them but this communion of souls, this harmonious beating of hearts. To make sure that hers beat in unison with his he pressed his ear against her chest. It wasn't his fault if her budding breast happened to be in the way . . .

It got him another slap and another lecture.

Life at Brailov, however, was not all slaps and love in the bushes. There were the early-morning rehearsals with his two fellow musicians, Sonia's piano lessons, the afternoon concerts in Madame's drawing room.

He played Piotr Ilyich's music better every day, and his employer was delighted with him.

"You are playing with much feeling and sensitiveness, my little Bussyk. In a few years, if you work hard, you will play like our great Russian pianists."

In her mouth there was no higher praise.

Occasionally she inquired about Sonia's progress at the piano. Without batting an eye he replied that Mademoiselle Sonia was doing very well.

"How is her French?"

"Getting better and better."

It was true. As summer advanced, her French greatly improved. So did her knowledge of the French character. In her opinion it left much to be desired. Claude, she found, had no inclination for the communion of souls.

One day, as his hand wandered far afield, she snatched it back with the startling remark, "We'll do those things when we're married."

"Married?"

"Of course. We love each other, don't we, Volinchka? Then we must get married."

This came as a surprise to him, but he said nothing. She had it all mapped out. They would be married in four or five years and live in Moscow. Moskva, as she called it.

"But not in Maman's house. In a house of our own. I saw one I liked very much on Tverskaya Street. I'll ask Maman to buy it for us. If she says no, I'll ask my brother."

"It sounds nice," he said. "But wouldn't you like to live in Paris? It's a beautiful city."

She waved the suggestion aside. Paris was fine for two weeks in the spring to buy clothes, but it simply did not compare with Moskva.

"Oh, Volichka, you'll see how beautiful it is! Especially in winter when the snow crackles under your boots and you can skate on the river."

She would show him the Kremlin, where the Czar stayed when he came down from Saint Petersburg. They would visit the wonderful Pokrovsky Cathedral that had towers of every color and shape. One looked like an onion, another like a melon, another like a pineapple, and so on. They would drive to Kitay Gorod, with its wonderful bazaars, dine and drink champagne in elegant restaurants where they played gypsy music.

"One day we'll go to Tolkuchy Rynok, that's the thieves' market."

There was no stopping her. Silently he said good-bye to Paris, the chestnut-lined avenues, the sidewalk cafés, the bookstalls along the quays . . .

"I hadn't thought of living in Moscow," he said when she paused to take a breath, "but I'm sure I'll like it very much."

Well, that was settled. Now all he had to do was to learn about Russia and become a Russian.

"I'll teach you," she said.

Slowly summer was reaching its zenith. In the August sunshine the wheat stood ripe and golden in the fields. Claude lived enchanted days. Never, since the Aunt Tavie years, had he been so happy. Soon he would be nineteen. He was in love. And each afternoon, in their secret hideaway, the object of his love went on with his Russian education.

First he must learn that Russians loved to cry and they cried most when they were happiest. Didn't Maman cry when he played Piotr Ilyich's music? They also loved to dance and get drunk on vodka. When angry they spat in each other's faces, but this applied mostly to uneducated people, like *muzhiks* and monks. Gentlemen killed each other in duels, like the great poet Pushkin, who had been killed in one. Or they played Russian roulette, a very dangerous game.

"If you meet a priest in the street you must spit three times over your shoulder to avert the Evil Eye."

Another thing. Russians loved tea and traveled with their own brand. Also, their own sugar. Also, their own bed linen, for they hated to be bitten by other people's bedbugs.

"Now you must learn to speak Russian. You'll see, it's very simple."

And so it went. Around them all was peace and sunshine. Time, it seemed, had stopped. But it hadn't. It slid on, silently, furtively, like a thief. In a slow arpeggio of luminous days and star-studded nights September went by. Again it was time to say good-bye.

Now, in the mossy nook, Sonia wept, and he learned that Russians cried not only when they were happy, but also when they were not. Their last meetings were tender and sad. She had no heart to teach him Russian any more or he to misbehave.

"We will love each other always. Won't we, Volichka?" she said the day before he left.

"Always."

Always . . . It became their secret password, and she breathed it in his ear as they said good-bye at the station and he climbed into the train that was taking him back to faraway Paris.

♦

Autumn had laid its golden mantle over Paris. In the parks, the russet trees looked like giant chrysanthemums, but he did not see them. Nor did he see the people in the streets, faceless strangers among whom he passed, lost in dream. At the Conservatoire he gazed out of the window, thinking about Sonia, or stared at the ceiling, patiently waiting for the recess bell.

When it rang on that particular morning he rushed to go out, but was called back by Monsieur Guiraud.

"How long are you going to act like an idiot and look like a lovesick calf? If you are fascinated by the cracks in the ceiling, you may come here and gape at them to your heart's content, but not during my class, while I'm killing myself to teach you how to write music."

"Yes, Master."

"Now go home and get to work or I'll break your neck."

"Yes, Master."

Monsieur Guiraud's words had no effect on Claude. His heart and mind remained in Brailov. When he should have been doing his homework, he copied the Russian alphabet. Instead of studying his counterpoint manual he lay down on his cot, remembering the summer days.

Six weeks after his return he still was in a daze. Even Madame Moreau-Sainti was beginning to lose patience.

"What's the matter with you? You didn't fall in love with one of those Russian girls, did you?"

He gave her a fey smile and said nothing.

"You're still a little young to fall in love. Wait a few more years. You have all the time in the world to be miserable."

A few days later she rustled into the studio escorting a blond, slender, extraordinarily beautiful woman in a gray dress and modest fur piece. He rose from the piano stool and bowed. She nodded back while removing her gloves. The lesson began. When it was over, she said, "Thank you, Monsieur," and walked away.

"Did you ever see anyone so beautiful?" cried Madame Moreau-Sainti excitedly, after seeing her to the door. "How old would you says she is? Twenty-nine . . . thirty. Now why on earth should a woman like that want to study singing?"

For an instant she paused, lost in speculation, a finger tapping her chin.

"Bored, I suppose," she muttered to herself. "Her husband is quite an old man."

The new pupil came twice a week. Claude noticed that her hair was not really blond, but tawny. Her eyes, which he had thought brown, were hazel. When the light touched them they turned chartreuse, almost amber. She practiced her scales dutifully but did not exert herself. She had a high soprano voice that was naturally pure and required little training. When she received a compliment she smiled in a calm, faintly amused way. Toward him she remained polite, but somewhat distant. He decided that, like all beautiful women, she must be cold and rather stuck-up.

"She came to see me in my office the other day," Madame Moreau-Sainti remarked one evening, as they were dining together. "We talked about you."

"Me?"

"I told her you're preparing for the Grand Prix de Rome, and she said what a good accompanist you were. She asked me if you could coach her privately for some kind of musicale or concert her husband has arranged."

"I don't have any free time, except on Sundays."

"That's what I told her, but you aren't doing anything particular on Sundays are you? And you probably could use some extra money."

"Yes, I guess we could."

"Well then, go and see her next Sunday afternoon and bring your songs with you. I told her you've written some very nice ones and she said she'd like to hear them."

The following Sunday he called on the new pupil. She opened the door and peered inquiringly in the dimness of the landing.

"Oh, it's you." She smiled, recognizing him. "I wasn't sure you'd come. Please come in."

It was the first time he had seen her without a hat. In her simple blouse and skirt she looked younger. And even more beautiful.

She led him into the drawing room and waved him to a chair.

"I see you've brought your songs," she said, noticing the roll of music paper in his hand. "Perhaps you will play one for me later on?"

He did not reply, but remained motionless in his chair, overwhelmed by the multitude of paintings that blanketed the walls, frame to frame, up to the ceiling. There were thatch-roofed farms in the sunset, stormy waves crashing against cliffs, plums spilling out of baskets, cherries spilling out of baskets, strawberries spilling out of baskets; cavalry men charging joyously to their death, sabers high and a song on their lips; cardinals sipping port, cardinals playing chess, bishops dozing in their chairs; naked young women with eyes turned heavenward and the palm of martyrdom in one hand; naked young women with flowing blond hair doing nothing; naked young women reclining on pillows, lust in their eyes and a rose between their teeth; sloe-eyed odalisques about to enter the harem bath; kneeling nuns; Italian beggars in tatters; tense Spanish women, skirts awhirl and castanets in hands, dancing the fandango. And over the mantelpiece, a large canvas showing Napoleon in his tent, alone and gloomy, peering down by candlelight on a map, presumably before Waterloo.

"I see you're looking at our paintings," she said with a smile. "The effect is rather staggering, isn't it?"

"I've never seen so many paintings in one room."

"None of them is very good, but the frames are superb. Once I told Pierre, my husband, that if we ever became very poor we could live off them for a while." She chuckled softly. "He was furious and said I had no appreciation of the arts."

He looked at her, surprised to find her so different from the reserved, rather cold woman who came to the studio.

"You see," she went on, "Pierre knows a great many artists, and artists are very touchy. If they give you a painting they expect you to look at it for the rest of your life." She paused hesitantly. "Would you play one of your songs before my husband returns?"

He walked to the upright piano in the corner and she sat next to him on the bench. As he started playing she leaned forward to read the words. Soon she hummed fragments of the melody. Then, encouraged by his smile, she began to sing. To him it was an ecstatic revelation. No one had ever sung his songs. They had echoed in his head like the sound of waves in a shell. And suddenly this one was coming to life on the lips of this lovely woman.

"It's beautiful," she murmured when he finished playing. "What's the title?"

"*Nuit d'Etoiles.* I dedicated it to Madame Moreau-Sainti."

"Please play it again."

He did. Then another, then another, until they no longer could read the music. Around them the room had become dark and shadowy, cloaking them in a suspect, almost guilty intimacy. For an instant they were acutely aware of their nearness.

She sprang to her feet. "Please forgive me for making you play so long. I can't image what's happened to Pierre, he should've been home an hour ago. If you want to go now, please don't hesitate to say so. Unless—unless you wouldn't mind having a cup of tea with me. Surely he'll be back by then."

They passed into her sitting room. "Make yourself comfortable while I go and prepare tea. The maid is out with the children. Every Sunday they visit their aunt."

She went out and he looked about the room. It was small, sparsely furnished, with none of the artistic pretentiousness of the drawing room, but it had an air of genteel, lived-in intimacy, which the drawing room did not have. In the fireplace two logs were burning silently.

She returned carrying a tray, which she set on a table, and took her place by the fire. "Pierre says this room is a disgrace, but I like it better than the drawing room."

"So do I," he said sincerely. "I like it very much."

The visit was not turning out at all as he had expected. To his surprise he found he was enjoying himself. It was nice sitting here in this cozy little room, having tea with this beautiful and friendly woman who sangs his songs so well.

She asked him about the Conservatoire. How long had he been there? Was he a good student?

"Are you really preparing for the Grand Prix de Rome, as Madame Moreau-Sainti says?"

"In theory every composition student is preparing for the Grand Prix"—he gobbled another biscuit—"and in two or three years I may have a try at it, but I'll never make it."

Why? Was it so very difficult? . . . Difficult! You practically had to be a genius to survive the elminations. Let alone the final test.

"In the eliminations they lock you up in a room for a week and you're supposed to write a fugue and a small cantata. But in the final they really crack down on you. This time you're locked up for three weeks and you must write a long dramatic cantata with solo voices, choral ensembles, full orchestration. Practically the Ninth Symphony."

"Why is it called Grand Prix de Rome?"

"Because the winner is sent to Rome, where he lives three years at the taxpayers' expense with nothing to do but breathe the creative Roman atmosphere and write each year a large composition. Something really big and boring, like a mass or an oratorio."

In this way another hour passed. The clock on the mantelpiece chimed.

"I really don't know what's keeping Pierre, he was so anxious to see you."

"It's about some sort of musicale, isn't it?"

"If it were, I wouldn't mind so much. In a musicale you are among friends and they can do nothing but applaud. But it's a public concert at the Flaxhand Hall with the critics and everything. I didn't want to do it, but I was forced into it."

A friend of her husband's, Monsieur Thieberg, a concert violinist, had come to dinner a few weeks ago and told them he was in a serious predicament. He had reserved the Flaxhand Hall for his spring concert, and suddenly the vocalist who was to share the program with him had announced she was unable to do so. A few other professional singers he had approached had commitments on that date. There he was with a concert hall on his hands and no singer.

"He then asked me if, as a favor, I would help him. Naturally I told him I was only an amateur and never had sung in a concert. But he and my husband pleaded so long I finally said I'd do it. The next day I told Pierre I wouldn't sing unless I had a good accompanist, and since he didn't know any, I suggested he might ask you whether you'd come here and help me with those songs."

For an instant she gazed down at her hands. Then, raising her hazel eyes, she looked full at him. "Would you?"

♦

Thereafter he came every Sunday afternoon. He played his songs for her and she loved them. He met her husband, a friendly, loquacious, white-bearded architect, and her two small children. He learned that her name was Alix.

"Not Alice, but Alix—with an x. Father had a weakness for sixteenth-century names."

He also met Monsieur Thieberg. A general conference was held and the concert's program discussed. Alix agreed to sing an operatic aria after the first violin number, but she insisted on singing two of Claude's songs. "If I sing songs people have never heard, they won't pay so much attention to my voice." Monsieur Thieberg hesitated, then gracefully gave in.

A sort of routine established itself. He arrived early, as early as he dared, and for an hour or so they practiced in the drawing room.

Occasionally her husband made an appearance, looking very dapper in his double-breasted redingote, effusively polite, showing his yellow teeth in his white beard. He would listen for a few minutes, a finger to his temple, in an attitude of total absorption; then, mentioning some unavoidable social engagement, he would be off in a cloud of compliments and good wishes.

The rehearsal over, they would go into her sitting room, take their places by the fire and have tea. This was the part he liked best. Over their cups they would chat about all sorts of things: the man who had fallen into the bear hole at the zoo, the journalist who had traveled all the way from Vienna in a cab, the scientist who had discovered that Paris was built on a volcano and might explode at any moment.

Before long he told her about Aunt Tavie. For years he had longed to talk about her. Twice he had gone to visit Madame Mauté, but his former teacher was too ill for conversation. For a minute she had held his hands in hers, smiled at him with her eyes, then fallen back on the pillow. Now he had someone willing to listen, and he poured out his childhood memories. How lovely she had been, their games in the garden at Cannes, their walks, hand in hand, on the boulevards.

"During our last summer together we used to sit in public squares," he said one afternoon. "The sunshine did her good."

She saw that his eyes were moist. "Did you ever hear from her?"

He shook his head, fighting back the tears. "No, but I still dream about her sometimes."

Gradually he began telling her about his family, his father and his Mozart dream, the piano lessons to neighborhood children, the lonely Sundays in railway stations with a book, the two wonderful summers he had spent with Madame von Meck.

At last he could not hold his secret any longer and told her about Sonia.

"I didn't tell anyone about her, but I feel I can trust you."

She was touched by his naïveté, his faith in her. "I'll never betray your confidence."

That was all he needed. He plunged into his story like a retrieving dog into water, starting with the early piano lessons when she called him *Monsieur le Professeur* and the croquet games in Florence; then Brailov, their French conversations on the river bank, her slaps, her lectures on the communion of souls.

"She said all Frenchmen were lewd and disgusting, and I was like the rest of them."

She smiled over her knitting. How young and naïve he was! Poverty had done that to him. He had been too busy earning money to think much about women, and he had been spared the usual initiation with hardened prostitutes or the backstairs rendezvous with neighborhood girls . . .

"We plan to be married. We've discussed it seriously and decided it was the best thing. Not right away, in four or five years."

"That's very wise," she murmured, relieved.

"We'll be living in Moscow. She has already found the house for us. But she said we'd come to Paris every year for two or three weeks."

She was on the verge of warning him that fifteen-year-old girls said many foolish things, but she did not have the heart to spoil his happiness. Let him have his dream.

"I think you have the whole thing very well planned."

He thought her the most wonderful, most understanding woman in the world, and because she was wonderful and understood everything he also told her about his classes at the Conserv, his teachers, his classmates. She became acquainted with the rivalry between the three composition classes for the annual contest of the Gand Prix de Rome and grew familiar with the school's slang. She learned that a professor was a prof. If he were a severe prof, he then became a "cow" or a "camel." A hard-working student was a "beaver."

But most of all he told her what he thought of harmony, counterpoint and all musical rules.

"Perhaps you think music is something you write with your heart, but it isn't. It's nothing but rules. Everything that's nice is forbidden. Take parallel fifths, for instance—"

"What's a parallel fifth?"

Impatiently he explained. "A succession of fifth-degree chords."

"Thank you. You've made it very clear."

"Anyway, they're forbidden. And why? Because some old peruke, like Bach or Beethoven, didn't like them. So nobody can use them. In modulations alone, there are enough rules to drive you crazy. And the modes!"

"What's a mode? After all, I haven't been at the Conserv."

He gave her a long-suffering look, as though everyone in the world knew what a musical mode was. "It's the various arrangements of the diatonic tones of an octave."

"I see." She decided not to ask any more questions.

"There are three great modes: Greek, Gregorian and Modern. Well, just to give you an idea, the Greek mode alone is divided into Dorian and Hypodorian, Phrygian and Hypophrygian and Mixoledian."

"How interesting!"

"Once Monsieur Durand, the harmony prof, a regular camel, tried to trick me. He asked me to explain the Hypomixoledian mode. He must've thought I was an imbecile. But I just laughed, because obviously the Hypomixoledian is the same as Dorian, so the joke was on him and everybody laughed. But he gave me a demerit just the same."

One by one she learned the names of his favorite schoolmates: Gabriel Pierné, Paul Vidal, Georges Marty. All terrific beavers who could recite the modulation rules in their sleep, all preparing for the annual contest of the Grand Prix de Rome.

"That's why I'll never win it, but I don't care. It doesn't mean anything anyway."

Although they were beavers, they were nice fellows and it was fun having a beer with them, going together to the Opéra in the students' box without paying a sou. But, of course, with them you never could talk of anything intimate or personal, like Aunt Tavie or Sonia . . .

"That's why I'm so grateful to you for letting me come here on Sundays." Suddenly his bashfulness had returned. "To you I feel I can say anything . . . Since I've known you, I'm not lonely any more. Sometimes I feel so happy I'd like to do something silly, like climbing a lamppost or dancing in the street . . ."

She watched his handsome, happy face, his gleaming black eyes. Yes, she had done that for him, she had given him friendship. That was all he needed. Someone to talk to, someone who would listen. Now he was bursting with high spirits, like a frisky colt that rolled in the grass, just for the fun of it. Well, let him climb lampposts, if he wanted to. One of these days he probably would do some foolishness, but even that would be better than spending his Sundays in a railway station . . .

So she was not overly surprised when, one Sunday, he told her that he had been thrown out of the Opéra.

"It wasn't my fault," he began defiantly. "I was in the students' box with my friends and those stupid gendarmes picked on me."

"Why did they pick on you rather than on someone else? And what were the gendarmes doing at the Opéra in the first place?"

"You see, it was the première of *Namouna,* and some jealous imbeciles were trying to ruin the performance. So, after the curtain rose, they started laughing very loud, calling each other across the room. Naturally I couldn't sit there and do nothing, could I? After all I was entitled to see a performance, wasn't I?"

"Go on," she said quietly.

"Well, I leaned over the box railing and spotted one of them, an old man, a big fat pig that was laughing like a hyena, and I shouted at him that he was a German spy, a cuckold, and that his mother had been scared by a horse and that's why he looked like one, and if he just waited a minute I'd come down and spit in his face. I was right, wasn't I?" He looked at her with eyes of grieved innocence. "After all, he was disturbing the performance."

"Never mind. Then what happened?"

"Just at that moment two gendarmes burst into the box, grabbed me under the arms and dragged me to the director's office. I fought all the way, but they were big, husky brutes and you know how *flics* are . . . Anyway, they threw me into the director's office and said I was making more noise than anyone else, which was not true. It was a lie. I assure you, I wasn't—"

"And what did the director say?"

"He said I was a ruffian and I had disgraced the Temple of Music— that's what he called the Opéra, the Temple of Music!—and dishonored the Conservatoire, and a lot of hogwash of that kind. Finally he took my name, said I would hear from him. Then he told the *flics* to throw me out of the building."

Again the two brutes had seized him by the arms, and despite his resistance, hauled him all the way down through the building, along the carpeted corridors, across the foyer, down the monumental marble staircase, and finally bounced him out of the building into the rainy night.*

"They wouldn't even let me go back to pick up my hat," he said indignantly.

"And then?" she asked, fearing the worst.

Well, as he had expected, the following morning he was summoned to the office of Monsieur Ambroise Thomas, director of the Conservatoire.

"He looked at me as if I were some disgusting insect, then he said the same thing as the director. I had disgraced the Conservatoire and the Opéra and brought shame on everybody, and his duty was to expel me from school. But Monsieur Guiraud, my teacher, had come to see him and begged him to give me another chance. And so he only gave me ten demerits."

"I hope you thanked your teacher properly."

"Naturally. I went to see him immediately, but he didn't even let me speak. He only said I was an idiot and I should settle down to work, instead of making an ass of myself."

Alix let out a sigh of relief and remarked that Monsieur Guiraud sounded like a fine man.

◆

Spring came early that year. By mid-April, every tree in Paris was pimpled with green buds.

"My God!" Alix exclaimed one day. "Do you realize that our concert is only three weeks off?"

* Many years later Debussy wrote an amusing account of this youthful incident and tendered his belated apologies to the director, Monsieur Vaucorbeil.

There was no more time for leisurely teas and idle chats by the fire. Now Monsieur Thieberg attended the rehearsals, which became long and strenuous sessions with only short pauses between songs. In addition to accompanying Alix, Claude also assisted the violinist in the rendition of the various piano-and-violin compositions included on the program. At the last moment he even wrote a *notturno* and a scherzo, especially for the occasion.*

The concert was a success. Alix's husband had marshaled his numerous friends. Monsieur Thieberg had some reputation as a concert artist. And he, too, had many friends. Together they filled the Flaxhand Hall. After each number there was much applause. At the end, Alix received a large bouquet of yellow roses, and Monsieur Thieberg gallantly kissed her hand on the stage. Claude took a few awkward bows as composer as well as accompanist. Critics wrote the indulgent, meaningless compliments they write on such occasions. Of Claude's songs they said nothing. Two days later the whole thing was forgotten.

"You were wonderful," Alix told Claude on the following Sunday, "and I am ever so grateful to you. But I am glad it's over. Now I can prepare for our summer in the country."

The country—she laughed—was only Ville d'Avray, a small town half an hour from Paris.

"But it's quite rustic. And, of course, it's very convenient for Pierre, who must go to his office every day. We have a little house there, and I love it. I hope you will come and visit us."

"When are you leaving?"

"Probably next week."

At this point her husband entered, gloved and top-hatted, his silver-knobbed cane tucked under his arm. Ceremoniously he kissed her hand and said he would join them for tea, as soon as he had changed his clothes. He returned a few moments later and at once monopolized the conversation.

"I can't tell you, my dear Claude, how much obliged I am to you for helping my wife with this concert. It was a great success, wasn't it?"

Without waiting for a reply, he turned to Alix. His face creased into an indulgent grin.

"You may not believe it, but this sort of thing is most helpful in business. Only yesterday the president of one of our most important banks told me how much he enjoyed your singing. He also mentioned

* Neither the *notturno* nor the scherzo has been published. In fact, these two compositions are not even included in the definitive catalogue of Debussy's work and we know of their existence only by the program of the concert, which took place on May 12, 1882.

he was planning to build a branch in Clermont-Ferrand and suggested I come to see him at his office for a little business talk. You see, my dear, this concert was not as silly as you thought."

Still smiling, he took a sip from his cup, delicately rested it on its saucer, and with a graceful gesture of his free hand he elaborated for a while on the importance of social contacts in business.

"My wife is very shy," he said, addressing Claude in a man-to-man sort of way. "She doesn't take enough part in social life. I wish you could persuade her to give a few musicales next winter."

"We'll talk about it," she said with a shade of impatience. "I told Claude he must come and see us at Ville d'Avray."

That was enough. At once the elderly architect launched into a lecture about the charms of the little town and its bucolic countryside. He told how Balzac had built a house there, drawing the plans himself.

"But the poor man forgot the stairs! So he had to climb to his room by a ladder."

This brought forth much mirthful chuckling and amused remarks about people who tried to be their own architect. He then talked of the numerous artists who had made Ville d'Avray one of their favorite subjects.

"Corot was one of them. All those lovely silvery ponds you see in his pictures were painted there."

On and on he went, speaking with the ease of the born talker, enjoying his own conversation, glad to have an audience.

He really was a nice old man, Claude thought. He just talked too much. There was something faintly theatrical about the way he clipped his words and waved his shapely blue-veined hands. With his long white locks brushed back from his forehead, his white beard, his studiously "artistic" tie, he did not look so much an old artist as an old actor impersonating an artist.

"Yes, our little town has been made immortal by its artists. Forever it will live in the enchanting canvases—"

Claude glanced at Alix. She was looking down at the rug, lost in thought. How had such a beautiful woman come to marry this foppish, chattering old man who was neither very rich nor very successful? With surprise he realized he knew nothing about her. Like her husband, he had done all the talking while she listened. Perhaps some day she would tell him about herself, perhaps he would get to know what sort of woman she was behind that calm, lovely face of hers.

At last the subject of Ville d'Avray was exhausted and the architect complimented Claude once again on his talent, both as a composer and singing coach.

"I imagine how busy you must be at this time of the year, what with examinations and such things. But I do hope you will find a moment to come and see us in our little villa."

He rose, shook hands, and with a flash of his yellow teeth he hurried out of the room.

Alone, Claude and Alix remained silent for a while. Then she gave him a soft, coaxing smile.

"You'll come, won't you?"

Paris seemed empty after her departure, but he was too busy to brood. At the Conservatoire the year-end examinations were on, and as usual he squeezed through them. Then there was the excitement of the approaching contest for the Grand Prix de Rome. Who would win this year? A fever descended upon the school. Everyone had his favorite candidate. Bets were made.

"I want you to try next year," said Monsieur Guiraud. "You won't even pass the eliminations, but it will be good practice."

At the singing studio pupils now arrived dressed in their spring ensembles, flowery hats and cotton gloves. Like Alix, they were anxious to leave town for the summer.

Madame Moreau-Sainti asked him to dinner, and over the dessert told him she was definitely closing the studio.

"I'll miss you, but it's time I retire. I'm getting old and I want to start working on my garden before it is too late."

She told him of the house she had bought near Dijon. It was small and cozy and it had a charming little garden. "I'll grow the prettiest roses, and my neighbors will be green with envy."

After a long pause she reached for his hand. "It was sweet of you to dedicate your song to me. I'll play it and sing it to myself. Oh, yes, I can sing . . . I even used to have a nice little voice, a long time ago."

She smiled dreamily, and in the lamplight her poor ugly face looked for an instant almost beautiful.

Three days later he received the usual letter from Madame von Meck's secretary. He was instructed to take the Nord Express to Moscow.

There he would board the train for Plescheyevo, where Madame was residing at the moment. He was to advise by telegram the day of his arrival. Someone would meet him at the station.

On the following Sunday, Claude went to Ville d'Avray. He had hoped to spend the afternoon with Alix. But her husband was there and he talked all the time about Byzantine architecture.

Claude left without having had a chance to be alone for a minute with Alix.

◆

On and on and on, interminably, the Nord Express raced across Europe toward Moscow.

For two and a half days there was nothing but the clatter of wheels, the gentle swaying of the red-plush compartment, the unrolling of landscape in the window. Eighteen hours after leaving Paris, he had a glimpse of Berlin in early-morning mist. That evening he arrived at Warsaw, mid-point of the journey. Then, again the slamming of doors, the piercing whistle of the stationmaster, the answering hiss of the locomotive, the stretching of steel muscles under his feet; and, once more, the panting heartbeat of the train boring through the night into the flatness of Russia.

He slept until Minsk and part of the way to Smolensk. Afterward he was too excited to do anything but gaze out the window and think about Sonia. Would she be glad to see him again? Would she rush into his room as she had at Brailov . . . ?

By noon the following day he finally reached Plescheyevo. His two colleagues were waiting for him at the station.

"A long trip, wasn't it?" said Pahulski, taking one of his bags.

Danilchenko, the cellist, grabbed the other. All talking at once, the three young men piled into the waiting *troika*. On the way to the von Meck estate Claude was told the news. Everybody was well. Ostap still played his Cossack songs on his balalaika and drank vodka in his room. Mademoiselle Sonia was getting prettier every day. Only Madame was nervous and irritable. Frankly she made life difficult for everyone around her. Her terrible three-day migraines had returned, and while they lasted the whole household lived in terror. Then her railroads were giving her a good deal of trouble. She had bought the Plescheyevo domain to be near Moscow and remain in close touch with the central office.

But most of all she had been terribly shaken by the Gretener affair. Herr Gretener, a handsome young Swiss who was Sonia's German tutor, had been foolish enough to fall in love with his pupil and dared ask for her hand. Naturally he had been dismissed at once. But the incident had opened Madame's eyes. With a jolt she had realized that Sonia was almost sixteen and might fall in love with some unsuitable young man. She was determined not to let this happen.*

"Since then she has Mademoiselle Sonia watched as if she were a convict on the way to Siberia."

Despite the summer heat Claude felt beads of cold sweat prickle his forehead. He struggled to conceal his emotions from his friends, but his fears were confirmed as soon as he stood before his employer. She was sitting in the shade of an awning on the balcony adjoining her

* In a letter to Tchaikowsky, Madame von Meck wrote: "Any man would choose Sonia. She is young, beautiful, and, as women go, well educated. But most of all, she is an heiress. If I opened my door to her suitors, there would be so many I never could get rid of them. I don't want a man of Sonia's choice. *I want one I shall appoint, and Sonia will like him.*"

apartment, dressed as usual in black taffeta, a book open on her lap, her dog crouched at her feet, very much as she had been, two years ago, at Interlaken. But her expression had changed. Her thin face had grown hollow-cheeked, furrowed with lines of bitterness and pain.

She watched him in silence for a moment, and he had the feeling that she regretted having sent for him. She did. He was handsome, much too handsome for her liking. With his mane of black hair and long-lashed eyes, he looked like a poet. Just the kind some silly sixteen-year-old girl might fall in love with . . .

"This summer you will discontinue your French conversations with my daughter," she said at last, "and confine your relations to giving her piano lessons."

With the familiar motion of the hand, she waved him out of sight.

Not until he returned to his room did he feel the full impact of her words. He had just traveled the whole breadth of Europe to be reminded he was nothing but a piano teacher. No doubt he would be watched and dismissed at the first infraction.

He stood at the window, gazing at the garden below, when he spied Sonia cantering toward the house, followed by a groom in livery. How grown-up and lovely she looked in her riding skirt and glossy top hat! With pounding heart he measured the abyss between them. How could he even think of this girl as his wife!

He watched her being helped down from her horse by the groom. As she was entering the house, a knock on the door made him turn around. Ostap, huge and bearded as ever, handed him a letter and without a word walked off.

"Volichka, my dove, light of my heart . . ." the letter began.

It was impossible for her to come and see him, for she was being watched every minute, but tonight, at ten o'clock, she would be waiting for him at the stables.

There was a full moon that night and it helped him make his way to the stables, which were located far from the house, behind a screen of pine trees. At last he distinguished the pale blur of her face, as she stood in the doorway, waiting. He ran to her, but before he could utter a word she clamped her hand over his mouth, pulled him inside, shut and bolted the door.

Then she flung her arms around him and kissed him on the lips.

"Volichka, my pigeon, soul of my soul, do you still love me? Did you miss me as I missed you?"

Without waiting for a reply, she took his hand and led him through the dimness to an empty stall at the end of the stables, directly under the flickering glow of a wall lantern. She lowered herself on a bedding of fresh hay and motioned him to stretch down at her side.

"It isn't as nice as our little nook by the river, is it?" she said ruefully. "But it's the best I could arrange."

He was too happy to speak and gazed at her, drinking in the loveliness of her young face.

"You are even more beautiful than last year," he finally said. "And you know, I've learned the Russian alphabet."

She looked at him in dismay. "My Volichka, I love you, but you are a *dourak,* an imbecile. You talk to me of the alphabet when we are in terrible danger."

Suddenly she broke into gasping sobs. This poor stupid Herr Gretener had spoiled everything! They wouldn't be able to meet any more, except here and at night. And even this would be difficult.

"But we love each other, don't we, Volichka? And if Maman wants me to marry someone else, well, we will kill ourselves, like Romeo and Juliet. Won't we, darling?"

He tried to cheer her up. Perhaps her mother would have a change of heart. In France people believed there was a special providence that watched over people in love.

"You'll see, everything will be all right."

Sonia had no faith in that French providence and preferred her pure Russian gloom. She saw no other escape but in a double suicide. To please him, she swallowed her tears and pretended to share his hopes. For two hours they lay side by side, kissing, whispering, savoring the melancholy rapture of their reunion.

"Now you must go back to your room," she said with a sigh.

Again she warned him to be on his guard. They would be watched all the time, but somehow she would communicate with him through Ostap, who was her slave and had given her his soul.

She was right. Already the following morning he saw they were being watched. Sonia came to her piano lesson escorted by a governess, who pretended to read but darted covert glances at them over the rim of her book. During the afternoon concert he did his best and played as never before, but try as he might he could not wrench a single compliment from his employer. When he came into her sitting room to receive her orders for the next concert he found her at her desk, poring over bulky ledgers through her steel-rimmed spectacles. She scarcely lifted her head to give her instructions and returned to her work without a glance at him. Every day grave gentlemen carrying leather cases arrived from Moscow and remained closeted with her in lengthy conferences. Twice, because of these visits, the concert was abruptly canceled.

During his stay at Plescheyevo, Claude saw little of Sonia, except at lessons, which was the same as not seeing her at all. Only once did he receive another note and meet her again at the stables. In the yellow haze of the lantern they clung to each other, swearing that nothing would tear them apart.

Tearfully she admitted that her ingenuity was being foiled by her governess' constant surveillance. It had taken all her cunning to arrange this meeting.

"Let's go away," she suggested. "Now, this minute."

He shrugged hopelessly. Where would they go? In an hour the police would have them back at the house and he would be dismissed, like Herr Gretener.

"Volichka, what are we going to do? We are trapped. And things are going to be even worse when we move to Moscow next week."

Again she was right. They moved to the fifty-two-room mansion on boulevard Rodjestvensky, and things got worse. He was allocated a dingy, airless room on the top floor in the servants' quarters. The afternoon concerts were suspended and so were the piano lessons. Every day he expected to be sent back to France.

Sonia was nowhere to be seen. She might as well have dwelt on another planet. It was torture to know that she was here in the same house, yet as remote as a star. No note came from her; but he remained in his room, always hoping for Ostap's knock. From despair he lost himself in work and sketched a symphony full of somber chords and *nitchevo*.*

Finally he accepted the fact that he would not hear from Sonia any more, and he began going out of the house and wandering at random through Moscow. Thus he saw in the swelter of summer the city that he had seen in his mind blanketed in sparkling, crackling snow and which was to be his home. Alone he visited the places he had dreamed of visiting with her. He saw the pink, blue, yellow wooden houses, the marble palaces and the onion-steepled churches. Idly he stood on the Kinietsky Bridge and gazed at the reflection of the Kremlin in the glassy waters of the Moskva. He shambled through narrow streets where children played as they did in Naples, sat on public benches, glanced into bazaars, feeling more than ever his solitude among this good-humored but foreign crowd of men in blue blouses and red leather boots, yellow-braided women and itinerant monks in their three-cornered hats and verminous robes.

Days dragged by, bringing no hope. There was no lovers' providence after all . . . Soon he would be back in Paris with nothing but the memory of their two meetings in the stables. Apparently Madame had lost interest in music and would not send for him again. He would not see Sonia any more. The fairy tale that had begun at Interlaken was coming to an end.

* A fragment of this Symphony in B was found forty years later in a Moscow market and published by the Soviet State Publishing Company.

Then one afternoon Ostap brought him another note.

This time he met her after midnight in the cellar of the house amidst tubs of lard, mountains of red cabbage, rows of smoked hams hanging from the beams. She was waiting for him, her face drawn and pearl-white.

"Oh, Volichka," she cried, rushing to him. "I'm so afraid. Yesterday at dinner Maman said, 'It's time for you to marry. Soon I'll choose a husband for you.' "

"She can't do that!" he exploded.

She placed her hand over his mouth. "Like the parrot you speak, but you don't know what you say. If Maman chooses a husband for me, I will have to marry him. There is only one solution."

Modestly she turned around, lifted her skirt and brought out of her petticoat a long, narrow object which he recognized with horror as Ostap's dagger.

"First I kill myself," she said with tragic calm. "Then it's your turn."

He saw that she meant what she said. Panic sent a flash of inspiration through his brain.

"Wait, Sonitchka, wait!" he cried, snatching the dagger from her. "I have a better idea."

Excitedly he explained there was another solution. One that was pleasant and sure-fire.

"We are engaged, aren't we?"

She nodded, and he plunged on. "That means we're almost married, doesn't it?"

"But we aren't."

"Let's imagine we are."

"But we aren't."

He looked at her with impatience. What was marriage, anyway? A mere ceremony, a silly convention . . . "In France thousands of people make love every day without bothering about getting married."

Comprehension dawned upon her at last. "You want us to make love—all the way?" she gasped. "And what if I have a baby?"

"All the better. Oh, Sonitchka, my love, don't you see, don't you understand?" He spoke in low whispers, hugging her, his lips almost touching hers. "Then your mother will be forced to let us get married."

She pulled herself away and glared at him with horror. Only a disgusting Frenchman could think of such a thing! . . . "You sing like the nightingale but your heart is as black as that of a snake. I hate you!"

Already she was running toward the door.

"I'll never speak to you again," she cried over her shoulder.

Suddenly he was alone, the sound of her words pounding in his ears. He had lost her . . .

For the next few days he lived in a sort of stunned and shamed grief. He had lost Sonia. Both her love and her esteem. He was a cad. The worst kind—an unsuccessful one . . .

He was thinking of resigning and returning to Paris, when the news came of their departure for Vienna.

In the haze of August, Vienna was all smiles, waltz music and *Gemütlichkeit*. But to him it was a town full of beer-drinking ghosts. Like a lost soul he wandered about, ignoring the brightly lit Kärntnerstrasse, the lovely Prater, the terrace at the Sacher's where officers in dolmans and monocles loitered, sabers between their legs, ogling women. He went to the Zentral Friedhof, Vienna's cemetery, and stood bareheaded before the graves of Beethoven and Mozart, two fellow musicians, who like him had suffered much from women.

Then, as if by magic, all was changed. One afternoon, as he was returning to the hotel, he was informed by Madame's secretary that the concerts would be resumed the following day. He nodded and made his way to her suite to take her orders for the musical menu.

To his surprise she was in excellent spirits.

"My little Bussyk, I've missed your playing." She smiled. "You really play the piano very well."

"Thank you, Madame."

He had never seen her look so well or act in such a friendly manner. For the first time she seemed relaxed, almost happy, amidst her knickknacks and the silver-framed photographs of her children, of her late husband and, naturally, scattered through the room, of Piotr Ilyich Tchaikowsky.

"I am quite pleased with you," she went on. "You are a sensible young man, not foolish like so many of them."

He gathered that he was no longer suspect. His assumption was confirmed when he learned that he was to resume giving lessons to Sonia.

The following morning Sonia arrived, unescorted, for her lesson. It was the first time he was seeing her since their disastrous meeting in the cellar, and he clung as best he could to his professorial dignity.

"We shall begin by a few scales, Mademoiselle."

Dutifully she began playing, only to stop a moment later.

"I still love you," she said in a whisper, "and have forgiven you. We can see each other again. Maman said so. She thinks you're wonderful."

From then on everything went well. Madame could not do enough for him. After the concerts she complimented him on his playing, asked his opinion about composers, his plans for the future. On his birthday she gave him a splendid gold watch with his initials set in rubies. A truly magnificent gift. He now enjoyed complete freedom. He met Sonia in one of the innumerable little salons scattered throughout the hotel; and if it happened to be occupied, in a large broom closet she had discovered on the second floor.

It could have been heaven, it was hell.

She gave him no peace. Maman was in a wonderful mood, she thought the world of him.

"You must go and ask her for my hand."

He recoiled at the thought, pleaded for a delay. "Wait till next year, darling. I'll do anything, even win the Grand Prix de Rome for you. Then perhaps your mother—"

It would be too late. He must act and act now . . . "Now, Volichka . . . Next year I'll be married."

Finally he could not stand it any more.

One day after the concert he went into Madame's sitting room, as usual. She smiled at him.

"Madame," he said before she could speak, "I have the honor of asking you for the hand of Mademoiselle Sonia."

She blinked. "What did you say?"

He repeated the sentence as before, all in one breath. Her eyes hardened, her face creased into a mask of anger. He thought she was going to order him out of the room. For an instant they looked at each other.

Abruptly her frown vanished, her mouth relaxed. Then she did something he had never seen her do.

She laughed. Shrilly, uncontrollably.

He felt the blood draw out of his cheeks, turned around and walked out of the room.

That evening he was aboard the Orient Express, on his way back to Paris.

♦

"Did you see Sonia again?" Alix asked, without taking her eyes off her knitting.

Around them the garden bathed in the September sunshine. Three hours ago he had arrived from Vienna and come directly to Ville d'Avray, driven by a compulsive need to be near her. Now he had come to the end of his story. He felt drained of words, almost of feeling, and was slow to reply.

"Yes," he said at last in a flat, toneless voice. "As the fiacre started moving away from the hotel, I turned around and saw her. She was standing at a window, weeping. She waved at me and I waved back."

The words died in his throat. "Well, that's all. Forgive me for talking so much and thank you for listening to my silly story."

"Pain is never silly," she said, going on with her work. "And you are in pain. I would be disappointed if you weren't. You loved each other."

"We did," he said after a pause. "And I'll never love again."

She did not have the heart to smile. He really meant it . . . "Of course, you won't," she said soothingly. "Although in time you may find it difficult to live without love."

"It brings nothing but pain. I don't ever want to love again."

"We can't always command our heart . . . Do you know the tale of the man who had sworn never to love again? No? . . . Well, this man was so afraid to love again that he remained locked up in his room, seeing no one. One day there was a knock at the door. It was Love. Our man opened it, but quickly slammed it back, bolted and nailed it shut. He was pounding the last nail when he saw Love coming in through the window. Fast as lightning, he rushed and closed the shutters, which he fastened with a heavy iron bar. At that very instant he spied Love smiling at him from the chimney. This time he lit a big fire that sent Love up the flue, black with soot and half roasted. Already he was rubbing his hands when he noticed Love squeezing through a rat hole in the floor molding. He closed that, but Love slid through the shutter slats; then through a crack in the ceiling. Even through a worm hole in the oak flooring. By now our man was exhausted, but he had won. He had sealed every hole, every crack and cranny. Love could enter no more. But neither could air. A few days later they found him lying on the floor, dead."

"It's a nice story. But what does it prove?"

"Fairy tales don't prove anything. They aren't supposed to. But sometimes they point out some little truth."

"If this one is supposed to show that we need love as much as air, it's very silly."

"Not silly, only slightly exaggerated. No doubt you may live without love, but you live much better with it. Just as you may live without arms or eyes or legs, but you live better with them. Don't you agree?"

He didn't, he certainly didn't . . . Eyes, legs, arms were useful, but what could you do with love? Nothing . . . It merely made you miserable, lost you your job and broke your heart. Love was the most useless, the most stupid, the most—

Quietly she went on with her knitting and let him talk, drain out his pain in words. More than ever he was going to need companionship and understanding. This Russian puppy love, foolish as it had been, would leave its mark on him. He had had his first sentimental disappointment, and like many sensitive young men, he might easily turn into a cynic. And then these embraces in stables and cellars had aroused his manliness. It would burst out at the first opportunity. With his looks he would have no trouble finding women. He would neglect his studies, become one of those pampered, jaded ladies' men whom women love, spoil and in the end destroy. It would be a pity, for he had talent, great talent . . . Yes, he was going to need friendship, understanding, discreet guidance. And he had no one to give him these things. No family, no elder sister . . .

He was still talking. "Love may be a rose, as poets say, but it is full of thorns, while friendship—"

From cliché to cliché he went on, not remembering what he was trying to prove, happy to be near her, surprised to find her looking younger than he remembered.

"Perhaps you're right," she broke in. "Friendship is a precious thing, and I hope we'll always be good friends. Now, tell me, what are your plans?"

He shrugged evasively. "I don't know. I'll try preparing for the Grand Prix, I guess. But it will be almost impossible. Madame Moreau-Sainti has closed her studio and I'll have to start giving lessons again."

"Perhaps you won't have to. All summer my husband has been after me to give a few musicales this winter. I am sure he'd be grateful if you would coach me, as you did last year."

CHAPTER

3

IN OCTOBER, CLAUDE RETURNED TO HIS COMPOSITION CLASS. BUT NOW he did not stare at the ceiling cracks or wait for the bell. He studied his counterpoint manual, did his homework and avoided parallel fifths. In short, he applied himself.

So pleased was his teacher that one day he took him to lunch. They went to the Brasserie Pousset, a bustling café which catered to a colorful clientele of newspapermen, novelists, playwrights, stage people and even stockbrokers from the nearby Bourse.

"I like this place because it has good food and the best billiard tables in Paris," said Monsieur Guiraud, as they took their places in a quiet corner. "Do you play billiards?"

"No, Master."

"It's a wonderful game. I love it, and Shakespeare must have loved it, too, for he has Cleopatra play billiards while waiting for Antony."

During lunch he put Claude at ease by talking about New Orleans, where he was born. Even after many years in Europe he still remembered the French Quarter with its wrought-iron balconies, the flowered patios, the pretty octoroon with whom he had been in love at sixteen.

"Then my father packed me off to France and the Conservatoire. He had won the Grand Prix de Rome and had a notion that I should do the same. To oblige him, I did. Which proves that with a little application almost anybody can win the darned thing. Even you."

"You make it sound easy, Master, but you know it isn't."

"Nonsense." He took a sip from his cup of coffee and went on in a brisk, businesslike tone, "Listen. Now that Pierné and Marty are safely in Rome, your only serious rival is Paul Vidal, and you can beat him."*

"I'll do my best, Master, but he's a real beaver."

"You, too, could become a beaver. It wouldn't kill you to do some real work. Study Bach, write a fugue every day, cram your counterpoint. And for God's sake, stay away from those parallel fifths."

"But, Master—"

"I know they sound well sometimes, but get into your head they're forbidden. Don't you think I know what you're trying to do? You're groping for fresh harmonies, new combinations of chords. It's fine, but you are not ready. Win the Grand Prix, and when you are in Rome you can do all the groping you want."

He lit a cigarette and let out a long plume of smoke. "Ah, Rome! . . . I spent three happy years there. I remember when Bizet and I were together at the Villa . . ."

The villa, of course, was the Villa Medici, the magnificent ocher-walled palace where the laureates of the Grand Prix de Rome for Music, Painting, Sculpture, Architecture and Engraving lived and worked for three years at the government's expense.

"What talent he had! You should've heard him improvise at the piano. We used to dream of the operas we were going to write on our return to Paris, we were going to set the world on fire."

Lunch was over and he was slipping into a mellow digestive mood.

"Georges did set the world on fire. He wrote *Carmen!* I—I became a professor at the Conservatoire. Well, we can't all have talent."

A shadow passed over his face and he let out a sigh. For an instant he gazed wistfully ahead; then turned back to Claude.

"But *you* have talent, you have something to say and you'll never have a chance to say it unless you win the Grand Prix. And you are going to win it, if I have to pound counterpoint into your head with a mallet."

"Yes, Master."

"Now, please do me a favor. Don't get into any more trouble. Don't get yourself thrown out of any theatre, don't make an ass of yourself. And above all, don't fall in love. At least not before the contest."

* That year Gabriel Pierné and Georges Marty had both received the Grand Prix because no award had been given in the previous year.

"Don't worry about that, Master. I won't. I've learned my lesson."

"You haven't. Nobody ever learns that lesson. But, please, keep away from women for a few months. You'll have time for that in Rome."

He paid for the lunch and together they walked out of the café. On the sidewalk they shook hands.

"Good-bye, Claude. Go home and write a nice fugue."

"Yes, Master. And thank you for the lunch."

He slammed his slouch hat low over his forehead, raised the collar of his overcoat and walked away. Thoughtfully the professor watched him thread his way through the crowd. He had talent, that boy. Perhaps more than talent. It was still too soon to tell.

Only then did he notice it had started to drizzle. A cold, forlorn November drizzle that slid down your neck. Perfect weather to stay by the fire and correct students' homework. Oh, the dreams of long ago in Rome! . . .

With a sigh Ernest Guiraud opened his umbrella, crossed the street and started in the direction of rue Pigalle, where he lived.

Claude did not go home; instead he went to see Alix. He found her reading aloud to her two children from a large illustrated book.

"Make yourself comfortable," she smiled, "and don't pay any attention to us."

He sat down at his usual place by the fire, pulled his book from his pocket and plunged into the intricacies of the harmonic minor. Now and then he peeped at her over the rim of his manual. Once their glances met. Her lids narrowed into the swiftest of smiles, yet long enough for him to know she was glad he had come.

He went back to his book. Gently her voice seeped through his thoughts. He heard her say, "The boy-rabbit bowed deeply and said to the girl-rabbit, 'Mademoiselle, have no fear. I shall defend you with my life.' "

Suddenly his heart swelled with gratitude for this woman who had given him affection and understanding and had removed financial worries from his life. Quietly she had taken Madame Moreau-Sainti's place and become his employer. Under the pretext of coaching lessons he received the same wages that he had as an accompanist, and could go on giving money to his mother.

At first he had protested he could not accept so much money for so little work, but she had cut him short. "It would cost me much more to take lessons in a singing studio, and I should have the bother of going there. So stop worrying. You aren't taking advantage of me, I am taking advantage of you." In this way she had silenced his qualms and made him feel that his good fortune was in fact his good deed.

Having no set schedule he always had an excuse to see her. Two

or three times a week he would drop in, dutifully suggest they rehearse this or that song. She would claim a headache or a slight cold
that made singing impossible. The rehearsal would be forgotten—but
he would stay. Thus they spent many hours together, sometimes
alone, sometimes in the company of her children, to whom he brought
candy and who climbed on his back and called him "Uncle Claude."

She went on reading aloud, her voice droning into the silence of
the room.

" ' "All is well," said the boy-rabbit to the girl-rabbit. "I am glad I
saved your life. My wound is slight and of no concern to me. Please,
Mademoiselle, give me your hand, and let's go for a stroll in the
woods." ' "

She closed the book and hugged the small boy and girl. "That's
all for today. Now, give a kiss to Uncle Claude, then run to the
kitchen and play with Madeleine."

When they were gone, she poked at the fire for a while, then took
her knitting from the basket at her side.

"What are you reading with such a deep frown?"

He raised his eyes and smiled.

"I'm trying to learn about harmonic minor. Do you want to hear
the sort of thing we must learn?" She nodded, and he began reading
aloud and very fast: " 'It is true that the use of harmonic minor is
calculated to impress the learner with a sense of the real character-
istics of the minor mode, but its merits are counterbalanced by the
awkwardness arising from the augmented second between the sixth
and seventh notes while it is difficult to regard it as a diatonic scale
at all, in spite of its theoretical correctness.' "

Teasingly he glanced up. "Would you like to hear some more?"

"No, thank you. I think I'll leave you to your book and see how
Madeleine is doing in the kitchen." At the door she asked, over her
shoulder, "Of course you're staying for dinner?"

Thus the afternoon went by.

Later he told her about his lunch with his teacher. "He really
wants me to try for the Grand Prix this year. He thinks I can win it.
I don't."

"Yes, you can, but you must work hard. Wouldn't it be wonderful
if you did! Imagine living in Rome in that nice Italian sunshine—"

She stopped, for her husband had swept into the room, in a state of
jubilation.

"My dear, it's done!" he said, even before kissing her hand. "The
contract has been signed today."

After many delays the bank had finally entrusted him with the
building of their Clermont-Ferrand branch.

"We'll start as soon as I complete my plans."

All evening he discoursed about the project and the fine architectural points it aroused. Bank building, he explained, required a delicate blend of the artistic and the functional. What style was most appropriate to a bank? Neo-classic with a few Doric columns? The warm provincial that appealed to farmers and modest depositors? What about a discreet reminder of church architecture? A Gothic window in the manager's office, for instance? . . . After all, wasn't a bank some sort of a church? The Temple of Money, you might say . . .

It was all terribly challenging. His enthusiasm was a joy to behold, he looked twenty years younger. At long last he was going to have a chance to show what he could do. The bank was contemplating the erection of several other branches in various provincial towns, and already he saw himself traveling all over France, supervising building squads. And, of course, besides the pride of achievement, there was the sizable financial reward. Yes, this time fortune had knocked at his door.

"And to think it all started with that concert last May! . . . Which proves how important these social functions are."

He was about to elaborate on the subject, but Claude excused himself, explaining he still had a fugue to write before going to bed.

◆

The following Sunday, Claude and Alix talked about the bank her husband was going to build.

"Pierre is terribly excited about it," she smiled. "All week he's been telling me how rich we're going to be. Already he wants me to look for an apartment where we could entertain in style. He loves social functions."

"And you?"

"Not much. Frankly I find these things rather tedious. At the beginning he used to beg me to go out with him. I did at first, then I suggested he go alone. I'm afraid I've been a great disappointment to him in that regard."

She paused as though she had said too much, and quickly added, "Anyway, I am not convinced he's going to make as much money as he thinks. Somehow I feel that banks must be rather cautious about spending money, and Pierre is a good architect, but not a shrewd businessman. He should have been a college professor and lecture on church architecture. That's one thing he knows well. He even wrote a book on the subject."

She took a long sip of tea, uncovering her throat. The gesture had an unaware sensuality that brought a flush to his cheeks. He fought back an impulse to rise and kiss her.

She rested the cup on its saucer. A slow, wistful smile spread over her face. "I married him because of that book."

"Just because he wrote a book?"

"No. But I wouldn't have met him if he hadn't written it. Strange, isn't it, how little things can affect your life? One day he came to visit Father about a certain Pinaigrier."

"Who?"

"Don't rack your brain, you've never heard about him. Neither has anyone else for that matter. All we know is that he lived in the sixteenth century and made the wonderful stained-glass windows in the Church of Saint Etienne du Mont. And we aren't even sure about that. But Father had written a monograph about him. He loved to write about medieval artists, but not the famous ones. He always picked up some obscure craftsman, some stonemason or wood carver no one cared about. He loved to discover geniuses three hundred years after their death. He had been a judge, and he used to say that it was his duty to correct miscarriages of artistic justice."

For a while she spoke about her father in a tone of loving tenderness and teasing reverence.

"He was such a wonderful man! Brilliant, witty, kind. A bit eccentric at times."

Claude felt she was enjoying talking about him. It was the first time that she was abandoning her reserve, taking him into her confidence. He sensed that she, too, had longed for someone to talk to. In a flash it struck him that this beautiful, reticent woman was lonely.

"You were lucky to have such a wonderful father."

She nodded. "When my mother died, he retired from the bench and devoted himself to the history of art, which had been his hobby. I was his only child and we were very close. We worked together and I enjoyed every moment I spent with him, for he had a way of making the dullest subject become adventurous and exciting. Anyway, he decided to write a monograph on Panaigrier. For months we explored old churches, consulted parochial registers in ice-cold sacristies. Back home he would dictate to me. I still see him sitting by the fireside, smiling at me from his green leather chair."

Suddenly her eyes welled with tears. She turned aside and gazed at the burning logs. "You must forgive me, its been so long since I spoke about him . . ."

She turned back to Claude and went on, "Well, when we finished the monograph, I corrected the proofs and mailed the usual complimentary copies to critics and historians, who tossed them in their trash baskets. But Father did not mind. He was one of these rare men who expect no reward for their work. By chance, Pierre happened to read it. He was writing his book on church architecture at the time and he came to ask Father for some information. He returned the following week, and in time they became friends. Then, one day, Father died. In his sleep, thank God. To me it was a shattering blow. Somehow I believed he would live forever and I would spend the rest of my life at his side."

Abruptly, at twenty-four, she had found herself alone, with little money, without friends or family, except some distant cousins.

"Didn't you ever go out with young men?"

"Oh, yes. Father urged me to marry, and to please him I entertained several eligible bachelors. Unfortunately I was used to his brilliant mind and I found them cocky, shallow and utterly boring."

"I am young, too. Do you find me boring?"

"You—you're different." Quickly she went on, "Pierre called on me several times. He was kindness itself."

He had cheered her solitude, shared her grief and shown his love in many delicate ways. Gradually she had come to accept the idea of marrying this elderly man, who, like her father, was a widower and a scholar, kindly and rather helpless.

"He told me he wanted me to help him with his book. He made me feel needed. This, to a woman, is a great inducement. Anyway, I married him and helped him finish his book. But to him work is not an end in itself, as it was to Father. He wants approval, the congratulations of friends, social success. He had hoped his book would make him famous. When it went almost unnoticed, he was deeply disappointed. He never wrote another one."

In a faintly mocking aside, she added, "Perhaps it's just as well."

She seemed about to go on, but she held herself in check. Again she looked at the fire. An uneasy silence fell over the room, a silence of unsaid things made more intense by the patter of the autumn rain against the window. Her face had lost the animation of a moment ago and turned as expressionless as a cameo. Yet he read on it her disappointment at having married a second-rate opportunist instead of a man of talent and character, as her father had been.

As though she wanted to close the intimacy of the moment, she remarked what an excellent man Pierre was. At some length she expatiated on his kindness, his erudition and various other qualities. She stressed her devotion to him.

"He is a fine husband and an excellent architect," she said, a trifle too emphatically. "I'm sure he will build a nice bank in Clermont-Ferrand and give full satisfaction."

She held out the biscuit tray to Claude. "Here. Eat this last biscuit and finish your tea. Then let's go to the living room and do some work. My first musicale is in ten days."

♦

She regretted her confidences. They had aroused memories she wanted to forget, awakened a bitterness which she had thought extinct. She had resigned herself to the mediocrity of her fate. She had no taste for extra-marital adventures. The inviting glances she had caught among her husband's friends had left her indifferent. After an initial rebelliousness, she had slid into acceptance of the fact that she would never know the rapture of passion or the excitement of living in contact with a brilliant mind. At thirty-one she felt detached, passive and old.

Claude's entrance in her life had come as a pleasant diversion. Like her father she had a flair for discovering and recognizing talent, and since that Sunday afternoon when he had first played his songs for her, she had known that he was no ordinary youngster. His loneliness had stirred her compassion. She had wanted to give friendliness to this adolescent who was thirsting for it, and the gentle guidance he did not find in his family. Once again she had felt needed. Not by an elderly commonplace man this time, but by a gifted, neglected and lonesome boy.

And this time there had been no disappointment. He had returned her affection, opened his whole heart to her. It was to her that he had come after his Russian misadventure. She was touched by the songs he wrote for her, his piteous five-sou bouquets. Even more by the look of gratitude she read in his wonderful black eyes.

It had all been pleasant and innocent, but since the day she had told him about her marriage she had caught other glances. Shy but unmistakable flashes of desire, little leaping flames of lust she had pretended not to see. Twice, at the piano, he had rested his hand upon hers, as if by accident. She had felt a strange thrill at the contact of his young smooth flesh. Now and then she found herself musing how it would feel to be kissed by him. Once she had dreamed they were making love . . .

Perhaps, she wondered, it would be wiser to send him away? . . . But what a cruel thing to do to a youngster who had placed his trust in her! And how lonely she would feel without his visits, their friendly afternoon teas . . . Besides, it would mean the end of those musicales she had promised her husband. What excuse would she give to explain the disappearance of Claude, who had become almost a member of the family. Pierre looked on him as a son, the handsome, talented son he would have liked to have. He loved talking to him at dinner, displaying his erudition before him. And then the children adored him . . . Anyway, in a few months he probably would win the Grand Prix and leave for Rome . . . Until then, it was simpler to let things go on as before, avoid further confidences, be friendly but distant. And watch him . . . and herself.

She tried to re-establish their relationship on its former basis, that of a kindly woman toward a poor, friendless music student. It was too late. The wall of her aloofness had been breached. She had taken him into her confidence, told him things about herself, let him guess many more. He had felt her gaze on him, heavy with longing tenderness. With the impetuosity of youth he took advantage of the situation.

Boldly one afternoon he told her she had beautiful eyes. "And not only your eyes, but your nose, your lips, your ears—everything."

"Stop talking nonsense."

"It's true. You're very beautiful."

"That's the most banal compliment you can pay a woman. Either she is and she knows it, or she isn't and she knows you are lying." She frowned, tried to sound annoyed, and for an instant she reminded him of Aunt Tavie when she was displeased. "Besides, I hate flattery."

"It's not flattery, it's the truth."

"Whatever it is, you can dispense with it."

"I thought we were friends and I could tell you everything."

"We are friends, but I am eleven years older than you and— Well, tell me what you've been doing at school today."

She used the word "school" instead of "Conservatoire" to mortify him and remind him that she looked upon him as an insignificant schoolboy. It was intended as a punishment and as such it was effective, for the young hate nothing more than being reminded of their youth.

It squelched him, but not for long. A few days after the musicale, he mimicked one of the guests, an elderly gentleman who had kissed her hand with a flowery, courtly gesture.

"Like this," he said, clamping a long kiss on her wrist.

"That's enough," she snapped, trying to pull back her hand.

He tightened his grip, gently bit her flesh.

Impatiently she jerked her hand away. "You are a very silly boy."

"That's how he kissed your hand."

"It was not. Sometimes you act like a ten-year-old. Now go back to your chair and try to act like an intelligent young man."

"You mean you think I am an idiot?"

"Sometimes."

Despite their difference in age she found herself sliding into a teasing, arguing comradeship. She became a sort of elder sister whose authority was always accepted, but not without protest. Sometimes she herself forgot the years between them and felt young enough to be the elder sister of this unruly, enterprising youngster.

Now Pierre seemed older, his face more wrinkled, his handsome hands less handsome. His garrulity became harder to endure. Impatience seized her in the middle of his effusions. Once or twice she cut him short. "Yes, Pierre, you have already told me about it, several times . . ." She saw the hurt look in his eyes and she reproached herself for her nervousness. At night she felt restless, paced the floor of her room. Occasionally she awoke with a start, moist and tense with desire. Her youth, which she had thought gone, was rushing back, imperious and demanding.

One day Claude kissed her. In the middle of a sentence he got up, walked to the engraving hanging on the wall behind her chair and admired it at length. Then, swooping down, he kissed the back of her neck.

She was furious.

"I am very much annoyed with you, Claude. I don't ever want this sort of thing to happen again."

"If you were my sister you wouldn't be mad at me for kissing you."

"But I am not your sister."

"To me you are."

Anger faded from her eyes. "I, too, am fond of you, but you must promise never to do this again. It isn't right."

"Why?"

"Because it isn't, that's all. And I don't wish to talk about it any more."

"I am sorry," he said, lowering his eyes. "I won't do it again."

But he did, less than a week later. They were sitting at the piano and she had just finished singing one of his songs. Without a word he seized her shoulders, turned her around and kissed her on the lips.

"That's because you sang so well."

It had happened so fast that it took a few seconds before she was able to speak.

"I won't have this sort of thing," she said at last. "Do you hear? I won't tolerate—"

"I'm sorry. I really am."

"You are not. Let me warn you—"

"I swear I lost my head."

"You seem to lose your head quite often these days. Let me warn you—"

"I know. You'll send me away."

"That's what I should do if I had any sense. Perhaps it would be best—for both of us."

Her expression betrayed her. He saw the longing in her eyes. Something snapped in his mind. Roughly he pulled her to him, clasped her against his chest and kissed her again. This time with the fierce hunger of his youth. He felt her lips slacken and part under his, her arm coiled around his shoulders and her fingers clutched his neck. For a long time they clung in silent embrace.

With an effort she pulled away and rose from the bench.

"I am sorry this happened," she said in a toneless voice.

This time he knew he had gone too far. "I wish I could say I am sorry, but I am not. I've been wanting to do that for a long time."

"I think you'd better go."

"You mean we won't see each other any more?"

"I think it's better if we don't. I am a married woman. True, my husband is old, but he is kind and considerate. And he is my husband."

In silence they crossed the room.

"Well, good-bye, Claude," she said at the door. "I am sorry, but it is better this way."

In the dimness of the landing they looked at each other. For an instant he thought she was going to fling herself into his arms. He gulped, tried to speak, but no word came.

She lowered her lids—and slowly shut the door.

♦

Now that he had lost her, he could not get her out of his mind. He berated himself for what he had done, but did not feel any remorse. They hadn't committed any crime. She wanted him to kiss her, her lips had told him that. Then what was wrong? Because she was married? . . . Married to an old man she didn't really love. There should be a law forbidding old men to have beautiful young wives . . .

He found some relief in recriminations, but they did not bring her back. Twice he went to her house, started to climb the stairs, ready to beg her forgiveness, promise anything so long as she would let him come and see her again. His courage had failed, his hand had not rung the bell.

During the day his classes kept him from brooding. But at night his restlessness became unendurable. He stayed away from home as late as he could, afraid his parents might ask embarrassing questions.

He was walking at random one evening, an unusually mild January evening, smoking, strolling along a deserted ill-lit street, when he heard a whisper coming out of an arched doorway.

"Where're you going like that, by yourself?"

He tried to push on, but a little hand, not much bigger than a child's, shot up and clamped on his sleeve.

"Let me go," he said. "I have no money." This was his standard excuse and usually effective.

He shook off her hand and hurried by, followed by a patter of high heels.

Halfway down the street he stopped under a lamppost. "What do you want?"

"What's your hurrry?" she said, a little breathless, as she caught up with him. "Going to a fire or something?"

"I told you I have no money." In the glow of gaslight he saw that she was pretty and very young, despite her heavy make-up.

"You've got a cigarette, don't you?"

He looked at her, surprised at her extreme youth. Often, on his way home at night, he had been approached like this by streetwalkers, hard-eyed, aggressive women much older than himself. They frightened him a little, but this girl was too small and too young to frighten anyone.

"What's the matter with you?" she asked petulantly. "Cat got your tongue?"

He fumbled in his pocket and brought out a rumpled cigarette.

"Got a light?" she asked.

He struck a match. She leaned down and for an instant she sucked the flame in his cupped hands.

"Thanks."

He took a few steps and again she ran afer him.

"You can stay a minute, can't you? It gets lonesome waiting all night by myself."

"What's your name?" he asked.

"Irène. I don't like it. Some day I'll get me another one."

"How old are you?"

"Sixteen almost. That's why I can't do the boulevards. I'm too young to get the Prefecture card and the *flics* are always pouncing on the girls without it. And you, how old are you?"

He told her while lighting a cigarette. For a while they faced each other, talking easily with the comradeship of youngsters.

"If you really don't have any money, you can pay me some other time," she said, taking a last pull on her cigarette. "I trust you."

"I have two francs," he admitted.

"All right." Already she was taking his arm. "You'll give me one and keep the other."

They walked to a shabby hotel nearby, with a gas jet in a globe of frosted glass over the entrance. In the hallway a night clerk squinted at them over his newspaper but asked no questions. Together they started up the creaky stairs to her room.

A paper-shaded lamp was burning on the nightstand, making a yellow haze of light. He could distinguish a washstand, half hidden behind a screen, a pink wrapper hanging from a nail in the wall. On the dresser was a small alcohol lamp and an orange spilling out of a paper bag. A rose was dying in a glass of water.

"Get undressed," she said, as she disappeared behind the screen.

Later that evening, she cuddled to him, her head nestled in the curve of his shoulder.

"I like you," she murmured. "If you want, you can come to see me again tomorrow. It won't cost you anything."

Thus she slipped into his life, became a small part of it. Neither had time for love, only love-making. Yet their relationship had a tenderness of its own, the innocence of youth. They almost loved each other without daring to say the word. He only spent an hour or so every evening, but during this time he did not think about Alix. When he returned to his room he felt relaxed and worked hard and well.

It lasted two weeks.

Then, one day, as he started climbing the stairs he was stopped by the night clerk.

"No use going up. The *flics* have nabbed her. It was bound to happen. No card, you see . . ."

No, he didn't know where they had taken her. Probably to some house for minor delinquents, outside Paris . . .

It was as simple and final as death. For two days he loved her desperately, wanted to rescue her, even marry her to get her free. Less than a week later he could not remember the exact color of her eyes. Since she had given him only pleasure, her imprint was not deep. Soon she was only a memory. Then, not even that.

◆

One morning, as he was coming out of the Conservatoire, he was handed a letter by the concierge.

"A lady brought it."

Eagerly Claude tore the envelope open. Alix was asking him to meet her at three o'clock that afternoon in Parc Monceau.

A few minutes before three he was entering the park. At once he saw her, sitting on a bench at the end of a deserted alley, pensively gazing down at the ground. He broke into a run. She raised her head at the sound of his footsteps and smiled.

"It isn't three yet," he gasped, coming to an abrupt stop before her. "Your note said three."

"I came a few minutes early. Sit down and catch your breath." Then, softly, "How have you been?" Behind her veil her face was pale and drawn.

"Fine. And the children?"

"They miss you. I told them you had gone on a trip but would be back soon . . . Is Monsieur Guiraud satisfied with your work?"

For a moment they asked each other questions to give themselves time to adjust to the strangeness of their surroundings. It was a blustery February day, with gusts of wind sweeping dead leaves down the alley.

"How's your husband?"

"He has never been so busy. Several times he has gone to Clermont-Ferrand to supervise the construction. It seems that the bank is planning to open another branch and he thinks he will get the contract. He asked about you and I told him you couldn't come for a while because of an examination you must prepare. He wants to know if you'll be able to coach me for my next musicale."

"Of course." Impulsively he took her hands. "Oh, Alix, I missed you so."

"I did, too," she said slowly. "Couldn't we be friends again, as we used to?"

"Is that what you want?"

She nodded, averting her eyes. "It's better than not seeing each other."

"All right. We'll be friends."

They tried. Bravely they played their parts. Again she became the kindly lady, affectionate but reserved; he slipped back into his role of singing coach and friend of the family.

At the end of the month Alix gave her second musicale. Again the living-room furniture was pushed against the walls. Chairs, rented for the occasion, were set in orderly rows. Again Pierre's friends came, duly applauded after each number. By eleven o'clock, to everyone's satisfaction, it was over.

"I hope my last musicale won't interfere with your work," she said the following afternoon.

It was scheduled for April and the contest for the Grand Prix de Rome began in May.

"I can cancel it, if you wish," Alix said.

He protested that the musicale took little of his time, which was true.

"Besides, I wouldn't then have any excuse for coming here."

They often spoke of the Grand Prix contest. He insisted that he did not have a chance to win against Paul Vidal, who knew all the forms of counterpoint backward.

"Even if I pass the eliminations, I'll never make the finals."

In his opinion the whole thing was a monstrosity, something invented by sadistic academicians for the torture of poor music students. The eliminations were bad enough, but the finals were inhuman.

"How would you like to be locked up in a room for three weeks, like a criminal, and write a whole cantata on some stupid subject? I tell you I'll never make it."

She quieted his fears, assured him he would win the contest. "I'll be so proud, if you do."

"Don't count on it."

"Of course you will. And think of living three years in that beautiful Villa Medici, with no financial worries and all the time in the world to write music."

"Yes. In prison, also, I would have time to write music! Do you realize they don't give you any vacations? Once you are inside their confounded Villa you have to stay three years! . . . Three years without seeing you . . ."

There it was, the crux of the matter. Each time they spoke of the Grand Prix, their discussion ended there. Why should he want to win a prize that would keep him away from her for three years? . . . Feebly she protested he must think of his career, prepare for his future. He shrugged. Career, future—what did they mean if he must spend three years away from her? . . .

"Wouldn't you miss me at all?"

She nodded, keeping her eyes on her knitting, and changed the subject. She mentioned the construction of the Panama Canal, in which millions of Frenchmen were keenly interested. Or the war in Indochina, or the opening of the Brooklyn Bridge, at which a number of persons had been crushed to death.

It was no use. Their pretense at friendship was becoming each day harder to maintain, a pitiful sham that convinced neither of them and reminded him of the game of make-believe he had played with his aunt in their last summer together. They watched themselves so much that now they found less and less to say. Conversation dwindled to a trickle of words or stopped altogether with half-spoken words ebbing into silence.

Sometimes, when her husband was out of town, he dined with her and the children and spent the evening with her. Then their pretense became torture. Her knitting needles clicked in her fingers like miniature dueling swords. He tried to read. But their glances met now and then and betrayed their longing. After a while the atmosphere became electric.

By the end of April he couldn't stand it any more.

One evening he suddenly pushed back his chair and got up. "I think I'll stop coming here. You've given your last musicale and there is no more reason for me to come."

"Please, darling—" The word escaped her. "Don't leave me. Your friendship is so dear to me . . . In a few months you'll be going to Rome and I won't see you again."

"What's the sense in tormenting ourselves, saying what great friends we are when we know we are long past being friends?"

"Please—"

She bit her lower lip, but it was too late. A tear fell on the back of her hand. Quickly she rose and ran out of the room.

For a moment he stood motionless, waiting for her return. A minute passed. Then, as in a trance, he went to her room. From the threshold he saw her silhouette haloed in lamplight. She was sitting on the edge of the bed, sobbing quietly, a balled handkerchief to her lips.

He walked to her, gently lifted her chin and kissed her mouth.

"Don't," she murmured. "Please don't."

In love who pleads is lost. He kissed her again, and this time she returned his kiss with a surge of passion. For a moment they clung to each other. With welded mouths they pitched down on the bed. Her hair came undone in a puddle of spun gold. Slowly her arms slid down his sides, then opened in a cross of surrender.

She had come to the end of her struggle. It was too soon for remorse, too late for regrets. Now, breathless and disheveled, she waited for the reward of her defeat.

◆

A week later he took part in the contest of the Grand Prix de Rome and behaved with his usual unpredictability. He almost failed at the eliminations; then passed the finals brilliantly and almost won the Grand Prix.

Almost . . .

He won the Second Grand Prix. Paul Vidal won the First, the only one that mattered.

He was prepared for anything but that. The award plunged him into deep brooding.

After a night of self-searching introspection he called on his teacher, Monsieur Guiraud, who received him in the small, cluttered den of his bachelor's apartment.

"I am proud of you," said the teacher, shaking his hand. "I've seen your cantata and it's very good. A member of the jury told me that they almost decided in your favor. Don't worry, you'll make it next year."

Claude received these compliments with a doleful smile.

"I thank you, Master. I know you're trying to encourage me, but I have no illusions. I know I'll never be a first-class musician. I love music, but as you said the day we had lunch, we can't all have talent. I might as well face the fact before it's too late. I've decided to change my profession."

"You—what?"

"Yes, Master. I've decided to become a painter."

He had given the matter much thought, and his mind was made up. To win the Second Grand Prix was evidence of mediocrity. It proved that you were second-rate. Better give up and start on a new career. Already he had bought a palette.

"I merely came to thank you for your patience and kindness. I'll always be grateful to you."

Monsieur Guiraud considered him in silence, his hands joined before his face.

"I'll be sorry to see you go," he began, "but I'm sure you will be an excellent artist. Will you be a portraitist or a landscapist?"

Claude hadn't thought of that. "Both, I guess."

"Excellent! Of course you will want to win the Grand Prix de Rome for Painting."

"I suppose so," said Claude evasively.

Well, then all he had to do was to enter the Beaux-Arts School. Of course, he would have to pass the entrance examinations. They were very similar to those of the Conservatoire. But never mind, where there was a will there was a way . . . After passing the entrance examinations he would then be enrolled in a class of elementary drawing. Something like the solfeggio class. There he would be among twelve- and thirteen-year-old boys . . . Then, year after year, he would pass from one class to another, just as he had at the Conservatoire.

"In about ten years you should be ready to compete for the Grand Prix for Painting," he wound up with a cheerful smile.

Claude had listened with growing despondency to the general schedule described by his teacher. Obviously there was more to becoming a painter than buying a palette. His resolution to become a painter wavered.

"I wouldn't mind being a musician," he said at last, "if I knew I had real talent."

This time Monsieur Guiraud exploded. "You half-wit! Of course, you have talent. Great talent . . . Why do you think I begged Monsieur Thomas not to expel you from school? Why did I pound counterpoint and orchestration into your head all these months?"

It took some time for him to restore Claude's self-confidence as a musician. He pointed out that most great musicians had failed the contest in their first attempts.

"Do you know how many times Berlioz tried before he made it? Five times! Now, have a good summer and enjoy yourself. And next

October I want to see you back in my class, or I'll go and get you wherever you are and break your neck."

By now Claude had not only regained his assurance but had swung to a brimming optimism. "You'll see, Master. I'll write you the best cantata ever written. I'll show the jury—"

"Please, don't show the jury anything. Just win the Grand Prix, that's all I ask."

As for Alix, she was radiant with happiness.

"It means you won't have to go to Rome! It means we have a whole year to ourselves!"

She then told him she had found a new pretext to continue paying him wages and having him come to Ville d'Avray every day.

"You'll give piano lessons to Marguerite. Of course, she is only a child, so the lessons will have to be rather short. Say, ten minutes . . . Pierre thinks it's an excellent idea."

And so it was arranged. Every day he took the suburban train and thirty minutes later arrived at Ville d'Avray. He walked the short distance to the villa, pushed open the rusty gate, crossed the garden and climbed the perron stairs that led into the house. Amidst much giggling, kissing, frowning and wagging of fingers he gave the little girl a brief lesson that neither took seriously. The lesson over, Madeleine, the maid, appeared in white coif and apron and escorted Marguerite and her brother Maurice to some neighborhood villa, where they played all afternoon. Soon the sound of their voices faded away, and the two lovers remained alone in the house.

Sometimes he played the piano for her or she sat beside him and sang one of his songs. But their flesh was too restless, and music merely needled their desire. His arm came around her waist; her head leaned against his shoulder. With kisses and caresses they goaded their desire until, by unspoken accord, they rose and walked up the stairs to her room. There, in the dimness of half-closed shutters they made love. With the voracity of his twenty years he mauled and ravished her splendid body that should have been fondled with expert tenderness. Her ardor matched his own, for passion was also new to her. In love they were the same age.

Sometimes they sat in the garden under the linden tree by the house and chatted like old friends. But, most often, they walked hand in hand through the fields to their favorite place on the edge of a pond, one of those Ville d'Avray ponds that Corot had loved so much. There they spent the afternoon hours, feeling the ripeness of summer around them, dozing or gazing at the sky until they heard the whistle of the Paris train.

"What are you thinking about?" she asked one afternoon, rising on her elbow to kiss his cheek.

"Nothing," he said, still munching his blade of grass. "Just listening."

"To what?"

"The sounds of summer."

She gave him a languid smile, which he did not notice, and lay back on the ground. Only an hour ago he had loved her joyously, hungrily; now he was a thousand miles away, unaware of her presence, lost in a world where she couldn't follow him. Where no woman ever would. He had forgotten her, and like this he would forget all the women who would come after her. It wasn't his fault: he was born that way. He would lure them with his gentleness, his wonderful eyes, and make them happy; then escape into music, leaving them empty-handed and waiting . . .

"Do you know what I wish?" she said another afternoon. "I wish this day would never end, and all the clocks in the world would stop and we could stay on like this forever."

She sat up, looked at the glassy pond turning rose in the sunset. Another perfect day was coming to an end. Time, alas, did not stand still. Already August was half gone. Another six weeks and they would be back in Paris. What then? How would they meet? . . .

She looked down on him. He was stretched out on the grass, watching her with a smile.

"What are you frowning about?" he asked. "Something's worrying you?"

"I was thinking how we'll meet when we're back in Paris in October."

"We'll find some way."

She smiled at him. He was content to enjoy the moment. Somehow things would take care of themselves. Perhaps it was the privilege of extreme youth not to worry about the future . . .

The whistle of the Paris train wafted to them across the fields.

"I think we'd better go," she sighed, plucking the twigs from her hair and skirt.

She glanced once more at the pond. "Good-bye, lovely day!"

They reached the station as the train was arriving. He watched her greet her husband with wifely affection, marveling at the naturalness of her deceit. Could a man ever be sure? . . .

During dinner he listened to the architect's long-winded dissertations on the Grand Prix de Rome, which had become one of his favorite subjects.

"How often have I wished I had competed for the Architecture Grand Prix in my youth!" he would sigh. "I would be a rich man by now."

No question about it, the title of Grand Prix de Rome was the magic word that opened all doors, the key to success. All government contracts—city halls, prefectures, post offices—were invariably awarded to some former laureate. It was the same in music. Opera conductors, professors at the Conservatoire, academicians were all former Grand Prix.

"This is why, my boy, I conjure you to do your utmost to win it next year."

Claude had grown fond of the kindly, tireless talker who looked at him through his red-rimmed eyes full of affection and almost fatherly pride. Now and then he experienced some small qualm at being his wife's lover.

"Do you think he suspects anything?" he asked Alix one afternoon.

She gave him a rueful smile. "No, darling. He doesn't and he won't. It is not that he is stupid, but he is extremely vain, and that makes him blind. He truly believes that he holds me under his spell with the brilliance of his conversation and his lovely fluttering hands. A man as vain as he is, will not see anything. And then, he is old enough to be your father. To him you are a mere schoolboy. The idea of a schoolboy making love to his wife is inconceivable."

And so the wonderful summer wore on, each day happier than the one before. On his twenty-first birthday they took the children on a picnic in the Saint-Cloud forest. He played hide-and-seek with them. All afternoon the woods resounded with their tinkling laughter.

Early in September, Alix and Claude took the river boat to Saint-Germain. He showed her the house where he was born, the church where he had been baptized, the crockery shop his father had lost. They were in a gay mood, and went everywhere, arm in arm, like young lovers. They bought gingerbread for the children.

On the way back they leaned on the deck railing at the stern of the ship and watched the reflections of sunset in the churning wake. Their gaiety of a moment ago had vanished. Already the melancholy of autumn hung in the air.

"September already!" she murmured to herself.

He slipped his arm around her waist.

"Darling," he began hesitantly, "I hate to bring this up, but I won't be able to come so often any more. I must start coaching my cantata for the Public Session."

The Public Session, he explained, was a pompous, very social affair and the concluding ceremony of the contest for the Grand Prix de Rome. The cantatas that had been awarded the First and Second Grand Prix were performed in the Great Hall of the Palais Mazarin before the joint academies, the critics and an elegant audience.

"Madame Gabrielle Krauss, of the Opéra, has agreed to sing

mine. Also Taskin and Muratet for the tenor and baritone parts. I'll
have to rehearse with them. You understand, don't you?"

"Of course, darling."

She understood, she understood only too well . . . Life was wedg-
ing itself between them. This concert was only the beginning. Tomorrow it would be his classes, his friends, his books. It had been like
this last winter, but now it was not enough. Already she resented
every hour he would spend away from her. And then there was a
new problem. Where would they meet to make love. He had no
place of his own. Then what? Some *garçonnière,* some furtive love
nest where they would meet for one hour? Some dingy room in a
shabby hotel where no questions were asked?

The thought made her wince. She must . . . must find some way
to share every minute of his time that could be shared. Time went
so fast when you were in love. She wouldn't be cheated of that short
year of happiness for which she had sacrificed her honor as a wife.
She must find a solution . . .

And one day she did.

"Pierre is going to be very busy this winter," she remarked one
afternoon.

They were at their favorite place, lying side by side on the edge
of "their" pond, as they called it. Around them all was peace and
sunshine.

"He said he would be out of town a good deal," she went on,
"because of that new bank he's building in Moulins. And it gave me
an idea."

He turned on his side and smiled at her. "What kind of an idea?"

"You know I've been worrying where we could meet this winter.
Well, I've found the solution. You can come and live with us."

"With you? In your apartment?" Stupefaction widened his eyes.
"Are you crazy?"

"I am not. On the contrary, it's the simplest, most natural thing
in the world. We have a guest room and you can use it."

"And what will you say to Pierre? What sort of an excuse can
you possibly give him for my moving into his house? He may be vain
and think I am five years old and all that, but he is no fool."

"He won't suspect anything. I shall say that I am afraid at night
to be alone with the children."

"What about the maid?"

"She sleeps at the other end of the apartment and wouldn't even
hear me if I called. Besides, she wouldn't be of any use in an emergency. Don't worry, darling. He won't have the slightest suspicion
or make any difficulties. He's always telling me about robberies.
Every night he checks the bolt on the door before going to bed. Not

only is he afraid for us, but for his famous paintings, which, he thinks, are worth a fortune."

He remained silent. The plan did not seem preposterous any more. She was right, it was quite natural and Pierre wouldn't suspect anything. And how wonderful it would be to live with Alix, be with her all the time! . . .

"The only possible obstacle may come from your parents," she went on. "Do you think they might object to your moving in with us?"

He gave a short, bitter laugh. "My parents wouldn't object if I moved to the North Pole. On the contrary, they'll be delighted to give my room to my sister and have one less mouth to feed."

"Then there won't be any trouble. As you know, Pierre is very fond of you and wants you to win the Grand Prix next year. I'll tell him that you're miserable at home and can't work properly there. He'll be delighted to help you and at the same time acquire a free watchman. He thinks he is very shrewd, and this will appeal to him."

She paused to watch a robin flash in a flurry of little wings. A slow smile spread over her face.

"It's rather funny, isn't it? Almost like in a play . . ." She snuggled against him. "Do you think you will like living with us?"

"I'll be the happiest man in the world—if you can arrange it."

"Don't worry, I will. And I won't have to force his hand either. He will think that the whole idea comes from him. In fact, he himself will invite you to move in. Don't forget to look surprised."

"I won't."

They felt like two accomplices who have put the final touches to a promising plan. Already they were savoring their future happiness. For the first time she looked carefree, as though a weight had been taken off her mind.

"I love you so," she breathed. Her lips reached out to his in a light kiss. "Now you'll be near me until it's time for you to go to Rome."

Tenderly she ran her fingers through his hair. She had won. Life would not wedge itself between them. They would remain together, as close as they were now. For them it would be summer until the end.

◆

As she had predicted, Pierre swallowed the story of her nocturnal fears and was quick to see the advantages of a companion, protector and home watchman during his absences. In no time he made the idea his own, and with his usual floweriness he broached the subject to Claude one evening while Alix was upstairs tucking the children in bed.

"I was distressed to learn of your working problem, my boy. I know how much an artist needs peaceful and congenial surroundings. It occurred to me that perhaps you might consider coming to live with us."

Great show of surprise on Claude's part, followed by just enough hesitation to make the old man become anxious and eagerly explain the advantages of his plan. Finally, surrender culminating in a flow of verbal gratitude.

"Don't thank me, my boy. It will be a pleasure having you with us. I've grown very fond of you and regard you as—how shall I put it?—a member of our family."

Claude's parents raised no objection. When he announced he would try to find a part-time job and contribute to the family budget, indifference turned to appreciation.

"Real nice of you," said his father. "We'll sure appreciate it."

The years had not been kind to Manuel Debussy. He was nearing fifty and had grown stout and withdrawn. At meals he spoke little, chewing his food and drinking his wine in a sort of sullen reverie. He had never recovered from the brief mirage of riches, and knew that he would go on emptying trash baskets and sticking stamps on envelopes for the rest of his life.

"Remember you can come back any time," he said at the door.

Suddenly Claude felt sorry for him. He would have liked to say something nice, show that he harbored no resentment for the slams of a ruler on his knuckles. But it was no use. There was no bond between them any more, not even that of hatred.

"Thank you, Papa, I'll remember."

Thus the incredible came to pass. Claude moved in with his mistress and her husband.

His room was small but cozy. Alix helped him tack his Japanese prints on the walls, arrange his books, hang his meager wardrobe in the armoire. The children greeted his installation with squeals of pleasure. Even Madeleine, the maid, gave him a welcoming smile. A week after moving in, he felt more at home than he ever had with his family.

His cantata, *Le Gladiateur,* was duly performed at the Public Session and warmly received. Critics frowned on his "rather exaggerated craving for originality" but forgave it as an evidence of youth. All in all, they were rather complimentary.

A few days later another stroke of good fortune came his way. Before leaving for Rome, Paul Vidal, his friend and successful rival, recommended him to Monsieur Gounod as his successor to the post of accompanist and chorus master of the vocal society Concordia.

"Go to see him. You'll see, he's a nice old codger. Tell him you're crazy about *Faust*. He'll like that."

That afternoon Claude went to rue Montchanin, a short and opulent street favored by bankers, senators and millionaire industrialists, where Gounod lived. His two-story mansion had a wrought-iron gate, a stately porte-cochere, silk curtains at the windows and that air of elegant aloofness that comes with money.

He rang the bell and was ushered by an elderly gibbous butler into the composer's study: an enormous room decorated with carved bookcases, a number of gold-framed paintings and a huge pipe organ.

"I liked your cantata, my boy," said the composer of *Faust,* who among other dignities was president of the jury for the Grand Prix de Rome. "We almost gave you the prize, but don't be discouraged. I tried three times before I finally made it. That was in—let me see, in '39. God, how time flies! Ah, Rome! . . ."

He crossed his hands over his paunch and launched into a flow of reminiscences about his years at the Villa, the evening musicales with Monsieur Ingres, the director, his long walks in the Campagna Romana, his friendship with Felix Mendelssohn.

"He was about thirty at the time, and you have no idea how handsome he was. A real *grand seigneur*. And what a musician! The moment he sat at the piano—"

It was impossible not to like this plump, apple-cheeked old man, with his wide snowy beard spread like a bib over his chest, his velvet skullcap and quilted smoking jacket. He was brimming with friendliness. He even tried to be modest, which was very hard when you were France's Great Old Man of Music, member of every possible academy, decorated by every government, foreign and domestic.

The stream of memories dried up at last.

"So, you want to take Vidal's place, do you?" he said with a benign smile. "Could use a little money, couldn't you? Don't be ashamed to be poor, my boy. I, too, was poor once. Some day you also may write an opera—"

"Not like your wonderful *Faust!*"

The composer made a deprecatory gesture. "Today I'm detached from all worldly glories. I devote myself to singing God's praises in my music."

He studied Claude for an instant, and went on, "Yes, I think you will do very well. Vidal told me you were an excellent accompanist and won first prize in sight reading. This will be useful. The salary is one hundred francs a month. Come next Saturday evening at eight, and we'll drive to the rehearsal together."

The following Saturday he was waiting at the Gounod mansion, and thereafter he regularly escorted the composer to the weekly rehearsals. He became accompanist, chorus master, librarian and general handy man of the Concordia Vocal Society. He gained valuable experience in the handling of choral music and was able to give some money to his parents.

At the Conservatoire he now was regarded with the reverence due his standing as winner of the Second Grand Prix. When he entered the courtyard in the morning, the pupils of the elementary classes pointed at him from afar and gazed at him with awe, just as he had done in his solfeggio days.

In the evening he did his homework under Alix's loving eye. If he still indulged in a few parallel fifths and strange combinations of chords it was in a prankish spirit and no longer from repression and rebelliousness. In class he applied himself. He even became something of a beaver.

In a flush of enthusiasm he enrolled in the organ and fugue class of Monsieur César Franck, Papa Franck, as he was called at school.

Every Tuesday he made his way to the huge classroom with its dilapidated organ, a wreck of an instrument which had come from the Tuileries seventy years before. In his black redingote, white tie and gray trousers, César Franck was already waiting at his desk, impatiently plucking at his bushy side whiskers.

"Hurry up, children, hurry up . . ." He would fret while the students hung their mackintoshes and pelerines on the wall and took their places on the wooden benches. "We have a lot to do this morning."

Gradually silence would fall over the room and César Franck would begin his lecture.

"Gentlemen, this morning we propose to study Johann Sebastian Bach's immortal Fugue in E flat."

Or in G minor, or Beethoven's C sharp minor Quartet . . . He always began like this in a solemn professorial tone. "This is one of those supreme compositions in which inspiration and technique are blended in the most felicitous—"

But already his decorousness was crumbling. The sentence remained unfinished, and he began searching through his pockets. Surreptitiously at first, then in frantic dismay, muttering to himself, "Now where can they be? I am sure I had those notes when I left the house . . . *Saperlipopette,* they must be somewhere . . ."

By now he had lost all restraint, forgotten his dignity, and was emptying the contents of his pockets on the desk, pulling drawers open, peering under his chair, rifling through stacks of music, red-faced, disheveled, his white tie askew. The students were accustomed to such scenes and exchanged amused winks. Papa Franck's absent-mindedness was legendary in a Conservatoire full of absent-minded professors.

Finally he gave up the search.

"I had prepared a few notes on this fugue, but I have misplaced them. That's what happens when you get old, you forget things. It's terrible to grow old. Take me for instance. I was born in '22. Now 1822 is an important date in music. Can anyone tell me why?"

Smilingly, he ran his soft brown eyes over his students.

"Come on, children. What important event took place in 1822?"

There was something endearing about this short, excitable old man. He looked like a provincial lawyer, yet a simple majesty shone in his gaze, in the fatherly smile that rolled back his jowly cheeks. In fits of anger he turned beet-red and stamped his feet, only to apologize a minute later for his "awful disposition" and go off on some other musical dissertation. His students made fun of his umbrella, which he carried under his arm all year round, his worn top hat, his gray trousers hitched up high over his ankles, but they loved him. And he loved them back. He did not remember their names or faces, could not follow any pedagogic plan, lost himself in digressions and anecdotes, yet his teaching was extraordinarily fecund.

"Come on, come on," he went on, taunting his audience. "Do you give up? Well, it was in 1822 that Beethoven wrote his last sonata, Opus 111. What a masterpiece! As you know it is in C minor and begins with—"

He was off. Forgotten was Bach and his immortal fugue. For the next ten minutes the students were treated with the most lucid and penetrating analysis of Beethoven's last sonata. From there he swayed into an appraisal of the man. He described how he flew into rages, fell constantly in love with young ladies, who laughed at him, and dined at the houses of rich men he despised.

"He was vain, miserly, rude and at times unethical—he sold his *Missa Solemnis* to two publishers—but his faults only bring him closer to us. And, above all, he wrote some of the greatest music ever penned by man."

From his pocket he pulled an immense handkerchief and blew his nose. "But let's be methodical. We are not here to talk about Beethoven, we are here to study Bach's Fugue in E flat. Before we proceed, let's make sure we understand what a fugue is. We know it isn't an invention, a variation, an episode or a development. Then what can it be?"

At random he pointed to a student. "You, my boy. Tell us what a fugue is."

"A polyphonic composition developed according to strict counterpuntal rules."

"Very good. No, don't sit down. Please, tell us how a fugue begins and develops." He turned to the others. "Listen carefully. This is very important."

"It begins with a theme or subject, first given by a one-voice part which proceeds with its own counterpuntal development while the subject, now called the answer, is repeated at an interval of a fourth or fifth degree—"

"Remember that," interrupted Franck. "An interval of a fourth or fifth. Go on."

"—until all parts are answered one by one combining their melodies in one complex whole in which the theme is often entirely lost only to reappear at some unexpected time."

"All this, of course, is elementary and familiar to you." He was beaming with pleasure. "Excellent, my boy. You can sit down."

He then proceeded to analyze some famous classical fugues by Haydn, Handel, Bach and Beethoven.

"Now let's study Mozart's fugue in his wonderful *Requiem*," he said, chalking the theme on the blackboard behind his desk. "Here you notice that the subject with its various counter-subjects is presented in double counterpoint—"

For a while he lingered over the fugue, went into raptures over Mozart's genius and told a few anecdotes about the composer.

He described the concert which Mozart, aged seven, had given at Schönbrunn before the Empress of Austria and the Court. "After playing his last number, he took a deep bow. Then, stepping down from the platform, he got entangled in his tiny sword and fell flat on his face. One of the little archduchesses rushed to help him up. She was three months older than himself. Her name was Marie Antoinette."

In broad strokes he depicted Mozart's short and piteous life, which had begun so brilliantly.

"He died on a stormy December night. At the theatre, they were playing his opera *The Magic Flute*. He knew he was dying. 'It's all over for me,' he said. 'Already I have the taste of death on my tongue.' The next day it was snowing so hard that, after the service, his wife and few friends decided to go home. Only his little white dog followed his coffin to the cemetery. A week later, he would have been thirty-two."

Suddenly he returned to his train of thought. "Well, now that we know what a fugue is, let's see what it can become in the hands of a master."

He walked up to the organ and began playing Bach's Fugue in E flat. The main theme rose, filling the room like an unearthly presence. Then, in stately order, other themes appeared, coiled into one another, vanished, reappeared, twined again and unraveled once more with the grace of ribbons waving in the breeze. Steadily the fugue swelled into an increasingly beautiful and complex web of sound until its majestic end.

"This, children, is the kind of music you must hear in Heaven," said Franck, returning to his desk.

The class went on. Several students played the Bach fugue while the teacher listened, pulling on his gray side whiskers, interrupting now and then to explain some marvel of counterpoint, point out the perfection of a phrase. By the time the recess bell rang the young men had been made to feel the grandeur of the humble choirmaster who was the greatest of musicians. For César Franck taught more than music, he taught the love of music.

◆

Back in his little room Claude told Alix about his classes, mimicked his various professors to make her smile. In the evening, when her husband was out of town, she came to knit by his table after tucking the children in bed. Now that they spent so much time together, their passion had spent some of its violence. They still yearned for each other, but now tenderness tempered their sensuality. Silently she savored each moment of her year of sin.

As for him, never had he been so happy.

"I wish the contest were ten years from now," he remarked one day. "So we could stay on together like this."

"So do I." She smiled ruefully. "But it can't be. Let's be thankful it is still a long way off."

Thus winter went on, with its flurries of snow, its gusts of wind that rattled the windows, its endless rains. Then, unexpectedly, toward the middle of March the weather turned arctic. The Seine froze solid. A *midinette* who tried to drown herself merely sprained an ankle. The cold became unendurable. Couples who had not exchanged a kiss in twenty years now clutched each other in bed to keep warm. Reporters interviewed Madame Labourette, a rag picker who was a hundred and three and the oldest living Parisian. They found her in her hovel, toothless, disheveled and blind drunk. Yes, she hiccuped, this was the worst one yet, but it had a good side. The cold killed the bedbugs. As her recipe for a long and happy life she recommended rum for breakfast.

At the Observatory, Professeur Gratin, the eminent astronomer, held one of his rare press conferences. The cold wave, he explained, was due to cosmic changes, interplanetery upheavals, sun spots and the fact that the Gulf Stream had left its bed. He predicted a return of the Ice Age, backed his prophecy with a swarm of figures and confused everybody with his explanations. His advice to the Paris population was to prepare for a long polar siege.

"If possible, move to Algeria, where it's warm," he said as the journalists walked out of his office.

Two days later the temperature rose, the Seine started flowing again and spring breezed in, premature and unannounced. Along the quays bookstalls reopened, trees swelled with sap and the first lilies of the valley appeared in the flower carts around the Madeleine Church.

Claude, also, felt the surge of spring. It expressed itself in greater sensuality and a change of hairdo. His exalted status at school demanded, he felt, a more sedate coiffure than his present tousled mane. He did not mind being regarded as a revolutionist, but he did not want to look like one. Moreover he had long been dissatisfied with his enormous forehead, which, he thought, made him look like Beethoven. He did not want to look like Beethoven. He wanted to look like a romantic young genius.

He spent several anxious hours before his mirror. Finally, by brushing his hair down and cutting it in a straight fringe an inch over his eyebrows, he achieved the effect he sought. The new hairdo concealed most of the embarrassing forehead and made him look like a dashing Renaissance artist. Give him a doublet and a plumed toque and he would have passed for one of Raphael's students.

Another important factor in his transformation was his beard. At long last it had made its appearance. A black silky down that darkened his chin and upper lip and the line of his jaw. Now he looked his age, twenty-one. Nobody would insult him any more by thinking he was eighteen or nineteen.

When he appeared at school with his new Renaissance coiffure he created a sensation. With his pale, handsome face and his jet-black eyes he did look romantic and faintly tenebrous. He was dubbed the Prince of Darkness and the nickname stuck. He made no protests. There was something rather flattering in being compared to the beautiful and defiant angel who had tried to be God.

By now the annual fever which preceded the annual contest for the Grand Prix de Rome was beginning to show itself. In the bistros surrounding the Conservatoire, students argued heatedly over the merits of the various candidates. Claude as usual was pessimistic. He told Monsieur Guiraud that he had won the second prize by a fluke and never would win the first. Anyway, the whole thing was a barbarous invention of the Academy.

"You're an idiot," said his teacher as they were lunching together. "Your only serious rivals are Xavier Leroux and Charles René, and you are better than they are. Now stop worrying, will you, and please, win the Grand Prix."

And sure enough, that year, Claude won the First Grand Prix.

Only then did he realize the plight he was in. He would have to leave Alix . . .*

Like a poisoned arrow, the thought imbedded itself in his mind. The congratulations he received now sounded like mocking jeers of his secret despair. What was he going to do? . . . From then on he knew no peace. Apprehension kept him awake at night. He lost his gaiety, barely touched his food.

Alix read his wretchedness in his eyes and easily guessed its cause. With a pang she measured the involuntary cruelty of her selfishness. To keep him at her side she had given him a home. Now she saw that this was the worst thing she could have done to a youngster who had known no real home since his childhood days. During the months he had lived in her house his youthful carnality had turned into a deep, dual love. Unwillingly she had become for him not only a loving mistress, but a sort of second Aunt Tavie. In his mind the two had become inextricably entangled. It would be hard to make him see reason, understand that the time had come for him to go and be alone again.

How hard, she did not know . . .

"You don't want to go to Rome," she said one day. "That's it, isn't it, darling?"

He looked at her, his mouth clamped in a line of stubbornness.

"You knew that some day you would have to go," she went on.

"I don't have to go anywhere. Nobody can force me to go where I don't want to."

"Of course," she said soothingly. "Still it's regulations."

"I don't care."

She did not insist.

Early in June the whole family moved to Ville d'Avray for the summer. Again Alix's husband commuted every day to town; again Claude pretended to give piano lessons to Marguerite. Again the lovers spent much time together, walked hand in hand through the fields, sat by the edge of their pond. Yet things were not the same as the year before. The shadow of his approaching departure fol-

---

* Eighteen years later Debussy described that fateful morning of June 27, 1884, when he stood on the Pont des Arts, "fascinated by the exquisite play of sunlight on the rippling waters" and waiting for the decision of the jury. "Suddenly someone tapped me on the shoulder and said breathlessly, 'You've won!' . . . People may not believe me, but nevertheless it is a fact that at once all my joy was over . . ."

His winning cantata, The Prodigal Son (L'Enfant Prodigue), is dedicated to his teacher, Monsieur Guiraud. It received twenty-two of the twenty-eight votes.

lowed them everywhere. Sometimes they lapsed into brooding silence, gently squeezed each other's hands in silent anguish. Both became acutely aware of the passing of time, but in different ways: she, with resignation to the inevitable; he, with revolt.

"Listen, darling," he said one afternoon, as they were walking along a narrow lane. "I've thought it all out. In October, after the Public Session, I'll get a doctor's certificate saying I am ill and I'll resign the Grand Prix, supposedly for ill health."

He waited, proud of his ingenuity, a satisfied smile on his lips. "In this way I won't have to go."

She looked at him, stunned by the havoc she had wrought. She was prepared for tirades against the Academy, against the regulations, against everything under the sun. But she had not foreseen he would be willing to throw away his Grand Prix.

"They can't send me to Rome if I am sick, can they?" he said in the silence.

"No. I suppose they can't," she said at last. "But first, how will you get this certificate?"

For an instant he was at a loss for an answer, but caught himself. "I'll just go from one doctor to another until I find one who gives it to me."

"And then what will you do?"

He laughed. "Stay with you, of course. That is, if you want me. You do want me to stay, don't you?"

"Yes, darling, I'd like to, very much. But it's impossible. Please, try to understand—"

All summer she tried to make him see the absurdity of his plan. Even if he were mad enough to resign his Grand Prix he could not live in her house. Why? . . . Because of a lot of reasons. The excuse of his working problem at home no longer existed. Then, Pierre had had a disagreement with the bank's president and was not likely to receive any more contracts. He would be home all the time. The fable of her nocturnal fears would become senseless.

"No, darling. It's no use. We've been lucky all these past months. Let's not ask for the impossible."

Still he clung to her. Even after their return to Paris and the Public Session he continued to implore and argue. Now their discussions often degenerated into quarrels that rekindled their passion. For a moment they forgot their disagreement in the pleasure of their flesh. He tried to win her to his side through lustfulness, and at times he thought he had succeeded. She would look at him through eyes full of tears.

"But, don't you see, darling, that it is just as hard for me as for you? . . . Please, don't make it more painful than it is already."

December came, and still he would not go. By now, in addition to his arguments with her, he had to fight the authorities. He was summoned to the office of Monsieur Thomas, director of the Conservatoire. He explained he had just lost a dear relative.

"Your grief does you honor," said the official skeptically, "but you can mourn your relative in Rome as well as in Paris. I want you to leave by the end of the week."

Three weeks later he was still in Paris. This time it was his teacher, Monsieur Guiraud, who made him feel his displeasure.

"Are you going to stop this nonsense? Naturally you have a girl and hate to go. I did, too. Every Grand Prix has some girl he hates to leave. But, damn it, he leaves her. And you'd better do the same."

The trap was closing. Like a cornered animal he looked for some way out, but there was none. Even Alix's husband was becoming pressing. "You should already be in Rome. What's holding you back, my dear boy?"

The Christmas holidays came and went. Paris fell into the gloom of a slushy January, and Claude slid into hopelessness.

He still held on for two more weeks.

By mid-January he finally admitted he had lost and gave up the fight. With a leaden heart he began the round of farewells. First he called on his former teachers. Then on Monsieur Gounod, beaming in his broad white beard. "Congratulations. It was a very good cantata . . ." Then Monsieur Guiraud, frowning and grinning at him at the same time. "Well, better late than never. Now you can write all the parallel fifths you want. Come and see me when you come back." His parents; his sister and brothers. "Send us a line when you can . . ." Then Alix's husband, loquacious as ever. "Don't forget to visit our Embassy, the Palazzo Farnese. It was built by Cardinal Farnese, whose sister Julia was the most beautiful woman in Rome and the Pope's mistress. He wasn't a very good cardinal, and later, he was an even worse Pope, but he had good taste in architecture. He got Michelangelo to supervise . . ."

Then Alix . . . Her clear eyes smiling behind their tears. The last caresses, the last kiss. "Good-bye, my Claude . . ."

CHAPTER

4

ON JANUARY 27, 1885, SEVEN MONTHS TO THE DAY AFTER WINNING the Grand Prix, Claude finally set out for Rome.

At the Italian frontier the Paris-Rome express got a new locomotive, a new engineer, a new conductor with a gold-striped cap—and became a *rapidissimo*. And a *rapidissimo* it was indeed. It plunged on its way down the peninsula with much vigor and whistling, rattling merrily over the rails, ignoring small stations, flashing through the countryside with its mane of black smoke down its jostling spine. This went on for miles, during most of the afternoon. Then, as it neared Rome, it seemed to lose zest, began stopping more and more frequently and for less and less reason. First in towns of three thousand inhabitants. Then two; then one. Then five hundred; then three, then two. Finally, any hamlet with a church, a fountain, a tobacco shop and a post of *carabinieri*. Never was there a train so reluctant to reach its destination.

By now Claude was too tired to care. His slouch hat over his eyes, his frozen hands deep in his coat pockets, bouncing on the third-class wooden banquette with every jostle of the train, he waited for the ordeal to end. The rain, which had stopped at dawn, shortly before Marseilles, had caught up with them and was now coming down in buckets, pelting the metal roof of the train, sluicing in translucent curtains down the compartment's windows. A flash of lightning scribbled its hieroglyph on the slate of the sky, and the *rapidissimo* came to a shuddering halt, like a frightened horse, waiting for the thunderclap that followed.

Then the locomotive sent up a feeble squeak, and the trip was resumed at an even slower pace. After another kilometer, there was another halt. Through heavy lids Claude distinguished the dripping outline of the station of Monte Rotondo, a distant suburb of Rome.

Stolidly he was waiting for the jolt which would announce the next departure, when he heard urgent knocks on another window of the compartment. Turning his head around he recognized his former schoolmates Gabriel Pierné and Paul Vidal, who were signaling to him. At the same moment a group of noisy and very wet young men burst into the compartment, shook his hand and seized his two suitcases.

On the station platform he found himself surrounded by a group of fellow Grand Prix, who, following the venerable tradition of the Villa Medici, had driven all the way to Monte Rotondo to greet him and drive him back in style to Rome.

"First let's eat," said Paul Vidal. "There must be a restaurant somewhere. Wait here."

He dashed off and returned a minute later with the station master, a heavily whiskered man in a red soft-crowned kepi with much gold lacing.

A *ristorante!* Of course there was a *ristorante* in Monte Rotondo. And what a *ristorante!* People came from miles to eat there. Nowhere in the whole of Italy would they taste such ravioli, such lasagne! It belonged to his brother Giuseppe. His mother was the *cuoca.* And what a *cuoca!* No one in the whole of Italy could cook like her.

"But the *ristorante,* it is not here." With a sweeping gesture he pointed to a handful of houses a half mile up the hill. "It is there!"

Monte Rotondo, they learned, was divided in two parts: Basso Monte Rotondo, which did not amount to anything, and Alto Monte Rotondo, where all the important buildings were located—the church, the *municipio* or city hall, the post of *carabinieri,* the piazza with its beautiful fountain and the single hotel which also included his brother's restaurant.

There was an effusive exchange of thanks, waves and smiles. Then the young men clambered into the cart and started on the long trek up the hill. Half an hour later, drenched to the bone, they entered the Piazza del Popolo. Without difficulty they located the hotel, which stood right in the center of the square.

During dinner Claude was asked a thousand questions. The young exiles hungered for news of Paris. How were things there? . . . And the weather? . . .

"Awful, as usual. It was snowing when I left."

"Here, of course, we're enjoying perpetual sunshine," laughed Paul Vidal between two mouthfuls of ravioli.

And how were things at the old Conserv? . . . Was Durand, the harmony prof, the same old camel? And Papa Franck? Did he still say, "Hurry up, children?" Did he still forget his notes?

He became acquainted with Marcel Baschet, Grand Prix of Painting, who declared he would do his portrait. "Something in the style of Caravaggio . . ." Gaston Redon, Grand Prix of Architecture, introduced himself with the mention that he played the flute and the guitar.

"And both as badly," shot Georges Marty.

This brought forth much laughter. The powerful local wine was beginning to be felt around the table. After dessert, long clay pipes appeared and the conversation proceeded in a cloud of tobacco smoke.

"You don't look any too happy," remarked Gustave Popelin, also Grand Prix of Painting, grinning in his blond beard. He was the eldest of the group, a sedate old man of twenty-five and in his last year at the villa. "I know how you feel. I, too, hated to come to Rome, But it isn't so bad, really. I'll be almost sorry to leave. If you feel lonely, drop in at my studio."

Claude was told at great length about the life at the Villa Medici: the meals in common, the regulations, the authorities. The director, Monsieur Cabat, was a nice old codger who dozed in his beautiful office most of the time and did not bother anybody.

Then there was Monsieur Brondois, the general secretary. A real friend, that one. He closed his eyes if a girl happened to spend the night in one of the studios. Never reported you if you stayed out a few days . . .

"So long as you stay in Rome, it's all right."

At this point Giuseppe, the owner, emerged from the kitchen, wiping his hands on his apron. Like his brother, the station master, he had a fine mustache and a winning smile. He inquired if they were satisfied. The raviolis, they were delicious, no? And the wine? Velvet on the tongue, was it not? A ray of sunshine in the bowels . . . Not like the *vino* of Rome, which was indigestible, heavy, *molto pesante,* and lay on the stomach like lead . . .

Paul Vidal explained in his faltering Italian that it was late and still raining and they were too tired to go back to Rome. Could they sleep in the hotel? . . . Certainly they could sleep here. There was a beautiful room.

"Only one?" The seven young men looked at each other.

Yes, only one, but what a room! It had the most beautiful view and two big beds with soft mattresses of fresh straw. Why, seven could easily sleep in such beds. Three in one, four in the other . . .

"You'll see, you'll sleep like *bambini*."

They did. Claude slept flanked on both sides by Vidal's and Popelin's feet. The others managed as best they could. They awoke next morning, feeling refreshed and hungry. The rain had stopped. Sunshine wafted through the window.

After a copious breakfast they piled back in the cart, waved good-bye to the owner, his wife, his mother, his children and half the population of Monte Rotondo, who had come to watch them leave.*

It took them all morning and part of the afternoon to return to Rome, but at last the carriage came to a halt in front of the Villa.

"Well, here it is," said Vidal, pulling up on the reins.

At the sight of the huge ocher-colored *palazzo* that was to be his home for the next three years, Claude felt his throat contract. He braced himself, climbed down from the cart, and with pounding heart, walked through the arched doorway of his prison.

◆

And so it began.

He was allocated a studio, a huge cavern of a room that was called, nobody knew why, the Etruscan Tomb. It was painted a bilious green and was so large that the few pieces of furniture in it floated like islands in a far-flung archipelago. Besides the iron bed, the washstand, the unpainted table and armoire, there was a wheezy, arthritic grand piano and a pot-bellied stove with a long flue that jerked its way up almost to the ceiling. The single window offered a splendid view of Saint Peter's dome and a vast expanse of sky.

On the day after his arrival he was received by the director, a frail, white-bearded academician with narrow shoulders that stooped from the weight of years and official honors. Claude's entrance awoke Monsieur Cabot, who straightened up in his carved red-damask chair and looked at him for a moment through sleepy, blinking eyes.

"I was beginning to think you would never come," he said at last.

With a weary hand he waved aside the explanations Claude was about to give and proceeded with a description of the joys that awaited him at the Villa. Here he would find the peaceful surroundings propitious to creativeness.

"Also the companionship of outstanding young artists who, like

* The hotel is still there, very much as it was when Debussy and his six companions spent the night in a single room.

you, have won the supreme award in the various branches of art. I have myself spent many happy years in this house and I grieve to think that soon I shall have to leave it."

Slowly he gazed, as if in farewell, about the dim, sumptuous room with its glassed book cabinets, its velvet drapes and the marble fireplace in which burned a cheerful fire.

With a sigh, he returned to Claude. "I hope you will enjoy your sojourn with us, and if you have any problem, contact the general secretary, our dear Monsieur Brondois, who will do his best to help you and will acquaint you with the regulations."

This brought the interview to an end. He smiled, made a feeble dismissing gesture and relapsed into a doze.

Thus Claude became one of the twenty-odd *pensionnaires* who lived in the old palace. Like them he appeared in the dining room at mealtime, ate spaghetti and drank the heavy Roman wine under the fixed stare of the portraits of former Grand Prix laureates who looked down from the walls.

As a rule there was much banter about art and women during meals, but now little talk arose at the huge oval table. Everyone at the Villa was busy on his *envoi,* the work that was required from them after their first year in Rome. The young men wolfed down their food in absorbed silence; then scurried back to their studies to toil over the painting, sculpture, engraving, architectural drawing or musical composition that was to be sent to Paris in the spring.

Having no *envoi* to prepare, Claude remained amidst the general activity as the sole champion of idleness. He usually finished his meal alone, smoked a leisurely cigarette over his demitasse; then he shambled back to his Etruscan Tomb.

There he stood at the window, endlessly brooding over Alix. She had made him promise to try to forget her, but never had she seemed so near as now when she was so far. Her presence haunted the silence.*

Sometimes he sat down at the piano and played Tristan's Liebestod, or some other emotional page from Wagner's operas, for which he had recently developed an unbounded enthusiasm. He wallowed in the stormy music, churning his longing with its desperate crescendos. After a few hours of this he would walk away from the instrument, feeling more miserable than before. Or he read poetry. The more desperate, the better. He felt as one with the poets who had bewailed the wretchedness of love and life. With moist eyes he read their poignant strophes and wished he were dead.

* It must have been on one of these despondent afternoons that he scratched the inscription, *"Ce qu'on peut s'emm—ici!"* on the drainpipe that ran alongside his window.

Sometimes he stretched out on the bed and gazed at the ceiling, thinking about Alix, wondering where she was at the moment and if she thought about him. He cursed music, which had taken him away from her. If he hadn't studied music he wouldn't have won the Grand Prix and would not be a thousand miles away from the woman he loved.

Sometimes he dropped in on Popelin. Love is a vocal disease that craves expression and sympathy. In the blond-bearded painter he had found a patient listener. He would sit down on the edge of the bed and talk about Alix, happy to pronounce her name, recalling episodes of their relationship while the artist walked back and forth from his easel, pulling on his pipe.

"I'll never forget her," Claude remarked one day with a hopeless sigh.

"You don't even try. Go and get yourself a girl. This town is full of pretty women."

"I hate women."

"That's what I used to say when I came here, but I've changed my mind."

"I'll never change my mind," said Claude with finality.

"Then try working. You've been here six weeks and haven't done anything."

"I can't think of anything to say, I can't create without her."

"Well, then go on being miserable and enjoy yourself."

The idle, empty days dragged by. By the middle of March, spring arrived—the early pine-scented Roman spring, languid with desire and approaching summer. Now Claude began taking long solitary strolls in the Villa's magnificent gardens. He sat beneath some rose-entwined statue, doing nothing, weaving his forlorn reverie on the gentle splashing of the Bologna fountain. Or he ambled along the cypress-lined alleys. Soon it grew warm enough to lie on the grass. Under the parasol pines he took long afternoon siestas. He did everything but work. After two months at the Villa he had not written a single page of music. Not a line, not a note.

"At this rate, you'll soon turn into a complete idiot," Popelin remarked one day.

He was putting the finishing touches to his *envoi,* a large canvas entitled "The Temptation of Saint Anthony." It showed the bald-headed, long-bearded hermit, haggard from fasting and meditation, struggling against the advances of a luscious young woman, entirely nude except for her gold earrings. Why this gorgeous wanton should want to force herself on this decrepit and obviously very poor old man was not clear, but art can dispense with logic, and the merits of the picture lay in its rich coloring and its dramatic play of light and shade.

Claude did not reply to the painter's offensive remark and sat moodily on the edge of the bed.

"You look like hell," the artist went on with the frankness of true friendship.

"I can't sleep."

"And I know why." This time he exploded. "For God's sake, get that woman out of your mind!"

"I can't."

"What you need is a girl."

"I told you I don't want to meet any girl."

"Listen." Popelin's patience was wearing thin. "When I came here three years ago, I couldn't get my girl out of my mind. I couldn't sleep, just like you. I wanted to jump out of the window. Then it dawned on me that love and love-making are two different things, and I still could love her while making love to someone else."

"You couldn't have been truly in love," said Claude harshly.

"I tell you, I wanted to jump out of the window. What more do you want? But at least I had some sense. So I got myself a girl and after a few days I felt wonderful. I wrote to my girl in Paris and told her how wonderful she was and what great friends we'd always be, but if she found someone who wanted to marry her, please not wait for me and grab him."

"What happened?"

"She did. She has two children now."

"I'll never betray Alix. She's faithful to me and I'll be faithful to her."

"Of course, be faithful. Be faithful as much as you like, but in your heart. That's enough."

"You're disgusting."

The painter chortled in his whorly blond beard. "Perhaps. But you have no idea how much better you'll feel and how much clearer you'll think after a few nights with a pretty girl. Let me introduce you to Angela."

"Who's she?"

The painter pointed to the temptress in his canvas. "This is Angela. Look at her."

Claude did—at length. His eyes ran over the smooth, amber throat, the firm breasts, the lean curve of her thighs which the hermit found so hard to resist. He felt a general tightening of his muscles and his mouth went dry. Bravely he turned his head aside.

"I don't want to meet her."

Popelin rested his palette on the stand near the easel and came to sit next to Claude.

"Let me introduce you. She is beautiful and awfully nice. She's helped me a lot and I hate to leave her. But I must go in August. Also, a dealer has arranged an exhibition for me as soon as I return, and I'll have so much work until then, that I can't spend any time with her."

Claude was adamant. Love was a sacred thing. There was no compromise in love.

"Real love, that is," he said pointedly.

"Come on, don't be such an ass. Let me introduce you to her. You'll thank me for it. After a while you'll be able to think more clearly about this woman of yours, see how hopeless the whole thing is and turn your foolish love into real friendship. Which is what she wants, anyway."

"She does not."

"You told me she made you promise to forget her."

"She did, but she didn't mean it."

Popelin gave a defeated shrug and rose. "Have it your way."

He did. He remained faithful and miserable. He lost his appetite, slept badly and brooded himself into a fever. At last he fell ill.

At once his hopes revived.

◆

He had read that the first *pensionnaire* of the Grand Prix of Music, a certain Androt, had died at the Villa, almost a century ago, from an attack of the Roman fever, a form of malaria.

"I think I've caught the Roman fever," he told Popelin, who had come to visit him."

"You haven't caught a damn thing, you aren't sick. You just sulked yourself into a temperature."

"I tell you I have malaria, like Androt."

Surely the authorities would not want the blood of another Grand Prix of Music on their hands, would they? No doubt they would send him back to Paris to recover or die. In either case he would see Alix again.

"You'd better tell the secretary to call a doctor."

The doctor came—a friendly Roman physician with a bulbous nose, a bristling goatee, and a small leather bag which proved to be an arsenal of medical instruments. He peered into Claude's throat, tapped his abdomen, pressed his ear to his chest, poked a thermometer into his mouth, and finally looked at him with the grave and knowing look doctors assume when they have not the faintest idea of what is wrong with their patients.

"You are sick," he said at last in Italian, for he spoke no French.

Popelin, who acted as an interpreter, informed Claude of the doctor's diagnosis.

"Ask him if it's the malaria," whispered Claude, delighted. "The Roman fever."

The doctor's reply was an emphatic shake of the head. There had been no malaria in Rome for the last thirty years.

"Anyway, tell him I am very unhappy here and he must send me back to Paris."

"You mean you're unhappy here, in Rome?" the doctor gasped. "In this most beautiful of all the cities in the world?"

Claude nodded and the doctor exploded with civic indignation. The Roman air was the most salubrious in the world, people practically never died in Rome. While in Paris, *Parigi,* as he called it, the air was so foul people died like flies. Sputtering in his beard he slammed his instruments back into his bag, shoved his top hat down on his head and stormed out of the room.

Claude's hopes crashed to the ground. His spirits sank while his fever rose. His condition grew so alarming that the director himself came down from his office to investigate. He sat by the bedside, his scaly hands crossed over the knob of his cane, and asked a few questions. Claude replied in a feeble voice. Yes, he was very ill. Only in Paris would he have a chance to get well. Monsieur Cabat did not take the hint. In his whispering voice he pointed out that the doctor's report dismissed any suggestion of malaria. It merely prescribed two weeks in bed as a sure cure for whatever was ailing Claude.

"I also think that rest will do you a lot of good," the director went on with an imperceptible smile in his filmy eyes. "You will remain confined to your room for the next fortnight."

Then, with a comforting smile, he left.

During his two-week confinement Claude had time to reflect on his situation and women's selfishness. He had written Alix describing his illness and sufferings, and she had replied with a friendly but brief note of sympathy. She did not appear overly alarmed over his Roman fever and urged him to make the best of things, get well and work hard. This seemed to him both unjust and cruel and proved that already she had forgotten him.

He recalled Popelin's offer to introduce him to Angela. After seeing her picture he felt he already knew much of her, and was eager to know more. All right, he would make the best of things, as Alix suggested. He would keep his promise and forget her. He would wipe her from his mind.

"When I can get out of this damn room, I'd like to meet Angela," he told the artist one day, somewhat sheepishly.

"Oh, you do? I thought you hated women."

"I've been thinking."

"And you've changed your mind, that's usually what comes from thinking."

Finally he took pity on his young colleague and promised to arrange a meeting.

"But now you'll have to wait till she returns. She went to Sicily to see her mother. She told me she'd be back early in June. You'll meet her then."

And now it was April. Swallows nested under the eaves of the Villa. From the gardens came the fragrance of roses. After weeks of furious activity life had resumed its easy routine. The *envois* had been collected by the "dear Monsieur Brondois," and were being put on display in the Salon d'Honneur for the traditional exhibition that preceded their shipment to Paris.

This exhibition was one of the fashionable events of the Rome spring season. The King and Queen of Italy never failed to attend its opening, as well as members of the Court, the local artistocracy and the diplomatic circles. And even two or three art-loving cardinals. It also was the signal for a round of social functions at the Villa Medici.*

Having decided to put Alix out of his mind, and having no inclination to work, Claude had little to think about. Time weighed on his hands. Fortunately, illness is a short cut to popularity. His colleagues, who had paid no attention to him when he was well, took to dropping by his studio now that he was sick, at least officially. Singly or in groups they arrived, bringing French newspapers, cigarettes, fruit which they filched from the dinner table. One gave him a copy of Casanova's Memoirs, which Berlioz used to read in one of the Saint Peter's confessionals. Claude received them in bed, playing the part of the grateful patient.

Soon the enormous Etruscan Tomb became an after-dinner gathering place. Vidal or Pierné played the piano. Gaston Redon followed on his guitar or his flute. Lombard sang obscene atelier songs. Sculptors came dressed in their corduroys, marble dust in their beards, bringing their models with them. Filled with smoke, laughter and the strains of Offenbach's galops, the studio turned into a place of revelry. As night progressed the singing became louder and the dancing more lascivious. Clad in his long nightshirt, Claude attended to his duties as a host and joined in the carousing.

---

* The tradition of this annual exhibition is still being observed. Only once were the King and Queen of Italy not invited to it by Monsieur Cabat, who judged some of the *envois* too indecent for Their Majesties.

It was good to feel young and carefree again, freed from the Alix obsession. This illness, he decided, had done him a world of good.

♦

He was well enough to attend the director's final reception in the last week in May. At Monsieur Cabat's request he accompanied a few ladies who had volunteered to brighten the occasion with their artistry. Graciously he assisted them in their renditions of songs and operatic arias.

During the intermission he was introduced to various guests, among them Count Primoli, a distinguished music-loving Roman aristocrat.*

"I understand you have been ill," said the count, smiling in his gray beard. "Why don't you come and spend some time with me at my villa in Fiumicino. Summer is almost here and Rome will be unbearable. The sea air will do you good."

The director approved. Claude prepared to leave.

"Enjoy yourself," said Popelin. "Eat well, sleep well, swim a lot and don't brood over that woman in Paris."

"Have no fear," Claude said with a reassuring smile. "She means nothing to me any more. I have made up my mind, and I wouldn't cross the street to see her. Now what about Angela? You won't introduce anyone else to her, will you?"

The painter grinned through a cloud of smoke.

"Don't worry. You'll meet her when you come back."

A few days later Claude found himself in Fiumicino, one of those tenacious villages that dot the Italian coastline and with no apparent means of survival manage to endure for centuries. The count's villa stood on the beach at the edge of a pine forest. During the day Claude saw little of his host, who had the rare gift of leaving his guests alone. In the evening they dined together on the terrace, eating leisurely in the Roman fashion, talking and smoking far into the night. Sometimes, after dinner, they went into the drawing room and Claude played some of his compositions. He felt at ease with this amiable soft-spoken man, who reminded him of his Godfather Arosa. Soon they were friends.

One day the count announced he was called away and must leave at once.

"But, of course, you can stay as long as you wish," he added.

And so Claude remained at the Primoli villa, enjoying its luxuriousness, its works of art, its library and the attentions of a staff of well-trained servants. Without effort he slid into a millionaire's life, breakfasted in bed, swam several times a day and sun-bathed on the beach.

* Count Joseph Primoli was the nephew of Princess Mathilde Bonaparte, herself the niece of Napoleon.

His natural talent for idleness grew to staggering proportions. He spent hours stretched on the hot sand, dozing, gazing at nothing, listening to the gentle breathing of the sea. For a few days he was the happiest of men. Heaven, he felt, must be an eternal Fiumicino.

Then, suddenly, *she* was back, nearer and yet farther away than ever. Now it was Alix's voice he heard in the sighing of wavelets on the sand and the murmur of parasol pines at night. Her face looked down at him from the blue emptiness of the sky. The sound of cicadas brought back memories of their summers at Ville d'Avray.

He made some feeble resistance, tried to cling to his newly won freedom. He read Flaubert's *Salammbô* and promised himself to turn it into an opera on his return to Rome. He went to the village of Fiumicino, spoke as best he could with the fishermen repairing their nets, drank wine at the local *trattoria*. It was no use. She wouldn't let him alone. His good resolutions collapsed. It was better to think of her and be miserable than not to think of her at all. Happily, he plunged back into his misery.

◆

He returned to the Villa, in a summer-broiling Rome. During the afternoon the city turned into a ghost town of empty, sun-baked piazzas and shuttered houses. The population vanished from the streets and took refuge in long siestas behind airless mosquito nets. The Tiber dwindled to a rivulet. Even the birds did not venture long out of their nests.

Claude remained closeted in his Etruscan Tomb, avoided the company of his colleagues. In June he had written to Popelin of his heartbreak and now he could not bring himself to face the artist.* He did not want to meet Angela any more. He only asked to be left alone with his longing and tormenting memories.

During the day he lay on the bed, smoking, dozing, brushing off flies in his sleep. At dusk he sneaked out of the Villa for a solitary meal in some distant restaurant. He had seceded from the human race.

At last Popelin learned from the concierge that Claude was back, and sought him out.

"I should've known something like this would happen," he said,

---

* In this famous letter—dated June 24, 1885, from Fiumicino—Debussy poured out his heart to Popelin: "Do I have to tell you that these last months have done nothing but exasperate my feelings. I must admit their strength, for in the absence of the one who inspires them *I cannot live* . . . As I told you, I've taken the habit of wanting and creating only through her . . . As you see, I am far from doing what you advised me to do and reduce to friendship this mad love [. . . *cet amour qui est fou*]. I know that it is mad, yet its very madness prevents me from reasoning . . ."

looking down at the prostrate form on the bed. "Solitude is for happy, intelligent people, and you are neither."

"Leave me alone. I'm perfectly happy."

"That's the trouble. You're like the monk who can't live without his hair shirt. Come on, get up."

"Go to hell."

"Come on. I'm going to take you to meet Angela."

"I don't want to meet her."

Calmly Popelin walked to the washstand, returned with the water jug. "Now are you going to get up?"

"I told you I don't want to see her."

"Well, you're going to whether you like it or not. Now get off that bed. Comb your hair and put on a tie, I want you to make a good impression."

They went to the *trattoria* where Angela worked as a waitress when she did not pose for artists. It was still early in the afternoon and she came to sit at their table and helped them drink their bottle of Chianti. She had the blue-black hair of Sicilian women, moist brown eyes and cherry-red lips. Briefed by Popelin on the piteous state of his friend, she had from the kindness of her heart promised to do her best to cheer him up. After a few minutes of conversation and several long glances at Claude she was eager to keep her word.

A moment later Popelin excused himself on the pretext of an urgent appointment. Angela remained alone with Claude.

"Tell me about the sadness in your heart." Like many Italian country women she had a natural poetry of speech. "Tell me why you look as sad as a fly in October."

He told her that he loved a woman who was far away, and she became even more solicitous.

"Absence makes the heart very heavy, *molto pesante,*" she said, reaching for his hand across the table. "I, too, love a man who is far away. But soon I'll go back home and marry him."

"What does he do?"

"He is the postman," she said simply.

The similarity of their plight seemed to strengthen the bond between them. Soon they confided in each other. When, in answer to her questions, he told her he had known no woman since his arrival in Rome more than six months ago, she was incredulous at first, then sympathetic. It was a terrible thing for a young man to live without a woman's caresses. It was against nature. It made the heart weep in the chest and set the flesh afire. Such a man suffered the torments of the damned. He agreed.

After their third meeting she saw to it that he no longer suffered the torments of the damned.

Thus Angela entered his life at about the same time as Popelin went out of it. Having completed his three-year sojourn, the painter returned to Paris. Claude and Angela escorted him to the Termini Station and stood, hand in hand, under his compartment window until the train started to move away.

"Take care of him," said the painter, as he receded in a cloud of steam.

She did. She was kind, sensual and expert. Now he slept better, no longer brooded over Alix. At least not so much. He even tried to work, and returned to his Fiumicino idea of turning *Salammbô* into an opera. He discovered he could not write about what he did not feel, and he felt nothing about the Carthaginian war machine. Beethoven could be inspired by Coriolanus; he couldn't. He set *Salammbô* aside and instead started writing the opening number of a four-hand Petite Suite.*

Meanwhile, all sorts of things were happening at the Villa. Monsieur Cabat called himself to the attention of the Paris government by his resignation. A new director, Monsieur Ernest Hébert, arrived from Paris. Like his predecessor he was an elderly white-bearded man, an academician, a former Grand Prix and a painter.

Then there was the Brondois affair. It was found that dear Monsieur Brondois, the general secretary, had embezzled twenty-six thousand francs from the Villa's treasury. He had lost the money in unwise speculations in rosaries and religious objects. He had ordered crates of them from France, hoping to resell them at a profit in Rome. This was like bringing coals to Newcastle. A last shipment of Saint Josephs did him in. The theft was uncovered. There was talk of sending him to prison. Instead he was permitted to resign. Thus he departed without scandal. But the shock had been too great, he could not tear himself away from the building where he had left, besides a large deficit, his heart. Every morning Claude could see him from his window, sitting on the low wall of the Piazza dell'Academia, gazing mistily at the Villa. Now and then he went down and tried to cheer him up. After all, righteous people have the comfort of their conscience in their hour of trial, while crooks do not have even that. One day he did not see Monsieur Brondois at his usual place. He had died during the night.

Summer came to an end. Autumn arrived veiled in gentle rains. Rome, so regal a few days before in her make-up of sunshine, now looked like a tired old actress after the show. Tourists had gone, and she could relax. Oddly, Claude found her more beautiful in her sodden rags than in her summer regalia. The grayness of October enhanced the perfection of the Campidoglio, the sweep of the Spanish Steps,

* This piece, *En bateau,* has become one of Debussy's most popular melodies.

the noble melancholy of the *piazzette* where marble fountains gurgled the years away.

In the course of his wanderings he entered a few churches, not the stupendous basilicas that are God's Versailles, but the slum chapels redolent of prayer and incense, still echoing the sobs of long-gone generations. In the Church Maria dell'Anima he heard Masses by Palestrina and Orlando di Lasso that moved him by their simple grandeur and depth of feeling.

With the advent of autumn, the Villa entered upon a new cycle of social functions. Unlike his predecessor, Monsieur Hébert loved society. He set out to dispel the gloomy formality that had been a feature of the official receptions. Under his impulse they turned into lively evenings of music and light-hearted dancing that made them popular among the younger members of the aristocracy and diplomatic corps. Now when ambassadors retired, their attachés remained; when duchesses drove home, their daughters stayed behind. Sometimes these affairs lasted far into the night, ending in an exuberant cotillon that snaked its way through the old *palazzo's* corridors.

At one of these receptions Claude met a ravishing Parisian socialite, who, with her husband—a prominent financier—was the director's house guest. She was much impressed by Claude's compositions and decided to know their author better. The party over, she eluded her husband's surveillance and threaded her way to the Etruscan Tomb. She knew what she wanted and had come prepared. When, in reply to her knock, Claude opened the door, he saw that she was nude under her fur coat.*

In November, at another of Monsieur Hébert's receptions, Claude was introduced to Franz Liszt.

All his life he had heard about him. His piano teacher, Madame Mauté, had told him how handsome he looked when he casually strolled onto the concert platform in his green frock coat and green gloves, his blond shoulder-length hair framing his angelic face; how he shattered keyboards with his gigantic hands and how women swooned at his concerts.

The man Claude saw that evening was a seventy-four-year-old cleric in a black cassock who smoked an enormous cigar. Time had finally ravaged the face that had ravaged so many women's hearts. The lips so often kissed had receded in a thin scar between sunken cheeks. The shoulder-length hair was still there, but hanging in gray, lusterless strands over his ears. Only his hands, his incomparable hands, still moved with youthful grace.

---

* Many years later Debussy mentioned this fleeting adventure to René Peter, giving it as an example of forthright purposefulness in contrast to the well-simulated qualms with which many ladies preface their surrender.

"I understand you were a pupil of my dear friend Monsieur César Franck," he said, addressing Claude.

He removed the cigar clamped between his gums and his clean-shaven face rippled into a smile.

"What a great and humble man!" he continued in his cracked old-woman's voice. "All his life he has toiled without glory in the Vineyard of Music, but he will receive his reward in Heaven, for it is written that the last will be the first and the first the last."

Perhaps he meant what he said and perhaps he didn't. He seldom meant what he said and seldom did what he preached. His attempt at priestly humility was awkward and touching. The most-acclaimed pianist in the world and the greatest Don Juan of his time was now trying hard to be a saintly man. He did not quite succeed.

All his life he had been torn between the flesh and the spirit, shuttling endlessly from bedroom to confessional, fleeing women yet unable to resist the caress of their hands, the worship in their eyes. Now in the shadow of death he still fought his ever-losing battle. Everyone in Rome knew he spent hours in church on his knees, read his breviary, visited the sick and gave princely alms to the poor. Yet everyone smiled and no one was convinced, except perhaps of his good intentions. For everyone knew that he had taken the cloth to escape a princess with whom he had been living for years; that, in his piano class at the Budapest Conservatory, maiden pupils clustered around him during recess and slipped violets into the buttonholes of his cassock; that he drank brandy with the best of them and played cards until all hours of the night, never failed to attend an aristocratic function or to pose for his portrait, lived at the palace of Cardinal Prince Hohenloe and employed a valet to help him dress.

He replaced the cheroot in his mouth, sucked on it like a child on a pacifier and let out an aigrette of ill-smelling smoke.

"My young friend, won't you please play for an old and weary man?"

Claude did not dare to play alone for the greatest of pianists. He signaled to his friend Paul Vidal, and together they performed Chabrier's *Valses Romantiques*.

Liszt congratulated them with effusiveness, predicted a great future for them, as he did to almost everyone who played for him.

Before leaving he invited them to a musicale at the home of Giovanni Sgambati, a few days later. Claude went, and for the first and last time he heard Liszt play. He watched him walk to the piano, spread his clawlike hands over the keyboard, strike a long, echoing chord. And suddenly there was no more pose or posturing and senile lecherousness, but only a grand old man, genial and foolish, who was going to die and prayed in the only way he knew to the only God he truly loved—Music.*

Liszt's visit concluded the cycle of autumn festivities at the Villa. Peace and dust settled back over the Salon d'Honneur. In their studios the *pensionnaires* began thinking about their next *envois*. Claude worked on the Petite Suite.

Then, one day, Angela came to tell him she was returning home.

"My heart cries at the thought of leaving you," she whispered the following morning, "but my fiancé misses me and suffers the torments of the damned. I must go and make him happy."

Thus she drifted out of Claude's life, leaving behind the fragile memory of her kindness, her gleaming smile and soothing hands. Oh, that love could be only this! An innocent copulation, a kiss of lips and bodies. Without jealousy, without possessiveness, without torment . . .

◆

Now it was winter. In the Etruscan Tomb daylight seeped like a grayish fog through the rain-streaked window. It got quite cold in the enormous room and Claude shivered at his work table. The small stove did its best, sent out billows of smoke but very little heat. He complained to the new general secretary, Commandant Delaitre, a retired major, who, from force of habit, did nothing about it.

Finally a heating specialist came. He looked at the stove, took measurements, scratched his head and declared the problem insoluble.

"Just kick it from time to time," he said, as he was leaving. "But not too hard."

Claude did that and it helped. Now there was a little heat with the smoke.

But nothing could help his mood. Since Angela's departure solitude had closed in again. Popelin was not here any more to listen and give advice. In solitude his longing swelled, turned into a throbbing ache. Once more Alix filled his thoughts. Despite himself memories returned, like air bubbles rising to the surface of a pond. Now it was their afternoons by the fire that he recalled, their first love-making on the coverlet of her bed, their evenings in his little room when she knitted by his side.

A few days before Christmas he received a letter from her. Innocuous, chatty, full of trifling news. She had started taking singing lessons again. She had participated in various musicales and sung several of his songs, and they had been well received. She was now posing for her portrait by Monsieur Paul Baudry, the celebrated artist

* Debussy never forgot this occasion. Many years later he wrote about Liszt's masterly pedaling "as if the piano itself were breathing." This was Liszt's last visit to Rome. He died a few months later, July 31, 1886.

and one of Pierre's friends.* The children missed him. They had begun going to school . . .

He read and reread the letter, seeking in it some hidden message of love, some assurance of her faithfulness. He was not long in finding it. Why, it was all clear as day . . Why had she started taking singing lessons? Because she wanted to remember their coaching sessions in the drawing room. Why did she sing his songs? To show him that after eleven months she had not forgotten him . . . To proclaim their love through his music. Why did she pose for her portrait? This was a little more subtle, but to him it was plain. He knew her too well to think she cared a hoot about having her portrait painted. She wanted to show him that she kept busy in order to fill her loneliness . . . Sweet, brave, clever Alix! She had managed to tell him everything in this apparently insignificant letter. She longed for him as much as he did for her.

Again she became an obsession. There was nothing in his mind but the thought of seeing her again. Nothing but his yearning. He wanted to make love to her again. Feel her, the whole of her . . .

Somehow he must . . . must find a way to elude the regulations and go to Paris. If only for a few days.

One afternoon, as he was pacing back and forth the length of his studio, there was a knock on the door. Lorenzo, the concierge, removed his cap and informed him that the director wished to see him.

He followed Lorenzo through the corridor and up the marble stairs that led to the office.

Monsieur Hébert came to him, smiling, his hand extended in welcome.

"I wanted to tell you how sorry I was to hear about your stove," he said, walking back to his desk and waving Claude to a chair. "I wish something could be done about it, but you know how those ancient buildings are. Beautiful, but rather uncomfortable."

Claude noticed the director's office was both beautiful and comfortably warm, which proved something or other. He had no time to delve into the question, for already Monsieur Hébert was telling him how much he had enjoyed his piano playing during the recent musical functions.

"Although I am a painter by profession, I adore music." He made a deprecatory gesture. "I even play the violin, like my illustrious predecessor, Monsieur Ingres. A mere hobby, of course . . . But I wondered if once in a while, after dinner, you might—"

The gist of the matter was that the director wished Claude to be his accompanist. It was the kind of wish that was almost a command. Claude said he would be honored.

* This portrait remained unfinished, interrupted by the artist's death.

The director gave him a delighted smile.

"Perfect!" he said, clapping his hands and rising from his impressive chair. "When would it be convenient for you to start? Let's say—tonight at eight?"

Thereafter Claude saw a great deal of the director. In the library adjoining his office they spent many hours playing one sonata after another. Monsieur Hébert did love music, even though his playing left much to be desired. Joy suffused his face as he ran his bow over the strings, pressing his violin to his cheek like a doctor auscultating a patient.

"I can't tell you how much I'm enjoying this," he said after each session, "and how much obliged I am to you."

Between numbers they would sit down in the capacious leather chairs, sipping cognac or benedictine. Monsieur Hébert was a delightful, erudite old man, a brilliant conversationalist and a man of many loves. He loved painting, he loved music, he loved Mozart, he loved Rome.

But, most of all, he loved the Villa.

"Architecturally it is one of the finest buildings in Rome, perhaps in the world! There are many fine *palazzi* in Italy, but few are set in such exquisite surroundings. It was sheer genius on the part of Lucullus to build his villa here, on this enchanting Pincio Hill. Did you know that in Roman days, the Pincio was called the Hill of Gardens? Yes, we do owe a great debt of gratitude to Lucius Licinius Lucullus. What a remarkable man! Did I ever tell you about him?"

Well, to begin, Lucullus was the richest man in the Roman Empire. He also was a man of culture and taste. It was here that he had built his princely house and planted his fabulous gardens, because there was no finer site in Rome. Here, on this very hill where they now stood, he had walked with his friends Cicero and Pompey, shown them the palm trees he had brought from Africa, the roses that scented the air with a fragrance like that of woman's flesh, the beehives that were his pride and joy, the alabaster basins in which revolved rare Persian fish and poisonous murenas wearing gold earrings in their gills.*

"And so much history has taken place on this hill! I couldn't begin to tell you."

But he tried . . . Here Messalina had pursued her lusts and plotted her crimes. Here Nero, the all-around artist, painter, sculptor, engraver, architect, musician, had sung his songs and plucked his turtle-

---

* Lucullus' gardens extended over the entire Trinità dei Monti district; the Sistina, Gregoriana, Due Macelli, Capo le Case streets; and reached to Piazza Barberini.

shell lyre, while Christians, living torches soaked in resin, blazed on pedestals and made the night bright.

"In time it all passed away. Lucullus' palace crumbled to ruins, his gardens fell to the weeds. For many centuries the Pincio was left to itself, the sunshine and the cicadas. Now and then Cesare Borgia and his father, Pope Alexander VI, came here to find privacy and discuss family matters."

Then a cardinal of simple tastes had built here a modest country house. A few years later, another cardinal, a sixteen-year-old youngster by the name of Ferdinando de' Medici, had bought the house, practically razed it to the ground, rebuilt it, spent a fortune on it and created the Villa Medici.

For two centuries it had remained in the Medici family, until the day, in 1804, when Bonaparte—who else?—had wrenched it away. Since then it had been the Académie Nationale de France à Rome, the Villa.

Monsieur Hébert did not tell the story of the Villa at one session. He told it in installments, one period at a time while sipping liqueur.

It was in the course of one of these lectures that one evening, in a sudden blinding flash, Claude conceived the plan, the wonderful plan which would get him to Paris and Alix ... It sprang from his mind, clear, whole and perfect. Like Minerva from the brow of Jupiter.

The following evening, when they reached the end of the first sonata, Monsieur Hébert rested his violin on the piano and, as usual, suggested a little brandy.

Claude declined the brandy.

"Some benedictine, perhaps?"

Claude declined the benedictine.

Monsieur Hébert frowned with anxiety. "Nothing wrong, I hope."

Claude remained silent, his gaze fastened on the carpet.

"There is something wrong," insisted the kindly old man. "I can see it on your face. Are you, by chance, in some kind of trouble? Money, or perhaps a girl? ... You can trust me. Once I, too, was young."

Claude lifted his eyes, slowly turned them on the director. "I wouldn't say it to anyone, but I know I can trust you, *Monsieur le directeur.*"

"Of course you can. What is it?"

"Well, this morning I received a letter from my mother and she tells me my father isn't well." A pause, a sigh, a gulp. "I hope he'll be all right."

"I hope so, too." Another pause. Then, in a tone of deep affection, "You are very devoted to your family, aren't you?"

"Oh, yes, *Monsieur le directeur.* Very."

"I am glad to hear it. Nowadays children are so inconsiderate, so ungrateful. They seldom appreciate what their parents do for them."
The opportunity was too good to resist, and he delivered a short homily on parents' sacrifices and children's lack of appreciation.

Claude listened to it in silence, with an occasional nod of approval. "I hope Papa gets better," he said, forcing a brave smile. "I really do." He felt that for the first evening he had said enough.

At their next meeting Monsieur Hébert could see that Claude was much distraught. Even his piano playing was not up to par.

"I have no wish to pry into your affairs, but I can see that you are seriously worried. It's your father, isn't it?"

Claude nodded and let out a sigh at the same time.

"What's wrong with him?" pursued the director. "A serious cold, perhaps?"

"It's not a cold, *Monsieur le directeur.*"

"What is it then?"

"His heart."

Monsieur Hébert took a quick breath. "My poor boy! . . . But don't lose hope, remember we are in 1886 and medicine has made immense progress."

"That's what I keep telling myself. But if something happened to my poor papa—" He stopped, unable to continue.

Thus the plan went into full swing. With his talent for self-delusion Claude soon believed his own lies. His father's illness became real to him. Tears would gleam in his eyes as he told the director endearing episodes he invented on the spur of the moment.*

"If only I could see him," he risked a week later. "Just for a few days. I know he'd get well."

Monsieur Hébert was sympathetic, but he explained that a trip to Paris was out of the question. The regulations were formal on this point. Claude gulped, nodded and did not insist.

Back in his studio he surveyed the situation. His campaign was bogging down in a quagmire of sympathy. He must act, bring things to a head. By now his impatience to see Alix had become unbearable. And what if Monsieur Hébert wrote the authorities and asked them to check up on his father's illness? . . . There was no time to lose.

Without hesitation he wrote himself a heart-rending letter, purportedly from his mother, imploring him to rush home before it was too late. The doctor had given up hope and hinted that the end was near. A week at most, perhaps less . . .

"I can't tell you how sorry I am," sighed the director that evening after reading the letter.

* Debussy could cry at will, an achievement of which he was inordinately proud.

He fell silent, his conflicting thoughts mirrored on his kindly face, one hand clasped to his beard as if for support.

Now was the time to strike.

"Please, *Monsieur le directeur,* I beg of you . . . You can see my poor papa's dying and he wants to see me once more before he dies."

He was telling the truth. In his mind he distinctly saw his father in his nightshirt and nightcap breathing heavily through his mustache, asking for him in a wheezy rattle.

"Please, *Monsieur le directeur.*" Genuine tears brimmed out of his eyes. "Please, let me go and see him or I'll . . . I'll do something desperate."

"Now, now, calm yourself. Let me think . . . Of course, the regulations are very specific, yet this seems to be a genuine emergency. Perhaps . . . perhaps I could . . . a short compassionate leave . . . a few days, a week . . ."

"Oh, thank you, *Monsieur le directeur!*" The words exploded out of Claude's mouth. Instantly the tears stopped flowing. "Thank you!"

With bated breath he watched him write the leave of absence, sign it and apply the official seal of the Villa.

"There, my boy." With a fatherly smile Monsieur Hébert held out the paper. "As you see I've made out the leave for two weeks. This should give you ample time to visit with your family and rest your mind at ease."

At the door he shook hands with Claude. "I hope everything will turn out all right. Now, go back to your studio and try to sleep. You have a long journey ahead of you."

The following day Claude had to elbow his way through merry crowds in masks and dominoes. It was carnival time, and before shrouding herself in the purple veil of Lent, Rome was enjoying a few days of pagan revelry. The Corso bustled with carousing mobs. At last, sprinkled with confetti, he reached the Termini Station.

Clutching his bag, he crossed the enormous waiting room, ran onto the train platform and climbed into the *rapidissimo.**

---

* Some biographers state that in the course of his imploring interview with Monsieur Hébert, Claude knelt down, brandished a revolver and threatened to kill himself, and actually frightened the kindly official into granting the leave of absence.

It's possible. He was twenty-three, madly in love, foolish and desperate enough to do anything. Even that.

CHAPTER

ALL THE WAY TO PARIS HE CONGRATULATED HIMSELF. HE HAD BEEN clever, that's why he had succeeded. The idea of his father's illness had been a stroke of genius, and his acting superb. Those tears! . . . When he did not congratulate himself on his cleverness, he congratulated himself on his luck. Two weeks! He had hoped for five days, at most a week, and there he was with a two-week leave of absence. Good Monsieur Hébert! Kind, generous, wonderful Monsieur Hébert! . . .

When he couldn't think of anything more to congratulate himself about, he thought about Alix. Oh, that first instant when she would see him! Incredulously she would stare, open-mouthed, too startled and too happy to smile. Then she would say something; he didn't know what, but something tender and wonderful. And all of a sudden she would be in his arms, sobbing, laughing, her fingers in his hair, her mouth against his. Then, hand in hand, they would run to her bedroom or perhaps to his old room, and they would make love. Make love as never before.

He arrived in Paris the following morning. Someone less clever or cautious might have raced up the stairs to her apartment, rung the bell and said, "Here I am!"—not he. Craftily he waited at the street corner until the maid came out of the house with the children skipping about her, on their way to school. A moment later Pierre appeared, pulling up his gloves, dapper as ever in his topper and fur-collared overcoat.

Now she was alone.

He climbed the stairs slowly, forcing himself to pause for breath at each landing. At last he reached her floor and pulled the bell. He waited, his heart pounding against his chest. Silence; then a faint sound of footsteps, growing nearer and more distinct. Now the key was being turned in the lock . . . the door was opening . . . and there she was!

"You!"

He'd known she would be surprised, and she was. Thunderstruck . . . For a second he thought she was going to throw herself in his arms. He caught the flash of joy on her face, the forward surge of her body.

"Yes, darling. It's me."

"What're you doing here?" Already she was regaining control of herself. Now there was only anxiety in her eyes. "Shouldn't you be in Rome?"

"It's all right." Why didn't she fling herself in his arms, instead of staring at him as if he were an escaped convict? "I have a leave of absence."

"Well," she said hesitantly, "come in."

She didn't take his hand, didn't run to the bedroom, but turned around and preceded him through the corridor. As she opened the drawing-room door he saw the outline of her body through her wrapper and a gust of desire flushed his cheeks.

She made him sit on a chair while she lowered herself onto the sofa. "Now, tell me how you happen to be in Paris."

"I wanted to see you and asked for a leave of absence."

"What reason did you give?"

He sensed her suspicions. She didn't believe him, he could see it in her eyes. "I have it with me, if you want to see it."

"May I?"

He got up and walked to her. From his coat pocket he pulled the folded paper. She took it and began to read. He watched her through tears of fatigue and disappointment. Was this why he had come to Paris? Traveled almost thirty hours? To have his credentials checked when they should be kissing and making love? He felt himself tightening into a rage.

"I guess it's all right," she said, folding the letter.

It was too late. He swooped down on her, catching her unprepared, stifling her protests with his mouth, pushing her backward on the sofa with all his weight. She fought back, managed to utter a few incoherent words. Her nails dug into his wrists and the pain merely needled his lust. With his knee he forced her legs open. Her head rolled back on the pillows, and her hair fell undone. For an instant she lay half naked and unresisting. Gradually, as he possessed her, her breathing quickened, swelled, and finally broke into the moan of rapture he knew so well. In rhythmic shoves his anger flowed out of him into her. With a last quiver, he sagged and toppled down on her, his face pressed into the curve of her shoulder.

Eyes closed, they remained welded to each other for a long time. Then he said, "I'll go now, if you want."

She did not reply. Her arm encircled him. Everything was all right . . .

He took a room in a discreet hotel, far from where she lived. There she came to see him every afternoon. From his window he watched her step down from a fiacre at the street corner, walk the short distance to the hotel and duck into the entrance hall. Eagerly he waited for her on the second floor, held out his hand to help her up the last steps and into his arms.

For two weeks they were happy, happier than he had dared to hope. Never had she been so tender and loving. Or so understanding. Even when he finally confessed his lies about his father's illness she did not reprimand him, but merely looked at him, shaking her head as if he were a mischievous, irresponsible boy.

"You're mad, darling, absolutely mad . . . Will you ever grow up? . . . But what will the authorities do if they find out your father isn't sick?"

He shrugged the question aside. First, they wouldn't find out because Monsieur Hébert wouldn't say anything. And if they did, what could they do? Give him a lecture, insert an official reprimand in the *Journal Officiel.* "At worst they'll cut off my allowance for a month or two, that's all."

Cautiously he avoided mentioning they might also expel him from the Villa, revoke his title of Grand Prix. No use worrying her, spoiling their wonderful time . . .

His explanations did not quite set her mind at ease, but she accepted them, hoping for the best. After all he did have some sort of a leave . . . How he had obtained it was another matter, and she preferred not to think about it. It was enough that he was here, that somehow he had managed to wrench these two extra weeks for them to be together once more.

"It's been wonderful," she murmured on their last afternoon. "Forgive me for being so unfriendly when you arrived. I was afraid you'd done something crazy and run away."

He was to leave in the morning. A moment ago they had made love, and now they lay side by side, smiling at each other, their heads on the same pillow.

She went on, "I'm glad you came to Paris, even if you had to deceive this nice Monsieur Hébert and tell a pack of lies." For a moment her eyes rested on him, soft and sad. Then, almost inaudibly she said, "You'll never know how much I've missed you."

"No more than I did."

"Perhaps not, but in a different way. There is a longing of impatience, and a longing of regret. You looked forward to the time we would be together, I looked back to the time we had been together. At night I'd lie awake and think about our days at Ville d'Avray, our walks through the fields, our place by the pond. And I'd say to myself, 'It's over . . . it's over . . . it'll never happen again . . .' I tried to be brave, but it's hard to be brave when you are alone in the dark."

She saw he was about to speak and gently pressed her finger tips over his lips. "You see, darling, I didn't expect to see you until you'd finished your term at the Villa, and by then it would be too late. Three years is such a long time. At my age it means forever. A woman can change so much in three years. I knew I'd look old and you wouldn't love me any more." Suddenly her face creased with pain. "Oh, darling, you can't imagine how hard it is for a woman to see herself grow old. She's afraid to look into a mirror, afraid to find a new wrinkle, a new gray hair—"

"But you aren't old! You're beautiful—"

"To you perhaps." A melancholy smile brushed her lips. "For a short time."

"It's not true!" Impulsively he raised himself on his elbow and avidly began kissing her face. "You're young and beautiful," he protested between kisses. "More beautiful than any other woman . . . and I love you and always will . . . and I never want to leave you . . . never . . . never . . ."

"What did you say?" Already her expression had changed.

He had not planned to blurt it out like this. Now he had no choice but to go on. "It came to me last night that there's really no reason, no reason at all why I should go back."

"What!"

"Honest, Alix. It's so simple and logical, I don't know why I didn't think of it sooner."

"Is this another of your plans? Like those doctors' certificates you were going to get last year."

"This is different. It's solid, based on facts." She made an impatient gesture, and his voice grew urgent and beseeching. "Please, darling, please listen."

She remained silent while he explained how in a flash the realization had come to him that he could earn a living in Paris.

Publishers would certainly buy a few of his compositions. And then, if need be, he could always do transcriptions, arrangements.

"And don't forget, I can also give piano lessons."

She gazed at him with a mixture of compassion and anger. "And for that you'd throw away your Grand Prix! Will you be a child all your life?"

This stung deep and spurred him to more frantic protests. First, he wasn't a child, he was twenty-three. And the Grand Prix wasn't half as important as she seemed to think. Many musicians who hadn't won it were very successful. They made a good living and there was no reason why he couldn't do as well.

Patiently he began again. "Publishers are in business to publish music. You'll admit that, don't you? They need new music. Well, then it's obvious they'll buy a few of mine, isn't it?"

"And what if they don't? What if they don't like it? What if you don't get lessons? Oh, my poor Claude, don't you see you will starve. Anyway, whether or not you can make a living isn't the point."

"Then what is it?"

"The point is that you will have sacrificed your career for a foolish, rather pathetic love affair with a middle-aged woman."

"Don't say that. You aren't middle-aged."

"Yes, darling, I am middle-aged." Her words came in a whisper. "And you're barely more than a boy. This is the point, don't you see? In a year, perhaps two, I'll look old. And one day suddenly you'll see it. But by then it'll be too late. You will have wrecked your career, ruined your life on my account. And I can't let you do it. Please, Claude. Please, go back to Rome."

He would have none of it. She was imagining things. She wasn't old, she was young and beautiful and he would love her always.

From then on they knew no peace. Each day that he overstayed his leave she grew more frantic. By now the authorities must be informed of his presence in Paris, and she saw him apprehended by the police, brought back to Rome between two gendarmes. He laughed. First they must find him, and he'd taken the precaution of registering under another name at the hotel. Oh, he was clever, he'd thought of everything . . .

Because she held herself responsible for his aberration she still came every afternoon and pleaded with him. It did not good, and one day she threatened to stop coming. Brazenly he threatened to walk to the Conservatoire and hand in his resignation. Thus he forced her to come. When she did, he refused to discuss anything until they had made love. And so their most furious disputes took place in bed, in an atmosphere of love and hate: he, kissing and caressing her; she, remonstrating in half-sobbing pleas, with tears of rage and supplication in her eyes.

It went on like this for two weeks. At last he surrendered, but first he imposed his conditions.

"You'll write me. At least once a month."

"Yes, darling, yes."

"You'll think of me every day."

"Yes, yes. Every day, I promise."

"And you won't fall in love with anyone else?"

"No, darling. I swear I won't."

Another thing . . . On his return she'd still love him and come to see him and never . . . never speak about being middle-aged and all that nonsense?

She promised everything, swore anything he wanted.

Finally, a month after his arrival, having extracted her promise, oath and sacred word of honor on everything he could think of, he returned to Rome.

◆

As he expected, he was summoned to the director's office the moment he entered the Villa. Dutifully he followed Lorenzo up the worn spiraling stairs.

From his damask chair Monsieur Hébert surveyed him across his desk for a while.

"I should be very angry with you," he said at last. "You've given the Paris authorities and myself a great deal of trouble. You are a very trying young man. An unmitigated liar, a forger and all-around imposter. Needless to say, there's been much correspondence between the Academy and the Villa about you and your family, especially that poor dying father of yours. At one time there was talk of sending the police after you. Myself, I've been on the verge of requesting your expulsion from the Villa. Do you know why I didn't?"

"No, *Monsieur le directeur.*"

"Because you're young, and much must be forgiven to the young, for they are so incredibly stupid. Since most people must do a few stupid things in their life, they might as well do them when they have the excuse of youth. And then I received a letter from your composition teacher, Monsieur Guiraud, pleading on your behalf. The opinion I gather from his letter is that you are extremely gifted as an artist and at the same time deprived of common sense. A sort of half-wit who can't be held responsible for his misdeeds."

He let that sink in and slowly ran his slender hand down his white beard.

"Finally, I realized you did it all because you are in love, and therefore even less responsible for your actions. Hector Berlioz did exactly what you did. He, too, escaped from the Villa. And since he was forgiven, I guess I'll do the same and forgive you."

The old man waved a weary hand. "Please, don't thank me. You thanked me enough for your leave."

"I'm sorry, *Monsieur le directeur,* but I had to go."

"We always have excellent reasons for doing what we want to do." He paused, his fine, thoughtful face etched in lines of patience. "Now, go back to your studio and get busy on your *envoi.* Remember, it must be ready next month."

And so Claude set to work on his *envoi.* The regulations required some large orchestral work: symphony, Mass or symphonic suite. Since he could not possibly compose an original work in such a short time, he dismantled *Zuleima,* an ambitious effort he had started when he was still at the Conservatoire, and patched it into a fluid and shapeless musical oddity which he called *Ode Symphonique.* As prescribed by the regulations he had the manuscript bound and handed it to the general secretary.

With the coming of spring the Villa entered its usual round of social festivities. Once again the King and Queen came to the exhibition of the *envois.* There were receptions, concerts, one or two gala soirees. By June it was all over. Summer returned. Romans left Rome to tourists and foreign priests. In his Etruscan Tomb, Claude lay on his bed, feeling hot and lonely. There was no Fiumicino that year, the Primoli villa was closed. Popelin wasn't there to talk to, nor Angela to spare him the torments of the damned. Only the ghost of Alix remained, and it brought him no comfort. A few letters had come from her. Friendly, almost motherly letters preaching patience and fortitude. Not at all the kind of letters she had promised to write.

He played Wagner's operas and found some relief in their exalted lyricism. Tristan's Libestod became his favorite composition. Some day he, too, would write operas that would bring comfort to unhappy lovers all over the world.

Finally he couldn't bear it any longer. He must get away. Regulations permitted traveling. In Italy, of course. It was supposed to broaden your artistic education. All right, he would travel in Italy. Living was cheap. For one lira or two you could get a bed in an inn. Food cost very little. With his monthly allowance of a hundred and sixteen francs he could wander from town to town, see the country, escape from his studio and his thoughts.

Monsieur Hébert was sympathetic.

"It'll do you good. Italy is a land of incredible beauty. Not only natural but artistic beauty. I'll give you a few letters of introduction."

Then, as the interview was coming to an end, "You aren't going to slip away to Paris, are you?"

Claude shook his head. "No, *Monsieur le directeur,* not this time. I'll be back in October."

The general secretary obligingly advanced him his allowance for the next three months. The following morning, bag in hand, Claude set out on his tour of Italy.

First he went to Naples. It was every bit as hot as Rome, but at sunset the sea breezed a pleasant coolness upon the town. He roamed through the colorful, slovenly town, with its full-breasted women, its streets full of song and swooping laundry lines. Nowhere had he seen such poor and yet contented people. The Neapolitans were the only Christians who had come to an understanding with God and themselves. When they were sick they prayed, wept and repented; at any other time they did exactly as they pleased. Life was wonderful and the after-life even more so. Since God was a fine, understanding Neapolitan Signore and Heaven another Naples, eternity would be spent eating pasta, drinking wine, making love and playing the mandolin forever and ever and ever.

Leisurely he resumed his wanderings. He sailed to Capri, climbed the hills of Anacapri on the other side of the island.* Then he went to Ischia, enchanting Ischia, a flouting emerald gem on the blue bosom of the sea. He returned to the mainland, retraced his steps to Naples, and then by easy stages made his way northward through the peninsula.

He halted in out-of-the-way hamlets consisting of a handful of houses clustered around a steepled church. He watched the men till the fields or play cards in rustic cafés, and the women walk to the fountains, clay jars on their heads, black-shawled and stately like Biblical figures. He discovered the innate kindness of the Italian people, their courtesy, their patience and wisdom. In Orvieto he spent a few days enjoying the view, the food, the incredibly beautiful church and the masterpieces that glutted that small town. He wandered through Umbria, passed through Florence, which brought back memories of Sonia and his first summer with Madame von Meck. Finally he reached Milano.

He called on Arrigo Boito, to whom he had a letter of introduction. They talked about Paris, where Boito had spent some years on a musical scholarship. "Strange, isn't it?" He chuckled. "Our government sends its music students to Paris and yours sends its to Rome." In the course of the visit he urged Claude to go to Sant'Agata and meet the famous composer Verdi.

"I've just written the libretto of his new opera and I'll give you a

* In 1910 he wrote the famous prelude The Hills of Anacapri.

letter of introduction. It may not do any good, for he's a crotchety old man and loves to play the bear. But it's worth taking a chance, for then you will have met our greatest musician."

Two days later Claude rang the gate bell of the Verdi estate. A servant appeared and blandly informed him that "the Maestro" was not at home.

Claude pointed to a white-bearded old man in shabby clothes who stood in full sight a few yards away humming to himself and watering his salad patch. "Isn't that the Maestro?"

"*Si, signore.*" The servant nodded. "It is the Maestro himself, but officially he is not at home."

He went on to explain that the Maestro liked privacy. *Dio mio,* if he received all the people who came to see him, all the journalists who pestered him for interviews, he wouldn't have a minute to himself. In his faltering Italian, Claude replied he was no journalist and slipped Boito's letter through the gate. The servant disappeared and returned a minute later, grinning under his wiry mustache.

"Now the Maestro is at home," he said, opening the gate.

The composer of Aïda greeted Claude with well-rehearsed gruffness and in excellent French. "How'd you like it if I barged in on you like this? What do you think I am? A curiosity, like the Leaning Tower of Pisa . . . Don't you see I'm a poor old man and all I ask is to be left alone?"

For a while he grumbled under his breath while holding the watering can over his heads of lettuce. "Oh well, since you forced your way in, you might as well stay for lunch. You're young and must be hungry. I always was hungry when I was your age."

They repaired into the spacious country house and walked to the dining room, where an elderly lady in old-fashioned clothes welcomed Claude with smiling graciousness.

"Don't believe a word my husband says," she remarked, taking his hands. "He really is delighted you came. And so am I. We're old and we like the company of young people."

During lunch she asked the Maestro to speak about his experiences as an opera composer. At first he refused. Couldn't an old man eat *risotto* in peace! Whereupon he plunged into a stream of talk.

"The only thing you must expect, if you ever write an opera, is trouble," he began, refilling his glass. "First with your librettist. Composers and librettists are natural enemies. Once I wrote an opera, *Ernani,* adapted from a play by Victor Hugo, and he challenged me to a duel. Poets are a bloodthirsty breed. They always want to kill people, especially musicians. Then you have trouble with the orchestra, starting with the conductor, who thinks he knows more than yourself and doesn't follow your indications. The piccolo player says you can't write for his instrument and your music is unplayable. Then the singers. They are very sensitive, which is fine, but alas, most of them sing off key. If you mention it, they stomp off the stage and go to weep in their dressing rooms, saying you are a heartless brute. Then you have the problem of the authorities and the Church. In every opera there is something that displeases the government or the clergy. Two days before the première of my opera *Nabucco* the Cardinal of Milano condemned it as immoral, sacrilegious and revolutionary. Mind you, he hadn't seen it, but cardinals are like that. And then you have the critics, who hate you for keeping them out of bed and making more money than they do. Take my advice, don't ever write an opera."

After lunch he excused himself. Yes, he must go back to work. A peasant could enjoy a nice siesta, but not he, not Giuseppe Verdi, a feeble seventy-four-year-old man! . . .

"And you know why?" Dramatically he addressed Claude as he rose from his chair. "Because this confounded Boito wrote such a marvelous libretto that I couldn't resist setting it to music, and now I'm trapped!"

Yes, trapped . . . Contracts had been signed. La Scala had announced the première of *Otello* for the next season. Costumes were being made, scenery painted. And so a poor old man could not have his siesta.

"But, on my word, this is the last opera I'll ever write! Never will I write another one . . . Never!"

He walked away, muttering in his beard. His wife watched him go with a smile and eyes full of love.

"*Mio Verdi!*" She sighed, turning back to Claude. "Each time it's his last opera. When this one is finished, he'll pester Signore Boito till he writes him another libretto. And we'll go through the same thing all over again . . ."*

Claude's visit to Sant'Agata was the high point of his Italian tour. That same afternoon he returned to Milano, where he spent a few days. Then he took the train back to Rome. He arrived just in time for the autumn rains.

◆

Two letters from Alix had arrived during his absence. Full of the usual admonitions and good advice. He must be patient and sensible, use his time productively, serve the full regulation term. He read them through blurred eyes and felt as lonely as before.

A few days later a bundle of books he had purchased in Paris was

---

* Verdi did write another opera. At eighty he wrote *Falstaff*, probably his masterpiece, which, like *Otello*, was adapted from Shakespeare by Arrigo Boito.

delivered to his door. It contained a French translation of Shelley's complete works in a handsome leather-bound set. Also a few literary magazines and, finally, a just-published French translation of Dante Gabriel Rossetti's poems. One of these, in particular, enchanted him. It was called *The Blessed Damozel*.* For a moment he considered setting it to music: a huge symphonic work with a chorus of women's voices and two solo singers. His enthusiasm did not last long. The more he thought of it, the more the size of the project filled him with awe. The darned thing would take months to write, and he just didn't feel up to such an undertaking. Some day, when he felt in the right mood and everything was going well, he would have a go at it. But not now. He couldn't even stir himself and start work on his *envoi,* let alone plunge into a work of that magnitude.

And so, like slowly-turning pages of a book, the autumn days went by, one by one, in mournful idleness. Dutifully he attended Monsieur Hébert's receptions, took a more active part in the social life of the Villa. Sometimes, on rainy afternoons, he played cards with the concierge. He read a little, slept a lot.

Shortly before Christmas it snowed, and half of the Roman population thought the end of the world had come and rushed to confession. Claude spent a melancholy Christmas in his cold and cavernous Etruscan Tomb, which looked and felt more and more like one. He did, however, receive a sweet New Year's letter from Alix, in which she assured him of her affection and that of her family. She also mentioned that he now had been almost two years in Rome and had only a little more than a year to go.

This convinced him that she, too, was counting the days and it cheered him considerably. His heart surged with love, and in the subsequent flutter of energy he even began thinking about his *envoi.*

His *Ode Symphonique,* which had been his previous year's offering, had been reviewed with severity by the jury, who had declared it "bizarre, incomprehensible and impossible to execute."† This time, he decided, he would redeem himself and write a large symphonic work for voices and orchestra. It would be called *Printemps.* For no particular reason, except that spring was a nice season and he liked thinking about it. He started by drafting the work in a four-hand piano version. The orchestration he would tackle later. After all, the *envoi* was only due in April, more than three months away, and there was no reason for him to kill himself, was there?

* *The Blessed Damozel* was written by Rossetti for his beautiful and consumptive mistress Elizabeth Siddall. At her death he placed the manuscript in her coffin; it was removed when, several years later, the publication of his complete works was undertaken.
† *Journal Officiel,* December 31, 1886.

In February he received no letter from Alix. At once he was assailed by a thousand anxieties. He tried forgetting them in work and made great progress in his *envoi*. But *Printemps* grew less and less springlike. By the end of the month it was finished but had turned into an autumnal lament.

March came, and again there was no letter. Now work stopped. The very thought of starting on the orchestration was more than he could bear. He felt miserable enough without worrying about combinations of instruments. His life became a silent and inconclusive debate that went on endlessly, whether he lay on his bed or paced the floor. Even reading offered no escape. Hour after hour he stood at his window watching the rain fall from sodden, lumpy skies on Saint Peter's dome. Now and then he played Tristan's Liebestod: it gave voice to his wretchedness and increased the confusion of his already confused mind.

All the time he thought about Alix. His opinion of her changed with his mood and his mood changed every hour. One moment she was mortally ill, dead perhaps, and she had asked that the news be kept from him as long as possible, so that he wouldn't again escape from the Villa. The next, she was in perfect health, a heartless, deceitful woman who had betrayed his trust. Her promises and sacred words of honor had been lies intended to send him back to Rome. Women lied disgracefully when it suited their purpose . . .

Finally he stumbled on the truth. She was sacrificing herself! She loved him as much as he loved her, but because she imagined herself to be old she was renouncing him, withdrawing from his life. That was it. How stupid of him not to have guessed it sooner! Now, in retrospect, it all became clear. Her constant references to her age, her insistence that soon she would look old were warnings he had failed to understand until now. When she begged him to stay his full term at the Villa, she only wanted time to do its work and give him a chance to forget. Noble, wonderful Alix! It was just like her to stifle her feelings, break her heart with her own hands, fade out of his life without a word. In a splendid, silent gesture of self-renunciation.

Well, he wouldn't let her . . . And since he couldn't hope to obtain another leave of absence, he had no choice but to resign and return to Paris. Surely in a week or two he would sell a few pieces, enough to rent a litle studio. And there she would come as she had to his hotel room, last spring. They would make love and gradually she would forget her silly fears about being old—and all would be well.

From that moment on there was no hesitation in his mind. At times, however, the gravity of the step he was about to take forced itself upon him. Resigning the Grand Prix would entail some serious sacrifices, no doubt about that. Not only would he lose the financial security of the

Villa, his rent-free studio, his monthly allowance; but, most important of all, he would forgo his festival.

Every winner of the Grand Prix was entitled on his return from Rome to a festival—a concert dedicated entirely to his compositions— given under the patronage of the Academy, with the co-operation of the orchestra and chorus of the Conservatoire. It was a gala affair attended by critics, music publishers, conductors, theatre directors, famous artists and fashionable hostesses. To a young and unknown musician it was an opportunity without equal, a splendid introduction to the artistic and social world of Paris.

Well, he would have to give up his festival, that's all. It was a small price to pay for seeing Alix again, bringing her back into his life.

By now it was mid-March. The rains stopped and spring arrived, on schedule. The sun went to work on Rome's ancient, crackled face, and in no time the old girl was herself again, rouged and smiling, her ruins in perfect condition, ready for the onrush of tourists. In the gardens of the Villa roses burst into bloom and the Bologna Fountain splashed happily in the sunshine.

Claude prepared to leave. Of course, there could be no question of writing the orchestration of his *envoi*. He had neither the time nor the inclination for it. Anyway, who cared about a silly old *envoi* when Alix was at stake. Each additional hour he stayed in Rome took her farther away, made it more difficult to bring her back.

He took the piano version of *Printemps* to the binder, and a week later, handed the beautifully bound score to the general secretary. Also his letter of resignation.

This done he went back to his studio and started packing. Soon there was a knock on his door and his friend Lorenzo informed him that the director wanted to see him at once.

"I see you've decided to leave us," said Monsieur Hébert with a sigh. "To tell you the truth I have expected it since your return from Paris last year. I know you've tried to adjust yourself to the life at the Villa, but obviously it is beyond your strength."

He leaned forward on his chair and took the bound score of *Printemps* from his desk.

"Now about this *envoi* of yours," he went on, thumbing through the score. "I am no musician, but it seems that you've neglected to write the orchestration. As you know, the regulations insist on an orchestral work."

Claude had come prepared. Yes, he knew that the regulations demanded an orchestral work and he had obeyed them to the letter. He had written a wonderful orchestration on a separate manuscript, which somehow had gotten burned at the binder's. "Burnt to a crisp."

The elderly man gave him a glance of total disbelief. "This is indeed the most extraordinary mishap in the entire history of music. I've heard of lost or stolen manuscripts, but never of a manuscript being burned to ashes while being bound. The jury, I am sure, will be as surprised as I am."

Wearily he closed the book and placed it back on his desk. "Since you've resigned I don't suppose it makes much difference."

He twined his fingers over his chest and considered Claude in thoughtful silence. Then, with an effort he continued, "I'm sure that you've reflected on the consequences of your decision, and nothing I would say could possibly change your mind. And so it remains only for me to wish you God's speed and good luck."

He rose, extended his hand and the interview was over.*

That evening Claude leaned on the window sill and for a long time gazed into the spring night. Before him Rome slept, watched over by a skyful of stars. How many times had he stood like this at night gazing at the old city that held him prisoner, cursing the venal necropolis that lived off her ruins, like a beggar from his sores. But tonight he felt no hatred, but rather a belated, vaguely apologetic regret. Rome had been kind to him. It had offered him the splendor of its treasures, the poetry of its narrow streets, the good humor of its people, the liquid murmur of its fountains. But he had seen none of it, for the eyes do not see when the heart looks elsewhere. All the time he'd been looking to Paris, because Alix was there.

Well, he was going back to her—and this time forever. He wouldn't risk losing her ever again. If Rome had taught him anything, it was that he couldn't live without her.

He pulled himself from the window, looked once more at the dark starry sky.

"Good-bye, Rome," he whispered under his breath.

Then he turned around and hurried on with his packing.

◆

He arrived in Paris on a perfect April morning. At the station he climbed into a fiacre, gave the address of the hotel where he had stayed the year before, and settled back on the worn leather seat.

As the carriage jostled along he looked about, wide-eyed, his heart swelling with joy. He was back in Paris. Paris where Alix lived . . . Nothing had changed. The green vapor overhanging the parks . . . Barelegged children racing their hoops, sailing their toy boats . . . The grayness of old stones after the tawniness of

---

* In its official report on *Printemps* the Academy referred with transparent skepticism to the binder's accident.

It was a final evidence of Monsieur Hébert's kindness that he had Claude driven to the station in his own carriage.

Rome . . . Notre Dame standing between the two halves of the city, like a mother between her two children. The bookstalls along the quays, the Seine fishermen, the gendarmes, the *midinettes* who smiled as they pattered by. Nothing had changed. It was good to be back . . .

That evening he had dinner served in his room. A trifle extravagant, but after all it was his first evening in Paris and he must celebrate. Over his demitasse he decided he would take a stroll up to Alix's house. No, of course not, he wouldn't go up and see her. But there was no harm in looking at her house, was there? Perhaps he might catch a glimpse of her behind a lighted window.

There was no light in Alix's window, and after a long wait he returned to the hotel feeling disappointed and vaguely afraid. Not that there was anything to be afraid about. He simply had picked a night when she and her husband happened to be out.

Despite the fatigue of the journey he slept fitfully. The following morning, instead of starting on his round of publishers as he had planned, he went back to rue de Constantinople. This time he stood at the street corner and waited for the maid to appear. But she didn't, and neither did the children, nor Pierre. In a gust his old fears were back. She was sick! Terribly sick, perhaps dead . . .

Finally he could no longer control himself and dashed into the house. He was halfway up the stairs when the concierge called him back.

"No use your going up," she said from the threshold of her lodge. "They moved out three months ago."

He felt his knees sag, but he turned around and managed to ask, "Where?"

The woman shrugged. "They didn't say."

Then, with a shake of the head, she shuffled back to her lodge.

CHAPTER

6

HE WENT TO VILLE D'AVRAY, AND SHE WASN'T THERE. THE HOUSE, he learned, had been sold.

He returned to Paris and for two days remained in his hotel room in a state of half-conscious bewilderment. Then gradually the shock wore off and pain set in. It came in waves of pure grief, a mumbled litany of unanswered questions that trailed into silence. Why? Why had she moved away without letting him know? Why hadn't she left an address? Why had she been so unfair and cruel? . . .

Disappearance has the finality of death and thus brings its own relief. He finally stopped asking questions he could not answer. Pain subsided into a dull ache and he began surveying his situation. It was simple, and frightening. He had thrown away his Grand Prix and was now in Paris with very little money, no purpose and no prospects. Oh, yes, he had talked a great deal about the compositions he would sell, the transcriptions he could do, the lessons he could give. But, suddenly, none of these things seemed assured. What then? What if he didn't sell any music, what if he didn't find any transcription or lesson?

Now fear was closing in on him. There no longer was time for the luxury of grief. Anxiety over money brushed aside his anguish over Alix. As usual his apprehension was tinged with remorse. On one of his extravagant impulses he had traveled first class from Rome, and when he asked for his bill he found that room service was a costly indulgence. Sweat broke out on his forehead when he discovered he had already spent more than half his money.

That day he moved out of the hotel. Near the Sorbonne he rented a dingy room left vacant by a student. The following morning, with his manuscripts under his arm, he started on his round of publishers. A week later he had seen them all, at least those who would receive him. They were impressed by his title of Grand Prix de Rome, glanced at his compositions, declared them unusual and interesting, but not commercial. When he asked for work—transcriptions, arrangements, anything—he was told to return in September. "We may have something then."

As the days, the weeks passed and he still found no work to do or lessons to give, he began pawning things. First, the birthday gold watch Madame von Meck had given him. He got a goodly sum for it, but had a hard time proving he hadn't stolen it. Then went the de-luxe Shelley set. He didn't get much on that: books were a drug on the market and the clerk did not appreciate hand-tooled bindings.

Life became a nightmare. To save a few sous he did his laundry in his washbasin, dined on a roll and a stick of chocolate. He learned to eat slowly, chew each mouthful, drink a great deal of water. The secret was never to leave your stomach empty . . .

Then it was summer. His room turned into an airless oven. At times he felt faint from heat and hunger; yet, miraculously, his brain that had been stagnant in the security of the Villa, now rustled with music. Half naked, his face varnished with sweat, he tackled the staggering task of writing *The Blessed Damozel*. By the end of September he had drafted the whole score and begun the orchestration.

But still no job. The transcriptions vaguely promised in April did not materialize. He sold a song for twenty francs and ate almost the entire sum in one enormous solitary banquet. Things grew desperate. The landlady became unpleasant and muttered threats. Again he went to the municipal pawnshop, the Mont de Piété, and tried to pawn his beloved Japanese prints. This time the clerk laughed in his face. Now hunger became a presence that never left his side. For lack of food his brain blurred, his eyes did not focus. On the music paper the notes danced on quivering staves.

Then music stopped coming.

One evening he found his room padlocked. That night he slept in the waiting hall of the Saint-Lazare Station. The following morning he pawned his overcoat, wolfed down a fifteen-sou meal. With the rest of the money he persuaded the concierge to let him take out his manuscripts and meager belongings. Finally, swallowing his pride, he went to his parents. They saw him without surprise, asked no questions. His mother gave him a bowl of soup and let him sleep on the sofa.

Now he was not hungry any more, but he could not work. His family had moved into a smaller apartment on rue de Berlin. It was crowded, filled with talk. After a few days he gave up. This time he was beaten.

One afternoon, in a dismal autumn drizzle, he went to rue Pigalle to see Monsieur Guiraud.

The professor received him in his cluttered den. For a moment he remained silent, scratching his bearded chin, eying his former pupil with a perplexed frown. Leaning back in his red-plush chair he scanned the pale, almost haggard face, the rumpled clothes and battered shoes, the dripping rain-soaked hat.

"So, you finally came! I was wondering how long it would take you to come and see me."

"I wanted to, Master, but I didn't dare. I knew you must be angry at me for leaving the Villa."

"You're damn right I was angry. I still am, for that matter. I could wring your neck. I thought you were at last safely tucked away in Rome and out of mischief. But no, you couldn't stay put and behave. You had to resign, ruin your career before it's even started!"

"But, Master—"

"Shut up. And your little escapade last spring, that was another brilliant idea! And overstaying your leave, remaining two extra weeks, that was more clever still. Oh, you're a bright young man, no doubt about that!"

"I'm sorry, Master."

"I know. You're always sorry afterward, when it's too late. Why can't you be sorry before, when it would do some good?" He lit a cigarette without taking his eyes off Claude's face. "There are three excellent composition classes at the Conservatoire, why . . . oh, why did you come into mine? Why couldn't you inflict yourself on someone else?"

Angrily he pulled on his cigarette. "Remember a few years ago, when you were bounced out of the Opéra and Monsieur Thomas wanted to expel you from school? I wish I'd let him. At least I'd be rid of you." An involuntary gentleness crept into his voice. "And where's your overcoat? You had an overcoat, didn't you? What became of it?"

"I pawned it."

"I see." He still spoke gruffly, but his anger was ebbing. Compassion was getting the best of him. "Don't you even have an umbrella?"

Claude shook his head. For a moment they looked at each other in silence.

"Well, sit down and dry yourself by the fire. No use your catching pneumonia." Already a gleam of affection was stealing into his eyes. "What's this you have under your arm?"

"Something I started working on. It's called *The Blessed Damozel*."

"Let me see." He reached out his hand, crossed his legs and opened the manuscript on his lap. "Here." He tossed Claude a pack of cigarettes. "Have a smoke while I look at it."

Silence fell into the room. Outside, rain was now falling in a steady but soundless downpour, slithering down the windowpanes. In the courtyard the huge plane tree was losing its last yellow leaves. Claude leaned forward on his chair, smoking, letting the heat from the fire seep through his damp clothes. Small blue flames leaped along the burning logs. Now and then an ember plunged into the ashes, glowed like a gem for a while; then turned black. For the first time since his return to Paris he felt safe. Monsieur Guiraud had not thrown him out. Of course, he was still angry, but that would pass. And he *was* interested in his work. Perhaps he would help him, tell him what to do, how to go about making a living . . .

"Getting warm?" asked the teacher, glancing up from the score.

"Yes, Master." Then, anxiously, "Do you like it?"

"I'll tell you in a moment."

He resumed his reading, trying to conceal his excitement, his stunned admiration. Genius was an awesome word, not to be bandied about, but, by God, genius was there. It was there, radiant, gleaming in every bar . . .

"It's good," he said at last, closing the manuscript. "Very good. Now you must finish it."

"I can't. I live with my parents, but I have no room, no place to work. When I came to Paris I was sure I'd sell a few pieces or find work so I could rent a place of my own. But I didn't sell anything and couldn't get any kind of work. Believe me, Master, I tried. I went to every publisher, but they had nothing. I even offered to copy music, but they didn't even have that. Tell you the truth, I don't know what to do any more. I . . . I . . . ." His voice broke.

"Don't be ashamed. Cry your heart out if it makes you feel better. Of course, you're a damn fool and you've brought your trouble upon yourself. But what's done is done, and the question is, 'What are we going to do about it?' First let's have a drink."

He got up, opened the cupboard overhanging his desk and pulled out a bottle of brandy. He filled two liqueur glasses, handed Claude one and, holding the other, resumed his seat on the red plush chair.

"Now tell me everything. And start at the beginning, from the day you arrived."

"Well, I drove to a hotel. Then that evening—"

With surprise he found he could talk about Alix with detachment, as if the pain had burned out her memory, leaving only a scar that no longer hurt.

"You loved her very much, didn't you?"

Claude looked into the fire. "In Rome, I couldn't get her out of my mind, but now I don't know what I feel."

"Well, go on. Then what did you do?"

"I didn't have much money by then, so I left the hotel and rented a room. Very cheap—"

Monsieur Guiraud listened, absently twirling the stem of his glass, as Claude told his story, the familiar story he had heard many times. Repeatedly he had seen friends or colleagues defeated by poverty, their brains grown dull and sterile in the never-ending search for daily bread.

"I wish you'd come earlier to see me," he said when Claude stopped talking. "But perhaps it's just as well you didn't, for now you know what poverty, real poverty, means."

Claude gave him a rueful smile. "I really do and I don't like it a bit."

"You'd better learn to like it, for I'm afraid you're going to have a great deal of it." Thoughtfully he gazed at his glass. "I don't want to discourage you, but you must face facts. Music, at best, is a thankless profession, and composers are the waifs of music. Just remember that Bach, Mozart, Schubert and Chopin died penniless. Today there are perhaps four or five composers in France who earn as much as a moderately successful dentist. The others do as I do, they have jobs and write music in their spare time. Even a man like César Franck cannot support his family with his music. And so he teaches at the Conservatoire, plays the organ at Sainte-Clotilde's and composes every morning from five to eight before starting on his round of lessons."

He turned his gaze from the glass and looked at Claude. "Since you are Grand Prix de Rome I perhaps could get you a position as music teacher in a school or assistant editor in a publisher's firm. It would give you a small but regular income. Enough to eat and have a place of your own. Would you like that?"

"No, Master. I wouldn't."

The answer was so prompt that Monsieur Guiraud made a gesture of annoyance. "Think well before you speak, for this decision is going to affect your whole life." His face assumed an unusual expression of seriousness. "Now listen. You have talent, perhaps more than talent, but your music is too original to be commercial. It'll be a long time before it is appreciated and widely played. And until then, how are you going to live? You've had a small taste of poverty and seen how unpleasant it is. Do you want ten, fifteen years of it?"

"No, Master, I don't. Please don't be angry with me, but I couldn't work in an office or teach in a school and write my music in my spare time. I know others do and I wish I could, but I can't. Anyway—" A sudden smile illuminated his face. "I couldn't hold a steady job. I'd be fired the first week."

Monsieur Guiraud let out a long, defeated sigh. "I'm afraid you're right. Judging from your past performances you probably wouldn't even last a week. You're a born nonconformist and you'll pay for it, but you can't change yourself. Let's forget about the job."

He drained his glass, rested it on the desk and leaned down to prod the fire. Sparks flew from the protesting logs, and for an instant he looked like a benign sorcerer bent over a swarm of spiteful spirits. Then he settled back onto his plush chair, joined his finger tips before his mouth and considered Claude through half-shut lids.

"For the moment our problem is to find a publisher who will give you some work and if possible an advance, so you can get your things out of pawn and rent a place of your own. I'll see what I can do."

With a grunt he hoisted himself to his feet, and together they walked through the corridor.

"Come to see me in two or three days," he said at the door. Swiftly he pulled something out of his vest pocket and slipped it in Claude's hand. "And for God's sake, go and buy an umbrella."

Then, gently pushing Claude out on the landing, he closed the door and went back to his untidy den.

◆

Three days later Claude was the happiest young man in Paris. He had received his first commission, a four-hand transcription of *The Flying Dutchman* Overture, together with a generous advance.

He had redeemed his watch, his overcoat and de-luxe Shelley set, and he was now wandering through the lower part of Montmartre in search of a studio. The houses displayed their decrepitude with the tranquil absence of shame peculiar to the district. Long sooty smudges ran down their crackled façades, like mascara smears. Shutters had missing slats; in a few windows broken panes had been replaced with newspapers. Everywhere poverty showed its ugly, unwashed face. Even the air smelled poor.

At 42, rue de Londres, he noticed a To Let sign hanging down from a rusty nail. He entered the hallway, which stank of cabbage and fried onions. The concierge appeared, holding a long-handled spoon in her hand.

"If it's for the apartment, it's on the top floor," she said without preamble. She had gentle eyes in a gaunt, leering face. Her gray hair was pulled tight into a bun at the back of her head. "Want to see?"

She led him up the creaky wooden stairs, stopping between floors to puff out her cheeks and catch her breath.

"*Voilà!*" she said at last, opening a door. "This is it."

It consisted of a single spacious room located directly under the roof.

"The view is superb and you won't have to buy furniture. As you see, it's nicely furnished." With a wave of her spoon she took in the pot-bellied stove, the unpainted kitchen table and three straw-bottomed chairs, a mahogany washstand and, in a corner, a full-sized iron bed.

"And behind that curtain is the kitchen." She started toward a door at the end of the room. "Now come and see the toilet," she said as if suggesting a picnic.

They passed on to a balcony with an iron railing at the back of the house, and there stood the toilet, a flimsy wooden structure not unlike a sentry box, ventilated on all sides by large gaps between the boards. From it one commanded a panorama of leprous walls, grimy windows with flower pots on the ledges, laundry lines and the neighbors' outside privies. There was about it an air of informality and neighborliness.

"See? You don't have to share it with anybody," she went on. "Real privacy."

They returned to the room. Slowly he gave a last circular glance. It was pretty shabby, but it had charm. A certain subtle, beseeching charm. It had been allowed to go into disrepair, that's all. Places, like people, needed love and care, and he would give it both. A coat of paint, bright curtains at the window, a few scattered rugs, his Japanese prints on the walls and you wouldn't recognize the place . . .

"I'll take it," he said.

He paid one month's rent in advance and that afternoon he moved in.

◆

After one week it was clear that his new home would need all the love he could give. Several unsuspected features came to light. The view, as the concierge had said, was fine, but it consisted mostly of the sooty roof of the nearby Saint-Lazare Station. When the wind was right, billowing clouds of smoke rolled into the room, together with the piercing whistles of departing trains. The kitchen consisted of a sink flanked by a hand pump and, on a dusty shelf, an alcohol lamp abandoned by the previous tenant. The kitchen table that had seemed so sturdy collapsed the moment he set his music on it. He noticed that one wall of the room was built of whitewashed gaping boards, through which seeped every draft, sound and smell of the house. The washstand mirror was not only cracked but spotted. To look into it was a lesson in humility.

Finally, the roof leaked.

"I know," said the concierge calmly, when he informed her of the fact.

"Why didn't you tell me?"

"You didn't ask." She went on sweeping the entrance hallway.

Well, he was asking now and demanded to know when she was going to send someone to fix it. To this Madame Sénégal—this was her name—replied with a peal of laughter. Fix it! Why the whole roof was rotten. If you tried plugging one hole, two appeared. As a matter of fact, the whole damn thing might collapse at any time.

"Tell the landlord I want it fixed at once," he said with the imperiousness of a man who has paid a month's rent in advance. "At once!"

"Tell him yourself if you want, but you'll be wasting your breath."

She then explained that Monsieur Moulot, the owner, had tried for the last five years to get rid of the house and wouldn't hear of any repairs.

"If you want to fix it yourself, nobody's stopping you. I can loan you a ladder."

He protested, uttered vague threats of legal action and finally hoisted the ladder up to his attic. Hammer in hand he went to work and skillfully plugged the hole. As Madame Sénégal had predicted, two new ones appeared. He thought it prudent not to persist. At the hardware store he bought two large blue enamel basins and set them on the floor, directly under the holes. Now, when it rained, water dripped into them, making a merry chime. One hole, he observed, dripped in F sharp; the other in B flat. He also repaired the table, pounded the washstand drawer into sliding again, reinforced a chair's leg that was about to come off, washed the window, dusted the kitchen shelf and stuffed with newspapers the gaps in the pine-board wall.

This done, he set out to paint the room.

He decided on blue. But not just any old kind of blue. An unusual delicate Vermeer blue. Somewhere between sapphire and lapis lazuli. The color of Wagner's Blue Grotto bedroom in Venice . . . To get the right shade he mixed the paint himself. It took time, but he got it. Vermeer himself couldn't have done better. Now to work!

At first it was great fun. Joyously he climbed up and down the ladder and splashed away. Small blobs of paint flew in all directions. After a while rivulets of paint slithered down the brush handle to his fingers, then his palm, then his wrist. Finally his forearm. Curiously, the more he painted, the bigger the room seemed to grow. The fumes of turpentine made his eyes water, and tears streamed down his cheeks. Still he went on. Teeth clenched, he dragged his brush along the endless wall. At last it was done. He had his blue walls, and beautiful they were.

Because of the smell of fresh paint he slept that night with the window wide open. There was a breeze, the right kind of a breeze . . . By morning, his walls were smeared with long sooty streaks. Anyone else would have been discouraged or furious. Not he. The difficult child is always the best-loved one, and by now the garret had become his child. Difficult, disappointing—and much loved. With its blotched gray-blue walls it looked worse, if possible, than the day he had seen it for the first time, but also more piteous, more beseeching than ever. All right, it did look a little drab. Well, that could easily be fixed . . .

He bought curtains for the window and the kitchen, three scatter rugs, a few colorful pillows, a Venetian glass ashtray and a gorgeous yellow Japanese silk embroidery showing two carp swimming through an under-water growth of bamboo. He had seen it in an art-shop window and instantly lost his heart to it. For a few minutes he had struggled with himself over it. Was it reasonable to spend fifty francs for this useless trifle, when he hadn't yet bought an umbrella? But an umbrella wasn't beautiful, and this was. His studio was crying for it.

And so he bought the Japanese silk, and it did look beautiful. A frozen patch of sunshine on the wall . . . It brightened the whole room.

As a matter of fact his studio now looked so nice that he itched to show it to someone. At his invitation Monsieur Guiraud came the following Sunday afternoon, purportedly to have a cup of tea.

"Very . . . very nice," he said, standing in the middle of the room and glancing about.

He grinned at the sight of the rain basins on the floor, praised the Japanese prints and silk embroidery, the flowery window curtains.

"I see you painted it," he remarked, sniffing the lingering smell of paint. "I, too, painted my first studio when I came back from Rome."

A frightful room on the Left Bank, but to him it had been the most beautiful place in the world. "The first studio is like first love, there's nothing quite like it ever again. It's there you have your first love affairs, your first dreams of success. I was about your age when I returned from the Villa, and I was ready to take Paris by storm. In my valise I had a one-act opera, and I saw myself walking on the stage after the performance, receiving the applause. And naturally royalties were pouring in . . ."

He chuckled softly, under his breath. Things hadn't gone quite that way. Three weeks after his arrival he was playing the drum in a small theatre orchestra in order to keep alive, and when a year later his opera was produced it died after a few performances.

"It didn't discourage me," he went on in the indulgent tone in which aging men speak of the mistakes of their youth. "Right away I started on another one. It took five years before it was produced, and when it finally was it died even faster than the first one. Then came the war and there was no more time for music."

Claude's studio had put him in a reminiscent mood. While sipping tea he recalled the days of the Franco-Prussian War, the despair of going into battles that were already lost. "The French have an idea that wars are won with courage alone."

His words trailed into a sigh.

"Well," he went on, briskly changing the subject, "now that your studio is finished you should be about ready to go to work. By the way, you're going to need a piano. Before you go and rent one, let me see if I couldn't get the Maison Pleyel to loan you one of their instruments. The director is a friend of mine."

With a wave of the hand he cut short Claude's thanks. "Just write a few more things like *The Blessed Damozel* and I'll be satisfied. Incidentally, I want you to finish it and send it to the Academy in April, as if it were your *envoi* from Rome."

"But I've resigned."

"I know, and the Academy does, too. But according to the regulations you still owe an *envoi*, and it won't kill you to obey them for once. It'll show your good will and gratitude for the free education you've received and the trouble you've given everybody, including me. It will be a nice gesture and the Academy will appreciate it."

He took another sip of tea. "As for this *Flying Dutchman* Overture," he went on, resting his cup back on the table, "I am sorry the publisher didn't have anything else to give you. It's a very difficult and over-orchestrated number, like most of Wagner's music, but do the best you can with it. Regard it as a chore that must be done."

"Don't worry, Master, I'll put my soul into it."

"You needn't go that far." The teacher laughed. "Just do it carefully, but keep your soul for your own music."

To his astonishment, Claude went on in the same tone of religious fervor to say that Wagner was without question the greatest composer of all times and he felt honored to transcribe his sublime music.

"Besides it will be an invaluable experience when I write my opera."

"You're planning to write an opera?"

"Oh, I've been thinking about it for quite some time. Already at the Villa I toyed with the idea of turning *Salammbô* into an opera, but I was worried about other things at the time and I couldn't set my mind to it. But now I'm ready. I'm only waiting for the right libretto."

"And what sort of libretto are you looking for?" asked his teacher, now thoroughly alarmed.

"One that would combine Wagner's dramatic concepts and the French genius."

At great length and with increasing obscurity he elaborated on the requirements he demanded from the libretto he had in mind. "In short," he wound up, "it must blend Wagner's dynamism and French finesse."

"My God!" explained the teacher. "Don't tell me that you, too, are going to try writing the great Franco-German opera! For the last twenty years I've heard and read about that great opera that would blend the geniuses of the two nations. Don't you see it's impossible? Try mixing Beethoven and Verdi, for instance, and see what you'll get."

"But, Master, Beethoven is a symphonist and Verdi a composer of operas."

"All right. Both of them wrote masses. Try mixing Beethoven's *Missa Solemnis* and Verdi's *Requiem Mass*. Or, if you prefer, try mixing their operas. See what you can do with *Fidelio* and *La Traviata*. Don't you understand that each race has its own individual genius."

"But music is universal."

"Yes, but only in the sense that its alphabet is universal. Music itself remains the creation of a certain man with his background and nationality. Can you conceive Johann Sebastian Bach as a Spaniard or Rossini as a Swede? Wagner is German and his music is German. Not even he could combine the geniuses of two races. Look. *The Flying Dutchman* takes place in Norway, *Tannhäuser* in Belgium, *Tristan and Isolde* somewhere between Ireland and Cornwall, *Parsifal* in Spain. Yet there isn't a speck of Norwegian, Belgian or Spanish music in any of them. Tristan is English, yet he sings exactly like Siegfried. And Isolde, who is supposed to be Irish, exactly like Brünnehilde or any other Wagnerian soprano."

He paused, and his face relaxed into gentle anxiousness. "Listen, Claude. Wagner is a great composer, but he is the complete opposite of your musical nature. And he's written all the Wagnerian music we need. Please, don't try to write any more."

The discussion might have ended there, but Claude was not going to desert his favorite composer, even to please his teacher. "If he is a great composer, why aren't his operas given in Paris?"

"Because he was a mean, arrogant, treacherous and contemptible man who insulted France after the war, when she was down and defeated—"

"But this is no reason why we should hate his music."

"We don't hate it. As a matter of fact, at one time the French liked Wagner's music very much."

"Then why was *Tannhäuser* hissed at the Opéra?"

Monsieur Guiraud grinned patiently. "I knew you'd come out with that old story. *Tannhäuser* was hissed for a combination of reasons which had nothing to do with music. And the proof of it is that the year before its production, Wagner gave two concerts in Paris which included the Prelude to *Tristan,* three numbers from *Lohengrin* and four from *Tannhäuser.* They were so well received that they had to be repeated three times. Do you hear? Three times."

He lit a cigarette, blew a long plume of smoke and watched it dissolve. "But Wagner forgot about that. When his opera failed, after a hundred and sixty-four rehearsals and a two-hundred-thousand-franc deficit, he heaped sarcasms on France in her hour of sorrow. He was that sort of man. Since then the French have felt no great urge to listen to his music. Honestly, can you blame them?"

"No, but they deprive themselves of the greatest music ever written."

Monsieur Guiraud had a gesture of impatience. "Will you, please, stop talking in superlatives, as though Wagner were the Holy Trinity. He wrote some splendid pages and hundreds of others that were uninspired, repetitious to a degree and at times appallingly banal."

This outburst brought back his good humor. "But cheer up. The French are mending their ways. It's becoming quite chic to be Wagnerian. Everyone is singing the praises of the 'Meister.' Verlaine and Mallarmé have written odes to him. Renoir has painted one of his strawberry-and-cream portraits of him. Now the snobs are rushing in. At dinners, people who can't distinguish between a Bach fugue and the braying of an ass are discussing *Parsifal* like experts."

Still chuckling he pulled his gloves from his coat pocket and began slipping them on. "I wonder what will become of them in a few years when it won't be fashionable to be Wagnerian any more. I guess they'll find something else."

He was about to leave.

"But you are not a snob," he said with sudden gravity. "You are a musician and have something to say. Say it in your own way and don't try to imitate anyone."

He rose, and Claude helped him into his overcoat.

"Meanwhile," he went on as they started toward the door, "finish your *Blessed Damozel* and come to see me from time to time. Thanks for the tea."

◆

Claude was a little disturbed by his teacher's visit. The news that other musicians had previously attempted to write the Franco-German opera had come as an unpleasant surprise. On the other hand, it was reassuring to know that none had succeeded. It meant that the opportunity was still open.

Of course, it also could mean that it couldn't be done, as Monsieur Guiraud had said. But this Claude refused to admit. It was not a question of mingling Beethoven and Verdi, but adapting—that was the word—adapting the Wagnerian concepts to French sensibility. Could anything be clearer? Yet his good teacher had failed to understand. Well, after all, he was fifty and you couldn't expect a man of that age to keep much alertness of mind. By then the brain began to fossilize. His remarks about Wagner having written a few splendid pages and many tedious ones were evidence of this low disintegration. Anyone in full possession of his facilities could see that every note Wagner had written was inspired. But Monsieur Guiraud could not. That's what years of teaching in such a bigoted, reactionary school as the "Conserv" did to a man. Sooner or later a professor was bound to think like a professor. With Monsieur Guiraud it had taken longer than with most, but it finally had happened. And then there was this question of patriotism. In fairness you couldn't expect a man who had fought against Germans to be impartial toward a German composer. It was just too much to ask.

After much pondering Claude reached the conclusion that his master was the finest of men, a wonderful friend, a splendid teacher, a keen-minded adviser in all musical matters except one—Wagner and Wagnerian music. He would not mention his operatic plans any more, but some day when his opera was written he would bring him the score. Then his good old teacher would be overwhelmed, and with tears gleaming in his eyes he would clasp him in his arms and acknowledge his errors.

But this was still far in the future. He hadn't even found a libretto as yet, but never mind, he would some day. It all would come in due time . . . Meanwhile various matters were pressing for attention. His beautiful studio had cost him much more than expected and had swallowed most of the publisher's advance. Now, in retrospect, the purchase of the Japanese silk looked like a mad extravagance. Already next month's rent was almost due and not a note of the *Flying Dutchman* transcription had yet been written.

With panic he discovered he had just enough money left to buy food for about two weeks. All of a sudden disaster was closing in again, as in the summer months.

But this time it was winter.

To save money he lived on bread and tea, which he brewed on his alcohol lamp. He stopped buying coal for the stove, and it got so cold in the garret that he could not work at the table and took to working in bed, fully dressed and bundled in his overcoat, a wooden board balanced on his knees. In this fashion he managed to write the *Flying Dutchman* transcription, although he did not have time to put much of his soul into it. He paid the next month's rent with only one week's delay.

"I hate taking money from you," said Madame Sénégal, when he counted the francs into her palm. "I know you could use it."

She was feeling sorry for him. Gradually they were becoming friends. They exchanged smiles when he passed by her lodge, sometimes a few words.

The remainder of the transcription money gave him a short breathing spell. He bought a few paper bags of coal and the studio became pleasantly warm, if somewhat smoky, at times. He treated himself to a few meals at a local restaurant. And he went in search of a cat.

In a neighboring courtyard he found a beige and white kitten daintily picking at a heap of refuse. It had amber eyes, silky whiskers, and upon inspection proved to be a female. She let herself be caught so easily that one might have thought she had been waiting for just that. He slipped her into his shirt, next to his chest, and brought her home. Graciously she took possession of the garret and accepted him as her roommate. Five minutes after her arrival she had lapped a saucerful of milk and was asleep on his bed.

"What am I going to call you?" he murmured, gently stroking her fur.

He recalled the kitten he had played with as a child, when he lived with his aunt. "I'll call you Linne," he said.

For a few days he lived happily in his warm studio. He talked to his cat, played Wagner's music on the beautiful Pleyel piano Monsieur Guiraud had secured for him. And in one week he wrote two piano pieces which he called *Arabesques*.

"Delightful," said Monsieur Guiraud, when he finished playing them on his own battered upright. "That's your kind of music. Believe me, leave Wagner alone and keep on writing things like that."

It would have been fun to write a few more "things like that," but already there was next month's rent to think about, and money was disappearing at an alarming speed. Living in Paris was prohibitive. The price of coal, for instance, was outrageous. One franc and twenty-five centimes for a measly little bag . . . And food was getting out of hand. One franc and a half for a meal! Thirty centimes for a bottle of wine! It cost a fortune to keep your stomach halfway satisfied. Poor people should have been made in such a way they'd only have to eat once in a while, say, once a month. Rich people, on the other hand, could be hungry as often as they liked . . .

With these thoughts in mind he started looking for work. For that's the price you had to pay if you wanted to be free and not nailed down to some gruesome steady job. As soon as you finished a job you must start looking for another. Or you couldn't eat, couldn't pay your rent, and things got very unpleasant . . .

Once more he started on his rounds of publishers. In his thin overcoat he trampled all over town in the cold December rain, his slouch hat low over his eyes, his manuscripts under his arm. He became a familiar figure in publishers' antechambers. Some receptionists scowled at him for treading on their fine carpets in his muddy shoes and sent him back on his way with an impatient wave of the hand. Others took pity on him, let him sit down and warm himself at the stove.

When he finally was ushered into the publishers' offices, he was informed that business was slow at this time of the year. No, they had no transcription to give him. No arrangement either, not even proofreading. Sorry. Perhaps next month . . . If they let him play his compositions he was told they were too unusual and difficult and had no popular appeal. Some said it brutally, cutting him short in the middle of a bar, adding he needn't come and bother them again. Others said it kindly, with a tinge of regret in their voices.

Monsieur Fromont said it in the form of a lecture. He was a portly man, kindly and talkative, especially after lunch; niggardly in money matters but prodigal of advice. He had a florid complexion and a flowing white beard that streamed from his cheeks down to the middle of his chest, where it lost itself in the rotund expanse of his white-vested paunch.

Leaning back on his chair he would squint at Claude through the smoke of his cigar, running scales over his beard, as if it were some sort of musical instrument. Then, abruptly, he would begin, "Young man, if you think publishers are in business for their pleasure, you're very much mistaken."

A slap on the desk, a challenging frown—and he would proceed to say that publishers were in business to make money. And how could they make money unless they published music people wanted to buy? "Good commercial music. Easy to play, easy to sing."

He would expatiate on the risks and pitfalls of music publishing, which was the most dangerous and speculative of all businesses, forever skirting bankruptcy and requiring immense vision, acumen, daring and unerring judgment. This done, he would describe the beautiful relationship that existed between the publisher and the composer of good commercial music, ending with a homily on the virtues of hard work, thrift and early rising, to which he attributed his own success.

Patiently Claude would listen, nod, agree with everything Monsieur Fromont said, for sometimes the publisher would preach himself into a mood of benevolence and give him some work to do.

"Here," he would say, "make me a four-hand arrangement of this waltz. It'll show what I mean by good commercial music."

And with it, grudgingly and with many protestations, he would give a small advance on which Claude would live for a few days.

Shortly before Christmas it started snowing. Now two small stalactites hung down from the holes in the roof, like inverted candles. That month he had to pawn his watch to pay the rent. It was useless trying to find work at this time of the year. Except for a short and unsatisfactory visit to his parents, he spent the Christmas and New Year's holidays in bed with Linne cuddled at his side and his writing board propped on his knees, setting to music a few poems by Verlaine about the rain, trees along a river, fruits, flowers. One was about a carrousel and its wooden horses who galloped round and round to nowhere.*

It was like living in another world. A wonderful world of beautiful things and music, where there was no winter, no hunger, no rent to pay, no publisher to beg for a transcription. Now and then he would write a few lines of music, talk to his cat while blowing on his numb fingers. He would get up to boil some water for his tea or give Linne something to eat or rush to the outside toilet, from which he would return shivering, his teeth chattering from cold, and run back to his still-warm bed.

Soon it would be dark and he would light the lamp on the nightstand. Now a yellow haze would fall over the music paper, the coverlet, Linne digesting her dinner in contented sleep. Night would spread through the garret like a black fog, and all would be darkness except for the shaft of lamplight. Gradually the last noises of the house—footsteps on the stairs, the closing of a door, the whimpering of a child—would cease. After midnight, even the train whistles would become infrequent. The silence of night, so different from the silence of day, would descend into the room. And he would go on dreaming and writing music until sleep would blur his thoughts and pull down

---

* These are the six Verlaine songs published under the title *Ariettes Oubliées.* It is one of the mysteries of genius that Debussy could write the joyous Carrousel Song (*Chevaux de Bois*) at such a moment in his life.

his lids. Then he would push the board to the foot of the bed and happily slide down beneath the sheets. So long as music stayed with him, everything was all right.

A few days after New Year's he called on his teacher for the usual season's greetings. He played his Verlaine songs for him.

Monsieur Guiraud was very pleased. "You're getting better and better. Just go on like this and don't let anything sway you one way or another. You are on the right track."

Excitedly Claude announced he had already started working on another group of songs. "This time on poems by Baudelaire. One is about the sea, the second about a forest at sunset—"

"It's all very well," interrupted the teacher, "but where is my *Blessed Damozel*? Remember, I want you to send it to the Academy in April. If you don't I'll wring your neck." Fondly his eyes scanned Claude's face. "You look thin. Come on, let's go and have something to eat. Afterward we'll have a game of billiards."

The holidays were over and again it was time to start looking for work. Another rent day was approaching and the money from his watch had dwindled to less than fifty francs. He must . . . he must find some sort of a job. Oh, God, would there ever be an end to this? . . . Yes. When he wrote his opera.

Meanwhile he must find a transcription. Damn it, in a town like Paris, there should be someone who wanted a transcription or a four-hand arrangement. An orchestration. An original song for fifty . . . forty . . . twenty francs . . . Apparently there wasn't. He went to every publisher, even those who had told him to stop bothering them. Everywhere the answer was the same. No work . . . Now publishers did not even trouble to receive him and let him know by the receptionist "he might try again in about six weeks or two months." Even Monsieur Fromont shook his head. "Come back by the middle of March. I may have something then . . ."

But the middle of March was six weeks away. How was he going to live and pay his rent until then? He did not know and there was no use thinking about it. He still had some money, enough to eat for a while. Two, perhaps three, weeks . . .

He refused to despair, lived on boiled potatoes and even tried to work. For a while he was successful. He plunged into the orchestration of *The Blessed Damozel,* and by the end of January he had most of it written. But by then he was growing feeble for lack of food. At times his mind went blank. Music grew blurred and so faint he could no longer hear it.

This time he made the rounds of cafés, but no café owner needed a pianist. Then, by chance, he got a job as a *tapeur* in a dancing studio. Ten hours, ten francs a day. It lasted four days, until the regular pianist returned. Forty francs . . . You could hold on for a while on forty francs. But not very long, not after you had paid fifteen francs on account for the rent.

Now he stayed out as much as he could, shuffling along the streets, indifferent to the rain. Walking aimlessly, to keep warm. Hoping for a miracle: a banknote, a wallet in the gutter, a chance encounter with some former classmate who might invite him to lunch or dinner. Having all the time in the world he loafed, looked into shop windows, stood at the entrance of expensive restaurants. For no reason, except that he liked to watch elegant couples step out of carriages and rush inside. Sometimes the women left a trail of perfume in the air. His rain-soaked hat lost any semblance of shape, his clothes were creased and soiled. He became the derelict the liveried doormen wave out of sight and the gendarmes eye suspiciously.

He discovered the indifference of crowds, the abyss between people who rubbed elbows. But he also discovered the secret solidarity of the poor. Sometimes he would find a bowl of soup at his door, or a few slices of bread and *saucisson* left there by some anonymous neighbor. When, in February, he caught a cold that turned into bronchitis, Madame Sénégal installed herself at his bedside and started slapping hot poultices on him. They seared the skin off his chest and back, but they got him well.

"So long as you're sick in bed, the landlord can't throw you out," she said. "There's a law about that."

And so he stayed in bed, and there, one day, Monsieur Guiraud found him.

"When I don't see you for some time, I can wager you are in some kind of trouble," he said, pulling a chair by the bed, while Madame Sénégal discreetly withdrew. "Why the devil didn't you let me know you were ill?"

His gentle eyes belied the gruffness of his voice. For a while he examined his former pupil with affectionate concern. "Are you all right now?"

"Yes, Master. The concierge has taken care of me."

"Are you able to work?"

Claude nodded. "I've been thinking about a fantasy for piano and orchestra, a sort of piano concerto—"

"The devil with that. Haven't you finished that confounded *Blessed Damozel* yet?"

Two weeks later Claude brought the finished score to his teacher, who read it with great attention.

"Excellent," he said at last. "Now send it to the Academy and let's see what happens."

♦

Like an unclenching fist, winter's grip on Paris relaxed. Looking out of the window one morning Claude noticed that the swallows were back. The air had lost its edge. Blue puddles of sky showed between the clouds. Spring was on its way.

In the streets people looked less worried; the women prettier. Receptionists did not scowl any more. Even publishers had become human; they actually listened to his music.

In quick succession he sold his six Verlaine songs to Madame Girod, an elderly widow who conducted her late husband's publishing business. Another publisher bought two piano pieces he had written many years ago when he was still a student. Then, after a long lecture, Monsieur Fromont gave him an important transcription and, unexpectedly, a liberal advance. On top of all, the Maison Durand bought his two *Arabesques*.

Suddenly he was rich. But he had learned his lesson. Money was to be saved, not spent. No more Japanese fish for him, no more foolish extravagance. From now on, thrift was to be his rule.

And so he was thrifty and did not buy an umbrella, because it seemed foolish to buy an umbrella at this time of the year. What if it drizzled now and then, what were those puny sprinkles to a veteran of the winter deluges? Instead he bought a rare, pedigreed and expensive tulip plant guaranteed to bloom for months, which promptly died. He then went down to the corner flower stall, bought an unguaranteed, unpedigreed geranium, which he placed and forgot on the window sill, where it bloomed all summer.

Naturally he redeemed his gold watch and paid the arrears on his rent. Claude insisted on taking Monsieur Guiraud to dinner at Bignon's, on avenue de l'Opéra, one of the most expensive restaurants in Paris.

This was Claude's only serious extravagance. The rest of the time he still took his meals at the modest local *gargote*. Occasionally, he allowed himself a small cognac with his demitasse; Linne had sardines for breakfast. That was all: nothing reckless.

Then the Maison Durand bought his *Petite Suite,* and this was too much. At one stroke he purchased three pairs of button shoes, a suit and a beige overcoat with a wide black velvet collar. And two *lavallière* silk ties of that exquisite Vermeer blue he loved. And a hat. Not one of those enormous, shapeless felt hats worn by Montmartre bohemians, but a dapper, unusual, truly artistic hat. It had a flat rigid brim like a Spanish sombrero, and a soft malleable crown like a cowboy hat. Different, very different . . . And to go with the hat, a cane. Not just any ordinary cane. A blue cane. Blue, with some delicate carvings in the knob. "There isn't another one like it in Paris," assured the merchant. He was right. The blue cane created a sensation.*

With this change in his wardrobe came a change in his coiffure. He began parting his hair on the left, brushing it slantingly down to conceal as much as possible his embarrassing Beethovenian forehead. The new hairdo made him look, he felt, more sedate. Older, more serious. With his new button shoes, his sombrero, his beige overcoat and blue cane he now felt properly attired.

His living habits also underwent a change. Being now a young man of means, he saw no reason why he should not also be one of leisure. Since leisure consists in doing what one likes, he still worked, but only on his music. He wrote the last of his Baudelaire songs and drafted his Fantasy for Piano and Orchestra. As for Monsieur Fromont's transcription, no date of delivery had been specified. Therefore, there was no need to hurry. The weather was really too nice to sweat over someone else's music . . .

He got into the habit of quitting work by mid-afternoon. Around four o'clock he would rest his pen against the inkwell, lean back on his chair and stretch luxuriously. Then, while exchanging a few remarks with Linne, he would dress with care and start on a leisurely stroll.

Spring was unfolding over Paris, like a lovely song. The women's parasols bloomed along the avenues, and the air was full of music from the café orchestras. It was good to be walking on like this in the sunshine, with not a care in the world and money in his pocket. No question about it, money was terribly important. One must watch one's pennies. Thrift—that was the thing. Never buy anything useless . . .

With his sombrero at a jaunty angle, he would amble along the boulevards, twirling his blue cane, eying women's ankles as they sauntered by in a soft rustle of petticoats. Women . . . He had almost forgotten what pretty things they were. He'd been too busy to think much about them. One of these days he would have to do something about getting himself a girl. *Pour l'hygiène,* you know . . . Yes, women were nice. But for God's sake, stay away from love! That was truly dangerous. Remember Alix? God, what a woman could do to you! Remember the days at the Villa? The longing, the pain, the tormenting face always before your eyes . . . No, never, never again. Alix, beautiful Alix—where was she now? Strange how a woman who meant everything to you could vanish out of your life without a word,

---

* Through this "bohemian" period of life, Debussy's style of dressing was distinctly personal. In the portrait Paul Robert did of him just a few years later he still appears in the famous sombrero, flowing tie, black-velvet-collared overcoat. The French writer Curnonski wrote that he looked "somewhat like a Spanish pirate."

without a trace. Stranger still, how somehow you survived, even forgot in time . . .

Occasionally he would sit on the terrace of a café and enjoy the spectacle of the street with its back-and-forth weaving of carriages, horsecars crawling along the curb and tinkling their bells, the buses pulled by three percherons who almost crushed the wood blocks with their big hooves. The gendarmes, always gesticulating, always swearing at somebody; the newsboys yelling the evening extras, the old flower women sitting on their folding stools with their baskets at their feet. The trees that made lacy shadows on the façades of the houses behind. No question, Paris was a pretty town.

Sometimes he would ask the waiter for a newspaper and inform himself of the state of the world, which, as usual, was deplorable. In Russia revolutionists were throwing bombs right and left, trying to kill the Czar and always killing someone else. England was torn with labor riots; London's Hyde Park was alive with the twitter of birds and socialistic oratory. In Africa the poor savages did not seem to appreciate the benefits of civilization and had to be killed in large numbers. In Paris, of course, there was talk only of the Great Exposition Universelle—"l'Expo," as people called it—scheduled for next spring to commemorate the centennial of the storming of the Bastille.

It was to be the grandest exhibition ever held, and work had been in progress for months. On the flat and empty acres of the Champs de Mars, right in the center of town, the government was building a replica of the French colonial empire, a make-believe exotic city of temples, bazaars, mosques, Tunisian coffee houses, Saharan oases, jungle huts; even a Tahitian palm-roofed village, complete with a lagoon. But the star of the show was to be that gigantic iron tower Monsieur Eiffel had been working on for more than a year. Already it was sprouting out of the ground, a four-legged monstrosity rising more than a hundred feet high in an entanglement of wires, steel cables and riveted beams. Newspapers said it would be the tallest thing in the world, attract thousands of tourists. Privately the Parisians felt that at the first stiff breeze the whole damn thing would collapse.

Sometimes, to pass a moment, Claude went to look at it. It was interesting to watch those hundreds of workmen crawling like ants over it, each one busy, apparently knowing what he was doing. Sometimes he spent hours browsing through the Seine bookstalls in the hope of coming across the libretto he was looking for.

Sometimes, like today, he strolled along the quays for no particular purpose and with no special destination in mind. Merely for the pleasure of walking along the river, watching the boats, the fishermen, the bridges' reflections in the water.

He stopped to look down on the embankment at a *clochard* sleeping peacefully, a bundle of rags under his head. What a wonderful thing sleep was! Hell must be a place where you couldn't sleep . . . He raised his eyes and with a start realized he had reached the Font des Arts. And behind it, in the middle of the Seine, rising like a stone-hulled caravel, was la Cité, the island which carried Notre Dame on its back.

Unhurriedly he walked alongside the Palais de Justice, with its spiked turrets, its stone walls black with age. Then Notre Dame came into view. Notre Dame, the heart of France, calm and golden in the afternoon sunshine . . . As he followed the quay he noticed that the narrow strip of water had itself become a liquid stained glass from the reflections of the cathedral's windows.

He took a few more steps, and on an impulse crossed Pont Marie. He found himself on Ile Saint-Louis, a smaller island trailing behind Notre Dame, like a dinghy after a clipper. From a blue-enamel street plate he learned he was standing on Quai d'Anjou. He sat down on the low parapet wall, removed his hat and gazed down at the river through the foliage of the overhanging trees.

At once he felt the tranquillity and eerie detachment of his surroundings. This was a Paris he did not know. A Paris incredibly old, cut off from the hustle and bustle of the encircling city by only a moat of water, yet a thousand miles away from it. A Paris of silence and peace turned toward the past, frozen in the stillness of places where time has long ceased to run.

"Claude."

The voice wafted from behind and he recognized it at once. Alix!

He rose, turned around—and his breath caught in his throat. It wasn't . . . couldn't be Alix! The woman in the fusty dress and old-fashioned hat, who stood a few feet away, smiling, a little breathless, did look like Alix. But older, much older . . .

She caught the expression of shock in his eyes. "Have I changed so much as that?"

There was no resentment or bitterness in her voice; only helpless resignation as though her changed appearance were an affliction, some unsightly rash she could not conceal.

"After all, it's been a long time, hasn't it?" she went on with a piteous, apologetic smile. "More than two years, isn't it, since we last saw each other? A woman can change a lot in two years, especially at my age. Remember, I'd warned you about it, but you wouldn't believe me."

Yes, she had warned him. Many times. He even remembered her words, "In a year, perhaps two, I'll look old, and one day suddenly you'll see it . . ." In that, as in everything, she had been right. And he, as usual, wrong . . .

Despite himself he continued to scan her face. Her eyes had not changed, but the skin around them had become crisscrossed with thin lines. Her cheeks had begun to sag, and underneath the dowdy hat her hair had lost its sheen. Yet she was still beautiful. But her beauty was no longer naked and startling. It had grown blurred, a sort of inner radiance that became noticeable only after a while.

"But you haven't changed at all." Her pleasure at seeing him made her eyes gleam. "A little thinner perhaps. Didn't they feed you at the Villa?"

He was about to say he had left the Villa more than a year ago, but she gave him no time and went on happily. "You know, I almost didn't speak to you. You seemed so lost in thought I didn't want to break in, but I had to. I was so pleased to see you I just couldn't pass by without talking to you." Irrelevantly she asked, "Do you come here often?"

"It's the first time."

"Lovely, isn't it?"

He nodded. "And what're you doing here?"

"Why, we live here!" She laughed, and her laugh had not changed. Already she looked younger than a moment ago, almost as young as he remembered her. "Don't look so startled. Quite a few people live here, you know. This isn't exactly a deserted island. We've lived here for over a year now and we love it. It was one of Father's favorite spots. We used to come here and walk around. Then we'd sit on the wall, as you were doing a moment ago, and he'd tell me about the time when Paris was a village in the middle of the Seine."

She paused, and again he noticed the gleam of pleasure in her eyes. They might have been two friends meeting after a long absence.

"Would you like to walk around my little island for a moment?" she asked.

Side by side they started walking along the quay. Below, the river stirred and flowed slowly in the opposite direction.

"People liked living here," she went on, "because they felt safe and snug with water all around. And when you've been living here awhile you feel the same. When I cross the bridge to go shopping I feel as if I were going into some foreign, bustling town full of noises and buses and agitated people rushing about, not knowing where. I can't wait to come back."

Lovingly she smiled at the stately old houses with their wrought-iron balconies and carved archways.

"Here everything's so quiet you imagine yourself living in another world. A world of friendly ghosts who once had the same problems, the same joys and pains as we have and who have found peace. And their peace hangs in the air, you almost can feel it. Little by little it seeps into you." Her voice dwindled to a murmur. "It's a nice place to grow old in."

He asked about her children, and she said they were well.

"And so grown-up you wouldn't recognize them. Children are like clocks that remind you of the passing of time. You turn around, and when you look at them again they've shot up an inch. Marguerite is a real little lady now and very helpful. She gives me a hand with the housework. We don't have a maid any more."

"And Pierre?"

He was fine. But he, too, had changed a great deal. "He never goes out any more. In the morning he sits on the balcony, reads a little, dozes in the sun. It does him good."

The accent of tenderness in her voice was unmistakable. She spoke of him as of a child or some beloved invalid. Claude felt a prick of resentment. The old man had won.

"Shall we sit down?" she said.

They sat down on the parapet wall. With a languid gesture she removed her hat and set it at her side. Then she turned her head aside and gazed down at the river, her hands folded in her lap. For a while they remained silent, not touching each other, lost in thought. The sunniness of a moment ago was ebbing out of the sky, turning into the lavender dust of twilight. Two white-coiffed Sisters of Saint Vincent passed by, eyes down, in a rustle of voluminous skirts.

"Strange, isn't it, our running into each other like this?" she said, without looking at him. "I thought I'd never see you again."

"I went to your house, but the concierge told me you had moved and she didn't know your new address."

A shadow brushed over her face. She kept her eyes fastened down on the river. "I had asked her not to give it to you."

The words struck him like a blow. For an instant he hated her with his whole being. Then the pain returned, as hot and sharp as it had been fifteen months ago.

"Why?" he asked.

"Because it was the only way to put an end to it." Slowly she took her eyes away from the river and looked full at him. "You see, Claude, I loved you very much, and when it comes to love, nobody is strong. I was afraid of what I might do if I still saw you. Or what you might . . . Anyway, I thought it was best for all of us. Yes, all of us—the three of us. For then Pierre had found out about us."

"How? You said he never would."

"He didn't. Not for the longest time. Even when you were living with us, even after you'd gone to Rome and I'd lie awake or pace the floor of my room thinking of you. On the contrary, he would show me your letters and tell me about the great advantages you would

draw from having won the Grand Prix. He was very fond and proud
of you."

She paused. In the approaching dusk her face had regained its
former perfection. Now it was the Alix he remembered who was looking at him, leaning slightly forward in pleading urgency.

"Then you got that leave of absence. Every afternoon I went to
your hotel—and still he didn't suspect. It never crossed his mind to
follow me or doubt my excuses. Then you returned to Rome, and I
almost went crazy. I knew you still must remain there another two
years and I knew that by then I would look—well, as I look now, and
you wouldn't love me any more. Oh yes, I know I could've let you
resign and kept you near me. But I couldn't bring myself to do it, I
knew I would never forgive myself and some day you'd hate me. And
so I promised everything you wanted and you went back and I told
myself I'd done the right thing. But doing the right thing can be a
chilly comfort. For a few months it went on like this. Each day I'd
write you to come back and then burn the letter. I became so nervous
and irritable that Pierre wanted me to see a doctor. He offered to take
me to the country, he suggested my taking a trip. He was patient and
kind and I hated him for it."

She took in a deep breath.

"Then, one day, by chance, he found out."

Around them silence was deepening, hushing the sound of her
voice. The color was going out of things. Below, the river was turning dark gray and across the bridge the first lampposts were being lit.
On the other island Notre Dame had become a blurred silhouette of
spikes and steeples and towers, a shadowy monster kneeling down in
sleep.

"It was a Sunday, I remember it well. A dreary winter day, shortly
after New Year's. The children had gone to visit their aunt, and
Pierre, as usual, was out at some reception. I was alone in the house,
sitting at the piano, trying to play one of the songs you dedicated to
me. Pierre came in earlier than I expected. I heard the door open and
turned around. He was holding flowers in his hand and started toward
me. Then he saw I was crying, and he stopped dead, as if he'd been
nailed to the floor. I'll never forget the expression of shock and desolation in his eyes. I could easily have invented some excuse, but I didn't
even try. Perhaps I was tired of pretending, or just didn't care. For an
instant we looked at each other and he read the truth on my face.
Then, quietly, he asked where he could find a vase for the flowers, and
I said, 'In the kitchen,' and he went out without a word. I watched him
go, and at that instant something happened which I can't understand
or explain. I didn't love you any more and I loved him instead."

Again she paused. Her gaze went down to her hands. She seemed to have forgotten Claude's presence and he knew she was living the memory of that moment.

"As I said, I can't explain it, or even understand it." She spoke half aloud, eyes down, as if to herself. "They say you can fall in love instantly, at a glance. Perhaps you can fall out of it the same way. Who knows at what moment the leaf stops clinging to the tree? Suddenly something inside me relaxed, gave up. I stopped clinging to you, to love and youth. I accepted my fate, and at once I felt at peace."

He listened, smiling at his naïveté, at the disenchanting prosaism of life. So, that's how it happened . . . She hadn't sacrificed herself, broken her heart with her own hands, as he'd thought. One day she'd grown tired of it all. Tired of longing, clinging, wishing, remembering —the whole exhausting gamut of emotions which go with loving. And he, the clever one, the builder of plans, had thought of everything but the obvious. And true to form, he had plunged ahead and made a fool of himself.

Gently he asked, "And Pierre—what did he do?"

"He never mentioned the incident, but from one day to another he became a different man."

He had crumbled before her eyes. In a few weeks the dapper, almost foppish man-about-town had turned into a frightened, troubled-eyed old man. He who had walked straight and fast now stooped and took short shuffling steps. All pose and posturing had gone out of him. Gone, also, the flowery chatter, the fluttering gestures of hands. He was old; in less than a month he had become very old.

"He still went to his office, but he no longer cared for his work. Back home he'd sit and gaze into the fire. Then one day he turned to me, took my hand and said, 'Forgive me, Alix.' Strange, wasn't it, his asking me to forgive him? But I understood what he meant. He meant to say he was sorry he had lured me into marrying him with his talk about the books he was going to write and how much he needed me, when all he wanted was a handsome wife to show off to his friends. He was looking at me, waiting for me to speak, but I didn't. Instead I knelt down by his chair and pressed his hand against my cheek. And so, without a word, we forgave each other. Perhaps two people must forgive each other at least once before they can be sure of their love."

Her face relaxed into a slow smile. "From that moment on we felt truly married. More than that—like newly-weds. I know it sounds absurd, but I can't express it any other way. We were newly-weds starting life together.

And like newly-weds, they had started making plans. She had suggested he retire from business. She'd shown him that by selling the Villa d'Avray house, dispensing with the maid, discontinuing musicales, receptions and such mundane nonsense, they could live modestly on their savings. Their lease was almost up and she proposed taking a smaller apartment. She had found one on the island. "And so we moved in here. But, as I told you, I was still afraid I might lose my head and do something crazy if I saw you again. I didn't want to take any chances. That's why I asked the concierge not to give you our new address. You understand, don't you?"

He nodded. "And now—you aren't afraid any more?"

She shook her head. "No, darling. No more . . . I'm happier than I've ever been. The children, too. They love it here and don't miss the country at all. They go down and fish on the embankment just below the house, and Pierre and I watch them from the balcony. With their friends they play in the street, for there's practically no traffic. In summer they go swimming at the little establishment up the river. They're happy, and so is Pierre. He's even started writing another book, and I help him with it when I have a moment. It'll never be finished, but who cares? . . . We're happy."

Suddenly they were strangers, like travelers on a wharf after a cruise. Several years ago, because she'd come to a singing studio, their lives had entwined. Now they no longer did. Nothing remained of their lust, their longing, all the pains and joys they had given each other. Nothing remains of a dead love affair, except a few bewildered, incredulous memories. And after a time, not even that.

"And you?" she asked. "Are you happy?"

He nodded, and she went on, "Did you just return from Rome?"

"No. I resigned and came back last year."

"Mon Dieu!" Her hand went to her mouth. "I was afraid you'd do something like that. At first I wanted to write and tell you what had happened between Pierre and me, but I was sure you'd run away and take the first train for Paris—and without leave of absence this time. If I didn't write I knew you'd be hurt, but by then you had only one more year to stay in Rome and I hoped you'd see the wisdom of finishing your term." Impulsively she clasped his hand. "Oh, my poor boy! It's my fault."

She looked so distraught that he broke into a smile. "Don't blame yourself," he said. "I wanted to resign anyway."

"At least have you found work, have you sold some of your compositions?"

Yes, he had. Several of them . . . Oh yes, he'd had a few difficult moments, but nothing serious and now everything was fine. He elaborated, improvised a few details as he went along. The over-all impression was one of great prosperity. Prospects, he suggested, were most encouraging.

"And one of these days I'm going to write my opera," he said casually. "Then I'll be established."

She knew him too well not to discount much of his boasting. But his new shoes, the expensive blue cane, the silk tie, the dashing sombrero confirmed some small measure of affluence. At least he wasn't starving. She felt relieved.

"I'm glad you're doing so well." Gently she pulled her hand away.

"And what about love? Have you found some young girl you like?"

No, he hadn't. He'd been too busy to think about girls. Besides, they could be such a bother . . . Some day, he probably would get interested in a girl.

She repressed a smile. Why were the young so ashamed of their youth, always trying so hard to pass for cynics? And he, of all people! . . . "I hope you find one soon. Everyone more or less wants love, but you need it. Although—" She broke short.

"Although what?"

"Although I don't know whether I envy or pity the girl who will fall in love with you."

"And why?" Now he was offended. "What's wrong with me?"

"Nothing, darling. Except that with you music will always come first. Remember that day at Ville d'Avray, we were lying by our pond and you were nibbling a blade of grass, and I asked you what you were thinking about and you said you were listening to the sounds of summer? That's the kind of thing that hurts a woman."

"But it was true," he protested.

"I know, and that's what hurts. A moment ago we had made love and I wanted you to hold me in your arms. But no, you were a thousand miles away, listening to your sounds of summer. That's what I mean, music will always come first. Be careful. No woman likes playing second fiddle to a lot of notes on a page of paper."

She saw he did not undersatnd, and soothingly added, "Don't worry, darling, she'll forgive you and learn to love you as you are. For even with your music, she will still have more with you than with most men. She will know some wonderful . . . wonderful moments."

Somewhere a clock struck the hour.

"It's getting late," she said.

Night was closing in, spreading her dark veils, chasing away the last gleams of twilight. Over Notre Dame the sky was green. Already the first evening star hung directly above the nave.

She reached for her hat and absently began putting it on. As she did so she turned again into the dowdy, middle-aged woman who had called his name two hours ago.

Suddenly she froze into motionlessness, and for an instant she remained lost in thought, her face bent down, her arms still raised.

"Strange, isn't it, that it was because of our affair that Pierre and I finally found each other? . . . I sometimes wonder how things would have turned out if I hadn't been crying that afternoon when he came into the drawing room."

Her smile spread, turned into a glow that incandesced her face. She leaned forward and kissed Claude on the cheek. "Good-bye, darling. Please, don't rise. I'd rather go home alone."

She started walking away. He watched her figure recede along the quay in the deepening night.

Then she turned into an arched doorway—and out of sight.

Book Two

GABY

"Love is a devil: there is no evil angel but Love."
SHAKESPEARE

CHAPTER

7

A FEW DAYS LATER, IN THE COURSE OF ONE OF HIS AFTERNOON strolls, Claude happened to stop in front of a small bookshop on rue Chaussée d'Antin. For a while he examined the books in the window, then casually pushed the door open.

He was greeted by a goateed rosy-cheeked old man who tipped his skullcap and informed him that he was at his service and his name was Edmond Bailly.

"But my friends call me 'Père' Bailly, and you may do so, for we're going to be great friends. I see it in your aura."

Claude refrained from comment. "As you know," the bookdealer continued, "the presence of spirit forms in the human body creates a mysterious radiance which is the aura. It is invisible to the vulgar, but not so to the initiate." His blue eyes smiled behind the steel-framed spectacles. "Yours is unusually brilliant and harmonious. Therefore, you may come and browse in my shop as much as you like."

He stopped, quickly glanced at the door, and his voice dwindled to a whisper. "Excuse me, but Voltaire just came in. He often drops in like this to see if his books are properly displayed. You know how authors are!"

With a hasty wave he dashed away to wait upon the distinguished visitor.

Claude left the store that day with the suspicion that his new friend was a little touched in the head. Subsequent visits left him no doubt about it, but did not lessen his sympathy for the eccentric and genial old man. On the contrary, he grew very fond of him.

In a world full of normal and tormented people Père Bailly radiated happiness. One day he told Claude how he had found peace and contentment.

"As a young man," he said, "I was most unhappy. I believed in brotherly love, I dreamed of a world in which there would be no more frontiers, no more wars, no more hate. As the world happened to be just then in a state of great strife, I felt it my duty to promote universal understanding."

To this end he had dabbled in politics: the humanitarian, well-meaning, dangerous kind, with the result that after the fall of *la Commune* he had been thrown in jail, tried, condemned and only by a miracle escaped being shot.

The nervous shock of his narrow escape had unhinged his brain and opened his eyes. In a few lucid flashes he had realized how useless it was to insist on understanding people who insisted on not understanding you; how unwise to try changing anybody's ideas and how presumptuous to think that you alone were right and everyone else wrong. It also had dawned on him that all religions had their martyrs, all political parties their heroes, and throughout history brave, admirable people had died for the most conflicting principles.

He had found it all very educational. The more he thought of it the less he felt inclined to die for something as fragile and uncertain as a social theory, even his own. As his reason collapsed he had acquired common sense. In a great burst of enthusiasm he had decided to mind his business and let the world go to hell.

Since then he had been a little mad and very happy.

"I found peace in books and the companionship of the dead," he told Claude. "That's why I became a bookdealer and an occultist."

He had resigned from the society of the living and entered into communication with illustrious and long-departed men of letters. In his shop he received the visits of Voltaire, the Encyclopedists, Montaigne and, occasionally, the great Molière himself. On Sundays he engaged in long and friendly conversations, through table rappings, with Plato, Dante, Goethe, Shakespeare and other foreign authors, who replied in fluent, colloquial French.

Besides selling books, Père Bailly engaged in publishing in a small, unprofitable way. He put out limited editions of slim *plaquettes* of verses, erotica and short uncommercial novels that had been turned down by every publisher in Paris. As a rule they languished on his shelves, but he usually got back his investment, for the authors themselves bought the whole editions to present autographed copies to their friends and admirers.

"For some reason a writer's friends never buy his books. Somehow their friendships do not stretch quite that far, and you have no idea how many friends an author can have! That's why most writers are poor."

He also published a magazine, *La Revue Esotérique,* for the benefit of his fellow occultists and esotericians: most of them, Claude noticed, ladies of advancing years and receding looks who dressed in flowing veils and enormous hats and floated into the shop like ectoplasms and in whispers informed Père Bailly of their latest supersensorial experiences.

In addition to mediums, astrologers, fortune tellers and kindred spirits, a number of other people frequented the bookshop. Preoccupied-looking men, some with manuscripts jutting out of their pockets, came in singly or in couples late in the afternoon, waved absently at the bookdealer and in quick strides made their way to the back room, where they disappeared.

"They are writers," explained Bailly. "They meet there to discuss."

"About what?"

"Anything. Writers love to talk, some even more than write. Would you like to meet them?"

Claude was duly introduced and, since he was a musician and therefore no rival, heartily welcomed. He found that Père Bailly was right. Not only did writers love to talk, but they hated to listen. Never had he heard so many people talking at the same time. Mostly about the deplorable state of belles-lettres in France; publishers' greed, critics' incompetence and the public's indifference to great literature, by which they meant their own. He watched them pull nervously on their cigarettes, wave their expressive hands and slash one another with razor-sharp repartee, while observing the rules of the most flowery courtliness. He thought them fascinating. They, in turn, appreciated his reverent attention. His silence was the foundation of his popularity.

There he made his first literary friend, Henri de Régnier: a twenty-four-year-old, prematurely bald poet who looked like a diplomat. He wore a black-ribboned monocle, a high collar and had a blond drooping mustache. His manners were exquisite; his speech refined. There was about him none of the bohemian untidiness so common among writers, especially poets. He was emphatically a gentleman-poet, as some people are gentlemen-farmers. Like them, he was primarily a gentleman.

He wrote Symbolist poetry; and it, too, was very refined. Much too refined, in fact, to be appreciated by the average public. The poet, he sighed, must be resigned to toil in obscurity for his own delight and that of a small, discriminating elite.

Claude agreed. Yes, it was the artist's lot to be unrecognized for a long time. But if he had real talent, success was bound to come his way.

"Look at Wagner!" he said one day as they were sipping their *apéritifs* on the terrace of a café. "For years he was laughed at. He, the greatest musician who ever lived! Yet in time people began to recognize his genius."

"Since you are a Wagner admirer, you must come with me to Monsieur Mallarmé's reunions," said the gentleman-poet, polishing his monocle with his handkerchief. "You will find yourself among friends. At Mallarmé's everyone admires Wagner."

And not only Wagner, but Symbolist poetry and literature, for it was Paris' finest intellectual and artistic elite that met every Tuesday evening at Monsieur Mallarmé's. And composed not only of professional artists and writers, as one might expect, but also of enlightened art-loving amateurs of great means and high social standing.

"I particularly want you to meet Etienne Dupin and Prince Poniatowski. They are about our age and will like meeting you. Etienne Dupin, as you know, is enormously rich, and he loves Wagner almost as much as you do. Every summer he goes to Bayreuth to hear his operas."

As for André Poniatowski, he was a young financier and one of the best gentlemen-jockeys in France. Monsieur Degas, the artist, had made innumerable sketches of him for his race-track pictures. But André wasn't only a financier and sportsman. He also loved Wagner's music, Symbolist poetry and avant-garde literature. And with that, was always willing to do you a good turn. In short, a prince of a fellow.

"And, of course," Régnier wound up, "you will have the honor of meeting Stéphane Mallarmé, head of the Symbolist School and probably the greatest poet France has ever produced."

The following Tuesday evening the two friends went to Monsieur Mallarmé's. They filed into the already crowded dining room, and Claude was presented to the host.

The poet was seated at a large round table in the glow of the ceiling lamp, nibbling the edge of his voluminous, graying mustache while waiting for the twenty-odd guests to finish taking their places. Although he was only forty-six, the weariness of his expression and the fringed Scotch plaid he wore on his shoulders made him look much older. Between his long bony fingers he held a cigar, which he brought now and then to his lips with an absent, almost automatic gesture.

He greeted Claude with courtesy, murmured a few words on the kinship between music and poetry and urged him to look for a vacant chair. "If you still can find one," he added with a doubtful smile.

Claude did not find a seat and had to stand against the door jamb, but he was too excited to care. Here he was—he, who had never gone to school—a member of the Paris intellectual elite rubbing elbows with eminent writers, poets and artists . . . From his end of the room he watched Mallarmé rest his cigar in the ashtray, riffle a sheaf of manuscript paper and discreetly clear his throat.

This, apparently, was the signal that the session was coming to order, for instantly silence fell in the room and the guests assumed attitudes of utmost concentration, chin in hand or hand over eyes. In a soft, euphonious voice the host began reading his unintelligible poems. Claude could not make head or tail out of them, but this he attributed to his deficient education.

An hour later the reading came to a halt. With a tired smile the poet announced there would be an intermission. Refreshments were served. Everyone came out of his trance and started talking at once, but in a more restrained fashion than in Père Bailly's backroom. The gravity of the gathering called for ponderousness, not vehemence. The air was heavy with profundities.

"Master, I just can't tell you what these reunions have done to me," Claude told his teacher a few weeks later, as they were dining together. "They've given me a whole new set of literary values."

Throughout the meal he expanded on the exciting theories he had heard at Mallarmé's, the great writers he had met, the new friends he had made.

"And then," he went on, "it's such a thrill to hear Monsieur Mallarmé read his poems. Of course, they are too cryptic for the average public, but what depth, what mastery of language!"

"Also what nonsense!" added Monsieur Guiraud, who had been silent for a long time.

Claude let out a gasp. "You don't think that Monsieur Mallarmé is one of our greatest poets?"

"Since I can't understand what he writes, it's difficult to say. But whenever I've been able to get the glimmer of the thought behind his poems I found that it was neither original nor profound. You see, Claude, a platitude remains a platitude, even when twisted beyond recognition. Perhaps future generations will recognize Mallarmé as an unfathomable genius. I'm inclined to think they will rather remember him as a nice, modest man who found time to pose for innumerable photographs and portraits, worked very hard to express commonplaces in a complicated way, and also wrote a hand-ful of simple and beautiful verses which somehow escaped his passion for turning French, the most lucid of languages, into gibberish."

Claude rushed to the defense of his literary friends and his new set of literary values. He duly repeated the various aesthetic formulas he had heard at Mallarmé's, displayed his fresh vocabulary of cryptic words. Like a brave and faithful Symbolist, he insisted the purpose of poetry was not to express ideas but to make music with words.*

To his dismay, Monsieur Guiraud received this pronouncement with a burst of laughter.

"I'm going to tell you a great secret," he said, his face still creased into a grin. "The way to make music is with music. Just as the way to walk is with your feet and not on your head. I know it sounds old-fashioned and not at all avant-garde, but I think that in time you will agree. Now drink your coffee"—still chuckling he signaled to the waiter—"and let's have a game of billiards."

Claude was distressed by his teacher's pedestrian remarks. It was tragic to watch creeping old age wither and paralyze a man's brain. Already his good teacher could no longer see that Wagner was the greatest of all musicians, and now he showed the same lack of perceptiveness toward literature. There was no use trying to discuss such matters with him. You just couldn't bridge the chasm between generations . . .

He decided that in the future he would avoid mentioning Mallarmé to his teacher, as already he avoided mentioning his operatic plans.

◆

With everyone else he talked a good deal about his operatic plans. At Mallarmé's his prestige as Grand Prix de Rome had brought him an audience to which he discoursed at length about musical matters and the opera he was going to write some day. "As soon as I find the right libretto."

One evening, as he was pronouncing these words, a stout man with a streaming beard and a gray mane of hair spoke.

"I have it," he said.

This was Catulle Mendès. He was nearing fifty, and his face—once extremely handsome—had grown swollen and flabby. Thirty years of bohemian living had left their mark on him. There were spots on his vest. Dandruff speckled his shoulders. He had done too many things and lost himself along the way. The everlasting need of money had

---

* This was the main tenet of the Symbolist School of poetry. A famous anecdote illustrates this point. One day the painter Degas told Mallarmé that he had been trying all day to write a sonnet, but couldn't get an idea. "But, *mon cher*," replied Mallarmé, "one doesn't write a sonnet with ideas, one writes a sonnet with words."

dulled both his ethics and his esthetics. Gradually his facility had smothered his talent. He could write anything: poems, essays, critiques, plays, novels, librettos. Name it, and Mendès had it. If by chance he did not have it, he could produce it in a few days. Sometimes in a few hours. He had two specialties. One was salacious literature, for which he had been condemned by the courts; the other was Wagner. In both fields he was regarded as an expert.

"Yes," he repeated, "I have the libretto you've been searching for. I wrote it only a few months ago and it has all the qualities you require. For the moment let me just tell you that it's called *Rodrigue et Chimène* and that it takes place in Spain—like *Parsifal*."

He now was in command of the situation and told Claude the glory as well as the enormous financial rewards that awaited the composer who would blend musically the French and German genius.

"And don't forget that I am an intimate friend of the director of the Opéra," he went on with a meaningful wink. "Therefore, we are assured of an immediate production. How long do you think it'll take you?"

"I don't know. Eight or ten months, I'd say. Perhaps a year."

By then they were surrounded by a number of attentive listeners. Etienne Dupin turned to Claude. "Why don't you come with me to Bayreuth this summer? As my guest, of course."

Yes. What better preparation for writing this opera than to attend a few performances of the Meister's works in the theatre that he himself had designed for that purpose?

And so, three weeks later, Claude formally promised Catulle to make *Rodrigue et Chimène* into an opera and went to Bayreuth with his wealthy young friend, Etienne Dupin. Together they climbed the steep hill to the Festspielhaus, where they listened to the Wagnerian music billowing out of an invisible orchestra while on the stage storms raged and awesome happenings took place. During intermissions they raced to the buffet for a plateful of wurst or cold chicken, washed down with delicious Bavarian beer. Then, at the summons of trumpets blaring the Walhalla theme, they rushed back to their seats for more and still more Wagnerian rapture.

Claude returned to Paris, like a Moslem from Mecca.

"I'll never thank you enough," he said to his genial host. "This was just what I needed. I am now ready to start on *Rodrigue*."

But summer was still on and it was hot. Much too hot, he felt, to tackle such a vast undertaking. Instead he finished his Fantasy for Piano and Orchestra and Monsieur Fromont's transcription. Meanwhile he spent every possible moment studying Mendès' libretto, outlining some of the scenes in his mind and conditioning himself for the task ahead.

A few days before the reopening of the Conservatoire he called on Monsieur Guiraud, who had just returned from his vacation. On the way to his teacher's home he reminded himself to avoid any reference to *Rodrigue,* but five minutes after his arrival he inadvertently mentioned Bayreuth. This led to an explanation about Etienne Dupin, which in turn led to an explanation about the purpose of the trip, which in turn led to Catulle Mendès' libretto—and the opera.

"And so you're going to write an opera," said the teacher, consternation in his eyes.

"Yes, Master."

"It sounds most interesting," said Monsieur Guiraud with a forced smile. "What is the libretto about?"

"About Rodrigo del Bivar," said Claude importantly. "You know, the great Spanish hero."

Some historians called him Rodrigo del Vivar; others El Cid. Rodrigo had the burning ambition to free Spain from the Moslems, push them back in the sea and plant the Cross on the tip of their mosques. Everyone in Spain urged him to go ahead and do it, but Rodrigo was more anxious to spend time with Chimène, Ximena, as they said in Spanish. He loved her madly, and she, too, loved him madly, but at the same time she hated him because he had killed her father in a duel.

"Naturally there are complications and secondary plots, but roughly that's what it's about." He waited for his teacher's reaction.

"You're aware, I'm sure, that your libretto is merely a variation of Cornielle's *Le Cid,* but this is not important. You seem quite excited about it."

"Oh yes, Master, I am. Very much."

"You have no doubts, no doubts at all, that it lends itself to your kind of music?"

None whatever. He had thought it all out. His head was full of musical ideas. Already several scenes were blocked out in his mind. "All I have to do is jot them down on paper."

"Well," said Monsieur Guiraud, "then everything is fine. I don't want to detain you from your work any longer. Don't forget to come and show me the first act as soon as it is written."

◆

Claude returned home in an eager mood. He climbed the stairs two at a time, addressed a few cheerful remarks to Linne, who quivered her whiskers in reply; then he sat down at his table.

Now to work! . . .

The first act shouldn't take him more than a month. Six weeks at most . . . From the ream of music paper he took a blank page and wrote in large letters:

"RODRIGUE ET CHIMÈNE. OPERA IN THREE ACTS."

On the following page, in smaller characters he wrote:

"Act One. Prelude."

This done he looked out of the window.

The Prelude . . . Yes, the Prelude . . . It should begin with a solemn fanfare, a few blasts of trumpets to indicate the general character of the work. Something like the Walhalla theme, but with a Spanish flavor. After all, the story took place in Spain. How about a few guitars? . . . A distant clatter of castanets perhaps? . . . No, no castanets. Only brass. Very loud and solemn.

He waited, straining his ear for the sound of the opening fanfare.

It did not come, and after a while his mind wandered away from the Prelude. Slowly his eyes traveled over the mottled sky. The day was gray, with the portent of approaching rain. Soon the roof would start leaking again . . . A cloud was lumbering across the sky, ready to burst into millions of raindrops. Raindrops made a lovely sound on the leaves . . . It would be fun to catch the sound of rain in music . . .

The whistle of a departing train brought him out of his musings and back to the Prelude. Oh, yes, the Prelude . . . Perhaps it should begin with a fiery Spanish dance. A habañera or a fandango . . . After all, it was a Spanish story and Spaniards loved to dance. Perhaps this fandango could become Ximena's leitmotiv. Now that sounded good . . . Each time she came on the stage you'd hear the distant strains of the fandango. Yes, that's what he needed. Some colorful, sensuous melody. Something that would suggest whirling petticoats, castanets, tambourine and tapping heels. Passionate, but tender . . .

Again he waited. This time he losed his eyes for greater concentration. The fandango failed to appear.

He was about to try a third approach to the Prelude when he realized that he was ravenous.

He would go and have dinner; then he would return and try again. Surely, this time the Prelude would come . . .

It didn't.

Nor the next day, nor the next. Three weeks he waited. No Prelude came. Finally in a fit of exasperation he wrote a brief opening number that began with a somber churchlike fanfare and developed almost immediately into a spirited Spanish dance.

It was almost November. At Mallarmé's, his friends were impatient to hear excerpts of the opera. Catulle Mendès wanted the first act. "You see, if I could show the first act to my friend, the director of the Opéra, I could get a sizable advance . . ." To all, Claude replied with a friendly but firm shake of the head. No, no private auditions. Not even the Prelude. No excerpts either . . . About the date of completion he was optimistic but evasive. *Rodrigue* was advancing steadily, but they must understand that an opera took time . . . much time . . .

Back in his garret his optimism would change to a feeling of grim determination. He must, simply must write *Rodrigue*. Yes, it was difficult. Much more difficult than he had anticipated. It only meant that he must work harder, lash himself into a creative trance . . . To do this he gorged himself on Wagner's music. He played his operas on the piano, pored over the scores, analyzed the instrumentation, dissected the dramatic structure. When at last he thought he had churned himself into creativeness he would rush to bed—for now it was winter and the garret was ice-cold—set his writing board on his knees, and wait.

And so a few more weeks passed.

On that memorable December afternoon he was still waiting, trying to project himself into medieval Spain, straining every cell in his brain to "feel" Rodrigo's lust for Ximena, when there was a knock on the door.

"Come in," he shouted, furious at the interruption.

An elderly gentleman in a top hat and heavy overcoat shuffled in, leaning on a cane. As he neared the bed he looked smilingly at Claude sitting up with his board on his knees and Linne cuddled at his side.

"What an inspiring sight!" he exclaimed. "I, too, used to work like this when I was young and poor. Youthful hardships make sweet memories in old age. Mark my word, young man, some day you will look with emotion on these poverty-stricken years."

Claude was in no mood for chatter. What did the old codger want? "What's on your mind?" he asked ungraciously. "You can see I'm busy."

From then on, the interview was doomed. Stiffly the visitor informed him that the Academy had been gratified by his *envoi* of *The Blessed Damozel*. As a mark of its appreciation it had decided to overlook his resignation and grant him his Grand Prix festival.

"There is, however, a small condition," he went on between tight lips. "The Academy expects you to write an overture for the graduation exercises of the Conservatoire next July."

"What! Here I am working on an opera and you come to bother

me with some silly school piece! Do you realize what this opera means to me? Everything, yes, everything. And you come to pester me about that measly, insignificant—"

The old gentleman did not wait for the end of the tirade. Without a word he turned on his heels and shuffled out of the room.

Monsieur Guiraud was furious.

"You fool, do you realize what you've done!" He was pacing up and down his study, clasping his hands, almost choking from anger. "You've ruined your chance to have your music played. But no, you don't realize it. You're too stupid to realize anything."

"But, Master, I was working on my opera—"

"Your opera!" The words burst out in an explosive snort. "Don't you see that you can't write this absurd opera of yours, that it isn't your kind of music, that you're only wasting your time and hurting your brain? But no, you don't see it, you're too stupid to see anything. Oh, get out, get out of my sight!"

A sudden weariness seemed to fall upon him. He stopped pacing and lowered himself into his chair by the fireside.

"No, don't go," he said quietly. "Let's see what can be done—if anything."

He ran his hand over his eyes, and he looked so discouraged that Claude felt pangs of remorse.

"I'm sorry, Master. If you want, I'll write this overture."

The teacher shook his head. "It's no use. I've seen a few members of the Academy and you could write twenty overtures and they wouldn't give you your festival again. Do you realize that in almost a hundred years, since the Grand Prix de Rome was founded, no other laureate has ever been given a second chance to have his festival. And you—you threw it away!"

His anger was returning, but he held it in check. "How's your music ever going to be played?" he said half aloud.

Broodingly he rubbed his chin for a while. Then with a sigh he went on, "You have no other choice but to join La Nationale. They are the only people now who will give you a chance. But they need help, and you must tell them you're willing to do anything. They may ask you to address envelopes or send you out to hang posters, but at least they'll play your music from time to time. It won't be anything like your festival, you can be sure of that, but it'll be better than nothing. Right after the New Year go and see the secretary, Monsieur Chausson. Tell him I sent you."

♦

Early in January, Claude went to the office of the Société Nationale de Musique, better known as La Nationale. It was a dingy

room with a single curtainless window, an inffectual stove that made
noises but gave out practically no heat. Yellowing posters of long-
forgotten concerts hung on the walls. On a corner shelf stood a plaster
statue of a nude woman plucking at a lyre. Presumably Euterpe, the
muse of music.

Behind a desk cluttered with stacks of circulars, ledgers, printing
proofs, clipping scissors and pots of glue sat Monsieur Ernest Chausson: a bald, bushy-bearded man in his middle thirties, looking
harassed and overworked.

"Indeed we need your help," he explained after listening to Claude.
"As you know this is a volunteer organization—which means that
nothing works and nobody does what he promises to do. Our accompanist hasn't shown up for the last two rehearsals; our singing
coach pretends she has laryngitis and can't go out of the house, and
our musical librarian has left town. And for almost twenty years
things have always been like that. Nobody knows how our poor
Nationale manages to survive."

It was in a permanent state of bankruptcy. The sale of tickets did
not even cover the rental of the hall. Nobody wanted to do the chores
associated with the preparation of concerts. And yet La Nationale
went on year after year. Why?

"Because it fills a need, and we can't let it die. It's the only group
in Paris that will play new music and compositions by unknown
musicians. In fact, if you have a few songs I may be able to have
them sung at one of our February concerts. Meanwhile could you
possibly come tomorrow night and help us with the rehearsal?"

And so Claude joined La Nationale and took part in its activities.*

He did not hang posters in the street, but he coached singers,
played accompaniments, became assistant librarian. He made himself useful. He attended the Saturday night concerts, which were
makeshift, rather pathetic affairs. La Nationale was so poor it could
afford an orchestra only once a year for one symphonic concert in
the spring. The rest of the time the performer—usually the composer
himself—walked onto the small gaslit stage, played his piece on the
upright piano and walked off in a patter of applause. If the composition happened to be a vocal one, he brought along a friend who sang,
or the society provided him with a singer—and that's all there was
to it.

In this fashion Claude's Verlaine songs were performed in Feb-

* Debussy's application was formally accepted by the committee on January
28, 1889. On this occasion Chausson wrote: "We can depend on him for accompaniment or voice coaching or any other artistic chore, but I don't quite
see him addressing circulars or ordering posters."

ruary, with himself at the piano and Edmond Bagès as the vocalist. They were received with polite indifference.

"Don't be discouraged," said Monsieur Chausson. "Next year we shall include one of your orchestral works in our symphonic concert." "That'll be wonderful."

He appreciated the gesture and tried to sound enthusiastic, but could not feel much excitement at the prospect of another performance at La Nationale. A half-empty hall, a drizzle of applause, compliments from the committee. Perhaps a line or two in a critic's review . . . And then next year was a long way off. By then *Rodrigue* would be finished—

Or would it?

He still clung to his operatic hopes, spurred himself with visions of enthusiastic audiences and golden streams of royalties, but the pretense was becoming increasingly difficult to maintain. His opera wasn't going well. The few scenes he had written had cost him an immense amount of effort and, he knew, weren't any good. Worse, he was losing interest in his personages. Each day he cared less whether or not Rodrigo married Ximena, whether or not the Moslems were pushed back into the sea or remained in Spain. So far as he was concerned they could stay there forever.

He did not yet give up. Through the late winter and early spring he grappled with *Rodrigue,* tormented his brain to lure music that refused to appear. In despair he turned again to Wagner for help. For hours on end he sat at the piano, playing his operas. With sudden frenzy he plunged into the study of his scores. But something had happened. The heavenly music now sounded merely noisy. At times even trite.

Finally by the end of April he conceded defeat. He would never write *Rodrigue,* and at once the consequences of his failure loomed ominously in his mind. It meant he would never escape poverty, never get out of this hand-to-mouth existence he had led since his return from Rome. It meant the loss of his prestige among his Mallarmé friends. It meant a breach of contract with Catulle Mendès and possible legal unpleasantness.

With his chronic incapacity to face reality he did not even attempt to solve these problems; he merely pushed them aside.*

Like a man coming out of a trance he looked about him and discovered that spring had come and the Eiffel Tower was finished. The

---

* Debussy's lack of practical sense and "irresponsibility" were main traits of his character. They explain the reckless, at times nearly self-destroying actions of his life in later years. He was aware of this psychological failing and often deplored that he could not bring himself "to being responsible." In a letter to a friend he wrote: "I only face reality when it is forced upon me, and then it is insurmountable."

Exposition was on. Paris was bursting at the seams with tourists. Bearded, onyx-eyed men in fezzes and turbans sat on the terraces of cafés. From all over the world people came to see the Eiffel Tower, this iron giraffe nine hundred feet tall. At the Exposition crowds milled before exotic booths and pavilions. Frenchmen could at last fulfill their dreams and survey their overseas empire without leaving home. Snake charmers tooted their flutes to attentive cobras; blue-veiled Tuaregs looked down on the crowds from the height of their camels, ebony bare-breasted women wove straw hats in front of their thatch-roofed huts. Wares and attractions of all sorts lured the visitors. For the ladies there were oriental rugs, perfumes, ivory bracelets; for the children donkey and elephant rides; and for their fathers belly dancers from mysterious palm-fringed oases.

At night Paris turned into a fairyland of light and music. The Eiffel Tower became a gigantic French flag made of twenty-two thousand gas jets, each in its blue, white or red glass globe. Notre Dame glowed in the dark, and so did the Arc de Triomphe. On the Seine the river boats were festooned with paper lanterns, and as they sailed by, accordion music floated out to the quays.

In this strange and wonderful Paris, Claude forgot about *Rodrigue* and escaped from his thoughts. He was momentarily in funds, for the Maison Durand had commissioned him to do a transcription of Saint-Saëns' opera *Etienne Marcel* and advanced him a goodly sum on account. He spent much time out. He strolled along the boulevards bustling with elegant carriages, he sat on the terraces of cafés and listened to the buzz of foreign tongues. And like everyone else, he visited "l'Expo." He meandered through Tunisian bazaars and attended pseudo-voodoo rituals. An old mulatto woman in a yellow bandanna told him his fortune and predicted that in three years a very beautiful woman would come into his life, would love him very much and make him very unhappy.

One day, as he was crossing the Esplanade des Invalides, a long way from the Exposition grounds, he noticed a delicate toylike pagoda with a multiple tilting roof of green tiles. It was the An-namite Pavilion. He brought a ticket and found himself in a colon-nated theatre. On a minuscule stage six young girls dressed in stiff gold saris and steeple-like headgear were performing a grave and sensuous dance. Like glittering animated dolls, they whirled rhythmically on the balls of their feet to the accompaniment of bamboo flutes, muted drums and odd-shaped guitars, undulating their slender pale-bronze arms, clapping and twirling their gold-nailed hands before their round doe-eyed faces.

To Claude the performance was a revelation. He often returned to the green-roofed pagoda and each time the magic reappeared. The fragile dissonances of the gamelang orchestra opened up to him a bewitching world of sounds, poignant and subtle. Here was an art of restraint that he understood and loved. A muted roll of drums, a few notes on a flute could be more frightening than a blast of trombones. Real grief made little noise and passion needed no trumpets.

He was mulling over these thoughts one afternoon when he was hailed by his friend Etienne Dupin.

"Where have you been?" asked the young millionaire. "We haven't seen you at Mallarmé's in ages. Are you still working on your opera?"

Claude told him he had given up *Rodrigue,* at least shelved it for a long time. His mind was tired and confused. Even Wagner's music had become alien. Perhaps, Dupin suggested, it was only a temporary crisis.

"Come again with me to Bayreuth," he said. "It'll help you clear up your mind."

To Bayreuth they returned that summer. Again they panted their way up to the Festspielhaus, heard billows of sound swell out of the invisible orchestra. Again they wolfed down sausages during intermissions, and at the trumpeting of the Walhalla theme, hurried back to their seats. Claude did his best to recapture his former enthusiasm, but the Wagnerian world had lost its magic. The supercharged instrumentation left him groggy after each performance. The libretto which had seemed so inspired the year before now seemed absurd. Try as he might, he no longer cared about the problems, the rages, the lust of these corseted warriors in kilts and winged helmets, these pilgrims, magicians, bouncing nymphs, charging Walkyries in yellow braids and spurred boots.

"Thank you for giving me a second chance," he told Dupin on the train. "But I'm afraid I don't feel Wagner any more."

Paris was gay and crowded as ever. "L'Expo" was still on. Already more than one million visitors had climbed to the top of the Eiffel Tower. In cafés industrious young ladies engaged in polyglot conversations with foreigners. For their benefit they had become linguists and money changers. At a glance they could spot "ann Amerikhan dollaaarh" and remember it was worth five francs, a ruble four, and "an Angleesh pooound" twenty-five.

It went on like this for three more months. Each week brought its contingent of royalty and celebrities. From India came maharajahs in bejeweled turbans. The Shah of Persia arrived with his favorite page, Kiki, who got lost and almost caused a diplomatic incident. From Russia grand dukes and Tolstoy. Also Rimsky-Korsakov, who gave two concerts of Russian music at the Trocadéro. Now it was Buffalo Bill with his cowboys and Indians. Then Monsieur

Edison, the famous inventor who had to be restrained from doing acrobatic turns on the top railing of the Tower.

In November the Exposition closed. Tourists departed: rich in memories, poor in cash. The magic city of domes and minarets was dismantled, baring its piteous innards of plaster and papier-mâché. One day Claude's little pagoda was ripped open; its green tilting roofs lay in a heap on the ground. Lights went out. Notre Dame no longer glowed at night. On the Seine the boats no longer pulled multicolored wakes. Only the Eiffel Tower was allowed to remain as a memento of an unforgettable summer, a perfect moment in French history. Gradually Paris resumed its familiar aspect. People went back to their daily routine.

And one day Claude braced himself to do what he had not dared to do in several months, and went to see his teacher.

"You were right, Master," he said humbly. "I can't write *Rodrigue*." Then, after a pause, "But I can't write anything else either. I don't hear any more music in my mind. It's as if I had become deaf."

Monsieur Guiraud looked at him with grave eyes. "I was afraid of that," he said at last. "The human mind is a delicate instrument, and you have abused and mistreated yours for months. You've crammed it with Wagner's music, which is foreign to your nature, and in the process you've pushed away your own kind."

"Does it mean I'll never write music again?" Claude asked, trying to conceal the anguish in his voice.

"I hope not . . . But it means you must be patient. It's going to take a long time for your brain to get well and be creative again."

"How long?"

"I don't know. Two—perhaps three years."

◆

For the next two years Claude lived in an almost complete musical vacuum. He convinced himself that out of kindness his teacher had lied to him and that he never would write music again. Coming on top of his disappointment over *Rodrigue,* this broke his spirit.

Music had been the unfaltering friend. It had filled his loneliness, given him moments of indescribable joy. In the most arduous days of poverty it had made him forget cold and hunger and kept his hopes alive. Now hope went out of his life. Outwardly his existence remained unchanged: the same never-ending search for money, with its round of publishers, a few piano lessons, now and then an odd job as an accompanist. As before, flashes of opulence followed long periods of near-starvation when he pawned his watch, lived on bread and boiled potatoes and an occasional meal with his teacher or some friend.

None of this was new. He had lived in this fashion before and had survived. But now there was a difference—an immense difference. He knew it would go on like this forever. He was not a composer but a hack. He never would write great music, never have money to buy beautiful things, never be able to marry and have a home. All his life he would live in leaky garrets, transcribe other people's music, plead with the landlord, cook his meals on an alcohol lamp. And how long could this go on, how long could a man subsist on a diet of bread and boiled potatoes? What if he ever fell ill, what if one day the landlord got tired of waiting for his rent? What then? . . . He did not know the answer, or rather he knew it only too well. And it was no use thinking about it. There was always time to face unpleasant facts . . .

And because he did not want to think, his life assumed a new quality of aimlessness and all-embracing indifference which at times could pass for gaiety. Now that music no longer filled his free time he found himself with a good deal of leisure; and leisure meant thinking—the very thing he did not want. And so, whenever he stopped searching for work, he started searching for escape. Since he had neither money nor taste for liquor he could not seek oblivion in absinthe, as so many artists did.

Instead he turned to women.

All kinds. *Midinettes,* artists' models, actresses between engagements, occasionally a married woman whose husband was out of town for a few days. He met them accidentally, on buses, in restaurants, in cafés. Sometimes along the quays, in the course of his afternoon stroll; in summer on park benches. Life, he found, was full of such hazards, and Paris was full of girls and young women who were just as lonely, as lost and as eager to avoid thinking as he was. They gave him their youth, their caresses and the illusion of companionship. On the soft pillow of their breasts he found the oblivion he sought.

They insisted on telling him the story of their life and they did this with immense relish, tears and a complete disregard for truth. Most of them attributed to themselves prestigious backgrounds. Their fathers were colonels, high government officials, titled landowners living in ancestral castles. At thirteen they had been raped by their uncle or a friend of the family. "A real nice monsieur with the Legion of Honor." Or they had been cast out of their home because they had become pregnant, or their stepmothers had been envious of their youthful beauty. Some were more cynical and more truthful. They had gotten tired of slaving ten hours a day in the back room of a dress shop for a franc and a half.

With patience and sympathy he listened to their plans. Some dreamed of becoming music hall stars, becoming the toast of London and marrying *un chic milord.* Apparently young earls could not resist French music-hall actresses. The others longed to find some rich and generous "gentleman friend" and become one of the elegant demimondaines who supped at Weber's and paraded in shiny carriages on the Champs Elysées. On and on they talked to give themselves confidence, escape the gnawing fears of their probable future with its gradual descent into prostitution; and at the end, a black lamppost at night in some narrow street.

To them he brought a brief illusion of romance. Their common fears created the semblance of a bond between them. For a few days they contrived some pathetic mirage of carefree bohemian love and made brave, half-hearted attempts at living together. Soon they found out that two could not live where one could barely subsist. One morning, while he slept or was out on an errand, they vanished, leaving a tender, mispelled and tear-stained farewell note pinned on the pillow.

Early in 1890 he had an affair with a society lady, "Madame V."

He called her "Madame V" because on the night they met she refused to tell him her first name, except that it began with a V. "As a matter of fact," she had added, "I am not sure I should be talking to you at all."

The meeting took place in a sumptuous drawing room of the Etoile district, where he had played his *Petite Suite* with his friend Jacques Durand, the publisher's son, who had arranged the performance. The composition had made no impression whatever on the audience, but he did not mind. The buffet made up for the lack of artistic appreciation. Such caviar, such pâté de foie gras!

And there he was in his rented formal suit plucking canapés from silver trays and gobbling them at vertiginous speed, when he heard behind him the soft ripple of a woman's laughter. Turning around he saw two brown almond-shaped eyes smiling at him over the crescent of a lace fan.

"So it's true what they say about musicians being always hungry," she said. "Come on, let me help you fill your plate."

They talked. She said she had enjoyed his composition, and he said she was lovely and what was her first name. She tapped his knuckles with her fan and replied that he was much too forward and shouldn't presume to ask a lady her first name on a first encounter, and as a matter of fact she wasn't sure she should be talking with him at all. He said he did not have the plague, but if she didn't want to talk to him it was all right, and started to leave. She held him back by his sleeve, apologized for being rude, and wouldn't he like another plateful of those delicious canapés. He said he would, and after that they were friends.

That was how it began, with polite banter coming out of their mouths, while a tender, sensuous debate went on silently between their eyes. Their affair was one of those irrational, compulsive entanglements that are doomed from the start, yet have to come to life, like those plants that insist on growing in wall cracks or between cobbles. She was Belgian, from Antwerp; beautiful, rich, Jewish and married. In Paris, for a visit with relatives.

Entertained a great deal, she was also aware of being watched, and laughingly she would tell Claude of the ruses and maneuvers she must adopt in order to come and see him. She was not a frivolous woman, much less a promiscuous one. She respected her husband, even loved him in some ways. "I love him with all my heart," she would say, and that was the trouble, for love is not of the heart alone. In Claude she had a glimpse of the man she could have loved in every way. She, in turn, delighted him with her beauty, her understanding, her culture, her elegance, the abandon of her love-making. Everything in their natures pulled them toward each other, and everything was against them. It was the age-old tug of war between life and love, which love always loses.

Foolishly they fell in love, with the result that after her return to Antwerp they were miserable. She more than he, for being rich she had more time to think and suffer. He, as usual, had to think about food and next month's rent. It kept his mind occupied.

Then he received the visit of Catulle Mendès, who vigorously objected to the delays in the completion of "their" opera and reminded him that a contract was a contract. This also kept Claude's mind occupied.

Finally, with his flair for doing the wrong thing, he committed another blunder. The incident brought him so much unpleasantness that he did not have a minute left to be heartbroken over "Madame V."*

This time he got in trouble with La Nationale. He had maintained good relations with the group, rendered many services. In appreciation the committee had included his Fantasy for Piano and Orchestra in its annual symphonic concert. At the last rehearsal Claude became dissatisfied with a group of variations in the last movement. Since the concert was scheduled for that evening, there was no time to make

---

* Despite its briefness, his affair with "Madame V" had a lasting effect on Debussy. Seven years later he dedicated to her three of his most famous songs.

the necessary changes. He did the next best thing. While the orchestra was out to lunch, he walked up to the stage, removed the parts from the racks and went home, his score under his arm.

This whim of his almost wrecked the concert. The committee was furious. There was talk of expulsion from the society, legal proceedings to recoup the cost of rehearsals. Even Monsieur Chausson urged him to stay away for a few months.

"Give people time to forget," he said.

As for Monsieur Guiraud, he merely shook his head. "Tell me, Claude, is it your intention to alienate *everybody?*"

There was no Exposition that spring and Paris felt listless. People missed last year's excitement, the exotic carnival on the Champs de Mars, the Eiffel Tower draped in her luminous flag, the colorful tourists. Newspapers commented on this general feeling of nervousness. As an example they cited this young bride, a wisp of a girl, who became so annoyed with her husband that she had picked him up from the floor and hurled him out the window. The number of duels grew alarmingly. Matters of honor were settled in meadows at dawn and munching cows were killed by stray bullets.

For Claude life went on as before. Often, after his discouraging tours of publishers, he would drop by Père Bailly's bookshop. But he no longer sought the company of the writers in the back room. The old bookdealer was as mad and cheerful as ever. He had established contact with famous men of letters from the most remote antiquity and was now trying to reach King Solomon. "Ah, Monsieur, this Solomon, what a poet! What a man! A thousand wives, and all happy . . . It makes you wonder when he found time to write his Song of Songs, doesn't it?"

He sensed Claude's despondent mood and did his best to restore his self-confidence. "Remember that you are a genius," he would say in his high-pitched voice, "and all geniuses have known these periods of sterility. Why, only the other day Plato was telling me that for years he couldn't think of anything to say . . ." He did more than talk. He arranged to publish Claude's Baudelaire songs, which had been turned down by every music publisher in Paris.*

Summer came, bringing no change in Claude's precarious, aimless existence, except that now it was stiflingly hot in the garret. He talked to his cat, washed his shirts, swept the room, made up his bed,

* This de-luxe edition of one hundred and fifty copies was, unbeknownst to Claude, partially financed by Etienne Dupin and Ernest Chausson. It met with no success whatever until many years later when each copy became a collector's item. The old bookdealer was among the first to guess the young composer's genius. At a time when Debussy was absolutely unknown he would predict his forthcoming recognition. "He is the greatest," he would say in his effusive way, "the most noble, and he is going to be the most illustrious of all."

watered his geranium on the window sill, wiped the dust off the piano's lid. He slept a great deal. Occasionally Madame Sénégal came to visit him, bringing a bowl of soup or a plateful of stew. While he ate she entertained him with her views on politics and her opinion of the tenants. On the first floor rear lived Monsieur Tricout, "a perfect gentleman," she said, although a mere lavatory attendant. Madame Marcelle occupied the third floor front. She was a whore. Claude had met her a few times on the stairs and thought she looked like an aggressive cow, but the concierge assured him that she wasn't "a bad sort" when you got to know her. The others were humble, honest people who worked hard, raised their children and paid their rent on time. "Which," she would add with a kindly leer, "is more than you do."

In the afternoon he walked through the city at random, watched children play in public parks, listened to street singers. Sometimes he walked as far as the Jardin des Plantes and yawned at yawning lions in their cages. He had a few brief and inconsequential love affairs. Mere genital greetings between strangers that brought little satisfaction and left no regrets. Now and then he thought of "Madame V," but her memory only sharpened his loneliness.

Thus summer shambled on, one hot, lonely day after another. Then, one afternoon, occurred one of those microscopic incidents that change the pattern of a life.

His precious alcohol lamp fell apart.

He took it for repair to a nearby plumbing shop on rue d'Athenes. A stout round-faced young man, with a curled-up mustache and a black derby set far back on his head, was standing at a workbench peering into a short length of pipe, like an admiral through a spyglass. At the tinkle of the doorbell he turned around.

"It only needs soldering," he said after examining Claude's cooking apparatus. "Do you want to wait or come back tomorrow?"

"I'll wait."

"It won't take long."

He went back to his work. Idly Claude glanced at the kitchen sinks, toilet bowls and water tanks that cluttered the shop. Between two *bidets* a fly-specked calendar showed a beautiful young women rapturously sniffing a rose.

Suddenly the young plumber broke the silence. "Aren't you the musician who lives on rue de Londres? . . . I, too, am an artist, but only in my spare time."

His name was Vital Hocquet. Their friendship was instantaneous, as often happens between young men of about the same age. Chance had brought them together when they needed each other most. In Claude, Vital found the confidant he had been seeking; in turn he opened to Claude a new field of escape by introducing him to the bohemian world of Montmartre.

For Vital was both a plumber and a poet. During the day he went about the district unclogging pipes, repairing leaky faucets, kitchen sinks and defective toilets, bringing joy and relief to harassed housewives. At night he became Narcisse Lebeau, poet, songwriter and one of the volunteer entertainers at the Chat Noir, Montmartre's most famous cabaret.

They were a joyous and motley crew, these young poets who, like Vital, produced themselves nightly on a small stage at the end of a long smoke-filled room, dimly lit by pseudo-medieval oil lanterns; and for the sole reward of applause recited their tender or naughty verses, sang their songs to the accompaniment of a rickety piano and performed short dramatic sketches. For this they had come from near and far, in some hazy hope of fame and fortune. One by the name of Papadiamantopopoulos had come all the way from Greece.* Several had braved the wrath of their families, abandoned promising careers. Some lived in unspeakable squalor. Others, like Vital, compromised. They clerked in government offices, wrote their sonnets on letterheads of the Préfecture de Police or the Compagnie des Omnibus. Some practiced a trade. There was a pharmacist; another, a one-eyed colossus, was a butcher.

Under Vital's sponsorship Claude was accepted at once. His sombrero, his flowing tie, his awesome title of Grand Prix de Rome and his obvious poverty created about him an aura of congenial prestige. He dined with them in an upstairs room before the evening performance, watched them argue across the table with their mouths full, their beards jutting, waving their knives and forks. He joined in the lusty chorus that saluted the arrival of some favorite dish. Once, in a fit of exuberance, he climbed on the table and conducted the singing, using an asparagus as a baton.

Next to poetry, Vital's other avocation was women. They fascinated and distressed him at the same time. Their deceitfulness came to him as an ever-fresh surprise. Once he had attempted suicide over a young Polish singer and had been rescued just in time by Maurice Donnay, a fellow poet from the Chat Noir. Despite these setbacks he still hoped to find "the perfect woman," and Claude escorted him in his wanderings through the Montmartre dance halls and cabarets and other unlikely places where he expected to find her. Together they climbed to the Moulin de la Galette, where the local thugs in sideburns and striped sweaters waltzed between holdups. They also went to Le Mirliton, where Aristide Bruant, in black velvet

---

* Under the name of Jean Moréas, Papadiamantopopoulos became a celebrated French poet.

suit and high boots, sang his poignant ballads about streetwalkers. And naturally they went to the Moulin Rouge, a new dance hall where a bevy of young sluts danced the cancan in their frilly bloomers —and sometimes without.

The noise, the laughter, the women—it all helped. At times Claude almost forgot that once music had flowed through his mind. Winter, that year, seemed less cruel; its hardships easier to bear. His comradeship with Vital made up for the drudgery of piano lessons and hack work, the inner barrenness. Vital, on the other hand, dreamed of love and a pretty wife who would wait for him after a hard plumbing day with a kiss on her lips and dinner on the table. Both found relief in explosive arguments or riotous gaiety. They disagreed about everything, broke off relations—for a difference of opinion over Beethoven they stayed two days without speaking—and always returned to each other. With brotherly casualness they filched things from each other. Claude appropriated Vital's favorite tie; Vital retaliated by stealing Claude's precious Japanese silk.

"You're a thief!" yelled Claude, bursting into the shop.

"How about my tie?"

"It's not the same thing. My fish are a work of art."

Finally a bargain was struck. In addition to the tie, Vital presented him with a superb ebony-handled umbrella. All was well again.*

Then one day Vital found "the perfect woman," and on a fragile April day he married her. Claude acted as his best man, and after the ceremony, signed the city hall register, listing his profession as "gardener." The wedding dinner in the sun-flecked back yard of a Montmartre restaurant was a joyous bohemian affair. Vital's fellow poets sang songs and proposed innumerable toasts. Claude did his best to join in the general gaiety and only succeeded in getting drunk. To him Vital's marriage marked the end of their friendship. He knew they wouldn't see much of each other any more. He was right: they didn't.

A few days later, on the twenty-first of April, Monsieur Guiraud was elected academician, and Claude called to congratulate him.

The teacher gave him a wistful smile. "The trouble with honors is that they come too late, like wisdom. You become wise when

---

* All his life M. Vital Hocquet treasured Claude's Japanese silk, as well as a copy of the Baudelaire songs inscribed "To Vital, who stole my fish . . ." In 1931 he gave an interview, which appeared on the day of his death, about these early obscure years of Debussy's life, of which he was the most intimate witness. To him we owe the description of the garret as well as several revealing anecdotes, like that of the umbrella. That Debussy should have lived through four Parisian winters without an umbrella gives the measure of his poverty.

you've made about every possible mistake and it no longer matters whether you're wise or not."

Claude had not seen him in a long time and found him aged and looking tired. With the candor of youth he told him so.

"I do feel a little tired. I'll be glad when July comes and school is over. Well, after all, I am fifty-four . . . How old are you?"

"I'll be twenty-nine in August."

"Twenty-nine in August," he repeated the words under his breath. "How wonderful it sounds."

For an instant he looked out the window at the budding tree in the courtyard. Then he turned back to Claude. "How are things with you? Still no music? . . . Be patient. It'll come back, you'll see . . . Any work?"

"I just wrote a military march for a British general. A four-hand arrangement. Monsieur Fromont gave me the job."

"It sounds interesting. Tell me about it."

Well, the general's name was Meredith Read, and beside being a general he was an earl and the head of the Ross Clan, in Rosshire County, up in the Highlands of Scotland. There were other clans, too, and apparently they all had terrible feuds that went on for centuries and over which they brooded during the long winters. As soon as spring came and the fog lifted enough for them to see a few feet ahead, they went to war and killed one another. The Ross Clan had an old family tune they liked to fight by, and this was the march Claude had arranged into a four-hand piano version. The general had been delighted and proved most generous.

"It's really a very pretty tune," he said.*

Once again it was spring, and someone introduced bullfights in Paris. But the ignorant Frenchmen cheered the bull and hissed the matador. The fights had to be discontinued. One morning Toulouse-Lautrec's Moulin Rouge poster appeared on the walls and rocked the city. Moralists said the streets were unfit for French maidenhood. Then the first pneumatic tires were installed on bicycles; even women rode in shameless calf-revealing knickers. Now moralists said that the streets were unfit for everybody but the blind.

It could have been a happy spring, but Claude missed Vital, their arguments, their free and turbulent comradeship. He went back to the Chat Noir, but now the place meant little to him. As for the other cabarets and dance halls, he had frequented them only to assist his friend in his search for the perfect woman. The idea of visiting them alone did not even cross his mind.

* This Scottish march remained one of Debussy's favorite works. In 1908 he wrote it for full orchestra and it was published under the title *Marche Ecossaise des Comtes de Ross*.

He did, however, drop in occasionally at L'Auberge du Clou, a bistro-restaurant on rue Trudaine, where he spent a few moments with a young eccentric by the name of Erik Satie, who was the pianist of the establishment and a composer of sorts. With this one exception he withdrew from the Montmartre world, to which he had never really belonged.

During the summer he tried his hand at writing short prose poems in the Symbolist style, which he called *Proses Lyriques*. Thanks to the general's money he was free from financial worries and he spent his time in morose idleness. Once more he turned to women for escape, this time from boredom. With dismay he discovered that one navel looked astonishingly like another and kisses could be as tasteless as water. Without love, women weren't really much fun.

He was glad when the first autumn rains came and his roof started leaking again.

Sometime in November he decided to go back to work on *Rodrigue* and get it finished, if only to get rid of Catulle Mendès, who was becoming increasingly unpleasant. He worked on it in his spare time, in the evening, while the winter squalls shook the window. Now that he no longer cared or tried to "feel" his personages, music came without effort. It wasn't good music, but it was better than no music at all.*

And so the year drew to an end. December was marked by a series of tragedies. A typhoon swallowed a number of fishing vessels, mostly Chinese. In Japan an earthquake destroyed six thousand homes and killed seventy-five thousand people. At once charity balls sprouted all over Paris. News of fresh disasters kept society dancing all winter.

Late one night Claude felt something stirring in his mind. For the first time in two years he heard music again . . .

◆

"How many bars did you hear?" asked Monsieur Guiraud eagerly. "And what kind of music?"

"About eight or ten. Very soft."

"Was it a theme?"

"Yes, Master."

"You're sure it wasn't just a modulation or a resolution of chords?"

They were talking fast, sharing the same feeling of excitement. To Claude, last night's experience had been an unforgettable moment, a minute of heartbreaking joy, and he had not yet recovered his self-control.

* Early in January of the following year—1892—he wrote to a friend that he had already written two acts.

"I'm sure. It was a melody. Of course, it lasted only a few seconds."

"Never mind how long it lasted. What did you expect—a symphony? The essential is that it came. It means your brain is getting well and becoming creative again. One more thing—did you hear it distinctly?"

"As if someone had played it on the piano. It was in D flat and 9/8. And I recognized it right away. It was the beginning of my *Clair de Lune.*"

"What *Clair de Lune?*"

Claude explained that several months before, he had thought of writing a few piano pieces in the style of the Italian comedy. He had even thought of a pretty title, *Suite Bergamasque.* One of these pieces was to be *Clair de Lune.* But no music had come . . . "That's why I never mentioned it."

The teacher pointed to the piano. "Do you think you could play those few bars?"

Claude played them. His teacher was delighted.

"That's your kind of music. Now, for heaven's sake, don't start straining your brain and trying to force music back. Be patient. It'll come of its own accord."

"When, Master?"

"How should I know? When it feels like coming back."

Work was scarce that winter. Claude was back to his diet of bread and tea. Once more he was in arrears on his rent and he was obliged to pawn his watch to placate the landlord with something on account. As usual he had neglected to buy coal during the summer months when it was cheap, and now he froze in his garret.

Yet nothing could dent his optimism. Hope had returned to his life. Music was coming back—that's all that mattered. Of course it wasn't yet the steady flow it had been in the days of *The Blessed Damozel.* But wisps of melody came to his mind more and more often, like the first halting heartbeats after an agonizing pause. As Monsieur Guiraud had said, he must be patient.

Every morning he started out on the familiar round of publishers. Sometimes he tramped halfway across the city to give a piano lesson, but now he had Vital's umbrella and it was almost a pleasure to be out in the rain . . .

In the evening he worked on *Rodrigue,* and one day in February he actually finished it. He brought the score to Catulle Mendès, played for him some of the scenes; then told him he did not want it produced.

"Why?" asked the librettist.

"Because it isn't any good. I wrote the damn thing to keep my promise. That's enough."

He had braced himself for a scene. To his surprise Mendès surrendered without difficulties. *Lohengrin* was about to be produced at the Opéra. A Franco-German opera had lost much of its meaning now that the public could hear the works of the Meister himself.

They separated on cordial terms. The *Rodrigue* nightmare was over at last.*

A few days later Claude received a visit from Monsieur Chausson, who told him that the Fantasy incident was now forgotten. "As usual our poor Nationale is in a state of utter confusion. Please, come back and give us a hand."

Claude said he would, and Chausson went on, "By the way, I went to see Monsieur Guiraud the other day and he mentioned you'd written a lyrical oratorio called *The Blessed Damozel*. It sounds like an interesting work and I would like to read it. Would you mind lending me the score?"

Monsieur Guiraud was pleased to hear that Claude had resumed his activities. "But, please, behave yourself."

Claude said he was almost thirty, the threshold of middle age, and no longer the foolish youngster he had been two years ago. The teacher said he hoped so.

Early in April, Prince Poniatowski invited Claude to lunch at his club. Over the hors d'oeuvre he announced he was about to leave for New York. "Perhaps I may be able to interest someone in your compositions," he said. "Who knows? You may come to America yourself. An artist has many opportunities there."

During lunch Claude listened to the opportunities that awaited him in the New World. By the time they had sipped their coffee, he had drunk three brandies and felt ready to sail. Already he saw himself playing his compositions in Fifth Avenue drawing rooms, dining with Monsieur Carnegie, a great music lover, and flirting with ravishing heiresses.

"Please, write me as soon as you can," he beseeched the young prince as they were saying good-bye at the club's gate. "But it'll be safer to address your letters to Bailly's bookshop. I never know when my landlord may get it into his head to throw me out."

For a few days Claude's mind was filled with radiant American visions. But as usual, urgent problems of food and rent demanded

* For a long time it was believed that Debussy had burned the the score of *Rodrigue*. He did not. The manuscript exists in its entirety and is the property of Monsieur Alfred Cortot. At the composer's request, the opera has never been produced.

his attention, and he forgot all about America, its millionaires and heiresses.*

This time he was lucky. Monsieur Fromont gave him a long and difficult transcription to do. Even more wonderful, he did not haggle over the price.

"But I want it in two weeks, understand?" he said, handing Claude a fifty-franc advance. "And no excuses."

Claude was so pleased over the commission that he hurried to an antique shop on rue des Saints Pères and paid thirty francs on account for a delicate ivory figurine he had long admired.

"Just to make sure you don't sell it to anyone else," he said to the merchant.

No sooner was he out of the shop than he berated himself for his extravagance and irresponsibility. He was three months in arrears on his rent and here he was buying an ivory figurine! . . . Oh well, he would work harder and finish the transcription in a week, that's all . . .

He plunged into work. Day and night he sat hunched over his table, filling page after page, stopping only to eat or snatch a few hours of sleep.

By the third night he was almost half through. Fatigue came in waves, closing his lids. Vigorously he rubbed his eyes and returned to his task. It was long past midnight. No noises rose from the street. Everyone in Paris slept, except him . . . Under the green shade the lamp made a circle of yellow light. On a chair Linne slept, crouching like a sphinx.

Then it happened.

His hand froze on the sheet of music. Stealthily the *Clair de Lune* melody floated into his mind. Like a night butterfly it wafted and soared and glided in solitary rapture. Then, swiftly, it vanished.

Many times that night it came and vanished, but finally it unfolded from beginning to end, each note etching itself on his brain.

The windowpanes were hemmed with dawn when he finished jotting down the melody on paper. He rose and for a while stood at the window. He no longer felt tired. His whole being throbbed with joy. Nothing, absolutely nothing, was as wonderful as that! . . . In his net of little notes he had caught the moonlight.

He slept twelve hours without stirring. When he awoke, the afternoon was ebbing into sunset, the dawn of night. Instead of returning to Monsieur Fromont's transcription he made a clean copy of *Clair*

---

* In his delightful memoirs, *D'un siècle a l'autre,* Prince Poniatowski tells the details of this American project that failed through Debussy's absent-mindedness.

de Lune. Then, unable to wait any longer, he brought it to his teacher.

As soon as he entered the den he rushed to the piano, sat down on the red plush stool.

"I have it, Master," he said, flattening the manuscript on the rack. "Listen."

When he finished playing he waited for Monsieur Guiraud to speak.

"It's beautiful," said the teacher quietly. "It's full of new harmonies, but it's well built. Solid. It will last. You're back on the right road. Don't ever leave it."

They went to a small restaurant on nearby Place la Bruyère, one of those small squares so numerous in Paris, peaceful and planted with old trees, that are like bits of country in the middle of the city. It was late and the restaurant was deserted, except for an elderly gentleman with a goatee who was sipping his demitasse while reading the newspaper.

A tubby woman with flabby jowls greeted Monsieur Guiraud with affectionate reproaches. Had he been ill? Didn't he like her cooking any more? It was more than a week since he had come last.

"Tonight I give you a nice *estouffade de boeuf*," she announced, setting the bread basket on the table.

"No use asking for a menu," he said when she was out of earshot. "You eat what she gives you or you eat somewhere else. After all, you don't have a menu at home either. And this is as near to a home as a bachelor can have." A shadow passed over his face, and quickly he changed the subject. "I'm glad you finished *Rodrigue* and can now forget about it. Did you learn something from it?"

Oh yes! . . . First of all, that he never wanted to write another opera. But if he ever did, at least he would know all the things he would avoid. No involved libretto with great political or religious issues at stake. No battles, no chorus of soldiers drinking from cardboard steins before going to war. No arias, no great howling duets between tenor and soprano. A simple love story set in no particular country, no particular period.

Monsieur Guiraud broke in with a chuckle. "For someone who will never write another opera you seem to have done an amazing amount of thinking on the subject."

The chuckle ebbed into a lingering smile. He looked at Claude across the table with almost fatherly fondness.

"It's good to see you in shape again," he said at last.

Excitedly Claude told about his plans. First he was going to set to music his *Proses Lyriques,* those short poems he had written last summer. Then he was going to tackle a symphony. Yes, a symphony.

"One evening I heard Monsieur Mallarmé read one of his poems, and it would make a wonderful subject for a symphony. It's called *The Afternoon of a Faun*. It's about a faun stretched out on the grass on a hot summer afternoon and dreaming about love."

"Fauns don't dream about love," grinned Monsieur Guiraud. "They dream about love-making, which isn't the same thing."

"That's just it. Wouldn't it be wonderful to see if music could express desire, heat, the stillness of the afternoon?"

"I see. A sort of phallic pastoral symphony . . ." He took a sip of wine. "It would be interesting," he mused. "Come to think of it, music, which is supposed to be the most sensuous of arts, has expressed about every emotion except pure sensuality. It would be a curious experiment . . . But meanwhile do you know what I should like you to write? A quartet."

A quartet! Claude made a face. What could one say in a quartet? It was the most rigid, most classical of all musical forms.

"I know," said Monsieur Guiraud. "The very name sounds musty. Immediately you imagine four old men in white perukes playing Haydn. But don't you see, that's the challenge. Could you say something new in such a strict, purely classical form?"

"I don't know. I never thought of it."

"Well, think of it sometimes. Read Beethoven's last quartets. They are the finest things he wrote."

They had finished dinner and were lingering at the table in congenial silence.

"Master," Claude began hesitantly, "I'd like to tell you that I appreciate everything you've done—"

"Just write some good music," cut in the teacher with a pretense of gruffness. "That's about the only thing you're good for." While speaking he glanced at his watch. "I must go back," he said with a sigh. "I still have homework to correct. You know, a professor is a perennial schoolboy. He spends most of his time in classrooms, his schedule is regulated by the clatter of a bell, and when he goes home he does his homework, except it consists in correcting that of his pupils'. It's not a bad life. You have two months of vacation in which you can try writing something of your own. It gives you a feeling of security, a sense of usefulness. And once or twice in your life, when you run across some exceptional student, real happiness and pride. But it deadens the mind. I'm glad you didn't take a steady job after all. You've chosen the hard way, but for you it's the right way."

They went out of the restaurant and walked side by side in the deserted street, their footsteps echoing in the soft May night.

"This weather reminds me of spring in New Orleans," said Monsieur Guiraud after a silence. "You can't imagine how beautiful it is in Louisiana at this time of the year. I remember one day—"

He was off again, Claude thought. Lately Monsieur Guiraud had been talking an awful lot about New Orleans. Sometimes, when they played billiards or discussed music, he would suddenly launch into reminiscences about the Vieux Carré, the old houses with their wrought-iron balconies, the patios with bougainvillaea foaming purple over the walls.

"Each year I promise myself to go back for a visit," said the teacher as they were approaching the house. "But always there is some confounded thing that stops me from going. Next year I won't let anything stop me."

They came to a halt in front of the arched doorway.

"Next spring I'm going to take a leave of absence and go. Well, good night, Claude."

With a grin and a little wave he opened the door and stepped into the darkness of the house.

"Good night, Master."

♦

Three days later Monsieur Guiraud held his morning class as usual. Then he dropped into the office of the administrator, Monsieur Réty; and there in mid-sentence he died of a heart attack.

The news struck Claude with such force that for several days he felt no pain, only a stunned bewilderment. Even after the requiem Mass, the cemetery speeches, the shovelfuls of earth on the coffin— even then it did not seem true. More, it seemed impossible. It just couldn't be that he would never see his teacher pluck at his beard again, hear him say, "I'd like to wring your neck. Get out of my sight! . . ." And further back: "So, you've bought a palette and plan to become a painter? An excellent idea . . ." And still further back, in the early composition class days: "Monsieur Debussy, before you start changing the rules of harmony, don't you think it would be a good idea to learn them first?" Strange, that all that remained of a ten-year relationship was a few fragments of sentences, the memory of some familiar gesture, an inflection of voice, the quiet amusement of a chuckle.

And now that it was too late, you thought of a thousand things you could have said and done that would have made him happy. And you wished he could come back for a minute, just long enough to tell him how grateful, how very grateful you were for letting you sit at his fire when you were wet and tired and desperate, getting work for you, taking you to dinner when you were hungry . . .

Monsieur Guiraud's death had been so swift and sudden that

Claude came to believe that his teacher had merely gone away on a long journey. Perhaps to New Orleans, as he had hoped to . . . His teacher's memory did not turn into a haunting shrouded ghost, but a familiar presence, smiling, frowning, affectionate, at times reproachful.

With a jolt he remembered Monsieur Fromont's transcription and his long-overdue rent. Again he plunged into work and by the end of the week the transcription was almost finished. But sometimes in the middle of the night, his lids began to close in spite of himself. Desperately he would rub his eyes, try walking. He only shambled as far as the bed, onto which he tumbled, reeling with fatigue and already fast asleep.

Toward noon one day he was awakened by an insistent pounding on the door. Groggily he got out of bed and shuffled to the door.

Swift as an arrow Madame Sénégal darted in.

"This time you've done it," she squeaked, her voice shrill with drama. "The landlord came up a moment ago and knocked on your door and you didn't even answer—"

"I didn't hear him. I was asleep."

"How could he know that? Anyway, he said that it was bad enough not to pay the rent, but when a tenant refuses to see his landlord it's time to throw him out. He said if you don't pay at least half by tonight, he'll padlock the door." She looked at him, concern on her hatchet face. "What're you going to do?"

"I don't know," he said, slumping down on a chair. He was still only half awake and blinked his eyes into focus. "I'll think of something."

An hour later he was ushered into Monsieur Fromont's office. The publisher had just returned from lunch and sat behind his desk, flushed and frowning, caressing his beard.

"Where's my transcription?" he asked, removing the cigar from his mouth. "It was to be ready a week ago."

The transcription was finished. Well, almost . . . "But something came up that will interest you. I've written my first piece of commercial music—a piano number called *Clair de Lune*—and I want you to be the first to hear it." He spoke with the urgency of someone who doesn't quite believe what he says. "Before anyone else," he added, implying that other publishers were frothing with impatience to secure this valuable composition.

"Is it easy to play? I don't want any of your fancy music."

Easy? . . . Why, a child could play it.

"Let me see it."

He took the manuscript, forked a gold pince-nez on his nose, glanced at the opening bars and tossed it angrily across the desk.

"Five flats at the key and you call that easy! You'll never write commercial music. You'd better go home and finish my transcription."

That was just it, Claude explained. He couldn't go home and finish the transcription because the landlord was going to padlock his room. "If only you would give me another advance. Let's say—a hundred francs."

Monsieur Fromont sprang from his chair. "A hundred francs! What do you think I am? A charitable institution?"

Finally he capitulated, and reluctantly pulled his wallet out of his coat pocket. "Now go straight home, understand?" he said, handing Claude a hundred-franc note. "And finish this transcription."

"I am on my way," said Claude, already halfway to the door.*

Outside, his good resolutions began to melt. The prospect of sitting at his table, hunched over Monsieur Fromont's transcription, looked unattractive. It was such a nice afternoon. Tonight would be time enough . . . Besides, he was hungry.

He made his way to the Café Weber, almost deserted at this hour. With the assurance of a man with money in his pocket he selected a prominent table, set his sombrero on the leather banquette at his side and beckoned to a dreaming waiter.

"A *thé complet*" he said casually.

The waiter gave a start. A *thé complet* constituted almost a meal in itself and was rarely ordered by a single person. It included, besides tea, an assortment of biscuits, brioches, canapés, macaroons and pastries, and was served with an elaborate array of silverware and on trays of all sizes. It was also about the most expensive thing one could order.

"Just for Monsieur?" he asked with a lift of eyebrows.

"Certainly."

With a flip of the wrist he dismissed the waiter. This done, he leaned back, lit a cigarette and contentedly glanced about the room.

Then he saw her.

* Thirteen years later, in 1905, the Fromont firm did publish *Clair de Lune*.

CHAPTER

8

LIKE MOST YOUNG MEN, CLAUDE FANCIED HIMSELF A JUDGE OF feminine beauty. It was his considered opinion that few women could be called beautiful. Pretty, yes. Piquant, intriguing, exciting, provocative—but not beauiful.

The girl across the room, staring musingly at the door, could be called beautiful.

He estimated her age at about twenty-three, the shade of her hair as somewhere between darkish-blond and auburn. Her mouth was somewhat large and full-lipped. Parted in smile it must be irresistible; in repose, as it was now, it suggested sensuousness and vague discontent. As for her complexion, it was peachlike, perfect. So perfect that he felt sure she must come from the country. City girls simply didn't have complexions like that.

At this point she turned her head and slowly brought her gaze to rest on the chandelier hanging down from the ceiling. With a start he observed that her eyes were green. Not turquoise or aquamarine, but green. This, of course, he dismissed as an optical illusion; nobody had green eyes. Nevertheless, hers did look green.

Regrettably she was not alone. Next to her sat a middle-aged, corpulent man engrossed in the reading of a newspaper. Her father? Certainly not. No family resemblance whatever. Husband? Gentlemen did not bring their wives to cafés . . . It was only too plain that he was her lover, and judging from her expensive clothes, a generous one. Since he paid for everything else he must also have felt that his money gave him the right to be rude and read the newspaper in her presence. Pretty disgusting, that's all that one could say.

The arrival of his *thé complet* brought him out of his thoughts. For a while he was too busy to think about the girl. After disposing of the macaroons and cream puffs he poured himself a second cup of tea and between sips resumed his observations.

Yes, pretty disgusting, yet she did not seem to mind. There was about her an air of placid indifference. What a depressing sight! Two people handcuffed together by sordid motives of lecherousness and self-interest . . .

For now he saw it all. Each piece of the jigsaw puzzle was falling into place. She was one of those unfortunate farm girls who every year flocked to the Big City and usually wound up walking the streets. This one, because of her beauty, had fared better. She had caught a steady, wealthy, in fact a rather distinguished-looking lover. Being cold-blooded and calculating, like all women of her kind, she knew a good thing when she had it and was perfectly content with her lot. But then, why the wistful expression on her face, the discontented curve of her lips? Perhaps she was dreaming of the beautiful things in life she was missing, of the love that could give her some fine, understanding, virile young man. He, for instance . . .

The girl stirred out of her reverie. Reluctantly she took her eyes off the chandelier and looked about the room. The gaze of her green eyes brushed over him with the indifference of a lighthouse beacon.

Now, that would never do . . . As a rule women took notice of him. In the street they often turned around to glance at him over their shoulder. Of course, he was too modest to pay attention to such trifles, but it proved he was not insignificant-looking. She certainly could have shown some flicker of interest . . . Perhaps she was absorbed in grave personal matters and had inadvertently failed to notice him. He would give her another chance . . .

He waved to the waiter and in a loud tone ordered another tray of macaroons.

"Also, another pot of tea," he added, still louder. "This one is getting cold."

She couldn't have helped hearing him, yet, with typical womanly mulishness, she insisted on looking away. But by now the semblance of a smile trembled at the corners of her lips. She was aware of his presence. Not only aware, but amused. She was ignoring him, that's what she was doing. Damn it, this girl was infuriating.

He cleared his throat: lightly, at first; then raucously. Soon he was coughing his lungs out, peering at her over his hand. At last, with a slow, rotating motion of her head, she looked in his direction. Their gazes met in mid-air, clung for an instant, her face softened into a half-annoyed, half-amused smile. As he was about to flash back his most seductive grin, her escort crumpled the newspaper into his lap and turned to her. With exquisite timing she gave him the remainder of her smile.

It was a masterpiece of womanly guile, and again he marveled at women's genius for deceit. From his seat he watched them exchange a few cordial remarks. Her expression that had been vacant and bored a moment ago was now gay and affectionate. She reminded him of Alix at the Ville d'Avray station greeting with tender warmth the husband she had betrayed two hours before. Could a man ever be sure? . . .

She slipped her pink cotton gloves on while her gentleman friend paid the waiter. Then, gallantly, he helped her to her feet, and together they walked out of the café. Claude watched them cross the sidewalk and climb into a waiting victoria drawn by two shiny-coated horses. She opened a pink parasol. He thought he saw her look back into the café through the plate-glass window, but he couldn't be sure. A footman shut the door and ran back to the box. At the flap of the reins the horses shuddered their rumps, rose their front hooves in perfect unison. The carriage slid out of sight.

"Well, that's that." Claude sighed, half aloud, biting into another macaroon.

She was gone and he'd never see her again. Like those lovely places you glimpsed from the train and which were out of sight before you'd had time to look at them. Well, at least she had smiled at him, and for that he wished her well. Good luck, little country girl! . . .

Suddenly the café seemed an empty, depressing place. Even his jubilation at getting a hundred francs from Monsieur Fromont was beginning to fade. With alarm he surveyed the various trays on the table and tried to compute how much money he had already spent. Quickly he stuffed the remaining biscuits into his pockets, brazed out the waiter's look of astonishment at the sight of the empty trays and handed him his hundred-franc note.

Then, having pocketed the change, he picked his sombrero from the banquette and left.

◆

Early in June the weather turned very hot. A heat wave sent everyone scurrying to the beach or the mountains. Except, of course, the poor devils who couldn't go anywhere and had to take their town in all her moods, good or bad, as if they were married to her. Claude spent the following three weeks in pleasant idleness, musing about various compositions he planned to write. In the afternoon he some-times went to the Parc Monceau and spent an hour or two on a bench in some shady alley, read the newspaper on the terrace of a café. Occasionally he still thought of the green-eyed girl and returned to Weber's in the hope of seeing her again. She never appeared, and he concluded that, like everyone else, she had left town.

Then one afternoon he collided with her as she was coming out of Jouvin's, the fashionable glove shop on Place de l'Opéra. In the impact of encounter the dainty box she was carrying slipped down onto the pavement.

"Pardon," he said, coming out of his thoughts.

Simultaneously they recognized each other. He, with delight; she, with annoyance.

"Do you always walk like this, Monsieur," she snapped at him, "with your head in the clouds? You'll get killed one of these days."

As he stood motionless, grinning at her, unmindful of the traffic, she went on, "At least you could pick up my package."

Of course. How rude of him! . . . Now he was all speed, confusion and apologies. In the space of a few seconds he had retrieved her glove box, remarked it was intact, stopped an approaching carriage with his raised hand, seized her by the elbow and helped her back to the safety of the sidewalk.

Without a pause he went on to say that she looked even more beautiful than he remembered her, how often he had thought of her and how pleased he was to see her again.

"Not only pleased, but surprised. I would've wagered you had left town."

"Good thing you didn't or you would've lost."

How true! But he wouldn't have minded losing the bet, for he was overjoyed at seeing her again. "I can't tell you how many times I thought of you."

"You already said that and it's all very interesting and I'd simply love standing here and listening to you, but I must go."

She took a step forward, but he blocked her way. Go! . . . Why, this was unthinkable! Just when he had met her! Where could she be going that was so important and so urgent?

"If you must know, I'm going to the Magasins du Louvre to buy a garden hat." She smiled. "We're leaving tomorrow."

Tomorrow! *Mon Dieu,* this was terrible. "At least permit me to drive with you to the store. Please . . . Just to show you've forgiven me for bumping into you so rudely."

She hesitated, but already he was waving to a fiacre. She started climbing in, her foot already on the carriage step.

"Please," he repeated.

She turned around, gave him an uncertain glance over her shoulder. "I think I'd better not."

"You're leaving tomorrow and I won't see you again—"

Her eyes lingered on him for a few seconds. Then, swiftly, in grudging acquiescence, "All right." She nodded. "Come in."

In a leap he was at her side on the tufted leather seat.

"Magasins du Louvre," he flung. "And don't drive too fast."

As the fiacre started moving across Place de l'Opéra, she turned to him with the same half-annoyed, half-amused smile she had given him at the café.

"I am not sure at all I should be driving with you," she said. "That little comedy of yours at Weber's was very silly. All that coughing and throat-clearing to attract my attention—"

"Forgive me, but you looked so sad—"

"Sad? I was thinking about the dresses I should take to the country with me."

"I thought you had some terrible problem and I wanted to cheer you up."

She shrugged. "All you wanted was to flirt with me, while my gentleman friend was reading his paper."

Her directness unsaddled him, but he did not give in. Flirt? Why, nothing had been further from his mind. "Of course I couldn't help responding to your beauty—you are so lovely, so—"

"Never mind the flattery." In spite of herself, laughter was coming to her eyes. "Don't think I don't know your kind. You'd flirt with anything in a skirt."

He protested. He wasn't the flirtatious type at all. As a matter of fact he seldom paid attention to women, but she happened to be so striking, so unusual-looking, so—

"You certainly can sell a pig." Now she was laughing, and her laughter enchanted him. It was full-throated and sensuous. "You've never heard that expression, have you? It means you're a good talker. It's one of our sayings in Lisieux, where I come from."

"Where's that?"

"In Normandy."

"Ah, Normandy! The loveliest region of France. Meadows, cows, apple trees—"

"Have you ever been there?"

"No. But I read about it."

"Did you also read about Lisieux?"

"Naturally. It's a lively little town with a wonderful old church, some very fine monuments and a public park with a bandstand and public benches on which people sit."

She saw he was improvising as he went along and took pity on him.

"You don't know what you're talking about. You never read about Lisieux, never even heard about it. It's a sleepy little town where you die of boredom. But that's where I was born and where my family lives—and I love it."

"The moment I saw you I knew you were a country girl."

"Country girl!" She flashed him a glare and he realized he had said the wrong thing. "Do I look like a country girl? See any hay in my hair? Who do you think—?"

"It's your complexion," he said, frantically trying to retrieve his blunder. "It's so fresh. I knew you couldn't be from Paris. . . . Besides, there's nothing wrong with being born in the country. I was born in the country myself. Well, almost. A little town called Saint-Germain. I bet it's even smaller than Lisieux. Ever been there?"

"Yes, I have. And that's no lie, like your story about Lisieux. I drove there with my gentleman friend. There's a beautiful forest and a big castle with a park. But you haven't got anything like our cathedral. It's almost a thousand years old."

"Yes, but who was ever born in Lisieux? Somebody important, I mean."

"Jean Lefèvre," she boasted feebly. "He was an astronomer."

"Who's ever heard of him? Instead, in Saint-Germain, we have Louis the Fourteenth. Now, that was somebody."

Suddenly they no longer were strangers, but two small-town people brought together by fate in immense, alien Paris.

The fiacre came to a stop in front of the store.

"Come with me and help me choose a garden hat," she said impulsively. "I'll see if you have good taste."

They entered the vast department store, and in their mood of gaiety everything became an occasion for laughter: the multi-branched gasoliers that looked like octopi; the prissy salesladies in their whalebone collars; the vacant-eyed dummies. They lost their way, tittered while asking a pompous floor manager for directions and finally reached the right section.

She sat down at a small *table d'essayage,* and he stood behind her chair, watching her reflection in the mirror as she tried on various garden hats. At moments she reminded him of his Aunt Tavie at her vanity table, studying her beauty spots. After each hat she would search his eyes in the looking-glass and with an inquiring glance ask for his opinion, which he expressed with a wince, a shake of the head or an indifferent shrug.

Finally she tried on a wide-brimmed straw hat with a thin green ribbon. The kind his aunt had worn in Cannes . . .

"That's the one," he declared. "No argument about it."

She hesitated. "Do you think so? It's rather old-fashioned."

"Old-fashioned! Why, it has more chic, more dash than any of them."

For an instant she gazed, undecided, at her reflection. "You're sure?"

"Of course I'm sure. Just look at yourself. You never looked prettier."

"I guess you're right," she said, brushing away her last doubts.

On their way out of the store they passed by the fan counter.

"I think I'll buy a fan to go with my hat," she said. "Tell me the one you like best."

Fans being an essential accessory of ladies' apparel, a vast selection of them was on display. Of all sizes and shapes, for all purposes and every conceivable occasion. Morning fans, afternoon and evening fans. Fans for travel, street, theatre, summer resorts. Wedding fans with Cupid darting arrows; black fans to be used at funerals. Ballroom fans with attached *carnets de bal*. Fans for gala functions and fans for informal gatherings. Exotic fans made of thin bamboo reeds, military fans with portraits of Napoleon. Church fans inscribed with New Testament quotations, philosophical fans garlanded with lofty maxims suitable for dinner conversation. Flirt and courtship fans that unfolded on teasing vignettes calculated to intrigue, encourage and trap the pursuing male. Fans of all prices, from the sumptuous ivory-handled fans made of Venice lace, ostrich feathers, brocade or just silk, down to the humble North-Wind that was made of paper and cost only one franc.

And at last, at the very end, the rustic or garden fans with handpainted pictures of thatch-roofed cottages or sunsets over peaceful landscapes.

He pointed to a parchment fan decorated with a composition of green leaves and field flowers. "That one."

"That's the one I was going to pick," she cried, her face bright with pleasure.

She opened her purse, but already he was forcing money into the saleslady's hand.

"Permit me to present it to you," he said as they started away from the counter. "For letting me come with you."

She took the slim, narrow box, but to his surprise she resented his gesture. "You shouldn't presume to give me presents," she said, walking faster.

Their comradeship of a moment ago was gone. Obscurely he sensed she regretted having invited him into the store.

"Won't I see you again?" he asked, as they came out in the street.

"I told you I'm leaving tomorrow."

"But later—when you come back?"

"I don't see why we should." While speaking she crossed to the edge of the sidewalk and glanced about for a fiacre. "We'd better leave things as they are."

"Won't you at least tell me your name?"

"Why?"

"I could say it to myself."

He looked so meek and despondent that her manner softened. A gentleness came into her eyes. "All right. It's Gaby. Mademoiselle Gaby Lhéry."

"Gaby—it's a pretty name. Mine's Claude Debussy. Couldn't I write you?"

"Certainly not," she said, waving to a fiacre.

"Then perhaps you'll write me?"

She shrugged in reply and with one hand began gathering her skirt as the carriage pulled in. "It's been nice meeting you. Now if you'll excuse me—"

He seized her elbow. "In case you change your mind, my address is—"

Irritably she freed herself and stepped into the carriage. "Drive on," she told the cabby.

The fiacre entered the traffic, and only then did she notice that Claude was running alongside.

"Get back!"

"I just want to give you my address. It's 42, rue—"

"*Get back!* . . . You're going to get killed."

The carriage was gathering speed, but he was still clutching the door handle. "Remember, 42, rue de Londres, near the Saint-Lazare Station . . . Say you'll write. Please—"

The horse broke into a lively trot and he lost his grip. For an instant he remained motionless in the middle of the bustling traffic. He had a last glimpse of her frightened face, then she was gone. Suddenly he noticed a gendarme shouting and waving at him from across the street and realized the dangerousness of his position. In a few nimble leaps he wove his way back to the sidewalk and contentedly resumed his stroll.

"Gaby," he said half aloud to himself. "Gaby."

Yes, it was a pretty name . . .

♦

During the days that followed he thought constantly about her. This in itself was unusual. With the exception of Alix and "Madame V," the women he had known had left no deep impression. Even those who had given him a great deal of pleasure had vanished from his mind almost as soon as they vacated his bed. He deplored this trait in his character and accused himself of fickleness and want of sensitivity. Sometimes he wondered whether he had not lost his capacity for love in the Alix-tormented days at the Villa. Some illnesses, they said, left you impotent; perhaps some love affairs left you emotionally inert. Perhaps Alix and "Madame V" had done this to him, made it impossible for him to fall in love.

Thus he was surprised to find himself thinking so much about Gaby. He repeated her name to himself, recalled their visit to the store, heard the sound of her laughter in his mind. How gay and simple she had been. And how beautiful! . . .

At first he felt for sure she would write. Every morning he clattered down the stairs and asked for his mail. There never was any, and as the month wore on he finally admitted that she must have found him neither attractive nor interesting and did not want to see him again. This deflated his ego and changed his opinion of her. She became a mean, selfish woman. She lacked intelligence: her conversation was deadly dull. Her laughter was no longer tinkling and brooklike, but raucous, unpleasant to the ear. She was unbearably affected. Also callous and calculating. As for the name Gaby, it was cheap and whorish. The only thing to do was to forget about her. After all, there were other women.

He stopped inquiring about his mail and tried forgetting her. Then one morning, on the last day of June, Madame Sénégal brought him a note. It came from Clairvaux, a small town in the Aube *département*. In it Gaby informed him that she was going to Lisieux for her mother's birthday and would spend a few hours in Paris between trains. And would he like to meet her at two o'clock that afternoon at the Café des Voyageurs, on rue de Clichy? . . .

With pounding heart he reread the letter and for a moment savored the rapture of vindicated pride. She wanted to see him again . . . He had known all along that she liked him. She really was a very sensitive, beautiful and intelligent girl. And he knew why she wanted to see him. After all, he wasn't exactly naïve and she certainly did not plan to spend those few hours sitting in a dingy bistro and making conversation . . .

He glanced at his watch. It was past noon already. He had no time to waste.

He ran down the street to the Saint-Lazare Station, where he was told that the only afternoon train for Lisieux was at five-thirty. This, he calculated, gave him about three hours to bring their encounter to a happy conclusion. On the way back he stopped to buy some flowers. At the wine shop he bought a bottle of port. It was after one when he returned to his garret. In a frenzy of activity he set the flowers on the table, the bottle of port on the nightstand, swept the room, hid the shirt that was hanging in the window, changed the bedsheets. Hastily he washed, combed his hair, knotted his Vermeer-blue tie. This done, he raced down the stairs and ran all the way up to the Café des Voyageurs, which he reached, panting and drenched with sweat, on the stroke of two.

She was not there.

At three o'clock she hadn't yet arrived, and it started to drizzle. A few tepid drops that turned to steam and made the heat still more oppressive. There were two or three thunderclaps followed by flashes of green lightning.

In the bistro it got so dim that the owner stirred himself from behind the counter and lit a gas jet. But the storm did not break and the rain remained a sprinkling of large hot drops splashing on the pavement. From his table at the end of the room Claude watched the doorway and the clock on the wall, his mood growing more churlish as time passed and his plans crumbled in his mind.

Bitterly he was reflecting he might have saved himself all this trouble and expense, when shortly after four o'clock she hurried into the bistro.

"I'm sorry," she called from the door, shutting her parasol. "My train was late."

She sat across the table, breathless, smiling at him while removing her gloves. A light suntan suffused her face with a pale amber glow. She looked more beautiful and desirable than ever.

"I don't know what the trouble was," she went on. "But it kept stopping every few minues. Then, with this damn rain, I couldn't find a fiacre at the station, and it took me at least twenty minutes to walk here."

"It's all right," he said coldly. "You don't have to explain. What will you have to drink?"

She gave him a startled look. "What's the matter?"

"Nothing."

"Yes, there is. I can see you're angry. Honest, it wasn't my fault."

"I didn't say it was."

"But I feel you think so. Please don't be annoyed. I was so much looking forward to seeing you again."

Her pleasure at being with him in this dingy bistro was so real that it almost brought him out of his surly mood. For an instant he was on the verge of telling her how glad he was she had come and that he understood it wasn't her fault if the train was late and his plans had gone awry. Had she sat next to him he would have slipped his arm around her shoulder, kissed her, and everything would have been all right. But she sat across the table and he could not even touch her. This became the symbol of the day's frustration. Nothing was right. Even her gentleness sounded ironical. How easy it would have been to take her to his studio. Now it was too late . . .

"And all the time I was in the country I was wondering if you had gotten out of the traffic. You sure frightened me."

"Thank you for your concern." His disappointment found an outlet in sarcasm. "But if you hadn't been in such a hurry to go, I wouldn't have had to run after you. But you couldn't wait to get away."

"I'm sorry, but I was afraid someone might see us and tell my gentleman friend."

At once he pretended alarm. "Maybe someone is spying on you now? Are you sure it's safe for you to be here?"

A flash of anger passed through her green eyes, but she held herself in check. She even forced a little laugh at his suggestion of a spy. "Nobody's going to look for me here," she said. "Do you know why I chose this place? Because when I first came to Paris I used to work in a modiste shop a little further up the street, and when we worked late I'd come here to get coffee."

Silence fell between them. She waited for him to say something friendly, show in some way that his ill humor had gone.

He did not speak, and finally she asked, "How have you been?"

"All right."

A pause.

"What've you been doing?"

"Same as usual. Writing music."

"So that's what you do! I thought you must be some kind of an artist, but not a musician. More like a painter . . . Do they play your songs?"

She was referring to the barrel organs that wandered through the streets, grinding out popular tunes. Any other day he would have laughed, today he was offended.

"I'm sorry," he said stiffly. "I don't write that kind of music."

That did it.

She blanched under her tan, and he knew he had gone too far.

"How in hell am I supposed to know what kind of music you write?" Suddenly she was hard-eyed and loud-mouthed, the veteran of street brawls, unafraid of him or any man. "I don't give a damn what kind of music you write or what you do. You can jump off a bridge for all I care."

"Please, Gaby—"

She didn't let him go on. "And who the hell gave you the right to call me by my first name? We haven't slept together, have we? And it don't look like we ever will." She laughed, and her laugh also had changed, become shrill and vulgar. "I know why you're cross. Because I was late and you won't have time to get me into your bed. I wager you've got your place all spruced up, with fresh bed linens and a bottle of port handy . . . Men are so stupid, it makes you cry. You don't even give a girl a chance to know and like you, all you want is hop in bed with her, and show her what great lovers you are! Look, I'm a professional, and I can spot the likes of you a mile away. The moment I saw you at Weber's I knew I shouldn't have anything to do with you. You haven't a sou, don't know where your next meal will come from, but because you're handsome you think you can get any girl. Well, this is one girl you won't get, I don't need you, see? I've got what I want. He may not be the youngest or most handsome man in the world, but he's rich and kind and he treats me nice. And that's enough for me."

She stopped. For an instant she studied him from across the table. Her anger had burned itself out. Only the sadness and disappointment remained and they showed in the slow shaking of her head, the lidded heaviness of her green eyes.

"And I was so sure you must be different," she murmured to herself. "Not like the rest of them."

She let out a brief self-mocking snort. "Shows you how wrong a girl can be, doesn't it?" With a shrug she picked up her gloves.

"Please, let me explain—"

"Don't trouble yourself," she said, pushing back her chair. "Save it for some other girl. Well, good-bye. I have a train to catch."

As he was rising to escort her, she motioned him to remain seated. "Stay where you are. I can find my way to the station."

◆

The storm broke during the night. He could not sleep and stood at the window watching the flashes of lightning, waiting for thunderclaps and all the time thinking about Gaby.

That meeting at the café had been a disaster, and he for one was sorry it had ever happened. Everything had gone wrong and it had been his fault. He had no right acting as he had, being rude and sarcastic when she was only trying to be friendly. After all, she couldn't help it if her damn train was late, if it was hot and it rained. He wished he could apologize, tell her he was sorry. Truly sorry.

But, on the other hand, women could really be infuriating . . . They spent hours making themselves desirable, yet you were supposed to be enthralled exclusively by their minds and the charm of their conversation. Woe if you showed you liked their looks! Then they turned prudish on you, called you stupid and a sex maniac. Gaby's lecture about his wanting to get her in bed was a typical example of that peculiar attitude of women toward men. You'd think he was a criminal because he'd bought a bunch of flowers and a bottle of port and hoped to bring her to his studio. Of course he wanted to get her in bed. What did she expect him to do? Sit three hours in this stinking bistro, gazing into her eyes or reading her fortune in the palm of her hand?

To hell with it! . . . The whole episode had been a mess, and the only good thing that had come out of it was that he now knew it was better for him if he never saw her again. Not that there was any chance of it, but even if there were he would make a point to keep out of her way. Oh, yes, she was beautiful, no argument about that, and she could be very nice. But they had nothing in common, lived in worlds thousands of miles apart. And then she was a professional—she had said so herself—and he didn't like women who sold themselves to the highest bidder. And what a temper that girl had! If she could work herself into such a state over a little vexation, he'd hate to think what she might do if she ever got *really* mad! And, finally, she had a man. A gentleman friend, as she said. And she liked him—at least that's what she said . . . Whatever way you looked at it, any relationship with her could bring nothing but trouble, and personally he was glad she had walked out on him.

He found comfort in these reflections and went to bed. He slept like a child. The storm spent itself at dawn, and morning arose bright and sunny in a sky scrubbed clean.

From then on, summer behaved itself. Paris became a sleepy provincial town of green-leafed boulevards, sun-flecked sidewalks and white-trousered gendarmes. Ice cream vendors pushed their brightly painted carts, blowing their horns. Along curbs, cabbies snoozed on their seats.

Claude was now up to his neck in music, writing a quartet. And no one was more surprised about it than he. He had not planned to write a quartet, he had planned to write his symphony, his *Afternoon of a Faun* symphony he had told Monsieur Guiraud about during their last dinner together. It was to be a large work in three movements: Prelude, Interlude and Paraphrase. He saw it all very clearly in his mind and nothing remained to do but write it. But no music had come. For hours he had focused his thoughts on his faun stretched on the grass and dreaming his naughty dreams, but, mulishly, music had declined to appear. It was *Rodrigue* all over again.

Instead a lively eleven-note theme insisted on prancing all over his brain, and something had to be done about it. Since the only way to get rid of it was to put it down on paper, and since it couldn't be expressed in any other way but a quartet form, there was nothing to be done but postpone the symphony and write a quartet. At times Claude could have sworn that his teacher was behind it all, making him do whatever he wanted, as he had when he was alive.

Soon he had fallen under the spell of the quartet medium, this most exacting of musical forms. No cheating was possible in a quartet, as it so easily was in a symphony. No sweeping of musical dust under the rug of brilliant instrumentation. It demanded perfect craftsmanship, flawless melodic line. And if, in addition, you tried to say something new within this ancient and rigid frame, then you really had a problem on your hands. Monsieur Guiraud had said it would be a challenge, and indeed it was.

But what a fascinating one . . . By the end of July, Claude could not tear himself away from it. He discontinued his afternoon strolls, stopped dropping in at Père Bailly's for a chat. He saw no one, went nowhere and stayed home with his quartet, as happy as a dog with a bone.

Summer swelled into August. On the window sill Linne squinted at the sun. Newspapers said it was the hottest summer in years, but Claude was not aware of it. Coatless, the collar of his shirt open, he remained at his table, oblivious of the world, hunched over his pages of music paper.

So absorbed was he in his work that he almost failed to notice his birthday. Suddenly, in the middle of a bar, it flashed through his mind that he was thirty years old. He rested his pen against his inkwell, overwhelmed by the solemnity of the occasion. Thirty. He was thirty. My God, where had the years gone! His youth was practically over and he hadn't yet made his mark. All his former classmates were well on the way. Organists, assistant conductors or chorus masters. Only he was lagging behind. It was time to take stock, make a complete survey of the direction, purpose and aims of his life. Yes, he must do that. Without fail. He must go over the general situation and make some important decisions. But not now. Later, when his mind was free. At present he was more interested in getting this quartet finished . . .

Naturally he made no survey, no decisions. Everything went on as before. But he kept on writing his quartet.

September arrived, cool and luminous, interrupted by an occasional avant-garde shower from the approaching autumn. Claude was now working on the last movement of his quartet.

That afternoon he had reached the final allegro, weaving the various themes into a last intricate pattern, when there was a knock on the door. As the concierge sometimes came to visit him at this hour, he called, "Come in," without looking up.

When he finally did, he saw Gaby standing on the threshold.

"May I come in?" she asked hesitantly.

His first reaction was one of annoyance, but he rose politely. "Please do."

"You're sure I don't disturb you?"

"Of course not."

"I won't stay long," she said, starting to walk into the room.

Quickly he waved Linne off a chair and brought it to the side of the table. She sat down, and for an instant they looked at each other in smiling uneasiness.

"I'm glad you came," he said at last in a conversational tone of voice, "for I've been wanting to apologize for my behavior at the café."

"It wasn't your fault."

"Oh yes, it was—and I'm sorry."

"No, it wasn't." This with a small gesture of protestation. "You'd been waiting two hours and you had a perfect right to be annoyed."

"Just the same, I never should—"

"I was the one to blame."

"You? Who gave you this silly idea?"

"Yes, I was and I'm sorry for what I said."

"Please, don't mention it."

"That's what I came to tell you. How sorry I am."

Magnanimously he waved to signify that he refused to accept her apologies. "As a matter of fact it was nobody's fault but that of the damn train—"

"And that stupid rain."

"And then it was so miserably hot—"

"And so damp, too."

Suddenly they realized they were trying to apologize and save face at the same time, reciting the excuses they had given themselves. They laughed.

"Oh, let's forget it," he said.

"Yes. Let's be friends."

"How about a cup of tea? I'm the greatest tea brewer in the world."

This time everything went well, just as at the bistro everything had gone wrong. It was pleasantly cool in the room. Through the open window a breeze wafted in, gently rippling the curtains. The sky was turning mauve; only the tip of the Eiffel Tower still gleamed with sunshine. There was no more awkwardness between them. They were happy to have made peace, to be seeing each other and drinking tea like old friends.

She looked with curiosity at the unfinished page on the table. "I'm afraid I disturbed you from your work."

"Not at all. It's almost finished, anyway."

"What is it?"

"A quartet."

A quartet—what was that? . . . It was a composition written for four instruments. If one of them was a piano, it was a piano quartet. If, on the other hand, they were all stringed instruments, then the composition was called a string quartet.

"What's yours?"

"A string quartet."

"Good. Is it difficult to write a string quartet?"

Yes. It was. Much more difficult, in fact, than writing for a full orchestra, because you didn't have the resources of instrumentation to fall back upon . . .

He felt she was scarcely listening to what he said, but he did not mind. He was content to make conversation, have an excuse to look at her. He had almost forgotten how lovely she was. And desirable . . . But, of course, she would be going any minute now, and this precluded any thought of love-making. Too bad . . . Well, at least she had come back, they had apologized and she had given him a chance to remember her as the beautiful, friendly girl she was.

"Thank you for explaining everything to me," she said when he finished talking. "I had no idea it was so difficult to write a string quartet." She picked up one of her gloves from the table and began slipping it on. "And the tea was very good."

She glanced around the room, congratulated him on his Japanese prints, asked the name of his cat. "How long have you been living here?"

"Almost five years. It's getting pretty shabby. I'm going to paint it again one of these days."

"It looks nice as it is. But isn't it awfully cold in winter?"

He grinned philosophically. "A little, but you get used to everything."

She was putting on her other glove and he noticed the deliberate slowness of her gestures. Obviously she hated to leave as much as he hated to see her go.

"I suppose you're going back to the country," he said to fill the silence.

"Yes. I just came to town to do some shopping."

"At what time is your train?"

"Nine-thirty."

He jolted on his chair. Nine-thirty! Why, it wasn't even seven o'clock. They could have dinner and return to the station with time to spare. She hesitated, looked at her watch. He insisted. She needn't fear, he would see to it that she wouldn't miss her train.

"You're sure?" she asked, tempted but still concerned.

He gave her his word. She could rely on him and stop worrying. "We'll go to a little restaurant where we can dine outside. Nothing fancy, but it has a nice little garden."

He had dined there a few times with Vital in the days of their Montmartre wanderings. The food was good and cheap, the wine smooth and powerful. Behind the two-story ramshackle house there was a cobbled courtyard with a linden tree in the center, where in summer and early autumn a few tables were set.

"Do you like it?" he asked after they sat down.

She nodded eagerly. "It's like being in the country, isn't it?"

The owner came out of the kitchen in his shirtsleeves and blue apron, carrying a small paper-shaded lamp, which he set down on the table. He wished them a good evening, called them *m'sieu-dame,* pretending to believe they were married, and wasn't it a balmy night they were having, and personally September was his favorite month of the year. This done he recited the list of the dishes that were available, stressing the particular excellence of the *navarin,* which, he swore, was famous all over Montmartre.

They said that after the *potage du jour* they would have the famous *navarin.*

"Now for the beverages." His tone dwindled to a confidential whisper. "I have a little wine . . . one of those little wines . . ." Words failed him and he blew a kiss. "And so cheap! . . ."

He told how one day, by pure chance, he had taken a sip of it and ever since had been unable to drink anything else. Judging from his varicosed cheeks it was plain that he drank a good deal of it.

"Have a bottle. Just as a personal favor to me." Then, with dramatic suddenness, "And look! To show you the kind of man I am, if you don't like it you don't have to pay for it."

Could anything be fairer? he asked. Claude and Gaby agreed that nothing could and they would try his "little wine."

After the man had returned to his kitchen they exchanged a few amused remarks about him, his famous *navarin* and his wonderful wine.

"He, too, can sell a pig, can't he?" Claude smiled teasingly.

"Oh, you remember . . ." For a few seconds the memory of their drive to the Magasins du Louvre hung between them. Indulgently she shook her head. "You sure were full of nonsense that day. I'd never heard anyone talk so much."

"I was so happy, I said anything that passed through my mind just to keep you interested."

"You certainly did. Ah, Normandy!" She mimicked his voice, his lyrical gestures. "The loveliest region of France. Meadows, cows, apple trees—"

"Well, they do have cows in Normandy, don't they?"

"And your description of Lisieux! A lively little town with a wonderful old church—"

"I was right. There's an old church in Lisieux, isn't there? And a public park with benches and a bandstand? Every city has them, so I knew Lisieux must have them, too."

"Do you always tell lies like that?"

He smiled, a little sheepishly. "Only when I have to."

Soon they had exhausted their few common memories; and since they did not wish to revive that of their meeting at the bistro or reveal their thoughts, they talked during dinner about the quietness of the place and the softness of the night. They discussed the lamb stew, the celebrated *navarin* which was famous all over Montmartre, and she said she could cook one that was every bit as good, if not better.

During courses the owner inquired about the wine, and wasn't it the best they'd ever tasted? He assured them he would rather cut his throat than recommend a wine that wasn't up to his standards and the reputation of his restaurant, and they nodded approvingly.

Dinner over, he brought a blue-enamel coffee pot and filled their demitasses. By now the last customers had left. Except for the pool of yellow light on their table, the back yard lay in darkness. The linden tree had turned ink-black. Now and then a cricket squeezed his small jet of sound.

They no longer tried to make conversation and leisurely sipped their coffee. Now and then their eyes would meet over the rims of their cups and they would smile. He had lit a cigarette and was watching her across the table. Lamplight stenciled her face in a pattern of shadows and salmon-colored flesh. Beneath the long lashes her eyes gleamed large and green.

"What are you thinking?" she asked.

"That they're really green."

"They really are, aren't they?"

He sensed she was pleased he had remarked about the unusual color of her eyes and had often been told about it.

"At school they used to call me 'Cat's Eyes.' And you know, they change with the light. In the morning they're kind of turquoise, but sometimes they get real dark. Like mint."

And the funny part of it was that no one else in her family had green eyes. Neither her father, nor her mother, nor her sister Blanche.

"Hers are blue," she said a little deprecatingly. "Although she's very pretty just the same. The most beautiful complexion you've ever seen. People used to say we were the two prettiest girls in Lisieux. But we're so different you'd never think we're sisters. Black and white."

Blanche was a year younger but terribly serious. Church every Sunday, confession every month. Never let a boy touch her, or anything. The kind that wanted nothing but a quiet life with a husband

and a flock of children. Even when they both were little tots in pig-
tails they already were different as night and day. Blanche was the
one who got all the good marks at school, while she had barely
learned how to read and write and just enough catechism to do
her First Communion.

"And I always was in some sort of a scrap. Our teacher, Sister
Gertrude, used to say, 'Gaby, why can't you be like Blanche?' Funny,
isn't it, that two sisters can be so different."

But that didn't stop them from loving each other. On the contrary, there couldn't be two sisters that were more affectionate. They
loved being together, and there was nothing one wouldn't do for the
other. Between them there were no secrets.

"She is the only one who knows what I'm doing. Naturally she
thinks it's wrong and I live in mortal sin and all that. But Blanche
would rather die than say a word to anyone. Especially to my parents.
You see, they don't suspect anything. I know it's hard to believe, but
it's the truth."

Five years ago she had come to Paris to work in the fashion business, and so far as they were concerned she still was in the fashion
business. Oh yes, it demanded quickness of mind, but up to now,
thanks to Blanche's complicity, she'd been able to keep up the pretense. Her father was no problem. Like all men he didn't notice
things. He was glad to see her whenever she came home for a visit,
and asked no questions. But with her mother it was another story.
Maman had sharp eyes, and it took a bit of doing to maintain the fic-
tion of the virtuous, hard-working girl.

"Naturally I don't put any mascara on and I don't use any perfume, or anything. But she knows clothes, for she's a seamstress. And
the best in Lisieux, too. Women come from miles to have her make
them a dress. So I tell her I work as a mannequin in a chic dress
shop and they give me my clothes after I've shown them."

"And she believes you?"

She gave him an embarrassed nod. "Yes, she does. And you know
why? Because she can't imagine that her own daughter would tell a
lie. When I was a child she used to tell me that each time someone
told a lie it made Our Saviour's wounds bleed all over again."

For she was very pious, Maman was. Always talking about Our
Saviour and how He'd been crucified so that people could go to
Heaven. Every morning at five she went to Mass and then worked
like a slave all day. Even found time to visit neighbors when they
were sick. A saint, that's what she was. The best mother anyone
could want.

"Poor maman, she'd die if she knew what I'm doing."

"Aren't you afraid she'll ever find out?"

"Not a chance."

"What if she ever comes to Paris?"

No danger of that. She had never left Lisieux and she was as likely to come to Paris as to take a trip to the moon. "Besides, I don't use my real name."

Her real name was Dupont, not Lhéry, as she had told him. Plain Gabrielle Dupont. Gaby Lhéry was something she had invented for business reasons. Her professional name, you might say.

"My parents aren't rich or anything, but they're fine people," she said with humble pride. "I wouldn't bring shame on them for anything in the world, and I love them."

Her attention was caught by a moth whirling around the lamp. Repeatedly it hurled itself at the flame and fell down on the table-cloth, only to start again a moment later.

"Isn't she silly?" she said. "She gets burned each time but she goes on trying. What do you think makes her do that?"

"Probably can't help herself." He pulled out his watch. "And if you're going to catch that train we'd better start for the station."

She crinkled her nose in a childish gesture of distaste. "It's so nice here, I hate to go."

"I do, too, but we only have half an hour."

"Perhaps—" She hesitated, then plunged in. "Perhaps I could take the eleven-twenty. It's much faster and it gets there only forty minutes later."

He gasped with joyous surprise. "Why, that'd be wonderful, but won't you get in trouble?"

She wouldn't. Several times she had taken the eleven-twenty and her gentleman friend had never made any trouble . . . "But I wouldn't want to take your time," she added with apparent concern. "You must be anxious to get back to work on your string quartet. See? I remember what you taught me."

He smiled. Yes, she was an excellent pupil and it was a pleasure to explain things to her. But she needn't worry. His quartet was practically finished, and besides, he seldom worked at night.

"I'll tell you what we'll do. We'll stay here a little longer, and then if you like, we could go back to my place. It's nearer the station anyway . . ."*

---

* Gabrielle Dupont, alias Gaby Lhéry, was born in Lisieux on June 11, 1866. Recent documentation has brought full light on her life as well as on her character. Because of the extraordinary color of her eyes she was known in the fashionable Parisian demimonde as Gaby-aux-yeux-verts: Gaby-of-the-green-eyes. When she met Debussy she was twenty-five, and had been living for two years with a certain Comte de Villeneuve.

Her sister Blanche was also born in Lisieux, on August 11, 1867.

CHAPTER

IN THE BRIGHTNESS OF EARLY AFTERNOON SHE SLEPT, HER MOUTH
almost touching his chest, a thigh flung halfway across his loin.
Smilingly he scanned her face, innocent, almost childlike, in sleep,
a wisp of hair twirled upon her cheek, the edge of her teeth gleaming
white between her parted lips.

Gaby, darling Gaby . . .

For three days they had lived in a world of their own; a topsy-
turvy world of laughter and caresses, sandwiches at three o'clock in
the morning, breakfast on a tray in mid-afternoon; a world in which
time did not exist, or day or night or work or people. Only themselves and their hunger for each other. It had been something new—
this ever-fresh thrill at fondling her, watching her grow taut with
desire, trailing his fingers up her thighs and learning by touch, like
a blind man, the secret map of her body. He would not soon forget
this girl and their three-day affair. It had been one of those madcap
adventures you read about, but which never happened in real life.
Well, it had happened to him—and now it was about to end.

Her train was leaving at four; and judging from the patch of sunshine on the wall it could not be much later than one o'clock. In
three hours they would say good-bye. She would return to the country,
her lover, her way of life; and he to his music. They were to forget
each other, never try to meet again. She had insisted on that. He had

suggested that perhaps they could see each other occasionally during the winter. She had been adamant and quite blunt about it. Fun was fun, but life was a serious business and neither of them had time for romance or any such foolishness. Their little affair had been very nice and all that, but it had been a whim, a caprice—nothing more.

Since she felt that way, there was no point in discussing the matter any further, and he had not insisted. And now that their "caprice" was almost over he hoped she would go on sleeping through their last moments together and be spared the sadness of farewells.

Drowsily she stirred beneath the sheet.

"What're you thinking?" she murmured.

"I thought you were asleep."

"I am, but I can hear you think."

"I see." He smiled and leaned down to kiss the pink shell of her ear. "And it keeps you awake, I suppose. Well, if you must know, I was thinking how wonderful it's all been."

"Nice, wasn't it?" she murmured. "Remember how I fooled you at dinner with my story about the eleven-twenty?" Softly she tittered to herself.

"Yes. And you should be ashamed of yourself for deceiving a nice man like me."

It seemed there was no eleven-twenty train. Nor nine-thirty either. Nor had she come to Paris on a shopping tour, as she had said. The truth was that she had been on her way to a three-day visit with her family, and between trains she had come to see him, without knowing exactly why. Perhaps to make sure he was as ungracious and conceited as he had been at the café. Then she would brush him off her mind once for all. But things had turned out unexpectedly. She had never gone to Lisieux . . .

"It's that *Clair de Lune* of yours that did it," she said. "It made me feel nice and sleepy."

"I'm glad my music is good for something. Want me to get your breakfast?"

"I want you to stay here and keep still, so I can kiss you."

He felt the nibbling of her lips on his chest, like that of some languid and amorous squirrel.

"Stop eating my nipples, will you?"

"I'm not eating them. Besides, I have the right to do anything I want with you."

"Not to chew me alive. If you're hungry, eat the pillow."

"Anyway, you don't need those things."

"Come to think of it, they're rather useless. But they're decorative, and I'd like to keep mine. Now, be a good girl and try to sleep for a while. It's still early."

"All right."

The nibbling stopped. She nestled her head into the curve of his shoulder and pretended to sleep.

"Will you miss me a little when I'm gone?" she asked after a while.

"I thought we were supposed to forget each other."

"Oh, that's true."

"You know I'll miss you," he said, gently stroking her hair. "Terribly so. And I think you'll miss me a little too. That's why it seems so foolish for us not to see each other." He had promised himself not to bring the matter up again, but the words had come out of their own accord. "At least once in a while."

"I'd like to, but it wouldn't be right." Previously her denial had been brusque and emphatic, now it came in whispers. "Please, darling, try to understand. I have my career to think about."

"What career?"

She caught the irony in his voice, but kept herself in check. "The one I'm going to make for myself."

She raised herself on her elbow and looked down into his eyes. "You think I'm silly, don't you? Yes, you do, I can see it. But if a lawyer or doctor spoke about his career you wouldn't laugh, would you? Well, let me tell you something."

He opened his mouth but she pressed her finger tips to his lips. "Have you ever heard of Fanchette Dupin, Judith Widmer, Reine Romani, Caroline Otero, Emilienne d'Alençon, Alice Howard, Léonie Closmenil?"

"I've seen their names in the papers," he said evasively.

"Each one of these girls earns ten times more than any lawyer or doctor or banker in Paris."

They were *les grandes biches,* the stars of the demimonde. All of them had their own houses, servants, carriages, jewels that a queen might envy. Their gentlemen friends were the wealthiest men in Europe and America. Sometimes a grandduke or visiting king would ask for "a favor," and the favor would cost his treasury fifty thousand francs.*

"How many years would it take a lawyer or a doctor to earn that much?" Amusedly she smiled, waiting for his reply. "Mind you," she went on when he failed to speak, "I don't say I am one of these girls yet. But I am not far behind. I've done pretty well for myself since I came to Paris. My gentleman friend is a count. Rich, generous, easygoing. I like him, but I've had some wonderful offers lately and one of these days I'm going to make a change. In this business you must go up, or you go down. Give me another year or two and I,

* The financier Berguen paid twenty-five thousand gold francs (five thousand dollars) for *half an hour* of privacy with Caroline Otero.

also, will have my own house, my carriage and everything. And in five or six years I can save enough money to be rich for the rest of my life and do all the things I want to do. Now tell me, darling, don't you think it would be rather stupid of me to spoil my chances by coming to see you?"

She gave him a tremulous smile, then suddenly her eyes filled with tears. "I know it's going to be hard not seeing each other any more, but it won't be so hard if we stop now. A lot of people live without love and they get along. I lived without it before and I guess I can live without it again. Right now you think you won't forget me, but you will. You'll go back to your music, get yourself another girl and in two or three weeks you won't even remember I ever came here."

"It's not true, and you know it."

"It *is* true. Anyway, it's no use arguing. That's the way things are and we can't change them. We've had three days, three wonderful days together, and that's more than most people have in their whole lifetime."

He watched her wipe the tears from her cheeks with the back of her hand. She was right, and it was no use arguing. Life was the enemy of love. Life did not want them to see each other again, and for that it was creating obstacles, spoiling things as it always did. With Sonia it had been her mother, with Alix their difference of age, with "Madame V" her husband. This time it was a career, a demimondaine's career . . .

"You're right." He smiled. "Let's not talk about it any more."

"I'm glad you understand." Then, to show that the discussion was closed, she went on in a brisk tone of voice, "Now tell me, what're you going to do after I leave."

"First, catch up on my sleep," he said in an attempt to bring back the bantering mood of a moment ago. "With you around I haven't slept a wink."

"I don't mean that. I want to know what you're going to do, who you're going to see, where you're going to go?"

"I'll start looking for work, as usual."

"What kind?"

"Any kind. Anything that will buy food and pay the rent. Piano lessons, transcriptions. If I'm lucky I'll sell a song or two."

"What else?"

"I'll finish my quartet. Then—" He let out a gasp. "Oh, my God, I forgot about America!"

At once she was full of questions. America? What had he got to do with America? He told her about Poniatowski and his offer to interest some American conductor in his music.

"I'd asked him to write me at Bailly's bookstore, but I got busy on this damn quartet and forgot to get my mail. Now it'll be too late. I always do stupid things like that."

Tenderly she comforted him, assuring him he was much better and safer in Paris than in a country full of howling, scalping Indians. When he remonstrated that there were a few civilized people in America, she cut him short. Three years ago, at the time of "l'Expo," she had attended Buffalo Bill's show and she knew what she was talking about.

"Then what else?" she pressed on to divert his mind from America.

"Monsieur and Madame Chausson have invited me to spend a week with them in the country."

This brought forth a swarm of new questions. This Madame Chausson, was she young, was she pretty? . . . No, she wasn't young, about thirty-three or -four. And she wasn't what you'd call pretty, but very nice and intelligent. Also, she played the piano very well. He had met her in the course of his visits to her husband at their house on boulevard Decourcelles.

"What does he do?"

"He writes music."

"I don't mean that. What kind of business is he in? He must have some sort of business to have a house on boulevard Decourcelles."

No. So far as he knew Monsieur Chausson didn't have any business. "He just was born rich, I guess. That's why he can write music and give so much time to La Nationale."

"La Nationale—what's that?"

She wanted to know everything, expected him to explain in a few sentences the musical world of Paris and his place in it. Of course, it could not be done, but it made time pass and kept her from thinking about their approaching separation. Patiently he explained to her that La Nationale was the only musical group that would perform the works of unknown composers.

"You mean you're an unknown composer?"

He was touched by her bristling loyalty. "Yes, darling. I'm afraid I am."

"What's wrong with your music?"

"Nothing, except people don't seem to like it."

She frowned at his light-heartedness. "Do they play it often?"

"Oh, yes. All the time." No work of his had been performed since the regrettable incident of the Fantasy two years ago, but he felt it unwise to go into details.

"How much do they pay you?"

"Well, you see, darling—"

It took some time to explain that La Nationale was running at a deficit and could not possibly pay royalties to composers. "It's admirable they go to the trouble of performing our works at all."

This failed to move Gaby. She felt that Claude was being exploited because of his good nature, and for an instant she considered him with the annoyed indulgence of an elder sister toward a helpless, rather stupid but much-loved brother.

"When it comes to practical matters you aren't very intelligent, are you? You can't help it, I guess. All artists are pretty dumb when it comes to money."

Suddenly she was weary of musical talk. She slid down to her former place, her cheek pressed against his shoulder.

For a while they did not speak; then in a whisper she asked, "What time is it?"

"It's still early." He tightened his arm around her and glanced at the moving patch of sunshine on the wall. "Around two, I should say. Try to sleep for a moment."

"I'll have time to sleep in the country."

With a creeping motion she brought her face level to his on the pillow. In silence they gazed into each other's eyes. In an hour it would be time for them to start for the station. Helplessly they listened to their heartbeats that ticked away the end of their affair.

"Kiss me."

The words breathed out of her lips, half in command and half in plea. Gently he kissed her. Then again and again. Soon nothing existed but the caressing of hands and mouths over their bodies. This was the last time they would ever make love, and their despair goaded their lust. They loved as though they wanted to sate their hunger once for all. Their desire rose into a searing impatience that tautened their muscles and swelled their loins until it could no longer be denied, and found release in a flowing climax that brought him toppling down on her, mouth to mouth, his spine still shuddering with soblike, dwindling spasms of pleasure.

At last he reeled onto his side of the bed and lay panting, his eyes closed, face turned to the ceiling.

Stealthily she scanned his face. Claude, darling Claude . . . Only three days ago they had been strangers, now she hated the thought of leaving him. How could a man come to mean so much in such a short time? Yes, he was handsome, but she had known handsome men before. He was gentle and gay, helpless and sensitive. So were hundreds of other men. Then why . . . why was he like no one else?

She knew. She had known since their first night together. He had given her such pleasure as she did not know existed, and because of that he was like no other man. Before him love-making had been something to be endured because men made much of it and paid well for it. She had laughed when she heard about girls losing their heads and ruining their lives over some man. She had called them fools. Now she knew better. She understood that a girl might grow to crave and need that kind of pleasure till she'd do anything for the man who gave it to her.

Thank God, she was no fool. These three days had been fun. It had been thrilling to be loved and caressed and to love and caress in return. But what did it get you? Nothing. It was nonsense and she had no time for nonsense. In her business you kept your eyes open or you wound up at the foot of a lamppost. Nothing like that was going to happen to her. She was on her way up and she intended to get to the top. And no man was going to stand in her way. No penniless musician was going to be the ruin of her.

♦

On the way back from the station Claude stopped at Bailly's book-shop, where he found a six-week-old letter from Prince Poniatowski, urging him to send his compositions to New York. Anton Seidl, the conductor of the Philharmonic Orchestra, was anxious to see them and might include some in his winter programs.

Claude read the letter with a sinking heart. It was too late. Once again he had lost a splendid opportunity. And, as usual, through his fault . . . He returned to his garret in a flagellant mood. Would he be a fool all his life, would he ever do anything right? . . . Coming so soon after Gaby's departure, this mishap sent him into the throes of discouragement. Finally he stirred himself and wrote a long apologetic letter to the prince.*

Then he went back to his quartet, and once again lost himself in music. Less than a week after Gaby had gone, he had completed his score and forgotten about America. Remembering Chausson's in-vitation, he packed up his bag and left for Luzancy.

As the country train puffed into the station he spied his host, baldheaded as ever and grinning in his reddish beard, waving at him from the platform.

"I'm afraid you're going to find the house rather crowded," said Ernest Chausson, as they walked to the tilbury waiting outside the station. "My wife adores the solitude of the country, but she loves it most when she can share it with ten or twelve people."

With a chuckle he climbed into the two-wheeled carriage, gathered the reins in one hand and with a flourish of the whip launched the

---

* In this letter—the longest he ever wrote—Debussy asked his friend to address all further correspondence to 42, rue de Londres. But, as he feared, the winter programs had been arranged and it was too late to include any of his music.

mare into a placid trot. For a while they jostled along a dusty road in easy companionship, exchanging an occasional remark, enjoying the peacefulness of this late-summer afternoon.

"Also, I must warn you that all our guests are married and you're going to find yourself the only bachelor among them," Chausson went on, as they neared the house. "As you know, married women look with suspicion upon bachelors and fear that their presence might arouse regrets in their husbands' hearts. So watch your step and try not to look too happy."

The house stood at the end of a long poplar-lined alley: a rambling two-story building stubbled with climbing roses and adorned with wooden balconies, scalloped eaves and a pigeon coop on the roof. It had an air of opulent and studied rusticity.

Madame Chausson saw them arrive, waved from the living-room window and went down to greet her guest.

"Now don't expect to be entertained," she told Claude, as she led him to his room. "Here everyone is supposed to provide his own fun. Just remember lunch is at one and dinner at eight. The rest of the time you may do whatever you like."

She had a pointed, yet kindly face with sparkling beady eyes. She spoke fast, as though she were in a hurry, and usually she was. Had she taken the trouble she could have been enticingly pretty, but life had given her everything she wanted and she had no more use for womanly weapons than a soldier for a bayonet after the battle has been won. Wife, mother, hostess, she was happy with her lot, content to take care of her husband, her children, her guests and the elaborate households in town and country, which she ran with formidable yet discreet efficiency.

"Let's go back," she went on, breezing out of the room. "I'm going to introduce you around, and after that you will be on your own."

During his week at Luzancy, Claude had little time to himself. He took part in the afternoon croquet games and the evening discussions on the terrace. He played with the guests' children, carried them on his back and had as much fun with them as they had with him. He also fed the goldfish in the pond, tossed rubber balls at dogs, played four-hand piano with Madame Chausson and spent pleasant moments with her brother, Henri Lerolle, who had set up his easel in the garden. One morning he went to the village and bought a fisherman's hat: a parasol-like piece of headgear made of woven straw with a crown like a truncated cone and an immense brim that flapped up and down when he walked. His sombrero had already been much remarked; his fisherman's hat created a sensation.

At dinner he was, as Chausson had predicted, the ladies' target for barbed hints on the shortcomings of bachelorhood and the advantages of married life. Take home cooking, for instance. Was there anything so delicious as a home-cooked meal? According to these ladies, the most precious cooking ingredient was love. The greatest chefs' delicacies could not compare to a stew prepared by one's own wife—with love. He agreed and truthfully declared he often had wished for a home-cooked stew.

"And what about illness?" another lady would ask across the table. "What if you ever get sick?"

Yes, what if he were stricken ill in the middle of the night? Alone, helpless and feverish, deprived of a wife's loving care, how would he manage? . . . He wouldn't, he admitted. He would die. Purely and simply. The thought often crossed his mind and filled him with dread. There seemed to be no other solution but for him to stay healthy . . . And what about loneliness? they would ask. Didn't he feel lonely sometimes, without the tender companionship of a wife? . . . He certainly did, he agreed. Especially at night. Sometimes he awoke with a start from sheer loneliness and was grateful for the presence of his cat at his side. The bachelor's lot was a wretched one, indeed.

"You've been a great success," said Chausson, when he drove him back to the station. "The ladies feel you've helped them in convincing their husbands of their good fortune to be married to them. Everyone hopes you'll be able to come back next summer. I am only sorry we didn't have a chance to be alone and talk about music. I wanted to tell you that at our last committee meeting there was much talk about performing your *Blessed Damozel* at our next symphonic concert in the spring. How do you feel about it?"

With more enthusiasm than he really felt Claude replied he would be delighted, of course, and grateful. "But how can you hope to present a work that requires not only a full orchestra, but a women's chorus and two solo singers?"

"We'll manage somehow. We'll have a good orchestra and an excellent chorus which Madame Pauline Roger has volunteered to coach. Of course you know who she is."

"I'm afraid I don't."

Madame Roger was the widow of an army officer, Chausson explained, and probably the finest singing teacher in Paris. Her pupils came from the highest society. She was enthusiastic about the score and had promised to secure Julia Robert and her own daughter Thérèse for the two solo parts.

"Both are concert singers and accomplished musicians, but your music is quite unusual and difficult and I'm afraid you will have to coach them yourself."

Claude hesitated. It would take a lot of work and time. And for what? One performance that would pass unnoticed and be forgotten the next day. Yet he could not refuse. Especially after the trouble Monsieur Chausson had taken, for obviously it was he who had arranged the whole thing. And since the committee was willing to forget and forgive the painful Fantasy episode, the least he could do was to co-operate and show his appreciation.

"I'll be glad to. When should I start?"

They had reached the station. Chausson reined in the mare and brought the cart to a stop.

"Sometime after New Year's, I would say. The concert is scheduled for April, and this should give you ample time. Don't you think?"

On the journey back to Paris, Claude tried to muster some enthusiasm over the prospect of the performance of *The Blessed Damozel.* He merely succeeded in stirring up his admiration and gratitude for his kindly host, who had gone out of his way to give him this opportunity. At last the train arrived and jolted to a stop with a great hiss of exhaustion. Valise in hand Claude started for home. It was early evening when he finally climbed the stairs to his garret.

The moment he opened the door Gaby's memory sprang at him with the suddenness of a leaping puma.

In the country he had been able to keep from thinking about her. Here she was everywhere. The scent of her perfume still hung in the air. He found one of her hairpins on the floor, and it brought back a swarm of memories.

Two days after his return the autumn rains began and the roof started leaking again. The blue-enamel basins went back to their appointed places. The sun vanished from the sky, and daylight became a gray mist that dribbled down from the window and left most of the room in shadows. One by one his three pupils returned to town and informed him of their arrival. His life resumed its pattern of lessons and visits to publishers. But no transcription or arrangement was to be had, and in October he was unable to pay anything on his rent. He had a painful encounter with the landlord, who muttered fresh threats of eviction.

He took them in his stride, went back to his diet of bread and tea, cut down on his smoking and waited for something to turn up. In the evening he went over the score of his quartet, made a few changes, then a few more—and finally started rewriting it. Things would not have been too bad, but for Gaby's persistent memory. He felt annoyed with himself for not forgetting her and tried to reason himself out of his melancholy. As days went by, his longing, instead of vanishing, increased. It seemed incredible that a little three-day affair could leave so much pain behind. He took refuge in work; usually it helped, but sometimes it didn't. When he looked at the bed, he would see her sprawled on it, nude and wanton, or cuddling against him, limp and disheveled, smiling her drowsy, contented smile. Then work would become impossible—and something had to be done.

He went in quest of women and found some, only to discover they did not help at all. She had been a sensual banquet to their meager table d'hôte. For it was of women as of restaurants: in most you merely ate, while in some you dined. In sex, as in everything else, you quickly got used to the best. He found that in three short days she had spoiled him for any girl who would come after her. Thus there was nothing to do but wait for his yearning to pass. It would in time, as it had for Alix and "Madame V" . . .

October dragged on in a drizzling wretchedness that sieved down from mud-colored skies. The everlasting search for work continued. Again there were good days when he brought home some small job with a twenty- or thirty-franc advance, and bad days when he returned bringing nothing but his tiredness, his dripping umbrella and spongy-soled shoes.

November arrived in a tantrum of northerly winds that sent the rain pelting against the roof and filled the room with icy drafts. The dripping from the roof became a rapid pizzicato. One afternoon, as he was sewing a button on his overcoat, he heard the rush of footsteps on the stairs.

The door opened.

Suddenly there she was, swathed in furs, running to him, her face flushed from the climb, her arms outstretched.

"Oh, darling!"

◆

He flung his coat aside and ran to her. They collided midway across the room and for a long time remained clasped in a silent, hungry embrace.

At last they disentangled and started talking at the same time.

"I . . . I can't believe it—"

"I didn't want to come back—"

"I almost didn't recognize you in your fur coat."

"You look terrible. Don't you eat anything."

"You'll never know how much I—"

"Me, too. I couldn't stand it any more."

They had too much to say and could not wait to say it. Later they would speak.

Now they clung to each other, motionless but for their avid, groping lips. Then, once more, they separated and tried to speak, but again they spoke at the same time, and their words mingled in a confusion of gasping, unfinished sentences. Talk could wait . . . Already he was pulling off her fur coat, tossing it on a chair, unfastening her blouse with fingers clumsy from cold and impatience.

"Here"—she laughed—"let me do it."

Without another word they undressed and slipped into bed. The coldness of the sheets choked the breath in their throats. Shuddering they pressed against each other to get warm.

"How can you live in this place?" she stammered through chattering teeth.

"Imagine it's summer and very hot," he said, pulling the sheet over their heads. "In a minute you'll be all right."

Gradually their shivers subsided. They felt warm and buoyant. Soon they were kissing again in a ravenousness of suckling mouths and darting tongues. But their desire was too pressing for caresses.

"Take me," she begged impatiently.

Although they loved in haste their pleasure was as great as in the September days. For a long time afterward they lay side by side, inert but smiling, floating on the cloud of their bliss.

The liquid plucking of raindrops in the basins made her open her eyes.

She peeped up at the roof. "Does it always rain like this in your room?"

"Not always, only when it rains. I like it, it keeps me company." Lazily he turned to her. "You're even prettier than you used to be."

"You should get the landlord to fix it," she went on, ignoring the compliment.

He broke into a soft chuckle. "I tried, but he said I should pay my rent before asking for repairs, and I couldn't think of an answer."

"You'll catch your death of cold in here."

"I've been here five years and I'm not dead yet."

"But you will be very soon, if you don't take care of yourself." Tenderly she scanned his face. "You look awful."

"That's what I like about you." He slipped an arm under her shoulders and drew her closer to him. "You always say the nicest things."

Instinctively they had fallen back into the gentle teasing and bantering mood of September, as though they had never separated. They were drowsy with the joy of being together again, in each other's arms, and had forgotten the things they wanted so much to say a moment ago.

"You look like you haven't eaten for a week."

"That's not true. I ate yesterday."

For an instant she studied him with a frown of dismay. "You're really awfully poor, aren't you, darling?" she murmured. "Even worse than I thought."

"I wouldn't say that," he protested cheerfully. "You just happened to drop in when things are a bit tight, that's all. But usually I'm quite comfortable."

"You're a liar."

"Now look here." With a great show of indignation he raised himself on his elbow and looked down on her. "You haven't even been here half an hour and already you're insulting me, calling me a liar. You, of all people! You who invented the eleven-twenty train, and the nine-thirty and God knows what else! Just for that I'm going to kiss you."

He bent down and kissed her. They smiled into each other's eyes, their faces almost touching.

"Oh, darling," he murmured, "you'll never know how much I missed you."

"Me, too. I didn't want to come back. Remember how I said we should never see each other again. I meant it, and I fought as long as I could. But I kept thinking of our three days together and I wondered if you were sick and needed anything. And also—" She stopped.

Gently he prompted, "Also—what?"

She hesitated, then rushed on, "I wanted to see if it really was as wonderful as I remembered it. Our loving, I mean . . . I thought perhaps I was imagining it was nicer than it really was. You know, how sometimes you think about a party or a trip and you say it was wonderful, but it wasn't wonderful at all . . . So I thought that if I came back to see you and we made love again, it wouldn't be the same as it was in September and it'd be easier to forget."

"And now?"

The question hung in the air for a few seconds and in that time the expression of her face changed. Her eyes turned hard and glittering, her mouth twisted in sudden fury.

"Now I know I should've stayed away. I was a fool to come back. I knew it would be like it was, but I wanted an excuse to see you again. Damn you, why don't you leave me alone! Why don't you get out of my life!"

He stared at her, spellbound, as if she had gone mad. She was spitting the words at him as she had done at the bistro, finding some sort of frelief in the shrillness of her voice, her gush of profanity and incoherence.

He opened his mouth to speak, but she did not give him the chance.

"Yes, what's so special about you? What's so wonderful? You're nothing but a down-and-out music writer that can't even sell his music and earn enough money to eat. You've got nothing, you'll never have anything, never amount to anything, then why, goddamn it, why can't I get you out of my mind?" Her voice rose into a heart-broken wail. "Oh, God, why did I come back, why did I—"

"You didn't have to, if that's the way you feel."

"You're damn right, I don't have to." She sprang out of bed and hurriedly began to dress. "And that's just what I'm going to do. I'm no fool. I know trouble when I see it, and to me that's what you are—trouble. It's not your fault, but to me you're poison. Yes, poison! ... I won't let you ruin my life. If you think you've got me with those soft black eyes of yours, you're very much mistaken."

She laughed uproariously and finished dressing, oblivious of his presence, talking to herself in a scowling mutter. He was too angry and hurt to argue with her and watched her from the bed, leaning side-wise on his elbow.

At last she walked to the washstand and peered into the broken mirror, trying to adjust her small fur toque.

"Goddamn it," she raged under her breath, "there isn't even a decent mirror in this place."

He laughed. "What can you expect from a down-and-out music writer?"

She gave herself a last look and turned around. "Well, at least I know now what I wanted to know."

"And what's that?"

"That I'll never . . . never see you again."

"Suit yourself." He shrugged. "Incidentally, you don't make any sense, you know."

"Maybe to you I don't," she flared back, "but I make sense to myself and that's all I care about." She gave him a long look, then briskly went on, "Well, I guess I'm ready now. Good-bye."

"Good-bye."

He heard the slam of the door, her racing footsteps down the stairs. Then all was quiet. Quiet and gray, like the wintry twilight outside.

♦

Once again Claude decided women were exasperating. One moment they loved you, couldn't live without you; the next they loathed you. You were nice, did your best, made love to them, gave them pleasure and for a moment you floated in Heaven together. Then, five minutes later, just when you were resting, they decided they hated you and you were poison to them and they never wanted to see you again. He had had enough of it.

It did not stop him from thinking about Gaby, but it gave him some feeble satisfaction to think how bad she was. Self-pity is the cousin of self-esteem, and it was better to recriminate than to regret.

Then, three days after her visit, as he was returning to his garret, tired and disgruntled after another unsuccessful round of publishers, he found her sitting on the stairs in the flickering glow of a gas jet.

"What on earth are you doing here?"

"Waiting for you."

"How long have you been sitting like this?" While talking he opened his door.

"About an hour."

He stepped aside to let her in. Neither of them spoke while he lit the lamp. She sat down by the side of his table, lifted her hat veil, pulled off her gloves and folded them on her lap.

"Well," he sighed, taking his place at his desk, "what do you want to see me about?"

"To tell you I'm sorry for the things I said the other day."

"So you've decided I'm not poison to you any more?"

"I'm sorry, darling. I was angry. Not at you but at myself. I didn't know what I was saying."

"For someone who didn't know what she was saying, you certainly had a lot to say." He let out a small, cruel chuckle. "Quite a speech."

"Please don't be mean." Her voice was humble, her eyes moist and pleading. "I'm sorry. Please forgive me."

"All right, you're forgiven," he said coldly. "You really didn't have to wait an hour on the stairs just to tell me that. A note would've done just as well."

"I—I wanted to see you."

She looked so repentant and so desirable that he fought back an impulse to take her in his arms. He held himself in check. She must be taught that she could not insult him, bang the door, then trot back with some sort of an apology and expect him to forget everything. A man had his pride.

"Well"—he clapped his hands to intimate that the interview was at an end—"you've seen me and you've been forgiven, now you can go back with your mind at rest."

"You mean you aren't mad at me any more?"

"No. I am not mad at you any more."

"Everything's all right again?"

He did not quite know what she meant, but he nodded. "Yes. Everything is all right. Now if you'll excuse—"

He was about to rise, but already she was sitting on his knees, her arms around his neck.

"Oh, darling, you're so good, so kind, so wonderful," she said while covering his face with kisses. "And I thank you for forgiving me and not being mad at me any more and saying everything's all right."

She had said these things before, but now their impact was infinitely greater. The very weight of her proclaimed her gratitude. Her perfume stressed her sincerity and blurred his thoughts. He tried to retain his dignity, but it is difficult to be dignified with someone on your lap. When he urged, then ordered her back to her chair she kissed half the words off his lips so that his command was unintelligible and remained unobeyed.

She was a demonstrative, nervous girl and her joy at being forgiven seemed to have given her two pairs of hands and three mouths—two to kiss with, one to talk. Somehow one of her hands had made its way inside his shirt and was slithering down his chest, somewhere around his waist. And all the time she went on kissing him and talking. But now she no longer talked of her gratitude, but of her appreciation. Even in his confused state of mind he gathered that she thought him a superb lover, loved everything he did to her, and that there was nothing that he did that she did not like. While she talked her green eyes swiveled in the direction of the bed like a cat's toward a saucerful of cream.

"And, darling, I've been thinking and I have something to tell you—"

By now he no longer cared whether or not she had anything to say. He was responding to her kisses. His hands wandered and probed wherever they pleased. Soon things began to whirl in his head and he lost all clear notion of what he was doing.

Later he dimly remembered swooping her up in his arms, dumping her on the bed, tossing off her garments onto the floor, groping at hooks and corset laces; then nothing but the tautness of her, the rush of his desire and finally his flowing into her, like a wound bleeding into warm water. And then the lucent blankness, the floating peace, the slow return to reality, the amused surprise at finding themselves together in bed again, their faces close, almost touching on the same pillow.

"We always seem to wind up in bed, don't we?" she whispered with a little sheepish smile.

"Looks like it." Drowsily he grinned back. "Now I suppose you're going to say I am the bane of your existence and you never want to see me again and stomp out of the room. If you do, please, darling, this time don't slam the door."

"Don't worry. I won't." She cuddled to him, gently wedged her knee between his thighs. "And I've got something to tell you. I've been thinking—"

"About what?" he muttered, half asleep.

"What you said in September, remember? About our seeing each other from time to time—"

"—and you said it would be wrong and you had your career to think about and couldn't possibly waste your time on a man like me. Yes, I remember. I was a little bit hurt at the time, but I had to admit you were right."

"I wasn't," she said hotly. "I was stupid. There's no reason why I can't go on with my career and see you once in a while. Not a reason in the world."

"I'm glad to hear that. But, knowing you, you'll probably change your mind again tomorrow."

Instantly her lips were upon his. She couldn't change her mind, she had thought the whole thing over and it was no problem. No problem at all. The trick was to be sharp and not get caught.

"And I'm not going to get caught."

"How about your gentleman friend? Will you be able to get away?"

She shrugged. He was no problem. In the past he had watched her, but now he almost never asked her where she went or what she did. She wouldn't have any trouble sneaking away once in a while.

"And don't worry, I'll be careful," she went on. "I won't come often. Only once a month. It's not much, but it's better than nothing, isn't it?"

"Definitely." A last doubt crossed his mind. "You're sure you won't change your mind again?"

"Never. I swear."

He kissed the tip of her short straight nose. "All right. I believe you."

It sounded simple and reasonable—and very nice. It would be wonderful looking forward to her monthly visit, counting the days, having a pleasant little affair with such a beautiful girl . . .

"But an affair, do you hear?" he said, wagging a finger in her face. "Not a Greek tragedy. No more nonsense about my being poison to you and that sort of thing. Let's try being sensible for a change."

Yes, yes . . . She would be sensible, never give him another moment of trouble. And she was sorry for the things she had said, but from now on, everything was going to be different. They would laugh and make love and have fun.

"You'll see, we'll be the two happiest people in the world." She pressed herself against him. "Oh, darling, I love you so!"

◆

During the days that followed, Claude felt pleased that his relationship with Gaby had finally settled on a basis of common sense. He only regretted that she had taken so long to come to his way of thinking and adopt the plan he had advocated in September. But she was a high-strung, impetuous girl and she had to have things her own way before she would admit her mistakes. Now everything was fine. A monthly visit wasn't much, but it certainly was better than no visit at all.

He began to feel happier. Even the December cold, the discomforts of his garret failed to dampen his spirits. His former despondency gave way to a cautious optimism. He went over his second draft of the quartet and was almost satisfied with it. This cheered him up. The forthcoming performance of *The Blessed Damozel* in April, which he had regarded until now as something of a chore, now appeared as a God-sent opportunity. People might like it. Monsieur Guiraud had often said it was an unusual and beautiful piece of music. It might create a sensation. Perhaps one of the great Paris conductors, Monsieur Colonne or Monsieur Lamoureux, might take a fancy to it and wish to perform it. If so, London would certainly follow. Then Berlin, Amsterdam, Leipzig, Vienna . . . Those great foreign orchestras were always on the alert for interesting novelties. Why, even New York might want it for their next winter season . . . Things were going to improve; he could feel it in his bones.

And sure enough they did.

He acquired a new piano pupil—a freckled, pigtailed girl who instantly fell in love with him—and thus increased his income by twenty francs a month. Then he wrestled an important transcription from Monsieur Fromont, together with a sizable advance. Finally his friend Jacques Durand dropped in to see him, took the manuscript of the quartet to his father and returned three days later with the news that the Maison Durand was ready to publish the work. More wonderful still, they would pay him two hundred and fifty francs for the privilege of doing so.

All these sums of money falling on him at the same time hit him with the impact of brandy on an empty stomach. At once several exciting projects came to his mind. He would have the roof repaired at his own expense and shame the landlord for his miserliness. It then occurred to him he might also shame him into raising the rent. Better let the roof leak . . . He toyed with the idea of redecorating his room. A complete overhaul. Calking all cracks, plastering the pine-board wall. New paint, new curtains, new stove—new everything. On her next visit Gaby would be stunned, but she also would find the room full of unromantic bags of cement and pots of paint. Better leave the room as it was . . .

Suddenly it struck him that Gaby's next visit would coincide with Christmas. What if she brought him some little present and he had nothing in return? He recalled the ivory figurine and the thirty francs he had paid on account. Where was the damn receipt? Frantically he searched his room, but could not find it. He went to the antique shop on rue des Saints-Pères, explained his predicament to the merchant, who could not remember either the figurine or the account. Words passed between them. Claude called him a crook, and the merchant threatened to call the gendarmes. By chance, Claude spied his statuette on a shelf, half hidden behind a pewter mug, grabbed it and shook it in the face of the dealer, who now remembered everything. It all ended amicably. Claude paid the balance—ninety francs —and got his figurine.

As Christmas approached he started counting the days before Gaby's visit. In case she came unexpectedly, a few days before the month was over, he paid his traditional visit to his parents earlier than usual. He dreaded these reunions that revived painful memories for all of them. Manuel Debussy was still emptying paper baskets and stamping envelopes at the Compagnie Fives-Lille. He had grown stouter, his complexion wine-red. Victorine looked much as she always had, only a little grayer of hair. The children had gone away and left Paris. Only their eldest, Claude, had remained in town. He had proven the greatest disappointment of all. After the flurry of expectations from winning the Grand Prix, he had sunk into a penniless, bohemian obscurity from which it seemed unlikely he would ever emerge.

He read their rancor on their faces. He could have made them rich and he had failed them.

"We're getting old, me and your mother," his father said after a silence. "At our age most parents can rest, but we'll have to go on working till they cart us to the cemetery."

"I'm sorry, I wish I could help."

"We wouldn't need anything if you'd become a pianist, like I wanted you to."

For an instant the memory of the "Mozart dream" hung in the room. Claude looked at his parents. They would never forgive, never forget . . . Quickly he rose, slipped some money into his mother's hand and with a hasty *"Bon Noël"* hurried away.

Christmas came and Gaby did not show up. She did not send a note of excuse, not even a greeting card. He stayed home, pacing the floor or gazing at the ivory statuette on the table, holding his breath whenever he heard footsteps on the stairs. It was one of those lugubrious winter days which, like hopeless cripples, should never have been born. By three o'clock in the afternoon, night arrived and the gray slab of the sky began to crack in a dust of snow. He went to a café, did his best to get drunk and succeeded only in getting a migraine.

His disappointment spoiled the Christmas holidays for him. On New Year's Eve he went to the Moulin Rouge in search of noise and gaiety. The place was a bedlam, the noise deafening. He sat down at a table, blew a paper trumpet and felt worse than ever. Even the cancan failed to arouse his lust. For a while he exchanged serpentines with a young and heavily made-up woman with a plumed hat and around her neck a fur piece that looked like the tail of a Shetland pony. When she winked at him to come and sit down at her table, he got up and pushed his way out of the dance hall.

The night was clear and cold, with a sliver of moon. He took a deep breath and started down the Montmarte hill. The garret was pleasantly restful after the Moulin Rouge fracas. He lit the nightstand lamp and went to bed. Now and then the muted blare of a horn rose from the street, then silence closed in again. Sleep would not come, and he stared at the ceiling, his hands crossed under his head, Linne coiled at his side, and thought about Gaby.

Where was she now? Probably in some *restaurant de nuit* laughing and drinking champagne. Why not? That was her business, wasn't it? Part of her "career," for which she had come to Paris and which meant more to her than anything or anyone else. And justly so . . . At first he had been angry with her, but he no longer was. She had been right from the start; she had no business wasting time on a music writer like him. He saw that. Even the monthly visit, which had seemed so reasonable, now looked foolish, possibly dangerous. He understood all this. What he did not understand was that she had not written him, paid him the courtesy of a few lines, a farewell note. After all they had been lovers. He would have thought he deserved that much, but obviously she did not think so.

Now sleep was stealing over him, closing his lids. A few last thoughts drifted through his mind as it slurred to a halt. Another year had gone . . . another year very much like the ones before, except that now he was thirty and Monsieur Guiraud was dead and Gaby had come into his life.

And out of it . . . and it was better that way. It really was. She was a very beautiful girl and could be very nice, but too emotional and complicated. She changed her mind too often. Besides, they lived in different worlds and had nothing in common, except that they made love well together . . . It wasn't enough for the trouble she brought, the pain she left. They really were better off apart . . .

He reached out for the lamp, turned down the wick and fell asleep.

◆

The year began with a snowstorm and the explosion of a political scandal.

The affairs of the Compagnie du Canal de Panama were brought out in the open and filled the air with the stench of a bursting sewer. It was shown that a score of *députés* and senators and even the

Minister of Public Works had pocketed millions while hundreds of thousands of investors had been brought to ruin. With stupor Frenchmen discovered that their *belle République* was chock full of crooks. Newspapers broke into a delirium of polemics and sold daily extras. Everybody accused everybody else. Gleefully the royalist press pointed out that every one of these corrupt *députés* and senators had been freely and democratically elected. This, they said, was another evidence of the People's infallible wisdom: the "Majestic, Sovereign People," as it was called at election time, which was none other than the same poor brainless mob who, through the ages, had been at the mercy of any smooth-talking rogue, changed its mind like a weathervane with each puff of wind, waved palms at Christ on Sunday, crucified Him on Friday, and was incapable of thought, let alone of self-government.

Amidst the general turmoil Claude's existence went on, obscure and prosaic as ever.

He had about given up hope of ever seeing Gaby again, when early in January she rushed in one afternoon, breathless and gleaming-eyed, a powder of snow on her shoulders and the brim of her hat.

"Oh, darling, please forgive me, but I just couldn't come sooner. A thousand times I tried to sneak away, but something always happened."

She did not give him a chance to speak and between kisses explained that her life had been a whirlwind. The Christmas holidays had left her without a minute to herself. It had been an unbroken merry-go-round of parties, theatres and late champagne suppers.

"I just couldn't get away. You understand, don't you?"

He nodded ruefully, and she went on. "After all, I have my career to think about and I must go out a lot. But everywhere I went I thought about you and wished you were with me."

She nestled against him. "And you, darling, what did you do?"

He told her about his going to Moulin Rouge on New Year's Eve, and at once she was on the alert.

"Did you have a good time?"

"No."

"Did you find a girl there?"

"I wasn't looking for one. I just didn't want to be by myself, but the place was so noisy I only stayed a moment."

"Where did you go after that?"

"Nowhere. I came home."

She gave him a tender, approving smile. He sensed that she would have been hurt if he had spent the night with a woman. The fact that she herself had spent the night with her gentleman friend had no sig-

nificance in her eyes. With her it was business; with him it might
have been pleasure . . .

"I don't want you to make love to any girl but me," she said.

"In that case you'd better come here from time to time. I'm not
made of cast iron, you know."

"I will, I promise." Kittenishly she nudged closer to him. "Things
will be a little easier from now on and I'll be able to sneak away more
often."

They were still lingering in bed when she remembered her Christmas present. She ran to the table where she had left her purse and
returned with a small jewelry box.

"Open it," she smiled.

It was a pair of gold cuff links made especially to her order. One
face was cut in the shape of a grand piano with its lid open; the other
resembled a minuscule page of music with neatly etched staves and
notes and the title *Clair de Lune*.

He gazed at them, then smiled at her in silent gratitude.

"They're beautiful," he finally managed to say.

"Look at the back," she cried, enjoying the expression of pleasure
on his face.

He pulled out a cuff link, turned it between his fingers. There it
was, engraved into the heavy clump of gold: "September, 1892."

"You see, I really did plan to come at Christmas."

For a while they reminisced about their September affair and how
happy they had been during those three days. They smiled, kissed
and grew very sentimental.

"I, too, have something for you," he said.

It was his turn to jump from the bed, rush to the table and return
with his gift. She held the small ivory figurine in her hand and declared it was the most beautiful thing she had ever seen. But her tone
belied her words and he felt she wanted to scold him for spending
money on such a useless thing.

"I'm afraid I can't keep it with me," she explained. "My gentleman friend might see it and ask questions. Won't you keep it for me?
In this way you'll be able to enjoy it and I'll look at it each time I
come here."

They made love again; then quickly she dressed. Together they
went out on the landing and kissed once more.

"Now I must be going," she said, lowering her hat veil.

He watched her start down the stairs. When she reached the lower
floor she looked up, gave him a little wave.

"I'll be back soon," she cried, and disappeared.

Gaby's visit brought him back his optimism. Again he felt that things were going to improve. Even the beastly weather failed to dampen his spirit.

He began coaching the two young ladies who were to sing the solo parts in *The Blessed Damozel*. Julia Robert, he found to be a vivacious brunette and a superb musical technician who could master the most arduous passages of his score without much effort. Thérèse Roger, in turn, possessed a finer voice and greater sensitiveness, but was much slower at learning. He soon realized the futility of coaching them together. It was agreed that he would come to Julia's house twice a month, and to Thérèse's twice a week.

At first he felt some reluctance about the coaching sessions with Thérèse. Like most composers he was an impatient teacher, especially of his own work. Soon, however, he found himself enjoying the hours he spent with her. Her application made up for her lack of brilliance. He was touched by her good will, her eagerness to please him. Most of all, by her understanding and admiration of his music.

"I hope I'll do it justice," she remarked one day. "I want people to realize what a great artist you are."

He, in turn, liked the frankness of her gaze, the slenderness of her waist, her refinement, her intelligence. Everything about her was dainty and pastel-hued: her blue eyes, her pink lips, her blondness. Although they called each other Monsieur and Mademoiselle there was between them the comradeship of people engaged in a common task. They were young and laughter came easily to them. They enjoyed being together. Thus their friendship was born.

He did not speak to Gaby about her, for there really was nothing to say and he doubted whether Gaby would understand his friendship with another woman. It was simpler to keep silent. Anyway, Gaby was in a state of jubilation these days and whenever they were together she had so much to say that he barely could slip in a word edgewise.

He had told her the hours of his lessons and the afternoons when he stayed home, and she fitted her visits into the pattern of his life. She came whenever she could, without schedule or notice. Sometimes for only a few moments, just long enough for a love-snack and a hasty good-bye; sometimes for the greatest part of the afternoon. Then she would bring pastries and they would have tea and she would chat away while munching chocolate éclairs. And they still would have time to make love leisurely, as it should be made.

Never had she been so happy. Excitement had come into her life. She was engaged in a thrilling and dangerous game: the simultaneous pursuit of her career and her love. She knew it was usually fatal, but she welcomed the risks and accepted the odds. Other girls had tried to "play double" and wound up at the foot of a lamppost, but not she.

"I told you I wouldn't be caught, and I won't. And d'you know why? Because I'm sharp and I use my head."

These other girls hadn't used their heads. They had been stupid; they had moped over their champagne and brooded, like cows, when they should have been dancing and laughing. Another thing. They had talked too much. In no time a dozen friends knew about their *petit homme,* how wonderful he was and how he had a way of doing it that was just delicious. And sure enough, pretty soon, the gentlemen friends learned about him—and that was the beginning of the end.

"But I watch my step. I laugh and I dance and tell jokes, and nobody would ever suspect I'm thinking about you. Only the other day my gentleman friend told me it was a pleasure to be with a woman that was so gay."

Her eyes sparkled with triumph. She savored the fruits of her deceit and wallowed in her own cleverness. With the glee of a truant schoolgirl she told Claude of the ruses she employed to sneak away and come to see him.

"Isn't he getting a little suspicious?" he asked one day.

"Why should he? I told you he trusts me."

"Yes, but there're limits to a man's blindness. Doesn't he find it strange that you should disappear like this for several hours? Haven't you run out of excuses yet?"

She laughed. Excuses! . . . Why, she had enough excuses to last her ten years! There was the hairdresser, the modiste, the dressmaker; the pair of gloves she needed for that evening and which she had forgotten to buy; the visit she had promised to her ailing friend Léonie . . .

"She's my only girl friend. We've known each other a long time. She's older than me and she's got a good head on her shoulders. I always come to her when I need some advice."

Léonie had modest origins—her father was a butcher—but she was sharp and she had made a success of herself. She owned a house on avenue Malakoff; she had her own carriage, servants, jewels—everything. Her current gentleman friend was an "Angleesh milor," and you couldn't ask for anyone better than that, could you? Yet she had remained simple. Not stuck-up like most successful demimondaines. She was a good sort and you could trust her.

"She's the only one I told about you."

"And what does she say?"

"She thinks I'm a damn fool." Her eyes danced with laughter.

"But she sees how happy I am and she just tells me to watch out and be careful. And don't worry, I am."

Slowly winter was wearing on. After a freezing spell in February, the weather turned unseasonably mild. Some cafés unrolled their terrace awnings, and Frenchmen could now discuss the scandal of the Panama Company while sipping their *apéritifs* on the sidewalks. At La Nationale, the rehearsals of *The Blessed Damozel* began. From the start they proved a strain on everyone's nerves, especially Claude's. The musicians declared the score unplayable; the singers, unsingable. He had to intervene, explain, coax, soothe ruffled tempers and bruised egos.

"Sometimes I feel like telling them all to go to the devil," he told Gaby one day.

She comforted him with kisses and caresses, pleaded with him to be patient. Surely the performance of this composition would make him famous . . .

"You'll see, darling, everything will turn out all right."

He smiled, knowing that she had not the faintest idea of what she was talking about, but touched by her loyalty. It was enough that she came to his dingy studio, brought him her sumptuous body, the diversion of her chatter. As he listened to her he forgot the annoyance of rehearsals, the dreariness of lessons. Through her, he had glimpses of a glittering night world of crystal candelabra, soft music, champagne and whirling skirts.

"Guess what?" she would say excitedly. "The other night at the Café Anglais I saw Max Lebeaudy!"

Everybody in Paris knew about Max Lebeaudy, probably the richest man in France, his racing stable, his thousand-franc tips.

"I hoped he would look at me, but he was so busy eating his salad of violets that he didn't take his eyes from his plate."

Other gentlemen, however, did look at her, and their glances did not go unnoticed, for the time had come for her to make her next move up the ladder. An operation which, she explained to Claude, called for prudence, discretion and skill.

A young millionaire by the name of Gontran seemed to have the edge over his rivals. He combined great wealth with an ancient title and was known to be generous, even lavish on occasion. At the death of his aunt, an elderly, feeble countess, he would be still richer—and presumably still more generous. The fact that he was stupid, conceited and extremely unattractive did not enter into such serious and businesslike considerations. After all, no one was perfect.

"I saw him again at Larue's the other day, and he couldn't keep his eyes off me . . . I'll go and ask Léonie's advice. She knows him well, she'll tell me what to do."

The only shadow in the picture was that her gentleman friend had fallen in love with her. Oh, he hadn't come out and said so, because he was a quiet, rather reserved sort of a man. But she could see it in his eyes. He had changed in many little ways. For instance, he had developed a distaste for night life. All he wanted now was to spend the evening at home with her. Why, if she was going to stay home at night she might as well marry and be done with it . . . It was like moving a mountain to get him to put on evening clothes and take her out to dinner, then to the Folies Bergère or some other music hall and afterward to supper.

"He's selfish, plain selfish," she remarked with some asperity in her voice. "After all, how am I going to do my next move if I stay cooped up at home all the time?"

She looked at Claude with eyes full of injured innocence.

"Besides, at his age he should know that a gentleman friend isn't supposed to fall in love with the girl he keeps," she went on. "Mind you, he's a nice man and he's given me a lot of things and I'm grateful and I feel sorry for him and all that, but it isn't my fault, is it, if he falls in love with me? Just because someone loves you doesn't mean you can love him back, does it?"

She paused, gave him a slow, wistful smile. "Anyway, how could I love him, when I already love you?"

◆

By mid-March the rehearsals of *The Blessed Damozel* began to improve. Gradually his score was coming to life. Somehow the unplayable was played and the unsingable sung. Under the tireless coaching of Thérèse's mother, the women's chorus coalesced into a vocal ensemble. Best of all was Thérèse herself. Not only did she sing her part faultlessly, but in time of crisis she remained smiling and placid. Now and then her eyes met Claude's and he read encouragement in them. It was good having her near. She reminded him of those Swiss lakes that are calm and deep and ice-blue.

At last on the evening of Saturday, April 7, 1893, the annual symphonic concert of La Nationale took place. Many of the lady singers had brought friends and relatives and the Salle Pleyel was nearly filled. Several critics had troubled to come. Even the terrible Monsieur Willy was there, his flat-brimmed top hat perched over his bald pate, his enormous mustache twirled like a ram's horns over his rosebud mouth.*

* Willy (Henri Gauthier-Villars) was for many years an influential music critic. Not only did he know nothing about music, but he never wrote the reviews he signed. About Claude's famous Baudelaire songs he expressed this memorable opinion, probably the all-time low in music criticism: "Monsieur Debussy had thrown the *manure* of his music over Baudelaire's 'Flowers of

The Blessed Damozel came last on the program and was performed without incident. It was received with polite applause spiked with a little hissing. Nobody cared much about it one way or another. Monsieur Willy was magnanimous. He informed his readers that it was "a somewhat perverse symphonic stained-glass window by Fra Angelico-Debussy" and let it go at that. Others described it as a pagan oratorio. Again they remarked that Monsieur Debussy's music was sensual, decadent, perverse and terribly . . . terribly *moderne*. Now, of course, it was all right to be *moderne*, but Monsieur Debussy was too much so. He would do well to curb those modern tendencies of his in the future.

A few people were deeply moved, but they did not write in newspapers and their opinions went unnoticed. Vincent d'Indy, the president of La Nationale, congratulated Claude, and so did the members of the committee. Ernest Chausson went further: he secretly financed Père Bailly to publish a piano-and-voice reduction of the work. Claude was touched by his friend's generosity; but neither compliments nor publication could disguise the fact that *The Blessed Damozel* had been a failure.

"The public isn't ready for your music," said Thérèse, when he called to thank her and her mother for their help. "But don't be discouraged, some day people will understand."

He smiled wryly. "Yes, some day—when I'm dead and buried."

For the next few days he slipped back into a state of discouragement, but then something occurred that took his mind off *The Blessed Damozel*.

Catulle Mendès paid him a visit.

"How would you like to play the piano at the Opéra?" he cried from the door.

He had grown fatter and more untidy since Claude had seen him last. Dandruff lay thick on his shoulders, crumbs clung to his Biblical beard and spots constellated his vest. But his ebullience and capacity for work had not diminished. He still could dash off an article on the corner of a café table between sips of absinthe and snatches of conversation. As always he was engaged in ten different projects, rushing from one appointment to another, manuscripts jutting out of his pockets, his pudgy hands fluttering in perpetual motion.

"Yes, at the Opéra!" he repeated.

Like many stout men he was surprisingly nimble on his feet and he hurried toward Claude's table in a bouncing tiptoe, with the grace of an aging and overweight ballerina.

Evil.' " He even appropriated and published under his name the first books written by his wife, who, ironically, happened to be France's greatest woman writer, Colette.

"Think of the publicity," he said, slumping on a chair.

Still panting he began to mop his face with a large and none-too-clean handkerchief. Then he launched into the subject of his visit.

In a few weeks *Die Walküre* was to be presented at the Paris Opéra. To mark this memorable event he had been commissioned to deliver a lecture on the sublimities of Wagner's music and the profundities of his philosophy. It was to be given on the eve of the performance, and by special dispensation, in the hall of the Opéra.

"To enliven my talk, I'm planning to have a two-piano medley of Wagner's operas," he went on. "Raoul Pugno, the famous pianist, has already consented to sit at one of the keyboards, and I'd like you to sit at the other."

"Me? But I'm no pianist."

Catulle clucked his tongue disapprovingly and made a few deprecatory gestures.

"Now there's no need being modest. Everybody knows you are a splendid Wagnerian pianist."

Claude protested that he was very busy, that he had lost much of his former enthusiasm for Wagner's music and, finally, that he did not even own a formal suit of clothes.

Mendès swept these objections aside.

"Whether or not you personally like Wagner's music is of no importance. A pastry chef doesn't have to eat his own cakes, does he?"

As for the evening clothes the matter could be settled at once. The management of the Opéra had shown itself to be liberal. There was to be a fee, a sizable one.

"Here," he said, slamming a hundred-franc note on the desk. "Go and buy the proper clothes."

He then informed Claude that the lecture was scheduled for the middle of the next month. This done he gave him a beaming flash of yellow tobacco-stained teeth and with a hurried little wave bounced out of the room.

Mendès' visit and the prospect of playing at the Opéra sent Claude's mind into reminiscences of his student days and that particular evening when he had been thrown out of the building by two muscular gendarmes. It all seemed far back in the past and made him feel seedy and middle-aged.

The following day he began rehearsing with Raoul Pugno and together they arranged a colorful medley of Wagner's operas. He also ordered a *habit de soirée* from a tailor on rue Vivienna. His name was Victor Hugo.

"Yes, Monsieur, like the poet," he said, grinning modestly. "We're probably distant relatives."

As his shop was located in the financial district, the conversation veered to the Panama scandal, and while taking his measurement Monsieur Victor Hugo informed him with discreet pride that several of the bankers arrested for graft were customers of his.

"And you know why people trusted those crooks?" he asked while stretching his tape measure across Claude's back. "Because they dressed well. Nothing like a good suit to inspire confidence, any thief will tell you that. Yes, Monsieur, if you want to be successful, you first must look successful."

To Claude this seemed logic itself. And so, in addition to his *habit de soirée* and evening cape, he ordered an expensive business suit. Then it occurred to him that if one suit could make him successful, two would do twice as much, and he ordered another one. Monsieur Hugo congratulated him on his foresight.

"Believe me, Monsieur, you're making an investment."

A moment later he also let him know that his investment would amount to slightly over three hundred francs. Claude gulped but said that it sounded "quite reasonable" and would a hundred do on account. It certainly would, cried the tailor, snatching Mendès banknote. He then reminded Claude that gentlemen's tailoring was a gentleman's business conducted mostly on trust. Claude said he liked his business methods.

"From now on," he declared as he was leaving the store, "you can count on my patronage."

He looked successful indeed in his satin-lapeled tail coat on the night of the Mendès lecture. With Raoul Pugno he came out onto the stage, bowed to the audience and walked to the two pianos, standing with their lids open like some gigantic butterfly in the beam of the spotlight. Together they flipped back their coat tails, sat down at their respective keyboards and tore into the Ride of the Walkyries. The public loved it. The evening was a great success.

Four days later he again was wearing his handsome evening clothes. This time he was attending the première of a much-heralded play, *Pélléas et Mélisande.*

The author, a young Belgian by the name of Maurice Maeterlinck, had been hailed a few years before as a dramatic genius by an influential Paris critic. Since then a sophisticated public had found rare and cryptic beauties in his very long and very boring plays.

That evening the curtain rose in an atmosphere of great excitement; but even snobbism has its limits, and an hour later people were beginning to steal away from the theatre singly or in groups. By the middle of the second act the play was gasping its last. Rigor mortis set in at once. The performance turned into a wake, the flight of spectators swelled into an exodus. By the end of the fifth act the actors were half asleep on their feet, staggering about the stage in a daze, mumbling their lines for an audience consisting of a few elderly gentlemen asleep in their seats, dozing lady ushers, and upstairs, in the balcony, alone, breathless and wide awake—Claude.*

He left the theatre like a man in a trance and for hours walked through dark and empty streets. It seemed that all his life he had been waiting for this moment. He heard chimes in the air and the night breeze trailed soft fingers on his face. He felt the strange and silent exultation which poets describe as love. And indeed he had fallen in love—with a play. And what a play! Probably the worst ever written . . .

It had no action, no suspense, no dramatic structure—nothing. The plot, if you could call it that, was the triangle, this hoariest, tritest of all plots. A young woman, lost, afraid, battered by life, married a kindly middle-aged man she did not love; later she met his younger brother and fell desperately in love with him. It all ended badly, as such things usually did. The husband discovered the romance and in a fit of jealousy killed his brother, only to discover that his deed solved nothing. His wife did not love him any better than before, and she died, leaving him shattered with guilt and broken-hearted.

As a play *Pélléas* was about everything a play should not be. In fact, it was no play at all but an admirable prose poem in which unreal people expressed real emotions. But music, not words, was the true language of emotions, and that was why *Pélléas* was a lifeless work. It should be sung instead of spoken. It was an opera; not a play. It was waiting for music to bring it to life.

Dawn found Claude sitting in his evening clothes on a park bench. Above, the sky was pink. In the trees, birds were babbling from branch to branch, like housewives across the street. For a while he watched a *jardinier municipal* water a flower bed, and it reminded him of Verdi in his salad patch.

With a smile he got up and went home.

That afternoon he went to Bailly's and bought a copy of the play, which had been published the year before. During the next three days he remained plunged in work, shortened a few scenes, deleted others and slowly built up the draft of a working libretto. By the time he was through he was sure that this was the work he wanted to set to music.

Without hesitation he went to see Henri de Régnier, who, he had learned, was Maeterlinck's close friend. He told him he wanted to

* Catulle Mendès' lecture took place on May 13, 1893; the première—and only performance—of *Pélléas et Mélisande* on May 17. In memory of that fateful evening Claude treasured his ticket all his life.

turn *Pélléas* into an opera and asked him to obtain for him the author's permission.

"He'll be delighted to give it to you, I'm sure," said the poet, polishing his monocle. "The play was such a fiasco that no one is likely to be interested in it. I'll write Maeterlinck today, but I warn you that he usually tosses his mail into a drawer and forgets it for a few weeks. So don't be surprised if you don't hear from him for quite some time."

Back in the street Claude congratulated himself. For once he had been efficient and businesslike.

"I've done all I could," he told Gaby when he next saw her, "now there's nothing to do but wait and hope for the best."

"That's right. Just be patient, darling, and you'll see everything will be all right. You'll be able to write your opera."

She had never heard an opera, hardly knew what one was, but it made no difference. She wanted whatever he wanted, and if his dream was to write an opera, well, then an opera he must have . . . Deep in her heart she wished he were a salesman, a plumber, a storekeeper—something solid and reliable. But he was a music writer, and that was all right. It wasn't his fault if he was born like that, with a passion for writing little notes on sheets of ruled paper . . .

She had seen much of him in these last few months, and each time she felt closer to him. She loved the smile of his black, impenetrable eyes, the gentleness of his hands. Even his helplessness, his lack of practical sense aroused her pity as much as her exasperation. Casually, without trying, he had taken possession of her heart, and now she carried the thought of him wherever she went. Sometimes, in the crushing boredom of a "gay" night, she would feel her heart flutter in her chest and she wanted to shout out her love.

And now that the time had come to leave him she could not brace herself to do so.

"What is it, darling?" he asked, noticing the sadness of her face. "Did anything go wrong?"

Imperceptibly she shook her head and went on gazing at the wall across the room in wistful concentration. She was sprawled on her belly over the coverlet, nude and pensive, her chin resting on his chest, one leg rising and falling in a rhythmic motion of its own. This was her favorite position for "thinking," and he could almost hear the workings of her brain.

"It's just that I don't want to go, that's all," she said at last.

He did not speak at once and slowly raked the fingers of one hand through her disheveled hair.

"I guess we've been too happy this winter," he murmured. "Nothing ever stays as it should. But we knew you would have to go for the summer, so it doesn't come as a surprise." Then, to cheer her up, he added, "Anyway, soon it's going to be awfully hot in town and you'll be glad to be away."

"I suppose so," she said without enthusiasm. "And it'll be more fun on a yacht than buried in the country."

During the previous weeks she had kept him informed of the "negotiations" with Gontran, the young millionaire. These had taken place at Léonie's house under the guise of intimate afternoon teas at which Gaby happened to drop in, as if by accident. Over genteel *langues de chat,* various business details had been brought up for discussion and satisfactorily arranged. Gontran had agreed to provide Gaby not only with her "carriage and pair," but also with a luxuriously furnished apartment in the Etoile district. Of course, this was not yet the supreme objective—the mansion, the *hôtel particulier,* which was the dream of every demimondaine, but, as Léonie had wisely pointed out, it was the next best thing.

It only remained to decide the date of transfer, so to speak, the day on which Gaby would leave her present gentleman friend and join Gontran. This last pressed for an early decision, for he was impatient to have Gaby for himself and wanted to take her on a cruise aboard his yacht.

"Ever heard of a place called Scotland?" she asked unexpectedly. "That's where he wants us to go. He says it's beautiful in June."

She was silent for an instant, then burst out in a peal of gigglish laughter. "Did you know that men wear little skirts in that part of the world?"

Of course he did . . . He told her about the piece of Scottish music he had written for General Meredith and discoursed about the Highlanders, who not only wore kilts but loved to fight to the sound of their family songs. She enjoyed his explanations and said she hoped she would attend one of those clan battles. It would relieve the tedium of the trip with Gontran.

"When are you to give him an answer?" he asked.

"By the end of the week."

She relapsed into her morose broodiness, and he went on stroking her hair.

"This gives us only a few more days," he said after a long pause. "I'll miss you."

She did not speak, and he added, "When are you planning to tell your gentleman friend?"

"When I feel like it," she snapped with sudden irritation. "He's beginning to get on my nerves, that one. All he wants is to stay home with me, smoke his cigar and tell me how pretty I am."

Swiftly she raised herself on an elbow and looked at him with glaring indignation. "Do you know that he almost didn't take me to the opening of Maxim's! I was so mad I wanted to walk out on him. Can you imagine staying home on a night like that?"

The little restaurant on rue Royale had just reopened with considerable éclat as an all-night establishment. In Gaby's world the event had created a sensation. Not to attend such an opening would have been an irreparable loss of prestige.

"I told him I'd never forgive him, and finally he reserved a table. But I tell you, it was like pulling teeth." She was still incensed at the thought of his cruelty and selfishness. "Even then, I didn't really enjoy myself because at three o'clock in the morning he already was grumbling that he was tired and we should go home."

It had been a memorable evening. The luxuriousness of the place, the quality of the cuisine, the ceremonious courtesy of Benoit, the maître d'hôtel, the welcoming smile of Gérard, the head *chasseur,* an apoplectic little man with drooping mustaches *à la chinoise* who wore a monocle—these things had left on Gaby a vivid impression. And, of course, everybody who was anybody had been there that night. Not only Max Lebeaudy—the one of the salad of violets—but the brothers Hennessy, the Duke of This and the Prince of That, and Albert Meunier, the chocolate king, and so many others. Naturally all the *grandes biches* were there also. Alice Gaillard and her Russian prince; Maud Loty and her very, very rich American friend, Alain Soler. And Liane de Pougy and Cleo and Emilienne . . . All their hourglass dresses, diamond bracelets, jeweled fans, aigrettes and plunging necklines.

"I almost died of envy," Gaby said in a gush of candor. "But don't worry, in a year or two I'll be like them."

This brought her mind back to Gontran and her face darkened in thought.

"If only I didn't have to go with him so soon," she mused half aloud.

She remained motionless, nervously nibbling her lower lip. Then, like an uncoiling spring, she brought herself up to him, her lips level with his, her eyes mirrored in his eyes.

"Love me," she breathed.

Now there was no more thought in her, only the hunger of her youth, the impatience of her body. Love-making was to her the panacea that swept aside all problems. She plunged into it as she would have into prayer, with frenzy and faith in its power. As his hands slithered down her hips and his mouth drank from hers, a sort of animal exultation came over her, the joyousness of sex aroused and demanding. Her breath grew short, her loins taut with desire. Unconsciously they fell into a mounting rhythm and became the two halves of the same body, locking and unlocking, twining and untwining in a pattern of swelling lust, until finally they joined and were one in a moment of throbbing, moaning rapture.

She was slow to get up that day. At last she pulled herself away from him and out of the bed.

"I'm so happy when I'm with you, it gets harder to leave each time." She threw back her head and shook her loosened hair. "God, how I wish I didn't have to!"

He did not see her for several days; then, late one afternoon, she burst in.

"Guess what?" she cried breathlessly. "I don't have to go!"

She was too excited to explain and began swirling about the room to a tune of her own invention, repeating "I don't have to go! I don't have to go!" with the delight of a child out of school. Smiling, he watched her from his desk, still holding his pen in his hand, admiring the gracefulness of her motions.

"I'm free, darling. Do you hear? Free as a bird!" she said, coming to an abrupt stop.

She slipped between him and the table, sat down on his lap and clasped her arm around his neck.

"I don't have to go on his damn yacht," she went on between pecking kisses. "And I don't have to go to the country either. In fact I don't have to go *anywhere!* I can do anything I want, and d'you know what I'm going to do?"

He chuckled. "No, I haven't the faintest idea . . . I don't even understand how you got yourself free."

"Very simple. I just told him I couldn't go with him till September—"

There was too much to say and she wanted to say it all at once. It took her a long time to describe the day's events with a semblance of coherence.

Early that afternoon she had met Gontran at Léonie's house for a last interview.

"I swear I was ready to tell him I'd join him this evening after I'd talked to my gentleman friend, but suddenly I couldn't stand the idea of leaving you and spending the summer with him. The words just wouldn't come out of my mouth. So, in a flash, I told him I'd just learned that my mother was sick and I must go and stay with her, but I could join him in September when he returned to Paris. His jaw dropped and he was mad as a hornet, but I told him I couldn't help it and that's how things were and he could take it or leave it. And d'you know what?" Her voice rose in triumph. "He took it! . . . He said he was so crazy about me he would wait till September."

"And what did your friend Léonie think of it?"

"She came in after Gontran had gone and at first she said I was a damn fool and I'd muffed the opportunity of a lifetime. But I explained to her that everything remained the same and it gave me a breathing spell for three months and I was tired anyway and didn't want to go on his damn boat. Finally she said she understood and wished me luck . . . I told you she is a real friend."

Afterward Gaby had driven home and announced to her gentleman friend her decision of leaving him.

"I told him I appreciated everything he'd done for me, but I had found somebody else and naturally I had to think about my career. Well—he turned white as a sheet."

He hadn't, however, made a scene. On the contrary, he had recognized that she must look after herself and make the best of her assets while she was young. Then, without raising his voice, he had said, "But will you be as free with your new gentleman friend as you've been with me? Will he let you go and visit your lover as I have?"

"Can you believe it, he'd known all the time and said nothing!"

She could not take the wonder from her voice, hide the stupefaction she had felt at this announcement. Her gentleman friend, so easygoing, so blind and stupid, had known about her affair and kept silent. Why? Because he loved her, because he realized he was a dull old man and she was young and he did not want to lose her.

"He even promised that if I stayed with him he'd let me come and see you from time to time."

With tears in his eyes he had pleaded with her, offered her more money. She had felt sorry for him.

"But I just couldn't stand the idea of going to the country with him, seeing you only once or twice during the summer."

And so, bluntly, she had told him she wouldn't stay with him at any price.

"For a moment he just sat, looking at me and saying nothing. Then, without a word, he got up and went out of the room."

"And you?"

"I started packing, told the maid where to send my things and came here."

Again the jubilation of a moment ago was taking hold of her, almost choking the words in her mouth.

"And, darling, for the next three months, I'm free. Free as a bird . . . I almost can't believe it. And you know what I'm going to do? I'm going to take a nice little vacation."

"A vacation?"

"Why not? Since I came to Paris, I haven't had a day to myself. Why couldn't I have a vacation, like everyone else?"

He smiled at her aggressiveness. "Nobody says you shouldn't. I think it's a wonderful idea. Where will you go?"

"Go?" She laughed. "But, silly, I won't go anywhere. I'll stay with you."

It had never crossed his mind she might ever want to share the discomforts of his garret, but then everything she did was unexpected. If she felt like living with him for a few weeks, he certainly wasn't going to talk her out of it. Who wanted to argue with happiness?

"I think it's the most marvelous idea you've ever had," he said. "I'll do my best to make you happy."

"Oh, darling, we're going to have so much fun! Imagine, a whole summer together . . ."

She kissed him and nestled her head on his shoulder, but her happiness was too buoyant for her to sit still. She sprang to her feet, pulling him up after her by the hand.

"Come on, let's dance."

And, laughing, they plunged into a madcap polka to the beat of their foolish hearts.

CHAPTER

10

THE FOLLOWING MORNING, TWO BARREL-CHESTED MEN IN BLUE blouses delivered two large trunks. Also a shoe-case and several hat-boxes.

Gaby knelt down, unlocked the first trunk and started unpacking.

First, out came the dresses—of every kind, color and material. She handed them to Claude one by one and carefully he laid them on the bed.

"How many do you have!" he exclaimed a moment later, as the pile continued to rise.

She shrugged. "Why, that's nothing. You should see Léonie's."

Now it was the turn of the petticoats, and they, too, made a pretty rainbow on the bed. Then appeared the bustles, designed to defend a lady's honor from the rear; the corsets, formidable cuirasses, hard to put on but easily removed; the corselets, soft and stayless—no defense at all. Then the garters. A collection of them, from the plain everyday ones adorned with a mere knot of ribbon to the fancy ones for gala evenings, spangled with rhinestones and paste rubies.

This took care of the first trunk. Without pausing, she opened the second one. Out came the lingerie, an all-important item in her profession. Lace chemises consisting mainly of holes delicately hemmed by hand; bloomers diaphenous as cobwebs; *culottes,* practically invisible to the naked eye.

"Here, darling." She held out a stack of flimsy, neatly folded negligees. "Be careful, they tear easy."

He turned around, and his jaw dropped.

"What's that?" he asked, staring at the gun lying flat on top of the bundle. "Where did you get it?"

She glanced over her shoulder. "Oh, that," she said, plunging back into the trunk. "He gave it to me last year when we were in the country and he had to go away for a few days."

He set the bundle on the bed, picked up the revolver and laid it flat on his palm. It was a dainty, toylike weapon with a handle of mother-of-pearl and pretty designs engraved on the trigger. But there was nothing toylike about the short, sturdy muzzle of glistening steel.

"Do you realize you can kill somebody with that thing?"

"Sure." A soft chuckle rose from the depth of the trunk. "That's why he gave it to me. So I could protect myself if a prowler broke into the house."

"Nobody's going to break in here. Why don't you throw it away?"

"I will one of these days. Come on, darling." She handed him another bundle. "We're coming to the end."

She straightened up, puffed up her cheeks, brushed back a loose strand of hair and once more disappeared into the trunk.

For a while she worked in silence, rummaging methodically through her belongings, plunging in and out of the trunk, bringing up armfuls of lacy, perfumed things, like some deep-sea diver on a frivolous treasure hunt.

Handkerchiefs, fans, stockings. Gloves—dozens of them. Morning and afternoon gloves; evening gloves, almost as long as stockings, reaching to the armpits and designed to hide the vaccination scar. Pink, blue, violet gloves, fashionable at the races and sporting events. Net gloves that "let the hands breathe"; semi-formal gloves with a bit of lace at the cuff; winter calling-gloves, made of the softest kid, yet warm.

Deeper and deeper she foraged, her hair tousled, beads of perspiration gleaming on her forehead. At last she reached the layer of toiletries. Out came crystal bottles of Kiss Me Quick and other perfumes, jars of face cream, mysterious magic unguents, face powder, mascara for the lashes, kohl for the lids, rouge for the lips. And at last the humble hardware of a lady's toilette. Tweezers, scissors, hairpins, *bigoudis,* nail files, curling irons.

"Well, that's it," she said, handing him the last accessories. "It didn't take long, did it?"

"Now the question is, where the devil are we going to put it all?"

She gave him a glance of fond compassion. "Just leave everything to me."

She rose to her feet, retouched her make-up and went out. One hour later she returned at the head of a small quadron of men hoisting two oversized armoires, a huge chest of drawers, a vanity table with a three-sided mirror and a set of mahogany shelves.

"I also got a dining table, so we won't have to eat on your desk," she announced.

The room became a beehive. Gaby was everywhere at once, supervising the moving, cajoling the men into lugging the enormous armoires into a corner, then into another, then back to the first, flattering and teasing them into nailing the shelves on the wall, hanging her dresses, filling the drawers of the chest. With smiles and winks and quips she instilled in them such a fervor of work that they pushed Claude aside when he volunteered his services. Thereafter he watched the operations from his desk, cheek on hand, feeling useless and unwanted.

In less than an hour the dresses had been sucked in out of sight, the lingerie had disappered into the commode, everything was in order.

"I think you're wonderful," she said with a circular glance at them. "I don't know how I would have managed without you."

They stood around her, grinning, mopping their faces, ready to move mountains for her. She felt the impact of their maleness and she played with them, complimenting them on their muscles, saying how lucky their wives must be to have such strong men in their beds, slipping tips into their calloused hands. At last, reluctantly, they shambled out, doffing their caps and muttering their thanks. The room was quiet again.

"See how simple it is," she smiled.

"Why didn't you ask them to paint the room and scrub the floor while you were at it," he grumbled, still feeling the sting of their snubbing. "You should be ashamed of yourself."

She gazed at him, her face bland with innocence. "It worked, didn't it?"

He grinned, shook his head and motioned her to come sit on his knees. "Darling, you have the morals of an alley cat."

"Perhaps, but it gets things done. If we'd tried doing the whole thing ourselves, we would've been at it for a week."

She kissed him and leaped to her feet.

"Now I must go and buy some food. Tonight we're having dinner at home. You'll see, I am a pretty good cook."

She was—the best in the world . . . She had bought a three-burner alcohol stove and on this contraption she prepared a meal fit for a king.

"I had no idea you were such a wonderful cook," he said as they lingered over their demitasses.

"You should see my mother. There's a real cook."

"Will you cook again for me, once in a while?"

She pretended to hesitate. "I might, but it'll cost you a lot."

"How much?"

"A thousand kisses every day."

He choked over his coffee. "No cook is worth a thousand kisses a day."

"All right. You cook your own dinner."

"Come on, be reasonable. Seven hundred."

"Nothing doing."

For a while they argued. Tenderly, lazily, in the bantering tone of their September affair.

"Eight hundred and that's final."

"A thousand."

"Nine-fifty."

"A thousand."

"All right, a thousand. But it's sheer robbery."

They smiled at each other across the table in a languor of digestion and happiness. They liked their little kissing game. Of course it was silly, but happiness is not ashamed of silliness. It was a new language, a secret code they alone understood. Much could be said or suggested with it.

"And payable in advance," she said as an afterthought.

He had lost and was not going to haggle over details. "I'll even give you a bonus on special occasions. "Say, five kisses."

Outside, darkness was coming, but a glow of daylight still clung to the sky. Through the open window, a breeze gently fanned the silence and wafted away.

They did not feel like talking. It was their first dinner at home and obscurely they sensed that it marked a milestone in their relationship. Memories drifted through their minds. It was about this time a year ago that they had seen each other at Weber's—and now they were having dinner at home, like an old married couple . . . Of course it was make-believe and it would all be over in September. But for the moment it was real. And it would be real tomorrow and the day after that and the day after that for many . . . many days. September would never come.

"Happy?" she asked after a long pause.

He only nodded, but she understood the gleam of tenderness in his eyes.

"Me, too," she said softly.

◆

It had happened so smoothly and so fast that at times he wondered if he were not dreaming. A few days ago he had been living alone, cooking his own meals and doing his laundry, and now there was this gorgeous girl around. At meals, in his bed—everywhere and all the time. There was the joy of waking up and finding her at his side, her thigh wedged between his, asleep or smiling at him from the pillow; the pleasure of returning from a piano lesson and discovering that the room had been dusted and swept and his shirt was drying on the rear balcony. Flowers on his desk, the good smell of cooking coming out of the "kitchen" . . .

It was amazing how easily she had slipped into his life and he had become used to her presence. Of course it demanded some little adjustment. For instance, you had to learn to never be alone, have no privacy, no time to think or work or muse at the window as he used to. But who wanted to be alone when you could talk or take a walk or lie in bed with such a stunning girl? Anyway, what was there to think about? *Pélléas?* . . . Nothing could be done until he heard from Maeterlinck, and God only knew when that might be. As to writing some new large composition, the failure of *The Blessed Damozel* had cooled his creative ardor for the moment. He did not even feel like correcting the proofs of the voice-and-piano reduction Père Bailly had sent him. Most amazing of all, he did not even have to worry about money: he still had most of the Mendès fee . . . Come to think of it, he couldn't choose a better time for a little vacation, and what vacation could be more wonderful than three months with this baffling and adorable girl?

Each day he discovered something strange and unexpected about her. She could recite the *Lord's Prayer* in Latin, but knew the lyrics of every naughty song. She was an avid newspaper reader, not only of murders and *crimes d'amour,* but of society, sports, internal politics and foreign affairs.

"Where's the Bering Sea?" she asked one day during dinner.

"Somewhere around the North Pole, I think. Why?"

"England and the United States are fighting over the right to fish in the Bering Sea. Silly, isn't it?"

She also was intrigued by the World's Fair which had opened in Chicago, a large Indian village according to her.

In literature she had no patience with sentimental romance or salaciousness. To her love was something you made, but didn't write about. She had no use for vicarious excitement. "It's like trying to eat by reading a menu," she said. Her preferences went to wholesome stories of jewel robberies, opium smuggling and, now and then, plain murder. In politics she was an ardent republican and loyal daughter of the Revolution. When he told her there were only seven prisoners in the Bastille the day it had been stormed by the People, she point-blank refused to believe it, called him a liar and a "dirty royalist." Her religious convictions were both violent and vague. With God Himself she had little truck, but with the Virgin she was on terms of intimacy. Her faith was total, but tailored to her needs. She had no time to waste on saints, angels and other holy intermediaries.

"If the Mother of God can't get me what I want, nobody can," she declared with finality.

Modesty she had none. With the casualness of Eve strolling through the Garden, she walked about the room wearing only the mascara on her lashes. On the other hand, she said grace before meals, a childhood habit she had never lost. She had said grace—her own abridged version consisting of a closing of lids and brief quivering of lips—in the most unlikely places. Every midnight supper she had attended, every magnum of champagne she had helped drink had been duly blessed.

Her professional ambition was ferocious and candid. She wanted to become a *grande biche* and she did not care how many men she ruined in the process. And if one or two were kind and foolish enough to commit suicide on her account, that was all right, too. "Look at Alice Howard, the beautiful Angleesh girl. Two princes fought a deadly duel over her and now she has arrived . . ." Well, some day everybody in Paris would know about Gaby Lhéry. She, too, would give sumptuous dinners like Valtesse de la Bigne; she would have a bathtub made of solid silver, like la Paiva; and a gold tea service, like Judith Widmer; and a beautiful house, like Léonie. She would launch fashions, have a perfume named after her—even if she had to pay for it. Then, in about ten years, she would retire to some great big château in the surroundings of Lisieux with acres and acres of land and she would raise cows and pigs and chickens. Naturally she would buy a nice house for her parents, so they would be able to grow old in peace and comfort. And she would endow an orphanage. Marriage she did not want, but children she liked. Might even adopt one or two.

"I've got it all figured out," she said one day. "This summer with you will be the only vacation I'll ever take. It's a breathing spell, you might say. In September I'll be in fine shape and go back to work. And this time, mark my word, I won't stop till I reach the top."

Meanwhile, September was far away, and there was no sense in spoiling the present by worrying about the future, was there? Now was the time to be happy, as happy as she could. And she was. At times she almost felt her heart bursting in her chest. Her eyes sparkled; a smile clung to her lips, even in sleep. For no reason she would start to sing or launch into a waltz with her broom in her arms.

Her happiness was a simple, ebullient thing that demanded outlets of expression. She found them in sudden explosions of activity. One day she insisted on washing the window, climbed on the ledge and almost fell out. Another day she scrubbed the floor and waxed the furniture. The place stank with wax. She ran to the street corner and bought so many flowers that the garret looked like a funeral parlor and stank worse than ever.

A fortnight after moving in, she arrived one afternoon clasping an armful of wallpaper rolls, a bag of paste wedged under her chin, a brush tucked under each armpit.

"Look," she cried, dumping her load on the table.

Gingerly he peeked at a roll and shuddered. It showed, repeated in endless rows, Monsieur Sadi Carnot, President of the Republic, standing in a blue sky in his evening clothes with the red sash of the Legion of Honor across his chest, beaming in his square black beard, raising his top hat in cordial salute while, around him, doves flew in joyous white-winged garlands.*

"Nice, isn't it?"

He did not reply and she construed his silence as speechless admiration.

"I knew you'd like it. Let's put it up. The man at the store said it was very easy. I brought everything."

It was a memorable experience. They worked for hours: she kneeling down on the floor, splashing paste on the backs of the rolls; he, tottering on a ladder, wrestling with the twirling strips of paper, smacking them against the wall, grimly brushing them flat with his brush. When they finished, they slumped side by side on the edge of the bed, too exhausted to speak. From every angle Monsieur Carnot was beaming at them.

She was delighted. "It cheers up the place, don't you think?" she said after a while.

"It does. It really does."

He did not have the heart to spoil her pleasure and tried to sound enthusiastic. Why not? She loved the damn thing and after she was gone he would paint over it. Until then let her enjoy it . . .

"I think it looks just fine," he added for good measure.

And so it went: each day happier, sillier, more tender and playful than the one before. By now the kissing game was in full sway. Everything had its price payable in kisses. A small service—unfastening the hooks of her skirt, for instance—might be worth twenty kisses; a considerable favor such as breakfast in bed, one hundred. Soon they owed each other thousands of kisses, got entangled in their calculations, accused each other of cheating.

---

* In a letter written a few years later he still recalled "the wallpaper representing President Carnot surrounded by little birds."

"You don't know how to count, anyway," he would say. "You told me yourself you didn't learn anything at school."

"But at least I went there, which is more than you did."

Like all lovers they argued as to who loved most, each one insisting that he did. He said he was working on an invention, the lovemeter, based on the principle of the thermometer, which would conclusively prove his claim. She retorted that she did not need any silly instrument and she *knew* that she loved him more than he loved her. The discussion ended in a draw from sheer exhaustion. Another game of theirs was to pretend they could not think of any reason why they lived together.

"To think that at this very minute I could be on a yacht, enjoying myself with a handsome millionaire, and here I am, cooking and scrubbing for a down-and-out, unappreciative music writer." A long, hopeless sigh. "Why, oh, why?"

"And to think I could be free, shuttling gaily from one gorgeous woman to another, and here I am, tied for the summer to a country girl with lettuce-green eyes and a terrible disposition." A wheezy moan. "Why, oh, why?"

The dialogue proceeded along these lines for a while and finally they concluded they had been the victims of each other's tricks and sly maneuvers.

"It's those green snake eyes of yours."

"It's those sharp glances of yours."

"It's the spices you put in your cooking."

"It's the way you kiss. There should be a law against men like you."

Thus they argued and bantered and used their complaints to express their love, their joy at being together. And somehow their arguments always ended up in bed.

Their hunger for each other had not abated. Familiarity had not blunted their pleasure, but made it more intense. At times a shadow of anguish crossed her face. "Do you think I'll ever stop wanting you?" He reassured her. "After all we've been together only three weeks and we've barely got acquainted. But don't worry, by September we won't even want to look at each other. Everybody knows that sex burns itself out in a few weeks." Of course . . . Sex was fun for a little while, but one soon got tired of it. They laughed, and their gaiety returned.

One morning she treated herself to a home-bath, a *bain à la maison.**

---

* One of Paris' minor luxuries in the nineties was the *bain à la maison*. It entailed a costly and involved procedure. The tub, made of brass and mounted on casters, was brought in a cart with a built-in hot-water tank under the

On his return from a visit to the Chaussons' he found her in the middle of the room, humming and soaping herself in a tub, her head wrapped in a towel turban.

"What on earth are you doing in that thing!" he said, grinning.

"Don't you see? I'm taking a bath. You can't really wash yourself with a sponge. Some day I'm going to have the biggest, finest tub in Paris."

"And of solid gold, I suppose." He came to sit on the edge of the tub. "How long have you been in it?"

"I'll tell you when you give me a kiss."

"How can I? Your face is full of soap."

"All right. No kiss, no dinner."

Casually she lifted her leg out of the water, then slammed it down in a splash.

"Oh, I'm so sorry." She giggled. "My foot slipped."

"Think nothing of it, darling." He bent down as if to kiss her, then pushed her head down underwater. "Now are you going to be nice?"

Her reply was a gusher of soapy bubbles and a blind groping of hands. He released her, and she emerged, gasping, sputtering that he was a beast and wanted to drown her. While speaking she scooped a palmful of water and flung it at him. Before he could catch his breath she arched herself against the tub and sent it rolling across the room.

"Look!" she cried with childish delight.

By pressing herself against the sides she achieved some semblance of control and for a minute she gave him a demonstration of her skill, spilling a good deal of water overboard in the process.

"Isn't it wonderful?"

"If you don't stop, you'll be able to sail the damn thing! . . . At what time are the Auvergnats supposed to come back?"

"Noon."

He glanced at his watch. "It's half past. They'll be here any minute. Come on, get out of it."

She gave him a lidded smile. "It'll cost you two hundred kisses."

"Nothing doing. Do you want them to find you naked?"

"They won't mind."

"But I do. Come on, be reasonable."

She slid deeper into the water. "I think I'll have a little sleep."

As usual she had her way. After she had made him apologize for drowning her and promise to pay the two hundred kisses, she consented to get out of the tub.

---

seat, hoisted up the stairs and wheeled into the apartment. *Auvergnats* in yellow southwesters carried pails of hot water up the stairs and prepared the bath. At the appointed hour they returned and the procedure was repeated, in reverse this time.

"By the way," he said, while toweling her dry, "I went to see Monsieur Chausson, and his wife remarked how nice and well fed I looked."

"That's my cooking."

"That's what I told her, and she said she'd like to meet you before they go to the country."

Two days later he escorted Gaby to the house on boulevard de Courcelles. He felt considerable misgivings. He knew that the Chaussons belonged to the *haute bourgeoisie* and for all their artistic tolerance clung to the strictest moral standards. In their circle a divorced lady was quarantined; a woman of dubious morals was beneath contempt.

Thus it was with a flutter of apprehension that he gave their names to the butler, who ushered them into the drawing room. Madame Chausson walked straight to Gaby, and for an instant the two eyed each other as only women can. Madame Chausson had braced herself for some flamboyant hussy or bedraggled seamstress in home-made clothes and was startled by this beautiful and modest girl who wore no make-up and demure, elegant clothes. Gaby, in turn, had expected to be peered and sniffed at from behind a lorgnette and was won by the lady's bright and kindly eyes. They smiled at each other and impulsively clasped hands.

They were chatting like old friends when Claude and Ernest Chausson returned from the library, where they had repaired to discuss business.

"You two must come to see us at Luzancy this summer," said Madame Chausson when she escorted them through the foyer. "I'll never forgive you if you don't."

After their visit Claude and Gaby strolled along the sun-flecked boulevard.

"I am so glad you two got along," he said.

"She's a wonderful woman. I never expected her to be so simple."

"Real ladies usually are. Her husband is just as nice. He's helped me a lot."

"He looks like a nice man."

Her words ebbed into silence, and her face closed in thought.

"What's wrong, darling?" he asked.

She sighed. "I only wish time wouldn't run so fast. June's almost over already. How can a month go by so quickly! . . ." She turned to him. "I don't want to, but, darling, I must go to Lisieux. They'd be disappointed if I didn't come."

Her mother's birthday fell on the first of July and two days afterward her sister Blanche was to celebrate her engagement.

Again he was struck by her devotion to her family. Come what may, they would always be first with her . . .

"How long will you stay?"

"I don't know. Four, five days, I guess. Don't worry, I'll be back as soon as I can. Will you miss me?"

"And you?"

They smiled at each other, and for an instant they walked hand in hand, like children.

♦

Four weeks before it had been strange having a woman around; now it was strange being alone again. Cooking his own meals, sleeping without feeling the weight of her head on his shoulder, not haggling over kisses and whether or not they would have breakfast in bed. Strangest of all was the silence, the emptiness she had left behind. Thank God, it was only for a few days . . .

He started correcting the proofs of *The Blessed Damozel* and spent the first evening at home. It was the longest evening he had ever known. He had lost the practice of loneliness and he did not know what to do with himself. Time, which had run so fast when she was there, now did not move.

The following day he had dinner at the corner bistro and afterward he went to see his friend Erik Satie at L'Auberge du Clou.

He enjoyed the company of this witty and melancholy bohemian who was even poorer than himself—he slept on the floor of his room because he could not afford a bed—and still had enough energy left to stand the strain of an erratic love affair.

That evening Erik was in a state of total despair. He joined Claude as soon as he could leave the piano and once more unburdened his heart.

"Bigui has left me," he announced in a sepulchral tone and with eyes full of tears. "She's gone back to her lover."

"I thought you were her lover."

"I am, but so is he. You see, she shares herself between us. A few days with me, a few days with him. She is generosity itself."

Such had been the situation since that fateful night when he had seen Bigui for the first time. He was then assistant pianist at Le Chat Noir and she had come late, leaning on the arm of her current lover, Paul Moussis, a banker. Her entrance had struck Erik with the impact of a blow in the solar plexus. Ignoring the presence of her escort, he had run to her table and suggested they get married at once.

"She said it was impossible because it was two o'clock and the city hall was closed, but she had no objection to being my mistress. I tell you she has a heart of gold!"

The matter had been discussed between the three interested parties and finally agreed upon. For months Bigui and her two lovers had formed a united, happy triangle. With the banker she enjoyed the bourgeois comforts of wealth, slept in a feather bed, dined in the best restaurants; with Erik she slept on the floor, washed his shirts, mended his socks and ate shredded coconut.

In time, however, money had won over love; the banker's mattress had proven more attractive than Erik's hard floor. Bigui's absences had become longer and more frequent.

"Now she's gone," he said with a defeated sigh.

He removed his pince-nez to wipe off a tear that was trickling down into his beard.

"I shall hang myself as soon as I finish writing my ballet."

"How long do you think it will take?"

"I don't know. Two, three years . . ."

Relieved, Claude inquired about this new composition and learned that it was called *Uspud,* had only one dancer and was based on Flaubert's *Temptation of Saint Anthony.* The work was dedicated to the Holy Trinity. Soon Erik was talking with enthusiasm of its artistic and commercial possibilities. He had forgotten about Bigui and was again in high spirits by the time the owner of the establishment touched him on the shoulder and ordered him back to the piano.*

During Gaby's absence Claude called on Henri de Régnier, who informed him that no letter from Maeterlinck had arrived yet.

"Be patient," said the poet. "One of these days he will go through his mail and we'll hear from him."

Claude swallowed his disappointment and went home. He finished correcting the proofs of *The Blessed Damozel* and brought them to Père Bailly. In the bookshop he met a dashing young writer by the name of Pierre Louÿs, who was about to leave town for the summer. They had an *apéritif* together and promised to see much of each other in September, when Pierre would return.

At last Claude received a telegram from Gaby announcing her arrival and that same afternoon he went to wait for her at the station. He was there so early that he had to pace back and forth on the platform for almost an hour before her train came in sight.

At last he saw her leaning out of the compartment window and waving at him, and he ran to meet her as she stepped down. They fell in each other's arms and remained clasped in an embrace for a long time.

---

* Bigui, the object of Satie's passion, was Suzanne Valadon, a colorful Montmartre character, an artist in her own right and the mother of Maurice Utrillo.

"You'd think I'd been away for a year," she said when she disengaged herself.

"It seemed that long."

She straightened her hat and slipped her arm into his. "Oh, darling, it's so good to be back."

On their way home she told him about her sister's engagement. Everything had gone well and the betrothal dinner had been a great success, with many toasts and songs and all the cider one could drink. Personally she did not care much for her future brother-in-law, one of those priggish bigots who went to church all the time and always had a mean word for everybody. And with that, a widower with children and no money.

"I'll never understand what Blanche sees in him, but she loves him, and there's no use trying to put sense in her head."

She cried with pleasure when she entered the garret and saw the flowers and "Welcome Home" placards Claude had scattered about the room. They made love and only then did they feel they were back together, and everything was as before.

"I had almost forgotten how nice it is," she said, cuddling to him.

"That's what comes from going away. Until September you stay with me, do you hear? No more traveling."

She liked his possessiveness, his tone of gentle command. "Yes, darling. Anything you say."

That evening they had dinner at home. By the following morning it seemed that she had never left. Gradually they went back to their carefree way of life and before they knew, another week had passed and Paris was getting ready for Bastille Day.

"Let's go to Longchamps and watch the parade," she suggested.

That day he discovered still another Gaby. Gaby, the patriot, who yelled *Vive la France!* at each passing flag, waved her parasol at President Carnot standing in the tribune, blew kisses at the plumed generals and brave little *pioupious* as they stepped by in orderly rows. By the time the last "Marseillaise" had been played and the review was over, she was exhausted, almost voiceless, her boater hat askew on her head.

They were lucky enough to find place in an open-roofed horse-car and an hour later they were back in town. They spent the afternoon milling with the crowds on the sidewalks, listening to street singers, watching acrobats perform at street corners. They dined in a bistro full of men in shirt sleeves and girls in straw hats. Gaby felt refreshed and ready for more excitement. They visited small local fairs, shot at whirling pipes and rode carrousels. And naturally they danced.

"Come on," she cried, pulling him by the hand. "The government's paying for everything."

First they danced under striped awnings to the strains of apoplectic bands. Then, when the popular balls closed, they joined the couples who were still dancing in the street to the music of a single accordion.

It was early morning when they ambled back to the garret. Fully dressed they collapsed on the bed, too tired even to make love.

"I've never had so much fun," she sighed—and fell dead asleep.

It was now six weeks that they had been living together and the wonder of it had not yet palled on them. They remained locked in their enchanted world, indifferent to what went on around them. Even when she received a letter from Léonie saying she had run across Gontran at the Dieppe Casino and he had told her how anxious he was to return to Paris and set Gaby up in her new apartment, the news did not cloud their happiness for long. Wistfully she gazed out of the window, then with a shrug tore the letter up.

They still discovered things about each other. She was surprised at his sudden outbursts of boyish gaiety, his pranks, his laughter at the antics of clowns, as if a part of his childhood remained to be spent. She found he was as superstitious as an old woman and teased him because he would not go to sleep unless his shoes were set side by side with their tips outward.

He, in turn, never stopped marveling at the complexity of her nature, so shrewd and calculating one moment, so naïve the next. He learned that, like most women, she had no use for abstract speculation and gave a personal meaning to his most impersonal utterances. If he admired the blue summer sky she concluded that blue was his favorite color and he wished she had blue eyes. When one day he remarked at dinner that he liked his steak lean, it proved that he preferred lean women and she threatened to go on a diet until she was "a bag of bones" . . .

"Then you'll really love me," she said.

But most of all, he observed her gift for seduction and the tranquil cynicism with which she used it. He took her to Bailly's, and at the sight of her the old bookdealer removed his skullcap, kissed her hand, declared she had the face of a Greek goddess and offered to read her horoscope. She gave him the rapt attention which is the subtlest form of flattery and which in the hands of a lovely woman is a deadly weapon. In no time, Père Bailly fell into the trap of her adoring eyes. He dropped everything, neglected customers to take her aside and tell her about the joys of occultism. She hung on his words, gasped and finally gave him a kiss on the cheek.

"What did he say that was so fascinating," Claude remarked teasingly as they were walking home.

"I don't know, I wasn't listening."

"Aren't you ashamed to lead astray such a nice old man?"

She gave him a glance of flustered candor. "I did it for you. If he likes me, he'll help you more."

He gave her a sidelong glance and changed the subject, but her words lingered in his mind and made him uneasy. Never before had he found in a woman this readiness to serve, this intrusion in his affairs. It created between them a partnership, almost a collusion he did not seek. He wanted only a mistress, not a tool. But obviously love for her meant more than the gift of her body, it took in everything else. She was the kind of woman who would cheat, steal or walk the streets for her man; help him in a holdup or share martyrdom with him. It was a thrilling but disturbing thought; it revealed an intensity of passion that had no place in a light-hearted summer affair.

◆

Toward the end of July she had another opportunity to use her talent for seduction, this time on Monsieur Victor Hugo, the tailor.

Angrily he rapped on the door one afternoon and burst into the room in a sputtering rage. Nothing remained of the suave gentleman who had convinced Claude of the importance of looking successful.

"You don't believe in paying your bills, do you?" he sneered. "Well, give me back my clothes or I'll go to the police."

Claude gaped at him, too startled to speak. At this point Gaby intervened.

"You're absolutely right," she said. "And it was very nice of you to come all the way here and climb all those steps instead of sending the gendarmes. I always say you can recognize a gentleman by the way he behaves, and I am glad to see one. Please, won't you sit down and catch your breath?"

So saying, she pushed a chair under him and he jackknifed down onto it. Seated, he looked much less formidable.

"I was just about to have a cup of tea," she went on, "and perhaps you'll have one with me and tell me what this is all about."

She gave him a bewitching smile and turned to Claude. "You run down to the bakery and get some pastries," she snapped. "And hurry."

She winked at him and went to sit down close to the tailor. "Now tell me what this poor, stupid, irresponsible man of mine has done." Impulsively she took his hand into her own. "You know what fools artists are."

These were the last words Claude heard as he hurried out of the room. When he returned—and he took his time about it—he found

Gaby and Monsieur Hugo in pleasant conversation over their tea.
Now it was he who was holding her hand . . .

"What took you so long?" she cried with a fine show of anger.
"Monsieur Hugo is just about to leave. He is a busy man, you know.
And you're lucky you have to deal with such a fine gentleman."

Duly she berated him for his extravagance, his financial irresponsibility. It was a miracle that Monsieur Hugo happened to be such a
generous, understanding man. Not only had he consented to a substantial discount on the bill, but he had also extended credit for
another three months.

Thus the incident ended in smiles and thanks all around.

"Now let's sit down and eat those pastries," she said when the
tailor had left. "By the way, you owe me another five hundred
kisses."

"Here's one on account," he said, kissing her. "I don't know what
I would've done without you. Let's go to L'Alcazar tonight."

Her face flushed with pleasure. She loved music halls, in particular
L'Alcazar, a noisy smoke-filled establishment on the Champs
Elysées which remained open during the summer. She was the
perfect audience, laughing at the most inept jokes, gasping at the
acrobats and trained seals, joining in the refrain of popular songs.

After the show they went to a café and played their familiar game
of trying to guess the professions of the people at the neighboring
tables.

"I tell you he's a retired admiral," she whispered, glancing in
the direction of a decorous gentleman with clean-shaven cheeks and
the complexion of freshly sliced ham. "Look how ruddy his cheeks
are. You can see he's spent his life at sea."

"I wager he's a funeral director. He looks like a man who would
bury his best friend."

She hesitated. "Maybe he's a judge—"

Finally they agreed he must be a prosperous manufacturer of
toilet seats and fell into fits of irrepressible laughter which they tried
to conceal behind their hands as the gentleman eyed them severely
from across the room.

And so it went—because their hearts were gay, everything was a
pretext for fun. Each day brought a fresh supply of sunshine and
laughter. But each day rushed by faster than the one before, and one
morning, with a pang, she discovered that July was gone.

"Time goes fast, doesn't it, when you're happy?" she murmured,
clinging to him.

"How about going on a picnic," he said to change her train of
thought.

"Where?"

"Anywhere."

He suggested Asnières, on the banks of the Seine, only three miles from Paris. "We could take the boat."

At ten o'clock the following morning, they boarded *Le Touriste* at Pont Royal. It was a perfect summer day, all sunshine and blue sky. Gaby, who had never set foot on a boat, sat demurely on the deck bench, her basket on her lap, holding her straw hat with one hand, watching Paris slide by before her eyes. Soon she felt bold enough to leave her basket on the bench and wander about the ship. Now she felt like an old sea dog and went everywhere marveling at everything: the mossy bridge arches, the chugging of the engine, the gravity of the man at the wheel. Leisurely the river boat plowed her way from stop to stop and at last reached Asnières, where they disembarked.

The river bank was already crowded with fellow excursionists, but they located a few yards of vacant and weedy ground which they appropriated. They set down the tablecloth, emptied the contents of the basket and had their lunch in an illusion of complete isolation.

Afterward they felt drowsy with wine and sunshine and they lay side by side staring at the blue emptiness of the sky.

"I wish we could live on a deserted island," she murmured. "Just the two of us."

"And what would we do?"

"Lie on the beach, fish, eat bananas, make love." Her voice ebbed to a faltering whisper.

"Wouldn't you get a little tired of it after a while?"

"Never . . ."

He was going to ask her about the carriage, the house, the jewels she wanted so much, but glancing at her he saw she had fallen asleep.

He raised himself on an elbow and scanned her face golden in sunshine. Gaby, darling Gaby . . .

Her lips were parted in a smile and through the sheer material of the blouse her bosom made a pink translucent blur. Somehow it seemed natural that she should be sleeping like this on the grass, languid and lascivious like some antique nymph returned to life for one last summer afternoon, disguised as a French girl in a linen skirt and open-necked blouse.

Suddenly his breath caught in his throat.

Like a soft field breeze a melody lazed through his mind, a long sinuous chant played on a rustic pipe and trailing in the stillness of the hour. Then he heard the harps' echoing ripples and the sluggish stirring of the orchestra swelling by degrees into a sonorous wave of longing that broke at last in a wail of pleasure. Then, like desire itself, it dwindled slowly to its last perceptible drop of sound.

She woke up and saw him leaning over her, his eyes open and unseeing.

"What is it, darling?" she smiled.

He blinked, jarred out of his dream by the sound of her voice.

"I have it!" His lips were trembling. "I have it!"

"What?"

"My *Afternoon* . . . I heard it, clear as crystal."

She looked at him as if he had gone mad, but he did not notice it and went on, "It finally came! . . . It's taken time, but it finally did. And it's not a symphony as I thought, just a short orchestral piece . . . A single phrase that twirls and grows until it can't grow any more and bursts and crumbles . . ."

She watched him as he spoke. Never had she seen him so excited. He was breathing fast, almost panting, looking at her but not seeing her, unaware of her presence, lost in some remote world of his own.

"What on earth are you talking about?" She laughed.

The sound of her laughter brought him back to reality. He ran his hand over his eyes, let out a long sigh and grinned sheepishly.

"You must think I'm crazy."

"I wouldn't say so, but you surely sound like it."

"Forgive me, but it came so unexpectedly and I've been waiting for it so long."

He then told her about the Mallarmé poem he had wanted to set to music for more than two years.

"It's called *The Afternoon of a Faun* because the story takes place in the afternoon of a very hot summer day." And the story was about a faun who spied a nymph asleep on the grass, ran after her when she fled and finally caught her and made love to her. "To their mutual satisfaction, I hope."

He was trying to be flippant, but she did not smile. She still remembered how far away he had been a moment ago. It was a strange feeling to discover that he could escape into some secret world that was closed to her.

"Anyway," he went on, "I was watching you sleep and suddenly you had become the sleeping nymph. That's how it started."

The rest of the afternoon went by without incident. They returned to the boat landing and sailed back to town in a lilac haze of sunset. They stood together at the stern watching the foamy scar of the wake, chatting and laughing, their arms clasped around each other waists, but somehow their chatter and gaiety wasn't quite as spontaneous as in the morning.

The following morning she shrugged off her fears. What was she fretting about? Because he'd gotten an idea for some piece of music while she was having her siesta? Well, what of it? It only proved he was an artist and a bit touched in the head, like the rest of them . . . She did not mind. The thing to do was for her to show an interest in his music, make him talk about it. He would like that. Men liked to talk about the thing they loved . . .

That day she asked many questions about fauns and nymphs and pretended great interest in them. She stood by, very quiet and smiling, while he wrote the first draft of *The Afternoon of a Faun.* When he finished she had him play it on the piano and declared that she liked it very much.

A week later Henri de Régnier brought in a letter from Maeterlinck granting Claude permission to turn his play into an opera and make whatever changes he deemed advisable.*

Gaby went into transports.

"We must celebrate," she told Claude when they were alone. "Leave everything to me."

That evening they had champagne with their dinner. By the time they had had their dessert she was tipsy and in an uproarious mood.

"I wager you're going to write the damnedest best opera in the world," she said.

"I'll certainly try."

"Let's drink to that."

"Let's."

They drained their glasses and smiled at each other across the table. Her eyes had grown very large and blurry and she had trouble with her enunciation, but she went on in a long monologue to assure him that she was perfectly sober.

"Of course you're sober, but would you like to lie down for a while?"

"First we must finish this bottle," she said with a wide, all-embracing gesture.

For a while she gazed meditatively at her empty glass. "It's quite hot this evening, don't you think?" She opened her robe and fanned herself with the napkin. Suddenly her lips puckered into a silent kiss. "I love you an awful lot."

"Me, too."

"But you love that damn music too much. I love you more because I don't love anything else . . ." In the same breath she went on, "Let's have another toast. What shall we drink about?"

"I can't think of anything."

"I have it. Let's drink to President Carnot." She refilled their glasses, raised her own to her lips, then stopped abruptly. "For this

* This letter—dated August 8, 1893, and addressed to Henri de Régnier—was to play a decisive part in the stormy production of *Pélléas.*

one we must stand up." She tried to rise, but flopped back on her chair. "I guess I'm a little *pompette*," she admitted.

"I guess you are very much *pompette*." He smiled. "And you'd better lie down and sleep it off."

"Never."

"Yes—and right now," he said, rising.

Hurriedly she gulped down her champagne, let out a long, satisfied sigh and hiccuped. "Excuse me," she said politely, pressing her hand to her mouth. "Don't worry, I know what to do."

She tried various methods, all infallible according to her, but somehow none succeeded in stopping her hiccups. Finally she stretched out on the floor, raised one leg, went through complicated exercises, pinched her nose and almost choked herself. This brought no result either.

"I think it'll go of its own accord," he said, pulling her up to her feet. "Just lie down and you'll be all right."

She made no resistance and let him lead her to the bed.

"Kiss me," she muttered as he patted a pillow under her head.

He leaned down and kissed her, but already she was asleep. Gently he unclasped her arm from around his neck, and for a while he watched her sleep, peaceful as a child. Darling Gaby . . .

He tiptoed to the window, leaned on the sill and gazed at the purple sky pincushioned with stars.

Only now did he dare to abandon himself to his jubilation. He sensed that beneath her show of enthusiasm she resented his love of music, looked on it as on a rival. All evening he had kept his joy from bursting out, but now he could let it rise within him, fill his whole being. He had the rights to *Pélléas,* without supervision, reservation or control of any kind. He could do whatever he wanted with it.

Soon he would be able to start working. But not yet . . . As soon as Gaby left. It would fill his solitude, the loneliness she would leave behind.

CHAPTER

11

"PERHAPS YOU WANT TO START WORKING ON YOUR OPERA," SHE SAID the next day. "It's all right, I won't disturb you."

He protested that nothing was further from his mind. Just because he had received the rights to *Pélléas* he was not going to forget everything and bury himself in music.

"We still have a few weeks together and we're going to enjoy them to the last minute."

That evening he took her to L'Auberge du Clou. On the way to the cabaret he told her about Erik Satie and his love affair with Bigui.

"Last time I saw him he was thinking about committing suicide. He may have hanged himself by now."

But Erik was much too furious to think about killing himself. He had sent his ballet *Uspud* to the director of the Opéra for production and that disgusting man, that pig, had not even acknowledged receipt of the score.

"Imagine—a work dedicated to the Holy Trinity! But he will pay for it. I've challenged him to a duel. I'll carve him alive, slice him to ribbons!"

He was in a fine bloodthirsty mood and was about to go on when the owner of the bistro, with a stiff jerk of his thumb, sent him back to the piano.

"Well, what do you think of him?" Claude asked her as they were walking home.

"He's an idiot."

"I don't think so. He's very sensitive and an intelligent chap. Too bad he doesn't know harmony or composition, for he has talent. About two years ago I asked my teacher, Monsieur Guiraud, to let him follow his course, but the students laughed him out of the class. Just the same he'll make his way, you'll see. He has a flair for publicity and he's very shrewd. After all he is half Scot and half Norman, and you can't beat that for shrewdness."

"I still say he's an idiot."

"Let's say he's the kind of an idiot who makes other idiots think he is a genius, and that's a form of genius in itself, isn't it?"

August wore on, luminous and hot. Now and then he thought about *Pélléas,* but he did so furtively, when she was out. Their life remained unchanged. They breakfasted in bed, went out for afternoon strolls, spooned sherbets on the terraces of cafés and played their guessing game. Occasionally they dropped in at Père Bailly's, went to a circus, a small district fair or a music hall. On his birthday they had another picnic, this time in the Saint-Cloud forest. They kissed and laughed under the trees. After the siesta he told her about Aunt Tavie and the days when they had gone hunting for mushrooms together. She in turn told him about her fishing expeditions with her sister along the banks of the Touques River and how they always ran across Monsieur Martin, who was famous in town because his five daughters had all become nuns.*

"He spent all his time fishing, and every evening he left a basket of fish at the door of the convent."

This exchange of childhood memories brought them close in a tender, melancholy way.

"These are the happiest days in my life," she sighed as they were about to return. "I only wish time would stand still."

But it didn't, and August was soon over.

Just then Claude received a letter from Madame Chausson inviting them to spend a week at Luzancy.

"It'll give me a chance to wear my garden hat," Gaby said. "You know, the one we got at the Magasins du Louvre."

"And I'll show you my fisherman hat. If you like it, I'll rent it to you, for fifty kisses an hour."

She let out a hoot of protest. "Fifty! What d'you think I'm made of?"

They haggled over that while packing. He finally accepted a much lower rate.

* One of them was none other than Thérèse Martin, better known as Saint Thérèse de l'Enfant Jésus, who died in 1897, at the age of twenty-four in the Lisieux Carmel and was proclaimed the patron saint of France, with Joan of Arc.

"I hate doing business with you," he grumbled. "You always win."

As usual the big rambling house was full of guests, and again Claude had the opportunity to observe Gaby's uncanny flair for making friends. Madame Chausson's lady guests, who had greeted her at first with reserve, even a faint hostility, were quickly disarmed by her modesty and subtle compliments. When they felt sure she had no intentions on their husbands they forgot their prejudices and welcomed her in their group. Thereafter, Gaby, demure and chaste-looking in white organdy, spent her afternoons with them chatting and knitting under the large elm tree at the end of the garden.

As for Claude, he spent most of his time with Eugène Ysaye, a Belgian violinist who with his pretty wife and three children was enjoying a brief and well-earned vacation. Together they played a good deal of piano-and-violin music and during recesses they drank beer on the terrace at the back of the house while comparing notes on their respective careers.

Tall, bulky, clean-shaven and lion-maned, Eugène Ysaye looked exactly like the concert virtuoso he was. In a few short years he had skyrocketed to fame and at thirty-five he was regarded as the most brilliant violinist in Europe. In addition to his concert tours he found time to teach at the Brussels Conservatoire, give private lessons and conduct the Quatuor Ysaye, a chamber music ensemble he had founded and which was recognized as the finest of its kind. Exuberant, extravagant, generous to a fault, he worked from morning to night, spent money as fast as he earned it, helped poor musicians, collected rare violins and entertained lavishly in his handsome new house. He was the epitome of artistic success.

"When I am in Brussels I am on the go all the time, and when I am on tour it's worse. Of course, I earn a lot of money, but money isn't everything."

"That's what rich people say."

"I wish I had more time."

"And I wish I had more money. Which proves that nobody has what he wants."

In the course of their conversations Claude mentioned he had written a quartet which was being engraved at the moment.

At once Ysaye was on the alert.

"I'd like very much to see it. People are a little tired of the Haydn and Mozart quartets and it'd be nice to play something new for a change. I'm bringing my Quatuor to Paris for a concert at La Nationale during the Christmas holidays and perhaps we could present it then—if we have time to learn it. When could I see it?"

"As soon as the proofs are ready, which should be sometime in November."

"Send them to me as soon as you can and we'll start rehearsing."

"I might be able to bring them to you myself. You see, I'm planning to go to Ghent and show Maeterlinck the changes I've made in his play. On the way back I could stop in Brussels and give you the quartet."

On the day before they were to leave, Claude managed to see Gaby for a moment. "Madame Chausson would like us to stay another week."

"It's very kind of her, but we only have a little time left. Let's go back."

And so they left on the following afternoon amidst a cloud of good wishes and waving handkerchiefs.

Madame Ysaye made Gaby promise to visit her if she ever came to Brussels. "Remember our address," she cried as the carriage started rolling away, "48, avenue Brugmann."

On the way back to Paris, Claude complimented Gaby on her social success.

"You've made many friends."

"Everybody was very nice," she murmured, looking out of the window.

He saw she did not want to talk and watched her in silence. She was sitting on the opposite bench, swaying with the motions of the train, her face turned in profile. Again he was struck by her beauty. Slowly his eyes slid down her short straight nose that made kissing so easy, the full lips, the long fluid line of the neck.

Gaby, darling Gaby . . . Always he would remember this wonderful summer, the lovely demimondaine who had lived in his garret when she could have gone on a yachting cruise. It would be something to tell his grandchildren about, if he ever had any grandchildren . . .

It seemed incredible that September was here and in a week or two she would go out of his life. Oh, yes, he'd known all along she would leave, but until now it had been a dim, improbable eventuality like the notion that some day you must die. Now it wasn't dim and improbable but very real and the thought of her departure was almost unbearable. It would be hard learning to live without her, getting back to the old kind of life.

Even now, on their return, things wouldn't be quite the same.

"Darling," he said, and the sound of his voice made her turn around, "I'm going to have to start looking for work and giving my piano lessons again."

"I know that."

"It means I'll be out a good deal of the time and you'll be alone a lot. I'm afraid you'll be lonely."

"I won't mind."

"You say that to please me, but I don't want you to stay just because it makes me happy. Perhaps you'd better go to a hotel until your new gentleman friend arrives."

She shook her head. "Don't worry, darling, I won't be lonely. I'll find plenty to do while you're out. And by the way, I don't want you to take me out in the evening any more."

"Once in a while."

"No. I want you to start working on your opera."

"That can wait. I'll have all the time in the world, after you've gone."

She would not hear of it. He must work and write this opera as fast as he could so that he would earn some money. And she wasn't going to let him waste his evenings because he wanted to entertain her. Certainly not.

"I'll be just as happy staying home with you. So long as we are together, it's all I ask."

His heart swelled with love. Oh, Gaby, darling Gaby . . .

♦

Thus, on their return, their way of life changed. No more lolling in bed, no more picnics, no more guessing games in cafés. As he had said, he was out most of the day and she remained alone with nothing to do.

She tried to read, but her five-sou thrillers about jewel robberies and opium smuggling no longer held her attention. She scoured, scrubbed, moved furniture about, swept again the room she had swept a moment before. She got into the habit of spending an hour or so with Madame Sénégal in her lodge and they became friends.

Sometimes, in early afternoon, she went out for a stroll. Summer was dawdling along that year and sunshine sieved through the boulevard trees. Elegant and lonely, holding her pale-blue parasol, she walked on aimlessly, stopping to look in shop windows or at the posters on the kiosks. Inevitably she was approached by eager and grinning gentlemen who pretended to recognize her and attempted conversation. Wearily she waved them off and returned to the garret and diamond burglaries.

Somehow the afternoon would draw to an end. The moment she heard the sound of his footsteps, she would run out on the landing, fling her arms around his neck and they would kiss and kiss as if they had been separated for weeks.

"Lie down on the bed while I get dinner ready," she would say.

He would stretch out and forget the fatigue and disappointments of the day as he listened to her chatter and gazed about the room, saw the freshly laundered curtains, the flowers on the table. Each time he would feel a new surge of tender gratitude for the lovely girl who willingly shared his dreary life.

Then would come a delicious dinner, which he ate with a pang of conscience, knowing that he had not paid for it.

"I must owe you a lot of money," he remarked one evening.

"You don't owe me a sou, but you do owe me two hundred and seventy-eight thousand kisses, and what are you going to do about it?"

For a while they played the old game but it brought back memories of their carefree vacation days and stressed the differences between the present and the past.

"Let's forget about kisses, will you, and talk sense," he said. "How much do I owe you?"

"I told you, nothing. Don't you remember our agreement?"

In June, when they started living together, he had insisted at first that she was his guest and grandly announced that he would pay for everything. In a week her shopping habits had played havoc with his finances. She had forced him to accept an agreement. He would pay the rent and all entertainment expenses—café, theatre and so on; she would attend to groceries and household expenditures.

It had worked more or less equitably, except that now there was no more entertainment while he still continued to eat.

"From now on you'll jot down in a little book what you spend and I'll give you the money as soon as I can."

She promised and changed the subject.

"What did you do today?" she asked, coming to sit on his knees. "Did you see any publisher, did you have a hard day?"

"Not particularly. Mostly waiting in reception rooms. I'm used to it."

You sat down and waited and read a dog-eared magazine or watched the clock for an hour or two. Then a secretary came out and announced that the publisher had left for the day. If by any chance the great man received you he put on a show of feverish activity, barely took time to glance up from his desk to say that business was terrible and he had no work for you. "But come back in a week, I may have something then." And so it went.

"You're beginning to see what my life is really like," he went on. "The same endless grind every day. Not very cheerful, is it? But I brought it upon myself. My teacher warned me I should get some steady job. But no, I had to be free to compose . . ." He let out a low, mirthless chuckle. "And I've been free. Free to starve and half freeze to death in winter, but somehow it doesn't matter

so much. You get used to everything. It's you I'm worried about,
staying alone like this all day long. What did you do today?"

"Waited for you." She nestled against him. "Time goes so slow
when you aren't here."

Yes, time went slowly while she waited for him, but what made
the waiting so long was the conflict going on in her mind. She knew
that Léonie was back in town, yet she avoided going to see her, as
agreed. Each day the prospect of leaving Claude became more
painful. Her common sense told her she must go away, her heart told
her to stay.

At last a thought brought her a ray of hope. She was beginning
to see how dreary his life was and what it meant for her to go on
living with him. Waiting all day, washing, cooking and at night
watching him write his music, waiting for him to come to bed. What
girl would want this kind of life? If only she could stay on a few
more weeks she would have had her fill of it and nothing on earth
would keep her in this awful garret. She would run to Gontran, and
if he hadn't waited, well, she'd find someone else, just as rich, just
as generous.

All she needed was an excuse for staying another month or so.
Something foolproof that seemed perfectly natural and which he
would believe . . .

On his return home one afternoon Claude found her having tea
with her friend Léonie.

"I've just got some bad news," she said, walking to him. "Gontran
won't be back for a few weeks."

"One of those things that come up for no reason," Léonie stressed
with a philosophical shrug. "Like a hair in the soup."

She was a handsome, common-looking woman of ample proportions with a wide good-humored mouth and magnificent eyes. She
was dressed in purple velvet and a plumed musketeer hat. Her hands
were beautiful and she displayed them to advantage while she talked.

"All you can do is be patient and wait," she went on.

Gontran's aunt had died the week before in her château, somewhere
in the Cévennes, and there were some legal complications about her
will. Naturally he must stay on the spot and make sure his lawyers
didn't rob him blind.

"You know how they are." She smiled knowingly. "Regular
leeches."

"I hope it won't take too long," said Gaby.

Again Léonie shrugged. She had a wide assortment of shrugs and
could say or imply a great deal with each one. This time she implied
there was no way of guessing how long it would take.

"If you want my advice"—she addressed Gaby like an older and wiser sister—"you'll count on at least two months. Those legal things, you never see the end of it."

After her departure Claude and Gaby sipped their tea in thoughtful silence for a while.

"What're you going to do?" he asked at last.

"I don't know. But don't worry, darling, I won't stay here."

He was hurt by the emphasis of her tone. "Have you really been so unhappy?"

"On the contrary. I've never been so happy, but you probably want to be by yourself."

"What gave you that idea?"

"I can imagine what you're thinking."

"Oh, you do, do you? And what am I supposed to be thinking?"

"That I was to stay only till September and you don't want to be saddled with me for another month, perhaps two."

"Would you mind letting me do my own thinking? Did I ever say or hint in any way I wanted you to go?"

"No, but you suggested I go to a hotel."

"Because I didn't want you to be lonely."

"I thought perhaps you were getting tired of me."

"Why, you silly woman, I couldn't begin to tell you how happy you've made me."

"I love being with you too."

"Then why the devil don't you stay?"

"I don't want to be a bother. I know how much you like being alone."

"There you go again, knowing what I think, what I like, what I don't like. Well, do you know what I'm going to do right now?"

"No."

"I'm going to spank you. Come here." Imperiously he signaled for her to come and sit on his knees. "Come here and get spanked."

She obeyed. He made her bend down and pretended to spank her with great vigor.

"Now sit down," he went on, "and answer my questions. No speeches, just yes or no. Do you love me a little?"

"A lot."

"Are you happy with me?"

"Happier than I've ever been."

"Do you want to stay with me?"

"Yes, but only if you want me to."

"You know I do."

"Are you sure?"

"Of course I'm sure. Now look here, who's asking the questions?

You know damn well I want you to stay. I wish you could stay six months."

She laughed gaily. "I'm afraid I can't do that, but I'll stay as long as I can. That is, if you really want me to."

"I told you I do. What do you want me to do? Go down on my knees?"

A look of triumph flashed in her eyes. "No, but you can start paying back those two hundred thousand kisses you owe me."

◆

He was furious when, a few days later, she announced she must go to Lisieux for her sister's wedding.

"Again! And how long will you stay this time?"

"I'm not sure. A week or two. It depends on how much my parents will need me. It's going to be hard for them to get used to living without Blanche."

And he? Did anyone care about him? "Don't you think it's going to be hard for me living without you?"

Tenderly she soothed his feelings. "It'll do you good to be a bachelor again for a few days. Perhaps you'll like it so much, you won't want me back."

He did not like it; he hated it. It was no fun cooking your own meals, sleeping alone and in an unmade bed, waking up with Linne at your side, returning to an empty room at the end of the day.

With a shock he realized how much he had come to depend upon her and what an immense part she played in his life. Since she was gone, nothing seemed to go right. He could not find his cuff links, did not remember where he kept his shoelaces. Even the three-burner alcohol stove that performed miracles for her refused to work for him. He missed and needed her and wished she would hurry back.

Fortunately his finances had improved. From Monsieur Fromont he had received a transcription, together with a long homily on the virtues of thrift and work, and a respectable advance. He was able to make a payment on his rent and work on his opera in the afternoon as well as in the evening.

In a few days he finished a scene which he had begun three weeks before and brought it to Chausson for approval.*

"What do you think of it?" Claude asked when he finished playing.

"It's magnificent. But I don't see how you'll ever write a five-act

* Debussy began the composition of *Pélléas* with the second scene of the fourth act. The manuscript of this draft—the first of many—is at the Conservatory of Music in Boston (U.S.A.) and bears the inscription "September-October 1893." The singing parts are written in ordinary pencil, the orchestration is indicated in green pencil.

opera while doing transcriptions, giving lessons, and seeing publishers. You'll be dead in a year."

Absently he rubbed his chin for a minute.

"How would you like to give private auditions of Wagner's operas?
Many society ladies are planning Wagnerian musicales this winter,
and since you played in the sacred hall of the Opéra, you're regarded
as a Wagnerian specialist. I think my wife and I might be able to
get you a few engagements. It would pay better than piano lessons,
take only an evening now and then and leave you time to work."

Claude returned to his garret and found a volume of Johann
Sebastian Bach's fugues, which had arrived in the afternoon mail.
Inside was a card from Pierre Louÿs announcing that he would call
on him the following day.

"I sent you these fugues because you mentioned how much you
admired Bach," he began as he walked briskly into the room, his
cane tucked under his arm. "I do, too. Besides, I wanted to thank
you for the copy of *The Blessed Damozel* which you left at my place
while I was away."

He sat down at Claude's desk, rested his top hat on a stack
of music paper and finished removing his gloves. "Now let's be
serious. I want your honest opinion. Please don't spare me, tell me
the truth. How do I look?"

"Superb. The sea air has done you a world of good."

Pierre Louÿs let out a long, doleful sigh. "I was afraid you'd say
that."

Leaning forward, he held out a gold case across the table, then
took a cigarette out of it and struck a match.

"You see, my doctor—a very expensive, reliable one—informed
me six months ago I was consumptive and would be dead by the
end of next year."

He let out a double stream of smoke through his nostrils and went
on, "On the strength of his assurances I've arranged my life and have
been spending my inheritance at such a rate that I should be penniless
by the day of my death. I intend to be buried in potter's field, like
Mozart and other distinguished artists. By now, according to my
physician, I should begin to spit blood. Instead I feel wonderful,
eat like a horse, smoke like a locomotive and experience sudden,
almost uncontrollable urges to rape women, especially very young
ones." His voice throbbed with pathos. "Tell me, what am I going
to do?"

"I'm afraid you may have to go on living."

Pierre gasped. "Do you realize what you're saying? I may have
to go to work! Now, according to the Bible, work was intended as a

punishment, and I don't see why I should be punished just because my doctor is an ass."

He remained silent for an instant, broodily gazing through the smoke of his cigarette.

At last he emerged from his reverie. "Here I am, twenty-three, rich, talented and oversexed. I should be the happiest of men; instead I am a nervous wreck."

He also was hungry and suggested they go to dinner.

They went to La Maison Dorée, an elegant restaurant on boulevard des Italiens. While eating and drinking copiously, Pierre gave voice to another reason for his nervous collapse. This time it wasn't his health, but women. Especially a young lady who had attached herself to him with the dedication of a barnacle to the hull of a ship.

"I've tried everything," he said after ordering crêpes suzette. "I've told her I was a crook, a cardsharp, that I'd been expelled from my club and was wanted by the police. It didn't do any good. She suggested we hide together. Then I told her I sold drugs in my spare time, lived from the toil of prostitutes and was bound to wind up at the foot of the guillotine. She said she would pray for me. When I told her I had a shameful, contagious disease, she begged me to let her nurse me back to health. Have you ever had any such experience?"

Claude replied that he hadn't. The women he had known had left him after they had shared a few of his bread-and-tea meals and a few nights in his ice-cold garret.

"What a lucky man!" exclaimed Pierre.

For a while he watched the maître d'hôtel pour brandy over the crêpes suzette and send it into a blue burst of flame with the swift flash of a match.

He waited for the *entremets* to be placed before him, took an appreciative mouthful, complimented the waiter, who bowed and departed.

This done, he continued, "It is always difficult to reason with a woman; if she is in love, then it's impossible. The moment she falls in love she loses two-thirds of her intelligence, forgets all pride and modesty and whatever common sense she ever possessed and turns into one of those frightening half-witted heroines you find in Greek tragedies. A woman simply won't accept the fact that the man she loves may not love her back or may have stopped loving her. It shatters her vanity, crushes her ego, and she has no peace till she has made a mess of things."

He took a pensive mouthful, swallowed, dabbed his dashing mustache with his napkin.

"Experience has taught me that the only thing to do is vanish.

This is why I change apartments so often. I've learned it is easier to break a lease than a liaison."

He ate in dispirited silence, his eyes lowered on his plate; then, abruptly he leaned forward, fork in hand, as an inspiration flashed through his mind.

"You wouldn't consider moving and sharing a place with me, would you?" he asked. "Perhaps we could find one of those big old houses nobody wants and which rent for practically nothing. It would be fun."

Tactfully Claude declined. "I've become attached to my garret. It's full of memories and has become a part of me. I can't imagine living anywhere else."

During the remainder of Gaby's absence Claude saw Pierre almost every day, if only for a few moments. It was a trait of his nature that he needed the relaxation of male comradeship. He had been deprived of it since Vital's marriage; now he found it again in this loquacious and brilliant young writer. Although there was an eight-year difference of age between them and they held conflicting opinions on almost every subject, they enjoyed being together. Soon they were using the familiar *tu* and had no secrets from each other.

Inevitably Claude told him about Gaby. How lovely and tender she was, and how he had had to plead with her to stay with him a few more weeks.

Pierre went into transports of rapturous envy. "You don't know how lucky you are! Imagine, a beautiful girl who doesn't want to marry you, doesn't want to stay with you forever and ever, doesn't try to mother and smother you, reform you, turn you inside out and tuck you in bed! When may I have the honor of meeting her?"

"As soon as she comes back."

Gaby returned on one of those perfect October days that seem to bring summer back for a belated curtain call. She had much to say about her sister's wedding: the beautiful church ceremony, during which she had cried, Monsieur le Curé's allocution and finally the traditional Gargantuan dinner.*

"And you, darling, what did you do?"

"Almost starved to death."

He told her about his difficulties with the alcohol stove, and she was pleased when he said how much he had missed her tasty meals.

"I think that's the only reason you want me around," she teased.

He swore he loved her for a thousand reasons, but was it his fault if his stomach was also in love with her? Then he gave her an

---

* The wedding of Blanche Dupont to Jules Riffaut took place on September 25, 1893. Gaby returned to Paris on Saturday, October 7, in the afternoon.

account of his visit to Ernest Chausson. Finally he told about his
new friend Pierre Louys.

"He's anxious to meet you."

She said she would like very much to meet him, and the following
evening the three of them had dinner together.

As usual Gaby listened with breathless attention while Pierre
discoursed on various things and described the dramatic circumstances of his birth.

"I'll never forget it," he said. "It was during the war. My parents
had walked all day through mud and snow, fleeing before the in-
vaders. My father, a verdant fifty-eight, had maintained some measure
of vigor, but my poor pregnant mother was exhausted. As for me I
was all in, when, at last, we reached the Belgian city of Ghent on a
repulsive December evening. A few hours later I was born. It was
all I could do to bring myself to come out into the world."

The war over, his family had returned to Epernay, a small town
in Champagne, where his early childhood had been made miserable
by his father's intense dislike. At the age of nine he had lost his
mother. Mercifully his half brother Georges had arranged for him
to leave and take up his studies in Paris.*

"I was a brilliant student and would've won every prize but for
my classmate André Gide, my best friend, a horrible, priggish Protes-
tant boy who was even more brilliant than myself. Nevertheless, I
graduated with honors in Greek, Latin, ancient history and all the
useless branches of education. For a while I hesitated between music
and literature as a career. Finally I chose literature and have written
works of such excellence, both in prose and poetry, that they've met
with complete unsuccess. Now my only hope rests in posthumous
recognition."

It was a pleasant evening. On their way home Gaby told Claude
she thought his friend Pierre was a nice and amusing fellow.

♦

It was about that time that Claude began to notice a change in
Gaby. Almost imperceptible, yet undeniable.

Her laughter had an edge of shrillness it hadn't had before. At
moments she looked at him with wistful tenderness; at others with
sullen resentment. When he asked if she did not feel well or something worried her, she snapped back that nothing was the matter and

* Pierre Louys' biographer, Claude Farrère, hints that Pierre's real father
may have been his half brother, twenty-three years his senior. Whether he was
or not, Georges Louys behaved like one. A distinguished diplomat, he became
France's ambassador to Russia shortly before the First World War and died
in 1917.

she felt fine. He was struck by the asperity of her tone. Her reply made it clear that whatever her problem was she did not want to talk about it. He did not insist, but a vague uneasiness arose between them.

She still ran to meet him on the landing when he returned from work, but now the gesture had lost its spontaneity. Sometimes she pretended not to hear the sound of his footsteps and did not come out at all. Once, arriving unexpectedly, he found her on the rear balcony, weeping quietly.

Knowing how much she liked to go out, he suggested they spend the evening at a café or a music hall.

Bluntly she refused. "You've got to work."

But now he found it difficult to work with her in the room. Not that she talked or disturbed him in any way; on the contrary, she did not even clear the table or wash the dishes, but tiptoed about the room and soon went to bed. There she lay, silent and motionless, her eyes fastened on him, watching him as he sat in the lamplight hunched over the sheet of music paper, stopping now and then to nibble the end of his pencil.

The impact of her gaze would distract his train of thought, and gently he would ask her to go to sleep.

"I'm not sleepy," she would say.

"Then try to read for a while."

"I don't see you all day. Can't I even look at you in the evening? Don't worry about me, go on with your work."

"But, darling, it may be a few hours before I can come to bed."

"I don't mind waiting. What else have I got to do?"

Touching as it was, her patience became irksome, for he knew that it did not stem from any respect for his work. In this, she reminded him of his mother. She had the same plebeian prejudices against any work that did not entail physical effort and regular wages. To her, as to all women of the working class, a workman was a man who used his muscles and on Saturday nights brought home his pay. A man who toiled half of the night writing music was a fool, even if he was the man she loved.

"You think I'm wasting my time, don't you, darling?" he said one evening, coming to sit by her side on the edge of the bed. "You may be right. I don't know if I'll ever finish this opera, let alone if it will ever be performed. Then why do I do it? Because I can't help myself. You see, when an artist has an idea he is like a woman with child. He simply must express it, just as she must bring her child into the world. That's creativeness. If he doesn't feel this urge to put his thoughts down on paper or canvas or whatever his medium is, he is no artist, and that's all there is to it."

He saw she did not understand, but he went on, "Once there was a famous musician. His name was Beethoven. When an idea came to him he scribbled it down on anything he could find. Sometimes he wrote it in charcoal on the walls of his room."

She laughed. "He must've been real crazy, that one. I hope you'll never write music on my nice wallpaper."

It was no use . . . "Don't worry, darling, I won't spoil your nice wallpaper," he said—and walked back to his desk.

At times her mood changed. She would rush to him, sit on his lap, beg his forgiveness, and wearily he would forgive. All would be well and they would try to recapture the joyousness of summer. For a day or two they would know a fragile happiness.

Then the process of disintegration would start again. Irresistibly their gay and tender relationship was crumbling with each passing day, turning into the tense and morose cohabitation of two strangers. At dinner they avoided each other's eyes and fell into sudden and troubled silences. Locked as they were in a room that gave them no privacy, no escape from each other, they found a precarious refuge in a punctilious and insincere politeness.

Only during the day, when she was alone, did she give way to her mounting despair. A month ago she had been sure—at least she had pretended to be sure—that a few weeks of loneliness and hardships would bring her back to her senses. She had staged Léonie's visit and with her rehearsed the story of Gontran's legal tribulations. But her cleverness had been for nothing. October was coming to an end and still she stayed. Every morning she prayed for the courage to break away and every night she found herself waiting for him to join her in bed.

The bed! . . . That's all it was and no use calling it by any fancy name. For some reason this man emparadised her, and all day she waited for the moment when he would take her. And because of that moment she couldn't bring herself to go.

That's all there was to it, and it didn't do any good to say that it was only sex and sex was a pretty stupid thing. It was, but so was hunger when you came down to it. Nor did it help to say that any man could give her the same thrill. Might as well tell a mother that the kiss of her child was the same as the kiss of any child . . .

Oh, God, she was caught! It had happened to her. She had fallen in love, she now was one of those fool girls who lost everything because of some stupid man. She must . . . must do something before he ruined her whole life.

She did. She tried to choke her desire with surfeit, exorcise it out of herself by debauchery. Her sensuality, which had been the healthy pelvic appetite of a robust country girl, turned neurotic. She became the aggressor, lashed herself into an erotic frenzy that produced the climax but brought her no peace and sent her, limp and moist, into an exhausted sleep.

"What's wrong, Gaby?" he asked one day. "Are you sick—are you worried? Did I do something I shouldn't have done? Please tell me."

"Nothing's wrong. I feel fine," she said sullenly.

"You certainly don't act as if you did. You are tense, irritable. Perhaps it'd be better if we stopped living together."

"You yourself begged me to stay."

"I didn't expect things to turn out this way."

"What way? I don't know what you're talking about."

He gave her a long, angry look. Then, with a shrug, he got up, took his hat and umbrella and went out.

When he returned he found her, her elbow on the table, dozing in the lamplight. She was humble and repentant, full of promises. He was right, she had been a little nervous the last few days.

"But now everything will be fine, you'll see."

That night he held her close to him and she fell asleep with her head on his shoulder, as in the happy days.

But it took more than promises to close the gap between them. Soon she was unable to control her restlessness, even in his presence. The weather added to her irritability. The autumn rains, which had been slow to come, were now in full force. In the blue-enamel basins the dripping from the room went on night and day, without a stop. To him it was a familiar, friendly sound; to her it was torture.

"I can't stand it!" she screamed suddenly one evening, pressing her hands to her ears. "Why don't you get the landlord to fix that damn roof?"

"I tried and it didn't do any good."

"I'd like to tell him a few things."

"I hope you don't. We get along more or less and I'd like to keep things as they are. I'm always late with my rent and I can't expect him to make repairs."

"Why don't we move out? In two or three days I could find a better place than this one."

"I don't want to move. I like it here, I've grown used to it. Be patient, the rains won't last forever. Now, please, go to sleep and let me finish my work."

November came, bringing no relief, either in the weather or in their relationship. Each day revealed a new disparity in their natures. They found that after five months of common life they still knew nothing about each other. He, who had been such a lively partner in fun, was now a silent, withdrawn man who seldom laughed, scarcely listened to her and thought only about music. She, in turn, had become a beautiful stranger who cooked and washed for him but was entangled in some problem of her own that made life difficult for the two of them. Wistfully he wished their affair had ended in September, when it was supposed to. Now he could only wait for the day her new gentleman friend would return and at last she would leave.

One afternoon, on his return from giving a lesson, he found her smoking a cigarette.

"I didn't know you smoked," he remarked.

"I used to, but my gentleman friend didn't like it and to please him I stopped."

"Why do you start again?"

"Because I feel like it and it quiets my nerves. Any objections?"

He shrugged and walked to his table.

"Can't I smoke a *cibiche* if I want to?" she went on.

He winced at the word. Only streetwalkers called a cigarette a *cibiche*. "Got a *cibiche?*" was a standard introduction to a prospective customer. The word smacked of the gutter, night prowling in dark streets; it described a way of life.*

"By all means," he said. "Smoke all you want."

"By the way," she went on after a pause, "the landlord came while you were out and I paid the rent."

He frowned with annoyance and turned around. "Why did you do that? Why didn't you just tell him I was out?"

"Because he got on my nerves. I started telling him about the roof and he said he wasn't going to make repairs for a tenant that didn't pay his rent on time. I told him what I thought of him, and finally I said, 'Here's your damn rent and get out of here.' " She laughed. "You should've seen his face when I told him to get out!"

He did not join in her laughter. "I wish you hadn't done it. He isn't a bad man and he's been very patient."

"I knew you'd say that!" she shouted, striding to the table. "I'm always the one to blame, it's always my fault. I never do anything right. You worry about your landlord, but you don't care about my having to listen to that damn dripping all day." Suddenly her mouth sagged and her eyes blurred with tears. "Please, darling, let's move out of here. It's this place that makes me nervous and irritable. If we lived somewhere else we'd be happy again, as we used to. Remember?"

She looked pitifully tired and his heart swelled with compassion. Poor Gaby, she had a right to complain. He should have known she wouldn't be able to live in a place like this. A new apartment would

---

* Gaby became a chronic, compulsive smoker. The old-fashioned slang term is no longer in use.

be a diversion, give her things to do while he was out. Perhaps they would be a little happier. Anyway, she had spoiled his relationship with the landlord and sooner or later he would have to move. He might as well do it now before it started snowing.

"All right," he said. "I'll look for a new place."

A few days later he arrived earlier than usual and announced he had just picked up the first copies of the Quartet and was leaving for Belgium in the morning.

"And I've found the most beautiful place for us to move into," he went on in the same breath. "More exactly, it's Pierre who found it. We went to see it together and he is as crazy about it as I am. We could all live in it together, for there is ample room for everybody."

An enormous old house, a private mansion untenanted for years, with eight bedrooms—imagine, eight bedrooms!—each with its own fireplace. A gorgeous circular staircase, and downstairs a vast paneled drawing room with tall windows that opened on a small, lovely garden. Of course it was a little shabby but it positively oozed with charm and old-fashioned graciousness. And solid as a rock. The real estate agent who accompanied them had told them the house was about eighty years old and they knew how to build houses in those days.*

"I've personally inspected every ceiling—and not a leak anywhere . . . Besides, many rooms are half furnished with nice old pieces, draperies and even carpets."

He paused, waiting for some sign of excitement, but she remained silent, faintly sullen.

"Well, there it is," he wound up, somewhat deflated by her lack of appreciation. "It may not be perfect, but at least you won't have to listen to the dripping from the roof. It's located at 62, avenue Bourdon, in the Bastille district, and you can go and see it while I am away. I should be back in three or four days and we must give an answer by then. If you like it, you can start packing, and we can move in right away."

"What're you going to do in Belgium?"

"See Maeterlinck about his play. Also bring the copies of my Quartet to Ysaye. He may play it in December when he comes to Paris."

"You're going alone?"

"Pierre is coming with me."

"Why couldn't I go, too?"

Because it was a business trip, very dull and tiring and she wouldn't enjoy it at all . . . "Besides, I want you to see the house. Remember, 62, avenue Bourdon. I hope you like it as much as I do."

---

* In a letter to his brother, Pierre Louÿs mentioned his plans to live with Debussy and described the house on avenue Bourdon and its eight bedrooms.

◆

It was raining when Claude and Pierre started on their journey and it was raining when they arrived in Ghent. At the station they found an antiquated carriage, which drove them through the exquisite medieval town to a large square house where an old maidservant in a starched coif ushered them into Maeterlinck's study.

The author of *Pélléas* turned out to be a stocky, placid, pipe-smoking young man in brown corduroys and heavy boots who looked more like a Flemish peasant than a poet and playwright. The interview was slow in getting started. Both he and Claude looked at each other in smiling silence and the encounter might have ended then and there but for Pierre, who, sensing the danger, talked for the two of them.

He recalled his accidental birth in Ghent and his pleasure at seeing again his native city, even if only through a solid sheet of rain. He went on to praise Ghent as the perfect city for a writer, offering total solitude and the opportunity to pursue one's dreams. This led him to mention *Pélléas,* which he had not read but which he extolled as a masterpiece with tact and all the evidences of sincerity. Finally he mentioned his friend Claude, who was so enthusiastic about the work that he had come all the way from Paris to discuss it with him.

At last Maeterlinck stirred to life, and removing his pipe from his mouth, congratulated Claude on his undertaking.

"But you needn't have taken the trouble of making this trip," he continued in a slow drawl. "As I said in my letter, you may do anything you wish with my play. I don't know anything about music, and to tell you the truth, it bores me to death and puts me to sleep."

The three young men chuckled at the remark, which broke the ice. They started talking freely. Claude insisted on showing the changes he had made in the text of the play and Maeterlinck approved them all, even suggesting a few others.

An hour passed in animated discussion. By then the rain had stopped and they went out to visit the cathedral with its famous van Eyck altarpiece. This done they repaired to a café on the Place d'Armes and sipped beer while waiting for the Brussels train.

Claude and Maeterlinck were now conversing like old friends. They discovered they were born only a week apart and their parents shared the same total incomprehension of their work.

"I became a writer by the force of circumstances," said Maeterlinck, fingering the beer foam off his brown mustache. "To please my father I had become a lawyer, but when I lost all my cases, and all my clients, even the innocent ones, began going to jail, he felt I might as well turn to literature."

Neither of his parents had ever read any of his books or attended any of his plays. They regarded him as a harmless, daydreaming failure.

"As a matter of fact, everyone in town feels the same," he went on, a smile in his pale-blue eyes. "Which is all right with me, for people resent success in others—while they feel sorry about failures and expect nothing from them."

This left him free to dream to his heart's content, write his plays, translate Emerson's essays, putter in the garden with his roses and his bees, do carpentry work in the house's basement and go out for long hikes. He had found contentment in solitude, the friendship of books, the companionship of his dog, which he preferred to that of any woman. The chatter of literary cafés, the glamour of social functions had no appeal for him. Once in a while he went to Brussels, attended a reception at his friend Edmond Picard's and hurried back to his sleepy little town. He was happy.

"Much too happy!" protested Pierre Louys in the train. "It isn't fair, it's against nature. Artists were intended to be miserable. It is part of the over-all plan of Creation. Mark my word, one of these days some female is going to reach out her claws for him."

They reached Brussels in the evening. As the train puffed into the station Claude spied Eugène Ysaye pacing the platform, looking taller and bulkier than ever in his top hat and fur-collared overcoat.

"I received your telegram this morning," said the violinist, greeting Claude with a friendly bear hug. "Did you bring the copies of the Quartet?"

With typical Belgian hospitality he pressed the two young men to be his house guests, but Pierre declined on the pretext that he wished to study the city's monuments. Claude, however, accepted the invitation with pleasure.

"Then let's go home," said Ysaye, climbing into a fiacre. "You must be starving and dinner is waiting for you. Incidentally, I've arranged for a preliminary rehearsal of the Quartet for the day after tomorrow. Which means you'll be able to return to Paris the same day, if you are in a hurry—which I hope you aren't."

No sooner had they reached the house than he took Claude to his study and showed him his collection of rare violins.

"Here's my Guarneri del Gesù," he said, lifting the instrument out of its box as tenderly as if it were a baby. "There is no finer violin in the world. That's the one I'm going to take on my American tour next year. Listen to that tone."

He was about to play when Louise Ysaye entered the study.

"Oh, those old fiddles! They'll get us in the poorhouse yet. Come on, dinner's ready."

With a sigh he replaced the violin in its velvet coffin, and muttering under his breath he went into the dining room.

During dinner they recalled their pleasant days at Luzancy. Madame Ysaye inquired about Gaby, and Claude said she was well and sent her regards.

Ysaye discoursed about Ernest Chausson, for whom he had a deep admiration.

"If only he weren't so rich, he would be recognized as the great musician he is, but for some reason it is as difficult for a wealthy man to be accepted as an artist, as to enter the Kingdom of Heaven. Fortunately, when the time comes to make up the deficit of a concert or pay the mortgage on the church, then pastors and musical groups suddenly lose their prejudices against wealth."

After Madame Ysaye had retired, the two men lingered at the table in a mood of digestive languor, smoking and sipping their benedictine. For a while they talked desultorily about Charles Gounod and Tchaikowsky, who had recently died. Then the conversation faltered and silence fell between them.

The names brought to Claude memories of distant half-forgotten days. He recalled Monsieur Gounod, skullcapped and spade-bearded, playing the organ in his study, reminiscing about his years at the Villa, his discussions at the Café Greco with Mendelssohn . . . Then his mind drifted to Madame von Meck and her beloved Piotr Ilyich. Where was she now? Was she still alive, still having her afternoon concerts? And Sonia, darling Sonia, what had become of her? He probably would never know . . .

"What are you thinking about?" Ysaye smiled, pulling on his curved pipe.

"That life is a series of short stories without an ending. We meet, we part and then we never see or hear from each other."

"We even part from ourselves. We meet someone, fall in love and then one day we fall out of it. Why? Most of the time we don't know. Our heart does not ask our advice . . ."

He knocked the ashes from his pipe into his palm and let out a chuckle.

"If we're going to start philosophizing about life and love and that sort of thing, it's time to go to bed." He got up. "Please give me a copy of your Quartet and I'll read it before going to sleep."

The following morning he burst into Claude's bedroom and vigorously shook him out of his sleep.

"You've written a masterpiece!"

"What do you say?" asked Claude, blinking his eyes open.

"Your Quartet is admirable. I've read and studied it half the night. It's going to startle people out of their seats when we play it.

And the critics! Oh, my friend, what they're going to say! But, don't worry, your Quartet will be played long after they're dead. Now get up and come down to breakfast. We've got things to do."

From then on, Claude's visit became a whirlwind. Ysaye insisted on taking him on a tour of the city; then he introduced him to his colleagues at the Conservatoire and later that afternoon to various personalities, notably Edmond Picard.

"And tonight we're going to the Opéra," he announced during dinner.

On the following day the members of the Quatuor Ysaye gave the first reading of the Quartet. The rehearsal was followed by a general discussion that lasted until it was time for Claude to drive to the station.

"We'll see you in Paris the end of December," said Ysaye, waving his hat as the train started rolling.

On their way back to Paris, Claude and Pierre Louys had the good fortune to have a compartment to themselves.

Pierre was still moved by the sight of Brussels' architectural wonders. Although he had given them little of his time, the contemplation of Sainte Gudule, the city hall and the Maison du Roy had filled him with lofty resolutions. These noble buildings had inspired him to dedicate himself to some imperishable literary work.

"I'm thinking of some vast edifying opus," he announced with solemnity. "A treatise on God's sense of humor."

Theologians, he explained, had failed to stress this comforting trait among God's attributes. They had created a frightening picture of a cantankerous, perpetually angry Almighty. This, in his opinion, was the reason why so very few people, even among the most ardent believers, were really anxious to meet Him. He proposed to change all that.

"I shall begin with the wondrous story of Saint Paula the Bearded, a Spanish nun of great virtue, who grew a sudden and prickly beard just as she was about to be raped. I shall then proceed with an account of the death of Saint Denis, Paris' first bishop, who, having been beheaded, walked away from the place of execution with his head in one hand and the palm of martyrdom in the other."

These well-established facts pointed to a delightful, somewhat unexpected sense of humor in the Almighty. This trait became still more distinct in His supreme handiwork, the human body. Who but a jovial, faintly Rabelaisian Creator would have so deftly combined the organs of love and excretion together in one compact, space-saving unit? What about the mouth, so pliable, so versatile? The nose, this ornamental sewer, amusingly located in the middle of the face, for all to see? Those arms that were just a bit short, so you couldn't scratch your back? And those tufts of hairiness scattered in random whimsy throughout the human landscape? The manly mustache, the feminine pubic goatee, the armpits' fleece—weren't they like the inspired brushstrokes of an impish artist? Why, at every step one met with similar admirable evidences of God's comic genius! . . .

"Personally I am certain it was He who suggested to His Son the sublime prankish notion of a resurrection at night, without witnesses, thus mystifying millions of Christians for centuries to come."

He paused thoughtfully; then continued, "I feel confident that after reading my book people will lose much of their fears and will be eager to meet face-to-face, so to speak, such a playful Creator. Thus death will have lost much of its sting, and I shall have rendered a genuine service to humanity. What do you think?"

"It looks like an enormous work and you may not have time to finish it. Haven't you anything less ambitious?"

"Of course." Pierre Louÿs made a casual, dismissing gesture. "This is a mere novel. It's the story of Chrysis, a prostitute in Ancient Greece. I've never been to Greece, but then almost nobody else has either. And I know prostitutes well. They can't have changed that much in two or three thousand years. I think I can write it in about a week."

"That's the one you should tackle," said Claude without hesitation. "It won't be so much of a strain and you'll have time to move out of your apartment and escape from women."

They began talking about the house on avenue Bourbon.

"I hope Gaby likes it and we can move in right away," Claude said. "Perhaps we'll have some peace for the little time we still have."

"What happened? You seemed so happy the night we had dinner together."

"We were. I don't know what happened, but something did. I almost don't recognize her. One moment she's delightful, the next she's exasperating. There's been a good deal of tension lately."

"I knew it couldn't last, it was too beautiful . . . She's probably fallen in love with you and hates herself for it. And you, too . . . I know it doesn't make sense, but it happens all the time."

"Whatever it is, I wish she'd get over it, for it makes us both unhappy. I used to dread the day she would leave, now I'm looking forward to it. Why must love affairs always end badly."

"Only the sun sets in beauty and dignity. Lovers must part in tears or in a rage. It's been like this since the beginning of time. Happy the impotent, the eunuch, the heartless who is above sex, desire, love and all such nonsense. To him belongs the Kingdom of Peace."

It was late in the afternoon when they arrived in Paris. Even before the train stopped they could see the streets black and shiny in the rain, reflecting the carriage lanterns and café lights.

"That's what I like about this town," Claude grumbled, taking his valise down from the net. "When it comes to the weather, you always can expect the worst and sure enough you get it."

"I'll drive you home," said Pierre, as they were walking out of the station.

They did not speak during the short drive. When the carriage pulled up in front of his house, Claude picked up his bag and climbed down.

"Thanks for coming with me. I'll let you know what Gaby thinks of the house. We may be able to move in right away."

"Good luck."

The two friends waved at each other. Then Claude crossed the sidewalk, entered the house and started up the stairs.

He found Gaby on her knees before an open trunk, packing. His heart skipped a beat. She liked the house, everything was all right . . .

She glanced over her shoulder, sprang to her feet and ran to him. "Darling, I've found an apartment."

He stopped and stood stock-still. "You—what?"

"Just what we want. Three rooms and a kitchen. I signed the lease and paid two months in advance."

He stared at her, too stunned to speak.

Breathlessly she went on, "I said I was your wife and you were on a business trip. They said it was all right and we coud move in right away. You'll see, it's nice."

A sudden fury swept over him. "How dare you do such a thing!"

"It was the last one they had and I couldn't get in touch with you because I didn't know where you were."

"And what about the house on avenue Bourdon?"

She laughed shrilly. "You call that a house! . . . It's got no heat except those silly fireplaces, the floor is rotten under the carpets and the carpets have holes in them, and the banister needs repairs or somebody will get killed some day, and there's only one toilet for the whole house and the windows don't close tight."

She was right. She had not been taken in by the decaying charm of the place, but had seen it for what it was—a dilapidated, almost unlivable house. Yet her common sense merely fanned his anger; he did not want to forgive her.

"You had no right to do what you did," he shouted.

"I only wanted to please you."

"Please me!" It was his turn to scoff. "And what makes you think you know what I want?"

"Once you said you wished you had a room to work in, and there is one. Also a tiny bedroom and a real kitchen with a stove. And we won't have to eat in the kitchen because there's a dining room."

"And what on earth will I do with a dining room after you're gone? Serve my own meals in it? Or . . . are you planning to stay with me forever?"

She winced, and in a flash he knew he had stumbled on the truth. Suddenly everything was clear.

"You aren't going to leave, you're planning to stay forever. That's it, isn't it?"

"Just a little longer. Please—"

He did not listen, and now his voice filled the room. "That story about Gontran was something you invented to stay on, wasn't it? And you arranged for Léonie to come, so it would sound more plausible. Come on, speak up."

She made no attempt to deny it and nodded brokenly. "I only wanted to gain a little time . . . a few more weeks . . . I was sure I'd want to go then . . ."

"But you don't any more, is that it? . . . And what about your career and your carriage?"

"I don't care, I want to stay with you. Please, darling, let me stay until spring. I'll go then, I promise." The words came out in sobbing gasps.

"But you won't. Neither next spring nor next summer nor ever. You're out of your mind and you're going to ruin your life as well as mine. But I won't let you. I want you to leave. Now!"

As if wounded she wavered and slowly slid down to her knees.

"Please, darling, don't send me away."

Open-mouthed he stared at this disheveled, imploring girl who was clutching and kissing his hand. Was this the Gaby of a few months ago, who had giggled in her rolling bathtub and danced in the street on Bastille Day? Was this what love did to a woman?

He leaned down, gently tried to help her up to her feet.

"Come on, Gaby, get up."

She would not rise. His anger surged back.

"All right, stay on your knees," he shouted, "but crying won't change anything. You'd better finish packing and go." He wrenched her hand away and started to the door. "I'll be back in an hour and I don't want to find you here. Understand?"

She crawled after him, begging him to let her stay until spring, swearing she would go then, wailing her pitiful, senseless litany, "I love you . . . I love you . . . I love you . . ."

He did not turn back but walked out, slamming the door after him, followed onto the landing by the sound of her sobs.

Night had come and street lights glowed hazily through the rain. He went to a nearby bistro, made his way to the deserted billiard room and ordered coffee.

Like a nightmare the scene of a moment ago blanketed his mind. "I love you . . . I love you . . ."

He repeated the words half aloud in a derisive mutter. That's all she could think about, all she could find to say. Apparently this was the great unanswerable argument, the supreme reason that explained and justified anything. "I love you"—and this gave her the right to sign a lease behind his back . . . "I love you"—and she could install herself in his life and take his freedom away . . .

A convenient argument indeed, especially since only a woman could use it. When her gentleman friend had told her he loved her and begged her to go to the country with him, then the argument hadn't been effective. She had laughed at the fat old man and said that because someone loved you did not mean you must love him back.

Absently he turned the spoon in his cup, took a sip now and then. For an hour he spurred his anger with thoughts of her treacherousness. Imagine inventing this ridiculous story about Gontran so that she could stay on as long as she pleased . . . Casually renting an apartment while he was away . . .

He still could feel the pressure of her lips on his hands, but it only goaded his resentment. Perhaps she thought she could blackmail him with a few tears, a few kisses and her silly "I love you" . . . She would learn that he could be pitiless when he had to. He congratulated himself on his heartlessness. He had done the right thing. She would be the ruin of both of them if he let her have her way. But he wouldn't. No, he wouldn't.

He glanced at the clock on the wall and got up. He paid for his coffee at the zinc counter and slowly walked back home through the rainy night.

As soon as he opened the door he knew she was still there. He lit the lamp and turned around. Then he saw her, crumpled in a heap against the bed, weeping softly into her cupped hands.

So she hadn't gone . . . Well, he would pick her up and throw her out . . .

He took a few steps forward and stood in silence before her.

Suddenly his fists unclenched. Something held him back. He couldn't bring himself to use force on her. He had loved her too often . . . Frantically he called on his anger, but his anger had spent itself. He told himself that now was the time to be brutal, to put an end to their relationship. A strong man would pull her up, grab her shoulders and throw her out. Well, he wasn't strong. At least not that strong. Perhaps it was weariness . . . Perhaps it was pity at seeing her like this, degraded of all pride, waiting like an animal ready for slaughter . . . Perhaps it was desire, for even now she was still desirable . . .

He leaned down, picked her up in his arms, laid her down on the bed and sat next to her.

"Don't cry," he said, stroking her hair. "You won't have to go. Everything's all right. We'll make the best of it."

As he spoke he knew he was doing wrong, but he lacked the courage to throw her out, and there was no use trying to reason with her.

And so there was only one way out.

Since she did not want to go, all right, *he* would go.

CHAPTER

12

BUT WHERE? . . . ANYWHERE. SOME LITTLE TOWN FAR AWAY WHERE
he could work in peace and where she would never find him.

But it took money to go away.

Soon he learned that only the rich are free to go wherever they
want. The poor must wait and go only when and where they are
wanted. The few paltry jobs he could fill that were available in the
provinces required detailed applications, certificates, references and
would take at least two or three weeks of correspondence. Which
meant that there again he was beaten and he must stay in town for
that length of time. Meanwhile there was the matter of the lease Gaby
had signed, and nothing could be done about it.

So they moved out of the garret and went to live on rue Gustave
Doré, in a fifth-floor apartment at the end of a courtyard—one of
those bleak, cheap, functional units that boasted of a faucet over
the sink, gas light, an indoor toilet and "all modern conveniences"—
and which he hated at first sight.

He had to give up his piano, too big for his "study." For now he
had a study—a narrow room about the size of a large closet that was
intended for storage and constituted another modern convenience.
Linne also had to be left behind, or rather she declined to leave. As
soon as the moving began she went into hiding and was no more to
be seen. He made no serious attempt at finding her. She belonged to

the past, the carefree bohemian days, the memories, the part of himself he was leaving in the garret. The potted geranium had mercifully died a few weeks before and remained undisturbed on the rear balcony. When it was all over, Madame Sénégal stood in the doorway, dabbing her eyes with her apron as the moving cart disappeared down the street.

Gaby loved the new apartment. She pointed out how draftless and leakless it was and how much more comfortable than the garret —which was true. Wearily he agreed and continued to look for some position out of town.

He learned of an opening as conductor of the Casino Municipal's orchestra at Royan, a modest sea resort devoted to tourists in summer and to sardine fishing the rest of the year. Best of all, it was located in the remote Gironde province, several hundred kilometers from Paris.

At once he wrote applying for the job.

He was waiting for an answer when he received his first engagement as a Wagnerian pianist. The affair was a great success and in no time he gave several drawing-room renditions of the Meister's operas. And so he became a *pianiste mondain,* like Chopin. Like him, he entered the most sumptuous residences in Paris through the service entrance, appeared in his beautiful evening clothes at the appointed time, bowed, smiled and played to roomfuls of society ladies who chatted gaily while he played and daintily clapped their gloved hands when he finished. Just as their grandmothers had done for poor, great Frederic . . . For this he received from the hands of the head butler a discreet envelope containing his fee, slipped on his overcoat and walked back home in the winter night.

Suddenly he had money, more than he had ever had. He could give twenty-franc gold louis to Gaby for coal and groceries; he was able to rent an upright piano, buy a few pieces of furniture. Now when he came home the place was warm and welcoming. She had worked hard, sewn new curtains, painted shelves, waxed and scrubbed. She did her best to please him; she cooked his favorite dishes and kept flowers in his study. He was touched by her attentions and brought her little presents. Both tried to make the best of it.

Perhaps in other circumstances they might have been happy, but their mutual resentment was too deep. Words had been said that could not be unsaid and which still rang in their ears. She blamed him for making her fall in love and ruining her career; he blamed her for spoiling the memory of their summer and forcing herself into his life. She prayed for a miracle that would cure her of her need for him and send her back to her old life; he dreamed of escape and his little faraway Casino Municipal. Neither of them spoke his thoughts.

And so December went on. Eugène Ysaye arrived in Paris with his chamber music ensemble, and two days before the end of the year presented Claude's Quartet at La Nationale. As he expected, it did startle the critics. They wondered why such a famous violinist wasted his time and theirs on "Monsieur Debussy's meowing of cats." One of them timidly contended that it was an extraordinary work, called it "a quartet of guitars" and dared to compare it to Beethoven's "quartet of the harps." Despite the disparaging reviews an uneasy feeling grew in musical circles that a great musician was moving in their midst. Some people began whispering the word "genius."

Besides presenting the Quartet, Ysaye brought momentous news. La Libre Esthétique, Brussels' leading artistic club, wanted to give an entire concert dedicated to Claude's work. Not only his Quartet and his songs, but even *The Blessed Damozel.*

"We're going to give you the finest festival anyone ever had," Ysaye went on. "A full orchestra, a splendid chorus, my own ensemble, and for your songs our best baritone Demest. The only thing we don't have is someone to sing the soprano part of *The Blessed Damozel,* but I understand Thérèse Roger knows the part and she may be willing to come to Brussels, if you ask her."

It was tempting, yet Claude hesitated. The festival was scheduled for the first of March and he might be in Royan by then. Would he be able to leave his post and come to Brussels?

"I expect an answer any day," he told Ysaye. "I'll let you know at once."

The answer came on the day before the violinist was to return to Brussels. It was another disappointment. It seemed they didn't need a conductor in Royan after all. The Casino Municipal had been a mirage.*

"Then it's all arranged," said Ysaye when Claude brought him the news. "We'll start rehearsing right away."

Thus chance brought Claude back into contact with Thérèse.

Once more he sat with her at the piano, reviewed with her the score she had already sung the year before. Again he looked into her clear, open face; again he listened to her laughter and felt the warmth of her friendship. After each coaching session it became more difficult to return to Gaby.

Things were not going well on rue Gustave Doré. Gaby's excitement over the new apartment had waned. She no longer tried to make the best of it. There were no more flowers on his desk; dinner was

---

* In a letter to Chausson, dated January 8, 1894, Debussy tells of his disappointment over the Royan episode. In another, he describes his feelings as a *pianiste mondain:* "I don't recognize myself. I now may be seen in drawing rooms, smiling and bowing . . ."

not always ready when he came home, sometimes not even begun. Often he found her, cigarette in her lips, immersed in the newspaper or some murder story, or lying in bed, her hands knotted behind her head, her eyes filled with tears and staring at the ceiling.

Her restlessness had returned. At Christmastime, in an outburst of exasperation, she had spoken about leaving. She was tired of waiting for him all day and at night watching him scribble his "little notes." She wanted to go out and have fun. "I'm too young to stay cooped up in this place," she had said, but when he had offered to take her to a music hall she had refused. Patiently he had told her she could leave any time she wanted. He reminded her of her career, pleaded with her to go. Nothing had come of it.

"I can't go," she had said. "I can't live without you, but don't worry, I'll get you off my mind one of these days and then I'll leave and we'll both be happy."

But she remained, demanding his love, bristling with jealousy at the thought that another woman might take him away. "I'll kill you if that happens," she had said one day, and he couldn't decide whether she meant it or not. He simply could not reason with her. Immediately there were tears, pleas, shouts that could be heard throughout the house. He did not know what to do any more. Could you throw a woman out simply because she loved you?

The hours he spent with Thérèse became for him a restful pause. In her company he forgot Gaby's tears and tantrums, the increasing tension at home. It was nice to be with this lovely woman who was also cultured and intelligent, and, above all, sensible. How refreshing to be with someone who loved and understood his music. Gradually his friendship changed into love. Why hadn't he seen it before? Here was the girl he wanted and needed. Not for a few weeks or months, but forever.

Then one day their hands met on the keyboard and their fingers entwined. They looked at each other, smiling. She brought her face close to his. Her lips parted and they kissed.

"I've loved you since the first day you came here," she murmured.

Soon they were making plans. Of course he was poor, but not as poor as all that. He was earning good money these days with those drawing-room concerts. He had a few pupils and he would get more, many more. Then there was an occasional transcription, a song or a piano piece sold now and then for a hundred francs or so. And of course there was his opera, which would be finished in a few months. She, too, would earn money with concerts and lessons. Her mother would be glad to give her some of her pupils. They wouldn't be rich, but they would manage. And love would make up for whatever little sacrifices they might have to make.

"After our return from Brussels we'll announce our engagement," she said, "and we'll get married in June."

And what about Gaby, he thought . . . should he tell Thérèse about her? It seemed unwise. Also unnecessary, for Gaby was so unpredictable she might leave at any time. And if she didn't, well, then on his return he would tell her about his marriage and she would have to go, that's all.

And so he did not tell her about Gaby—and joyously they set out together for Brussels.

Claude's festival was not a great success, but it was the next best thing—a prestigious failure. To be sure, his music disconcerted the Belgians as much as it did the Parisians, but the applause was substantial. Everyone was infinitely gracious, even the critics were polite.

The social side of the affair left nothing to be desired. For three days Claude and Thérèse were wined and dined. On the evening after the concert a gala dinner was given at Edmond Picard's, one of those Belgian dinners that never end. At eleven o'clock the guests were still in the oak-paneled room, lingering over dessert. It was a scene à la Jordaens: a long table laden with fruit and silverware; vintage wines gleamed softly in long-stemmed goblets, like liquid tulips. The men, encased in their starched, pearl-studded shirt fronts, beamed in their beards; the women, flushed and bare-shouldered, looked pretty in candlelight. Now and then Thérèse glanced at Claude across the table, her pale eyes slightly blurred with love and champagne.

Contentedly, a little drowsily he watched her, admiring the grace of her gestures, the amiability of her replies. Her charm was not like Gaby's scheming flattery; she made friends simply because she liked people. She knew how to listen, but also how to talk. The most intelligent men at the table had enjoyed conversing with her during dinner.

He saw her turn her head aside as her neighbor congratulated her on her singing of *The Blessed Damozel*. She blushed at the compliment and said she was proud to sing such fine music.

"Perhaps that's why you liked my singing. I sang with my heart."

Then someone at the end of the table teasingly asked her if her admiration went only to the music or to the composer as well.

"Both," she said with a smile. She hesitated, then plunged in. "You might as well know it, Claude and I are planning to be married very soon."

Silence fell around the table. Then suddenly everyone was talking at once. The host sprang to his feet and proposed a toast. Men rose to shake Claude's hand; women kissed Thérèse on the cheek. Amidst the confusion Claude noticed that one of the guests, a journalist, was slipping out of the room, and his heart skipped a beat. My God, Gaby would learn of his engagement through the morning newspaper . . .

Later that night, after escorting Thérèse to her hotel, he ran to the Poste Centrale and sent Gaby a telegram.

Back at his hotel he stretched out, fully dressed, on the bed, unable to sleep, his mind throbbing with anxiety. What would she do? Erratic, impulsive, jealous as she was, there was no telling what might come into her head. And, as always, it was his fault. He never did anything right. Now that it was too late, he saw clearly what he should have done. He should have ended their relationship long ago . . . he should have thrown her out . . . he should have told her about Thérèse. At least he should have fled . . . He had tried and there also he had failed. Was it his fault if the Royan job had not materialized? Yes, it was. Everything was his fault . . .

On the train back to Paris he managed to conceal his anguish from Thérèse. He did not reproach her for her indiscretion at dinner, did not even make mention of it. What was the use? What was done was done . . . She talked gaily, and nestling her head on his shoulder, dreamed aloud about their future.

From the station they drove directly to her house, kissed each other good-bye in the carriage. He escorted her to her door; then, climbing back into the fiacre, he flung his address to the coachman.

"Please hurry!"

The apartment was empty.

Curiously he was not surprised, he had almost expected it. Wearily he passed into his study, sat down at his desk and lit a cigarette. There was nothing to do but wait for her return—if she returned . . . Quietly he smoked for a while, enjoying the soothing effect of tobacco.

He was about to crush his cigarette in the ashtray when he heard the door open, and almost immediately she was standing before him, her eyes hard as emeralds.

"Know where I come from?" She spoke in a shrill, derisive staccato. "From your fiancée's! I just had a little chat with her."

He turned white. "Didn't you get my telegram?"

"Of course I did! . . . And you thought it was going to fix everything, didn't you? Little Gaby would understand, give you her blessings and get out."

"I thought at least you'd give me a chance to explain."

"Explain!" She laughed the word out. "I don't need any explanations, I saw everything. You were too busy kissing her to notice me, but all the time I was behind the lamppost across the street. Oh, you were the perfect gentleman! Escorted her to the door and everything . . . The moment you were off, I followed her upstairs, and as I said, we had a nice little chat."

"Get out!" he said through clenched teeth.

"Did you really think you could throw me over and marry her?" she sneered. "How did you go about it? Did you tell her how lonely you were and how much you needed a sweet, loving wife? And by the way, how's she in bed? As good as me? Or shouldn't I mention it? Excuse me. You see I'm no lady, I don't know music, don't sing in concerts. I'm only a whore"—her voice rose to a shriek—"but even a whore can love and I wasn't going to let her take you from me. And she won't now, don't worry."

He could not stand any more of this. He rose and she stepped back, frightened.

"All right, I'll go," she said, walking back. "But I hope I've hurt you as much as you've hurt me."

Her voice broke into sobs. Like a demented woman she ran to the door and down the stairs.

Quietly he closed the door and returned to the study, still filled with the sound of her words. He sat down at his desk, trying to sort his thoughts, but fatigue was rising within him, numbing his brain, closing his lids. He was too tired to think or care about anything. You could think just so much, feel just so much; then you didn't give a damn about anything any more . . .

His head sagged. He slumped forward, and with his brow pressed on his arm, fell dead asleep.*

♦

She had her wish. He was hurt, brutally and in several ways at once.

From Thérèse he received a short, sad note ending their relationship. This was the first blow. He had expected it, yet he was hurt to be condemned without being given a chance to explain or make amends. The second blow came shortly afterward. This one was anonymous, therefore more cruel but just as predictable. Since the

* In his admirable study *"Tel était Claude Debussy,"* M. Pasteur Vallery Radot published Pierre Louys' letter, dated March 22, 1894, which throws full light on this hitherto obscure episode of Debussy's life. "He was tired of her [Gaby] and wanted to marry . . . He tried to rupture with kindness . . . If there had been less haste in publishing the news of his engagement, he would have been able to break away . . . He was unable to do so, or if you prefer he did not know how to do it, and has been savagely punished for it . . . As to the rumors circulating about him and his way of life, such men as M. Ernest Chausson and M. Ernest Dupin, who have known him for many years, will tell you what they are worth. I know nothing more cruel than to see a man dishonored [*déshonoré*] in one week and all the doors closed to him at the very moment when people begin to realize that he has genius . . ."

news of the engagement had been published, many people knew
about it. A few solicitous persons among Thérèse's friends and her
mother's pupils made it their business to discover the reasons of its
rupture. It did not take them long to learn about Gaby, and even
less to guess the over-all sequence of events. What they did not guess
they invented. Soon they had enough to start talking.

Gossip travels at the speed of sound. With righteous lifts of eyebrows he was condemned for his treachery toward Thérèse and his
heartlessness toward Gaby. Thérèse was highly commended for dismissing such a deceitful suitor. As for Gaby, she had everyone's
sympathy. The poor heartbroken and discarded mistress aroused the
warmest feelings; the beautiful demimondaine who had sacrificed
everything for the love of this penniless and cruel artist became a
touching, romantic figure.

No one could find a good word to say for him. He learned that
the world is full of strangers who only await an opportunity to be
your enemies. Suddenly people he had never met knew everything
about him. They were the most eager to speak.

"Do you know what those idiots say about you?" Pierre laughed
one morning as he prepared to shave. "That you hypnotize women
with a glance of your magnetic black eyes."

"What?"

"Yes. You hypnotize women and rob them of their will power.
Whereupon the poor dears become your willing victims. Naturally,
you enjoy their bodies for a while and toy with their hearts. Some
even hint you also take their money. Then, casually, you toss them
aside." He began lathering his cheeks and grinned over his shoulder
at his friend. "I was surprised to learn this, but apparently that's
the kind of man you are."

"Will you tell me why people say such things?"

"Because they're mean and stupid. Don't forget that man is the only
animal who torments and kills for pleasure. Gossip is the universal
pastime. If gossip died, the world would be silent."

"How can people believe such nonsense?"

"Because the more absurd a lie, the more easily it is accepted. Don't
ask me why, but it's true."

"The thing I don't understand is what people can find to say about
me. I am the most ordinary, most commonplace person in the world.
I am no exotic stranger, I've been here all my life. I don't do anything special. My existence is that of a thousand other artists who try
to make a living."

"True. Yet somehow the things that happen to you don't happen to
them."

"What do you mean?"

Pierre began honing his razor, then stopped to look at him. "Now please don't get mad, but try to understand. Try to see yourself as other people see you. You say there's nothing strange about you and you live like other artists. It may seem so to you, but not to others. For one thing you don't look like other peple."

"Is this my fault?"

"I don't say it is. I'm merely trying to make you understand why people say the things they say. Let's take your face, for instance. Whether you like it or not, you have an unusual face. I don't say it's the most handsome face in the world, but it is unusual, arresting. The kind women glance at twice. Then your forehead. Nobody has a forehead like yours, except Beethoven and a few other crazy people. Conclusion: people suspect you may be a genius or a madman. Both very dangerous and highly suspicious. From madman to evil man there's only one step. In the Middle Ages they would have said you looked like a heretic and hanged you as a matter of principle."

"But—"

Pierre raised his razor in a gesture of impatience. "Don't interrupt me. Let me finish, then you can talk all you want. Now let's take your eyes. You have the damnedest, blackest, deepest, steadiest, most probing, most disturbing eyes I've ever seen. People will believe anything of a man with eyes like that. I would. You would, too, if you weren't prejudiced."

"You're an idiot."

Pierre turned around to the mirror of his washing table and began shaving. "As a matter of fact I find it very odd that an attractive and sensible young lady like Thérèse Roger, a well-known concert singer, daughter of an eminent singing teacher, herself the widow of a high-ranking army officer, should even consider marrying a man with such microscopic means of support such as yourself."

"She liked my music."

"Don't delude yourself. Women love art as pigeons love statues in public parks, for a purpose. It gives them something to talk about with men and a chance to confound them with the breadth of their culture and the beauty of their minds. But you'll never catch two women alone talking about art. They'll talk about men, fashions, the price of salami, their operations, their bowels, their children, but never about art."

"You're a cynic."

"That's what people call you when they have no answer. But let's not digress. The other day at Weber's I heard about a certain society lady who came to visit you in your studio at the Villa Medici wearing nothing but her wedding ring and a fur coat. Now I ask you, do you know many people to whom this sort of thing happens? I myself am beginning to believe in this hypnotism nonsense. Finally, didn't they use to call you the Prince of Darkness at the Conservatoire? A rather unusual nickname, don't you think? Come on, my friend, confess. Admit that you're a vampire in human shape."

"You go to hell."

"That's the thanks you get for telling the truth." He remained silent while shaving his chin. "Don't be discouraged," he went on as he wiped the lather off his razor blade. "In a few weeks people will talk about someone else."

"Meanwhile they're taking my livelihood from me. I had several engagements to play in private homes; they've all been canceled. Three of my pupils have been withdrawn without notice. For your information, your hypnotist is starving to death." He walked to an easy chair in the corner of the room and sat down. For a moment he gazed through the tulle of the window curtains. A rueful smile formed at the corners of his lips. "And to think that all I wanted was to avoid hurting anyone. So much for good intentions!"

"Hell is paved with good intentions."

"Then will you tell me what is paved with the bad ones?"

"Instead of asking embarrassing questions, why don't you come with me to Weber's and tell your side of the story to a few people? How can your friends defend you, if you don't defend yourself?"

"I'm sorry, but I just can't bring myself to open my private life to strangers. Besides, I don't think it would do any good. With my face, my forehead, my eyes I don't stand a chance." He laughed. "People will always believe the worst of me. Well, let them say what they like!" He shrugged and let out a sigh. "I only hope they'll soon get tired of it."

And so Claude returned to his apartment, his work and his diet of bread and tea. Since he did not attempt to justify himself, his silence was taken as an admission of guilt and he acquired a small notoriety as a dangerous man and heartless Don Juan. Again he knew periods of complete indigence, pawned his gold watch and whatever else he could.

Days passed. He lived alone, seeing almost no one but Pierre Louÿs and Ernest Chausson, who discreetly helped him with small loans. As usual he went about his round of publishers. In the evening he worked on *Pélléas* and by the end of April he had the first act completed. As a breathing spell he began to orchestrate *The Afternoon of a Faun*. He longed for companionship and found a new cat which he called Linne. She kept him company and behaved very much like her predecessor. At times he could almost believe he was back in the garret.

Gaby's belongings were still in the apartment but she had given no sign of life. Where was she, what was she doing? . . . Curiously he felt no rancor against her. It is almost as hard to hate an absent person as a dead one, and he had no talent for hatred. It was so useless: it solved nothing, repaired nothing. Whatever harm was to be done had been done. Little by little he was forgetting their quarrels, her trickery, the shrillness of her voice in anger. Instead he remembered the sound of her sobs, the wailing plaint of her "I love you . . . I love you" . . . the sight of her tears streaming down her cheeks, the unconscious grace of her body in that awful moment when she had slumped down to her knees and kissed his hand.

Now he felt sorry for her—also for himself. He missed her caresses and love-making. Longingly his mind returned to the past summer with its haggling over kisses and long mornings in bed. He had resumed his bachelor's chores, and they, too, offered an opportunity for comparison and regrets. Once more he made his ineffectual attempts at housekeeping. While he washed his laundry in the basin, or swept the apartment or mended his socks, he recalled the days when there were flowers on his desk and clean shirts in the drawers. He struggled with the kitchen stove, which worked so well for Gaby, and came out of the contest defeated. To boil water for his tea he burned mountains of newspapers and blew his lungs out on the recalcitrant coals, all to no effect. Finally he went out and bought an alcohol lamp like the one he had used in the early garret days. With a sigh he admitted that women had their uses. If only they were reasonable, they would be perfect.

Gradually the gossip about him dwindled, then stopped. Other things were occupying the public's attention. The curtain was rising on a brand-new spring, and on the boulevards the first automobiles appeared. The horses that had just grown accustomed to bicycles, grew panicky again. So did the Parisians. These machines, they said, would poison the air; everybody would die of suffocation. The air resounded with the booming of Russian chimes and the chords of Rachmaninoff's Prelude. It also resounded with the booming of homemade bombs. Fortunately most of the anarchists who hurled them killed themselves in the process; the others were guillotined. People started breathing again. Anglomania became so acute that in chic districts panhandlers now begged in English. A philatelist killed a man over a stamp.

And Monsieur Fromont—dear, kind, wonderful Monsieur Fromont —gave Claude a small transcription and with it a sensational piece of news.

"Personally I don't think your music is commercial," he began, fondling his fine white beard, "but my partner seems to think it soon will be."

Claude pricked up his ears, for Monsieur Fromont had never before mentioned having a partner, but prudently he remained silent.

"After all," the publisher went on with a tolerant shrug, "everyone is entitled to his own opinion, even if it's wrong. Anyway, since nothing makes sense in this business, he may be right. The public's taste changes so fast you don't know what's what any more. Look at this Rachmaninoff Prelude! A piece written by a twenty-one-year-old youngster . . . Now why can't you write me something like that?"

"What about my *Claire de Lune*?" Claude ventured cautiously.

"Why don't you take a chance and publish it?"

Monsieur Fromont puckered his lips until they were like the end of a medium-sized funnel. "It's too fragile, too nebulous. It lacks a certain something."

"What?"

"That certain something a publisher recognizes at once and which tells him a piece is truly commercial. Your *Claire de Lune* simply doesn't have it."

He made the gesture of a busy man whose time is being wasted on trifles, and ruffled some papers on his desk. "Anyway, go and see my partner. His office is at the end of the corridor. His name is Monsieur Hartmann."

Monsieur Hartmann spoke with a faint German accent. He said he had been impressed by Claude's Quartet, which he had heard at La Nationale. He then explained that he was Fromont's partner in name only, an independent publisher who used the firm's printing and distributing facilities, and financed his own editions.

"Too bad the Quartet is already published," he sighed. "But no doubt you will write other things. What are you working on at the moment?"

"An opera and a symphonic piece called *The Afternoon of a Faun.* Also, I've begun jotting down ideas for a suite called *Nocturnes,* probably for violin and orchestra. Monsieur Ysaye told me he would play it as soon as it's ready."

"Excellent!" The publisher beamed. "I think you have talent and I see a great future for you. I'll drop in on you one of these days and you'll play for me some of your new compositions. By the way, could you use a little advance? Say a hundred francs?"

Claude signed a receipt and walked out in a daze. He felt he must tell someone of his good fortune. He went to Pierre Louys' apartment and found his friend at his desk, pen in hand, gazing at the smoke of his cigarette.

"What're you doing?" Claude asked.

"Can't you see? I'm waiting for inspiration. That's how writers spend most of their time. I've sat like this all morning. Writing is exhausting work, the tension is unbearable. You can't move, only yawn now and then. What brings you here?"

Claude told him about the transcription from Fromont and his encounter with Hartmann.

"This calls for a celebration," Pierre declared. "It's time for you to come out of your hole and see a few people. I'm going to give a small dinner and afterward you'll play for us what you've written of *Pélléas.*"

Excitedly he took his pen and began drawing up the list of his guests and selecting the menu.

"How about *poulet au champagne à l'Escoffier*?" he suggested.

Receiving no reply he looked up and saw that Claude was leaning back in the armchair, his eyes closed.

"What're you dreaming about?"

"Gaby. She'd be happy to know I've found a publisher."

"Are you still thinking about this girl after what she's done?"

"I'd like to know she's all right."

"Of course she is. A girl as pretty as this one doesn't have to worry. She's probably having a wonderful time and wondering what on earth she ever saw in you. You wouldn't be missing her, by any chance?"

"No, no. Of course not . . . I was just thinking how happy we were for a while."

"Well, forget about her and help me with the menu."

Thus Claude came out of retirement. The dinner at Pierre Louÿs' was succulent, the wines mellow, the conversation sparkling. Afterward he played the first act of his opera on a piano especially rented for the occasion. He received many compliments and returned home considerably cheered up.*

In high spirits he plunged into the second act. A few days later he was so engrossed in work that he did not hear Gaby enter the apartment until she was standing before his desk.

"Please forgive me," she murmured.

He looked at her, smiled and sprang to his feet. Without another word they fell into each other's arms.

---

* This dinner took place on May 31, 1894. It was on this occasion that Debussy met Thadée Natanson, director of La Revue Blanche, and his wife Missia, art patron and friend of Toulouse-Lautrec.

CHAPTER

13

THIS TIME THEY WERE GOING TO MAKE A GO OF IT. THE PAST WAS
forgiven and forgotten. They had learned how hard it was for them
to live apart and they were grateful to life for giving them another
chance.

Sometimes when they were in bed, their faces almost touching on
the same pillow, they talked in whispers of their feelings during
the weeks of their separation.

"I tried to hate you," she would say. "I swore I'd never come back,
but I couldn't get you out of my mind."

"And I used to tell myself I never wanted to see you again, but all
the time I kept wondering where you were."

"Darling, forgive me. I'll never hurt you again."

"It was my fault. I thought we shouldn't live together. I wanted to
get away from you, for your good as much as mine."

"It's so simple to be happy when you love each other."

They were full of good resolutions. They did not ask questions.
When she said she had gone to Lisieux, he pretended to believe.
Questions were dangerous. Happiness demanded discretion, trust,
good will. They would be careful. Watch themselves.

With delight he rediscovered her physical presence: the weight
of her head on his shoulder, her regular breathing when she slept,
the tiny mole under her left breast. He revisited the mounds and

valleys of her body. Again his hands slid down the slope of her loins and his fingers crept into lust's hideaways. Again she grew taut under his touch and her thighs opened before him, like a fan.

They had a tranquil summer: not as gay or foolish as the previous one, but tender and peaceful. They no longer kept count of their kisses; she no longer walked nude about the room. They were too sedate for that sort of thing. In the afternoon they paid a visit to Père Bailly or sat on the terrace of a café. Occasionally they spent an evening at the circus or at a music hall. There was nothing bohemian in their conduct. People in the district regarded them as a fine, well-behaved couple.

Thus summer wore on. He worked hard on *Pelléas.* Thanks to Hartmann's advances, he was able to dedicate most of his time to it and he made considerable progress. He also orchestrated *The Afternoon of a Faun* and drafted a new version of the *Nocturnes,* this time for various groups of instruments. As a diversion he would sketch a piano piece. Music flooded his mind. Gaby did not disturb him. She attended to the housekeeping, smoked her *cibiches* and read the newspaper. Now and then a letter came from Pierre Louys, who was in Biskra—of all places!—on the edge of the Sahara, half crazy with the heat and misbehaving with a young belly dancer. Tolerantly they chuckled over the account of his adventures. He was young; some day he, too, would settle down . . .*

At the end of August they spent a week with the Chaussons at Luzancy. With some surprise he noticed that Gaby's popularity had increased, especially among the ladies, while his had diminished. Of course no mention of the Brussels episode was made, but he sensed that their sympathies were on her side. He felt it in the severe glances they gave him, which contrasted with the effusions and marks of affection of which she was the object. Clearly everyone looked upon her return to him as a proof of her generous and forgiving nature.

At the same time Pierre came back to Paris, brown as a sheik, bringing back a burnoose, the memory of his nights with Meriem and the manuscript of *Les Chansons de Bilitis,* which he had managed to write in his spare time.

"I feel wonderful," he announced. "Only a little tired. Too much writing, no doubt."

Then it was autumn again, with its gray skies, gusts of wind, side-

* In July of that year, 1894, Pierre Louys had left Paris to attend the Wagner Festival at Bayreuth. On his way he stopped in Geneva, where his friend André Gide gave him an enthusiastic account of the beauties of Biskra, where he had spent the winter, and the charms of a certain dancer by the name of Meriem ben Atala. Forsaking Wagner, Pierre had rushed to Africa and in the furnace-heat of summer made contact with the exotic *ouled naid.*

walks flecked with dead leaves. One October evening newsboys shouted extras about the arrest of a certain Captain Dreyfus. With horror the French learned that this quiet, well-to-do family man had been selling military secrets to the German Embassy. Although the scoundrel protested—even in his sleep—that he was innocent, nobody believed him, for the army said he was guilty and that was enough. Therefore everyone approved when in December a court-martial condemned the traitor to public degradation and solitary confinement for life on Devil's Island. Many felt he should have been shot.

Three days after the verdict, on December 22, Claude's *Afternoon of a Faun* was presented at La Nationale.

To his surprise it was an enormous success. The hall resounded with applause. The entire piece had to be repeated. Even the critics were impressed. Grudgingly they admitted he had created a unique musical style and reached absolute mastery.

He had his first genuine taste of success, but his joy did not last long. Gaby was becoming restless again. He recognized the symptoms: the edge of shrillness in her voice, the sullen curve of the lips, her lidded glances of resentment. The conflict between her love and her career was stirring back to life. She uttered the same old grievances. Once again she mentioned the carriage and beautiful apartment she had given up "on his account." With consternation he realized the gravity of the mistake he had committed in taking her back. Nothing had changed: the chasm between them was as great as ever.

Even the triumph of *The Afternoon of a Faun* became a pretext for her gibes. Sure, he was famous now, but what good did it do them? Money was just as scarce as before and you couldn't eat applause. Her hostility flared up in sudden outbursts. "What does it get you, all this scribbling of little notes? . . . What kind of a profession is this where you get paid with applause?" At times she felt overwhelmed with remorse. She wept, begged his forgiveness for the pain she caused, and again he forgave. She even spoke of leaving, even started to pack up, but he knew she would not leave any more than he would order her out. They were bound together in chains of their own making which neither had the strength to break.

He would have liked to speak to Pierre, not only about Gaby but also about *Pélléas* and the music he was slowly weaving for it, but Pierre had again left Paris, this time for Seville and a survey of native cigarette girls.*

---

* Nothing illustrates better the differences of character between the two friends than their correspondence at that time. While Debussy wrote, "As for me I'm writing a kind of music that will be understood in the twentieth century," Louys wrote, "I continue to do nothing with my ten fingers, except un-

And so he sought refuge in work. All winter he worked on *Pélléas*. He spent nights at his desk. Dawn found him exhausted but happy, hunched over sheets of music paper. Gradually he withdrew into a world of sound and fantasy in which he forgot Gaby's recriminations and the absence of his friend. Once again music made up for everything.

Then one day in April *Pélléas* was finished. He almost did not dare to believe it. It had taken two years—and now it was finished . . . A gust of hope swept over him. Perhaps it would bring an end to his poverty, this hand-to-mouth existence he had led since his return from Rome. The end of piano lessons and odd jobs for publishers . . . Perhaps he would be able to take Gaby out to dinner or a show from time to time. For her, also, it had been a long and difficult period, but from now on, things would be better. They might even be happy again, for she did love him despite her moodiness and her tantrums. She didn't really ask for much: a little fun, a great deal of love and loving. Now he would be able to give her all that.

He brought the score to Hartmann, who was enthusiastic.

"You must hurry and finish the orchestration," said the publisher. "I'm anxious to submit it to the Opéra Comique."

Claude promised to write the orchestration during the summer. In September or October the work would be ready for production.

Hartmann gave him another generous advance. "With a bit of luck, we may have it performed next season," he said with his slight German accent. "And by the way, I saw Monsieur Colonne. He wants to play the *Faun* in October."

Claude gaped incredulously. This meant recognition. The Colonne Orchestra was one of the best in Paris; some said the best. Critics might sneer at La Nationale concerts, but they did not sneer at the Colonne concerts. Even Gaby was impressed when she learned that Claude's music would be performed in the huge hall of the Châtelet, and still more so when she was told that he would receive a royalty for the performance.

As if all this were not enough, his Quartet was again played at La Nationale, and this time quite a number of people liked it. One or two critics ventured to say that although it was a strange, hermetic work, it contained glimmers of great beauty.

To crown it all, Pierre Louÿs returned from Seville.

Nostalgically he recalled the tortuous streets, the glasses of manzanilla under the awnings of cafés, the clip-clop of shabby but proud Andalusian carriages along the Paseo and the local little sluts

---

mentionable things." When Debussy mentioned he was nearing the end of his opera and was "tremblingly [*en tremblant*] writing the death of Mélisande," Pierre Louÿs gave him the names and peculiarities of his various mistresses.

who had composed his Spanish harem. By now he had finished squandering his inheritance and was furious at his doctor for keeping him alive.

"He promised I'd be dead by now, and look at me! Solid as a rock—but not a sou in my pocket!"

With horror he faced the necessity of earning money. In his agitation a thousand projects formed in his mind.

"Why don't we collaborate on a ballet or an opera?" he suggested. "Something we could dash off in a few weeks that would make us rich."

Claude was all for it, and they discussed the opera they were going to write together. It was an adaptation of Grimm's fairy tale *Snow White* and was to be called *Cendrelune*. But soon Pierre's interest in the project began to wane. Their encounters grew less frequent. They took to sending little notes to each other and discussing the subject by correspondence as though they were living in different cities. Before long Pierre tired of *Cendrelune* altogether, and left for the country to write a novel which was to appear by installments in *Le Mercure de France*.

That summer Claude and Gaby went to Lisieux. She presented him to her parents as a fellow employee in the fashion establishment in which she was supposed to work. They looked just as she had described: her father, the aging small-town Don Juan still proud of his wavy hair and irresistible mustache, now a dull gray; her mother frail-looking and white-coiffed, with two gleaming blue eyes imbedded like precious stones in the wrinkled leather of her face. There he saw a Gaby who wore no mascara and did not smoke, who lit her father's pipe and ran out of the house to do errands for her mother. Without effort she became the adolescent she once had been, and even her lies had an undertone of innocence.

They went to Orbec, but there things were different. Gaby's brother-in-law did not approve of her and had forbidden his wife to receive her in his virtuous home. Thus the two sisters met furtively while Claude wandered through the Norman countryside or sat by the windmill on the pond of La Vespière, which reminded him of the silvery ponds at Ville d'Avray.*

They returned to Paris in good spirits that lasted throughout the summer. Again they tried to make a go of it, and for a while they achieved a semblance of happiness. They lived in an atmosphere of expectation. Success was around the corner, and success would bring money and make their lives easier. He was very busy with the re-

---

* Shortly before her death Gaby stated that it was during this visit to Orbec that Claude, caught in a sudden summer downpour, had sketched the famous prelude *Jardin sous la pluie*.

hearsals of the *Faun* at Colonne's. Naturally he hoped that Pierre, who was back in town, would attend the performance, but Pierre had another installment to dash off for the magazine and could not come.

"I am terribly sorry, but you understand, don't you?" he said.

"Of course."

Of course . . . He argued with himself that the matter was of no importance, but he felt the disappointment more keenly than he would admit. The performance of the *Faun* at Colonne's meant so much to him. He had been sure that his friend would want to share his brief moment of triumph. It came as a jolt that he had been wrong.

At about the same time he experienced another disappointment. This one of staggering proportions . . . While working on the orchestration of *Pélléas* he became dissatisfied with the opera. With desolation he realized that after two years of work, he had failed to say what he wanted to say. It was a crushing blow.

He went to see Hartmann, pleaded with him for an extension of time. "Only two or three months. I merely need to go over a few scenes."

The publisher retorted that the opera was excellent as it was. "Besides, what makes you think the new version will be better than this one?"

"I don't know, but I must try."

"You realize, of course, that the score should be submitted right now, if you want it performed this season."

"I do, and believe me, I am as anxious as you are, but I just can't let it go out of my hands until I feel I've done the best I could."

"Your artistic integrity is commendable, but also very foolish. You need money desperately and here you're refusing to release a work that is finished."

At last the publisher let Claude have his way. He even consented to continue his advances on future royalties.

"But for God's sake, hurry," he said as Claude was walking out of the office.

Claude started working again on *Pélléas*. At first he merely altered a few scenes, but before long he was rewriting the entire opera. To Gaby this was more than folly, it was perverse cruelty. She had lived in the hope that the production of the opera would improve their circumstances. Her hopes came crashing to the ground. Her disappointment vented itself in a flurry of sarcasm.

"You'll never finish it. Never!" she shrieked. "You'll always find something wrong with it. I know you, in twenty years you'll still be scribbling your little notes."

He snapped back that she did not have to stay and watch him scribble his little notes. The door was open, why didn't she go?

"Yes, why don't you go? Why don't you leave me alone!"

Now they were shouting, flinging their resentment at each other in words that hurt and were meant to hurt. Her eyes had grown opaque, her face chalk-white. Rage made her lips tremble and words came out of her mouth in a stutter. He watched her in a mixture of pity and desire; then, taking his hat, he went out.

Winter arrived. Their quarrels became a daily occurrence, almost their sole diversion, a cruel sport at which they became experts and which gave them a chance to vent their resentment and usually ended in savage love-making, sometimes on the bed, sometimes on the floor, which afforded them a few moments of bitter, exhausted peace.

To some, lust is food. Even in this climate of perpetual brawls and scorching sensuality they might have managed some sort of co-existence, perhaps even some kind of happiness. Gaby's jealousy spoiled this last chance. Like a throbbing disease it inflamed her mind and destroyed the last vestiges of her common sense. For both of them it made life an inferno.

Now when he came home she greeted him with suspicious glances and probing questions. "Where've you been? . . . Why didn't you come sooner?" Sometimes he patiently appeased her fears and the evening went by without incident. But jealousy feeds on its own torment and doesn't want to be cured. Soon she refused to believe his explanations. She did not want to listen, let alone be convinced. Now there was no more hope.

One evening he came home later than usual. He had had to wait for a pupil; the lesson had begun forty minutes late.

"And you expect me to believe that?" She laughed.

"I don't care whether you do or not. It happens to be the truth."

"The truth! Since when do you ever tell the truth! Why don't you admit you went to see a woman?"

"Because I didn't."

"Come on, tell me the truth. How was she? Did she make love well? As well as me?"

She was standing before him, staring at him through eyes that had turned a deep steely gray. The thought flashed through his mind that she had gone insane. No one but a mad woman could look as she did now.

"Well," she snorted. "I'm waiting. How was she? Did you enjoy making love to her?"

Suddenly her face went white, and it was a frightening thing this whiteness that rose from within and drained the blood from her veins.

"Some day I'm going to kill you, do you hear?" She spoke in low tones, almost in a whisper. "I'm going to kill you!"

"Oh, stop being melodramatic."

"You don't believe it, eh? . . . Well, you'll see, one of these days, I'll do it . . ."

With a shrug he turned around and walked to the door.

From the landing he still could hear her threats. Then she gave out a strangled moan and he heard her sob his name. For an instant he thought of returning, taking her in his arms. It was too late. She couldn't be helped. She was sick. Sick with love, with jealousy, with despair at her own weakness . . . Sick from loneliness and poverty, sick from loving a man she did not want to love . . .

She was asleep when he returned after spending half of the night in a café. She did not wake up when he slipped into bed at her side, and for a while he watched her tear-stained face, calm and golden in lamplight. Gaby, poor Gaby . . . Now, at least, she was at peace, free from her self-inflicted torment. Thank God for sleep . . .

But sleep did not last forever. Each day brought her fresh suspicions and new anguish. Their quarrels no longer ended in love-making but in explosions of senseless abuse that sent him stalking out of the apartment, slamming the door and rushing down the stairs. Thus she made it impossible for him to work and ironically achieved the thing she dreaded most. He stopped coming home after his lessons. He wandered through the streets, dined in unfamiliar *gargotes,* spent his nights in cafés. Now and then he went to L'Auberge du Clou and listened to Erik Satie's witty nonsense and bizarre compositions. And, inevitably, women reappeared in his life. Some gave him the solace of their friendship; others the momentary oblivion of their caresses. He returned home late at night to face a frantic Gaby who hurled threats at him. Without a word he locked himself in his study and worked for an hour or two before going to bed.

Gradually his life lost all purpose. Hope went out of it, like air out of a balloon. A tranquil despair settled upon him. He no longer had any faith in the future and accepted the certainty of ultimate failure and bankruptcy. He now knew that his father was right and that he would never amount to anything. Even the performance of the *Faun* at Colonne's had brought no commission from publishers, aroused no real interest in his music. Like all the other performances it had faded in a spatter of applause, a few lines in newspapers.

It was too late to change, but at least he had no illusions any more. Whatever he did, he would always be poor. He still worked on *Pélléas,* but without any serious hope of performance. Ruefully he suggested that his opera might perhaps be given in a puppet show.

When finally Hartmann lost patience and started to balk at further advances, his financial situation grew desperate.

Now even the pretense of a family budget had vanished. To avoid being evicted from the apartment, Gaby sold her dresses. He, of course, had pawned whatever could be pawned. They lived haphazardly from day to day, praying for a transcription, a loan from a friend, a fifty- or hundred-franc note that Chausson might slip into his pocket under some pretext or other.

Sometimes he watched her across the table over the remains of their pitiful meal. She had grown very thin. Her eyes had recessed into their sockets and glowed with a disturbing brilliance. It was strange to see her dressed in a cheap skirt and blouse, her shoulders wrapped in a fringed shawl. Strangely, she had become more beautiful. At times her face assumed a haggard loveliness that aroused his desire as well as his pity. Why, oh why did she go on living with him?

In June she would be thirty. Hadn't she wasted enough of her youth on him? Hadn't she yet had her fill of privations and grief? How much could a woman endure? How long could a woman flagellate herself for the love of a man?

A thousand times he had been on the verge of asking these questions, but he had learned that words merely confused things between them and he had kept himself in check. Anyway, he doubted that she knew the answers.

As for him, he had long stopped wondering how he felt about her. He only knew that at one time he had loved her very much. Now his feelings were entangled in a mesh of desire, pity, tenderness, anger, gratitude and exasperation. He was unfaithful to her, yet she was dearer to him than any other woman. Of such contradictions the human heart was made.

Weeks passed. Winter drizzled into spring. In cafés people had much to talk about. As usual, trouble was brewing in Africa. The Italians, who had gotten the colonialist bug, found Abyssinia a tough nut to crack and wisely returned to their beautiful country. The British were having difficulties in various places, but they were used to it and somehow muddled through crisis after crisis to their ultimate advantage. Luckiest of all were the French. Always successful with women, they persuaded the Queen of Madagascar to let them have her kingdom and thus acquired a splendid colony in a gentlemanly way. In Paris the Dreyfus Affair, which everyone had believed closed, flared up again. Disturbing rumors circulated about the way Captain Dreyfus had been convicted. Indignantly every general and the Secretary of War—himself a general—sputtered through their mustaches that everything had been perfectly legal. As proof, they offered their word of honor. Some people asked for something more substantial. A few even wondered if by chance Dreyfus could be innocent.

Amidst all this, Claude's condition remained unchanged. If anything it grew slightly worse. At the same moment Pierre published his novel *Aphrodite* and made a fortune.

It was the same novel which had appeared—with no success whatever—in *Le Mercure de France*. Anyone else would have been content to forget about it. Not Pierre. He had faith in his star. Borrowing money from his brother, he published the book at his own expense, made a shrewd contract with the printer and waited. At first nothing happened. Then François Coppée, an eminent critic, wrote a lyrical review and launched the book not only in Paris but all France and soon all over Europe. With ravishment the reading public discovered the splendors and vices of Ancient Greece. *Aphrodite* oozed sex from every page. In heady banquet scenes rose-wreathed guests reached for golden grapes on silver platters, and with the same gesture, for the naked slave girls who served them. Adolescent courtesans used their hands and tongues with consummate skill while shapely musicians— also naked—played caressing music on primitive instruments. It was all very exciting and artistic. Pierre, who had expected to be pursued by the authorities for licentious literature, found himself a celebrity and rich again.

Of course he enjoyed his success, but he did not let it go to his head. Despite the flatteries of society ladies and the congratulations of colleagues he remained simple, kind-hearted and as full of pranks as ever. Toward Claude he was generous. Many a time he helped his unfortunate friend with a discreet fifty-franc loan. He sincerely deplored that this brilliant musician, his elder by eight years and a former Grand Prix de Rome, seemed unable to make money and remained bogged down in poverty.*

Like most successful people he was inclined to give advice. "You see, the trouble with you is that you work much too slowly. Look at me, I wrote *Aphrodite* in a few weeks and people like it. Now take this opera of yours, you should've finished it long ago. Another thing, you don't know how to grab opportunities. You've had many chances and you've always muffed them."

Claude listened with attention, for when a friend has become your

---

* It has been stated that Hartmann paid Debussy a monthly pension of five hundred francs. This is hard to reconcile with Debussy's letters to Pierre Louys humbly pleading for loans of fifty francs, and even on an occasion the charity of *twenty francs!* Throughout the year 1896 Debussy's letters leave no doubt as to his destitution and despair. In one of them he mentions "the rarity of lessons"; in another he hints that soon he will have "to sleep under the bridges." In still another he speaks of suicide as the only way out of his difficulties.

creditor the least you can do is listen to what he says. Besides, Pierre was right . . .

"I wish I had your facility, but it's not in my nature. I write and rewrite because I always feel that I can make it better. I'm afraid I'll never change."

Pierre gave him a swift glance. No, he would never change. He simply had no business sense. With all his talent he was another of those poor devils who never become successful . . .

"By the way, I think I'll go and spend the summer at the beach, then I'll go back to Seville. Ha, Seville! There's a place for an artist! If I can find a moment I'll write another novel. Something with a Spanish background this time."

And so again Pierre went away, and Claude went on working.

Summer passed, then autumn. Winter came and nothing changed. Gaby remained with him. Week after week, month after month they remained together without joy or purpose, floundering from periods of relative calm, even doleful tenderness, to periods of open hostility.

Her jealousy was like a growing cancer that nothing could cure. Frightful scenes exploded unexpectedly between them. One word might send them shouting at each other. Her lovely face would contort into a mask of fury. Her mouth, her wonderful mouth that had been a fount of delight, would shriek incoherences that made him wince and threats that made him laugh. Then would come the tears, the promises, the solemn oaths that were never kept.

How long would it last? He did not know. He only knew that their relationship was doomed and rushing to some ineluctable, disastrous end.

◆

Now it was midwinter—Saturday, the twenty-third of January, 1897—and he was on his way to the branch post office on rue Bleue, slushing through the snow in his old overcoat, his green muffler and his dashing sombrero, which by now had lost most of its dash and had turned a muddy brown.

He looked poor and shabby and was aware of it, but he no longer attempted to hide his poverty. This was another thing he had stopped worrying about . . . When you were almost thirty-five and still couldn't pay your rent on time and had to ask your friends for fifty- and twenty-franc loans, there wasn't much use trying to look prosperous, was there?

He reached the post office, pushed the door open and walked to the general-delivery window.

"Anything for me?"

The clerk peered at him over his spectacles; then gave him a smile of recognition.

"Let me see."

Dexterously he rifled through a sheaf of letters, let out a hiccup of pleasure and pulled out a blue envelope, which he raised to his nostrils.

"Ha, heliotrope!" For an instant he sniffed the letter, like a wine taster smelling the bouquet of a rare burgundy. "You can tell a lot about a woman from the perfume she uses."

He handed Claude the letter and brushed aside his identification card. "No need for it. I know you well enough by now."

"Thanks."

Wistfully the old man watched him walk away. It must be nice to be young and receive perfumed letters from pretty women. He, who had delivered thousands of them, had never received any . . .

With a sigh he closed the wicket.

Halfway to the door Claude halted to read the letter. A smile came to his lips as his eyes coursed over the spidery writing. She missed him. She had a whole flock of new kisses to give him. She always was home between five and seven . . .

Still smiling he folded the letter, absently slipped it into the inner pocket of his jacket and resumed his walk.

Hélène . . . So pretty and blond and gay. Thank heavens, she was gay! She did not weep, did not scream, did not make scenes. Come to think of it, he hadn't seen her in more than a week and he did miss her a little. Well, later this afternoon, after the rehearsal he would stop and see her for a moment. It'd be nice to hear again the sound of a woman's laughter for a change . . .

Outside the post office he paused and glanced up at the sky. Little snowflakes fell on his cheeks, and he wiped them off with his sleeve. It was one of those miserable winter days that are born furtively, without dawn, as if against their will; struggle for a few hours to a sickly twilight and by early afternoon capsize back into darkness. Now, at three o'clock, the air was charcoal-gray. In a moment it would be night.

He shoved his hands into his overcoat pockets and started in the direction of the rehearsal hall, where he found his three colleagues sitting on the stage in front of their music racks, idly talking while waiting for him. He apologized for his delay, shook hands all around and sat down at the piano.

They played Lekeu's Quartet, which they all knew well. After the first reading the violinist suggested they cut short the rehearsal and go home.

"No use killing ourselves," he smiled. "Nobody will show up at the concert tonight, anyway. We might as well go home and sit by the fire."

"Go ahead," said Claude, "but I think I'll stay a little while longer."

It was still too early to go to Hélène's, and he did not like the prospect of tramping in the snow until five.

The others replaced their instruments in their cases, slipped on their overcoats and shuffled out of the hall.

Alone, Claude lit a cigarette and desultorily ran his hands over the keyboard. Then, striking a series of muted chords, he began playing and soon was lost in music.

A moment later he heard a voice behind him.

"Where are the others? Weren't you supposed to have a rehearsal?"

"It's over." He recognized Chausson's voice and went on playing. "We decided nobody would come to the concert and we know the Quartet by heart anyway. So they went home."

"I can't say I blame them. Just our luck to have a concert on a night like this. Why didn't you go?"

"I didn't feel like facing Gaby and her questions."

Chausson made no reply and for a few minutes he listened to Claude's playing.

"Is this from *Pélléas?*" he asked at last.

Claude nodded. "Yes, something I wrote last night. I was curious to hear how it sounds."

"It sounds very nice, and I wish you'd finish this confounded opera. You've written it twice already—why do you go on rewriting it?"

Claude swirled on his stool and grinned. "Because I'm an idiot. You should know that by now."

He looked at his friend standing before him in his top hat and double-breasted overcoat, and suddenly he felt a deep gratitude for this modest and generous man who had helped him so many times and in so many ways.

"Why do we do any of the things we do?" he asked. "For instance, why have you been so kind to me all these years? Why do you give so much time to La Nationale and do more work than anyone else? Why do you slave over music when you could enjoy yourself? Because that's the way you are, and that's all there is to it."

"At least I have more sense than to orchestrate silly pieces of music like those *Gymnopédies* by your friend Erik Satie."

"They are not silly. The melodies are beautiful."

"This is a matter of opinion. But don't you think you should finish your opera instead of wasting time on other people's music? Anyway, why doesn't he orchestrate his own work?"

"He doesn't know how."

"And so you played the Good Samaritan and did it for him. Incidentally, can you tell me what the word *gymnopédie* means? I couldn't find it in the dictionary."

"I don't quite know myself. I think it has something to do with barefooted children. He's probably coined the word, he likes to give strange titles to his compositions."

"Well, you can tell him that his two compositions"—he spoke the word with impatient sarcasm—"will be played next month."

"It'll make him happy to hear that."

"I hope he thanks you for it, for I don't mind telling you that the committee has approved the performance only because of you. I still can't see why you did it."

"I wanted to cheer him up. Since his girl friend left him he's been feeling very depressed. Besides, the religion he's launched hasn't been very successful. At one time he had twelve converts, but I think he's lost most of them."

Chausson gave him a long, searching look. "All I can say is that you are a very kind but very foolish young man. Now come on, let's get out of here and have something warm in a café."

Outside, they waited for a cab on the sidewalk, shivering in their overcoats, their breaths frosting before their faces, but none appeared and finally they started toward boulevard Clichy, holding their hats against the wind, leaving the imprint of their steps in the dirty, trodden city snow.

Now lanterns glowed at the sides of carriages. Snowflakes whirled through the lampposts' haze of yellow light. At street corners, news-boys cried the evening extras, running from one customer to another, snatching copies from the bundle under their arms, pocketing money or counting out change at top speed.

"Extra! Extra! Sensational revelations prove Dreyfus guilty!"

"Extra! Sensational revelations prove Dreyfus innocent!"

"Extra! Read the truth about Dreyfus!"

"Don't be misled by lies! Read the *real* truth about Dreyfus!"

Dreyfus . . . For months the name had volleyed back and forth across every Paris boulevard at this hour of the afternoon. Each week brought forth new revelations, allegations, documents, forgeries, confessions, retractions, charges and counter-charges. After more than two years *l'Affaire* was growing more confused every day. And the end was not in sight.

"Will there ever be an end to this Dreyfus business?" Chausson grumbled, as they passed by a cluster of yelling newsboys. Without waiting for an answer, he went on, "Let's stop in this café. I'm freezing."

They entered a crowded, brightly lit *brasserie* and made their way to the end of the room, where they hung their hats and coats on the pegs on the wall.

They sat down at a marble-topped table. "This will do very well," Chausson said, rubbing his hands together. "A crowd gives you as much privacy as solitude. How about a cognac?"

Around them people read newspapers, discussed the Dreyfus Affair, played cards or dominoes. Waiters snaked between tables, carrying their round trays high over their heads, calling their orders to the counter. In her wrought-iron cage the cashier pounded her bell incessantly. Although it was still early, a few women were already at work, seated behind untouched *cafés-crème,* their faces half hidden by their large plumed hats, their lustrous eyes darting here and there about the room.

Chausson signaled a waiter and ordered two brandies.

"And better make them double." Turning back to Claude he explained, "Nothing like brandy to take the chill off your bones. That's why the Saint Bernard dogs carry little barrels of it around their necks when they go out to look for snowbound travelers. If brandy doesn't revive them, they're dead. I feel half dead myself in this kind of weather. Next winter I'll go to Algeria."

"You say that every year." Claude grinned. "What would become of La Nationale?"

"I don't care." He almost chanted the words, stressing them with an emphatic gesture. "I don't care a hoot about La Nationale. From now on I want to spend my winters in the nice Algerian sunshine, like your friend Pierre Louys." He caught himself. "He is in Algeria, isn't he?"

"I think so. Last month he wrote me that Seville was getting too cold and he was moving south. He just sent Gaby a small crate of bananas from Algiers, so I imagine he is still there. Unless he's gone to Biskra or Egypt or Timbuktu."

"He is young, and travel broadens the mind."

"Perhaps, but it's hard on friendship. It's difficult being friends with someone who is always running off somewhere. Even when he is in Paris we see each other rarely, and when we do, we disagree about practically everything. We simply don't have the same tastes. He thinks Victor Hugo is the greatest man who ever lived, with Richard Wagner coming close behind, and as you know, I can't get excited over either of them. He likes fifteen-year-old girls and I don't. Even in politics we don't have the same ideas. He thinks Dreyfus is guilty and I think he's innocent. And so we really have very little to talk about and we exchange flippant little notes full of puns and witticisms of this kind."

He took a sip of cognac and absently held the glass in his hand.

"Yet we're devoted to each other. I'll never forget he was one of the few people who, like you, stood by me when Thérèse broke our engagement and people said such nice things about me. And the many times he took me to dinner and helped me with my rent. Which proves that friendship can be almost as baffling as love."

With a cheerless smile he set the glass back on the saucer.

"Almost, but not quite. Nothing can be as baffling as love."

They remained silent for a minute, each following his thoughts in the easy silence of true companionship.

"Yes," said Chausson at last. "Sometimes love expresses itself in strange ways."

"So strange that you wonder whether it wasn't invented just to see how much you can stand or how long it'll take before you'll go crazy and jump off a bridge."

"You know what Shakespeare said. 'Love is a devil: there is no evil angel, but Love.' "

"No, I didn't, but he must have had in mind someone like Gaby when he wrote it. Sometimes I could cheerfully strangle her, sometimes I feel so sorry for the poor girl it breaks my heart."

"She loves you very much."

"And I love her, too, in some ways. That's why we're both miserable. Neither of us can find the courage to part, as we should have done long ago. Oh, I tried in my own, ineffectual way. I tried talking to her, showing her the senselessness of the whole thing. It did no good. I tried running away. Remember when I applied for the job in Royan? . . . And I'm sure that she has also tried to get away from me. But as you see, we didn't. Why? I don't know. Perhaps because something held us together, because we loved each other in spite of ourselves. Have you ever heard of anything so silly? Two people loving and hating each other at the same time . . . Can you imagine two people living together year after year and both wanting to break away? Does that make any sense? Honestly, if you read about a beautiful girl living with a penniless artist, when she could have almost anyone she wanted, would you believe it? I know I wouldn't."

"If you love her, why do you have other women?"

Claude's face broke out into a smile. "Oh, you know that. Who told you?"

"My wife. She has a great sympathy for Gaby—"

"I know." There was a sudden tinge of bitterness in his voice. "Everybody has a great sympathy for Gaby. At the time of the Brussels episode, when she ruined my reputation and took away my livelihood, she was a great favorite. In summer when we go to your country home I have often felt that Madame Chausson and her friends regard her as a poor victim and me as a heartless brute."

"I shouldn't say that, but I must admit women do stick together."

"They certainly do—and usually their husbands stick with them. Which makes it unanimous."

His smile turned into a soft chuckle.

"And so my ever-loving little Gaby runs to your wife, sobs her heart out and tells her what an awful man I am!"

"I don't exactly know, but it must be something like that, because I get the second-hand account of your infidelities."

"You want to know why I am unfaithful to Gaby? Because I get tired of her shouts, her tears, her threats to kill me if I look at another woman. Because now and then I rebel against this girl who has installed herself in my life and expects to control every one of my thoughts. Because I am thirty-four and I'm not married to Gaby and she has not the slightest intention of ever marrying me, and I feel I have the right to do whatever I like. Finally, because once in a while I want to see if I still am a man and capable of a flutter of desire or if I'm drained out, emptied of all feelings."

They looked at each other; then for a moment they sipped their brandy in silence. Claude rolled a cigarette and looked around, taking a few puffs. Waiters still ran back and forth across the room. At the tables people were finishing their *apéritifs* and preparing to leave for dinner.

"It's all very sad and complicated," Chausson said at last. "I understand it must be quite difficult for you to write music in these conditions. I hope things get better between you two."

"I don't know whether they'll get better or worse, but one thing is sure, they can't go on much longer as they are. On top of all, Gaby's father, whom she adores, is seriously ill. I told her she should go and stay with him, but the poor girl is so insane with jealousy that she can't bring herself to leave. Naturally, she is full of remorse, which makes her all the more nervous and miserable. So there you are. One of us is bound to crack up before long. I, for one, am about at the end of my rope. As for her, God knows what she may do. Jump out the window or set the house on fire or put poison in my food or simply pack and go . . . Nothing would surprise me."

Wearily he ran his hand over his eyes.

"I don't know, I don't know anything any more."

Suddenly he was tired of talking. He felt no relief from this long conversation. Words solved nothing.

"What time is it?" he asked, suddenly remembering Hélène. "I don't have my watch with me."

"Where is it?" asked Chausson, pulling his own watch from his vest pocket.

Claude laughed. "At its usual place, the municipal pawnshop. Dear Madame von Meck, she didn't suspect what an important part her watch would play in my life. It has kept me alive many times. The clerk at the pawnshop has become very fond of it. He hopes that some day I won't be able to redeem it so that he may buy it himself."

"My God, it's almost six o'clock," exclaimed Chausson. "We just have time to go home and change our clothes for the concert. Even if nobody comes, we must be there by eight." While talking he pulled out his wallet. "By the way, I owe you tonight's fee and I might as well give it to you now. I probably won't see you after the concert, I don't think I'll stay until the end."

He placed a hundred-franc note on the table. Then, in order to cut short Claude's thanks, he quickly turned around on his chair and called the waiter.

◆

They parted in front of the Chausson home on boulevard de Courcelles, and Claude proceeded alone to rue Gustave Doré.

It had stopped snowing and the wind had died down, but the cold was becoming intense. The air had the immobility of the truly icy nights. In the sky a few stars glittered, like specks of mirror on black velvet.

At last he reached his house, crossed the snow-padded courtyard and climbed the five flights to his apartment.

Gaby was in the dining room, leaning forward on a chair and warming her hands at the small glowing logs in the fireplace.

At the sound of his footsteps she turned her head around.

"What kept you so long?" she snapped over her shoulder. "I thought you weren't coming."

"After the rehearsal I went out with Monsieur Chausson and we had a drink in a café."

"All this time?"

"Yes. We talked about the programs for the next concert."

As he spoke he watched her face tense with suspicion, her eyes purple-lidded from fatigue and sleeplessness. Yet her beauty remained unimpaired. For an instant he marveled at this loveliness which no privations or grief could mar.

"Which café?" she asked.

"Look, darling, I must be back at La Nationale at eight, and because of the snow the streetcars aren't running. So please, let's not have a scene. I don't know the name of the café, I forgot to write it down. You wouldn't believe me, anyway. Why don't you ask Madame Chausson next time you go to see her?"

He spoke with a mixture of weariness and impatience and sat down at the table.

"Is there something to eat?"

"I have some soup."

She disappeared into the kitchen and returned with a plate of steaming soup, which she set before him.

"At what time did the rehearsal end?" she asked, sitting down at the table.

He ignored the question and tasted a spoonful of soup. "Delicious. I've always said you were the greatest cook in the world."

"Cut out the chatter. At what time did the rehearsal end?"

"I'm afraid I can't tell you that, for I happen to be momentarily without a watch."

She did not seem to resent or perhaps did not notice the irony in his voice and looked steadily at him across the table.

"However," he went on between spoonfuls of soup, "I have several witnesses who are ready to swear I was at the rehearsal. For your information we played Lekeu's Quartet, which we're going to play again tonight before an audience of approximately six people. Anything else?"

She did not reply and watched him gulp down his soup. "Don't eat so fast, it's not good for you."

"I have to hurry. Chausson wants me back by eight." He put his hand in his trouser pocket. "By the way, he gave me this. You probably can use it."

She took the banknote and slipped it inside her blouse.

"Want some more?" she asked as he was finishing his soup.

"I have no time, but I'll eat one of these." He reached for one of the bananas in the compotier standing in the center of the table. "It was nice of Pierre to send them."

She nodded absently. "I laid your evening clothes on the bed and put the cuff links in your shirt."

"You did?" He smiled, touched by her attention. "Thanks. It'll save time."

He often had noticed this furtive, unexpected motherliness. After exasperating him with her jealousy, she would do gracious little things that allayed his annoyance and aroused his gratitude. With indulgent amusement she would watch him struggle with cuff links, shirt-front buttons or the knot of his tie, and a sort of maternal solicitude would come over her face. "I swear you're as helpless as a child." She would smile with a shake of the head. "Come on, let me do it. You'll always need someone to look after you." Perhaps it was true that a man was always a boy to a woman . . .

The tension between them had lessened, and to change the subject he asked, "Any news of your father?"

She shook her head.

"Well, perhaps that's a good sign. He looked very strong to me when I saw him and maybe he'll get well in a week or two. But, as I told you, if you want to go and stay with him for a while, don't hesitate on my account."

"So you can have women while I'm away?"

He jerked as if stung by a bee and sprang to his feet.

"Oh, go to hell!"

He crossed into the bedroom, slamming the door after him. A moment later she heard the sound of his footsteps in the vestibule.

"When will you be back?" she asked from the dining-room doorway.

He slipped into his overcoat and put his hand on the doorknob. "I don't know. I'll be back when I can. Good night."

She resumed her seat by the fire, idly prodded the poker at the logs until at last a small faltering flame leaped out. For a while she gazed at its jerky, stumbling dance. On the mantel a little ceramic clock dripped time into the silence of the room.

She'd been wrong, she shouldn't have made that remark about women . . . One of these days she would drive him away for good. Why did she always say stupid things? Why? . . . Because she loved him too much. When you loved too much you loved badly, you became jealous and stupid and did everything wrong.

She truly was sorry she had made that remark. Honest, she was—especially since he meant well and was right. She should go home. Her sister's last letter was urgent. "Papa's real sick and Maman is tired out. Please, Gaby, come." Yes, she should go and she wanted to, but—but she was afraid Claude would go and see other women. Or maybe it would be the other way around. Oh, yes—a lot of them were eager to go to bed with him, waiting to steal him from her, if she only gave them a chance. But she wouldn't. She would stay right here and keep her eyes open. Yet she should go home . . . she should . . . she should . . .

Tormentingly the dilemma swung in her mind.

"All right," she muttered at last, half aloud. "I'll wait till the next letter, and if Papa isn't any better I'll go."

The compromise brought her some measure of peace. Her breathing grew easier. She leaned back on her chair and for a few minutes fell into a shallow doze.

When she awoke she found she was hungry. She went to the

kitchen and returned with a plateful of soup, which she set on the corner of the table. For dessert she ate a banana, chewing slowly to kill time.

Dinner over, she lit a cigarette and smoked, hand on cheek, while musing about Pierre Louÿs. A card he was, that one—and sharp as a tack. With one little book he had made more money than Claude would in his whole life. And now that he was rich again he was enjoying himself in Algeria, which was only right. If Claude would only finish his opera or write a few easy pieces, he, too, would make money and could take a nice rest, instead of having to go out at night to play the piano in an empty hall. But he never would, he'd never make any money . . . It must be nice in Algeria. They said men wore long white robes and there were camels in the streets and oranges were as big as melons. And everywhere the sun—the warm, wonderful sun . . . Just the same it was sweet of Pierre to send her those bananas. One of his jokes probably . . .

On an impulse she decided to write him a note of thanks. She had nothing to do, it would pass a moment. She rose and stepped into Claude's study to fetch pen and paper. Back in the dining room she resumed her place at the table, pulled her shawl tight around her shoulders, and hunching over the sheet of paper, laboriously began to write.*

The letter was short and took less time to write than she had hoped. She read it over while smoking another cigarette, then once again she came to sit by the fire. Glancing at the clock she saw it was still early. Time simply didn't move when you waited . . . In the fireplace the little flame had vanished. Only a red glow, like a patch of raw flesh, marked the spot on the charred log where it had danced a moment ago. Her eyes fastened upon it as a symbol of her own defeat. Like this, a flame of happiness had burned for a while in her life and now it was gone. Nothing remained but the pain, the regrets, the fear of the future.

Suddenly her heart burst open with desolation. Her hands went up to her face. Uncontrollably, in nervous, racking spasms, she began to sob.

She had lost him . . . He had gone out without kissing her or

---

* This letter is dated January 23, 1897, "at nine o'clock in the evening." Its simplicity, its sadness and gentleness are indicative of her character and education, as well as her state of mind on that fateful night.

"Claude has gone to La Nationale, where he plays the Lekeu Quartet. I'm alone and sad, even sadder than the weather and that's saying a lot . . . Thanks for the bananas and for pampering my *gourmandise*, for I love this fruit very much . . . Write us and tell us if it's warm in Algeria. Here it's so cold that your letter will warm up our hearts . . . I kiss you on the left cheek . . . Your little friend, Gaby."

saying when he'd be back. That's the thanks she got for loving him, cooking and washing for him, letting him have his fill of her. A girl should never show a man how much she loved him, for he took advantage of it and became mean. Soon she'd be thirty, and what had she to show for the sacrifices she had made? Nothing. She had thrown away her best years, ruined her career, and now he was tired of her and didn't care whether she lived or died.

Her wretchedness was changing to anger. She took her hands from her face, irascibly poked at the fire. A log broke and fell in the ashes with a hissing of sparks.

Yes, that's the thanks she got after all she'd done, the carriage she'd given up for him, the beautiful apartment . . .

Nostalgically she recalled memories of her demimondaine career: gala nights at the theatre, the Longchamps race where she had displayed her pink gloves and spring finery, the opening night at Maxim's. In retrospect her former way of life appeared like an unbroken sequel of gay champagne suppers, whirling waltzes, visits to dressmakers. How wonderful it all had been, and now it was gone. Her lovely dresses had been sold. Even the lingerie, the hats, the fancy garters . . . Her friend Léonie refused to see her any more.

And all because of him.

If only . . . if only she could stop loving him and find the strength to pack up and go! Oh, she'd tried, more than once, but in the end she had stayed. Why? Because when you loved so much you didn't have any strength. Or pride either. You clung, even though you were not wanted any more. You lost every shred of dignity and self-respect. Even love-making became another humiliation, for now it was you who must do the loving and caressing until finally your master stirred himself enough to part your legs and deign to possess you. Yes, that's what happened when you were fool enough to love a man so goddamn much!

Now, in a fit of mounting resentment, she muttered her thoughts to herself, wincing at her own abjection. Her mind, blurred with fatigue and anxiety, floundered in a labyrinth of dazzling fancies. She did not love him any more, she was leaving him . . . now it was he who begged for her caresses and she who laughed at him . . . and the more he begged, the louder she laughed . . .

She heard the sound of her laughter, and it jolted her back to her senses.

"I'm going crazy," she said aloud. "I swear I'm going off my head."

Slowly she ran the back of her hand over her mouth to give herself time to think. But no thought came, and she sprang to her feet. With a start she noticed that she was trembling.

"Now what's the matter? Am I sick or what?"

No. She was tired. Just plain tired of being alone and waiting for him. Waiting, always waiting . . . And why the hell wasn't he back? They must have finished playing their goddamn quartet by now. Why didn't he come home? God, she was tired! If only she could sleep, forget about him, about her father and everything for a while . . . Well, she might try.

She turned out the ceiling lamp and went into the bedroom. It was still lighted, and petulantly she reflected on Claude's extravagance. You'd think he had money to burn, wouldn't you? She walked all the way across the district to save two sous on groceries, but Monsieur forgot to blow out the lamp when he went out! Then she saw his clothes thrown haphazardly over the bed and the sight infuriated her. Of course he was too much in a hurry to hang up his suit . . . And why should he, when he had a dumb maid of all work who cleaned up after him and attended to such things?

With a rebellious snort she picked up his jacket and started smoothing the creases with her hand.

Then she felt the rustling of paper in the inner pocket . . .

She hesitated for an instant, but the temptation was too strong. Stealthily her fingers reached inside the pocket and brought forth Hélène's letter.

Her eyes ran over the first lines, but her hand shook so much, she could not read further. She didn't need to. She now knew why he'd been so anxious for her to go home. He hadn't been kind, he hadn't meant well. He'd only wanted to get her away so he could run to this woman who was waiting for him . . . How long had he been her lover? How many times had he gone to see her under the pretext of going to a lesson? And this was the man she loved, for whom she'd given up everything!

She remained dry-eyed and motionless, still clutching the letter. Then slowly the room seemed to whirl and she thought she was going to faint, but at that moment she heard the sound of his key turning in the lock of the door.

She ran to the chest of drawers, frantically jerked one of them open.

Already he was walking through the vestibule, guided by the light from the bedroom. Gently he pushed the door and peered in the direction of the bed, hoping to find her asleep. Disappointed, he looked around and saw her. She was standing in a corner, rigid and white, her eyes enormous in the pale blur of her face.

And she was pointing a gun at him.

◆

"You love her, don't you?" She was half shrieking, half sobbing the words in a frenzy of rage and grief. "Love her better than me? . . . You haven't grown tired of her, like you have of me . . . Do you kiss her the way you used to kiss me? . . . Sure you do! And she likes it, eh? Likes it a lot . . . And she wants more. That's why she's waiting for you."

Tears streaming down her face, she lashed her jealousy with images of his love-making. The veins in her neck stood out, blue and taut. Clusters of foamy bubbles had formed at the corners of her lips.

"But she won't see you any more. Ever! . . . And you know why?" She broke into a strident laugh. "Because I'm going to kill you!"

He saw the madness in her eyes and held his breath, fear crawling up his spine.

"Yes. I'm going to kill you, d'you hear! I'm going to kill—"

She stopped in mid-sentence and stared at him, open-mouthed, as though undecided what to do next. She shut her eyes, brushed aside a strand of loose hair and wavered back and forth. He thought she was going to crumple to the floor and moved to give her support.

"Don't touch me!" she screamed.

For an instant time stood still. The room seemed to burst with silence.

"Come on, Gaby," he said at last, taking a step forward. "Give me that gun."

There was the whiplash of a shot; then a scuffle. With fury she bit, kicked and clawed, while all over the house doors opened and tenants rushed upstairs. Haggard and disheveled, she fought viciously, inexpertly, woman-fashion, with her whole body, shouting obscenities like a streetwalker caught in a police round-up. Together they stumbled on the bed. For a moment she held him back, her teeth clenched, her spine arched in a last spurt of effort. Then, abruptly, she turned limp and fell back, unconscious, on the coverlet.

By now voices could be heard on the landing. Fists pounded on the door. He did not move, but stood by the bed, in a daze, holding the gun in one hand, rubbing his scratched cheek with the other. A moment later he heard the concierge's panting cackle asking for explanations, then the grating of her passkey in the lock, and suddenly the room was full of people, excited and half undressed, gaping at Gaby, white and still as a corpse.

"Nobody must touch her," someone said.

A woman yelped, "You killed her!"

He did not reply. They turned away from him and huddled in a tight cluster, all talking at once: the women in wrappers, their hair in paper curls; the men in slippers, their nightshirts hastily shoved inside their trousers. He recognized Madame Turpin—third-floor-rear—who sometimes spoke to him when they met on the stairs; and holding an unlit candlestick, Monsieur Lepic, a dentist who lived directly below him. Covertly they watched him while they talked, ready to pounce on him if he tried to escape or kill anyone else.

"It's a matter for the police," said the concierge.

Madame Turpin turned to her twelve-year old son, who was standing at her side. "Get your overcoat and run to Place Wagram. There's always a *flic* there." As the boy dashed to the door, she called after him. "Tell him also to send an ambulance."

Fortunately Place Wagram was only a stone's throw from the house, and soon a very zealous and out-of-breath gendarme arrived.

"Where's my boy?" asked Madame Turpin.

"I sent him to get the ambulance," said the policeman, puffing through his mustache. "He'll be back soon."

He sized up the situation at a glance, walked to Claude and snatched the gun from his hand. Then he pulled a small leather-bound notebook from his pocket.

"Name, age and profession."

Diligently he wrote down the answers.

"How do you spell Debussy? . . . All right, that's enough for the moment. Sit down and don't try any funny business. And you'd better wipe the blood off your cheek."

He was middle-aged, short and stout, with bulging eyes and stupendous whiskers. His kepi, perched precariously on his bald head, gave him a rather comical air in contrast with his manner, which was ponderous, almost judicial.

"Let's proceed." He turned to the others. "Did anyone witness the crime?" He pointed a stubby finger at Madame Turpin. "You, did you see anything?"

She hadn't. Nor had anyone else, for that matter, but all had heard the shot. Yes, there had been quarrels before . . . The two didn't seem to get along . . .

The concierge volunteered the information that Claude was always late with his rent, and Monsieur Lepic explained at great length how he was about to go to bed when he had been alerted by a woman's cries followed by the report of a pistol shot.

"So I said to myself, 'I'd better go up and see what's going on.' "

The policeman cut him short and dismissed the tenants. Reluctantly they straggled out, disappointed to play such a small part in the drama. Even the concierge, who wanted to remain, was told to return to her lodge.

"Now let's have a look at the victim," he said when they were gone.

He knelt down by the bed, scanned Gaby's face and deftly ran his hands over her body.

"She's breathing, and I don't see any wound or any blood," he announced. "She must've fainted. Women do that all the time."

His voice had lost its gruffness. Obviously no one was dead, and he was relieved at the turn of events. What first had looked like a tragedy was becoming a minor matter, a mere lovers' brawl.

With a grunt he got back to his feet and turned to Claude. "Tell me what happened." He pulled up a chair and sat down. "Don't miss anything and start at the beginning."

He listened with attention and understanding. From time to time he nodded in silent agreement or interrupted Claude's account to express some sententious remark.

"So she found a letter in your pocket, eh? It was very stupid, Monsieur, very *imbécile* of you to forget this letter . . . Never mind. Let's proceed."

When Claude finished talking, the official pulled Gaby's gun from his pocket.

"I hadn't noticed it was a lady's revolver. Expensive, too. Look at this handle. Real mother-of-pearl."

For a moment he considered the gun in pensive silence. Finally he inquired, "Did she have a permit to keep a revolver?"

"I don't know. I imagine so."

"You see, legally it all boils down to that. If you were her husband, then, of course, you'd be responsible. But since she's only your mistress—" Perplexed, he lifted his kepi and scratched his bald head. "It's a delicate point."

Turning around he looked at Claude's cheek. "She gave you a real fight, eh? Amazing how strong women are when they're mad."

At this moment two ambulance men arrived, lifted Gaby on a stretcher and went out without a word.

The gendarme nudged Claude. "We must go with them. I need the doctor's testimony for my report."

Still dazed, Claude followed him out of the room.

From then on, it all became a blurred, trancelike sequel of gestures and motions. Later he vaguely recalled climbing into the ambulance wagon, the drive through the night, the horse stumbling in the snow, the arrival at the Clinique Municipale, Gaby being whisked away. Then the wait on a bench in an ill-lit corridor that smelled of disinfectant, with the gendarme at his side. At last, the sound of a door opening, footsteps, the night intern—a tired-looking young man with a short pointed beard. "No wound, no lesion. Only a severe shock, the result of a nervous collapse of hysterical origin. We'll keep her here for two or three days, then she must have a long rest. At least a month or two." A slow, reassuring smile. "She'll be all right, don't worry. Now go home and try to sleep. You look as if you could use some rest."

Then the return home on foot with the gendarme, now no longer a guardian but a comforting friend. "Women are very strange, Monsieur. Sometimes they do the damnedest things. You have no idea the things I see in my profession!"

On Place Wagram he said good-bye and shook hands. "Of course, I must make a report, but I don't think you'll have any trouble. After all she wasn't your wife. Only a guest, you might say . . ."

The weary trek alone across the empty square, the snow crunching under his feet. Then the house, silent again; the endless climb of stairs; the room quiet in lamplight.

At last the bed, darkness and sleep. Merciful, forgiving sleep . . .

CHAPTER

14

SOMEHOW THE NEWS SPREAD THAT GABY HAD ATTEMPTED SUICIDE.
She had shot herself and her life was in danger. Some said she was
dying.

The fate of this beautiful girl driven by love to the verge of self-
destruction aroused public sympathy, while Claude's behavior pro-
voked the most severe comments. The old scandal of his broken
engagement to Thérèse Roger was revived, as well as the rumors of
his evil power over women.

As before, he said nothing. He did not defend himself, did not
embarrass his critics by asking exactly in what part of the body
Gaby had shot herself. Was it through the heart, like a true romantic
heroine? Or in the mouth or through the brain or, more prudently,
in the arm? Nor did he inform them that a few days after supposedly
shooting herself the dying woman had found the strength to travel
to Lisieux, where she had arrived, unmarred by any wound or
bandage, in time for her father's funeral.

His silence was his undoing. When it became known that she had
been given refuge by Madame Chausson and later, in Brussels, by
Madame Ysaye, this was regarded as a formal condemnation of
Claude's conduct. People rejoiced that in her hour of trial, the poor
girl had at least found assistance and safety, away from her dastardly
lover.*

* During her father's funeral (February 7, 1897) Gaby lost all emotional
control. At the cemetery she engaged in hysterical manifestations of grief
which leave little doubt of her state of nervous collapse at the time.

They were still commenting on her good fortune in having such wonderful friends when, early in March, she returned to rue Gustave Doré.

"What're you doing here?" he gasped as he opened the door. "Haven't you done enough?"

"Please, Claude."

He knew only too well this broken whisper which had aroused his pity so many times. But not now . . .

"Why did you come?" he went on acidly. "Have you run out of friends? Aren't there any more ladies you might visit for a few weeks?" His irony broke into a cruel chortle. "Are you by any chance planning to stay here again?"

Two large tears rolled down her pale, grief-stricken face. "Where else can I go? I have no clothes, no money . . . Please, let me stay awhile. Just long enough to give me time to see what I should do . . . I won't give you any trouble."

How many times had he heard those words, how many times had he cursed them! Yet he couldn't bring himself to send her away. Once again her weakness was stronger than his strength, and pity became the substitute for love.

"All right," he sighed at last, letting her in. "Let's try again."

And so she stayed.

"Personally, I think you're an idiot," said Pierre when he returned in April. "How will you ever get rid of her if you go on taking her back?"

From Algeria he had brought back a luscious Arab girl by the name of Zorah, who was Meriem's sister and went about the apartment in native garments amidst the clanking of silver bracelets.

"Some day I'll give a little party and I'll have her do her belly dance," he went on. "You'll see, it's very educational . . . Now, how about that damn opera of yours, is it finished or not?"

"I couldn't think about music these last few weeks, but now I think I'll go back to it."

This fact, brought to light during an interview with Gaby shortly before her death and published in 1957, seems to dispose once for all of the tradition that she tried to kill herself. At no time did she ever say she had; nor did Debussy in his brief account of the event to Pierre Louÿs. "She found a letter in my pocket . . . Whereupon drama . . . tears . . . a real revolver . . . It doesn't change anything . . . yet I've been shattered [bouleversé]" (Letter of February 9, 1897). On the other hand, her jealousy is amply documented, as well as her threats to kill him if he were ever unfaithful.

The saddest consequence of this whole distressing episode was Claude's loss of his dear friends, the Chaussons and Ysayes. Although he continued to see Ernest Chausson and Eugène Ysaye occasionally, he never forgave their wives for interfering in his private life and publicly taking Gaby's side.

And he did go back to it, for now things were calm at home. Gaby
had kept her word and gave no trouble at all. Her jealousy seemed
to have vanished. He, in turn, now spent more time with her. After
dinner they would sit by the fire like an old married couple, sipping
their demitasses, listening to the pelting of rain against the windowpanes, for spring that year was rainy and cold. They talked little,
but sometimes their hands would touch or they would smile at each
other, then they returned to their thoughts. Slowly she was regaining
her strength and control. Her face had lost its pallor. For the
first time in months they felt close, almost happy. No doubt it was
only a convalescent happiness, fragile and still bruised, but to them,
who had not known any happiness for so long, it seemed wonderful.

She did, however, worry a great deal about her mother, and as
her own condition improved, her anxiety grew.

"She's too old to go on working and too lonely," she would say.
"I wish I could take her away from Lisieux and find her a little place
in Orbec. At least she'd be near my sister."

He listened, helpless and ashamed of being helpless, tasting anew
the bitterness of poverty. Cruel, hateful poverty that denied you the
joy of helping those you loved! . . . And to think that some fools said
money couldn't buy happiness.

Finally, one evening in May, she turned to him as he was working
a few feet from her, hunched over the dining-room table. "Darling,
I've just got to get money and help Maman. That's all there is to
it . . . You understand, don't you?"

He asked no questions, for he could read her thoughts in her eyes.
"I understand."

On his return from a lesson the following day, he found a flower
on his desk and a farewell note.

◆

Without warning she returned shortly before Christmas, pink-
cheeked and elegant in her new dress.

"Oh, darling, I missed you so!" she cried, clasping her arms
around his neck, as in the old days.

For a moment she stood arched against him, her lips pressed to
his. Then, swiftly, she pulled herself away.

"Now let me look at you." She ran her eyes over him while removing her gloves. "You're thin again, you always get thin when
I'm not around. You don't eat properly."

In a minute it seemed that she had never left. Already she had
forgotten the man who for six months had been her lover. She
scarcely had to forget him, for he had never existed for her. He
wasn't very rich, but rich enough for her purpose. From him she

had gotten a few dresses and money to install her mother in Orbec, which was all she wanted. He, in turn, had gotten whatever he yearned for. Now she had no more use for him, and the partnership had been dissolved. How simple human relations became when love did not intervene!*

"He didn't want me to go, but I was worried about you," she went on, smiling. "I know it's silly and you can manage without me, but I can't help it. Now, tell me. Did anything interesting happen while I was away?"

He shook his head. No, nothing of importance had happened. During the summer he had set to music two of Pierre's *Chansons de Bilitis* and had just written a third. Also, he had worked on the *Nocturnes*. A new version this time, for full orchestra.

"And, believe it or not, *Pélléas* is almost finished."

"I don't believe it."

"It's true. I only have to make a few changes and revise a few scenes. Hartmann is very excited about it, he thinks it's much better than the first version. As soon as it's finished, he wants me to play it for André Messager."

"Who is he?"

"The conductor of the Opéra Comique."

"Wouldn't that be wonderful!"

She tried to sound enthusiastic, but she had lost faith. He never would finish the damn thing. All his life he would fuss with it . . .

"What about Pierre and his Arab girl?" she asked, to change the subject. "How are they getting along?"

Not too well . . . Zorah had had enough of Paris, its gray skies and rainy days. She missed her nice Algerian sun, her camels and palm trees. Pierre was leaving for Egypt in a few days and he had agreed to escort her as far as Marseilles, where she would take the ship back to Algiers.

"I guess it's best for both of them."

Gaby remained silent, her eyes on the floor. Then, pensively, she murmured. "Yes. Perhaps they'll be happier apart."

He was startled at her remark. He sensed that it hinted at some secret thought. Did she mean that they, too, would be happier apart? Then why had she come back? He was about to ask the question, but kept himself in check. Time would bring the answer.

* Little is known about this ephemeral "gentleman friend," except that he was a man of means and an amateur artist. He painted a nude of Gaby, which she kept all her life. During the months of their affair she often visited her mother and rented a house for her in Orbec, on rue du Petit Four.

In September of that year her sister gave birth to a daughter, Gilberte. This event mollified her husband's antagonism toward Gaby, who, thereafter, was admitted to the Riffaut family.

Her hand went up to her blouse and she glanced at a gold watch he had never seen before.

"Mon Dieu!" she gasped. "I must go and get dinner ready."

Thus, without jolt, their lives joined once again and resumed their uneventful course through familiar hardships. His finances had not improved. Hartmann's advances helped a little. So did the lessons and occasional jobs. But poverty remained their faithful guest during the bleak winter months. Poverty and music—the two inseparable.

Outside, the city was in convulsion. The everlasting Dreyfus Affair was entering its final, hysterical stage. The ghost of the man on Devil's Island stalked the streets of Paris. Zola's article *"J'accuse!"* had begun the new year with a thunderclap. Cabinets rose and fell. At the Luxembourg Palace, snow-bearded senators shook their feeble fists at one another. On Sundays, preachers in surplice let out blasts of pulpit wind. The generals faced the mounting storm with the same arrogant flash of their monocles, the same inept lies and dramatic gestures. But their defenses were cracking. A few brave officers had risked their careers to tell the truth. Slowly, justice was on the march.

Amidst it all, Claude gave his piano lessons and worked on his opera. At his side, Gaby attended to the housekeeping and secretly tried to gather the courage to leave.

She had returned to Claude against her will, because she could not help herself. Her love was still too strong. But the six months she had spent away from him had given her time to think and measure once more the folly of her passion. With delight she had rediscovered the amenities of wealth. The softness of silk against her skin had aroused memories of her former way of life. Her ambitions had burst into blaze again, and with them a sense of urgency. She was thirty-one. If she were ever to be a successful demimondaine she must hurry.

Since her return she had reminded herself every day that time was short, but her good resolutions were crumbling. Common sense might warn her she must leave this man, but the prospect of living without him was unendurable. Her body still longed for the touch of his hands; her nipples still grew hard under the caress of his tongue. As weeks passed, she fell back into the grip of her weakness. She never would have the courage to leave him. So why make plans, why think of escape? Like a defeated drug addict she surrendered to her fate.

Because she no longer made scenes or harassed him with her jealousy he concluded she was cured and all was well. He mistook calm for peace and plunged headlong into music. For days at a time the outside world ceased to exist—and her with it. He still kissed her when he returned home after a lesson, talked during dinner, smiled at her over his demitasse and even now and then made her sit on his knees. But she sensed he did all these things in an absent, unfocused sort of way, while his mind remained turned to music. It was like living with someone very pleasant who couldn't quite remember your name.

Loneliness was bad enough, but she was used to it. For years she had known that two people can live side by side and yet be miles apart. But even in their darkest periods, sex had not failed them. It had been the refuge, the opium, the magnet that held them together. In anger or tenderness, in joy or despair they had made love. As they sometimes said, "We may not have much, but we have that!" *That* had made up for a lot of things.

Now a change came over him. In some obscure, vicarious way music seemed to satisfy his sensuality. When he shuffled to bed after a night at his desk, he no longer caressed her or noticed her advances. Peacefully he slept while next to him she lay awake and tense.

At times her amorous longing rose to a lancing throb. She then would walk to his study and try to coax him away from his work. "It's late, darling. Please come to bed." He would look up and smile. "All right, sweetheart. I'll join you in a few minutes." She would return to bed and wait, counting the minutes. Half an hour . . . one hour . . . Finally she would get up. From the darkness of the vestibule she would watch him, gazing unseeingly ahead, pencil in hand, his silhouette outlined in lamplight. He had forgotten . . . Stifling a sob, she would run back to the room.

Thus their sexual harmony, which had been their most precious and almost their sole asset, began to vanish. His love-making became hurried, spasmodic and left her unsatisfied. Already she was a lonely woman; she became a frustrated one. Insensibly she began nursing against him a woman's deepest, most unforgiving resentment: that of her slighted womanhood.

Then another thing happened. In April, André Messager came to hear the score of *Pélléas*. A handsome, dapper man with a brisk manner and a luxuriant mustache, the conductor of the Opéra Comique looked more like a cavalry officer in mufti than the brillant musician he was. As he listened to Claude's playing his face mirrored surprise, then astonishment, then admiration and, finally, unbound enthusiasm.

"I don't know if you realize it, but you've written a masterpiece," he exclaimed after the audition. "You've renewed the whole concept of the lyrical drama. There has never been an opera like this one. Now, let's talk business. Naturally I must ask Monsieur Carré, the director, for his approval, but I am sure of it and can promise we shall present your work next season. All you have to do now is finish the orchestration and let me have the score as soon as possible."

When Claude reported Messager's words to Gaby she was delighted. Like most people, she was awed by official titles. Although she had never set foot in it, she had seen the Opéra Comique—an enormous, stately, government-subsidized theatre on Place Boiëldieu. Surely the music director of such an establishment must be an important personage with almost unlimited funds at his disposal. At last Claude was going to make money, big money.

"You mean he really loved it?" she asked, still faintly incredulous. "You're sure he wasn't just talking?"

"I tell you he was crazy about it. And you could see he meant every word he said."

"That's wonderful! . . . How much of an advance is he going to give you?"

His jaw dropped. "Advance?"

"He promised to play your opera, didn't he? When you promise something you must pay a little money on account to prove good faith." Her voice became edged with impatience. "Or don't you know?"

"Well, you see, darling—"

"I see." Discouragement snuffed the joy out of her eyes. "You didn't ask him, did you?"

"I'm sorry, but I didn't think of it."

"Didn't think!" she echoed ruefully. "The concierge came up again this morning asking for the rent, I owe money to everybody in the district—and you didn't think to ask for an advance!"

She got up and walked away.

A moment later he went to the bedroom. She was sitting on the edge of the bed, weeping, her hands folded in her lap.

"I'm sorry," he said. "I really am."

"Never mind. You can't help yourself. Your head is so full of music, you can't think of anything else." She dabbed her eyes with her handkerchief and blew her nose. "That's the way you are, and you'll never change. Never!"

He protested he would. Why, tomorrow he would go to Messager and *demand* an advance of three hundred—no, five hundred francs! She listened, a tired smile on her lips.

Of course, he forgot about it. Things remained as they were. She sold her new gold watch and he got another hundred francs from Hartmann. The rent was paid, merchants were placated. Somehow they managed.

But the "advance" incident preyed on her mind. It had been the final disappointment, and she felt she couldn't go on any more.

Her body rebelled at being unwanted, her heart was bursting with loneliness. And then she was tired . . . tired . . . tired of being poor. Poor Claude, he never would have money . . . all his life he would live in a cloud . . . with him music would always come first . . .

And so, she was beaten at last.

It had taken seven years, but he had finally shown her the hopelessness of going on loving him. And he had done so without cruelty or violence, without even being aware of it. Simply by being himself.

His gentle, impractical, daydreaming, music-obsessed, exasperating self.

◆

Nothing remained but to get ready to leave and return to the old kind of life.

But she couldn't just say good-bye and walk away. Away to what? The street, the lamppost? No, sir! She wasn't going to start back at the bottom, she was going to start at the top. And for that, she needed clothes. Beautiful, expensive clothes. Then a bit of money to live on until she found the right man . . . All this would demand a good deal of planning and a few months of time.

All summer she mulled over these thoughts. Claude noticed nothing and went on revising his score, delighted to see her so calm and content.

One day at the end of August, she stepped into his study, lit a cigarette and casually announced she had gotten a job.

"What kind of a job?" he asked.

"Mannequin."

"That's nice."

"In fact it's you, darling, who gave me the idea."

"I?"

"Yes. Remember how you used to say I should do something, instead of staying home and brooding all day. Well, this afternoon I went to the place where I used to buy my clothes, and the director said he'd be glad to have me as a model."

For the thousandth time he marveled at her talent for secrecy. "I think it's an excellent idea. Does it mean you'll be living by yourself?"

Of course not. Everything would remain the same. "But would you mind if we moved nearer to the shop where I'm going to work?"

"Not at all. I never liked this apartment, you know that. It's full of bad memories for both of us."

"That's what I feel, too. The other day I happened to be walking on rue Cardinet and I saw a sign—"

"—and you signed another lease?"

She smiled. "No, darling, not this time, but it's a nice place. It's still on the fifth floor, but it has a nice little parlor. I think you'll like it."

He rose. "All right, let's go and look at it."

He liked the apartment, and they moved to 58, rue Cardinet. A new life began for them. Her work kept her out of the house most of the day. She returned late in the afternoon, tired but in good spirits. Again she wore lovely clothes, for the director of the shop had let her have an entire wardrobe at cost and on credit. "After all, my dear Gaby, you used to be a good customer, and who knows, you may still be one some day . . . Besides, a mannequin must be chic. It's good publicity . . ." Each week the cashier docked an installment from her wages. She had calculated that in six months she would be out of debt.

During dinner she told Claude about her work, the clients' remarks as she presented the various dresses, the people who worked at the shop: *petites-mains* who sewed and babbled in the back room; *vendeuses,* obsequious with customers, "stuck-up" with fellow employees; *habilleuses,* their mouths full of pins. In her colorful style she described Monsieur Flannel, the manager, a toothpick of a man who went about the shop in his cutaway and white vest, squinting behind his pince-nez, poking his nose everywhere, suspicious as a lawyer, but good-hearted; the cashier who spent his days in a cage like a monkey at the zoo; and Louis, the doorman, who looked like an admiral in his uniform and with whom she exchanged a few words whenever they met. "Imagine, he comes from Mezidon! That's only two steps from Lisieux . . ."

She amused him with the gossip of the models' dressing room—*la cabine,* as it was called—and the feuds among mannequins. "You should've been there this afternoon when Simone and Monique went at each other. It took four of us to pull them apart!" And sometimes she spoke of Rosalie Texier, another mannequin. "She calls herself Lily because it's more chic. I think it sounds better, don't you? . . . She's only twenty-four and very pretty, but the poor girl hasn't had much luck with men."

He listened, a smile on his lips. Sometimes with genuine amusement, sometimes not hearing a word of what she said. She knew it, but did not mind. Things that used to infuriate her did not even annoy her any more. As usual he was up to his neck in troubles of his own making. Now that *Pélléas* was finished, he was tormenting himself about the Opéra Comique. It was much too big, his music would get lost in that barrack . . . "You see, darling, *Pélléas* should be played in a small, intimate theatre. I wish I could meet Monsieur de Montesquiou. I understand he has a charming little theatre on his estate. About a hundred seats. That would be perfect . . ."

She nodded indulgently. "You're right, darling, absolutely right . . ." What was the use of arguing, reminding him, for instance, that this "charming little theatre" would mean no royalties? He probably had forgotten this detail . . . Another pet idea of his was to have *Pélléas* performed by puppets! He had nursed it a long time and was quite smitten with it . . . "I know it sounds a little strange, but it's perfectly logical. You must remember that the characters are mere symbols of emotions. I'm afraid that real singers may make the opera too realistic . . ."

And while he turned those grave problems over in his head he refused to release his score or finish the orchestration, and poor Monsieur Hartmann was cursing, cajoling, threatening, tearing out his hair. Which didn't disturb Claude a bit . . . "I realize he is anxious to get back the money he's advanced me, but we must be cautious, very cautious . . ."

Sometimes she wondered why she bothered listening to his non-sense, why she went on living with this impossible man. She now earned enough money to live by herself. Why then did she go on cooking for him, washing and mending on Sundays? Why? Because he was helpless and foolish . . . because he needed someone to look after him . . . because in some strange way she still loved him and felt toward him a sort of protective solicitude, a sort of mother-liness she could not explain. Perhaps, when everything was said, all forms of a woman's love were only variations of mother love? . . .

One morning he told her about a visitor he was expecting that afternoon, some playwright who wanted him to write incidental music to his play . . . "He's coming at six, and I forgot I have an appointment at five with Monsieur Messager. If I am not back, please ask him to wait, won't you? It may mean a little money . . ."

She was not sure she could leave the shop before six, but she said she would try.

♦

Monsieur Flannel eyed her suspiciously over his pince-nez. "This doctor's appointment, it's not a *blague,* is it? Some silly rendezvous?"

"Oh, no, Monsieur Flannel, it's the truth. You know I wouldn't lie to you."

Doctors' appointments made the best excuses. People were vaguely afraid, if they refused, you might drop dead at their feet . . .

"I'm very worried," she added, while he nibbled the fringe of his mustache.

"You aren't pregnant, are you?"

"I hope not."

More nibbling. "All right. You can leave at five-thirty, but don't let it happen again."

At five-thirty on the dot, Gaby crossed the carpeted reception room, smiled at Monsieur Flannel and stepped out of the shop.

Outside she waved at Louis, who beamed back.

"Leaving early, Mademoiselle Gaby?"

"Yes, and I'm late," she flung over her shoulder.

Already she was hurrying up the street, still slipping on her gloves—another elegant Parisian rushing off somewhere on her high heels in the grayness of the October afternoon.

Happily she rustled on toward home, holding up her skirt with two fingers, aware of men's appreciative glances as she passed by. It was nice being chic again, having men ogle you . . . Even Claude, when he came down from his cloud, remarked how attractive she looked these days. Why, sometimes after dinner he made her sit on his knees and slipped his hand inside her blouse, as in the garret days. Say what you wanted, there was nothing like a pretty dress to make men want to undress you . . .

She stopped at a sidewalk stall and examined the flowers on display. They were expensive; but this was an important occasion. It might bring Claude some money, and he certainly could use it . . . She selected a bunch of yellow chrysanthemums. As they were past their bloom, she asked for a discount and this led to a spirited haggling session with the flower woman. Finally she won, but by then it was past six o'clock. She was almost running when she reached the house. Puffing, she let herself into the apartment and lit the parlor lamp.

She had barely removed her hat and gloves when the bell rang. Grumbling under her breath, she went to open the door.

"Monsieur Debussy?"

"He's out, but he'll be back any minute."

She looked at the baldheaded, rather corpulent young man, smiling under his abundant blond mustache. His clothes were discreet but expensive. He should be able to pay Claude well . . .

"Please come in," she said, this time with a smile.

"Are you sure I shan't disturb you? I could come back at a more convenient time."

A real gentleman . . . "No, no. He said for you to wait. He'll be back soon."

He followed her into the small parlor and noticed that her hat and gloves were lying on the table.

"I'm afraid I am coming at a most inopportune moment," he said before sitting down. "Please don't hesitate to tell me if it is so. I have nothing special to do and I can return at a more propitious hour."

My, how polite he was, and what words he used! He spoke so well you practically didn't understand a word of what he said . . . "On the contrary, Monsieur. I'm the one to blame. I stopped to buy these flowers and it made me late. Please sit down, and do excuse the disorder of this room."

"It is charming as it is," he said, running his eyes over her. "Quite charming."

She caught his glance and coyly patted her hair. "Would you mind if I arranged these flowers? They'll die if I don't get them in water right away."

"Please, Madame, by all means. Flowers are so fragile! Their beauty is but of a moment."

"Isn't that a fact!" She sighed as she walked out of the parlor.

She went into the bedroom, where she hastily retouched her make-up; then to the kitchen, from where she emerged smiling and holding a vase in her hand.

"I can see you love flowers," she said, setting it on the table.

"How could it be otherwise? I am a poet, Madame. Or rather an amateur poet, for alas, I must attend to business."

She pricked up her ears. "Business, did you say?"

"Yes, Madame. When I return from the bank, tired and despondent after a long day's work, I love to sit down and chisel a sonnet."

"A bank?" she said, arranging the flowers. "You work in a bank?"

"No, Madame. I own one."

He said it so gently, so modestly that she could have kissed him on his glossy pink pate. "That's nice. And this bank, did you start it yourself?"

He made a deprecatory gesture. "Oh, no! My father did. He was born in France, but emigrated to Buenos Aires after the revolution of '48. He founded a bank there. When he died, he left it to me."

"Naturally."

She had finished arranging the flowers and came to sit opposite him. "Are you planning to stay long in Paris?"

"At least a year, Madame. I love Paris. My business is in Argentina, but my heart is here. Nowhere in the world is there such an appreciation of the arts."

"I understand you are a playwright."

Again he raised a deprecatory hand. "A mere amateur, Madame. In my spare time I do indulge in play-writing and I've written a tragedy in verses called *The Daughter of Pasiphaë*."

"How exciting! Won't you tell me about it?" As he appeared to hesitate, she added in a whisper, "Please."

He could not resist the entreaty in her voice, and clearing his throat, he began, "Since you insist, I should first tell you who was Pasiphaë. She was a legendary Greek character, the wife of King Minos, a woman of torrential, erratic sensuality. One day her husband received as a gift a magnificent white bull—"

She gazed at him with feigned attention, not listening to a word he said. There was something fetching about this baldheaded young banker. What if he was fat and wrote poetry? When you were a millionaire you could be as fat as you liked and write all the poetry you wanted . . .

"At the sight of this superb, extremely healthy bull, Pasiphaë was seized by a burning, unnatural passion. Just then, her husband was called away—"

With increasing pleasure, he orated before this lovely girl who listened with such enthralled attention. Here, at last, was a woman who was interested in something else besides his money . . .

"And so here she was, alone, with her husband away and nothing to do. More and more she thought about the bull. In my mind I see her, draped in flowing veils, ambling along the lanes of her kingdom, struggling with herself, a woman of surpassing beauty . . . like you."

He ventured the compliment, expecting a rebuke. None came. Soon he risked another, then another, which also were accepted without protest. Her hands were like the petals of some beautiful tropical flower. Her hair had the sheen of Flora's tresses in Titian's painting. Her lips— She did not reply, except with a flapping of eyelashes. Before long he had forgotten about Pasiphaë and her bull and was tossing at Gaby poetic flummeries which made clear that she greatly appealed to him.

"But above all, it's your mind I admire," he said, flushed with mounting lust. "It is so rare to find a woman with a true feeling for poetry."

"And still more so to find a handsome young man with such interesting things to say. I could listen to you for hours."

By now a definite rapport had formed between them. Beneath their verbiage, their minds stretched out exploratory antennae.

"How much I envy your wife!" she began. "What a lucky woman she is!"

"Wife? Alas, Madame, I have no wife."

A delicious shudder rippled up and down her spine. "But surely there must be a woman in your life? Someone to inspire you, encourage you in moments of depression?"

He shook his head. "I've found only rapacious women without a shred of interest in my writing."

"How dreadful!"

No wife, no mistress. This was too good to be true! Could it . . . could it be that the man she'd been hoping for was sitting there, before her eyes?

She had no time to pursue this line of thought, for it was his turn to grope for information.

"How lucky Monsieur Debussy is to have such a beautiful and understanding wife!"

"Wife!" She echoed the word in a sigh. "Alas, he never asked me!"

"What!" he exclaimed, much relieved.

She turned her head aside in a gesture of shame. "Oh, yes, he promised he would, and I was naïve enough to believe him. Then . . . he forgot."

With an effort she turned back to him. "I don't know why I'm telling you these things, but somehow I feel I can trust you."

"Please do." He leaned forward on his chair and extended his hand, which came to rest on her knee. "You can depend on my discretion."

"From the moment I saw you, I felt . . . I don't know how to put it . . . a warmth, a friendship, an attraction—"

"I did, too."

"I'm so unhappy!" She blinked back her tears. "So much in need of a friend!"

His hand cupped over her knee. "You've found one. But we can't talk freely here, for Monsieur Debussy may return any minute. Would you have lunch with me?"

She shook her head, but without conviction.

He pressed on. "I know a charming little place. Very discreet. And the food is delicious."

She still hesitated, and for a few seconds gazed pensively at the wall.

"All right," she said with sudden determination. "Wait for me tomorrow outside the shop."

She had just finished giving him the address when Claude stormed in, his sombrero low on his brow, the score of *Pélléas* under his arm.

"Would you believe it?" he shouted from the doorway. "Messager wanted me to give him the score as it is! We argued for two hours . . . I told him—"

He stopped, noticing the visitor.

"Oh, it's you," he said ungraciously. "You came about your play, didn't you? All right, let's look at it."

Gaby rose, smiled at the poet and went out of the room.

There was a long, tense silence; then Claude's announcement that he did not like the play.

"What did you say?" gasped the author, incredulous. "I've been told by experts that it is a masterpiece, and I am ready to give you half of my glory."

"You can keep it all." Claude rose, held out the manuscript. "I'm sorry, but you will have to find someone else to write music for it."

"I am prepared to pay whatever—"

"It's not a question of money. Your play is terrible. Now, if you'll excuse me—"

From the kitchen Gaby heard the scraping of a chair on the floor followed by brief salutations and rapid footsteps. She got a glimpse of the playwright as he slammed his top hat down on his head and dashed to the door.

Later, at dinner, she asked Claude how things had gone between them.

He shrugged impatiently. "I told him to take his silly play somewhere else. I'm not going to write music about a woman who slept with a bull."

"She did?" Gaby's curiosity was aroused. "And what happened?"

"She had a son from him, who was half bull and half man. He had the head of a bull and the . . . equipment of a man."

"What a pity! It should've been the other way around . . . Didn't she also have a daughter?"

"Not from the bull, from her husband. And she wasn't much better. She fell in love with her stepson, and when he refused to go to bed with her, she killed herself, leaving a note that he'd raped her."

"My God, what a family!" Her indignation was short-lived. "Just the same, you could've made a lot of money. I heard him say he was willing to pay whatever you asked. And he looked as if he could do it, too."

"Maybe, but there are other things in life besides money."

She smiled. Poor darling, he'd never snatch an opportunity.

But *she* would.

♦

The next day she had lunch with Monsieur Victor*

She saw him frequently after that, but always furtively and for

---

* In his account of his conversations with Gaby, Monsieur H. Pellerin merely identifies the South American as "Comte de B———." The financier-poet preferred, however, to be called "Monsieur Victor." In his apartment on Boulevard Hausmann he entertained the social and artistic elite of Paris. He was known for his enormous fortune. His play *The Daughter of Pasiphaë* was never produced.

brief periods of time after work or at lunch in small, expensive restaurants. Naturally she checked on his financial standing, and found it superlative. Besides a bank in Buenos Aires, he also owned a tobacco plantation in Cuba, a mine in Bolivia, a cattle ranch in the pampas. No doubt about it, he was very, very rich.

He was also very nice. She liked his modesty, his deprecating waves of the hand, even the long words he used and which she did not understand. Soon she realized that he was no ordinary "prospect," no cynical playboy. He was sensitive, cultured and a little naïve. He required, she decided, special treatment.

She played her cards with infinite skill. She gave him the breathless attention men crave, titillated his sensuality without quite satisfying it, refused his money, wouldn't even accept gifts. And she aroused his sympathy with touching accounts of her past. A virtuous, hard-working seamstress, she had made the mistake to believe in love and men's promises. Her affair with Claude had been a long martyrdom. She wouldn't go into details, but her expression told more than words ever could.

"You'll never know the things he's done to me!" she murmured one day as they were having lunch together.

"Oh, my poor, poor friend!" He reached for her hand across the table. "Why do you stay with him?"

She kept her eyes lowered on her plate. "Because I'm naturally faithful and I always hoped he would change."

"Do you still love him?"

"I thought I did, but since I met you—"

"Please go on—"

"Well, I don't any more."

"Then why don't you leave him?"

"Because all men are the same. They lie, seduce you and then break your heart. I am not the kind of girl to go from one man to another. If I can't have love, I might as well stay where I am."

She said it very well, with pent-up emotion. He was moved, and assured her that, although a man, he was an exception to the rule.

"I love you, Gaby," he said, patting her hand. "I really do."

She looked at him through troubled eyes. "Do you, Victor? Do you really?"

"Don't you believe me?"

"I'd like to, but I'm not sure yet. Men are such liars. Time will tell."

Thus, gradually, she changed the atmosphere of their relationship. He was tired of brash, predatory tarts; she gave him romance. They did the things lovers do. They held hands, looked into each other's eyes, kissed behind newspaper kiosks. What might have been for him another Parisian affair became a thing of tenderness and yearning. By Christmas he was head over heels in love.

With a great show of reluctance she accepted his first gift.

"Only because it is *Noël*," she protested, as he opened the jeweler's box.

"I chose something very discreet," he said, pulling out the strand of perfectly matched pearls. "Something that wouldn't attract attention."

"Oh, Victor!"

She kissed him through his bushy mustache and told him he was the most generous man she had ever met—which was true.

"I wish I could do something for you," she added.

"You can." He smiled at her surprise and took her hands into his own. "You can come with me to Buenos Aires."

She was stunned. "But you said—"

"I know. I had planned to stay in Paris at least a year, but something has happened and I must go." He smiled apologetically, "I may be a poet, but I also have a business to attend to."

Now questions rushed to her lips. How long would he stay away? Several months probably. He couldn't say . . . When was he leaving?

"There is a ship sailing from Marseilles in three days. We could leave Paris the day after tomorrow. Please, darling, come with me. You said—"

She was not listening. Three days! . . . It meant leaving Claude to himself, with no one to look after him, no one to send her news of him. He might be sick, he might die—and she wouldn't know . . .

Instantly her plan was made. It was a dangerous gamble, but she must take it.

"No, darling," she broke in softly, "I won't go with you. Not this time."

"What do you mean?"

She reminded him of their conversation at the restaurant three weeks before. He had said then he did not want their relationship to be a mere adventure, that he was not like other men, changing and deceitful. Now was the chance to prove it.

"If you return for me in the spring, then I'll know you love me."

"But I do, I do!"

She gave him a long-suffering smile. "You say so, but men change their minds. I want to be sure. If you come back in April, then I'll go with you wherever you like."

In vain did he plead and argue. She remained firm, but with a sad gentleness, and a finely acted show of despair.

"I must be sure," she insisted. "If you turned out to be like other men and broke my heart, I couldn't stand it. I think I—"

The sentence ended in a wince, but he caught its meaning. A

delicious panic overwhelmed him. At last he was loved! Now he was comforting her, drying her tears, assuring her that three months were but a short time, and he would be back in the spring.

"Shall I see you again before I leave?" he asked, anguish in his voice.

"Of course. Wait for me tomorrow after work."

"At our usual place?"

She gave him a long, promising look. "No, darling. Tomorrow we'll have dinner in your apartment."

Having told Claude that she had to stay with a sick friend—one of the girls at the shop—she spent the next night with Monsieur Victor and saw to it that he would not forget the experience.

He left for Marsailles the following day, still in a daze.

◆

Now she felt confident he would return . . . This gave her only three more months with Claude and she wanted to spend as much time as she could with him. Indifferent to rain or snow, she hurried home after work, rushing to his study the moment she arrived, happy when she found him at his desk scribbling his little notes or playing the piano. It no longer mattered if he wasted his time or did not make any money. It was enough that he was there and stopped working to pull her down on his knees and peck her face with little kisses while she told him the day's happenings at the shop.

The tense, angry silences of previous years had gone, and now, during dinner, they chatted of this and that: of Pierre, who was again in Algeria; of the weather, which was disgusting; of what people would do next year when the new century would begin. "They say the streets will be full of automobiles and there'll be no more wars . . ." They spoke about the government project to sell publicity on match boxes in order to balance the budget, and they spoke about Zizi. She was the hippopotamus at the zoo, and she had caught a cold. All Paris read with bated breath the daily bulletins of her condition.

And, naturally, they spoke of Monsieur Félix Faure, President of the Republic, who had just died in the . . . arms of Madame Steinheil, after receiving Cardinal Richard, Archbishop of Paris.

"That'll teach him a lesson!" she snorted over her demitasse.

"And one he will never forget."

"The newspapers say she was waiting in the alcove adjoining his office, and he rushed to her after seeing the cardinal."

"Which proves he was a serious man who put business before pleasure."

"If you ask me, he was an old *cochon*."

"*Cochon* perhaps, but not old. At fifty-nine a man is in his prime."

"Yes—and look what happened."

"Can you think of a better way to die?"

Peace had returned to them. More than that: a forgiving tenderness, a belated comradeship which occasionally swelled into laughter or a sudden itch of amorousness that sent them tumbling on the bed and left them smiling and a little sheepish. At times it almost looked as if they could fall in love with each other all over again; but, of course, it was too late for that. Too many years had passed, too much had happened; they had hurt each other too much and bore too many scars. Yet they still found moments of happiness, like those embers that continue to glow long after the fire had died.

They were becoming friends.

"You know, darling," she remarked one day after they had made love, "I like you an awful lot."

"I like you, too. Very much."

She snuggled to him. "Sometimes I feel as if I were"—she hesitated, groping for the right word— "as if I were your sister."

He grinned. "Sometimes you say the damnedest things!"

"You don't understand. I mean—"

She meant that she had emerged from the complications, the wretchedness of passion and rediscovered the clear pleasure of friendship and the simple enjoyment of sex.

"Maybe that's all love is," she mused, after a pause. "A whole panful of friendship with just a pinch of sex."

Whenever he had some money he bought her a package of *cibiches* or a new jewel-robbery thriller to read at the shop during lulls. She, in turn, bought flowers or *croissants* for their Sunday breakfast. She was right: except for a dash of incestuous love-making now and then, they were getting to be like brother and sister.

As winter wore on, she felt a mounting anguish at the thought of their approaching separation. Life would be awfully empty without him. The worst of it would be not to hear about him, wondering how he was getting along, if he had enough to eat . . .

One afternoon she arrived from the shop escorted by a tall, blond and very pretty girl. "This is Lily Texier. Remember, I told you about her?"

Lily spoke little during dinner and made no impression whatever on him.

"How do you like her?" Gaby asked when they were alone.

"She's all right."

"Don't you think she's pretty?"

"Yes, but she doesn't say anything. She has about as much personality as a clam."

"That's because she's shy. You'll see, she is very nice when you get to know her."

"Frankly I don't care whether I do or not."

But Gaby did. On various occasions she mentioned Lily and what a fine girl she was. "You've never seen anyone so obliging. Always ready to do you a favor . . ." He learned that, like Gaby, she came from a small town. "Maybe that's why we get along. She isn't stuck-up, like those Parisian girls that think it's something special to be born in this damn town . . . Her father is a railway telegraphist in some little village nobody's ever heard of."

One day she asked him to wait for her after work. She came out of the shop with Lily.

"Guess what?" she cried, rushing to him. "She's never been to a cinema! I told her we'd take her."

They dined in a modest restaurant, where the two pretty models attracted a good deal of attention. This time Lily overcame her shyness and asked Claude some timid questions about his opera. When would it be performed? Wasn't he proud to have written an opera that would be presented at the "Comique"? How did it feel to be a famous musician?

He decided she was more intelligent than he had first thought.

After dinner they went to the Salon Indien on boulevard des Capucines. They took their places on wooden benches and listened to the galop overture that opened the *séance cinématographique*. Gaby and Lily laughed themselves sick at the antics of a monocled gentleman in a straw hat and striped bathing suit who went about the beach, bowing and flirting, unaware of an enormous crab clinging to his *derrière*. A moment later, Lily almost died of fright and clutched Claude's hand when a locomotive came rushing at them out of the screen and almost crashed into the room. She did not faint, but several ladies did. The films lasted two minutes and were the last word in scientific progress.

"Lily wants me to tell you how much she enjoyed the evening," Gaby said the next day.

Winter ended early that year. After a few last downpours April arrived, bringing the first spring days. By the middle of the month, ladies wore linen dresses and cotton gloves. The streets were abloom with pastel-shaded parasols.

And Victor returned to Paris.

"You see, darling, your fears were groundless," he said, his mustache stretched in a smile. "I didn't forget you."

They were having lunch together, and she looked at him across the table. Sweet, dull, reliable Victor! He had kept his word, he always would . . .

"Now I know you truly love me, tomorrow I'll come to you."

That afternoon she gave her notice, said good-bye to everyone at the shop. The mannequins kissed her and wished her luck. Monsieur Flannel said they would miss her. The director guessed the situation at a glance. "Didn't I tell you you'd be one of our customers again?"

Outside, she exchanged a few words with the doorman.

He, too, wished her luck. "You've chosen a nice day to go, Mademoiselle Gaby. Though, between ourselves, spring in this town is nothing compared to our springs in Normandy. Some day I'll drop everything and go home."

"Me, too." She blew him a kiss and walked away.

Claude was not in when she returned. It was still early, and silence filled the apartment. She leaned on the window sill of his study and gazed down at the budding trees below. Well, it had come . . . A thousand times she had tried to imagine what her last day with Claude would be, and now she knew. A day like any other, a gentle April day. And memories, hundreds of them rising and crowding around her. And she, not knowing whether she was happy or miserable, whether she wanted to laugh or cry.

She pulled herself away from the window, went into the kitchen, slipped an apron over her dress and began sweeping the parlor. Then the study and finally the dining room. This done, she returned to the kitchen and ironed Claude's shirts, so that he would have a supply of fresh linen to wear after she was gone. Now, she thought, he would have to do his own laundry and iron his shirts . . . He wouldn't mind; he insisted he was an expert at it. Once he had given her a demonstration of his skill, and it was almost as bad as his cooking . . .

She was storing the shirts into the chest of drawers when Claude arrived, shortly before six, whistling between his teeth.

"Hartmann is really a wonderful man," he began, absently kissing her on the back of her neck. "Not only did he give me another advance, but he even got me a new pupil. And guess how much he asked? Hold your breath . . . Twenty francs!"

She glanced at him over her shoulder. He was as excited as a boy and had slipped his thumbs into the armholes of his vest to give more weight to his announcement.

"Do you mean twenty francs a lesson?"

"Yes, my dear Gaby. No more measly five-franc lessons for me. You may not know it, but I'm getting to be a fashionable piano teacher. I think this calls for a celebration. How about dinner at our little restaurant, you know, the one with the courtyard? It's warm enough to eat outside." Then, as the thought struck him, "Aren't you home early tonight?"

Yes. Monsieur Flanner had let her leave the shop early . . . "I'll tell you about it during dinner."

At the restaurant nothing had changed. In the courtyard the tables stood at the same places, with the same paper-shaded lamps and checkered tablecloths. The owner greeted them like long-lost friends, praised his *navarin* as he had in the past, and his "little wine" that was like no other wine in the world.

"And for dessert, I'll give you strawberries," he continued, lighting the lamp. "Not the big, tasteless kind you can have anywhere, but the small wild ones you find in the woods."

After he returned to the kitchen, Gaby told Claude she had given up her job.

"And, darling," she added softly, "I'm going away."

He had always known that some day she would say these words, yet now they struck him like a blow. For a moment he could not speak.

"I don't blame you," he said at last. "You must be tired of being poor. I'm surprised you stood it so long." Then, gulping back his emotion, "I hope you've found someone who will give you all the things I never could."

"Oh, yes, he can buy me anything I want. But this won't be a short affair. He really loves me and I like him and I think we're going to stay together a long time."

"But will you be happy?"

"Happy?"

She shrugged ruefully and turned to look at the lamp. Across the table he watched her face suffused with golden haze. The night was soft, quivering with small puffs of breeze. A last crescent of moon, like a wind-blown sail, floated high above the roofs.

"I've had with you all the happiness and all the misery I'll ever want," she murmured, still gazing at the lamp. "Now I'd like a little peace. We'll get along, I'm sure. It's easy to get along with a man you like. The trouble starts when you love." She turned her eyes back to Claude. "And thank God, I'll never love him!"

"How do you know he loves you?"

"Because I put him to the test and he came out all right."

He grinned. "I see you haven't lost your practical sense. From what you say he sounds like a nice man."

"He is. And I owe it to you that I met him." Softly she chuckled at his stupefaction. "Remember the man with the play?"

"My God. I would never have thought— Well, at least I did something useful in my life."

"My darling, you've done much more than that. You've given me the happiest days of my life. I'll never forget our first summer. Remember the garret?" Suddenly tears were trembling at the end of her lashes. "We were silly, weren't we?"

"We were happy. Perhaps the two go together . . . I don't think we'll ever be so happy again. At least not in the same way . . ."

"I know I'll miss you and worry about you. That's why I wanted you to meet Lily. She'll come to see you from time to time and write to me how you're getting along. You don't mind, do you?"

"Sweet Gaby! . . . I'll miss you, too. More than you'll ever know."

They looked at each other, trying to smile, fighting back the desire to rush into each other's arms. Memories from their long and tempestuous affair flocked back. Now it was all over . . . Slowly they were unmooring themselves from seven years of their lives.

"Are you going to join him tonight," he asked, struggling to make his voice sound natural.

"No, darling. This will be our last night, and it'll take us all night to say good-bye."

Book Three

HIGH COMBS
AND
WHITE CRESTS

CHAPTER

15

SHE HAD LEFT A FEW MINUTES AGO.

The side where she had lain in bed must still be warm. The pillow still bore the imprint of her head. It had been a night of passion with much underlying tenderness. Time after time they had clashed and tangled and made love to each other until, abruptly, they were spent and asleep, their lips still touching, without even having said good night.

Now, in his bare feet and wearing only his trousers, he stood at the window, not quite fully awake, breathing the fresh morning air and trying to get used to the idea she was gone. This time for good. Seven years was a long time, and she had left a lot of memories behind. Just as she had left her trunks, her dresses, her curling iron.

"I'll come for them one of these days," she had said at the door. "You don't mind, do you?"

No, he didn't mind. Not in the least. So far as he was concerned, she could leave them here forever. He liked having her things around. They would remind him of their good days together. And if by chance she had left them to make sure no other woman would move in, she needn't worry. He wasn't about to plunge into another affair. Anything but that! He had had enough of women and love and kisses for the next ten years. Well, let's say for two or three years. He wanted neither to love nor to be loved. Just to be left alone.

Alone with his music. This was the thing he really loved best. Even more than women. Mind you, it, too, could be exasperating, but it gave you the most wonderful moments. The only trouble was that it didn't bring you any money . . .

The following Sunday, Lily came to see him.

"Gaby made me promise to let her know how you are."

"My cooking isn't as good as hers, but except for that I'm all right."

"Do you miss her a lot?"

For an instant he gazed ahead, gathered his thoughts. Then with a nod of admission, he said, "Yes, I do. More than I thought I would . . . Have you heard from her?"

Yes. Gaby had written her a nice letter. She was fine, and her new apartment on avenue Niel was simply gorgeous.

"She said to tell you she has a wonderful bathtub and she spends half of her time in it."

He felt his eyes moisten as he recalled the *bain à la maison* and Gaby laughing and splashing in her rolling brass tub.

"She always was crazy about having a bathtub," he said with a smile. "This and a fine carriage were the two things she had set her heart on. I'm glad she's met a man who can give her both and many other things besides. Did you know she met him through me?"

He told her about the South American and his play. They laughed. Not much, not loud. As if Gaby were still in the room, watching them.

"Just the same it's rather funny, isn't it, when you think of it," he said with a rueful smile. "A perfect stranger comes to show me his play, I throw him out and he takes my girl away."

Which simply proved that life was made of the most unexpected, improbable accidents. For a while they talked about fate and the part it played and you never could tell what was in store for you.

He noticed she was very pretty. Not beautiful or exciting, like Gaby, but pleasant to look at. And it was nice having someone to talk to about Gaby.

"May I come again next Sunday?" she asked as she was leaving.

Of course. He'd be delighted if she did. "We'll have tea. You'll see, I make the best cup of tea in Paris."

The following Sunday they had tea and pastries. She said he was indeed an expert tea brewer. They still talked about Gaby, but less. There wasn't much to say, really, except that he missed her.

"When you've lived seven years with a woman, it's hard to get used to being a bachelor again. In the old days I didn't mind staying a week by myself; now I find it difficult spending even an evening alone."

Of course, he had his music. But somehow even music didn't give quite the same companionship that a woman did.

"But at least you're free," she said. "That means a lot."

Yes, it was nice being free. But it really didn't mean much. Free to do what? Have silly little affairs that brought you neither joy nor pain? No, thank you.

"I guess I'm getting too old for that sort of thing. I prefer staying home with a good book."

She felt the same way. She much preferred spending an evening by herself sewing or ironing, rather than going out with some man she didn't like.

"When I first came to Paris I used to go out a lot, but not any more."

That day she told him about her parents. She had still been a child when her mother died, and it was her father who had brought her up. She spoke of him with affection. After thirty years as a railway telegraphist he had just been pensioned off and was now living at Bichain, a village in the Yonne *département*.

"He owns a little house there. Nothing fancy, mind you. But it's got a nice garden."

She spoke of the fruit trees she used to climb as a tot and her father's vegetable patch which he tended with love and skill.

"We've got the best vegetables of the whole region," she said with pride.

At her next visit they went out to dinner. This time they did not mention Gaby. They talked of various things and enjoyed themselves.

"You're really a very nice man," she remarked over her demitasse. "I can't tell you how much I look forward to our little Sunday's together."

He said he did, too. Friendship was such a nice, relaxed relationship. You could be yourself, didn't have to watch what you said or did, as when you were courting a woman or simply flirting. Again he noticed how attractive she was. But for a country girl—for that's what she was—he thought her rather frail-looking. She was slender to the point of thinness. Even her make-up did not quite conceal the pallor of her cheeks.

"You're thinking I'm terribly thin, aren't you?" She smiled. "I always look run-down at the end of the season. It's the Paris weather. Don't worry. I'll go to Bichain this summer and I'll be all right."

After that they saw each other more frequently. He waited for her at the shop. Sometimes she came to see him unannounced. They admitted their loneliness and the pleasure they found in each other's company.

She had great faith in his future, and he asked her why.

"I don't know why, I just feel it," she said. "I'm sure you'll soon be famous."

He chuckled indulgently at her remark, and said she was talking nonsense. Nevertheless, he felt touched and quite pleased by her admiration.

One evening she arrived bringing groceries and announced she was going to cook dinner for him. She proved to be an excellent cook. He complimented her and remarked that this was the first delicious meal he had had since Gaby had gone away. Later he escorted her back to her house on rue de Berne. In the doorway they suddenly found themselves in each other's arms. Reluctantly she pulled away and slipped into the house.

The following afternoon he waited for her at the shop, and they walked together to his apartment.

Again she cooked dinner and again he complimented her. But that evening he did not take her home.

The following Sunday she moved in.

♦

He couldn't have said how it had happened . . . Only two months ago he was so sure no woman would ever live with him again, and there he was with Lily in his house! Which merely proved once more that you never could tell what would happen next . . . Neither of them had planned it that way. She had just come for a few visits to see how he was. They hadn't fallen in love or anything like that. But they did like each other. And both happened to be free and lonely. And it was June and the nights were gentle and—well, it had seemed like the natural thing to do. Anyway, there was no need to fret over it or fear he might trap himself again. Lily was nice and all that, but she was no Gaby . . . Besides, at the end of the month she was going to Bichain for the summer. They would probably forget each other.

Two days after Lily moved in, Claude received a note from Pierre Louÿs announcing his forthcoming marriage. The wedding was scheduled for June 24 in the elegant Saint-Philippe Church. And could he, please, dash off a wedding march for the occasion? Something pompous, lascivious, devotional and brief. Say, two hundred bars.

Claude replied with the usual compliments and said he would write the march. Their friendship had deteriorated to such a degree that he felt he was writing to a stranger.

That same week he learned of Monsieur Chausson's tragic death in a bicycle accident. The news brought back many memories and the usual flock of useless regrets. He was sorry he had not accepted his recent invitation to lunch, shaken once more the hand of this great artist who had been his benefactor and such a wonderful friend. And now it was too late: it was always too late.

Then, suddenly, Lily fell ill. The doctor said something was wrong with her kidneys. At the door, he added she should be taken to a hospital.

"He wants me to go to the hospital, doesn't he?" she cried the moment Claude returned to the room. "That's what he told you, didn't he?"

Her eyes were wide with fear. Like most country people, she had a terror of hospitals. They were the antechambers of the cemetery. In her mind she saw the lugubrious wards with their narrow iron beds lined against the walls, the huge black crucifix hanging down from the ceiling, the Saint Vincent sisters going about in their winged coifs, the priests in surplice and stole mumbling the last rites.

"Please, darling, don't let him take me away."

Gently he argued that in a hospital she would receive proper attention and recover much faster.

"I'll come to see you every visiting day."

She pleaded with him to let her stay in his apartment. She wept, pressed his hand against her cheek, promised to get well.

"You'll scc, I'll be all right in a few days."

He gave in. He nursed her as best he could, bade her take her medicines, rushed home after lessons to be at her bedside. He held her hand when she winced with pain, read the newspaper aloud when she felt better. He sat his work table in the bedroom. While she dozed he worked on Pierre's wedding march. He learned to sleep on a chair, like a professional nurse.*

He did not begrudge her his own discomfort, the cost of the doctor's visits. He did not even resent the irony of fate that was turning their little affair into a nursing ordeal. On the contrary, she became dearer to him in her helplessness and the humiliations of illness.

He had thought her pretty in her painstaking hairdo; now he found her pathetic and beautiful in the dishevelment of her blond hair and the pallor of her cheeks that her make-up no longer concealed. She needed him and he felt sorry for her. Compassion is one of the gates to love. This girl who was almost a stranger and had meant little to him until now, stirred up in him obscure capacities for devotion and sacrifice. By the time she began to recover, he was more than half in love with her.

---

* On June 15, 1899, he wrote Pierre Louÿs, apologizing for not having finished the march. "My *petite amie* is ill and I've spent two nights at her bedside . . ."

On the scheduled date, Pierre's wedding took place. It was a sunny late-spring morning and Paris smelled good from all the flowers stalls at street corners. The ceremony was a brilliant social function. An elegant audience filled the elegant church. Since the father of the bride was a member of the French Academy, a delegation from the illustrious assembly added the glamour and prestige of their green-and-gold uniforms. Even the officiant and his acolytes performed with exquisite drawing-room gestures. The altar blazed with burning candles and the wedding allocution bloomed with poetic metaphors. At last Pierre and his bride, ravishing in her nuptial veils, began the long walk down the red-carpeted aisle as Claude, sitting at the organ, filled the air with the joyous thunder of his march.

He hurried back to the apartment and found Lily waiting, bursting with curiosity.

"How was it?"

"Very nice, very *chichi*. Lot of people."

He let himself down on the edge of the bed, trying to catch his breath.

"You look good this morning," he said, scanning her face. "In a few days you'll be up and about."

She improved rapidly. Soon she felt strong enough to travel. Early in July she left for Bichain.

The apartment seemed desolately empty when he returned from the station. He tried working, but music eluded him and offered no refuge from loneliness. The long summer days went by in a slow, morose procession. Occasionally he thought about Lily, but it was Gaby he really missed. The sight of her trunks brought back happy memories but he found no joy in them. Instead they tormented his solitude. He refused to believe that a hundred times he had wished her to go and that he had let her disappear from his life without a word of protest. He felt listless, annoyed at himself, his lack of ambition, his brooding nonchalance. *Pélléas* was written, but he could not bring himself to orchestrate it. He lamented that its production was as uncertain as ever, knowing that he was the prime cause of the uncertainty. He was tired of being poor, yet did nothing to get out of his poverty. Time weighed on his hands.

Sometimes he dropped in at the Café Weber in search of companionship, but felt as lonely among friends as he did alone. He sought solitude and found it irksome. He floundered in a maze of contradictions.

"I don't know what I want," he told himself irritably.

He knew perfectly well what he wanted. A home, a wife, children . . . But these were out of the question. Never would he be in a position to get married. All his life he would remain as he was: obscure, alone and poor, writing music which would arouse polemics, perhaps some applause, but bring no material change in his life. At night he lay awake, reading to avoid thinking about the future.

He was filled with joy when, toward the end of August, Lily returned to Paris and resumed her work at the shop. This time she did not move in with him. By good fortune she was able to rent her former room on rue de Berne; and there one evening she informed him she would not be his mistress any more.

"I've had time to think in the country," she said, "and it's better if we're just good friends."

He was disappointed; as a lover his ego had been deflated, but he made no protests. He wanted companionship more than amorousness.

"At least may I come to see you?" he asked.

"As much as you want. I love being with you."

For a fortnight they saw each other every morning. They dined together. Sometimes at a restaurant, sometimes at his apartment and sometimes in her room. The country had done her much good. She looked healthy and even prettier than before. She was gay, but not too gay. When he told her about his forlorn summer and how much he had missed her, she said that she also had missed him a great deal. Sometimes he caught her eyes resting on him with lingering tenderness. He tried to kiss her. Gently but firmly she declined his advances. Now he found her extremely desirable. Especially when they spent the evening at her place and she changed her clothes and slipped into a loose wrapper.

He decided to bring the matter out in the open.

"Darling, don't you think this brother-and-sister game has lasted long enough? Why don't you be reasonable and move back with me?"

She looked straight into his eyes. "I like you a lot. I even love you, if you must know the truth, but I am not going to do what Gaby did. Give you the best years of my life and find myself with nothing at the end."

"She found a millionaire."

"She was lucky. But I don't count on any millionaire. I want security, a husband." She caught his blink of surprise, and went on, with a smile, "I don't mean you have to marry me. We can remain good friends, until—" She paused.

"Until what?"

"Until some man asks me to marry him."

Two days later she casually announced she would not be able to see him on the following evening.

"Albert asked me to have dinner with him."

And who the devil was Albert? . . . He was the shop's buyer. A nice-looking man, a widower, with a good solid position.

"Does he want to marry you?"

"I haven't the faintest idea."

As a matter of fact she knew very little about Albert, except that lately he had been quite attentive and had given her little bouquets and chocolates.

"Of course, these things mean nothing," she said.

To him they meant a great deal. He spent a miserable night, torn between jealousy and uncertainty. Curiously, he had never thought of Lily in connection with marriage. In his vague matrimonial musings his wife was always a person of elegance, charm, culture, refinement. And an excellent musician. Lily simply did not conform to this ideal. For one thing, she did not know anything about music. Then, she used too much make-up and had no flair for clothes, which was strange for a fashion model. As for culture—well, the less said the better.

"Did you enjoy your evening?" he asked when he saw her again.

It had been very pleasant. Albert had taken her to an excellent restaurant and afterward to a cinema. A perfect gentleman. In the carriage, on their way back to her house, he hadn't even tried to kiss her.

"By the way, I promised to have dinner with him again Thursday."

From then on he saw Albert quite often, and Claude lived through nights and days of anguish. As usual he was going to muff his chance and let this stupid buyer steal Lily right from under his nose. And then? . . . Then he would be alone. Completely alone—and forever. Panic gripped him at the thought. Already solitude was closing in on him. Monsieur Chausson was dead, Pierre was married, Gaby had gone out of his life. Was he also going to let Lily slip away? Here was a sweet, beautiful girl who loved him—she had said so herself —who was willing to share his poverty, make a home for him, give him the children he wanted . . . What if she didn't know music? Or have much education? On the contrary, it would be a joy to open her mind to knowledge and beauty . . .

That afternoon he waited for her at the shop. When she came out, he took her arm. She did not resist, and together they walked to her house.

During dinner he asked about Albert. She said he really was a fine gentleman, very serious and reliable. And he seemed quite fond of her.

"As a matter of fact, he asked me to marry him."

He gulped. Perhaps he was too late . . . "What did you say?"

"I told him I wanted to think it over for a few days."

"Are you going to marry him?"

"I don't know . . . I don't love him and I wouldn't think of marrying him unless—unless the man I love doesn't want to marry me."

That evening he asked her to marry him.

To his stupefaction she hesitated.

"I don't want you to feel you have to marry me."

"But I want to marry you."

"You say so now, but perhaps tomorrow you'll change your mind. Gaby told me how impulsive you are."

"Impulsive? Me? . . . Gaby doesn't know me at all. She never understood me. When I make up my mind, I never change it. Please say you'll marry me."

"Are you sure you want to?"

"Yes, I am. I beg, beseech you to marry me. What must I do? Go down on my knees?"

"All right," she smiled. "If you really want me to, I'll marry you."

◆

Early next morning he went to his district's city hall, where he was ushered into the office of the chief clerk: an amiable, corpulent man with an abundant mustache that billowed over his upper lip. In turn he was almost bald, and his few strands of carefully combed hair looked somewhat like the black keys on a piano keyboard. A cigarette stub dangled from the corner of his mouth.

With a cordial gesture he waved Claude to a chair.

"So, you want to get married, Monsieur? Permit me to congratulate you. Marriage is the cornerstone of our society. Without it, all would be chaos, social anarchy and moral collapse. This is why our Civil Code stresses its importance and describes it as a solemn contract." His voice turned grave, faintly ominous. "Notice the word solemn, Monsieur."

That morning Claude learned that marriage was not only a solemn contract, but a very public affair about which many people had much to say. You practically had to inform the whole world of your plans. Numerous documents must be secured, notices of "intention of marriage" had to be posted on the walls of the city hall.

"And, of course, you must obtain your parents' consent."

"What?" He couldn't believe his ears. "I am thirty-seven, and you mean I cannot get married without my parents' permission?"

"Exactly. If you were ninety, you still would have to have it. The law is formal on this point."

"And if they refuse?"

In this case, since he was over thirty, he still could get married, but he must send his parents a *sommation respectueuse,* informing them of his intention of overriding their veto and proceeding with his plans.

"In fact, you're lucky. Until three years ago you had to send two, a month apart. Now one is enough. But it is indispensable. Without it the wedding ceremony cannot be performed."*

He paused to remove the cigarette stub from his lower lip and crushed it into an ashtray.

"As I mentioned a moment ago, marriage is a solemn contractual obligation that engages not only the bride and groom, but their families as well, and even society at large. The law will not permit any trifling with it."

Claude stepped out of the city hall in a state of deep perplexity. He had the feeling his parents would object to his marriage.

And as he expected, they did.

With a wave of the hand his father cut short his explanation and announced point-blank that no fashion model was going to disgrace the family. Why, everybody knew those mannequins were only a step above cocottes. And sometimes not even that!

"Besides," Manuel went on, "how are you going to support her?"

"And if you have any children?" added Victorine.

Claude argued that Lily was a fine, honest and hard-working girl. He lied about his earnings, spoke of the forthcoming royalties from his opera.

He could have saved his breath. His parents remained adamant in their opposition. Yes, he could send them a *sommation respectueuse* and get married over their protests, but at least they would have made it clear they were against this marriage. In fact, they would not attend the wedding.

Claude left them in a rage, aggravated by the feeling that their objections were not entirely unfounded. How was he going to support a wife and children? He had told Lily that besides his lessons, he could depend on Hartmann's advances. And of course, soon there would be the royalties from *Pélléas.* It was technically true. But when would *Pélléas* be produced? How long would Hartmann continue to advance money on royalties that were growing steadily more problematic? . . . It was all quite complicated and rather frightening, if you stopped to think of it.

Another warning came to him a few days later, when Gaby paid him a visit.

"Lily writes me you want to marry her," she began with a faint, disapproving gleam in her eyes. "So I thought I'd better come and

* The law of February 2, 1933, abrogated the *sommation respectueuse.*

pack my things. After all, we don't want the bride to trip over my curling iron, do we?"

She looked more beautiful than ever in her blue taffeta dress, and he was so happy at seeing her that he scarcely listened.

"How have you been, darling? Are you happy?"

She shrugged and laughed softly. Happy? Who was really happy in this world? . . . She was well and satisfied. Victor was an angel, a regular angel, and just about as dull as an angel must be. God, what a bore he was! Except for that, he was perfect.

"But I didn't come here to talk about him."

She leaned forward and rested her forearm on his desk. "Tell me, darling, are you really going to marry her?"

"She wants to get married." He caught himself and continued in a bright, eager tone of voice. "And I also want to get married. Very much. I've thought it over and I feel I'm ready to get married. I am a family man at heart."

She smiled. "The funny part is that you really are, but—"

"But what?"

"Are you sure you're doing the right thing? Mind you, Lily is a fine girl, but she isn't the right wife for you. For some other man, yes. But not for you."

"What's so special about me?"

"You aren't exactly the average sort of man."

"I am like everybody else. You'll see, Lily and I will be very happy. We have the same tastes, we both want a quiet life and children." A crafty smile played over his lips. "I know what you're thinking. I have no money and I waste a lot of time dreaming about music and I have no practical sense. Don't you see that's the very reason why I need a wife! With Lily at my side, I'll settle down and work ten times harder than I ever did. The first thing I'm going to do—"

She no longer listened. From a gold case she pulled a cigarette and began smoking in silence, her thoughts weaving in her mind to the accompaniment of his words. Poor darling, he hadn't changed! . . . He believed what he said, really thought marriage was going to make a new man out of him. Here he was, about to make the biggest mistake of his life and there was no way to make him see it. He wanted to get married simply because he couldn't get used to being a bachelor again. In a sense it was her fault. For seven years she had given him the illusion of a home, and he just couldn't go back to the routine of the old garret days. Mend his socks, wash his shirts, cook his meals on the alcohol lamp . . . He was afraid to spend the rest of his life in loneliness. Most men, when they neared forty, fell into the same sort of domestic trance. Suddenly they dreamed of slippers, reading the newspaper by the fireside, having a woman around who wouldn't leave them if they were sick . . . He was in that mood, ready to marry the first woman who came along . . . Lily happened to be there, and he would marry her if she were deaf, blind and dumb. No use trying to open his eyes. He didn't want them open.

She came out of her thoughts and watched him through the smoke of her cigarette, a tender, wistful smile in her eyes.

He was still orating.

"Believe me, darling, I've studied Lily and I know she'll be the perfect wife for me. She has all the qualities I don't have." He was speaking fast, with the emphasis of people who are not sure of their arguments. "And she's the kindest, sweetest—"

"I hope you're right, and I wish you both all the happiness in the world."

She sighed, snuffed her cigarette in the ashtray and rose from her chair."

"I'd better get busy and start packing."

Again he saw the efficient Gaby he had known. In less than an hour everything was neatly packed, her trunks closed. Not a trace of her presence remained in the apartment.

"Well, I guess that's all," she said, giving a last glance at the room.

She walked to the armoire and stood before the full-length mirror while putting on her hat.

"You know, darling, I should've let you marry Thérèse Roger. She would have been the right wife for you."

He watched her reflection in the mirror and noticed that her eyes were brimming with tears.

"I should have," she went on quietly, as if speaking to herself. "But I couldn't see it at the time. I was jealous, I loved you too much. You hurt people when you love them too much."

He protested she had done him the greatest service.

"If you'd let me marry Thérèse, I wouldn't have had the chance of marrying Lily. Besides, I—"

Smiling, she turned around and pressed her fingertips to his lips.

"Keep quiet. You don't know what you're talking about. You're trying to sell yourself a pig." Slowly she scanned his face. "I love you and I guess I always will, but you have about as much sense as a flea."

She kissed him, just long enough to know that the old magic was still there.

"Damn you," she murmured tenderly. "I'd better get out of here before I make a fool of myself."

She started toward the door, but he tugged at her sleeve.

"Wait. I want to give you something. Something that'll remind you of our first summer. Remember our picnic at Asnières and how you slept on the grass after lunch and it gave me the idea for my *Afternoon of a Faun?* Just wait a minute. I'd like to give you the manuscript."

He began searching through his study, riffled through stacks of musical scores, opened drawers, even peered behind the piano.

"Damn it, I just had it in my hands a few days ago!" he grumbled under his breath. "It didn't walk away by itself, did it?"

Finally he found it in the bedroom under the bed, together with a pile of old manuscripts.

"I knew I had it somewhere," He beamed triumphantly. "I know where everything is."

He went back to the study, wrote a few words on the upper margin of the first page and handed her the manuscript.

"Here, darling. For old times' sake."

She read the *dédicace* and thanked him with a smile.

At the door they kissed once more, full on the lips. Swiftly she pulled herself away and started down the stairs. She waved at him from the floor landing below and he waved back. Then there was nothing but the receding sound of her rushing footsteps. And then, not even that.*

Thoughtfully he returned to his study, her words still echoing in his mind. Was she right by any chance? Was he making a mistake in marrying Lily?

For an instant he felt like a man tottering on the edge of an abyss. But already the moment of lucidity was passing. Merciful self-delusion was coming back.

No, he wasn't making any mistake. Lily would make a splendid wife. Anyway, it was too late for hesitation. Already the legal machinery was in motion. The *sommation respectueuse* had been duly sent to his parents. Notices of "intention of marriage" were posted at the city hall. Lily's father had written, announcing he would travel all the way to Paris for the wedding. Even the date had been set: the nineteenth of October. He had even bought a suit and a hat for the occasion. Lily had objected to his sombrero. Rightly so. Marriage was a serious, dignified affair, the first step into respectability. No more sombrero for him.

Suddenly, a week before the ceremony, Lily demanded a church wedding. She would not feel married unless she walked down the aisle

---

* Gaby kept the manuscript for more than thirty years, until forced by circumstances to part with it. It is today in M. Alfred Cortot's collection. The dedication bears the date of October, 1899, and reads, "To my dear and very good little Gaby, with the faithful affection of her devoted Claude Debussy."

in a white gown, like Pierre's bride. She, too, must have incense, oratory, organ music.

"I want God to bless our marriage."

Claude approached the curate of his parish and with dismay learned that the simplest wedding ceremony would cost eighty-five francs. He told Lily he simply could not afford the expense. God was beyond his means.

At last the great day came, a fine autumn day, wistful and pearl-gray. He got up early, put on his new suit and hat. He thought he looked very dignified. Then he searched through his pockets and discovered he had no money at all. As usual his watch had been pawned.

Luckily he had a lesson at ten o'clock that very morning.

He went to his pupil's house, and the lesson over, inquired if she could possibly pay him, since he was getting married in an hour.*

With his gold louis in his vest pocket, he ran all the way to the city hall, where he arrived perspiring and out of breath. Anxiously he glanced about, hoping that his parents might have weakened at the last moment and come to his wedding, but they were nowhere to be seen.

On the other hand, Lily was there with her father—ill at ease in his Sunday clothes and starched collar—together with the witnesses required by law.

At last they were ushered into a large and stately room. Behind a green-felt table stood a bearded official, a tricolor sash around his paunch. In a tone of unctuous and well-feigned emotion he delivered a few stirring remarks on the solemnity of the occasion. He reminded bride and groom of the responsibilities they were about to assume and the joys they would share throughout life. With a benign smile he said that in his humble person, France was actually present in the room, smiling on them, adjuring them to be good law-abiding citizens and give birth to numerous, healthy and patriotic little Frenchmen.

Then, in a voice of somber finality, he pronounced them man and wife.

* The pupil was Mademoiselle Worms de Reilly, who later confirmed paying Debussy his twenty-franc fee that morning so that he could get married.

CHAPTER

16

MARRIAGE WAS WONDERFUL. IT GAVE A NEW MEANING, A NEW DIGNITY
to life; a sort of spiritual glow that illuminated the humble daily
routine. It made everything simple. He was now a married man, and
all he had to do was to love Lily, love her more each day, work for
her, work very hard, provide for her, sacrifice for her—and this
to his dying day. In the past he might have recoiled at this prospect,
but no more. For marriage brought out the best in you; turned you
into the responsible, high-principled, hard-working man you should
be. No more daydreaming at the window for him, no more lolling
in bed in the morning or afternoon siestas in summer. No more squandering of money on useless trinkets, no more glances at pretty girls in
the streets. Work, thrift, faithfulness. These were now his mottoes.

While he remained in this exalted state of mind, the nineteenth
century was living its last days in the gloom of autumnal rains. The
Dreyfus Affair had at last come to an end. A devious, shameful end
that satisfied no one. Ten days after being tried and condemned once
again, Dreyfus had been unexplainably pardoned by the President
of the Republic. The poor man had been too ill and exhausted to
reject this final insult.*

As the year drew to its end, newspapers predicted the wonders
of the forthcoming twentieth century. It would be a century of scien-

---

* In July, 1906, eleven years after his degradation, Dreyfus was decorated
with the Legion of Honor.

tific miracles. Already Marconi had sent a wireless message across the Channel, and soon one would be able to send messages all over the world. Progress would wipe out poverty; science would wipe out disease. Above all, it would be a century of peace. That barbarous and obsolete institution known as War would be abolished.

Meanwhile it remained as popular as ever. But now men killed one another in the name of principles and human rights, usually freedom. The more principles a nation had, the more warlike it became. Having brought freedom to Cuba, American troops were now bringing freedom to the Philippines and getting slaughtered in the process. In China, natives were sniping at "foreign devils"; in the Sudan, civilization triumphed with the help of machine guns. In South Africa, Boers and British were at each other's throats. And France, having bought Russia as an ally, felt safe and smug now that the Cossacks were on her side.

In Paris elaborate preparations were being considered for the coming New Year's Eve. There was talk of great public festivities, with civic oratory, fireworks and the populace dancing from one century into another. But on the year's last afternoon, rain began to fall; by evening it was coming down in buckets. And so there were no speeches, no fireworks and no dancing. Cold and dripping wet, the twentieth century started on its long journey.

For Claude and Lily the early months of the new century were a period of mutual discovery and sober second thoughts. Like most people who have married in haste, they emerged from the nuptial raptures to find that they really did not know each other at all. In the cold gray light of married life a number of things big and small began to appear which had not appeared before.

He already knew she was an excellent cook; he learned she was also a thrifty housekeeper who could squeeze every sou and perform miracles with a two-franc coin. She prided herself on her bargaining talent. Sometimes, on her return from the market, she mimicked haggling scenes with fishwives and cart vendors in which she invariably achieved some small financial triumph. Clearly nobody was going to get the best of her.

This was all the more remarkable since she possessed little physical endurance. Even such a slight chore as the sweeping of a room caused her to pant and brought beads of sweat to her brow. Often, when he came back from giving a lesson, he found her stretched out on the bed, white-faced, wheezily trying to catch her breath. Also, she was, he noticed, uncommonly susceptible to colds and migraines.

Immediately after the wedding he had written a friend that she was "incredibly blond, as lovely as a fairy princess." Her blondness became less incredible when he saw that it came out of a bottle. At first he was delighted with her favorite song, a naïve roundelay about "a red-faced grenadier who wore his cap tilted over his ear." He found it touchingly inept. Then he discovered that it constituted about her entire musical repertory. After hearing it for days on end, he found it less touching and more inept. He wished she would learn another song or stop singing altogether. Preferably the latter, for he had noticed that her voice was somewhat grating and off-key.

Also, he was forced to admit that he had little to say to her. Since she knew or felt nothing about music, never read a book, had no views on politics or anything else, conversation required much ingenuity and effort. He smiled at the thought that only a few months ago he had fancied himself opening her mind to knowledge and beauty. How silly could a man be! What on earth had ever given him the notion that she wanted her mind open to knowledge and beauty?

No doubt many people found happiness in marriage. They were the lucky ones. For him marriage had turned out to be something entirely different from what he had expected. A complex, confusing way of life and state of mind that brought many surprises and quite a few disappointments. Perhaps it was its dailyness, its irrevocability, its damned confinement that made it so baffling. He did not know. But whatever it was it certainly called for a heap of adjustment, patience, good will, compromise, understanding and self-control.

No doubt many people found marriage a tender, hand-in-hand journey through life, the then-they-were-married-and-lived-happily-ever-after that ended all fairly tales. He hadn't. Instead he had found that marriage did not create companionship when there was no companionship to begin with. In order to share each other's thoughts, you first must have thoughts to share. If anything, marriage induced the kind of thoughts it was wise to keep to yourself . . .

Yes, his marriage had turned out to be a baffling, rather disconcerting experience. But the most baffling, disconcerting part of it had been to find out what marriage could do to romance. Mind you, everyone knew that romance was a bit of nonsense, a sort of mild, harmless delirium tremens that changed life into a gossamer enchantment. Nobody expected it to last forever. But it took your breath away to see how quickly marriage cured you of it. Nothing like marriage to take the stars out of your eyes . . .

Even love-making no longer felt the same . . . Even sleep had a new strangeness. It no longer was the contented rest of fulfilled bodies, the tangled stillness of passion spent. Now it was an escape, a breathing spell into oblivion. Sometimes, at night, he watched Lily huddled in slumber, not sleeping with her head on his shoulder as Gaby had done, but with her back to him. Perhaps all married couples slept back-to-back? After all, sleep was marriage's only privacy . . . Poor Lily! Occasionally he wondered whether she felt as perplexed at having married him as he was at having married her . . .

She did. She, too, was having private reflections about marriage in general and her husband in particular. She found it difficult to get used to his nonchalance, his time-wasting habits. She remembered his telling her how hard he was going to work as soon as they married. Now she found him at his desk, musing over a half-written page of music, and when she asked what on earth he was mooning about, he would reply with obvious sincerity, "But, darling, I'm working." Apparently this was his idea of hard work . . .

No wonder money was scarce. If it weren't for his lessons and the advances from his publisher, Monsieur Hartmann, they would starve. Not that he didn't think about money. On the contrary, he worried about it all the time, kept telling her how important money was and how they must start building a nest egg for the day when their first child would arrive. He always had some vague and promising project, usually a collaboration with some friend on a play or a ballet, that was going to make them rich. A week or two later he would forget about it, or for some reason the project would fall through.

Even his opera had turned out to be something of a mirage. Before their wedding he had told her about the royalties it was going to bring. Pencil in hand he had shown her how they could live in modest affluence on them alone. He had not lied. The director of the Opéra Comique had truly promised to produce Pélléas. Yes— eighteen months ago! And Claude had been content with this vague verbal promise and had not judged it necessary to ask for a written contract.

"If at least you had a letter from him," she had remarked, "you could go to court and force him to produce your opera."

Court! Why, he'd never think of doing such a thing . . . Besides —well, it was mostly his fault that Pélléas hadn't yet been produced. For many months he had had the ridiculous notion of having it presented in some small garden theatre or even performed by puppets. Silly, wasn't it? . . . And then—to tell the truth, he hadn't yet written the orchestration!

"But, don't worry, darling. At the first opportunity, I'll jump on it and dash it off."

He meant it, but he'd probably forget about that, too . . .

Mind you, he was a nice man and, when he thought of it, full of good will and sweet attentions. Often, after dinner, he offered to help her with the dishes. Sometimes, when he saw her sweeping the room, he took the broom from her hands and insisted she lie down and rest. Whenever he could afford it he took her to a café or a cinema. You couldn't help loving him and she did. But there was no denying it, in many ways he had been a disappointment.

At first she had been impressed by his title of Grand Prix de Rome, his forthcoming opera. Oh, yes, she had known he was a dreamer and had no business sense, but she had felt sure that all he needed was a good wife at his side and he would soon be a success. Vaguely she had fancied herself moving into a world of celebrities and famous artists as the wife of a brilliant composer, sharing his artistic triumphs, receiving distinguished friends, pouring tea on her day-at-home, like the society ladies she read about in newspapers.

Not that she had expected an overnight miracle. It might take a few months before he changed his habits. Well, she had waited; she had been patient. Nobody could deny she had been a good wife, squeezed every sou and given him a good home. It was he who hadn't turned out as she expected. He hadn't changed. Now, after six months of marriage, there was no material improvement in their condition, and none was in sight. At times she wondered whether he would ever be successful, whether she would ever attend a social function. Now and then she even asked herself whether she shouldn't have waited a little longer, gotten to know him better before marrying him . . .

And so, in the dawn of their discontent, they went on, neither of them speaking his thoughts, feeling no regrets as yet, only a vague uneasiness, a nebulous apprehension at the irrevocability of the step they had taken.

The year was coming into spring. Another Exposition Universelle opened, this time to celebrate the wonders of the new century. On rue Cardinet, the days followed without serious mishap, but without any noticeable progress either. Lily continued to wrench small rebates from cart vendors and save a few sous here and there; Claude to give his lessons, weave fanciful plans and muse over his music. And when, despite Lily's thrift, there was no more money in the sugar bowl, he again turned to his good and patient publisher for help.

But even Hartmann's patience was wearing thin. On this April morning it had about reached its end.

"Not another sou, not a pfennig will you get from me!" he exclaimed even before Claude had reached his desk. "No use coming to see me unless you bring the finished score of *Pélléas*."

"It's almost finished, Monsieur Hartmann."

"I don't believe you. That's what you said last year, that's what you'll say in ten years. I could've had it produced by now, if you'd written the orchestration instead of going crazy over those *idiotich* puppets of yours!"

"You're right, absolutely right! I was an idiot, and that's what I told my wife. But things have changed. I am now a married man and I finally pounded some common sense into my head. I swear I'll get back to *Pélléas*, as soon as I finish my *Nocturnes*. And they're almost finished."

"Almost!" The publisher's arms shot up in the air. "*Mein Gott*, that's all I hear! Everything is almost finished, almost ready, but I never see anything. How am I going to get back the money I've advanced you, if you don't give me anything to publish!"

"What do you mean? I gave you a lot of music!"

Hartmann made a conciliatory gesture. "*Ja ja*, you did. You gave me some *gut* music. But it's *Pélléas* and the *Nocturnes* I want."

If Claude would only orchestrate his opera, talks about production could be resumed in October. Perhaps presentation might be arranged for the next season. Then the money would really begin to roll in! As for the *Nocturnes*, the conductor of the Concerts Lamoureux was willing to perform them this winter. Naturally other orchestras would follow suit. Not only in France, but abroad. Already he had approached several conductors in Germany, Austria, England, and they had responded favorably.

"Your music is beginning to be appreciated, especially in foreign countries. Another two or three years and I'll have it played all over the world."

He paused, gazing unseeingly ahead, his eyes turned on some glowing inner vision.

"I'll make you rich yet! And me, too! But you must work."

"I will," said Claude with fervor. "My wife and I are going to spend the summer with her father in the country. There I will have time to work."

Time, peace of mind, no interruptions . . . He would work from dawn to dusk, and by October both *Pélléas* and the *Nocturnes* would be ready.

"I give you my word, my solemn word of honor."

"Just give me the manuscripts," said Hartmann with a perplexed, long-suffering sigh. "Well, I suppose you came to see me because you haven't any money, as usual."

He read the answer on Claude's face and wearily pulled open the drawer of his desk.

"I'm going to help you again, but remember this is the last time."

While talking, he counted three one-hundred-franc notes, set them on his desk and began writing in his receipt book.

"You couldn't make it three-fifty, could you?" asked Claude hesitantly. "I've had many expenses, and now that I'm married—"

"Marriage is a luxury, and you should've known you couldn't afford it. Any fool can get married. A composer should think about music, not marriage. Look at Beethoven, look at Brahms! Did they get married?"

"No, but Bach did. Twice. And he had twenty children."

"*Ach!* Think of all the beautiful music he could've written, if he had remained single!"

Petulantly, he pulled out another note from the drawer and held it out.

"By the way," he added as Claude was signing the receipt, "I've arranged to have some of your compositions played at the Exposition concerts this summer. It'll mean a little money for you and *gut* publicity."

Claude returned home brimming with gratitude toward his publisher and good resolutions for the summer. With a flourish he handed the money to Lily, and during lunch suggested they go to visit the Exposition.

They went that afternoon. With awe they gazed at a drop of water magnified ten thousand times and crawling with microbes. Enough to turn anyone into an alcoholic . . . They admired the moving sidewalks, the Swiss chalet with its bell-tinkling cows in front of it. Arm in arm, they strolled through the papier-mâché reconstruction of Paris' medieval streets. They sat in a dim, smoky tavern and drank beer from pewter tankards served by waitresses dressed in thirteenth-century costumes.

At the Russian Pavilion they gaped at the Czar's gift to the French nation: a map of France in precious stones with cities made of diamonds and rivers of platinum thread. The map itself rested on a large mantle of ermine. It was very grand. It had been made by political prisoners working in the Urals mines.

The visit to the Exposition marked a milestone in Claude's and Lily's lives, for two days later Monsieur Hartmann died.

◆

At one stroke Claude had lost a friend, a guide, a publisher; the only man who had faith in his music, the only man to whom he could turn for help. Whatever little security his life had had until now suddenly was gone. From now on he and Lily were thrown on the mercy of fate. What if money ran out? What if she got sick? These questions kept him awake at night. Finally he realized he had no choice but to hope that Lily would remain in good health until he had finished writing the *Nocturnes* and orchestrating *Pélléas*.

"I'll have everything done by October," he said with ill-feigned assurance. "Then I'll go to see the director of the Opéra Comique, remind him of his promise and demand he produce my opera."

She approved. *Pélléas* was now their only chance. Also, since

Monsieur Hartmann's last advance constituted their sole cash reserve, she suggested they leave as early as possible for Bichain, where they would be able to live on the products of the small farm and spend almost nothing on food. Because of his lessons, however, they must remain in Paris a few more weeks. During that time Lily did miracles of housekeeping. They still had about a hundred and fifty francs when, early in July, they arrived in the country.

He liked her father's house at once. It stood alongside a narrow country lane that twisted its way through meadows and vineyards. It was humble but inviting, with a white picket fence and unpainted shutters at the windows. The garden was as Lily had described it. Sunny, weedy, friendly with the cackling of hens.

The day after their arrival Claude installed himself in a dilapidated wicker chair under one of the fruit trees and plunged into work. By the end of the month the first two *Nocturnes* were written. Without a stop he rushed into the third.

Then Lily fell ill.

She complained of sharp pains in her back. The doctor came, prescribed barley *tisane,* which did no good whatever.

"It's her kidneys," he told Claude with a helpless gesture. "You'd better take her back to Paris right away and put her in a hospital. There they'll know what to do."

The trip to Paris in the sweltering August heat was agony for both of them. From the station they drove directly to the Clinique Dubois, where she was admitted as an emergency patient. This time she was in too much pain to protest.

The following day the resident physician informed him that Lily had kidney stones and must be operated on at once.

"In fact, she should have been operated on a year ago," he said, perusing the medical report on his desk. "Didn't she have these pains before?"

"Yes. About fifteen months ago, but she didn't want to go to a hospital."

Swiftly the doctor lifted his eyes and gave Claude a penetrating but not unkindly glance: "You should have made her go."

"We weren't married at the time."

"I see."

He returned to the report, absently tapping a pencil while he read. Then, with a sigh, he leaned back in his chair and considered Claude with mute sympathy, like a man about to deliver more bad news.

"Also, I regret to tell you that even after her release from the clinic, your wife will require medical attention for some time. Preferably in a sanatorium."

At length he went on describing Lily's medical condition.

"As you see," he concluded, "Madame Debussy is a sick woman and will be, I am afraid, for a few years. You must try to be patient and understanding."

Claude came out of the clinic, took a few steps on the boulevard Saint-Denis, then slumped down on a sidewalk bench. For a long time he remained there, stooped and motionless, his hands crossed between his knees, staring at the pavement in a sort of dazed bewilderment, unaware of the bustle of traffic around him. The doctor's words revolved in his mind, and little by little he felt their full impact, understood their disastrous portent. Lily was a sick woman. Not just a delicate woman susceptible to colds and other transient ailments, but a semi-invalid with defective kidneys and consumptive lungs who for a long time would need medical attention, expensive medicines, long periods of rest. His bride of less than a year was going to require his constant attendance and every sou he could earn. And how was he going to earn any money when neither the *Nocturnes* nor *Pélléas* was finished—and Hartmann was dead?*

His life became a nightmarish whirl of hack work for publishers, meals of bread and tea as in the garret days and, twice a week, visits to the clinic. From lack of sleep and insufficient food he went about in a light-headed dizziness that blunted his thoughts. His distress was so real that the district's merchants felt sorry for him and gave him some credit. Publisher's gave him small jobs as an excuse to come to his help.

In this way he was able to pay the clinic's twelve-franc daily fee. Somehow he managed to placate the landlord. On visiting days he even brought Lily small bouquets, for at this time of the year flowers cost almost nothing.

Ironically, at this very moment several of his compositions were performed at the Exposition concerts amidst growing appreciation. *The Blessed Damozel* aroused much favorable comment in foreign musical magazines. So did his Quartet. The small royalties he received from these performances helped pay the rent.

At last, in October, she was discharged from the clinic. On the way home Claude cautioned the cabby to drive slowly. He helped Lily climb up the stairs, made her rest between floors, almost carried

---

* In his letter of August 25, 1900, to Pierre Louys, Debussy announced that Lily had been successfully operated on for her kidney ailment. "But it seems that her whole system is in bad condition, and (this between ourselves) that she has a beginning of tuberculosis in both lungs. Something must be done immediately, she must be sent to the Pyrenees Mountains for three or four months. You can guess what this means, emotionally as well as financially, in the miserable condition I find myself at this moment . . . I am not a vindictive man, but honestly there are moments when I would like to slap Fate in the face . . . I don't know what to do any more . . ."

her up the last flight. When she shuffled into the bedroom she remarked with a smile about the flowers he had set on the chest of
drawers. It took some time to undress her, but finally he got her in
bed. For a moment she lay down flat on her back, smiling, whispering how glad she was to be back home, while he pulled up the
blankets and patted the pillows under her head.

"Now try to sleep," he said, kissing her forehead.

She closed her eyes, and fell into a doze. For a while he stood
by the bedside watching her sleep, listening to her short, faintly
wheezy breathing.

For a few days he thought it wonderful having her back in their
little bedroom, being relieved of the bi-weekly visits, their whispered endearments under the spying eyes of other patients. But she
was still very weak; her condition required her to stay in bed and
demanded constant attention. He found himself falling back into his
nursing role and sleeping in a chair, while still continuing to work
for publishers and giving his lessons. Her presence at home doubled
his burden. At times he could not keep up the pretense of cheerfulness
so desirable in a nurse and sat on the edge of the bed, too tired to
talk or do anything but hold her hand in silence.

Soon Claude discovered that illness seldom brings out the best in
people, but more often the opposite. Lily's ill temper became more
noticeable and trying than it had been during his short visits at the
clinic. She complained about her loneliness and lack of diversion,
the hours she had to spend alone when he was out looking for work
or giving lessons. At the hospital she had complained of the ward's
lack of privacy; now she missed its comradeship, the bed-to-bed
confidences, the excitement of the doctor's daily visit. She brooded
over the fact that no one in the house, not even the concierge, had
come up to inquire about her.

"In the country, when you're sick, people come to sit with you
and keep you company, but here you could be dying and not even
your next-door neighbor would ask about you."

He kept himself in check, concealed his impatience, attended to
her needs conscientiously and devotedly. But he no longer felt the
tender anguish with which he had nursed her in the days of their
brief love affair, when her pallor, her blond dishevelment had aroused
in him the first stirrings of love.

He tried to shame himself into a resurgence of his former feelings.
It was no use, and he felt too tired for self-delusion. His love for
Lily was oozing out of him as steadily as water from a cracked jug.
Strangely, her illness had nothing to do with it. He did not resent
her whining complaints or the long circular operation scar that
marred her lovely body. Nor did he begrudge her his sleepless nights,

the hours he spent at her bedside reading aloud asinine newspaper serials or the columns devoted to *mondanités*. "Yesterday Madame la Duchesse de—— entertained a few aristocratic friends in her exquisite mansion on rue . . ." No, it wasn't that. On the contrary, he felt sorry for this young woman with bad lungs and bad kidneys. He winced when he saw her lips twinge in pain.

But sorry or not, he no longer loved her, and that's all there was to it. He was tired of her grating voice, the emptiness of her mind, her lack of sensitiveness. His marriage had been a huge, a colossal mistake. He knew it now, had known it for quite some time. Just as he knew he had no one to blame for it but himself. He had begged Lily to marry him—and she had. She was his wife, his responsibility, and he would try to behave toward her as well as he could. And if this included sleeping on a chair, well, he would do that also. You didn't have to love your wife to do your duty by her. Marriage, like genius, was a long patience.

October wore on. Lily improved. As she regained her health, her disposition improved also. She complained less, thanked him for his nursing, even regretted her past fits of ill humor.

"You'll see, I'll make it up to you when I get well."

He did not care whether she did or not, but said that everything was fine and she had nothing to regret. He continued to be attentive and spent much time at her bedside.

One afternoon, as he was reading her the newspaper, the bell rang.

He went to open the door and saw Gaby, smiling, holding a box of pastries in her hand.

Her smile faded at once.

"What's the matter, darling?" she asked in a frightened whisper. "You look awful. Are you sick?"

No, not sick. Just a little tired . . .

"It's Lily who's been sick," he said, pulling her inside.

"I didn't know. Perhaps I'd better come another day."

"On the contrary. She always complains nobody comes to see her. She will love to visit with you. Wait here a minute. I'll go and ask her."

He walked to the bedroom, returned an instant later.

"She says it's all right for you to come in, if you just forgive her appearance."

The two women kissed and exchanged compliments with a little too much effusiveness, both talking at once about the joy they felt at seeing each other. Lily said that Gaby looked simply gorgeous, and Gaby declared that Lily looked fine. Nobody in the world would know she had been sick . . .

The amenities over, Gaby sat down on Claude's chair and began removing her gloves.

"I suddenly remembered it was your first wedding anniversary and I thought it'd be nice to have a little visit before I go away."

Go away? Where? . . . To Cuba! Where was that?

"Tell you the truth, I don't know." Gaby chuckled. "But Victor has to go there on business and he says Havana is wonderful in winter. So I thought I might as well go along. You never know. He might find some young little thing that will make sheep eyes at him and tell him he's the greatest playwright in the world and he might believe it."

Her chuckle swelled into her rich, throaty laughter.

"I know he would, because he did when I said it to him."

Still talking she turned to Claude and handed him the box of pastries.

"How about you making us a cup of tea, while Lily and me have a little visit?"

He went out, leaving the door ajar. From the kitchen he could hear the sound of their voices. How lovely Gaby looked, he thought. How radiantly healthy! She was thirty-four and each year she seemed to grow more beautiful . . . How sweet of her to remember their wedding anniversary and drop in like this. Now she was going away, and somehow Paris would be more lonely without her. Not that he ever saw her, but it was nice to know she was about, read her name in the *mondanités* now and then. It seemed that her receptions were much sought after. Diplomats, senators, even cabinet members attended them. Imagine Gaby giving formal receptions! Gaby, who had danced all night in the street on that Bastille Day! How long ago it seemed!*

They had tea in the bedroom. The conversation flitted from one topic to another while they munched chocolate éclairs and took sips from their cups. Lily seemed more alert and cheerful. With eyes shining with envy she said how much she, too, would like to go on a long sea voyage on a luxurious steamship. She laughed repeatedly, her nervous high-pitched laugh Claude had come to dread.

At last Gaby rose, pretending last-minute purchases. Again she kissed Lily, promised to come back as soon as she returned from Cuba.

Claude escorted her to the door in silence.

As they stepped out onto the landing she stopped and turned around. "My poor darling, you don't look very happy. Please, don't get sick . . . for my sake."

Their gazes clung for a few seconds, but they had too much to say and no time to say it.

* A frequent guest at the functions Gaby gave in her sumptuous apartment on avenue Niel was Aristide Briand, several times Premier of France.

Swiftly she brushed his lips with her own, and ran down the stairs. This time he did not stand at the railing to wave at her. With a sigh, he turned back into the apartment.

"It was nice of her to come, wasn't it?" Lily said as he entered the bedroom. "And look what she gave me."

From the nightstand drawer she pulled two one-hundred-franc notes.

"I told her I didn't want it, but she said it was only a loan, because when you're sick you have a lot of expenses, and she was sorry she didn't know I was ill and that's all she had in her purse."

For an instant she held the banknotes in her hands, looking at them with a thin, bitter smile.

"Imagine having *only* two hundred francs in her purse! . . . And to think that a few years ago she was just another whore walking the streets."

He felt the blood rush to his head and clenched his fists. Without a word he went out of the room. Oh, Gaby, darling Gaby . . .

♦

In the first week of November, Claude received a letter from Monsieur Chevillard, conductor of the Concerts Lamoureux, stating that before his untimely death Monsieur Hartmann had mentioned a new symphonic suite entitled *Nocturnes,* for which he had expressed the greatest enthusiasm.

At this point Claude permitted himself a small, reminiscent smile —the first one in a long time. Good Monsieur Hartmann! How like him to go about boasting about a work of which he hadn't heard a single note! There was faith for you . . .

He returned to the letter, which ended with an urgent request to bring the score to the conductor's office in view of a possible performance.

"Here it is," he said the following day, placing the manuscript on the conductor's desk. "It's a suite in three parts, but unfortunately the last one isn't finished."

In silence Monsieur Chevillard reached out to take the score and began reading it.

"It's a magnificent work," he said simply when he finished. "The two first pieces form by themselves a well-balanced ensemble and can be presented independently from the third."

He turned to a desk calendar and rapidly riffled through a number of pages.

"We can have the parts copied in ten days," he went on, as if thinking aloud. "Then we'll need another three weeks to learn and rehearse these two pieces. I think we could present the work at our regular concert on December ninth. Is this convenient for you?"

Claude found Lily sitting up in bed, her hair in paper curlers, reading the newspaper. He told her about his encounter with Monsieur Chevillard. She listened with patient indifference. Concerts didn't bring in any money . . .

"It's your opera you should work on," she said.

Her remark infuriated him.

"Thanks for your advice. But the orchestration of *Pélléas* will take several weeks—and the pharmacist won't wait."

At once he regretted his allusion to her costly illness and was about to apologize. But she had returned to her newspaper, and he saw that she had not even heard what he said. With a shrug he went to his study and resumed work on a publisher's transcription.

Around the middle of the month he received a visit from an elderly square-shouldered man dressed in a cutaway, with an enormous rosette of the Legion of Honor in his lapel, top hat and white spats, who introduced himself as General Bourgeat. His manner was brisk, his tone of voice imperious. Even his short-trimmed mustache had an aggressive prickliness about it.

"I am Monsieur Hartmann's heir and executor," he added, "and I should like to see you on a matter of business."

With a premonition of disaster Claude preceded him into the parlor and waved him to a chair. He sat down opposite him, conscious of his unmilitary slippers and the visitor's squinting disapproval of them. The incongruous thought flashed through his mind that the general probably breakfasted in boots and spurs.

"While putting in order the deceased's affairs," the officer went on, "I came across a number of receipts signed by you, spreading over a period of years, which amount to several thousand francs. I wish to know what you intend to do about these loans."

"They weren't loans, but advances on royalties. Monsieur Hartmann felt that some day he would be amply repaid."

"True. He seemed to have great faith in your music, especially your opera. But this was merely his opinion and I am not in a position to judge whether it was justified or not. Anyway, I am not in the music publishing business. I am a soldier, Monsieur—and I want my money."

This was real military straightforwardness . . . Nothing hesitant or ambiguous about General Bourgeat.

"If you just wait, you'll get your money back," Claude said. "Monsieur Hartmann was willing to, why shouldn't you?"

Obviously the general was not used to being questioned. His nostrils flared and his mustache seemed to bristle still more aggressively.

"I haven't come here to engage in a debate, Monsieur. I want to know when you intend to repay these loans."

"I already told you they were advances. Besides, you can see I haven't any money, can't you? But look around." He took in the room with a tired gesture. "I have some nice books, a few Japanese prints. You're welcome to them."

The general's face had turned brick-red. "Are you sporting with me by any chance?" He barked the words as if taking to task a delinquent sergeant.

"I'm just trying to show you I haven't any money."

"Well, go and find some!"

"Look. My wife is ill, I haven't had much sleep lately, I can barely buy medicines, please—"

"This is your affair, Monsieur. Not mine."

Claude blinked at him. Suddenly he had had enough of this yapping, brainless martinet. His spats and his mustache.

"Oh, go to hell, will you?"

He spoke the words softly, almost like a pleading request, in a muted explosion of weariness.

The general sprang to his feet.

"You'll hear from me! I'll make you pay for your insolence."

"Good. Do whatever you want, but for God's sake, get out."

From his chair he watched the general stomp out of the room. A few seconds later the slamming of the entrance door filled the apartment like the report of a pistol shot. Then silence returned like a soothing presence, but not for long.

Lily's voice wafted out of the bedroom.

"Claude!"

With a groan of fatigue he got up.

"What is it, darling?" he asked from the doorway.

"Please light the lamp. It's getting dark." Then, without transition, "I heard your conversation. How much do you owe this man?"

He struck a match, lit the bedstand lamp before replying.

"I don't owe him anything." While talking he adjusted the wick. "They were advances. If only he would wait, he'd get his money back."

"What is he going to do?"

"I don't know. Perhaps get a judgment against me."

"Hire a good lawyer and fight back."

"Lawyers cost money, darling . . . Anyway, even an idiot like him must realize that I haven't any money and no judgment will do him any good. My guess is that he'll wait till *Pélléas* is produced, and then pounce on me."

"You never told me you owed that much money."

"Please, let's not go into that again. I told you they were advances."

"Just the same you should've told me."

He looked at her, as though he had never seen her before. Had he really believed once that she would be a comfort in the days of trial and disappointment? . . .

"I didn't think of it, but you're right. I should have told you. Well, now you know . . . It's what makes marriage interesting. It's so full of surprises! . . . But in time you get to know all there is to know about each other and then there are no more surprises."

"What're you trying to say?" she asked, eying him suspiciously.

"Nothing. Now, if you don't mind, I think I'll go out for a while. A little fresh air will do me good."

On December ninth, as scheduled, the first two *Nocturnes* were presented at the Concerts Lamoureux. The performance was received with such an overwhelming ovation and deafening applause that Monsieur Chevillard, standing on the podium, baton in hand, could not believe his ears. His faithful but sedate audience was not given to noisy demonstrations. All he had hoped for was a polite success, and here he was with a triumph on his hands. Breaking all precedents, the performance was repeated and greeted with even wilder enthusiasm.

Claude, of course, was dumfounded by his sudden emergence into fame. Even the success of the *Faun*, a few years ago, could not compare with the present acclaim. For once, critics were unanimous in their praises. "The very exceptional, very strange, very solitary Monsieur Debussy," as one reviewer called him, was without a doubt the most original composer of his time.

The results of this outburst of eulogies soon manifested themselves. New pupils began to appear on rue Cardinet, eager to study piano or composition with such an outstanding musician. Soon Claude had all the students he could possibly teach. Money started coming in in a steady, impressive stream. He paid his debts in the district, settled the arrears on his rent. On top of all this, General Bourgeat did not follow up his threats and gave no sign of life. And Lily got well.

By the end of the year he dared to hope again.

The enthusiasm for the *Nocturnes* lingered through the winter. Brief but insistent notices appeared in newspapers demanding the production of *Pélléas*. The public was hungry for new music. How long would Monsieur Carré, the distinguished director of the Opéra Comique, delay the production of the opera on which "the very exceptional, very strange, very solitary Monsieur Debussy" was said to have toiled ten years?

In the spring, Monsieur Messager, conductor of the Opéra Comique, came to see Claude.

"Everybody is talking about your *Nocturnes*," he said. "As you know, nothing succeeds like success, and our good director is once again in a receptive mood about *Pélléas*."

"But I still haven't written the orchestration."

"Never mind. Until now I was the only one to tell him that your opera is a masterpiece, but now apparently everyone seems to agree that you are a splendid musician. Those little newspaper darts about your opera have been most helpful, and I've seen to it that they get on Monsieur Carré's desk. Now he is all excited about your opera. He wants to know why the devil you didn't show up in October, as you were supposed to. In short, he is ready to talk business. Come tomorrow to my house and play your score for him."

Claude did, and this time the official wasted no time on generalities.

"I'm going to present your opera next season," he declared. "It's a very strange work and we may end up with a dreadful fiasco, but I'm going to take a chance and present it. You have my word."

Then, as an afterthought, "Better still, I'll write you a letter about it."

Two days later, Claude received the written confirmation that *Pélléas* would be produced during the coming season.

This time there was no doubt. His dream was coming true . . .

As he held the letter in his hand, his heart swelled in his chest and tears of joy came to his eyes.

◆

Almost one year to the day after receiving this letter, at one-twenty in the afternoon of Saturday, April 28, 1902, Claude was standing by one of the two French windows in Monsieur Carré's office, his left hand parting the tulle drapes just wide enough for him to peer down at the restless crowd that filled the square in front of the Opéra Comique.*

It had come . . . In exactly ten minutes the curtain would rise on *Pélléas*. And the battle would be on, for there was going to be a battle. No doubt about that. For weeks discussions had been raging over his work, although no one but the theatre personnel had heard a note of it. For some unexplainable reason, *Pélléas* was no longer an opera to be judged on its artistic merits alone. It had become an issue. Moral, social, political, religious and God knew what else! Apparently it was the forerunner of Modernism, which was to engulf all traditions, sweep away all that was good and decent. As such it must be hissed off the stage. This afternoon's performance must not be allowed to proceed. At all costs the curtain must be brought down.

* This performance was the opera's *avant-première,* or public dress rehearsal. The première took place on the following Monday evening, April 30.

Yes, it had come . . . And of all days, it had to come today! On the eve of a general election, when people, nearly hysterical after weeks of political harangues, were seeking an outlet for their nervous tension, and their minds were on anything but music . . .

He looked aside at Lily, who was sitting in a corner, studying her reflection in a pocket mirror.

"We certainly picked the right day to present my poor *Pélléas*," he said with a dubious smile.

Before she could reply, Monsieur Carré burst in like a charging bull.

"We're prepared," he growled, while crossing to his desk. "If they want a fight, we'll give it to them. I've asked the Prefect of Police for another platoon."

He sat down at his desk and impatiently rustled some papers.

"I hear they're going to try to stop the performance," he went on with a defiant snort. "Well, let them try. I've given orders to the cast and musicians to go on whatever happens. Let them hiss all they want, our friends will only applaud the louder. I am not exactly an amateur at this game, you know. I have a few tricks up my sleeve."

A complacent grin crossed his pugnacious face. "Do you know what I did? I opened the galleries to the students. There must be a thousand of them. And with their girls, too. Not only from the Conservatoire, but also from the Sorbonne. The whole Latin Quarter is here. The young are with us, and let me tell you, they can outclap and outshout anybody."

"They certainly can." Claude smiled. "Once I was thrown out of the Opéra for doing just that. I wish I could sit with them."

"Some other day perhaps, but not this afternoon!"

With a hearty laugh the director leaped to his feet, grabbed a sheaf of papers and fled out of the room, his coat tails flapping after him.

Claude pulled out his watch.

"Five minutes," he said half aloud.

"Isn't it exciting?" Lily said, glancing at him.

Her eyes shone with anticipation. This was the moment she had dreamed about. Today Rosalie Texier was the queen of Paris. For the past few weeks she had lived in a whirlwind of excitement, talking to reporters, attending rehearsals, giving her hand to kiss. At last she was the wife of a celebrity. And this made her a bit of a celebrity, too, didn't it? To her this afternoon was more than the *avant-première* of Claude's opera; it was her social debut.

Yesterday she had spent hours at the hairdresser's, returning with a bright yellow pompadour that set upon her head like a golden turban. All morning she had labored on her face, before putting on her dress, the famous Mélisande dress, as she called it, which she had created for the occasion with the help of a seamstress. As a last inspiration she had crossed on the bodice two long-stemmed arums, which framed her face up to her cheekbones.*

"Don't you think we should go in?"

"Not yet," he said. "We still have two or three minutes. I don't want people to stare at us."

"I don't mind. Let them stare."

He made no reply and watched the crowd streaming into the theatre.

The door opened. André Messager came in, his face ashen from grief and fatigue. He had just arrived from his brother's deathbed, but had insisted on conducting. He walked up to Claude, placed a hand on his shoulder.

"The orchestra and the cast are with you," he said quietly. "We'll do our best. Some day we shall remember this afternoon as the proudest of our lives."

He turned around, bowed to Lily and went out.

"Let's go," Lily snapped, getting up to her feet. "I want to look around before they turn off the lights."

He looked at her, cringing inwardly at the sight of her greenish dress, her brassy hair and heavy make-up. She, who was naturally pretty, had managed to make herself ugly as well as ludicrous.

"I wish you wouldn't wear those flowers," he said. "Please take them off. I'm embarrassed to be seen with you rigged up like this."

"You don't have to look at me, if you don't want to."

"Don't you see they make you look ridiculous?"

"I don't tell you how to write your music. Leave the fashions to me."

"All right. Let's go."

The moment they entered their box all eyes turned on them. From the galleries came a spatter of applause that spread throughout the house. For an instant he stood up against the red plush ledge, smiling, half bowing, giving a small wave to the students in a sign of gratitude. His eyes swept over the audience. With a start of joy he recognized Gaby in a box across the room, clapping her gloved hands, nudging her gentleman friend to do the same. He had had a box reserved for her, but had not expected her to come. But she had. Gaby, darling Gaby! He caught a glimpse of Pierre Louÿs in another box, laughing, surrounded by friends. His gaze brushed over Missia Natanson sitting between Léon Blum and Georges Clemenceau. Other faces. Some friendly; others hostile. Critics, colleagues, gray-bearded Conservatoire professors.

* Lily's lilies and her "energetic" make-up caused a good deal of amused comment at the time.

Then he noticed that Lily was standing at his side, acknowledging the applause with smiles and repeated nods. Quickly he stepped back into the dimness of the box; as she sat down in front of him and began methodically unbuttoning her white gloves.

Messager appeared on the podium and bowed. Then he turned around, rapped his baton as the lights dimmed. Amidst breathless silence, the first chord rose from the double-bass and cello section.

Pélléas was coming to life.

He scarcely listened. He didn't need to. Since the garret days he had heard this music in his head. But now, for the first time, other people were hearing it, too. It no longer belonged to him alone. To the audience this performance was an introduction; to him it was a farewell. Farewell to countless nights spent over the score, countless changes, countless hours of torment and brief moments of ecstasy. Farewell also—and this was a blessing!—to the tumult of the last few months with its sequel of grotesque episodes in which he had found himself unwillingly involved. The sudden, vociferous enmity of Maeterlinck, who wanted the part of Mélisande sung by his mistress, for now the calm recluse from Ghent had moved to Paris and acquired a mistress who happened to be an opera singer . . . Messager's equally emphatic insistence that it should be sung by his . . . Carré's thunderous pronouncements and secret covetousness of the leading lady . . . threats and counterthreats of duels . . . the raging polemics in newspapers . . .

Thank God, that was over. Together with the back-breaking strain of writing the orchestration at full speed; the in-and-out rush of the theatre's errand boys snatching pages as soon as they were written; the correction of the copyist's innumerable mistakes; the aggravation of rehearsals; the discussions with set designers, costumes, electricians . . .

Yes, it took a great deal of work and from a great many people to get an opera ready. And *Pélléas* had taken more than the average. But finally it, too, had gotten ready.

And now it was being played and all was going well. Both the cast and the orchestra were doing their best, as Messager had said they would. Already the first act was halfway through and there had been no disturbance. Not a single hiss, hardly a cough.

Then, all of a sudden, bedlam exploded.

At once the hall was crackling with catcalls, yelps, whistles mingled with applause, shouts of approval, requests for silence. In the galleries students sprang to action, clapped their hands, pounded their feet, leaned over the railings to yell colorful invectives. Orchestra spectators quarreled across the aisles. Ladies hit their opponents with their fans and had their hats pushed down over their faces. A goateed baldheaded gentleman rose from his seat, shook his fist up at the students and shrieked, "You've been paid to applaud." A clay pipe whizzed down from the third balcony and hit him squarely on the nose. He had to be taken away, bleeding, screaming, held under the armpits by two gendarmes.

On the podium Messager remained impassive, waved his baton. The performance went on.

Time and time again, that afternoon, it seemed that the curtain would have to be brought down after all. Neither orchestra nor singers could be heard. When Mary Garden, who sang Mélisande, managed to be heard at all, her Scottish accent distorted some French words and elicited outbursts of hilarity. When laughter died, hisses started again. And so did the applause.

Through it all, Messager went on waving his baton and the performance proceeded without a pause. By the middle of the third act the opposition slackened. Since *Pelléas* could not be stopped, it might as well be heard. People began to listen. The last act took place amidst absolute silence. As the final notes were played and the curtain fell, a shudder ran through the audience. Then, in a surge of enthusiasm, they rose and applause filled the theatre as the curtain rose again and again and again.

Claude got up, took his hat from the wall rack.

"Let's sneak out of the theatre by the back door."

"Wait a moment," Lily said, still clapping. "This is the most exciting part of the whole show."

He felt she was taut with pride, as though *Pelléas'* triumph was in some way her own, and she wanted to stand on like this in full view in the hope that perhaps people would turn again toward their box and she might have to bow once more.

"Please come on." Impatiently he held the door half open. "Hurry up, so we can still get away before we get mobbed."

"Just one minute," she flung over her shoulder.

He pushed the door open. His nerves were aquiver from the ordeal of the performance. He was in no mood to be patient.

"Stay if you like, but I'm going."

He took a step into the vestibule, but it was too late. From right and left people were converging on him.

The first to reach him was a panting tousled-haired student.

"Master, you've won!"

It was the first time anyone had called him master and it gave him a little thrill.

"Did you like it?"

"Oh, yes! And your parallel fifths are wonderful."

He smiled at the youngster. Probably some composition student . . .

With his flashing eyes and floppy tie he might have been himself twenty years ago . . .

"Are you preparing for the Grand Prix?" he asked.

The boy nodded, and Claude went on, "Then stay away from them. The jury doesn't like them and they'll get you in trouble. Wait till you are in Rome . . ."

My God, he was talking like Monsieur Guiraud . . .

"Yes, Master."

Already the crowd was closing in on him, sweeping him back into the box, all talking at once, groping for his hand, brandishing programs for him to sign. "Please, Master, won't you autograph? . . . Please, Master, could you possibly give me an interview? . . . Master! . . . Master! . . ."

Fame had come.

♦

After years of obscurity he found himself in the limelight. Everywhere he felt the impact of his new celebrity. In the streets strangers raised their hats to him. If he stopped at the Café Weber he became the center of a group. Marcel Proust, with pleading in his slumberous odalisk eyes, asked him to let him give a reception in his honor with all kinds of titled ladies to pay him tribute. Unknown female admirers sent him little notes written in green ink on green paper, which he tore up and tossed into his wastebasket. As final evidence that he had arrived, caricatures of him began appearing in newspapers and magazines.

To his dismay he learned he had become the head of a musical movement called Debussysm. Young musicians aped his style and wrote music "à la Debussy" full of parallel fifths, unresolved sevenths and full-tone arpeggios. His self-appointed disciples called themselves Debussysts and proclaimed him as their leader. He appreciated their fervor, but found it irksome. Repeatedly he declared that he had no disciples and wanted none; this produced no effect whatever. Then, as they always do, the snobs came in. It became chic and avant-garde to love his music. Dreamy young men listened to *Pélléas* with eyes closed, brow in hand; soulful young women did the same. They sighed, they whispered, they fainted. Ladies drank vinegar to reduce and acquire the "Mélisande look." It was once again the Wagnerian neurosis of ten years ago. But now the Meister was French and his Festspielhaus was the Opéra Comique.

Claude's music was still highly controversial; and this, of course, made it all the more attractive as a topic of discussion. Defenders and detractors refuted one another for hours over their *apéritifs*. Newspaper editors added to the tumult by calling him a genius, but a pernicious genius whose music was revolutionary in its spirit and immoral in its effect. Mothers wondered whether their daughters could play *Clair de Lune* and still retain their innocence. Fuel was added to the controversy when it became known that the director of the Conservatoire had forbidden students to attend *Pélléas'* performances, and one of them was expelled for disobeying this rule.

Now, even at home, Claude had little privacy. Whether he liked it or not, he had become news. Even more than his music, his personality aroused the public's curiosity. His reputation as a ladies' man, Gaby's attempted suicide over him, his broken engagement to Thérèse Roger, his bohemian past, even his picturesque—now discarded—sombrero, had formed around him a volume of gossip which circulated with renewed vigor since the triumph of his opera. Newspaper stories about him found an eager public, and editors did their best to provide them. Reporters trekked to rue Cardinet, climbed the five flights of stairs to his apartment, paused to catch their breath and rang the bell.

"Is the Master in?" they would ask politely. "My newspaper—"

Lily greeted them with a bright, inviting smile. "Certainly. Please come in."

At first he had felt some little prick of excitement at being interviewed; but he soon had grown tired of reporters. They took his time, wearied him with their identical questions, sometimes annoyed him with their prying curiosity. Yet he still received them, for most of them were young struggling writers with unperformed plays or unpublished books in their drawers to whom he represented a chance to earn some money. An article about him meant a few meals to them, an installment on their rent. Such things were too familiar and still too recent for him to have forgotten about them. He was their transcriptions.

Excitedly Lily would peer into his study. "There's a reporter outside."

He would rest his pen against the inkwell and, with a sigh, "All right. Send him in."

After the usual amenities, the interview would begin.

"Master, how do you feel about the growing success of your opera?"

"Pleased, of course, and a little surprised. Again I wish to thank the persons who—" Here a few flowery compliments for practically everybody.

"You are aware, no doubt, that some critics have been severe in their reviews. How do you feel about them?"

"I try to bear up under their censure. Fortunately I have a gift of indifference and find it most useful. They have a right to their opinion and will continue to write what they want, and I shall continue to write what I want. In this way we'll all be happy."

"A columnist wrote that your music appeals only to perverts and depraved persons. Would you care to comment?"

"Just enough to say that there are people whose disapproval is a source of pride."

"What are your musical plans?"

"I'd like to write two more operas. One based on Shakespeare's *As You Like It,* the other on Edgar Allan Poe's story "The Devil in the Belfry." Also a symphony entitled *La Mer.* As I am a very slow worker, this should keep me busy for the next thirty years. At the moment I'm completing three piano preludes called *Estampes.*"

"Who are your favorite composers?"

"Bach—and Offenbach."

Then came the trivia that readers were supposedly dying to know. What was his favorite color? Green . . . Was he superstitious? Yes. Very much so and with good reasons.

"I see ill omens in everything and they usually come true."

Would automobiles replace horses as a means of locomotion? What did he think about women? They were charming creatures, and not only charming but indispensable . . . Did he prefer blondes or brunettes? These days most of them were both . . .

At this point the reporter usually would clear his throat and hesitantly begin, "Is it true, Master, that a few years ago a beautiful young lady tried to commit—"

Claude would rise hurriedly, pretend an urgent appointment, hold out his hand across the desk with a wide smile.

"Well, I guess you have about all you need for your article. Now, if you'll kindly excuse me—"

The young man had no choice but to rise, shake the extended hand. "Yes, Master, I guess I have. I'll send you my article when it comes out."

"Please do so. I'll read it with great interest."

From his desk he could hear Lily talking to the reporter as she escorted him to the door.

"I bet he didn't tell you how many times he was discouraged and thought he'd never get his opera produced. But I always had faith in his genius! Also, if you want, you can mention he still rolls his own cigarettes. A habit from the days when he was poor. For, believe me, we sure had some pretty hard times . . . Now don't forget to send me your article . . . Well, good-bye."

He had asked her to dispense with her remarks about his harrowing poverty.

"Everyone knows we've been poor, but this is no reason for harping on it forever. It is no crime to be poor, but neither is it any special achievement."

She had resented his remarks. She had created for herself the part of the artist's brave little wife who stands by her husband through thick and thin, and she had come to believe what she said.

During May and June, *Pelléas* was presented fourteen times. Box-office receipts increased steadily. Several performances were sold out.

"And next season we'll do even better," said Monsieur Carré, a few days before the annual closing of the theatre. "Try to have a good rest this summer, you look as though you could use it. But remember that in October I'm putting your opera back on the boards and plan to give it many times through the season. You'll be a rich man yet."

On July fifth the Opéra Comique closed for the summer. That same day General Bourgeat struck. Claude was awakened by a process server. Monsieur Hartmann's heir and executor had been a shrewd strategist. He had waited until all the season's royalties were in. Now he wanted his money. All of it and at once.

Claude discussed the matter with Lily.

"Get a good lawyer," she advised. "He'll drag this thing out for so long the general will be glad to settle."

She was right. Again he marveled at her combativeness. This was Lily with her claws out, Lily who could best fishwives in haggling contests . . . But a suit would mean long sessions with a lawyer, legal fees, his appearances in court. He had no stomach for a hard drawn-out fight. Besides, he did owe the money. It had kept him alive for years. He had told the general they were advances on royalties. Well, now there were royalties, and he no longer had any excuse. Better pay him off and have peace.

His royalties from *Pelléas* went to the general. As they were not enough, he turned for help to his old friend Jacques Durand, now an executive in his father's publishing firm.

For once he was lucky. Jacques Durand bought every manuscript still owned by Claude and paid generously for them.

"I only wish there were more of them," said the young publisher. "Now what about *Pelléas?* Are you willing to sell it?"

"No, not that. You've been more than generous, but it's all I have left. I plan to have it printed by subscription and publish it myself."

"I admit it's a tempting venture," said Jacques with a knowing smile. "Some composers have had the same idea, but none to my knowledge has ever published his own music successfully. However, I wish you good luck."

As Claude was about to leave, he added, "Should you ever change your mind, please let me know. Also remember we'll be happy and proud to be your exclusive publishers in the future."

And so the general was paid off and Claude got peace.

"Now we're poor again," said Lily ungraciously.

Yes, but only for a few months. In October new royalties would pile up. From lessons alone he could depend on a substantial income. And, of course, as soon as he had written *La Mer* he would start working on his new opera. Never had the future looked so promising.

July had just arrived when he received a letter from André Messager, who was conducting at Covent Garden, asking him to come to London and spend a week or two with him. "And I promise, you won't have to listen to a single note of music . . ."

"You go and enjoy yourself," Lily said, "but don't ask me to come with you. I'm no sailor girl. The idea of crossing the Channel doesn't appeal to me."

Claude went to London and instantly fell in love with it. Instead of the necropolis he had heard about, he found a bustling city in the throes of preparations for the coronation of the new King, a young man of sixty-one who embodied in his plump and jolly person the spirit of merry England. The gloom of the Victorian Age was dissolving in the sunshine of the Edwardian Era. The Queen—God bless her!—had died the year before. The nation had shed torrents of tears and breathed a sigh of relief. Soldiers who had fought in South Africa remembered with gratitude the boxes of chocolates she sent them at Christmas, but they were still more grateful that at last the war was over.

At the Cecil Hotel Claude saw little of Messager and Mary Garden, who were busy with their work and with each other. He did not mind. All day he roamed through the town, gaping at everything, peering into the strange shop windows, loving everything: the funny-shaped hansoms with the drivers bouncing at the rear; the bobbies in their ovoid helmets; the red double-decked buses. Like all good tourists he watched the Changing of the Guard and stared at the unblinking, monolithic sentries at the gates of Buckingham Palace. He gave pennies to sidewalk artists, saw the Thames turn gold at sunset and even ventured into a pub, where, in his best English, he ordered "oan bir, pleez."

The tenseness, the fatigue from months and months of strain and secret distress began rolling off him. His nerves relaxed, his brain seemed to cool off. At night he slept like a child. It was good to be free, have no rehearsals to attend, no music to write, no appointments to keep. To be alone for a change. Rapturously alone. Away from Paris, from home, from Lily . . .

"I've been here only three days and already I feel ten years younger," he told Messager, in one of their rare moments together. "By the end of the week, I'll positively feel like an infant."

The following morning the hotel clerk handed him a telegram. He must return to Paris at once. Lily was ill.

At the Clinique Dubois the doctor gave him a doleful smile.

"I'm afraid I must again give you bad news about your wife," he began. "New stones have formed in the kidneys and I simply don't dare operate. There is really very little we can do."

He was a soft-spoken man with compassionate, heavy-lidded eyes, which he held on Claude in a sort of silent apology for his helplessness.

"Take her to the country as soon as she can travel. At least the country air will do some good to her lungs."

Silence fell between them. Claude nodded repeatedly and absently, in resigned acquiescence. He had long ceased to revolt against misfortune. With a little practice you got used to being unhappy all the time, like those people who lived in constant pain day after day, year after year.

"Doctor," he asked at last, "will you tell me if my wife can have a child?"

Slowly, in a flat tone of voice, the physician replied, "She can't."

◆

At Bichain, Claude and his father-in-law relieved each other at Lily's bedside. The two men became friends in a shy, inarticulate sort of way. Sometimes, when she fell asleep, they went down to the kitchen, sat down at the rustic table and sipped a glass of wine in forlorn but congenial silence.

Toward the middle of August she began to improve.*

Her convalescence was rapid. On his fortieth birthday she was strong enough to come down to the kitchen and join them for dinner. Afterward they played cards. At nine o'clock he helped her back to her room. In a few minutes she was sleeping soundly, her face turned to the wall.

He tiptoed out and went to sit in the garden on the sagging wicker chair. The night was immense and calm; the sky cobalt-blue, teeming with stars. In sharp, three-dimensional clarity, scenes from the last few years of his life followed one another on the screen of his mind, like vignettes in a magic lantern show. Gaby saying good-bye on the

---

* In a letter from Bichain dated August, 1902, Debussy wrote, "It seems that my poor Lily has new stones in her kidneys. She has been in constant pain, but is now slightly better . . . Will this ever end? . . . Will she ever get well? . . ."

His London trip had lasted only four days, from Sunday, July 13, to Wednesday, July 17.

landing, smiling and weeping at the same time . . . Lily's Sunday
visits . . . their wedding . . . her first illness and his visits at the
clinic . . . *Pélléas'* first performance in a bedlam of hisses and applause . . . his recent trip to London . . . the doctor's announcement
that Lily could never have a child . . .

Here, in mid-chapter, the past became the present. He was back
in the garden with the night around him, surprised and a little sad
at being forty years old. No more vignettes came to his mind, but a
fog of confused thoughts. A jumble of feelings, regrets, apprehensions
that formed no picture, only an ominous blankness that was the future.

In October they returned to Paris, with Lily feeling and looking
better than she had in months. Again he was caught in a whirl of
rehearsals, lessons, interviews, business propositions and social engagements. *Pélléas* was back on the boards; many of his compositions
were included in concerts. In December *The Blessed Damozel* was
performed by the Colonne Orchestra, with overwhelming success.

The year 1902 ended for him in a drizzle of gold coins and a
thunder of applause.

In January he was decorated with the Legion of Honor. Hundreds
of messages arrived at rue Cardinet. Lily, delirious with pride, went
about the district telling every merchant about it. Even his father,
who had given no sign of life since the wedding, wrote to say he was
proud of him.

The following Sunday, Claude went to see his parents. They
guessed his marital disenchantment, but refrained from talking about
it, and he appreciated their reserve. The visit, which had begun in
an atmosphere of mutual awkwardness, grew more cordial and
ended in a semblance of conviviality. Before leaving he slipped a
one-hundred-franc note into his mother's hand, and went away happy.
Strangely, he felt closer to them than ever before.

A few days later he was offered the post of music critic on one
of the daily newspapers. His new functions required him to attend
many concerts and created another time-consuming chore in his
already crowded life. It did, however, give him an opportunity to
air his views about music and musicians. And, still more important,
another outlet for his growing restlessness.

He had long known that his marriage had been a mistake; the
knowledge that Lily could not have a child changed it into a meaningless, hopeless blunder that took the joy out of his success. He felt
trapped, and it made no difference that the trap was of his own
making. Beneath his apparent calm, his restlessness was rising, becoming more difficult to conceal. An evening at home turned into
an ordeal of twitching nerves and an exercise in self-control. He
now winced at the sound of her grating voice and shrill laughter.

Even work was made irksome by the strains of her everlasting grenadier song seeping through the door of his study. He kept telling himself she was his wife for better or for worse, with or without her rasping voice, but it brought him little comfort.

If they went out and attended some social function, her gaudy dresses, her tactless remarks sent flushes of embarrassment to his cheeks. She talked a great deal, not only because she was naturally voluble, but also because she was thrilled at finding herself in high society as the wife of a famous artist. Some obscure compulsion prompted her to want to share the limelight, claim for herself a part of his fame. Coyly she would hint that *Pélléas* was in some small measure her own creation. How well she remembered the hungry days of yore, the years of privation she had endured while watching over the birth of the masterpiece! She recalled pathetic episodes. "Remember, darling," she would fling gaily across the table, "the day the landlord came up for the rent and I told him you were out of town?" He wanted to shout back that his opera was written when he had married her and she had been too ill most of the time to see much of the landlord. Instead he nodded, tried to change the subject.*

Solitude, which had loomed so frightening that the fear of it had driven him into marriage, now seemed the most desirable blessing. He made a few ineffectual attempts toward it. One day he announced he could at last afford to send her to a sanitorium.

"Yes, darling." He smiled with a great show of relief. "Finally I can do what the doctor recommended. A few months in the mountains and you'll be in perfect health."

She laughed, said she was in perfect health now and was having much too good a time to leave Paris at the moment. Besides, he needed her. She was a good wife. She had promised to take care of him, cook and keep house for him, and she wasn't going to shirk her duty. He insisted that her first duty was to herself. He now could afford to eat in good restaurants and hire a part-time maid for the light housekeeping he required.

"I want you to take care of your health," he said as firmly as he could. "The doctor said—"

Point-blank she refused to go, and the discussion ended.

He did not reopen the subject. Instead he spent less and less time at home. Gradually he lost all ambition to compose. He spent time at his desk only to write his weekly musical review. A sense of futility and hopelessness descended upon him. Now that his marriage

---

* In his book of reminiscences, Monsieur Henri Busser, the eminent composer and conductor, recalls Lily's telling him (about *Pélléas*), "It is also my work, for I certainly encouraged Claude when he was despairing of ever seeing his score come to life!"

had become meaningless, his life became purposeless. Although very busy, he managed to waste a vast amount of time. He broke business appointments to go strolling along the quays or in the Bois de Boulogne. As an excuse for not answering important letters he simply stated that there was no more ink in his inkwell. Between lessons he browsed in bookshops and bought enough books to last him a lifetime. Now that he had money in his pocket, he gave free rein to his extravagant tastes and developed a fatal passion for fine bindings and first editions.

With the coming of spring his attention turned to sport, specifically horse racing. He became a sportsman, a turf enthusiast. Now he pored over racing sheets, lost himself in computations, calculations and statistics. Soon he regarded himself as an expert, a judge of horse flesh. He gambled. Worse, he urged his advice on his friends.*

As usual they spent the summer at Bichain. Lily was not ill that year. In the country her naturalness returned. Even her voice sounded less grating, her conversation less inept. Without make-up, with her chestnut hair casually pinned up on the top of her head she looked better than in Paris. At times, as he watched her going about the garden in an old straw hat and wooden shoes, tossing grain to chickens, he forgot his grievances. He even came to hope that perhaps if they spent most of the year in the country they might achieve some sort of companionship. Secretly he tried to buy a piece of land on which a house could be built, but the owner changed his mind and his price every day and finally Claude gave up.

They returned to Paris at the end of September. The moment he was back his restlessness flared up again. In a week she had shed her naturalness, her rustic charm. Her hair was brass-blond once more. Again she reminisced in public over her years of hardships. Each day he was startled anew by the mediocrity of her mind, her innate vulgarity, her flair for the cheap and the flamboyant. His exasperation did not yet explode in words, but he felt it simmering inside him, slowly rising.

Again he sought escape from it in wasteful and costly browsings through curio and book shops, with the result that sometimes he was unable to give Lily the money she required for housekeeping and her personal needs.

"I swear, if you were a millionaire, you'd still manage to be without a sou at the end of the month," she would rail. "That's another thing you forgot to tell me when you begged me to marry you. I

* On the eve of an important race he wrote to René Peter: "The horse's name is Brahma. You must, absolutely must, play it . . ." After the race: "I think Brahma used to be an omnibus horse . . . However, to his credit, it must be said that he was the first of those that didn't arrive. He'll get there one of these days."

need a new dress and here you go and spend a fortune on those damn stupid books!"

Her complaints fell on deaf ears. When he grew tired of them, he simply took his hat and went out for long aimless walks.

On this October afternoon, he had been wandering for more than an hour through deserted and unpathed sections of the Bois, when unexpectedly he found himself in the vicinity of the Allée des Dames. Already, through the russet foliage, he could catch fleeting glimpses of elegant carriages driving in the sunshine, and further away, the sparkling green mosaic of the lake.

He was trudging alongside the avenue when a stylish victoria slowed down at the curb and a teasing voice wafted up to his ears.

"Still going around with your head in the clouds, aren't you, darling?"

It was Gaby. Gaby reclining on the tufted green satin of her carriage, driving in solitary splendor behind her liveried coachman and footman. Gaby, dressed to the nines in pink silk, pink hat, pink gloves, holding a pink umbrella in one hand, looking like a pink praline and good enough to eat.

"Come in." She smiled, opening the door. "I'm dying to have a chat with you. Let's drive around the lake and show off together."

The carriage moved on. The two shiny-coated hackneys fell back into their prancing, trotting gait.

He sat at her side, grinning, too happy to think of anything to say. For a moment their gazes clung, as if in embrace.

Impulsively she grasped his hand. "God, I'm glad to see you! And so proud I could burst. I can't open the newspaper without reading your name. And I saw your portrait at the Salon. Real serious and important you looked with your hand on your lapel. And quite pleased with yourself, if you ask me."

"It wasn't my fault. He made me pose like that."

"Don't apologize, silly. He was right. You're a famous man now. Legion of Honor and everything! If you don't watch out, they'll make you President one of these days."

She paused. Then in her old tone of voice, the voice he had loved in the garret days, she murmured, "Oh, darling, I've missed you so!"

Swiftly she released his hand, almost tossed it away.

"I'd better stop holding your hand or pretty soon I'll start crying and my mascara will run down all over my face."

In a bright conversational banter she went on, "By the way, it was nice of you to send me that box for your opera. Did you see me?"

"Yes, and I was so glad you came."

"I wouldn't have missed it for the world. I wore out a pair of gloves applauding your damn music. Now, you know what I do?

Wherever I go, I lead the conversation to your opera, and if some-body doesn't like it, I murder him. I tell him he's just an imbecile who doesn't know a damn thing about music and he'd better go back and listen to it again.

"And you, how did you like it?"

"Nice. A little boring in places . . . Now, tell me, at least are you making money now?"

He nodded and she beamed.

"It's about time! Honest, I thought you'd never make it . . . What do you do with your money?"

"Spend it."

She clucked her tongue in rebuke. "You never had any sense when it comes to money. You should do the same as I do, buy Russian bonds. The government says you must. What kind of a Frenchman are you? Besides, they pay good interest."

"Didn't you see the map in precious stones they sent us at the Exposition? Why do we have to give them money?"

"To build trains."

"Why?"

"Don't you read the papers? Don't you know anything of what's going on? I'll tell you why we need the Russians. Because one of these days the German Kaiser is going to attack us, and when he does, the Russian Cossacks will come riding from behind, and he'll have to fight on two fronts. See?"

"If they come riding, then why do they need trains?"

"Oh, you don't understand anything!"

With an impatient wave of her pink gloved hand she dismissed the subject. "All right, go ahead. Spend your money. You'll wind up under a bridge and see if I care!"

For a few seconds she tried holding to her air of haughty in-difference, but soon her face softened and a smile returned to her green eyes.

"Oh, darling, I'm so glad you're here! I certainly didn't expect to see you today. The funny part is that I almost didn't go out, but the weather was too nice to stay in. Then Victor asked me to listen to his new play, and that did it. I decided I needed some fresh air."

"How is he?"

"He is the nicest, most wonderful man God ever made, that's all. So nice that I don't even get fun from sleeping with his friends any more. He'll make an honest woman out of me yet! He does everything I want, gives me everything I want, adores me, thinks I am the most beautiful thing that ever lived. Sometimes I think I've fallen into a barrel of whipped cream."

"Your mother and sister, how are they?"

"Everybody's fine. Maman is getting old though. But then who isn't? . . . ." Again she seized his hand. "And you, darling, how are things with you? How's Lily? I haven't seen her since my trip to Cuba. Is she all right now?"

"Yes. Much better."

"I'm glad. You looked awful that day I came to your place, and frankly you don't look much better now."

She scanned his face, frowning, her eyes grave with concern.

"You aren't very happy, are you?"

"No, I am not," he said quietly. "I shouldn't have married Lily. You tried to warn me, but I didn't understand at the time. Didn't want to, I guess. Now I know I've made a mistake and there's no way out."

Suddenly his voice grew tense. "Mind you, she isn't a bad woman. She keeps the house clean, squeezes every sou. She feels she is a wonderful wife, and in a sense she is, if all you want from a wife is a cook and a maid. I am sure she half believes the nonsense she spreads about the years of agony she went through while she helped me write my opera. The truth is that we only had a bad period, from April, when my publisher died, to December when the *Nocturnes* were presented. And she was sick most of the time! But even that doesn't matter. I don't care if she says she wrote *Pélléas* by herself! The thing, the dreadful thing, is that we have no companionship, no basic rapport, nothing. Perhaps it's my fault, perhaps I should try to find some common ground. But that's just it, there is none. I have nothing to say to her and I can't bring myself to listen to what she has to say. Sometimes the very sound of her voice infuriates me to such a point that I have to get out and walk till I finally cool off and can go back and listen to her again. That's what I was doing when you saw me a moment ago."

"Do you quarrel a lot, as we used to?"

"No. And that's another funny thing. People think we are a very happy couple. We don't quarrel because there is nothing to quarrel about. Our misunderstanding doesn't arise from what we do. That could be corrected. It arises from what we are, and that's what makes it hopeless."

"Nothing is hopeless if she loves you, and she does, I'm sure." As he remained silent, she frowned. "Doesn't she?"

"Perhaps . . . But not in the way you did."

He spoke slowly, searching his mind, trying to be fair and accurate.

"You, darling, loved me when I didn't have a sou, when you had a rich gentleman friend and you had everything to lose by staying with me. Lily had a room on rue de Berne, a rather precarious job and no generous friend. She was twenty-six, tired of working and anxious to get married. It seemed that she had a proposal from a widower she did not love, and I am not even sure about that. She married me after much hesitation, because she knew I had an opera that was to be produced and she took a gamble that I might be successful. For several months she thought she had lost, and complained bitterly that I had almost tricked her into marrying me. I don't think she loved me very much at that time. Then, just when she had about decided I'd never amount to anything, the miracle happened. *Pélléas* was produced, and there she was, standing next to me in the box, bowing and smiling. Since that day she's been living a dream and loving every minute of it. She loves my Legion of Honor, the reporters, the dinner invitations. Being Madame Claude Debussy, entering a drawing room with her arm in mine, giving her hand to kiss. Her gamble has paid off beyond all expectations. Sometimes, when we go to some reception, I watch her prattling away to a group of people and her face literally glows with excitement. I've never seen anyone who craves attention as much as she does. She'll do anything to be talked about. She can't help it, I suppose."

He paused. The carriage swayed gently under them as it rolled on around the lake in a drumming of hoofbeats.

He sighed; then in a calm toneless voice he went on, "I'm telling you all this to make you understand why she'll never let me go."

"I'm afraid you're right. But you could divorce her."

He gave out a short, bitter chuckle. "On what grounds? You can't divorce your wife just because you made a mistake and shouldn't have married her in the first place, can you? Or because you no longer love her and she can't give you the child you'd hoped for."

"How do you know she can't?"

"The doctor told me so . . . Funny, isn't it? You marry to start a family, then you find out that your wife—or it may be yourself—can't have any children, and there is nothing you can do but bear up and grin until death doth you part. As if you started mining for gold and you found out there wasn't any gold, but you must go on digging for the rest of your lives. This, apparently, is the ultimate in human wisdom, and marriage is the institution on which civilized society stands."

He looked at her, still smiling, as if he had told her some amusing little joke.

"As for leaving her and forcing her to divorce me, I've thought of it once or twice and frankly I shudder at the prospect of what she would do. If that woman ever had to renounce being Madame Debussy, she would turn into a fury from whom I could expect neither understanding nor mercy. She is naturally vindictive, always talks about lawyers, going to court, fighting to the death for your rights. I know what she would do. First she would retain the best attorney in Paris, at my expense, of course, and then begin harassing and tormenting me until I'd go out of my mind or throw myself in the river. Perhaps you think I exaggerate? Well, don't. I know her and I know what she would do. Not only would she ruin me, take the shirt off my back, but she would turn the divorce proceedings into a public execution, talk her head off, tell stories that would make a stone weep and spread so many lies that I wouldn't have a single friend left."

He shook his head and again let out a chuckle of mirthless jocularity.

"No, darling. I've done a few crazy things in my life, but I will not force Lily to divorce me. This is one mistake I shall not make. I have no desire to wreck my life. Not at this time, when I am successful and I'm beginning to earn money."

"Then what are you going to do? Stay as you are?"

"Exactly. No one could have put it better." A teasing gleam came into his eyes. "As they say in Lisieux, "When you've drawn your wine and filled your glass, you've got to drink it." And that, my darling, is what I propose to do. Drink it to the last drop. I'll do what thousands of unlucky husbands are doing. I'll try not to think. I'll buy books, bet at the races, spend as little time as possible at home, perhaps get a lady friend to while away a rainy afternoon now and then."

She did not join in his feigned jollity. Even his quip about Lisieux had not brought a smile to her lips.

"What if you really fell in love and wanted another chance to make a home, a real home, for yourself?"

He looked away at the sky turning hazy in the autumn sunset. All at once his weariness returned. Like a heavy cloak the sense of futility and hopelessness fell back on his shoulders.

"Look, darling, I've just told you what Lily would do if I ever broke up our marriage. The kind of love that would drive me to accept ruin and whatever else she would do would have to be such an irresistible love that I don't believe it exists. In books perhaps, but not in real life."

He reached for her hand, held it for a moment in his own.

"Listen. I don't want to be poor again, I don't want any more scandals. I've made a mistake and I will try living with it. I am forty-one years old, and I've learned that it is not enough to grow old, you must also grow up."

She hesitated. Then, slowly, "Are you sure?"

CHAPTER

17

THE FOLLOWING SUMMER PARIS WAS SHOCKED BY A RUMOR THAT
Claude Debussy, the famous composer, had left his wife and run
away with a married woman.

At first most people refused to believe it. It was too silly, it
couldn't be true. Only in romantic novels did lovers run away. Not in
real life, least of all in Paris, where people understood about *l'amour*
and were broad-minded about it. When two married persons took
a fancy to each other, they had a discreet affair, and everything
was all right. Appearances were saved, and that's what counted.

Why, there were thousands of such affairs! For instance, everyone
knew that Anatole France, the celebrated novelist, lived with Madame
de Caillavet. On the second floor of her avenue Hoche mansion, to
be exact. Yet every week he would appear, all spruced up in cutaway
and top hat, at her Sunday afternoon receptions, kiss her hand and
give her a bunch of violets (which her maid had gone out to buy
half an hour before) with the same, never-changing compliment,
"Madame, as I was passing by your beautiful home, I could not deny
myself the pleasure of calling on you and laying my respects at your
feet." Now, this was the way to handle things. But run away together—never!

Rumors, however, persisted. It became known that the lady was
a fashionable hostess and the wife of a prominent banker. In drawing

rooms incredulity turned to stupefaction. What was the world coming to if society ladies started running away with artists! How could an intelligent woman like Emma do such a rash, indiscreet thing! Had she gone mad? Of course, she was lonely, disappointed in her marriage. Her husband was a charming man, but—well, you know how husbands are . . . Nevertheless, this was no excuse for her to do what she had done. Defy conventions, ruin her social prestige, lose her beautiful home. No man was worth that. There must be some mistake, it just couldn't be true.

A few still clung to the theory that it was all malicious gossip, but soon they, too, had to surrender to the evidence. During the winter Monsieur Debussy had been a frequent guest at the banker's home. He was an attractive man and, of course, a great musician. Emma, for her part, had always been very musical. They were bound to be drawn together: she to his great talent; he to her exquisite singing voice as well as her charm and elegance. If you added that both were unhappily married, it was easy to understand how they could have fallen in love. Madly, desperately, as it happens in books. And one day they had lost their heads and run away.

Others were not so kind. That fellow Debussy had been dazzled by Emma's social standing, her poise, her glittering and delicious dinners. Her money . . . He, of course, had never had a sou. Even now that he was famous and his opera quite successful, he still had to give lessons to make ends meet, for it was no secret that in music the publisher became rich and the composer got the applause . . . In Emma he simply had seen a chance to crash society and live in luxury for the rest of his life. Being endowed with an uncanny fascination for women—remember that beautiful girl who had tried to kill herself over him a few years back?—he soon had added Emma to the list of his victims. This done, he had planned their flight together in order to create a scandal that would make it impossible for her to return to her husband. As for himself, he had simply and callously shed his wife—a common but brave little *midinette* who had slaved for him through his hungry years—and left her without a word. Then he had met Emma at some prearranged spot and they had skipped away together. Probably to Spain or Italy or some God-forsaken village in the Alps. But they could not stay away forever, some day they must return.

And then—

"They're going to make us pay for what we've done," he said quietly. "You know that, don't you, darling?"

She nodded, her head still turned to the sea.

They had not fled to Spain or Italy, but to the Isle of Jersey, a speck of an island between England and France. Here, for the last two weeks, they had hidden their sinful happiness. The trees, the grass, the sea had made no reproaches to them, asked no questions. The sun had shone on them as on the righteous. At night the stars had twinkled on their embraces. They had felt so safe and alone on their little island of green meadows and sandy beaches that, one morning, in a surge of gratitude he had jotted down a prelude which he called *L'Isle Joyeuse*.

Yet they could not go on hiding forever. Their mad, romantic escapade was coming to an end. Tomorrow they would sail back to France and face the consequences of their folly. But this evening was still theirs, and once more they had come to their favorite spot, a cow pasture on the top of a hill from where they could see the town of Saint Helier and the foam-fringed bays.

Now they sat on a low stone wall, watching the approaching night extinguish the last glimmers of sunset and invade the sky like a slow-spreading ink stain.

"Sometimes I feel I had no right to let you come here. Are you sorry you did, darling?"

She shook her head, her eyes still on the sea, remote in thought and unseeing.

Once again his heart swelled with love for the woman at his side. She was petite and dainty, with slender wrists and ankles; yet she had had the courage to join him without hesitation in this mad venture. Like him she had taken the irreparable step, knowing how high would be the price they would have to pay. And now she, too, was thinking about tomorrow, probing the future, bracing herself for the ordeal to come.

"Haven't you the feeling that it is all a dream?" His words dropped softly into the surrounding silence. "The feeling that it cannot be true, that we can't possibly have cut our bridges behind us, flaunted conventions and run away together? . . . Do you remember last November, when we used to meet at our little tearoom and we said neither of us wanted love, but only a little companionship, a little tenderness? And we believed it!"

His face relaxed in a slow, reminiscent smile and she turned to him, smiling also, waiting for him to speak.

"And then a few months later when we swore that we merely liked each other? And if, by any chance, we ever became infatuated we would have a polite little affair, but nothing more?"

Yes, they had been cautious, adult and civilized about the whole thing. They were not going to do anything foolish. Certainly not. They would meet in some discreet love nest for a few hours each week, then demurely return to their respective husband and wife.

"We had it all planned, didn't we?" His smile turned into a soft chuckle. "And look at us!"

One day in June it had burst upon them that they did not want a love nest, a polite little affair. With awe they had found they were in love and their love was total, uncautious and uncivilized. The kind that brooked no compromise. They wanted to start a new life together, never leave each other again. It was then that they had planned their flight to Jersey.

"I'm afraid it's going to be difficult for us to see each other for the next few months. We'll be watched and spied upon every moment, but somehow we'll manage to meet once in a while. It's going to be a bad period to go through, but it won't last forever. I am sure your husband will arrange for a quiet divorce. As for Lily, there's no telling what she will do."

Night had come. A ship went by. Already they could distinguish only the outlines of their faces. She groped for his hand. Neither of them spoke. And thus they remained for a long time, motionless and lost in thought. Two shadows holding hands in the darkness.

He returned to Paris prepared for the worst, but not for what was awaiting him.

He learned that Lily had tried to commit suicide and had been transported to the clinic on rue Blomet. As a gesture of sympathy toward the unfortunate wife and denunciation toward the infamous husband, a subscription had been opened to defray Lily's hospital expenses. At the clinic he was informed by Doctor Desjardin, who had operated on her, that Lily would soon be out of danger. The bullet, presumably aimed point-blank at the heart, had somehow deflected in the direction of the stomach.

After that there was no peace for him. To elude the pursuit of journalists he hid in a small apartment in the Passy district. In February, Lily started the divorce proceedings. She behaved very much as he had thought she would. She retained as her counsel one of Paris' most eminent attorneys and diligently assisted him in the defense of her rights. He knew he could not expect mercy from her, but he was not prepared for the savagery of her vengeance. She might have shot herself for love, but clearly she had changed her mind about him and intended to hurt him in every possible way . . .

Although he let her know he would not contest the suit, she insisted on suing him not only on the ground of adultery, which would have been sufficient for her to secure a divorce, but also for *injures graves,* which provided her with an opportunity to vent her grievances and reveal the abuses and ill-treatment she had endured during the four and a half years of her marriage.

Despite the secrecy of divorce proceedings, many intimate details leaked out: some shocking, others merely ludicrous. Lily attributed the desertion of her husband to his uncontrollable *gourmandise*. Apparently the composer of *Pélléas* had been unable to resist cuisine prepared by Emma's chef.*

Not content merely to pour ridicule on the man who had nursed her and spent sleepless nights at her bedside, she proceeded to try to ruin him and nearly succeeded. Harassed on all sides by orders of payment, injunctions and staggering legal fees, he was pushed to the brink of bankruptcy, from which he was saved by the generosity of his friend and publisher Jacques Durand, who bought *Pélléas* from him.

Having liquidated his last and only asset, he gave the money to his attorney, Maître Bourgoin, with instructions to settle all claims, offer no rebuttal to Lily's accusations and hasten the conclusion of the divorce proceedings. This done, he left for Eastbourne, a small English resort, where he finished writing *La Mer,* which he had begun at Bichain two summers before. There, early in August, he received notification from his lawyer that the divorce had been pronounced against him, with all costs and penalties provided by law.

After reading the letter he stood at the window of his hotel room, gazing out at the shimmering sea. At last it was over! Lily must be happy. She had made him pay, as she had said she would. He still recalled the morning of Bastille Day a year ago, when he had pleaded with her to give him his freedom, and finally, in despair, walked away. Yes, she had done all that she'd set out to do. She had pilloried him, ridiculed him, alienated his friends and ruined him. She had taken everything, even the little palette he had bought as a student. Her triumph was complete. But the poor fool had been so blinded with vindictiveness, so intent on hurting him, that she had also brought ruin upon herself. She had forced him to sell his opera, which could have maintained her in growing affluence for the rest of her life. Instead, the proceeds from the sale had gone to pay lawyers, solicitors, the rent of "the charming little apartment" on avenue Villiers, which she had occupied since her release from the hospital, and all the divorce expenses. Now almost nothing remained to be shared. She had avenged herself into poverty.

When the divorce became known, it aroused scant attention. The public was getting tired of Madame Debussy and her sufferings. It took her a little time to admit she no longer was news. She clung

---

* Lily's exact words were, *"Elle l'a pris par la gueule";* she (Emma) has taken him by the belly. It is one of those remarks that reveal an entire personality. Not only the vulgarity of the word *gueule* (which no lady would have uttered at that time) but the ineptitude of the statement itself give the measure of Lily's quality of speech and thought.

to the limelight as long as she could. In defiance of French law she continued to call herself Madame Debussy and visited her friends and champions until told by the maid or butler that they were not at home. Her moment had passed. Alone and deserted, she instinctively turned back to the country. One day she left for Bichain. Rosalie Texier plummeted back into obscurity.

In turn, her former husband was again being much talked about, this time as a musician. Two months after the divorce his symphony *La Mer* was presented at the Concerts Lamoureux. It raised such a storm of controversy that no one paid attention to his marriage to Emma, and their installation in a calm and secluded mansion located on a small square off the avenue du Bois de Boulogne.

Here, on October 30, 1905, a child was born. The most unusual, intelligent, beautiful, wonderful, adorable child in the world. She was named Claude-Emma, but to him she was Chouchou from the first moment he saw her.

Suddenly he was the happiest of men. The turmoil of the last twelve months was already fading into an ugly memory. It did not matter that his divorce had ruined him financially and lost him many friends. A few, however, had remained, and a man does not need many friends. Above all, he had a wife he truly loved and a child he adored. Whatever they had cost him, they were worth it a thousand times.

No, he had no regrets. He was still young, only forty-three and full of vigor. And his mind was brimming with music.

Now he could start rebuilding his life.

♦

Happy people, like happy nations, have no history. For the next few years Claude was happy and little happened to him. He all but withdrew from the world, wrote a great deal of music and became increasingly famous.

His habits changed. He no longer frequented Weber's. He was tired of those café friends who couldn't wait to be your enemies; tired of their smiles, their gossip and venomous quips. His fame discouraged him from strolling on the boulevards, as he had in the past. So many portraits and caricatures of him had been published that he was instantly recognized. Well-meaning admirers insisted on telling him how much they liked his music. Wanted to shake his hand, asked for his autograph. If, by chance, he and Emma ventured into a theatre or a music hall, heads turned in their direction. Sometimes, after the show, performers were presented to them.*

* Thus Charlie Chaplin, then a lad of seventeen and a member of a vaudeville act, was brought to his box after a performance at the Folies Bergère.

Gradually he avoided the city, took solitary walks in the nearby Bois de Boulogne. Most of the time he stayed home writing music, correcting proofs, answering his huge mail, coming out in the garden for a few minutes' stroll, spending his evenings with Emma by the fireside and ten times a day going upstairs to the nursery to peep down at Chouchou in her crib. With never-ending wonder he watched the wrinkled, gurgling, drooling, toothless old woman turn into a wobbly-legged infant that crawled on the lawn; then into a little girl with a heart-shaped face, sparkling black eyes and a genius for getting herself—and him—in trouble.

By the time she was four and a half she owned him, body and soul: used him as an accomplice in her pranks and as an ally in her war against Miss Gibbs, her English governess, a motherly spinster known about the house as "Miss." Miss had the patience of an angel and the fortitude of her race; she and Chouchou had different ideas on almost everything. Miss believed in little girls' brushing their teeth every morning; Chouchou did not. Neither did she believe in learning her alphabet, speaking only when spoken to and conducting herself at all times like a lady.

Petulantly she would complain to her father, "I don't want to be a lady."

"Why?"

"Because Miss says a lady shouldn't ride piggyback, and I want you to piggyback me."

"Miss is right, absolutely right." This firmly, to uphold Miss' authority. "You're much too old for this sort of thing."

"But I want to."

"Only babies go piggyback."

"Please, Papa!" This in a wail, with eyes lifted in supplication. "Please!"

"All right." Then, with finality, to save face, "But just this time, do you hear?"

With stupefaction he discovered that a four-and-a-half-year-old girl was a full-grown woman in miniature, as complex as a Swiss watch, already in possession of an arsenal of weapons of seduction of all kinds—tricks, blandishments, imploring glances which she used with consummate skill and no ethics whatsoever. He found out that to a female child the end justified the means, and any means was justified to get her end. Honor, sportsmanship and the like she regarded with scorn as silly grown-up notions. He also learned that —contrary to the saying—out of the mouths of babes came the most monumental fibs.

That spring the Ballets Russes made their debut. A troupe of fifty-five dancers from the Imperial theatres of Moscow and Saint Petersburg debarked on the quays of the Seine and took possession of the Théatre du Chatelet. For them the immense and shabby theatre usually devoted to blood-and-thunder melodramas was refurbished, repainted, recarpeted, its seats reupholstered, its stage refloored with special pine, kind to ballerinas' toes. In three weeks Paris' hoariest, most plebian playhouse was turned into her most elegant and aristo-cratic theatre.

On the evening of the première fifty-two among the loveliest and best-known cocottes—twenty-six blondes and twenty-six brunettes—were artistically displayed in the fifty-two front-row seats of the dress circle. This innovation—*la corbeille,* as it was called: the flower basket—received much favorable publicity. As for the spectacle itself, nothing like it had ever been seen. The audience was sent into con-vulsions by the savage lustfulness of *Prince Igor's* dances, the sudden entrance of a flock of goats in the *Pavillon d'Armide.* Never had there been goats in a ballet. Everything was new, daring, sumptuous. A collective gasp was heard when the curtain rose upon the exotic set of *Cléopâtre* and Ida Rubinstein appeared, sloe-eyed and sphinx-like, stretched out on a palanquin carried aloft by Nubian slaves and subsequently disrobed on the stage while a bevy of whirling maidens formed around her a living and inadequate curtain.

It was a triumph. The following day all Paris was talking about Anna Pavlova, Tamara Karsavina, the "almost-too-beautiful" Ida Rubenstein and the fabulous male dancer Vaslav Nijinsky, who could rise in the air and apparently stay there as long as he pleased. At once hundreds of overnight experts discussed *fouettés, entrechats, jetés, pirouettes, pas de deux, pas de trois* and *pas de quatre.*

Claude attended the première with Emma. For more than two hours he watched young men and women bounce about the stage, leap, crouch, run, bend, unbend, curve their arms in poetic gestures and do marvelously complicated things with their feet. He thought it all very fine and artistic.

But Chouchou could also skip and dance and run. She was espe-cially expert at running away from Miss, slipping into his study and hiding under his desk.

A moment later Miss would knock at the door, peer in and in her British-accented French politely inquire about Chouchou's where-abouts.

"Isn't she with you?" Claude would reply with well-feigned sur-prise. "I can't imagine where she may be. Have you looked in the garden?"

The door would close, and Chouchou would emerge from her hiding place, climb on his knees and give him a big kiss as a reward. She had long discovered she could do anything with him. While

Maman and Miss were on to her tricks and hard to deceive, Papa believed anything. He was wonderful, but not very intelligent, she thought. Just the same she loved him very much.

She loved him most when he told her about Monsieur Gros.

Monsieur Gros was a short, fat, baldheaded and funny-looking man with a big tummy and a round, red face. By profession he was a butterfly hunter. Naturally, to catch butterflies he had to live in a huge tropical forest that full of lions, tigers and crocodiles. His life was an unbroken sequence of desperate predicaments ending in hair-raising, miraculous escapes.

Claude had invented Monsieur Gros to beguile the tedium of a rainy afternoon. But, alas, Chouchou had taken a fancy to the funny-looking little man, and there was no getting rid of him. No day was complete without another installment in the endless saga of his adventures. Sometimes she would come into his study and ask him for another thrilling episode; sometimes when he came upstairs to kiss her good night.

And sometimes he told her about him when they went out hand-in-hand for their morning promenade: he, looking very dignified in black derby and starched collar; she, very stylish in a blue paletot, high-button shoes and round straw hat.

"Please, Papa, tell me about Monsieur Gros," she would ask, as soon as they had started down the avenue.

Sometimes he would tease her and pretend he had never heard of any Monsieur Gros, but she saw through his pretense and had no patience with it.

"You do know him! You said he was a friend of yours. Maman says you shouldn't tell lies."

"Oh, you mean my friend Monsieur Gros! Of course I remember him. Why, we used to go to school together. Now let's see. Where were we?"

"A lion was running after him."

He would begin, trusting to luck. "It was terrible. Here he was, running as fast as he could on his short legs, and the lion was getting closer and closer, already licking his lips at the idea of having Monsieur Gros for dinner."

She lifted her anxious little face to him. "Was he really going to eat him?"

"Certainly. He was a mean old lion, and Monsieur Gros was nice and fat."

"Why didn't he shoot the lion?"

"Because he had forgotten his gun. Don't you remember he was in his tent, brushing his teeth—for Monsieur Gros was a fine man who brushed his teeth every morning—when the lion came after him."

"I remember. Then what happened?"

"Well, here he was, running for dear life and the lion getting nearer all the time."

"He was in a pretty bad fix, wasn't he?"

"I should say he was! But luckily he spotted a big tree, and before the lion could catch him he climbed up, as fast as a monkey, to the top of it."

"How could he? You said he was very fat."

"Well, you see he was very scared and that made him hurry."

This made everything clear, and she nodded for him to proceed.

"Naturally the lion was furious. And you know why? Because lions can't climb tree. And so he fumed, and switched his tail back and forth and roared and scratched the bark with his claws. But Monsieur Gros was looking down on him, laughing and sticking his tongue out at him."

"Maman says it's not polite to stick out your tongue."

"She is right. It's very rude to stick out your tongue at people, but at lions it's all right. Anyway, here he was, up in the tree and the lion waiting down below to eat him."

He paused, stumped by his own invention. How was he going to get Monsieur Gros down that tree and safely back into his tent?

"Well, let me tell you he was pretty scared," he said to gain time.

"You said he was laughing."

Oh, the mental sharpness of children! . . . "Well, you see, he was laughing to annoy the lion, but deep inside he was worried. Wouldn't you be, if you had a lion waiting to eat you?"

"Go on."

In a flash the solution came to his mind.

"Then something wonderful happened. He noticed that the tree was full of coconuts. They look like walnuts, but much bigger. About the size of melons and very hard. This gave him a marvelous idea. He picked up a coconut and dropped it plumb on the lion's nose."

Her eyes widened. "Did it kill him?"

"No, but it made him a little dizzy for a while. He fell flat on the ground and went to sleep. And while he slept Monsieur Gros slid down the tree and ran back to his tent."

He sighed with relief. Monsieur Gros had had another miraculous escape . . .

"And then what happened?"

"Ah, my little Chouchou, the most exciting thing happened! Imagine, Monsieur Gros found a crocodile asleep in his bed! . . . I'll tell you about it tomorrow."

The Bois de Boulogne was their favorite spot. Sometimes they merely strolled along its sun-flecked alleys, discoursing on various things, like adults. Or they played hide-and-seek in the thickets, and when she ran into his arms to kiss him his heart welled with happiness. Now and then they stopped at a café, sat down at one of the tables on the lawn, and she sipped a grenadine through a long straw while he indulged in a glass of sherry. Occasionally they went as far as the Jardin d'Acclimatation, a small, elegant zoo at the edge of the Bois, where she had an elephant ride and—if she had been exceptionally good—a drive in a two-wheeled cart drawn by an ostrich.

These morning walks were his happiest moments. He loved the running stream of her chatter, the feel of her little hand in his own, the tingle of her laughter. There just was nothing like the love of a child . . .

◆

He had promised himself to rebuild his life and was doing so at a remarkable pace. Since he had found happiness, music literally flowed from his bamboo penholder. Songs, piano preludes, symphonic suites followed one another without interruption; and everything he wrote was successful. His fame was bordering dangerously on popularity. Compositions he had sold for a pittance in the garret days, and which had remained unpublished, now appeared in the windows of every music shop. To his despair *Rêverie,* which he had almost forgotten, was being played in every cinema and even on the terraces of cafés. *Clair de Lune* was maimed on a thousand keyboards. Even *Children's Corner,* six short piano pieces he had written for Chouchou, met with instant and almost embarrassing favor.*

As for his major works, they were being played all over Europe. The *Nocturnes* were acclaimed in Norway, with Edvard Grieg leading the applause. *Pélléas* continued its triumphant advance and was being presented in Frankfurt, Munich, Prague, Milan, Rome, even in New York. In London, where he had gone to supervise the production, the staid Covent Garden audience clapped for fifteen minutes, demanding his appearance on the stage until the manager sheepishly announced that *Mister* Debussy was at his hotel, asleep.

The spring of 1909 ended with the departure of the Ballets Russes. Like a flock of exotic birds the dancers returned to faraway Mother Russia. Their first Paris season had been an unparalleled triumph with every performance sold out. The receipts had been astronomical;

---

* Debussy regarded *Children's Corner* as such a trifling composition that he did not dare attend its first performance by the American pianist Harold Bauer, on December 18, 1908.

yet so lavish had been the productions that the venture closed with a deficit of sixty thousand francs. With a few sighs and clucking of tongues Henri de Rothschild, Basil Zaharoff and a handful of art-loving millionaires signed the necessary checks. Moreover, with additional sighs and clucking of tongues, they pledged their support for future annual presentations.

That summer Blériot flew over the Channel in thirty-one minutes, and Claude developed a passion for aeronautics. He read profusely on the subject and in no time at all became an armchair expert. He predicted that any day now airplanes would land on house roofs and he fretted about the coming traffic problems in the sky. So engrossed did he become in flying matters that he bought a kite, officially as a toy for Chouchou, in reality for himself. At dusk he sneaked out of the house and raced about the garden, tugging at his kite's string. Among the members of the household the opinion was that "poor Monsieur" had worked himself into second childhood.

Time seemed to fly. Suddenly Chouchou was five years old, and it was winter again and fires were crackling in every room of the house. The new year began in a downpour and wore on in a deluge. January was one long cloudburst. The Seine overflowed and rampaged through half of the city. At the Louvre, museum officials crossed the courtyard in rowboats and entered their offices through first-story windows. At last the rains stopped and gradually the river returned to its bed. Things went back to normal. Cabinets fell, railroads struck and politicians said the times were perilous. Fashions took a momentous leap forward. Women discarded their corsets and began breathing for the first time in years. Then, in May, Edward VII died. For once England and France forgot their bickering. Like his regal widow and beloved mistress, they joined in genuine grief over the stout and jolly man who had been both King of England and *roi de Paris*. His death sent a shudder of apprehension throughout Europe. For ten years this amiable *bon vivant* had been the symbol of reasonableness, order and peace. With him gone, nothing was the same any more. The future, which had seemed so safe, suddenly loomed dark and uncertain.

The present, however, remained cloudless and life went on as before. Since he had moved into his beautiful home Claude had grown to love it more every year. He had found happiness in it, but very little silence and solitude. Whenever he had a moment he worked on the libretto of his next opera, jotted down some musical idea; but there always seemed to be some urgent task that must be attended to at once. New batches of proof sheets arrived from the printer; conductors asked his advice on the interpretation of his scores; his publisher longed for his next composition. Distinguished foreign musicians called on him; a lady journalist traveled all the way from America for an interview. Success was pounding at his door, encroaching on his working hours. At times, he almost missed the tranquil obscurity of the garret days.

Despite the monthly allowance paid him by his publisher and the royalties from his compositions, he occasionally found himself in financial difficulties. Some were due to his incorrigible extravagance; some to the rising cost of living and mounting household expenses. As an emergency measure, he agreed to conduct a series of concerts in Vienna and Budapest that winter. The trip was a whirlwind of rehearsals, performances, ovations, banquets and speeches. Yet he found time to write Chouchou an entire children's story on five postcards.*

He who abhorred publicity, was pursued by it. Rumors about his romantic past, the scandals of his private life, the attempted suicides of two beautiful women on his account had woven around him a colorful legend which aroused public curiosity. It was with relief that he returned to the privacy of his train compartment and waved good-bye to his admirers.

No sooner was he back in Paris than he undertook a colossal task, also as an emergency measure. In four months he wrote the music and choral ensembles for *Le Martyre de Saint Sébastien,* a five-act religious tragedy by Gabriele d'Annunzio.

Even before it was presented, *Saint Sébastien* unleashed the most furious polemics. Editors sharpened their quills and plunged into battle. Some declared it sacrilegious that the saint should be portrayed by Ida Rubinstein, who was not only a woman, but also Jewish. Then the personalities of the composer and author came in for denunciations. Since neither of them was a practicing Catholic, it was deemed improper for them to approach a spiritual subject. In reply, others pointed out that few great artists had been ardent churchgoers, and that no painter, musician or writer of any stature had ever been elevated to sainthood. It was sad but true that most of the greatest religious paintings and much of the loftiest sacred music had been created by men of small faith and even smaller virtue. *Parsifal* remained a work of high spirituality, even though Wagner himself had been an unmitigated scoundrel. With the best will in the world Leonardo da Vinci, Titian, Rembrandt, Handel, Beethoven, Mozart, Shakespeare, Byron, Goethe and Voltaire could only be regarded as wayward Christians and chronic sinners. Morally speaking, geniuses were a sorry lot, and no mistake.

* Thanks to M. Pasteur Vallery-Radot, the letters, notes and telegrams Debussy sent his wife and daughter during this and subsequent tours have been published. More than any other documents, they reveal the depth and tenderness of his love for them.

Claude was much too busy to take part in the controversy or even pay much attention to it. But a few days before the première, he was jolted out of his detachment by the news that Cardinal Amette, Archbishop of Paris, had already condemned the play and forbidden Catholics to attend it, under threat of excommunication.

"Many years ago Verdi told me the same thing happened to him," he said to Emma. "Cardinals have a passion for meddling in theatrical affairs."

The two collaborators sent a joint letter to the newspapers in which they respectfully suggested that a little Christian charity might be in order and that a play, like an individual, should be regarded as innocent until proven guilty.

It had no effect whatever. The edict of excommunication remained in force. *Saint Sébastien* was no longer to be judged on its artistic merits. Like *Pélléas,* it had become an issue: this time a religious one. Doomed before its birth, the play closed after a few performances.*

"I only wish," he told Emma with a weary sigh, "I could have my music played without always having a scandal on my hands."

Apparently this was too much to ask, for the following year, at about the same time, he was involved in an even greater scandal.

This time it was not his music that caused it, but Nijinsky's interpretation of it. The piece was *The Afternoon of a Faun,* which had been announced by the Ballets Russes as their main novelty for the 1912 season. Nijinsky, who acted as choreographer as well as dancer, had devoted one hundred and three rehearsals to this twelve-minute pantomime. The night of the première was one of those gala affairs for which Paris prepares for weeks and churns itself into a fever of anticipation. Everyone who was anyone was there that evening: the men rigid in their snowy slablike shirt fronts; the women shimmering in their silk gowns, their shoulders bare, their jewels flashing off and on, like fireflies, every time they moved. In the first row of the dress circle, the cocottes of *la corbeille* sat in full view, all fifty-two of them, aigrettes up and bosoms forward. The curtain rose amidst a silence of breathless expectation.

The Afternoon of a Faun had been played countless times since its presentation at La Nationale almost twenty years before. In that time it had become a classic in France and abroad. Everywhere it was regarded as a miracle of orchestration and a masterpiece of evocative music. Its sensuality was exquisite and private, locked in

---

* Long regarded as "the unplayable masterpiece," because of its length and dramatic awkwardness, *Saint Sébastien* has been brilliantly revived at the Paris Opéra with the incomparable interpretation of the dancer-actress, Ludmilla Tcherina.

the hearer's mind. The ballet that Nijinsky presented that evening was a portrayal of bestial lust ending in a public orgasm.

As the curtain fell, an electric current ran through the audience. Suddenly the roof seemed to blow up. The formal audience of a moment ago turned into a horde of shouting, gesticulating men and women. In the middle of the pandemonium the curtain rose again and the ballet was repeated. The following day the press exploded into fireworks of conflicting statements. The *Faun* was an obscenity that should be stopped by the police; the *Faun* was a gem of plasticity, a splendid work of art. Auguste Rodin, the sculptor, wrote an article defending Nijinsky. *Le Figaro* announced that it would not publish any review of such a revolting spectacle. Everyone took sides; everyone talked. Every performance for the entire season was sold out.

Claude, as usual, said nothing. He granted no interviews, voiced no opinions. He was tired of public squabbles. Besides, it was spring and he had resumed his morning walks with Chouchou. They were more important to him than any controversy.

That year Monsieur Gros lived his last adventures, caught his last butterflies, eluded his last lions. His escapes became so miraculous and improbable that even Chouchou found them hard to believe.

"I think you're making it all up," she said bluntly one day as they were returning home.

He looked at her with a pang of sadness. It had come. The first moment of truth, the first disenchantment . . . She was growing up, already too grown up for Monsieur Gros. Poor Monsieur Gros, he would be the first myth to vanish. She was almost seven, emerging from the iridescent fanciful realm of early childhood. Her keen little mind was asking questions, her eyes were opening onto reality. Any day now she would take a good look at him and see him as he really was. No longer the glamorous friend of Monsieur Gros, the giant who swooped her up in the air, but a middle-aged man, nearing fifty, growing stout, a little stooped and flabby, with a beard turning gray.

Oh, that children would always remain children! . . .

◆

Another year went by. Much like the previous ones—in appearance. Happy, busy, productive. Many new compositions. Two ballets: both written in haste, without pleasure; both emergency measures.

It was in the spring of 1913 that he began to feel the first signs of lassitude. Emma had warned him against those eighteen-hour working schedules demanded by *Saint Sébastien*. He had laughed, boasted he was as strong as a locomotive.

"A young locomotive!"

Now the fatigue of this four-month creative debauch and eight years of unceasing toil was catching up with him. Music still came, but now it came in spurts. Occasionally his mind went blank. It worried him.

Something else worried him even more.

It was eleven years since *Pélleas* had been presented, and still his second opera was not written! Repeatedly it had been mentioned in the press that the Master was at work on it. He himself had complacently talked about it in the days when he gave interviews. It was going to be an entirely different sort of opera from *Pélleas!* An artist must not repeat himself. After all, a mountain climber didn't go on climbing the same mountain, did he? For the last several years every opera house in the world had been waiting for it. His friend Arturo Toscanini had asked him to do him the honor of letting him conduct the first performance. Signor Gatti-Casazza, director of the New York Metropolitan Opera, had already taken an option and forced him to accept an advance on it.

Oh, yes, he truly had meant to write it! In his plans he had always counted on this opera to assure the financial security of his family. Only the royalties from an opera which would be performed all over the world could make him feel tranquil about their future. But somehow the years had slipped by. Wonderful years. Successful, prodigiously active, but frittered away on a swarm of small compositions. Then there had been that exhausting four-month gamble on *Saint Sébastien,* which had turned out to be a failure. Somehow he had never been able to have the eighteen or twenty months of complete mental and material freedom he needed to write his opera. And now all he had was a nearly completed libretto and a jumble of musical ideas penciled down in his spare moments! . . . Until recently he had deluded himself, taken for granted that somehow he still would manage to write it; but now, in this spring of 1913, with a stab of anguish he began to wonder whether he *ever* would have the time— or the creativeness—for such a huge undertaking.

Meanwhile, the need for more money seemed to grow more pressing each year.

In her tactful, discreet way, Emma had suggested they move to a less expensive home, reduce the household staff. He had refused. Vehemently, obstinately. He could not tear himself from this house: its muted luxuriousness, the quiet beauty of the decor they had assembled, at great expense, together.

"Ask me anything, but not that," he had pleaded. "Every chair, every table, every knickknack has become a member of the family. A friend, humble but faithful." Then, with a little chuckle, he had added, "The more I know men, the more I like furniture! . . . Don't worry, darling. Somehow we'll manage."

Yes, they would, but not by his writing more songs or more preludes! . . . There was only one way out. He must accept the offers that came to him from every city in Europe to conduct his own works. Since his appearance in Vienna and Budapest he had declined many lucrative propositions of this kind, but still they came. He would no longer decline them, that was all. Of course, it meant leaving Emma, Chouchou, his study, his home. Long train journeys, hotel rooms, rehearsals, concerts, receptions. Standing on a podium, facing new audiences. All things he loathed. But it couldn't be helped. If he could not write his opera and secure his family's future with his pen, he must try doing it with a baton. Performers were always more highly paid than composers. Well, he would become a performer, an itinerant conductor. They wanted him in Russia, Italy, Holland, Belgium, London. Quite a bit of traveling, wasn't it? Come on, no use brooding over it. Better start writing letters of acceptance, making arrangements for dates, fees, accommodations and so on. The kitchen side of Art.

First came Russia. From Sergei Koussevitzky, conductor, publisher, double-bass virtuoso and husband of one of the richest women in Russia, had come an offer of a lavish, almost extravagant fee to conduct for three weeks in Moscow and Saint Petersburg. A brief exchange of letters brought the negotiations to a swift and happy ending. In Moscow, Claude would not be submitted to the indignity of going to a hotel. Koussevitzky's own home would be open to him, and an apartment placed at his disposal.

Claude left for Russia on December first. As he had thirty-one years ago, he found himself again in the Nord Express racing across Europe. But then it had been summer, whereas now it was the dead of winter. So he would finally see Moscow in winter. Moskva, as Sonia had called it, which was so beautiful with its wonderful snow that crackled under your boots! Moskva, where they were going to live as soon as they were married! . . . Little Sonia, what had become of her?

Endlessly the countryside unrolled outside his compartment window. After Berlin, it blurred into a flat expanse of snow that stretched out as far as the eye could see to the solid gray wall that was the sky. Then it was Poland. Then Minsk and the awesome emptiness of the Russian Steppes. Through a whirling blizzard he caught a glimpse of Smolensk's onion-shaped domes. Then the Steppes again, but now turning gray in the early afternoon dusk. Frozen rivers under wooden bridges, frozen fields. Now and then an isolated, thatch-roofed farm with an orange glow of candlelight in the window. On and on, for hours . . .

And, at last, at eight o'clock the next evening, Moscow.

As he climbed down from the train, he was surrounded by a group of bearded and voluble men in fur coats and caps who bowed to him, shook his hand with emotional reverence and addressed him all at once in excellent French through puffs of frosty breath. The gist of their compliments was that they greatly admired his music and were proud to welcome him to Moscow. After a while his host, who with his clean-shaven patrician face looked more like a British diplomat than a Russian musician, took his arm and led him to a *troika* sleigh outside the station. They ensconced themselves under a mountain of splendid furs, and at a crack from the coachman's whip the three horses spurted forward, sparks flying off their hooves, and launched into a fiery gallop through the snow-rutted avenue.

A few moments later they swerved into a vast courtyard and came to a halt in front of the stately entrance of the Koussevitzky mansion. There Claude was greeted by Madame Koussevitzky, daughter of Konstantin Ushkov, the multimillionaire tea merchant.

Thoughtfully she had arranged a small informal dinner for that evening.

"I thought you'd probably be tired and want to retire early," she said. "Please do so whenever you wish. Remember, this is your home as long as you stay in Moscow."

Under the influence of the superb French cuisine, the vintage wines and the cordial atmosphere around the table, Claude began to relax and forget the fatigue of his long journey.

Over his after-dinner benedictine he mentioned his previous visit to Moscow.

"It was many, many years ago. I was then employed as a pianist by Madame von Meck. She used to live on Rojdestvensky Boulevard. An enormous house—"

"I know it well," interrupted his hostess with a smile. "By a strange coincidence it now belongs to my father. Would you like to visit it?"

"Yes, indeed. I should like very much to see again the room where I used to give piano lessons to her daughter Sonia."

"You mean the former Princess Golizin?" inquired one of the guests. "She still lives in Moscow."

"Does she?" The words burst out of his mouth in spontaneous delight, as if he had come to Russia solely to see her. "Although I am not surprised, for she used to tell me Moscow was the most beautiful city in the world and she would never live anywhere else. If it could be arranged I would be happy to call on her any time, at her convenience."

He did not call on her. Two days later she came to see him.

He recognized her by her eyes. They alone had not changed. They still were soft and brown and impish, only now they were set in a web of fine wrinkles. The rest of her was that of a tallish, slender, almost angular woman who was a stranger to him. She was dressed carelessly, yet with elegance: the haphazard, involuntary elegance some unfashionable women achieve almost in spite of themselves.

She stood on the threshold of his sitting room, smiling hesitantly. "You've become so famous, I don't know what to call you. Master? . . . *Monsieur le professeur?* . . . "

He ran to her, hands outstretched. "Call me Volichka, as you used to."

"It isn't dignified enough for such a great musician."

"Stop talking nonsense and come sit here."

Already he was pulling her by the hand across the room toward the sofa in front of the blazing fire.

"Now let me look at you," he exclaimed, sitting down next to her and holding her hands. "I just can't believe you're here! . . . Most episodes in life have no ending. You meet, then life pulls you apart, you lose sight of each other. I didn't even know if you were still alive."

"Oh, I knew you were alive." She laughed softly. "I've heard your name many times. Once I said you used to give me piano lessons and nobody believed me. I almost wrote you a letter asking you for a testimonial, but I didn't know your address . . . Naturally, I've seen the posters announcing your concerts. I was planning to attend them, but I hadn't counted on seeing you. I wasn't sure you'd want to see me or even remember me."

"Remember you! Why, I remember everything. Our croquet games, Brailov, our meetings at the stable—"

While sipping tea they talked at random, each bringing forth little incidents they alone knew, chuckling indulgently, wistfully at their innocence, their adolescent foolishness.

"Remember that night in the cellar when I wanted you to be my wife in the eyes of God, and you slapped my face?"

"You should have been ashamed of yourself, you dreadful Frenchman . . ."

They tried to recapture the enchantment and despair of those days, but too many years had done by. They had become strangers, with nothing in common except the memory that once, long ago, they had loved each other.

Gradually the stream of their reminiscences dwindled down to a trickle.

"Would you like to see your old home?" he suggested to avoid falling into complete silence.

They drove to the former von Meck mansion. Despite its new furnishings they found it still haunted by the despotic ghost of her mother.

"She was a strange woman," mused Sonia aloud while glancing about the immense drawing room. "For a long time I couldn't forgive her for what she had done to us. Later I realized that she wanted me to be happy, but one shouldn't tamper with other people's lives. I married the man she chose for me and was miserable. Finally she ruined her own life. One day, nobody knows why, she cut off her relationship with Piotr Ilyich, and at the same time broke her own heart, for she loved him. She died only three months after he did."

"With all her faults, she did something for which your country will never forget her. She supported morally and financially one of your greatest musicians. And sometimes she could be very kind."

He pulled his watch out of his vest pocket.

"Look. This is the watch she gave me. I must have pawned it a hundred times, but you see, I still have it."

The visit through the mansion did them good. It relaxed their efforts to revive a past that had long crumbled to dust. Even the sight of the little music room stirred up nothing but a tender wistfulness.

By the time they drove back to her home, they had regained their naturalness and spoke with the ease of congenial acquaintances. He gave her a brief account of his life, grew lyrical over Chouchou. She mentioned her two unhappy marriages, which had both ended in divorce.*

Gaily she deplored the depletion of the von Meck fortune.

"Look at these sables!" she said, ruffling her jacket. "Five years old! In the old days I would have died rather than wear last year's furs. Now I don't care."

She did not mind being a pauper, as she said, and having only three servants. Nor did she mind being alone. She kept busy from morning to night and had found in politics a refuge from loneliness. She was that rare individual: a Russian feminist. She had become a leader in the crusade for women's rights.

"One of our great writers has described a Russian gentleman as a man who removes his boots before kicking his wife. Well, we're tired of being kicked with or without boots! We're going to change all that. We're holding meetings and preparing petitions to be presented to the Czar."

* Before marrying Prince Golizin, Sonia had married a distant relative of Rimsky-Korsakov.

Already night had come. Snowflakes flew in their faces, like white confetti. The sleigh glided to a stop before her small, unpretentious house. He escorted her to the door.

Gently she kissed him on the cheek. "Good-bye, Volichka," she whispered.

Smiling over her shoulder she disappeared into the house.

On the way back to the Koussevitzky mansion he almost regretted having met her again. Their encounter, he felt, had been like a stroll through a cemetery during which they had stood side by side before the tomb of their youth.

Memories, he told himself, should not be revisited . . .

He did not see Sonia again, did not know whether or not she used the tickets that were sent to her for his Moscow concerts. She was not among the persons who came to congratulate him afterward. It was better that way. She belonged to the past, and the past had no place in the present.

His last concert in Moscow ended in a sort of apotheosis.

Of course, that evening there was a farewell function. Caviar was plentiful and vodka flowed like the mighty Volga itself. As the ceremony progressed faces grew more flushed, eyes became moist and bloodshot. Emotions rose accordingly.

Claude, being the guest of honor, was offered countless toasts— to his health, his genius, his amiability, his modesty, his wife, his daughter, his country; then, the great French Army, the great Russian Army, the Franco-Russian Alliance, the President of the Republic and finally His Imperial Majesty the Czar. Dutifully Claude gulped down the toast in vodka.

By now everyone was swimming in brotherly love, and several of his admirers insisted on wrapping their arms around him and kissing him while tears of affection streamed down their cheeks into their beards.

It was then that he was presented with a parchment testimonial signed by twenty-five leading Russian musicians. It was written in oratorical French, the kind that is used in official functions and funeral eulogies.

It began:

Illustrious Master:
For a long time we awaited impatiently the moment when you would come and direct your works for us . . .

From there it rolled on eloquently to the ecstatic, transcendental climax:

The days spent with you will never be erased from our memory and they will dwell within us as the kindling of a light which will shine everlastingly upon our musical careers.

Claude rose and accepted the parchment with an allocution in the same exalted style, but suddenly he felt the floor moving under his feet. Quickly he brought his speech to an end and flopped down on his chair.

And then it was Saint Petersburg.

There, his success was, if possible, even greater than in Moscow. Twenty-five hundred people clapping at the same time could make a great deal of noise.

There was another function, with more vodka, more toasts and more oratory. It all was very nice and gratifying. But Emma and Chouchou were far away and he was getting homesick. Glory meant little when your heart was somewhere else.

He was back home in time for Christmas.

Chouchou, as usual, had written to Pére Noël and set her shoes in the fireplace; and once again Pére Noël had come during the night, squeezed down the chimney flue and left just the toys she had asked for.

"He must be awfully dirty when he gets home," she remarked on Christmas morning while unwrapping her presents. "Don't you think so, Papa?"

"He certainly is. As a matter of fact, he is as black as a chimney sweep."

"How does he get clean?"

"He takes a nice long bath and scrubs himself all over."

"Then what does he do?"

"He has a good dinner and goes to sleep for a week or two."

She threw him a doubtful glance. But she did not want to spoil *his* Christmas and pretended to believe what he said.

He, too, wished he could sleep for a week or two. But already he must prepare for his next tour. This time, Italy.

And so it went for a few months. Holland, then Belgium. In June he returned from London. A week later a student shot an Austrian archduke. In bewildered horror one nation after another found itself caught in the noose of its cleverly arranged alliances. By the end of July the situation was hopeless.

In a fracas of chiming bells, martial songs and trampling boots, war descended upon Europe.

CHAPTER

18

"WHEN I TOLD HIM I WAS FIFTY-TWO, DO YOU KNOW WHAT HE DID?"
He was so furious that he had forgotten to remove his hat, and he stood before his wife, panting, trying to catch his breath.

"He laughed! Yes, that whippersnapper laughed in my face and said I was too old and decrepit. It seems that fifty is the age limit and after that the army has no use for you. Apparently you must be young and in radiant health to stop a bullet and be killed! I told the idiot I didn't expect to go charging on a horse, but perhaps I could do something useful. Anything . . . Be a sentry, watch a bridge or even sit at a desk and do the same stupid work he was doing. He got very offended and said if I didn't stop insulting an officer—he was a lieutenant, I think—he would have me thrown in jail! . . . No wonder the Germans are already in France!"

For the next few days he was like a bear stung by a bee. Back and forth he paced in his study, gesticulating, mumbling to himself, refusing to answer the telephone or look at his mail. He growled at the maid when she entered to light the lamps in the evening, and glared at Miss as if she, too, were part of the conspiracy to keep him at home and stop him from doing his duty.

At dinner he ate in sullen silence, then exploded into ranting tirades against the stupidity of military regulations. Here he was, in the prime of life you might say, strong as an ox, eager to defend his country, and they laughed at him, told him he was too old and decrepit. Too old! . . . And General Joffre, the French Commander in Chief, was ten years older than himself! Yes, ten years! . . . In other words, a tired, fat, flabby old man of sixty-two, who went to bed at ten and could not be awakened afterward, was young enough to command armies, direct battles and assume the heaviest responsibilities, while he, Claude Debussy, a patriotic Frenchman still in the bloom of late youth, was cast aside like an old sock.

"Yes, like an old sock! Damn it, as a citizen I have the right to defend my country. After all, it's my France as much as General Joffre's that is being invaded. Isn't it?"

He bored everybody: the few friends who still called on him; the gardener, who was past seventy and came once a week to cut the grass and water the flowers; Miss, who fled at his approach. Even Emma, who had the patience of an angel.

Even Chouchou, who had the least patience of all.

"You won't talk about the war, Papa, will you?" she would ask before slipping into his study.

Although she was eight, she still sat on his knees sometimes; but usually she stood by his chair or hoisted herself onto the edge of his desk. She kept him informed of what was happening in the neighboring houses on the square. He learned that the old Monsieur who lived at number 18, the one who wore a top hat even in summer, was in bed with a cold. Funny, catching a cold in summer, wasn't it? . . . Madame Montagne's cat had just had a flock of babies. She wanted to take one, but Miss said no. Miss always said no. Occasionally she played the piano for him. The year before, she had started taking lessons and was showing exceptional abilities. Her teacher, she swore, smelled of moth balls, but they got along very well together.

And then, sometimes, in spite of themselves, they talked about the war. You couldn't avoid it. It was everywhere, affecting everybody's life, changing everything.

"Yesterday I saw Maman crying," she whispered to him one afternoon. "She was reading the newspaper, then she put it down on her lap and started to cry."

"That's because she has many friends and relatives in the war and she's afraid something might happen to them."

"Then why do you want to go? Don't you want to stay with us any more? Do you want Maman to cry for you, too?"

"Of course not. But you see, Chouchou, our country needs help and I want to do my duty."

Her brows knit as she tried to understand what he was saying, but his words had little meaning. Country was the house with its garden; the neighbors' houses on the square and the people who lived in them, their cats and their dogs; the elephants and ostriches at the Bois de Boulogne zoo; the carrousel Miss permitted her to ride if she had been good; the nearby Arc de Triomphe, and further away, jutting into the sky, the Eiffel Tower. These things were nice, of course, but not important enough to make Maman cry or take Papa away. As for this duty he was talking about, to her it meant even less. Duty was something you were *forced* to do. Like brushing your teeth or sitting straight on your chair. Nobody in his right mind wanted to do his duty . . .

"You mean you want to go to war?" she asked incredulously. "Like the little *pioupious* we saw the other day on their way to the station?"

She paused; then, before he could reply, she broke into a giggle.

"But, Papa, you're too old! You'd look funny!"

He gulped. Oh, the naïve cruelty of children! Her remark had pricked his martial delusions more surely than the lieutenant's sarcasms. Of course, he was too old . . . Two weeks ago they had watched a departing regiment and waved at the youngsters in red trousers and blue tunics marching by with flowers in the muzzles of their guns, singing, joking with the crowd. And it had struck him that forty-four years before, when he was about her age and on a similar summer day, he had watched their fathers march by, also with flowers in the muzzles of their guns . . . She was right. He would look funny and pitiable in red trousers, with a gun he wouldn't even know how to load. Why, he would only be a nuisance and get in everybody's way.

"I guess you're right," he said quietly. "My place is here at home. I'll try to take care of you all as best I can."

From that day on, a change came over him. He began thinking of himself as an old man, and almost overnight he began looking and behaving like one. His shoulders rounded; his step slowed down. He no longer ranted against General Joffre and the stupidity of army regulations. He still talked about the war; but now, like millions of other aging men all over Europe, he spoke of it as of some monstrous, unexplainable scourge he could do nothing about. But he was French and he thought only of France. To him, as to all Frenchmen, her cause was unimpeachably right; and like them he watched, aghast, the irresistible German advance spreading day by day, almost hour by hour, deeper into his country.

Like all Frenchmen he had thrilled at the news that the fearful Cossacks had galloped across the German frontier, two days ahead of schedule on their way to Berlin. He had remembered Gaby's predictions and felt shame for having scoffed at them. But the Russians had not gone very far. In the swamps of Tannenberg they had fought and died with futile courage. In a fortnight France had lost her muchvaunted and so costly ally.

By the first week of September, France was on her knees. Paris, silent and tense, its people quiet for once, had refused to become an open city. The governor, General Gallieni, stood ready to defend it district by district; blow up every one of its bridges, if necessary. Even the venerable Pont Neuf, the New Bridge, which was the city's oldest.

Then, on September 6, the French Army, which had retreated without a stop for ten days, suddenly turned back—and the miracle of the Marne began. That night, wave after wave of taxis, empty, headlights turned off in the moonlight and meters ticking, rolled out of Paris. In single file, like blind and obedient beetles, they crawled and rattled their twenty-seven-mile way to the front where they moved troops for the morning attack. The battle lasted three days. On September 9, French victory was assured and announced.*

Paris was saved, but active pursuit of the enemy was out of the question. On both sides, men had reached the breaking point. Less than a hundred kilometers from the capital, they tumbled down from exhaustion. And there they stayed—and dug in. The front, so fluid until now, took root in a muddy, bloody furrow that ran across France.

The war came to a stop, but not to an end.

Summer went by. Leaves started to fall. It rained night and day. From Switzerland to the Channel, millions of men, all longing for home, stood ankle-deep in mud facing one another behind machine guns and miles of barbed wire. Then rain turned to snow. In their respective trenches French and Germans wept from loneliness and cold. But orders were to hold on, hold on at any cost. And hold on they did.

The first winter of war began.

"Now, what kind of war is this?" Claude wailed at dinner. "I know I am only a civilian and have no right to speak, but just the same, couldn't those boys go home for the winter? Let them come back and kill each other next summer, if they must. But at least, don't let them die of pneumonia. You laugh, don't you? Well, our grandfathers thought it wasn't such a bad idea. In the eighteenth century campaigns came to a halt in winter. Soldiers sat around fires and got drunk until spring. And even in summer they didn't fight on Sunday. Now any old time is killing time."

Emma humored him with a nod and a smile, Chouchou looked at

---

* The ultimate verdict on the "miracle of the Marne" was pronounced by General von Kluck himself, who lost the battle. "That men will let themselves be killed where they stand, that is a well-known thing and depended on in every plan of battle. But that men who have retreated for ten days, sleeping on the ground and half dead from fatigue, should take up their rifles and attack when the bugle sounds, this is a thing upon which we never counted. It was a possibility never studied at our War Academy."

Incidentally, every taxi driver who went to the front was paid the regular fare and received one hundred and thirty francs.

him with tender indulgence. He was aware he was beginning to talk like those boring old men who always said how wonderful things used to be. But damn it, some things were better in the old days! Take the previous war, for instance, the old Franco-Prussian War. It had been senseless and horrible, but at least it had lasted only six months. While this one—why, from the way things looked, this one might last forever!

And there was nothing, not a blessed thing, he could do about it! As a matter of fact, if he really wanted to be useful, he should quietly die, get out of the way and let someone else have his food and tobacco. For these things were becoming scarce. Even bread. It seemed that bakers, at least those who knew how to bake a loaf of bread, made wonderful warriors and were all at the front. The clods left behind to attend the needs of the populace had no flour to begin with and wouldn't have known what to do with it if they had. And so they perpetrated something called war bread, *pain de guerre*. An infamous, gritty, grayish, ill-smelling, impossible-to-digest mixture of potato mash, sawdust, hay, soot, boiled cardboard, old buttons, chunks of cement and whatever else came handy. Oh, the delicious rolls of the garret days! . . . As for tobacco, it was all but unfindable. And if by chance you hounded out a measly pack, you had to coax, cajole, make eyes, make conversation, almost make love to those female tubs of lard that throned behind their counters. When it came to butter, milk, eggs—these things were fast becoming mere recollections from a dim, fabulous past.

Even Paris did not look the way it used to. Bags of sand were stacked against museums, churches and public buildings as a precaution against air raids. For now there were air raids! Another twentieth-century novelty! Why had Blériot ever crossed the Channel? Couldn't he have stayed on the ground, like everyone else? And those silly fools who went about in their paper-and-piano-wire machines, flying always higher and faster, what had they accomplished? Thanks to them, airplanes now came almost every night over Paris! Streetlamps had been equipped with blue-glass panels that let out a pretty moonlight glow, but no light whatever. You could get lost in your own district. Only burglars loved them . . .

But what changed Paris most was all those uniforms about. Streets were full of them. Of all kinds and colors, with all sorts of gold-plated hardware: buttons, emblems, insignias, medals, large-buckled Sam Brown belts. And of course, caps of every conceivable shape, all with chevrons, some even with tassels like nightcaps, all rakishly set at an angle. And glossy knee-high boots, some with spurs and some without.

Occasionally you spotted some Highlander in a kilt or some Indian soldier with a turban. Or some French officer in one of those dashing new horizon-blue uniforms that were beginning to replace the red trousers and kepis that had been the death warrants of so many little *pioupious*. No wonder women loved war. Men looked so devilish, heroic and handsome in uniforms. If he had anything to say he would insist on men fighting in their long woolen underwear. This would take the glamour out of war and mark a great step toward peace.

Whenever he ventured out of the house, he felt ashamed of his civilian clothes. They singled him out as a useless old man. He caught the pitying glances of the dapper young nurses who rushed about the streets in self-contained gales of flapping cloaks and flowing veils. Even the paunchy, gray-bearded reservists standing before public buildings in cast-off uniforms and holding empty guns seemed to look at him with scorn.

Finally, he almost stopped going out altogether and spent his days at home, fretting, grumbling about shortages, devouring the daily war bulletin, moving little flags back and forth on the huge map he had tacked up in his study, thinking of the hundreds, sometimes thousands, of young men who had died the previous day for a fifty-yard advance.

◆

In February, 1915, he began experiencing occasional stabs of pain. He tried deluding himself about them and almost succeeded—for a while. They were, he told himself, the result of war anxiety. Everybody was in poor shape these days. Some had terrible headaches; some, heart flutters. Others, stomach trouble. Well, he had these pains in his back, that was all. Where did they come from? He couldn't tell exactly. The kidneys, or perhaps the colon. Or maybe the bladder . . . After all, he was no anatomist, was he? Anyway, they were infrequent, and although sharp, not unendurable. They probably would disappear of their own accord one of these days.

Then, in a flash of lucidity, his pretense collapsed. His instinct warned him he was ill—had been for several months—and a premonition told him the name, the frightening name, of his sickness. Then, in the secrecy of his study, he would give in to fear, let his hands tremble and sweat come out in beads on his brow and the back of his neck.

He decided this could not go on. He was imagining things, and the only sensible way to set his mind at rest was to go and consult Doctor Desjardin about it.*

He did. That is, he walked as far as the physician's home and started to climb the stairs. Then, in an uncontrollable gust of terror, he turned around and ran out in the street until he reached the nearest

---

* Oddly, Doctor Desjardin, who had operated on Lily after her attempted suicide, had become Debussy's physician and friend. Besides, his functions at the clinic, he also had an important private practice.

corner. There he mopped the sweat from his face, for although it was a raw early March day, he was drenched in perspiration. Then he replaced his derby on his head and returned home.

Each step of the way he scorned himself for his cowardice. During the following days he did not relent, even for a moment. He shamed himself with wordless sermons on man's manliness, his fearlessness, his much vaunted capacity for looking death in the eye without flinching. They did little good; the highest-sounding maxims sounded the most hollow.

At last, from sheer weariness at this never-ending inner squabble, he went back to the doctor's house. This time he climbed the stairs all the way, rang the bell, gave his name to the nurse. With nonchalance he thumbed through a magazine for a few minutes before he was ushered into the doctor's office.

"Nothing wrong, I hope, my dear Master?"

"Nothing, thank heavens. Never felt better in my life."

He sat down, leaned back in the chair, his hands folded over his cane as for a social call.

"Of course, I have my good and bad days, but then—"

"I'm afraid you will always have them. You are a cyclothymiac."

"My God, what's that? It sounds dreadful."

"Nothing to be alarmed about. Cyclothymia is a mild neurosis involving recurring cycles of exhilaration and depression. Most artists have it in various degrees. In your case, it is particularly distinct." A reassuring smile appeared in his gray beard. "Don't worry, you'll never die of it."

"I'm glad to hear it." In a conversational tone he added, "Also, now that I think of it, I have an occasional little pain in my back, but it passes almost immediately."

"Fatigue, most probably. You spend too many hours at your desk, you work too hard."

"Exactly what I thought. I'll start doing some exercise."

"However, one cannot be too careful. Perhaps I'd better examine you."

He was about to rise, but Claude made an emphatic gesture of denial.

"Heavens, no! Besides, I wouldn't even have the time. I am due at my publisher's in a few minutes. I just happened to be passing by and on an impulse I decided to come up and see how you were. What with this awful war and all that!"

The doctor said a few words to the effect that war was a trial to everyone, especially to the few remaining doctors in Paris who had to assume the practices of colleagues in the army.

"But we try to do our part, as modest as it is," he wound up.

Despite his courtesy, he seemed clearly anxious to end this rather purposeless visit, and he went on in a brisk busy-man-who-has-no-time-to-waste sort of way.

"As for those pains in your back, try to take long walks and rest an hour or two after meals. And if you possibly can, try to go to the country this summer and relax."

"I'll speak about it to Emma," said Claude, rising. "She's always telling me I'm working too hard. Well, Doctor, I hope I haven't taken too much of your time."

Already they were walking together out of the office. At the door, the doctor extended his hand.

"It's been a pleasure, my dear Master. A real pleasure."

The doctor's words followed Claude all the way back to his home. My dear Master indeed! . . . If only good Doctor Desjardin could see his dear Master now, shuffling in the dusk, cloaked in his shame and his fears.

Back in his study he pondered his visit. It had been a narrow escape, but thank heavens, he had not let himself be examined. An examination could only be useless or disastrous. Useless, if the pains had no alarming cause; disastrous, if they resulted from illness, and this illness happened to be the one he feared it was. In this case, the doctor would certainly have felt duty bound to inform Emma and thus plunge the household into panic.

He, on the contrary, intended to keep the whole subject from her and Chouchou for as long as he possibly could. Which meant for as long as he would be able to conceal his pains. How long would that be? He did not know, but he hoped it would be at least a few months. And this would be that much time gained.

In the meantime, he must avoid brooding over his condition. He must work, keep busy every minute. And since he had no music in his mind, he simply would have to work on someone else's. The important thing was to do something, anything.

"Anything," he told his publisher the following morning. "Transcriptions, arrangements, orchestrations, I don't care. Please, Jacques, help me. I am in earnest."

Jacques Durand let out a sigh. "Since you insist, would you like to supervise our forthcoming edition of Chopin's works? It would be a great honor for our house."

"Never mind the honor. What do you want me to do?"

The work entailed comparing previous Chopin editions, checking discrepancies, making technical suggestions about the interpretation of some pieces, indicating the right fingering in some tricky passages, correcting printing errors, writing an introduction to the edition.

"As you can see, it's a long, delicate and tedious work."

"Fine. Give it to me."

"Now? But, my dear Claude—"

"Now."

Thereafter he remained closeted in his study, playing Chopin's music by the hour, studying every bar of his compositions. In this way he almost forgot about the war and himself. At meals he was pleasant, almost gay in an absent-minded sort of way. He no longer grumbled about shortages. Even the awful war bread wasn't so bad, he said, once you got used to it. His pessimism gave way to a wishful optimism. One of these days the Germans would come to their senses, get rid of their silly Kaiser, and this monstrous war would come to an end.

His appetite improved. He looked better than he had for months. Sometimes Emma would smile at him across the table. For no reason, just because she loved him. Because he was playing the piano again, which he had not done since the beginning of the war, almost a year ago. Because he seemed happier, more like his old self.

Only Chouchou was not taken in.

She was now going to school, a small private Institution pour Jeunes Demoiselles. On her return she never failed to drop in for a chat and a visit.

One afternoon she found him at the piano and came to sit at his side on the bench, but instead of babbling as usual, she leaned her head on his chest and lapsed into silence.

After a while she asked, without looking up at him, "What's the matter, Papa? Why are you so sad?"

Her question caught him off guard.

"Now what makes you think that? I am not sad at all, I am very happy."

Then, to change the subject, "Now tell me, what did the teacher say? What did you learn at school today?"

She remained silent, her head still on his chest, and suddenly from the shaking of her shoulders he knew she was crying. He put his finger under her chin, gently lifted her little face to him.

"Now, what do we have here? A crying baby, and I thought Chouchou was a big girl."

She looked at him, tears running unabashedly down her cheeks.

"I know you're sad, Papa. I can feel it."

For a fraction of an instant he longed to take her in his arms and unburden his heart to her of its gnawing secret.

But he held himself in check and said, "Yes, I suppose I am sad. Everybody in France is sad these days. Everybody in the world is sad. Now give me a big smile and run along. Papa still has a lot of work to do."

◆

The pains were becoming more frequent; also, they lasted longer. They came preceded by a slow contraction of nerves and muscles that served as a warning to his entire system. Then came the spasm itself: a knifelike thrust accompanied by a fit of nausea. For five or six seconds his upper body seemed to swell with pain and about to explode. Then his contorted face relaxed; air started flowing through his windpipe again. He opened his eyes, and after a minute or two all would be well—and so remain for the next three or four hours. He lived in terror that he might have one of these spasms during lunch or dinner and his secret would be out. But until now he had been lucky.

In the intervals between spasms he accomplished an enormous amount of work. By June he had finished the revision of Chopin's works, written the preface to the new edition.

Before leaving for the country with his family he asked Jacques Durand for another similar task.

"Something that will keep me busy all summer."

"I don't know why you insist on working yourself to death instead of taking a long rest," sighed the publisher. "But I've learned it is no use arguing with you. Would you be interested in revising Bach's sonatas for violin and clavichord?"

"I'd love it. Just the thing after Chopin."

At Pourville, a village on the Normandy coastline, near Dieppe, they rented a modest villa and moved into it at once. It was called Mon Coin—My Corner—and stood on the edge of the beach. Everyone in the household loved it, each for some particular reason. Emma appreciated its comfort and unpretentious charm; Chouchou, its attic full of intriguing things; Miss, its proximity to England. She swore that on clear nights she could see the lights of Brighton.

Claude was delighted with his study. An isolated, blue-papered room on the second floor, it was just big enough to accommodate his worktable, a rented upright piano and a cretonne sofa. Through its single window he could hear the lulling sound of breaking waves and the distant squeals of sea gulls.

There he began working on Bach's sonatas. And there, one day, Chouchou rushed in, clutching a toy soldier.

"Look, Papa!"

She came to a dead stop and gaped at him as she saw him sitting at his desk twisted with pain, his face ashen and distorted.

But already the spasm was over. He opened his eyes, tried to smile. "It's . . . all right . . ." He could barely form the words, but added in a panting mutter, "Please . . . close the door."

She did; then walked to him.

"That's what you didn't want to tell me, isn't it?"

He nodded. His breathing was still coming in gasps.

"You . . . mustn't tell . . ."

"I won't." She took his hand, gently tugged at it. "Lie down."

He rose, took the few steps to the sofa, slumped down on it. With quiet efficiency she made him recline, lifted his legs and set a pillow under his head. Then she knelt down at his side so that their faces were near, almost on the same level.

For a few moments he lay on his back, relaxed, smiling at her grave, unsmiling face.

"I feel fine now. These pains come over me once in a while. They really aren't anything serious, but you mustn't tell anyone about them."

His voice tensed into an urgent, imploring whisper. "You won't darling, will you? No one, absolutely no one. Especially Maman."

"I promise," she said quietly.

He looked at her through tears of gratitude. "It'll be our secret . . ."

She bent down over him, kissed his cheek, not in her usual pecking way, but with long and deliberate tenderness, in a gesture of innate motherliness.

"Yes, Papa. It'll just be the two of us . . . just you and me . . ."

No more needed to be said. They understood each other.

He asked about the toy soldier that lay on the floor next to her.

"I found it in the attic," she said. "And I was coming to show it to you."

It was an old linen doll, naïvely painted and filled with sawdust. It represented a soldier from Napoleon's Guard, with an enormous busby and the Legion of Honor on his tunic. The sawdust had seeped out of one of its legs.

"We'll fill it with sand when we go to the beach," he said. "And it'll be as good as new."

They did not refer to the spasm any more during the summer, but their secret always hung between them, bringing them together even more closely than before.

Occasionally he accompanied her to the beach and watched her run in and out of the surf. Tirelessly he filled his eyes with the sight of her reedy body, his ears with the sound of her happy cries. She still had the coltish, sexless grace of childhood, but before long she would fill out, curve into a demoiselle and one day she would be a bride in white veils and some young man would take her away. Then she would have a child of her own—his grandchild . . .*

Of course, all this was far in the future and he wouldn't see any of it. But a few dregs of the present still remained, and he still could see her as she was now, a little girl in a boy's striped bathing suit play-

---

* Mercifully, Claude Debussy was spared the knowledge that Chouchou was to die only a few months after him.

ing her teasing game with the waves. He wished these moments would never end. She seemed to grow more precious as time grew shorter. And time, he knew, was running out. Soon he wouldn't be able to conceal his pains any longer. Already he had had several narrow escapes.

She, too, seemed dimly aware of some approaching calamity. Unexpectedly, in the middle of some game, she would run back to him, wet and glistening in the sun, her hair flowing, her feet and ankles socked in sand. She would flop down at his side, lean her head against him and say, "Let's not talk, let's just be together."

Thus summer wore on.

He was plodding through Bach's sonatas one evening, when music —his music, this time—returned. Not in spurts, or tantalizing wisps, but in blazing, uninterrupted flashes. All of a sudden his mind was incandescent with them.

For the next few weeks, between excruciating spasms of pain, he wrote music like one possessed, without stop, almost without sleep, in a panic of urgency. First a two-piano suite, *En Blanc et Noir;* then six *Etudes;* then a sonata for piano and cello; then six more *Etudes*.

Now he had twelve, half as many as Chopin. He should have stopped to make a clear copy of them, for in addition to being incredibly difficult, they were almost illegible. But another sonata was throbbing in his brain. An unusual kind of sonata. For three instruments: flute, alto and harp. And so he had no choice but to write it. When he finished, September was almost gone. He wanted to write other sonatas—a third one for piano and violin, a fourth for English horn, oboe and clavichord. But now there was just enough time left to copy the *Etudes*. By the end of the month the work was done, the manuscript ready.*

When at last he wrote down the final chord, he rested his pen on the table, ran his hand over his face. Then he rose and went to lean on the window ledge. It was night, a night without moon or stars. He felt calm, mortally sad, and yet content. He had given Emma a good summer—thank God, he had been able to do that!—and he had written a great deal of music. More music than he had in the last two years . . .

For a while he stared into the void of darkness, listening to the murmur of the waves dying on the beach, ending their long journey with a sigh of fatigue and relief. Oh, if he, too, could only die now, this very minute, with a gentle sigh before the pain, the grief, the horror that was to come! . . .

---

* On September 30, 1915, he wrote his friend Jacques Durand: "Last night, at midnight, I finished copying the last note of the *Etudes*. Ouff! The most intricate Japanese woodcut is child's play compared to some of those pages, but I am content. It is a good work."

♦

In Paris, war had become a way of life.

People were getting used to the sight of men in uniforms, soldiers in wheelchairs or clutching the arms of their nurses, learning to be blind. Also, to waiting in line for a loaf of bread or a pound of meat, being jolted out of bed by the howl of sirens and the crashing of bombs, staggering down to cellars or sleeping in Métro stations.

November put an end to air raids, but tormented the population in its own way. With lashing winds and pelting rains. Then, toward the end of the month, it got very cold. In the houses as well as out, for neither coal nor firewood could be had at any price.

Emma caught a cold that threatened to turn into bronchitis.

"Surely there must be a pailful of coal in this damn town," Claude exploded one day, "and I'm going to find it!"

Before anyone could stop him he was out, hurrying in the rain, umbrella in one hand, in the other the drawing room's handsome brass coal scuttle.

He returned late that afternoon, wet, worn out—and without coal. Ignoring Emma's pleas he was out again early the following morning. On the third day he brought home half a pailful of English coke. For an hour he boasted about his feat. The imagination, the cunning, the patience it had required.

What he did not say was that he would have collapsed in the street, but for a public bench—one of the thousand wonderful, merciful Paris benches!—which he had reached in time. There he had sat until the spasm had passed, unnoticed by the hurrying crowd, clenching his teeth not to scream, his precious coal at his feet.

Once again he had been lucky, but the pains were becoming almost unendurable and he was bound to betray himself before long. Whether he collapsed in the street or at home, his secret would soon be out.

Chouchou sensed it, too.

He was not at his desk that afternoon when she came in, but sitting by the tall window in his study watching the winter dusk fall over the garden. She stood before him, unable to smile, finding nothing to say; then, without a word, she knelt down by his chair and laid her head in his lap, her eyes, wide and afraid, resting on him.

"I am proud of you," he said, fondling her black curls. "You've kept our secret well."

She did not reply, and they went on looking at each other: he, smiling, caressing her hair; she, gazing steadily at him.

After a while he went on, "I wish we could have held on to it until after Christmas, but I'm afraid I won't be able to. Oh, well, secrets have to come out sooner or later, I suppose."

She remained silent, but her eyes filled with tears. And he reflected that the cruelest thing about being ill was that you hurt those you loved.

All evening his mind returned to the picture of his daughter staring at him in loving, helpless grief. Because of him she would have an unhappy Christmas. Then he thought of the thousands of children who also would have an unhappy Christmas, because their papas were at the front or in hospitals or in shallow graves beneath wooden crosses. And those for whom there would be no Christmas at all.

They were the most pitiful, these homeless war orphans. The more he thought of them, the more his heart went out to them. He could see them wandering through the charred ruins of their villages, lost and cold and hungry. He could hear their piping trebles rising to Heaven in a bewildered whimper.

Why, he asked himself, why hadn't anyone written music about them? Theirs was the real voice of war. Not the fanfares, the bouncing marches and catchy tunes that made war sound so gay and dashing. War was an unspeakable horror. Like plague and famine, it might be inevitable. But, for God's sake, don't sing about it! War should be wailed about, not warbled about.

Now he had only one thought: put their cries in music. Frantically he searched for a suitable text and found none, for poets, like musicians, appeared to be enthralled only with the glamour of war. And so he wrote his own text. Childlike and tragic. Then, the music.

In two days he composed the *Noël des enfants qui n'ont plus de maison*.*

The next day was the first of December, and on that day he received an official notice to appear in person at the arrondissement city hall, avenue Henry-Martin, and receive his coal ration card. No servants or relatives could apply: only heads of families.

At seven the following morning, he was on his way. It had stopped snowing, but a few inches of snow covered the ground and outlined the avenue's leafless trees. It was a dour morning, shadowless, colorless, all black and white like a charcoal drawing. The avenue du Bois de Boulogne, usually so grand and bustling, looked bleak in its wintry emptiness.

Already a number of persons were waiting in line before the city hall. Elderly, obviously wealthy, stylish in an old-fashioned way: the ladies still in corsets and large feather hats; the men in silk hats and tremendously high collars, several flashing a monocle. There was about them an *air de famille,* the kinship of money, social standing and common prejudices.

* This *Christmas Carol of Homeless Children* is the most moving piece Debussy ever wrote, one of the most moving ever written. Speaking about it, he said, "It is my way of making war." It is justly regarded as the last spurt of his flickering genius.

Many had been neighbors all their lives; and from his place at the end of the line, Claude observed them as they cackled among themselves and damned the government in the mundane high-pitched voices. They were in their sixties, some even older, futile, ridiculous and pathetic; yet he felt one with them. He, too, belonged to a bygone gaslight era when there were no airplanes, no automobiles and the streets resounded with the clip-clop of hoofbeats; when lamplighters rushed about at dusk with their long poles on their shoulders; and straw on the pavement meant that, nearby, someone was ill and cabbies slowed down their horses and people spoke in whispers.

At last the doors opened. After a while his turn came. He was let inside the building, showed his identity papers to a clerk, who handed him his ration card.

"May I use it now?" Claude asked anxiously.

"Just go to the store indicated on the coupon and you'll get your coal."

It took him a few minutes to reach the shop, but there again he had to wait in line. Finally he was handed a good-sized paper bag filled with coal. Hugging it against his chest, he started on his way home.

As he crossed the avenue du Bois de Boulogne he noticed that it was still deserted, its snow still untrodden. He was only a few hundred yards from his house when he felt the symptoms of an approaching spasm. This time there was no public bench to sit on and he leaned against a tree for support, groaning and shaking in agony, a trickle of saliva and bile drooling out of a corner of his mouth.

When the pain receded he opened his eyes. With his handkerchief he wiped his lips and waited for his breath to relax. He felt very weak, but instinct warned him that another attack would come before long. He picked up his bag of coal and resumed his progress. He was panting as he turned into the alley that led to the recessed square on which his house stood. Luckily he had left the garden gate ajar. He shouldered it open and made his way to the entrance.

Miss opened the door, gasped incredulously at the bag of coal in his arms.

"How lovely!" she cried, clasping her hands and lasping into English as she always did when deeply moved. "I'm going to start a fire at once."

She took the bag from him and hurried away in the direction of the drawing room.

He still had time to reach his study, close the door behind him. But then another gush of pain surged through him, without warning and so excruciating that his legs gave way and he fell headlong on the rug.

There, a moment later, Emma found him, unconscious.

BEFORE
THE
NIGHT

FIVE DAYS LATER, ON DECEMBER 7, 1915, CLAUDE WAS OPERATED ON for cancer by Doctor Desjardin. The operation was successful, which meant that instead of a short agony he would have a long one.

When he came out of the hospital he had become very feeble and so thin that his clothes hung loose on him. At home the radium treatments, ruinous and painful, were begun, and for a few weeks there was a glimmer of hope. It vanished, and now nothing remained but to wait for death.

But cancer is a disease that takes its time. Weeks, months went by, and still he did not die. But neither was he truly alive. He had entered the forlorn world-wide brotherhood of incurable patients who dwell in a sort of no man's land between life and death, no longer living and not yet dead. His heart went on beating. For no reason, like those handless clocks that continue to tick. He could walk a little, eat a little, speak a little. He could smile, that he still could do. Only there wasn't much to smile about.

Thanks to sedatives he had moments when he was free of pain. Then he made great plans, wrote his publisher about all the music he was going to write. Several more sonatas. His opera. Yes, his opera . . . At last he had the quiet he needed to tackle the work. And he could work in bed. Why, in the old days, he had written reams of music in bed! . . .

These spurts of ambition did not last long. Pain would return. Unrelenting, pitiless, senseless. And with it his longing for a death that was certain, but would not come. At times his yearning rose in pleading sobs out of his lips. When, oh when would man win the right to die quickly, painlessly, decently! . . . Before he turned into a loathsome sight and a stench, before he ruined and harassed those he loved and earned their hatred . . . Must one commit murder to be given the mercy of swift death? When, oh when would man take the dying out of death!

Now and then he inquired about the war. It was now in its third year and still going on. As senseless as his pain, as endless as his disease. With millions of men still facing one another across strips of earth, white with snow or green with grass according to the seasons.

Whenever he felt a little stronger, his patriotism rekindled. Again he would orate about every Frenchman having to do his duty, and how he wished Doctor Desjardin would mind his business and stop telling him he was too weak to do anything, when, as a matter of fact, he felt perfectly well, and all doctors were tyrants at heart who only wanted to keep you in bed so that they could lord it over you.

And so, because his name would fill concert halls, he consented to appear in three war benefits. At the last one, on May 17, 1917, he had the joy of hearing his *Noël*. It electrified the audience and had to be repeated three times. When his turn came to appear on the stage he could barely stand up. As he finished playing and rose from the piano stool, Emma watched him with bated breath from the wings, praying they would stop applauding and let him go. But they wouldn't. The audience had risen and went on applauding in collective premonition that Claude de France, as he now was called, would never be seen again. He nodded, smiled, feebly waved at them, muttering words no one could hear. At last he signified he could not stand up any more and hurriedly shuffled off the stage into Emma's arms.

News of his illness had spread all over France and, despite the war, Europe. Messages of sympathy arrived from friends and strangers. Some people came to the house to inquire about his health and placed their calling cards in the silver tray at the door. Among them was a middle-aged, poorly dressed woman who never went farther than the garden gate, left a few flowers but did not give her name.

"Just tell him it's from an old friend," she would say.

For some time her identity remained a mystery, until Chouchou happened to answer the bell one day and opened the gate. A moment later she raced back upstairs, burst into her father's room with the visitor's flowers in her arms and explained in one long panting breath that she was quite an old woman but kind of nice-looking and she had big green eyes—"Honest, Papa, they're really green!"—and she had patted her cheek, asked her name, smiled at her for a moment and walked away.

Thus the mystery was a mystery no longer. It was Gaby. Gaby, alone now that her gentleman friend had returned to Buenos Aires at the start of the war . . . Gaby, poor again, ruined by her patriotism, and her Russian bonds.*

A few more months dragged by. Horrible months. For Claude, for everyone. A new year, 1918, began in a sudden fury of battles all along the front. In a last desperate offensive the Germans started bombing Paris with long-range guns. Every twenty minutes the monstrous shells came crashing through the sky with the clatter of a locomotive, falling at random, killing at random.

For Claude every hour now brought its torment, for cancer was also launching its final offensive and morphine became less and less effective. Sometimes, mercifully, he lapsed into unconsciousness and for a few moments he would know the peace of death. When he awoke, he always found Emma sitting by his bed. When did she sleep? Where did she find the strength to go on like this day after day, month after month? For no other reason but to give him a smile when he opened his eyes, let him know that she still was near and would remain until the end.

And she was, when at last the end came on March 25, 1918, at six o'clock in the evening.

The long range shells were thundering all over Paris, making big orange splashes in his bedroom window; and in her room, Chouchou slept soundly through it all, as twelve-year-old children will when they are very tired.

Suddenly Claude and Emma exchanged a glance, for both knew that at that instant Death had entered the room.

She rose and stood by his bedside, holding his fleshless, almost transparent hand. For a moment they gazed at each other, saying good-bye without words or tears, for they had no more words to say or tears to shed.

He looked at her once more, long and full as if he wanted to take her image with him.

She smiled, and his lips quivered in response.

And as he tried to smile, he died.

---

* After the war Gaby left Paris and was forced to find employment as a housekeeper. Finally she returned to Orbec, where she died on May 12, 1945, a month before her seventy-ninth birthday. In his searching study *Tel était Debussy,* M. Pasteur Vallery-Radot quotes a remark from the eminent musician, Alfred Cortot, who knew Gaby well in her last years: "She really loved him until she died."

ABOUT THE AUTHOR

From a letter by Pierre La Mure to his editor:

My second book (in French) had just been published; and I was living in America as the carefree, underworked correspondent of a Paris newspaper—no cables for me, but a leisurely weekly feature article—when the war broke out, France was invaded, my newspaper folded, and my budding career as a French writer came to an abrupt end.

Undaunted, I decided—please, don't laugh—I would thereafter write in English. It seemed so simple. I would merely translate my thoughts from French into English and—*voilà!*

Well, I had to learn and I did. The hard way, by myself . . . It took me a year to write the first hundred pages of *Moulin Rouge;* another to rewrite them; a third to tear them up and start all over again. And so on.

I've been at it ever since.

Take my word, English is a very difficult language. As a matter of fact, I never understood why William the Conqueror, who after all was a Frenchman, did not insist on the English learning to speak French. It would have made things so much easier for him—and me.

But he didn't; and this is why I, who was born with such genuine aptitudes for idleness, have had to work so hard. Each year I hope it will be getting a little easier, but it doesn't. You could ballast a ship with the drafts of *Clair de Lune*. Perhaps after my next book, it won't be so hard. At least, that's what I tell myself . . .